MW00857228

# FLOWER OF IOWA

by

Lance Ringel

Distant Mirror Press ★ New York

Published by Distant Mirror Press, New York
distantmirrorpress.com



This book is a work of fiction. While it has been carefully researched to include dates, places, and well-known historical people related to the chronology of activities of the U.S. 33rd and British 58th divisions in France in 1918, all other names, incidents, and characterizations are imagined creations of the author. Any resemblance to current events or living persons is entirely coincidental.

Cover Design: Minnie Cho, FUSELOFT, fuseloft.com

Cover photography: © Stephen Mulcahey (top) and © Sinisa Botas (bottom) from shutterstock.com

Book Design: Mark Pence

Maps courtesy Harry S. Truman Library & Museum, Independence, Missouri; and the Military and Naval Department, "Intelligence Maps," Record Series 301.110, Illinois State Archives.

ISBN: 978-0-578-64934-4
ISBN: 978-1-310-94060-6 (eBook)

# Contents

# Foreword by the Author

In my early teens, growing up in central Illinois, I first encountered the Great War through two excellent sources: Barbara Tuchman's Pulitzer Prize-winning masterpiece, *The Guns Of August*, and a CBS-TV series called *World War One*. Both made a considerable impression on me, and spurred a lifelong fascination with a conflict that, while it changed our world completely, remains mysterious to many, if not most, Americans.

More than three decades later, in the early 1990s, I found myself stuck in bed, recovering from a near-fatal bout of hepatitis. As a distraction, I re-watched the CBS series, then airing on PBS. At that same moment in time, Bill Clinton's campaign promise to repeal the U.S. military's ban on gay soldiers was stirring up the controversy that eventually would result in the infamous "Don't Ask, Don't Tell" policy. In the confluence of these events – one public, one personal – an idea came to me: What would life have been like for two soldiers of the First World War who found themselves falling in love… with each other?

Once I had recovered, I embarked on my research. Being an old-school journalist, I found myself spending countless hours researching in libraries and museums. But as much as I was enjoying being nestled elbow-deep in books, articles, and photos, it dawned on me: I could easily spend the rest of my life researching, and never write a page.

So, about six months into the process, I switched gears. I started writing *Flower of Iowa* while continuing to do research on both sides of the Atlantic. To tell this story properly, I needed to see with my own eyes the actual Great War battlefields of France and Belgium, as well as their surrounding towns. With the love of my life, Chuck Muckle, beside me, I scoured the state of Iowa to find the most suitable town to serve as Tommy Flowers' birthplace, ultimately choosing the village of Brooklyn. Wherever I went on this mission, serendipity seemed to follow me, in the guise of helpful strangers whose offers of information would me to enrich the narrative.

I was in midflight over the Atlantic, on a plane back from London, when I completed the first draft of *Flower of Iowa*. But being a perfectionist, I continued revising it for the next 17 years. Finally, with the centennial of the Great War looming, it was time to share the story of Tommy Flowers and David Pearson with the world.

When I published the novel as an eBook in the spring of 2014, I never could have imagined where the journey for the book, and for myself, would lead. To the top of the Smashwords charts for both Gay Fiction and Historical Fiction. To tea in London with the extraordinarily erudite, and incredibly supportive, actor-author Stephen Fry, who kindly tweeted, "Reading a truly wonderful WW1 novel" to his 7.7 million Twitter followers. To Ireland, where Chuck and I offered a dramatic reading of the novel to open the International Dublin Gay Theatre Festival. To the book's home turf, France, as part of the cultural portion of The Gay Games. And finally, to New York City's famed 42nd Street, where two remarkable young actors, Ben Salus and Bradley Johnson, brought Tommy and David to vivid new life in my staged adaptation, directed by Chuck.

Over the past six years, we have read from *Flower of Iowa* not only in the aforementioned European capitals, but also across a vast expanse of the United States, from Provincetown to Fort Lauderdale, from Chicago to San Francisco. A group of gay veterans in the Midwest was perhaps our smallest audience, yet their own stories from Vietnam and Iraq were powerful, and their response to the book was heartening. All of these in-person encounters have been gratifying, as has been the experience, in our wired world, of hearing from strangers, such as military history buffs in the UK and Australia, via cyberspace.

In all of our readings, the same matter inevitably arose: While some people eagerly went online to purchase the novel, many others said they loved what they were hearing, but simply could not get used to reading an eBook.

That matter has been rectified, as *Flower of Iowa* finally makes its appearance in print. And so the journey continues.

Lance Ringel
January, 2020

# ACKNOWLEDGMENTS

*Flower of Iowa* has traveled a long, long road from conception to publication. But it is a road that I have not traveled alone.

Any list of acknowledgments would have to start with three people: Chuck Muckle, the love of my life, who has been a tireless and enthusiastic source of strength and support, and the very first reader of the book; and my parents, Reg and Jane Ringel, who were always there for me. They did not live to see the novel published, but made the realization of my dream possible.

Renée Cafiero, as adept a copy editor as has ever plied that honorable trade, volunteered her skills in reviewing the manuscript word by word. If any errors remain, it is because a headstrong author failed to heed Renée's advice. Mark and Cheryl Pence, whom I have known since second and seventh grade respectively, are living proof of the value of childhood friends. Mark generously volunteered his considerable technical expertise to make both the electronic and print editions of this book a reality. Very early on, Cheryl, in her work at the Illinois State Library, was able to locate the 33rd's divisional history. Even more amazingly, she uncovered another self-published work, from the 1920s, by Captain Will Judy, who served with the 33rd. Captain Judy's account provided me with an invaluable real-life timeline to integrate with Tommy Flowers' fictional adventures.

And there have been many more, including friends, family, and to my astonishment, strangers who readily stepped forward to help, in ways large and small. A woman on the plane back from Iceland offered to share copies of letters from her great-aunt who had served as a nurse in France during World War I, thus helping me shape the character of Sister Jean Anderson. Earnest and attentive librarians and researchers at a host of institutions in Europe and the United States were eager to proffer assistance, nowhere more so than at the Imperial War Museum in London, simply one of the most marvelous repositories in the world, as well as an incredibly welcoming place for a writer from "off the street."

Publication of this book also would not have happened without the help of talented professionals, notably the energetic and astute Jay Blotcher and Alan Klein of Public Impact Media Consultants, and Minnie Cho of FuseLoft, who combined her deep, innate feel for this work with her formidable creative talents, culminating in a cover that captures the spirit of what lies within.

Finally, I would like to dedicate this book to the millions of men and women who suffered and lost their lives in the Great War, and to the gay soldiers of conflicts past whose stories have been erased from history. As gratifying as it has been for me to try to redress that balance, I wish the history of the early 20th century had never required me to do so.

# Maps

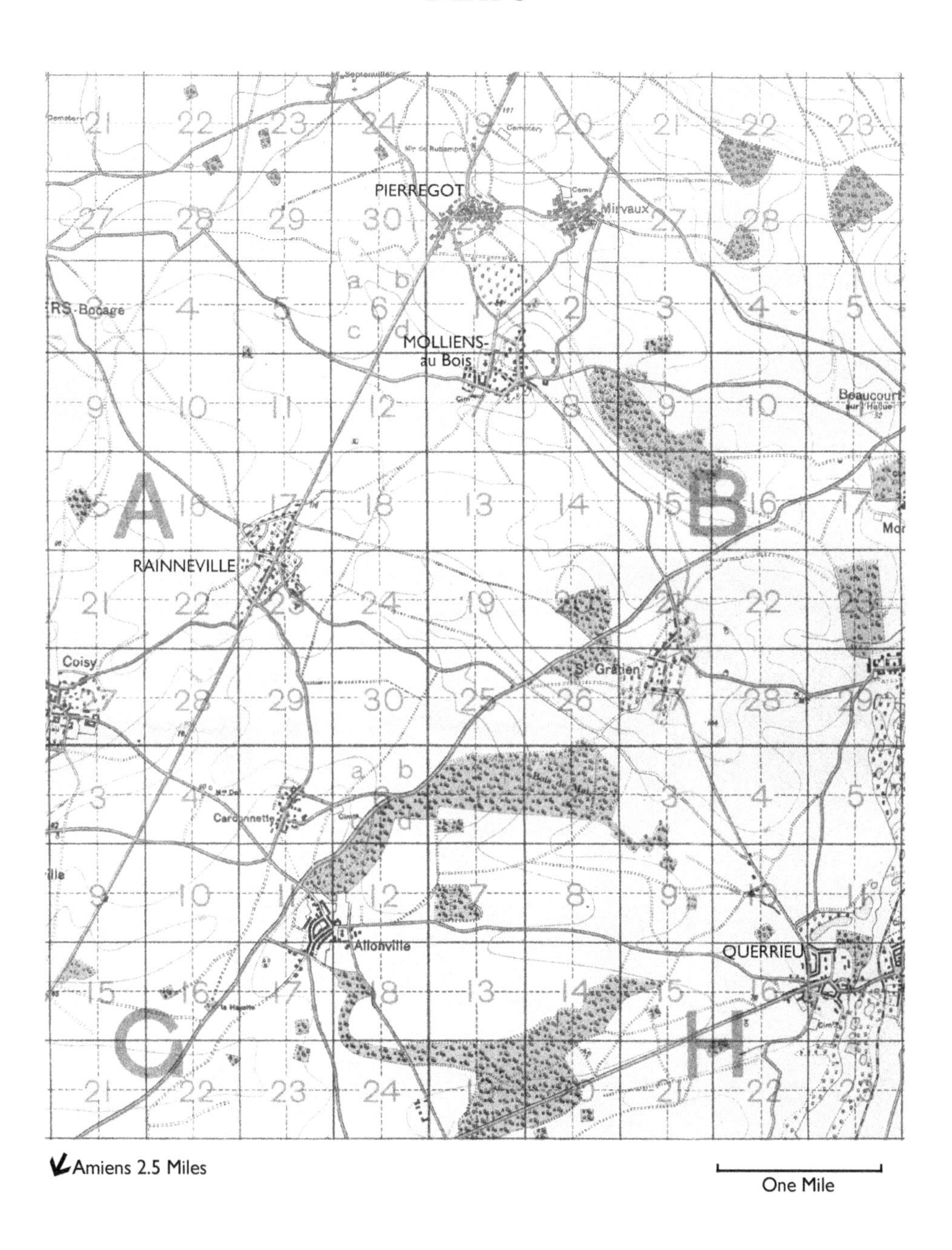


The Molliens area of Picardy, France

← Querrieu 4 Miles

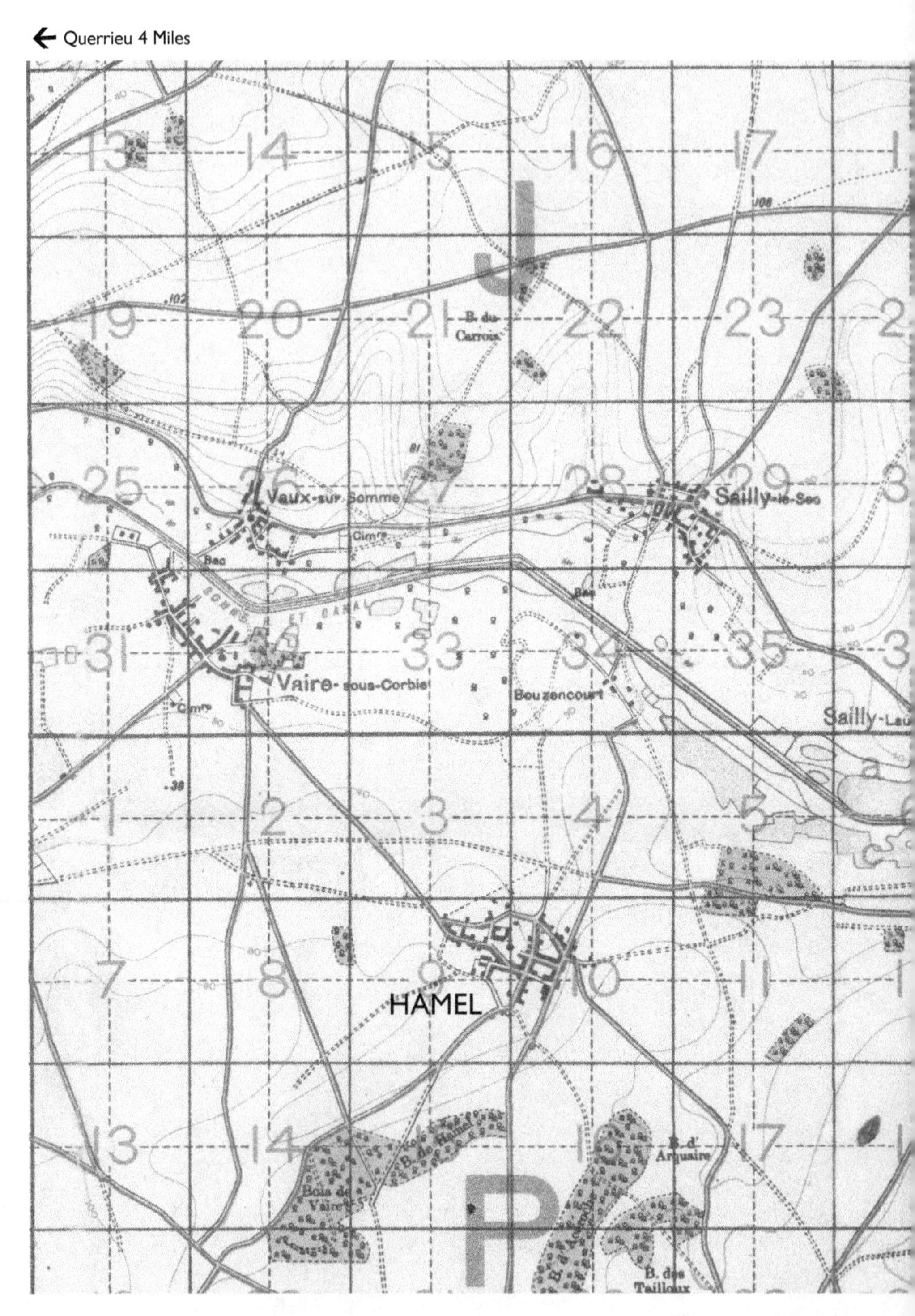


The Hamel – Chipilly area

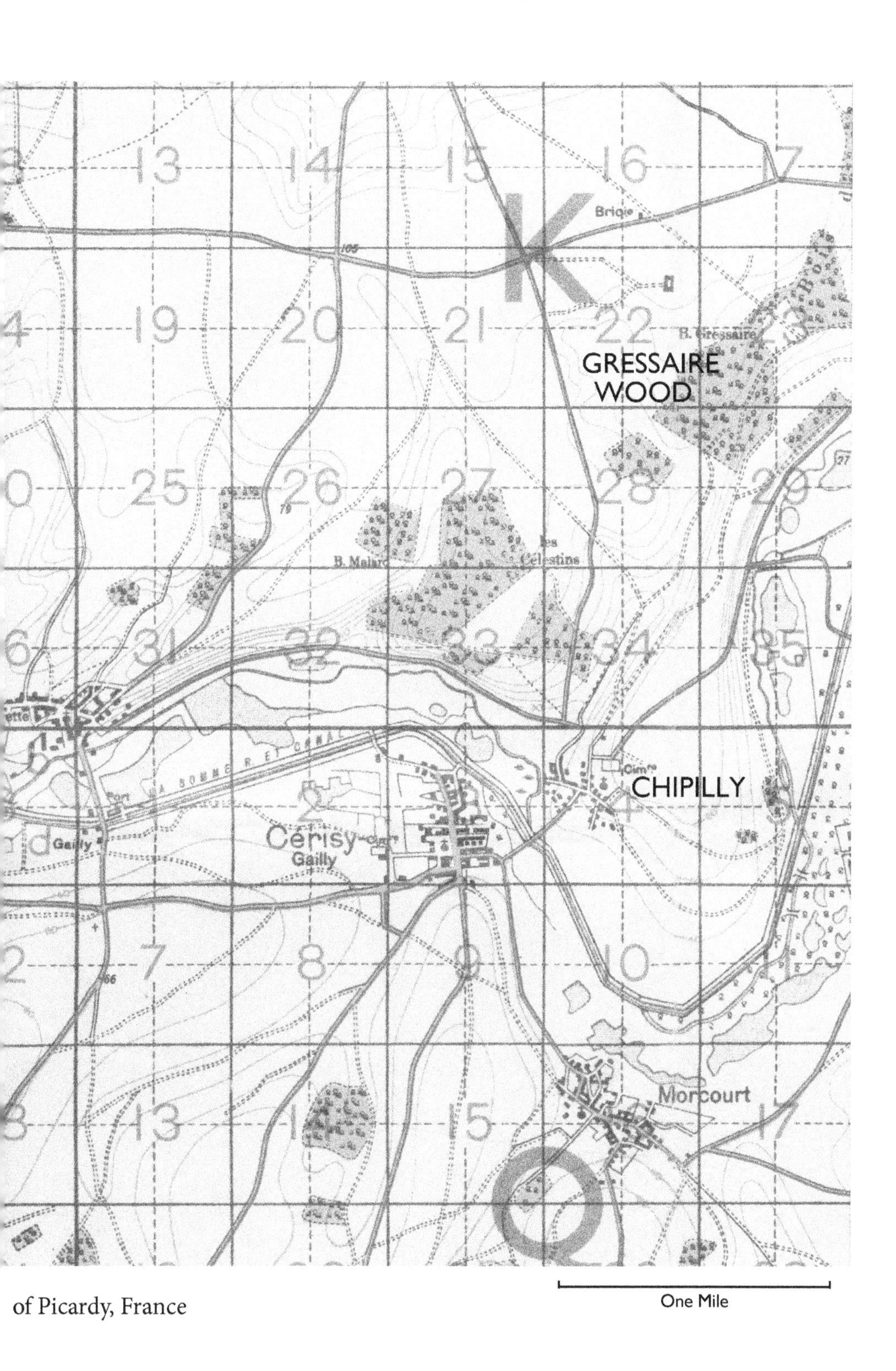


of Picardy, France

# JUNE 1918

# Chapter I

*"Hey, Tommy!"*

David Pearson, private in General Rawlinson's Fourth Army, stiffened slightly at the words, shouted clearly over the din of the humid, crowded *estaminet.* He'd been to the little public house before, but only once or twice, and then with chums from his company; everyone fancied the proprietress' niece, Nicole, who was rumored to be the only pretty girl left between Amiens and the front. Having just returned from a spell in the reserve trenches, he'd thought it a spot of luck to get a lift here in a lorry, but now...

"Tommy!" the loud voice insisted, and David, wary of its tone, lowered his eyes and started edging slowly toward the door. Before today, he'd never set eyes on a Yank, but now he found himself alone and adrift in a sea of Sammies – huge, all of them, and they seemed a mean and surly lot. He felt quite conspicuous, and a bit shabby, in his worn, dirty khakis, surrounded by the Americans' crisp, clean new uniforms.

"Tommy!" the voice repeated decisively, and abruptly David changed his mind and wheeled about. Like it or not, the honor of the British Empire was at stake. Why weren't they saving their energy for the Boche? He had nearly achieved the doorway, and thus escape from the heat, the smoke, and the press and smell of bodies, but now he faced back in the direction of his tormentor, a dark-haired giant who was staring intently his way.

"D'you mean me, then–" he began evenly, only to be drowned out by a cheerful, simultaneous *"What?"* from somewhere nearby, off his left shoulder. It was another Yank, rather different from the others – fair of hair and face, with large, deep-blue eyes and an open, pleasant look. He too was taller than David, though perhaps not by so much as most of his mates, and he appeared to be closer to David's age of eighteen.

The dark-haired Sammy continued to look David's way – or perhaps he was calling to the other man, after all. "I wancha ta meet somebody!" he shouted toward both of them, and David, still more hesitant, began again:

"Who–?" But the blond Yank pronounced the same word with far more vigor and volume. This time he noticed David, and explained "He means me" in the friendliest of fashions, with a hint of amusement.

"C'mon, Flower, get over here!" came the loud, persistent voice.

"I'm not over *here,* Carson," the fair Sammy retorted happily. "I'm over *there.*"

Then, to David's amazement, he began to sing, in a rich, clear tenor that carried over the hubbub:

*"Over there, over there,*
*Send the word, send the word, over there"*

The whole crowd of Sammies, and even Mme. Lacroix and Nicole, began to join in:

*"That the Yanks are coming, the Yanks are coming,*
*The drums rum-tumming everywhere"*

The tune was not an unfamiliar one to David; occasionally during the past few months he had heard his own fellow Tommies sing it, as if by so doing they could make their new allies materialize on the spot. But now that the Sammies at last were here in the flesh, it resonated differently. Although David was grateful for the respite from what he still regarded as a near row, he was in no mood to sing, much less linger. Seizing the opportunity to retire quietly, he squeezed out the door as the crowd concluded:

*"We'll be over, we're coming over,*
*And we won't come back 'til it's over over there!"*

and then started all over again.

David blinked momentarily, his eyes adjusting to the silvery light of the prolonged June dusk in Picardy. He thus was caught unawares when another huge Yank, who stood at the front of a line of still more Sammies awaiting admittance to the *estaminet*, shouted, "Hey, Tommy, what were *you* doin' in there?"

"Yeah, don't you know this is an *American* place tonight?" another one, two behind the first in the queue, demanded with a glower. He slurred the name of his home country so that it sounded like "Uh-m-u-r-r-i-kuh."

"Sorry." David shrugged, offering his most agreeable smile. "Di'n't know." He had as much right to be there as these Yanks, of course, and he wasn't afraid to fight if need be, but he wasn't up to a row. There were so many of them, all bigger and, apparently, older.

"Tommy's afraid to fi-ight," the head man said in a singsong. "That's why we had to come o-ver."

David, several strides past the Yank, turned round, gorge rising; nevertheless, he searched for the most neutral phrase he could muster: "You should save it for the Jerries, mate."

"Tommy's afraid to fi-ight." Now the third man in line, who stood nearer to David and may have been the largest specimen of humanity he had ever encountered, took up the chant, as well as a step or two in his direction.

"Aw, c'mon, Sanders, take it easy" came a cajoling voice from the doorway. It was the blond, singing Sammy, who jerked his thumb toward the interior of the *estaminet.* "Room for two more." The lead man in the queue, the one who had picked the quarrel with David, disappeared inside, along with the man who had stood behind him.

So, too, did David disappear, not wasting a second opportunity to withdraw. Seething, he walked briskly up the familiar rutted main street of Rainneville to the northern edge of the village, the laughter of the line of Americans burning in his ears, until a rumble to the east diverted his attention. Last light meant evening stand-to, and already the artillery was sounding. Not fifteen miles from here, chaps he knew were standing on the fire-steps of their trenches, peering out into no-man's-land. David had been up the line less than two months, but already he could tell the difference between artillery fire and thunder, even on a night like this.

"Tommy!" The pause to listen had proved fatal; one of the Sammies had come after him. David clenched his fists and prepared to stand his ground; but it was the friendly blond Yank, only him and no one else. He trotted to a halt just in front of David, breathing barely labored, and asked, "Why'd you run away?"

The tone remained amiable, but the choice of words revived David's intense resentment. Weeks of suppressed emotion erupted unbidden. "Run away? *Run away?*" he shouted with great agitation. "Tommy's afraid to fight? D'you not hear those guns?"

"Guns!" David could not tell if the suddenly bewildered Yank, who took a step backward, was stunned by his fury, the mention of artillery in the vicinity, or both. "Where?"

With the sure sense of direction that never deserted him, David pointed north and east, toward the River Ancre and Thiepval Ridge. "There! 'Tisn't thunder, Sammy. It's Moaning Minnies and five-nines. Our blokes are sitting under that. Tommy's afraid to fight?"

"It wasn't me that said that," the Yank replied, placating, taking a step back forward, but David didn't hear him.

"Run away? Tommy's afraid to fight? What d'you know about it? Why, Colin *died* under those guns–"

"I – I'm sorry. Who was Colin? A friend of yours?"

The simple decency of the question broke through David's rage. Trembling slightly, he turned away from the American. "It's not important." After a pause, he added, "See 'ere, Sammy, I must get on–"

"Don't go," said the Yank, cutting directly in front of him. "I've never met an Englishman before." David still looked down and away. "Who was Colin?" he repeated. "Your friend?"

David's throat constricted. "Me brother."

Reflexively the Yank placed a hand on David's shoulder, murmuring, "How can you say that's not important?"

David was still staring at the ground, fighting to keep control in front of this stranger, this foreigner. "'Cause in this bloody war, it's not," he replied bitterly. "'E was only one of many. Thousands – millions, per'aps." More softly, he added, "Even in me own family, 'e's only one of two we've lost. Now it's only me."

David heard a long, hard exhale and felt the Yank's hand grip his shoulder more tightly. "Two brothers dead? I'm… that's–"

Touched by the American's generosity, David looked him in the eye and simultaneously, briefly, patted the hand on his shoulder. "You've a large 'eart, Sammy."

The tall blond man smiled, and removed his hand. "Why do you call us 'Sammy'?"

"Why do you call us 'Tommy'?"

"You don't like it?"

"Gorblimey! We're proud to be Tommies!"

"Well, we don't like being called Sammies."

"You don't?"

"No. So how come you do it?"

David shrugged. "'Aven't a notion, really. Uncle Sam, I suppose. We mean no 'arm. 'Ave to call you something. Is Yank all right, then?"

"Yank's all right with me, but some of our Southern boys don't like it much. We're the Doughboys."

David snickered. "You're what?"

The taller man frowned and repeated, "Doughboys."

"D'you bake bread, then?"

"No!"

"But where would a name like that come from?"

"I don't know." The Doughboy's visible irritation abated. "Anyway, you can call me Tommy."

"But you're not a Tommy. You're American."

"It's my Christian name. Thomas. But everybody calls me Tommy." The Yank smiled broadly. "That's why Carson was calling me, when you thought he was calling you. Funny, huh?"

"But di'n't I 'ear 'im call you 'Flower,' too?"

"That's me, too," the American said with a nod, offering David the hand that lately had rested on his shoulder. "Tommy Flowers. Private, 33rd Division, United States Army. 66th Infantry Brigade, 131st Infantry Regiment–"

There was more, but David cut it off by grasping and shaking the proffered hand while responding, "David Pearson. Private, 58th Division, 175th Brigade, 12th London Battalion. The Rangers?"

The name of the Rangers meant nothing to Tommy, but he asked eagerly, "You from London, Dave?"

"It's David. Davey, I s'pose, if you must. I'm from a village called Dunster, in Somerset, though me mum's from Bristol, which you're more like to 'ave 'eard of, per'aps. But is your name 'Flower' or 'Flowers'? Di'n't your man Carson say–"

"That's what they all call me: 'Flower of Iowa,' 'cause I'm from Iowa. So I guess that makes you 'David of Dunster.'"

David scowled slightly in response as the village church bell, in defiance of its proximity to the front, began to peal. "Nine bells," he commented after they had silently counted it off together. "In 'alf an hour the just-a-minute will close."

"Just a minute?"

*"Estaminet."* When Tommy's look remained blank, David added, "The pub?"

"Oh, the tavern! What did you call it?"

*"Estaminet.* It's the French word."

"Before that. Didn't you say 'just a minute'?"

David gave a wry smile. "Sometimes we make our own words for things."

"There," Tommy said, jabbing a finger at him. "I knew you could smile. You should do it more often. You have a nice smile," he added, showing his own yet again.

David was glad the dimming light masked his schoolboy embarrassment. To cover it further, he said, "I 'eard you Yanks were coming to join our lot 'ere. From Chicago, though, not Ioway. Would that be near to Chicago?"

"Sort of. Chicago's in Illinois. Iowa's across the Mississippi River from Illinois. I'm from a town in Iowa called Brooklyn."

"But I thought Brooklyn was in New York."

"There's one there, too. But my Brooklyn's in Iowa. Most of the 33rd is Illinois National Guard, but I'm a replacement." It struck David as strange to be hearing famous American place names in connection with a real person standing right there in front of him. "So where's Somerset, and Dunster, and Bristol?" Tommy continued. "And what are you doing in the London Battalion?"

"I'm a replacement too," David answered, "from the South West of England. The Rangers were all from London to begin with, but after they lost so many of their men 'ere on the Somme, they cou'n't be particular about where their new men came from. And then Jerry made 'is big push, back in March, and all the King's armies needed replacements. So they lowered the age to go to France."

"So you were drafted?"

"Cor, not! I signed on as soon's I could!"

"With two brothers dead already?"

"More's the reason! I was afraid I might miss the war."

"Me too. But your mother–?"

"Me mum and me sis knew I 'ad to go. Me dad's dead–" David stopped short, suddenly ill at ease about volunteering personal information when it had not been requested.

But Tommy rolled right on. “I have a sister too. Three of them, in fact–”

“I ’ope you don’t think I’m being rude, Tommy,” David interrupted, “but it’s beginning to get darker, and it looks like rain, and we’re still standing ’ere. D’you know where your billets are?”

“Pierregot?” Tommy responded half questioningly, pronouncing it “Peer-gott.”

“Pierregot,” David corrected gently; though no expert on the French language, he pronounced it “Pyair-goh.” “I’m at Molliens. We’re neighbors, then. It’s the same way. We can walk back together a ways, if you like.”

“I do like, David of Dunster. I do like.” With the Briton taking the lead, they headed downhill in the waning light, on the well-traveled main road out of Rainneville.

# Chapter II

Flowers remained troubled by the scene at the *estaminet*, and especially by Sanders' taunting of Pearson.

"I'm sorry about Sanders and the other boys," he told David as they walked along, passing and being passed by a steady stream of mules, caissons, lorries, and men, Tommy loping to compensate for his longer legs. "We all just got here yesterday, and we were on buses all day and the night before–"

"Buses? Don't you mean lorries?"

"I guess, if that's what you call them."

"At least you di'n't 'ave to take one of those trains — '*Hommes 40, Chevaux 8*'."

"Oh, we already took one of those, too, to get to Abbéville. But tell me: does that mean they can fit forty men *or* eight horses in those cars, or forty men *and* eight horses?"

Although David knew full well it was the former, he answered, "No one knows."

"They smell like they fit in forty *chevaux*," Tommy quipped, pronouncing the word perfectly.

David laughed; but then his mood turned and he added, "They're as nothing to the smells at the front." When Tommy made no comment in reply, he said, "Your lot 'aven't been up the line yet then, 'ave you?"

Tommy shook his head, a little bit ashamed but even more excited. "No, though I hear we will soon. But you have, haven't you?"

David nodded. "Yes. I'm ready to fight Jerry, but… I can't say I fancy the life in the trenches much."

"How come?"

"It's more of a bore than anything, really. The mud, the smells, the noise - and you never sleep." David looked over at his companion. "Would you like to try a short-cut I know? It's a better short-cut for me than for you, really, but it's not so crowded as this road."

"I'm in no hurry. Lead the way." David did, cutting down a side path Tommy hadn't noticed. "You sure know this country well for being here such a short time," the Yank observed.

"I got a mem'ry for places. That's why they use me for a scout sometimes, on wiring parties and such. Someday soon, maybe, on a stunt."

"A stunt?"

"A trench raid."

"Oh." A loud clap and a sudden flash of light split the late twilight. Tommy looked to his newfound friend for reassurance. "That wasn't shells, was it?"

"No, thunder. Looks to pour buckets any minute now." With his head, David indicated a slight rise leading up off the side path they had taken. "There's an empty farm building up there – a stable, I think. We're still two miles, per'aps, from our billets. Shall we chance it this way, or go back to the main road, or ride it out in the stable?"

A few large drops already had begun to fall. "I say let's ride it out under cover if we can," Tommy answered, and they charged up the rise, with him leading, then abruptly coming to a halt as he realized he had no idea where he was headed. David caught up with him, nodded toward a clump of trees on their right, and Tommy took off again. When he drew close to the trees, there was no building in sight, and the copse suddenly loomed dark and dangerous. For a wild, unnerving moment in the now-pelting rain, Tommy thought he'd been led into a trap. Maybe David wasn't really a Tommy from Dunster, England. Maybe he was really a German spy, whose sole purpose that evening had been to lure away and murder a single Doughboy – him, Tommy Flowers.

The notion fled as quickly as it had arrived when David tapped him on the shoulder and pointed to a small mass just beyond and to the left of the copse. This time Tommy let David lead the way, to a windowless stone building which looked to be of a size to house about four *chevaux*.

In the deepening gloom and rain, David expertly located the door, pushed it open, and ignited a piece of straw with a tinder lighter, thereby revealing a section of stall with some old hay on the floor. The rest of the deserted stable, Tommy noticed as he followed inside, consisted of bare, hard ground, a few rusty and broken implements, and musty odors of livestock.

"It's lovely!" whispered David as he shook out the flaming straw and the place went dark.

"Why?" asked an unconvinced Tommy, standing stock-still as he heard David cross the room.

"A good roof, with cross-beams to brace it, a dry floor, and this." As David set fire to a second straw, Tommy could see he was using it to light an old oil lantern, something Tommy had not spotted during their first brief reconnaissance. "Not much in it, but it'll do for a while," David said, adjusting the lamp so it gave off the least possible glow without flickering out.

"Did you learn that trick at the front?"

"You wou'n't light a lantern at the front, mate. Blokes 'ave caught it between the eyes just for lighting a cig. 'Un snipers." With the rain now pounding heavily on the roof, David took off his cap and began to remove his tunic. "Poor devils up the line. What a night to be out in it."

"What are you doing?"

"I'm wet," David said simply. "That's why the cross-beams are a spot o'luck." He walked over to the hay, sat down, and began to remove his boots. Looking up at Tommy, he asked, "Will there be a roll call at your billets?"

"An hour before dawn," replied Tommy, still standing where he'd stopped.

"Morning stand-to," David said with an approving nod. "A good idea, to get you into the 'abit now."

"I guess so. Though the whole camp is still in an uproar."

"I should think so. Are you going to stand there all night?"

"You want to stay here the whole night?"

"Tommy, listen to that rain! We've a short walk when it lets up–"

"If it lets up."

"–and it's hours 'til dawn." As he spoke, David slowly unwrapped the puttees that ran from ankle to knee on both his legs.

"But why are you taking off your uniform?"

"You don't know, do you? In the trenches, they never let you take off your togs, ever. When they get wet – and they always do – they stay wet, and they stay on you. You're never dry." He gestured at the cross-beams. "This is 'eaven sent."

"Don't you think it's cool in here?" Tommy protested.

"Not after being outside in wet togs day after night," David replied, stepping out of his trousers and walking in his underclothes to one of the cross-beams, where he draped puttees, socks, and trousers next to his tunic and cap.

Barefoot, he padded back to the American and added, "And there's 'ay to sleep on. This is a bloody palace, Tommy. I thought you'd see that. I took you for a country lad. Are you a city boy, then?"

"No," said Tommy, finally removing his flat-brimmed field hat and beginning to unbutton his own tunic. "I told you, I'm from a small town in Iowa. I'm no city boy."

"Di'n't you at least go to Chicago to join the army?"

"No, I went to Camp Dodge, in Iowa. Then, when they needed replacements for the 33rd, they sent some of us down to Camp Logan in Texas. Then I was only there two weeks, and they put us all on a train to New York."

"Wou'n't know if you were coming or going by then."

"That's about right."

"Most of your chaps seem older'n you'n me. In their twenties, I'd say."

"They are. I lied to get in. I won't be nineteen 'til October, but I told them I was twenty-one."

"Most of our blokes are either very old, or more your and my age. There aren't so many of our lot left in their twenties, y'see."

"Oh."

David had removed his shirt, and was running a match up and down the seams. "Now what are you doing?" Tommy asked as he leaned up against a wall to remove his boots.

"Reading me shirt."

Tommy laughed. "What's the news?"

David smiled over at him and returned intently to his work. "Chats," he explained, and when he looked over again and saw Tommy's incomprehension, patiently added, "Lice?"

Tommy abruptly stopped uncoiling his puttees to recoil himself. "Lice?"

"You never 'eard of lice in Ioway?"

"Not on clean people – no offense meant."

"None taken. Clean people don't get chats in Blighty, either. But 'ere it's another story."

"Blighty?"

"England. You best get used to chats 'ere. You'll 'ave them soon enough. They di'n't tell you that in training? You cou'n't 'ave lived in trenches, then."

Tommy walked over to David and seated himself on the hay to remove his trousers, an amicable gesture that still kept him a safe distance from the Briton and his chat-infested shirt. "We had hard training," he replied defensively. "Good training. Back home, and here in France."

"When did your lot get 'ere?"

David's attention was still on reading his shirt. A surreptitious glance told Tommy that, small though David was, his upper body was fine, hard-muscled and healthy. "I told you, we just got here yesterday."

"I meant to France."

"Oh. We left New York the twenty-second of May, and we were ten days at sea." Tommy mimicked David by carefully draping his outer garments over the other cross-beam. Returning again to lie on the hay, he went on. "We took the *Leviathan.* I'd never been on a ship before, and this was a great big one. I heard it was a German luxury liner before the war."

"You were in a convoy, then?"

"Yes. And some U-boats came after us when we were practically to Brest. It was exciting, but we almost got tinfished. Felt like sitting ducks."

"Not a very good way to go under – torpedoed."

"I couldn't believe I'd come all that way just to drown with thousands of other boys, without ever even seeing France."

"You cou'n't be that unlucky." His "reading" finished, David shook his shirt vigorously to rid it of dead lice and, he hoped, eggs. "Damned bloody itching," he muttered as he put the garment back on. "D'you know 'oo it was your friend Carson wanted you to meet at the just-a-minute?"

"He wanted me to meet that girl – Nicole?"

"Blimey! You passed on the chance to meet Nicole?"

"Do you know her?"

"No one knows 'er, really. 'Er auntie watches over 'er like a 'awk. Wisht I knew 'er. 'Oo wou'n't want to chat up Nicole?"

"You mean make her lousy?"

As they both laughed, David reached over and gave Tommy a playful punch on the shoulder. "You're a funny one, Yank. But really, why di'n't you stay to meet 'er?"

"I've already got a girl, back in Brooklyn. Susan. I've known her all my life–"

"The girl next door?"

"Down the street."

"Really. What's she?–"

"–and I also wanted to talk to you."

"To me? You could 'ave met Nicole, but you wanted to talk to me?"

Tommy nodded. "I felt bad 'cause it seemed like the boys were insulting you. That wasn't right."

"That was right decent of you, mate. 'Twasn't your doing."

"And I've met a lot of Frenchmen, but like I said, I never met an Englishman before."

"Nicole's not a Frenchman, you silly bugger. She's a French girl. You're not just funny, you're daft. Barmy."

Tommy seemed taken aback. "Do you really think so?" he asked quite seriously, surprising David in his turn.

"No," the Englishman replied with another smile and an emphatic shake of his head. "No, Tommy, I don't. Don't take everything I say so to 'eart." David reached over to douse the light as the rain continued its steady thrum on the roof.

"Are we going to sleep already?" came Flowers' voice out of the ensuing blackness.

"We're going to try."

"But it's kind of early, isn't it? It still isn't even quite dark outside."

"So? Last light 'ere takes a long time. There's no such thing as too early for sleep. If you can rest, you rest. You'll see."

There was quiet for a minute; then Tommy said, "David? I'm cold."

"'Well, if you knows of a better 'ole, go to it.'"

"Hey, that's a cartoon! I've seen that."

"Brilliant, these Americans."

"I'm still cold."

"It's all right for you to move closer, if you like. Our bodies will keep us warm."

"But you've got chats."

"Oh, excuse me, then! Suit yourself."

"Don't be mad at me, David. I didn't mean anything personal."

"I know, Tommy. You wou'n't do that. But be a good lad now and keep quiet."

# Chapter III

Flowers had liked the dark-haired little Tommy with the soulful brown eyes from the moment he'd seen Pearson respond to Carson's call – although taking an instant liking to people was nothing new for him. Lying wide awake and as still as he could, his arms folded behind his head, he listened as his new friend's breathing quickly fell into the regular rhythm of sleep.

David had been right: Tommy was a farm boy, more or less. Though he had grown up in town, he knew his way around farms, and had slept in a barn more than once in his life. But this place looked, sounded, and smelled completely alien to him. In Iowa, everything smelled fresh, clean, and new: the hay, the wood used to construct the buildings, even the livestock. Here everything seemed musty, damp, and old. The hay was stale, and the walls were stone, cold and moist with strange, ill-smelling greenish patterns on them.

The steady rhythm of the rain finally began to lull him to sleep. Just as he was drifting on the edge of it, he distinctly heard a noise like crunching, and then another.

Instantly alert, he assumed a tense concentration, and was rewarded with two, then four more of the crunching sounds. He felt the hair on his neck, then his arms, then his legs, stand on end. An unreasoning fear swept over him: they were miles behind the line, but what if it was a Hun? He and David were only a couple of miles from their camps, but suddenly he felt as if they were far from anywhere.

You're a soldier, Tommy, he began to repeat silently to himself. You're a soldier, and you're here to fight, and die for your country if necessary. How can you be a soldier and be afraid?

Although he continued this voiceless chant, the fear, now verging on panic, still gripped him. Then, with no warning whatsoever, a shattering crash reverberated through the little stable, accompanied by a brief, brilliant flash. Tommy's taut senses snapped, and he screamed; at the same moment, David, ripped from a sound sleep, began to yell incoherently, until he rapidly reached total wakefulness.

"Wha–? What?" David finally began to form real words as, heart racing, he sat up, realizing and remembering where he was – and where he was not.

"David?" Tommy's voice came out of the darkness, barely above a whisper. "Was that a shell?"

Tommy could actually hear David sniff the air. "No. Thunder again. That loud, it would 'ave been close enough we could smell it." David lay most of the way back down, propped up only by his elbows. After a pause, he asked, "Are you all right, Tommy?"

There was another pause. "I think… I think I heard something outside."

David took a long moment to consider that. "I 'ear nothing but the rain. What was it?"

"It was… crunching sounds."

"Gorblimey!" Tommy heard David summarily reach over and strike his tinder lighter, then saw him flicker the lamp alive.

"Do you think someone's out there?" Tommy asked, still whispering.

David was up and stalking about the small space, peering carefully everywhere. "More like some*thing*. And in 'ere."

"Some*thing?*" In his mind, Tommy tried to picture French ghosts.

"Rats, mate."

Now the Yank sat up, startled. "Rats?"

"Yes. I've 'ad me bloody fill of rats, and you will soon enough, too."

"Any is enough."

"You best get used to them, too." David came back over and sat down, placing the softly glowing lamp between them. "But not 'ere. There's none 'ere."

"Then what was outside?"

David, unconcerned, shrugged. "Cow, per'aps. 'Oo knows?" He looked searchingly at the American. "Are you all right, Tommy? You're shaking."

"I'm cold," Tommy replied. There was a prolonged pause; then, in a very low voice, he added, "And I guess… I reckon I was just a little scared."

"It's too soon for you to be scared, or cold," David said jocularly. "Soon enough you'll be both all the time."

This did not have the desired effect of restoring Tommy to good cheer. Downcast still, he asked, "Do you think I'm a bad soldier, David?"

"Now, don't go getting the wind up. You'll be all right. You'll see." David lay back down in the hay.

Tommy, still sitting up, thought long and hard, then swallowed. "David? Can we sleep closer together?"

"I told you we could. You said I got chats."

"I don't care anymore. You said I'm gonna get 'em anyway."

"Well, come over 'ere, then," David said as he turned out the lantern. "I don't bite, even if me chats do." There was a rustling as Tommy pulled closer. Though they weren't quite touching, David said, "You're still shivering, Tommy. I can feel it." Without asking, and without saying anything more, he put his arms around the bigger man.

"You're shaking some, too."

"Per'aps I am." There passed a long minute as the heat of their bodies warmed them both, then David began slowly stroking Tommy's hair. "There, there. It's all right now."

Tommy said nothing, but wrapped his own large arms around David to pull him closer yet. It was a strange new sensation. As an only boy with three sisters growing up in a large house, he had always slept alone. Even in the army's close quarters he had, to date, always had his own bed. Now he could feel the bristles of David's cheek, the way as a little boy he had felt his grandfather's mustache and beard cutting into his face when the old man bent down to kiss him. But David's stubble was much lighter, like hundreds of tiny pinpricks that didn't really hurt at all. Thinking of the two or three times Susan had allowed him to kiss her, Tommy could remember the warm, soft feel of her in his arms, and her sweet, clean, vanilla scent. David was altogether different – not so sweet, hard here, soft there – but every bit as warm; indeed his breath, slightly sour with the wine he had been drinking at the *estaminet,* was hot on Tommy's neck.

For his part, David had grown up the youngest of three brothers, and the Pearson family was fortunate to have the small rooms over the storefront in the cottage they rented. He was well used to sharing a bed with other boys or young men. But Colin and Doug lived now only in his nightmares. He responded easily and in kind to Tommy's holding him close. Relaxing, the two of them fell asleep still intertwined.

Some natural ability that David couldn't explain, which had emerged only since he'd come to France, ensured that they did not oversleep. His still-tired eyes blinked open and traveled slowly to gauge the light in the room. He could discern, in a way that would have been imperceptible to him back home in Dunster, that the light in the windowless stable was changing, though he knew it was still dark outside. Dawn, he reckoned, was not two hours away. He and his companion needed to push on.

In moving his eyes to check the light, he had not moved his head. He couldn't, in fact, not very easily, because his head was effectively wedged between the powerful forearms of the slumbering American.

David's every muscle felt stiff. As his arms, which were free, moved slowly down his own body, he realized he was stiff elsewhere. David was someone whose prewar life had been spent poised between working-class matter-of-factness and lower-middle-class Victorian prudery. But on the business of a wake-up erection requiring a pee, the practicality won out. Far from being embarrassed, he just wanted to take care of the matter, and promptly.

There remained the issue of disengaging his head. He could shout or slap Flowers awake, and probably should, but depriving the Yank of even a few extra minutes' sleep in that way seemed a rudeness. He could try to push his way out, with probably the same result, or it might prove futile. Tickling Tommy seemed a kinder option; it might get him to relax without waking him. David slowly moved a hand up under the other man's arm and began to drum his fingers there, very lightly.

Whatever prompted the instinct, it worked. Tommy laughed out loud, sighed with extravagant luxury, and opened his arms, stretching them out wide. David quickly wriggled free, though as soon as he did, he found himself oddly sorry. Mostly it was a question of warmth; as he jumped up, he began to shiver from the lack of heat in the stable.

He tiptoed over to the cross-beams and felt his clothes – still a little damp, but drier than they'd usually been for much of the past six weeks. Next he took care of his most pressing business in the far corner; then he dressed quickly and relit the lamp. His ears and nose told him they were in luck; though the smell of fresh rain was omnipresent, the silence said that precipitation had stopped for the time being. "Tommy!" he whispered to the still-sleeping Yank. That had no effect, so he repeated the name in a normal tone of voice; still no movement.

He repressed a passing, peculiar urge to kick the American, and instead knelt down and regarded him in the lamplight. Flowers really was a charming fellow, like a very big boy. Without thinking, Pearson reached over and tousled the other man's blond hair. That caused Tommy to gradually waken. "It's time we pushed on, Tommy," David said quietly.

"Oh," Tommy said with a start. He sat up. "Sorry."

"No need to be sorry. Just get up."

With a powerful push of his hands, Tommy sprang into a standing position. Then he froze when he realized he had his own considerable wake-up erection, discernible beneath his underwear even in the dimness.

"Well, go on, get dressed," David snapped as he rose from his own crouched position.

"I–" Tommy said, scarlet in the lamplight, unable to stop looking at himself.

"Over there, in the corner," David said peremptorily. "That's where I did." Remembering his first encounter with Tommy, he suddenly sang, in a much better humor,

*"And we won't get going 'til you get going over there!"*

"Oh," Tommy repeated, feeling hopelessly foolish as they both laughed. Stumbling over to the indicated place, he caught the faintest whiff of urine. To his consternation, when he exposed himself to the wall, he started to get even harder. Interminable seconds passed. At length he remarked over his shoulder, "David, I can't, with you here."

"Oh, honestly! What are you going to do in a trench with a 'undred other men? 'Excuse me, I 'ave to go out to no-man's-land to take a pee, 'cause I can't 'ave no man around when I do'? Right!"

The scorn in David's voice stung, but the sound of the door closing behind him gave Tommy the immediate release he needed. Once he finished, he dressed in a rush, picked up the lantern, and pushed the door partway open, only to strike a startled David, who was standing just on the other side.

"What–?" David began; then, in a fury, he pushed the bigger man, lantern and all, back inside the stable with him. "What'd you do that for?" he demanded.

"What?" Tommy responded, angry himself. "What did I do now?"

"You took the light outside."

"I didn't know what you wanted me to do with it! Is it dangerous? Are there Germans?"

As tense as David had been a moment before, he suddenly went limp. "No. No 'uns 'ere. I don't know what got into me. You got me wind up, I suppose. But it's not a good 'abit to be prancing about in the open with lanterns."

Tommy replaced the lantern on the floor with great care, then straightened up. "I feel so stupid, David. You must think meeting me's been a complete waste of your time."

The straightforward statement caused David to respond with an equal, uncharacteristic directness: "Actually, I've been glad for your comp'ny."

At that, Tommy smiled a very large smile. "So, we can be buddies?"

David scratched his head, behind his ear. "I don't see why we cou'n't. For now, our billets are close by each other."

They looked at each other in mutually pleased surprise; then David, suddenly anxious, added, "You wou'n't tell anyone about this? That we stayed out?"

"Of course I won't! Will you?"

"Cor, not." They smiled at each other, co-conspirators. "All right," David said decisively. "Out with that light, then, and let's be off."

As they returned to the path, heading downhill again, Tommy's step turned noticeably jaunty. "What's got into you?" asked an amused David.

"I feel like the whole adventure's finally on!"

"What, the war, you mean? But why now? It cou'n't get any quieter than this."

"It's just that now it all seems real. Here I am, in France, close to the front, on my way back to camp with my best buddy – who's English." He put his hand on the back of David's neck and kept it there for a bit as they walked along.

"Cor, you are a loony, you know that? I think we're only chums so you can say your best pal's a Tommy."

"Not a chance."

For a few minutes they continued along in companionable silence, their senses stirred by the fresh smells of a rain-swept countryside in early-summer bloom.

Abruptly Tommy asked, "Hey, Davey! You killed any Jerries?"

"Killed a Jerry? I've 'ardly seen any!"

"But you said you've been in the trenches."

"I 'ave. That doesn't mean I've been over the top."

"But you said you scouted for wiring parties."

"And never sawr a Jerry when I did. A wiring party's not the same as going over the top. Mostly, you stay in your trench all day and all night, and they stay in theirs. You're not going to lay eyes on Fritz, except through your periscope, per'aps."

"So nothing happens at all?"

"Oh, I wou'n't say that. Things 'appen, all right. One bloke I knew 'ad 'is 'ead blowed off."

"You don't – really mean that – blown off."

"Don't I just? 'E was looking out from 'is firestep and 'e raised 'is 'ead up a little too far. Usually 'un snipers'll get you when you do that, but this time Jerry 'ad a Maxim working. Two sweeps o'that, and most of the poor sod's 'ead was gone."

Tommy was watching trees and bushes undulate in the pre-dawn dimness as they walked, inhaling the fragrance of – could it be lilacs? It didn't fit with what David was telling him. "That sounds horrible."

"You want 'orrible? *Shells* is 'orrible. Machine guns and snipers are bad, but if you use your 'ead, you can try to 'ide. Shells are the worst."

"There's no way to figure out how to hide from shells?"

"You 'ear that whistling, you 'it the ground and 'ope it's not too close. But that's not really 'iding, is it?"

"But – maybe there's less of a chance it'll kill you."

"They say you got a chance if you 'ear it. But the one that's got your name on it, you never 'ear it coming."

"But if you do?"

"You 'ope it misses you, or you 'ope for a Blighty wound."

"A… an England wound?"

"Bright lad! One what'll send you back 'ome without 'urting you too much."

"How do they know you never hear the one that kills you?"

David paused to consider that. "Don't know. 'Tis what they say, but 'oo can testify if it's true? They're all dead, aren't they?"

The two of them laughed, but Tommy's curiosity about trench life was sated for the moment. "What's Dunster like, Davey?"

"What, are you changing the subject?"

"Yes."

It was the kind of direct answer David seldom heard in the British Army. These Americans made it all seem so easy. You asked them a question and they actually told you what they were thinking. "All right, then, we'll talk about 'ome. It's a quiet little town, with a castle and–"

"A castle? A real castle?"

"Well, yes, but it's really quite an ordinary one."

"Ordinary! A castle?"

"Yes. 'Aven't you ever seen a castle?"

"Where would I, in America?"

"I know your country 'asn't got them, but they're all over France. Only they call them *châteaux* 'ere. There's some nice ones about – there's one in Molliens, in fact – but most I've seen 'ere 'ave been ruint by the war. It's sad, really." Tommy said nothing, and David added, "Tell you what, mate. If we live through this bloody thing, you should come 'ome with me to see Dunster. Then, when you go back to Ioway, you can tell your Susan you sawr a real English castle."

"Is that a deal? 'Cause I know we're both going to live through this war."

"Oh, you do? And 'oo told you that?"

Tommy shook his head. "Nobody needed to. I just know."

"It's a good attitude, you know. They say if you start talking like you're going to get kilt, then it comes true."

"'They say' this and 'they say' that. What else do they say?"

"They say it's rotten bad luck to get kilt on a Friday."

Fooled for a moment, Tommy pondered this, then burst out laughing. "You're a real card, David."

"I'm not a card. I'm a Tommy, Tommy." They both giggled over that, then David added, "Anyways, the offer stands."

"Good. I'll hold you to it."

"Look 'ere. We're back to a main road."

As they stepped out onto the wider thoroughfare, Tommy observed, "There's a lot less going on than before."

"The rain probably drove everyone off, if they di'n't 'ave to be out. Blimey, this road's turned to mud worse than the one we were on."

"I noticed that, too," Tommy said, looking with concern at his boots, now covered with a chalky slime.

"Anyways, mate, 'ere we are." David pointed to his left. "This road forks just down there. Take a right, and Pierregot's up the 'ill." Pointing to his right, he added, "I go that way."

"I guess this is good-bye for now, then. Do you remember how to find me?"

"You were 66th Brigade, 131st Regiment?"

Tommy's eyes widened and he smiled. "How'd you remember that?"

"I got a mem'ry for numbers like I do for places."

"It's also 2nd Battalion, Company E."

"Cor, your American divisions are big. What about me? 'ow are you with numbers?"

"Not that good. But I remember the London Rangers."

"That's all you'll need, then. Well, so long–"

Unexpectedly, David felt the bigger man's arms clasp around his body, not unlike the way he had spontaneously embraced the shivering American in the stable. But as the Englishman started to return the hug, an indeterminate sound down the road made them both jump, and break off quickly. Without looking back, Tommy headed up the road to Pierregot with a quickly muttered, "Goodbye, Davey."

"Goodbye… Flower of Ioway," David called softly after him, not sure if the Yank could even hear him.

# Chapter IV

The tiny village of Pierregot, nestled in precarious safety on a hilltop two miles across the valley from Rainneville and a mere dozen miles or so behind the front line, already had been quite overwhelmed by the British Army well before it had been selected to play host to the 66th Brigade of the 33rd U.S. Division. While the 33rd's officers mostly had managed to lodge in houses in town or on the closer-in farms, most of the privates, like Flowers, were sleeping on the ground in two-man tents, on the northern edge of town.

"Flower of Iowa!" Harry Carson hissed as Tommy tried unsuccessfully to creep unnoticed into the tent they shared. "Where have you been? We lost track of you at the tavern."

"Just-a-minute."

There was a prolonged pause, and then Carson whispered, "Yah?"

"Yah what?"

"You said, 'Just a minute.' What are we waiting for? Did you hear something?"

"No," Tommy replied with a laugh. "Forget it. Did you get to talk some talk with Nicole?"

"Not hardly. She don't know much English, anyway, and after three words between us, her aunt was shouting at her to pay attention to the other boys. Why didn't you come over to meet her?"

Tommy shrugged. "Doesn't sound like it would have done much good. Besides, I had other things to do."

"Oh?" Carson sat up further, interested. "Like what, for instance?"

"Just… things."

There was a short quiet, then Carson said, "You're never this mysterious, Tommy. What's got into you?"

"Nothing."

"Ain't you tired? It's almost time for roll call."

"No, Harry. I'm fine."

This produced a snort and a laugh from Carson, who lunged across the tent and punched Tommy in the arm, reminding Flowers of how Pearson had done exactly the same thing to him earlier that evening. "I knew it. Still waters run deep. You found another mam'selle and you're keeping her all to yourself."

Tommy just gave Carson a big, enigmatic smile. Let him think it.

★

Captain Henry Willnor was not pleased. The rotund, bespectacled West Point graduate sat at his desk – a teacher's desk at the old Catholic schoolhouse and *mairie* in Pierregot, a building from which students, teachers and the mayor had long since fled, and which was now functioning as part of brigade headquarters – and ruminated on the look of his soldiers at morning roll call several hours before. It already had been fairly clear to him that these boys were not really ready to fight, and the morning inspection had only confirmed that suspicion. But he'd be damned if a bunch of Redcoats (khaki notwithstanding, that was actually how he thought of the British) would show up the United States Army. Willnor deeply resented the 33rd being placed under that limey Rawlinson's command, and hoped fervently that the situation would prove as temporary as possible.

One of the problems the captain perceived in his men was an ongoing lack of spit-and-polish discipline. He was determined above all to maintain good order in the ranks, and was of the firm opinion that making an example of the occasional errant soldier was a mark of prudent leadership. An even better indication was the careful selection of that example; it was far more effective if he was somebody with real influence on the other men.

Thus Willnor had been both automatically annoyed and secretly pleased to note this morning the muddy boots of that fair-haired private the other men all fussed over, the one he'd heard them call "Flower of Iowa." The captain had seen it before: a soldier who was younger than his comrades, and possessed of an especially sunny disposition and/or unusually good looks, would become the unofficial beloved mascot of the company, the battalion, or even the regiment. Like the fine military mind he conceived himself to be, Willnor had carefully noted this recurrent phenomenon; examined it; and decided that, no less than singling out a company "goat," this was but one of the harmless methods by which men who knew very little about each other cohered into a formidable fighting unit.

So if such a "golden boy" (as the captain had dubbed the phenomenon to himself – and it seemed particularly apt in this case) could be made into an example when he stepped out of line, that was especially useful. Make someone like this Flowers toe the line, and all the rest would take even greater notice than they usually did in the gossipy life of soldiers on duty.

"Captain," came the voice of Corporal Daniel Dougherty, Willnor's indispensable adjutant (the captain's top aide should have held higher rank, but Willnor had found he could scarcely conduct business without the corporal). The officer looked up to see the dark-haired younger man with the steely green eyes snap a crisp salute. "Private Flowers is reporting as requested."

"Thank you, Corporal," Willnor replied with a desultory salute of his own, not rising from his chair.

Looking very much as he had a few hours earlier, the "golden boy" strode into the schoolroom and saluted. "Private Thomas Flowers reporting as requested, Captain, sir," he barked as Dougherty gave him a contemptuous look on the way out.

"At ease, Flowers." The private slightly relaxed his shoulders and folded his hands behind his back while otherwise remaining more or less at attention, a picture of correctness… at least from the knees up. "Do you know why I sent for you?"

"No, Captain, sir, I don't."

Willnor realized he should have given this scene more thought, for as he stood he attempted to pick up the nearest item he could find that resembled a riding crop or walking stick – and had to settle for a fountain pen. Sometimes, he thought, the airs the Redcoats put on were worth imitating. "Your boots, Flowers," he said sternly, shaking the writing implement as he pointed it, and thereby just missing staining the enlisted man's trouser legs, as several droplets of ink hit the weathered wood of the schoolhouse floor.

"Missed me, sir," the youngster said brightly. Momentarily dumbfounded, Willnor simply stared at the boy. It was such rank insubordination, talking to an officer in that manner (not to mention calling attention to a superior's error), but this Flowers did so with a smiling charm that somehow seemed to take the insolence right out of the remark. Small wonder he was a company favorite.

"Clean it up," the captain, recovering, ordered gruffly, and the boy snapped to:

"Yes, sir!" – but as Flowers looked around, equally frantic and dubious, for something with which to accomplish the task, the ink seeped into the ancient, cracked hardwood, leaving no wetness and precious little color change behind.

"Never mind about that," Willnor continued with a chop of his right hand, changing course and brooking no questions. "I was pointing out your boots, soldier. What do you have to say about them?"

For a moment, Flowers seemed to notice his boots for the first time; then he came stiffly to attention. "I'm very sorry, Captain, sir. It won't happen again."

"Why did it happen this time?"

"I – I have no excuse, sir."

"You didn't polish them and check to see they were clean before lights out?"

"No – no, sir. It was raining."

"In your tent?" Flowers started to speak, but the captain repeated more severely, "Never mind. You should be ashamed to answer roll call with muddy boots like those."

"I am ashamed, sir," the boy agreed much too readily.

"Be quiet!" Willnor shouted, noting that, far from acting spoiled because he was a company pet, this young man was responding exceedingly well to discipline.

"See to it that it doesn't happen again!" he added savagely, and Flowers appeared about to answer in assent, but remained silent as ordered. "I will give you a light punishment this time, Private," Willnor continued, "but not next time."

"There won't be a next time, sir."

"Didn't I tell you to be quiet?" the captain demanded, eliciting a satisfyingly intimidated look from the private. "You're damned right there won't be a next time! There shouldn't have been a first time!

"Now I have a mission for you," Willnor went on, and he saw the boy's eyes light up. No doubt Flowers thought he was about to be sent on some sortie behind enemy lines. "There's a major with the 175th limey brigade I have to send a report to, and I also have to send one to Colonel Cox. They're both at Molliens. Do you know where that is?" The soldier, tight-lipped, nodded. "Answer me, Private!"

"Yes, sir. I do know where Molliens is, Captain, sir."

"It's about 1030 hours now. You are hereby ordered to deliver these messages to Molliens, and be back here by 1200 hours."

"Sir?" Tommy asked, unsure he'd heard correctly.

"Are you deaf, soldier? I said be back here by 1200 hours. I don't care if you have to run double-time to do it."

"Done, sir," Tommy replied smartly, saluting and successfully stifling a smile of bewilderment.

"Corporal Dougherty will give you the messages. That is all."

"Thank you, sir." Tommy saluted again and strode out to Willnor's outer office – a passageway in the old school – where a smirking Dougherty handed him two sealed envelopes. Some instinct told Flowers not to confide in the corporal. But David had made it clear to Tommy that he had but a short walk to Molliens from the fork in the road where they had parted, so Tommy was bursting to ask someone how making a round trip of, he reckoned, about three or four miles on foot over the course of an hour and a half constituted any kind of punishment at all. He had no way of knowing that Willnor, newly arrived in the area like the rest of them, was a poor map reader, with an equally poor sense of distance and direction. Molliens was barely a mile from Pierregot, but the captain had read the kilometer figures on the local French maps as miles, and also had ignored the commas that functioned as decimal points in French numbers – therefore setting an example of Flowers by effectively giving him the better part of an hour free.

Impressed nonetheless by his interview with Willnor, Tommy rushed to his tent to clean the offending boots before setting off on his errand. Carson was there, already engaged in a cleaning task of his own – his Springfield rifle.

Tommy took a chamois cloth from his kit, wandered outside, and found a pail of muddy rainwater. He shook it gently so the silt sifted down, dipped the soft cloth into the relatively clear water that remained, and began to wipe down his boots just as Vernon Sanders came by. "Why are you bothering, Flower?" the big man asked. "Your boots are going to get muddy all over again."

"Captain noticed them at morning roll call. I'm not going to let it happen twice."

"You may not have a choice."

"What do you mean?"

"I hear we go up the line this afternoon."

"This afternoon? Today?"

Sanders nodded. "That's what I hear."

Tommy looked down at the two envelopes stuffed in his tunic. "I'll bet that's what these are about, then."

"What?"

"These messages I'm carrying to Molliens for Captain."

"We have wire and telephone contact with Molliens. Why would he send you there with messages?"

"I don't know, but he's sending me on foot. It's my punishment for the boots."

"Peculiar punishment," Sanders observed, and Flowers agreed:

"I thought so, too. But I'm sure Captain knows what he's doing."

"I sure would be interested to know what's in those envelopes."

"We aren't supposed to know. That's why they're sealed. They're none of our business."

"If it's orders for us to get killed, it's sure our business."

Tommy smiled, a look of deviltry spreading across his face. "You afraid of getting killed, Vern?"

"Watch it, Tommy. Afraid. Hm!"

Sauntering back down the main road out of Pierregot toward Rainneville and the fork where he had taken his leave of David, Tommy began to feel on familiar ground for the first time since his arrival in the area. Picardy really was a beautiful region, he thought appreciatively. Tall, sensuously waving bushes with dark-purple clusters of flowers told his eyes that his nose had been right the night before: lilacs were running riot over the countryside. Snowball bushes drooped under the fragrant weight of their own huge clusters of white flowers. The sky was of a shade like the blue of his mother's good china, and he could hear birdsongs altogether different from those he knew so well in Iowa. What a fine adventure to be here in such a country, on such a mission!

Tommy began to whistle as he marched along, first "Pack Up Your Troubles in Your Old Kit Bag," then an old song he had learned from his grandfather, which Grandad had told him he sang as he marched in the Civil War, the one that went, "Glory, glory, hallelujah." As he descended into the valley between Pierregot and Rainneville, the road was by no means empty, but he was blissfully oblivious of the other traffic – human, animal, and vehicular – concentrating instead on the sights, sounds, and smells of nature (though ignoring the considerable presence of horse and mule dung). His reverie, and his happy medley of humming, singing, and whistling, was broken suddenly when an Englishman in an odd-looking, partially upswept hat, approaching him from the other side of the road, shouted at him, "Hey, mate, don't you know any better songs?"

Tommy snapped out of his pleasurable trance and gave the man a closer look. He was old – probably thirty or more – with wavy, jet-black hair and deeply tanned and lined skin. "I'm sorry," the Yank said with an apologetic smile. "I'm American, and I'm new here."

"A Yank, eh? You should have learned some French songs by naow."

"I–"

"Haow abaout this one?

*Mademoiselle from Armentières, parlez-vous?*
*Mademoiselle from Armentières, parlez-vous?*
*Mademoiselle from Armentières,*
*She hasn't been fucked in fifty years!*
*Hinky-dinky parlez-vous?*

Tommy was struck speechless. He hadn't heard casual crude talk like that growing up. Of course he'd heard some – and even versions of this song – since joining the army; but this man was using such language in broad daylight, on a crowded road. Indeed, he was well into singing Tommy a second verse:

*Mademoiselle from Armentières,*
*Her pussy's the worst of all your fears!*
*Hinky-dinky parlez-vous?*

"Stop that!" Tommy cried impetuously.

"Eh? Do I sing that bad?" the Englishman asked, as Tommy realized to his horror that the man was a sergeant.

"Sorry, sir," Tommy said, snapping to and saluting. "I don't know what came over me."

The Englishman gaped at him, then burst into raucous laughter. "At ease, soljuh," he finally told Tommy, still chuckling. "You Yanks are a real piece o'work. What's your name, anywise?"

"Private Thomas Flowers, sir. 33rd Division, United States Army–"

"I know that."

"You do?"

"You're all 33rd, aren't you? Up here with Rawly?"

Tommy nodded, then asked, "Are – are you with the London Rangers, sir?"

"The – the London Rangers? Naow you *have* gone too far, mate. Calling me a Pom! I'm an Ozzie, you little bugger. You *have* heard of Australia?"

"Yes, sir. Sorry, sir. My mistake, sir."

"Certainly is. And stop callin' me 'sir,' Tommy – do they call you Tommy?"

"Yes, sir."

"Well, that makes for a good laugh, anywise. But I told you, it's not 'sir.' It's Jamie. Jamie Colbeck of the 11th Australian Brigade, Australian Corps, Gen'ral Monash."

"But aren't you a sergeant, Jamie?"

"Yes, I'm a sergeant. What abaout it?" Tommy, who could now hear how differently Jamie talked from David, just shrugged. Obviously this man had a much less formal bearing than his American NCOs. "Where you headed from, son?" the sergeant asked.

"Pierregot, sir – Jamie."

"That's where I'm headed naow."

"My captain – Captain Willnor – sent me on a mission to Molliens."

Colbeck smirked. "A mission, eh?" He peered quickly at a piece of paper in his hand. "So, tell me, Tommy, if you're goin' to Molliens, and you're comin' from Pierregot, what are you doin' on this road?"

"I'm – this is the way to Molliens. There's a fork, just down there–"

"But there's another road runs right from Pierregot to Molliens," Jamie said, pointing up the hill, then waving his arm to the right, where another town was visible on the ridge. "Can't you read a map?"

"Yes, sir, but–"

"Jamie."

"Jamie."

"Look at this, then." Colbeck watched as Flowers studied his map. "Are you shirkin' your duty, soljuh?" he asked, his voice suddenly stern.

"No, sir. Nobody told me there was another road. Captain told me I had to go to Molliens and back by noon. It was punishment."

"Punishment! And what was your crime?"

"My boots were muddy at roll call."

"Your boo–?" Jamie laughed again. "Oh, yes! I'm sure that'll cost us the war," he said, then, changing tone, added, "Bleedin' idiots."

Tommy felt compelled to defend his captain. "You shouldn't talk that w–"

"Don't tell me I shouldn't anything, Tommy. I don't give a fig for anyone above rankers. I've been in this war too long."

"And how long is that, Jamie?"

"More than three years." Jamie laughed yet again.

"Why are you laughing?"

"You should have seen your face, mate. Like you were lookin' at a bleedin' ghost. Which, maybe, you are. What's your battalion?"

"Second Battalion, 131st Regiment."

"Maybe I'll see you later, then. Run along to your errand naow. Sorry I int'rupted you."

"It was no interruption, sir," Tommy insisted as he saluted and turned with military precision back toward his intended direction.

"Tommy." The American turned back to look at the Australian. "You really didn't like my singin', did you?"

"You sing all right, Jamie."

"What, then?"

"I – didn't like those new verses very much, sir."

Colbeck grinned. "They're as old as verses can be, son. But I respect you for sayin' that. Be careful who you give an opinion like that to, though. It could get a lad like you in trouble."

"Thanks, Jamie."

"See you later, Tommy."

"I hope so."

"Hey. Try this one while you walk:

*Once a jolly swagman sat beside a billabong–"*

"Does that mean something indecent, sir?"

"You should know better than to int'rupt a superior officer, Private… A swagman is a drifter, like you and me. And a billabong's a water hole, like one a shell would leave, only there ain't no dead men floatin' in it to spoil the taste of the water."

That made Tommy gulp, but he asked, "How does the rest of it go?"

"I'm goin' to make you late for your big mission."

"That's not a problem, sergeant."

"If you call me Jamie, I'll sing the refrain."

"OK, Jamie."

Jamie recommenced:

*"Waltzing Matilda, waltzing Matilda,*
*You'll come a-waltzing Matilda with me–*
*And he sang as he sat and waited by the billabong,*

*You'll come a-waltzing Matilda with me."*

"That's real nice, Jamie."
The Australian winked at Tommy. "I'll teach you the rest of it later."

# Chapter V

Molliens – full name, Molliens-au-Bois – was a village about the same size as Pierregot, but a much better organized encampment, serving as it did as divisional headquarters for the Americans. Despite the greater complexity of the place, Tommy was able to locate Colonel Cox with dispatch. The colonel's adjutant took his envelope without comment, and tersely gave him general directions for finding the British major, who turned out to be attached to the general staff at the *château* of Molliens… which was on the way back to Pierregot, on the direct road Jamie had pointed out.

The *château* was the biggest building in the area, but rather plain, Tommy thought; if this was really a castle, he was not impressed. A stuffy little lance corporal staffing the desk of the major in question rudely snatched the envelope from Tommy's hand. When Tommy didn't immediately depart, he asked impatiently, "Well? What is it?"

"I was wondering if you could tell me where I might find the London Rangers, sir."

"If you have a message for them, I can take that, too."

"No, sir, there's no message."

"Then why are you looking for the Rangers?"

"I have a friend who's a Ranger that I'd like to see while I'm in Mol–"

"A friend?" the corporal interrupted sharply. "How is it you're friends with a Tommy? What kind of fraternizing is going on here? This isn't a tea party, Yank, it's a war. Who is–"

Luckily, at that moment a dignified older man with a white mustache came out the door of the office behind the corporal's desk. "What's going on, Jones?" he asked with a vague weariness that was reflected both in his voice and his eyes, which also showed a certain kindliness.

The corporal snapped to his feet and saluted, so Tommy saluted as well. "Major, sir! This Sammy brought you a message from his captain."

"A message from the Americans? What the devil?" the major muttered as he took the envelope, opened it, and scanned its contents. He looked up and over at Tommy, giving him a long, appraising glance. "I see your lot will be going up the line this afternoon, Sammy."

Tommy's heart leapt. "Will we, sir? I didn't know."

"Yes, well, no need to get too excited about it. It's just a test, in a quiet sector."

"But I want to fight the Germans, sir."

"Yes. Yes, of course, I'm sure we all want to fight the Boche. Don't worry, Private, you'll get your chance." While still gazing at Tommy, he shifted his voice back to the lance corporal: "And what were you discussing with the private just now, Jones?"

"Sir, I was reminding him of how serious the war is."

"Oh. Yes, I'm sure you were," the major said absently, still staring at Tommy. "Well, Private?"

Tommy hesitated. "Sir?"

"Is that all?"

"I – was looking for the London Rangers, sir."

"The Rangers? Why?"

"I have a friend with them, sir."

"A friend? You have a friend who's a Tommy?"

"Yes, sir."

"Oh, jolly good." The major turned to his aide. "Jones, kindly direct this soldier to the Rangers so he can find his mate." He turned back to Tommy. "We're awfully glad your lot is here with us, Yank."

"Thank you, sir," Tommy said with a smile. "It's good to be here."

"Yes, well. You'll excuse me, then." The major disappeared back into his office as the corporal grudgingly directed Tommy to the Rangers' encampment, the American thinking all the while about all the bad things he'd heard about British brass.

Following those directions, Tommy came upon a much less well put together area on the outskirts of the village, down the road from the *château* and in the direction away from Pierregot. Indeed, the place looked so shabby he thought maybe the nasty Corporal Jones had played a trick on him. While there were plenty of indications of human habitation, it currently seemed deserted. Finally he found one heavy-set, greasy-looking Tommy sitting by himself. It occurred to Flowers as he caught sight of the man that no one that short and fat would have been allowed into the American Army.

"'Ullo, Yank," the fat private hailed Tommy. "Whah ah yew 'ee-uh?" The man's accent was so thick the American could barely comprehend him.

"Is this where the London Rangers are?" Tommy asked.

"Ryne-juhs awwr-rawight."

"Where is everybody?"

"Naawt 'eee-uhhh."

"Did they go back to the trenches already?"

"Coah, naw'!" It sounded nothing like David's "Cor, not."

"Do you know where they've gone?"

"Thah aawull tykin' a baah."

"What?"

"A baah. Y'know, wi' waa'uhh." Tommy still couldn't understand him, so the man made scrubbing motions.

"Oh – a bath. Where?"

"Baah-'ouse."

Tommy got that. "And where is the bathhouse?"

"Tha-yeh." The man pointed to a nearby rise.

"Thanks." Tommy turned to go, then asked, mostly to be polite, "You don't get to go?"

"Doan' tyke baahs," the man said with a grin, showing a truly frightful set of teeth. "Bah fo' yeh." Tommy realized then that the man's statement had been unnecessary; his own olfactory had been telling him that all along, and now, suddenly, it registered to the point of near nausea. His fellow Doughboys had been complaining almost non-stop about the French since their arrival, but this man was as ripe as any *poilu.*

At the indicated rise, the mostly dusty and muddy terrain suddenly became verdant. As he approached the crest, Tommy began to pick up the sounds of many male voices, but also, he could swear, some feminine ones as well, which struck him as singularly impossible.

He was thus unprepared for the sight that greeted him as he reached the top: a green meadow filled with dozens of men, almost all of them naked, some lolling about in the grass, some standing in line at a large, windowless shed; and beyond that, another windowless building where women – some older, some closer to Susan's age, all of them fully clothed – were running in and out in full sight of the men, carrying armloads of clothes and laughing and giggling.

The men were a pretty scrawny lot overall; at best, some were slight of stature but sturdy, like David, whom Tommy was easily able to pick out, even from behind, in the line leading to, presumably, the bathhouse. Having found his friend, the American suddenly felt shy and awkward, standing there above the group so tall and so clothed; but one of the Tommies noticed him and pointed him out to the whole group, whereupon David shouted his name in recognition.

"Come on down!" his British pal called as an NCO in full uniform emerged from the shed and shouted, "Next group!"

In the time it took Tommy to amble down the hill to David, several men entered the first shed, including some of those who had been behind David in the line. "I've lost you your place" was therefore the first thing Tommy said when he drew up alongside David, avoiding an embrace this time, or even so much as a handshake.

"Oh, that's all right. I can get back in the queue," David said, unself-conscious as the sunlight and shade dappled his smooth, pale skin. "It's good to see you again, Tommy. But why are you 'ere?"

"I had an errand to run–"

"Splendid! D'you 'ave time for a bath, then?"

It occurred to Tommy that a bath might feel good at that. He hadn't thoroughly washed up since before boarding the bus at Eu, which seemed a very long time ago. "I've got probably half an hour or less."

"Well, come on, then – Poppert? Sergeant Poppert!"

The crusty-looking sergeant stuck his head back out of the bathhouse door. "Wot d'you want, Pearson?"

"Can me American mate take a bath with us, sir?"

"We've barely enough soap and water for usselves, Private."

"All right for that, Poppert. I can count. There's room for an extra. Be a decent 'ost."

"Wull, since we're near done, I s'pose it's awright. But mind your togs, Sammy, or someone'll run off with your nice clean unyform."

As Poppert disappeared back into the bathhouse, Tommy asked David, "Do people really steal uniforms?"

"Not 'ere they wou'n't. Maybe at the front, if someone got kilt wearing something too nice to bury."

Tommy didn't want to believe that; so instead he asked, "Then why did he say that?" as he began to remove his clothing. Ordinarily he'd feel a little strange about stripping out in the open, but in this case doing so made him like the rest of the men, and so more comfortable.

"'E means don't leave your unyform with the rest of ours, or it might get carried away. We get new underclothes after, and our tunics and trousers are cleaned."

"That's good, anyway."

"Not always. Sometimes what you get back doesn't fit, or it's got chats."

"I better keep an eye on my uniform, then, if I can."

"Just leave it out 'ere, Tommy. It'll be fine."

"How do you know?"

"I'll tell 'em not to take it."

"Tell them – tell who?"

"Why, the lovely ladies of the laundry, of course."

That was when Tommy, now naked like the rest of the men, noticed the washhouse women were only a few feet away – and they seemed to be staring right at him. "Now, ladies," David said to them with a wag of his finger, "don't be taking me chum's togs, savvy? 'e's not one of ours. *Non. Ne pas.*"

The women nodded, and covered their mouths and giggled, as Tommy colored – all over – in mortification. "Why are they staring at me, David?" he half whispered to his friend. "They weren't staring like that at any of you."

"Per'aps it's 'cause you're so much bigger, Tommy."

That comment only made it worse. "Would you – could you tell them to stop it?"

"Wou'n't know 'ow to, and keep it polite. But if you like, I'll stand in front – though I cou'n't cover much of the likes of you," David said agreeably, interposing his small, hard body between Tommy's and the prying eyes of the women.

"Who are they? Why are they here, with all of us with no clothes on?"

"Some are French, but most are Belgian. War widows, most. They've seen much worse than the lot of us as God made us." Somehow that made Tommy feel a little less self-conscious.

Suddenly Poppert reappeared and bellowed, "Last group!"

Tommy, David, and the remaining six men ducked out of sight of the women and into the shed. There Poppert handed each a tiny sliver of soap; then they lined up underneath a single, forlorn-looking, rusty iron pipe. "Soap up!" cried Poppert, and Flowers noticed a small metal bowl at his feet with slimy-looking liquid in it. The Tommies, each of whom had a similar bowl in front of him, began fiercely splashing the stuff on and soaping themselves.

"'Urry, Tommy, there isn't much time," David admonished as he noticed how leisurely his friend's lathering-up was going.

"How can you do that so fast?"

"I've 'ad more practice, and there's less of me. 'Ere, let me 'elp you. There's more of you to cover."

Once again, as in the stable, David didn't ask before touching Tommy. He started making wide circles on the Yank's back. The easy camaraderie of the whole scene he had stumbled onto had carried Tommy this far, but abruptly the feel of David's touch on his skin had a wholly unanticipated effect, generating a reaction that in turn caused him twice the humiliation he had just suffered with the laundry ladies. This was compounded when, inevitably, one of Pearson's colleagues noticed and shouted, "Look out! The big Yank's getting bigger!"

A couple of raucous follow-up comments were not even half complete before David sprang to Tommy's defense: "You would, too, 'Ardison, if you were thinking about all those ladies 'oo 'ad just been eyeing you in the altogether – but they wou'n't bother with the likes o'you."

"Bugger off, Pearson."

Before the discussion could proceed further in any direction, Poppert yelled "Water!" and Tommy, who had experienced showers as well as baths, tensed in anticipation of a warm spray. But what descended from the pipe onto each of the men in eight separate spouts was a thin trickle of ice-cold water. Tommy yelped in surprise and pain; even some of the others, presumably used to it, grunted at the contact with the frigid liquid.

David was whirling about like the toy top Tommy had played with as a little boy. "Got to 'urry this part, too," he called; and sure enough, the water had barely started when, just as suddenly, the trickling ceased.

Although half of Tommy was soapy and the other half was cold and wet, Poppert shouted "Everyone out!" and the group burst out the rear of the shed, back into the sunlight and the full view of the chattering women. All but Flowers immediately joined in a scramble for what they hoped would be clean underwear. When David turned around triumphantly with something that looked like it might even fit, he caught sight of his Doughboy friend and careened into laughter.

"You look like a beat dog, mate!"

"I'm *cold,* David."

"And you know I always take care of you when you're cold, don't you?" David said in a warm, intimate tone. "'Ere," he added, tossing Tommy a piece of cloth.

"What's this?"

"It's me towel. Don't worry. It's clean. No chats, I promise. Dry off, now."

As Tommy did, the sun suddenly felt warm and soothing on his body. He now saw why the other men had been lounging about; it was the most pleasant way to get completely dry. "D'you have time for a lie in the grass?" David asked him.

"Just a little."

"Come on, then," David said, clutching but not donning his prized new underclothes. They re-collected their uniforms, then lay down with their gear beside them, close enough to the other men to be part of the loose grouping, but apart enough to be by themselves.

"That was something," Tommy remarked.

"It's good to get a bath at all. Now you know what it's like, you'll 'ave the advantage over your mates their first time."

Tommy figured the American showers would be superior, but he didn't think that mentioning it was either wise or kind. Instead he said, "You're my mate."

"Right," said David with a grin.

At the sight, Tommy couldn't resist asking "David?" in a low voice.

"What?"

"How come you have such good teeth?"

"What, cor!" David flicked some grass at him.

"No, really."

David flushed, laughed nervously. "Why are you whispering? And why d'you ask me such a thing?"

Tommy looked uneasily toward the others, but they were paying no attention. "I – it's just – some of the other Tommies – and the French, too – they don't look like they've ever used a toothbrush in their life."

"Ah," David said with a nod, catching the Doughboy's meaning. "Probably 'cause most 'aven't, though they put one in our kits. Some of our lot think you

Yanks are strange, brushing your teeth all the time."

"But you must. You must not think we're strange."

David chuckled again. "Not for that, anyways."

"How come you use your toothbrush when most of the other Tommies don't?"

"I told you, me mum's from Bristol–"

"So people brush their teeth in Bristol?"

"No, but it's a port, y'see. People pick up foreign ways sometimes. Me mum picked up the 'abit as a girl, and she made us all do it – me brothers, me sis, and me."

"I'm glad."

"Now why would you be glad about something like that?" David asked idly, and Tommy was stymied; it sounded silly to say he wanted his friend to be better-looking than the others. When he failed to answer, the Englishman simply went on to something else: "'Ow about some dinner before you 'ave to go back?"

"I don't know. I already took some of your bathwater and your towel. I don't want to take food away from you, too."

"You wou'n't be taking it away. We'd share it."

"I've only got a little time left," Tommy demurred further, gauging the sun.

"It won't take long. Let's do."

As they dressed, then strolled back to the area where the fat Tommy had directed Flowers to the bathhouse, the American explained how he had come to be at Molliens.

"Maybe your captain di'n't really 'ave a mind to punish you, Tommy. Per'aps 'e was just saying that 'cause 'e needed someone to carry those messages."

"But why me?"

"Per'aps 'e liked that you said you were sorry and di'n't make excuses. Anyway, *I'm* glad you came – 'ere, 'ere's Muffett."

Muffett turned out to be the unlikely name of the obese Tommy. "Ahh s'pose yew uhll be wah-unh yew rahsh'n uhrr-ee, Pea'z'n," he said with a flash of his hideous grin.

"That's right, Muffett." David turned to Tommy with a conspiratorial wink and an altogether different sort of smile: "Muffett's our cook, y'see."

The thought of having to eat anything that this man had touched was too terrible for Tommy to contemplate. But the joke – he hoped it was a joke – became evident when Muffett handed Pearson a few tins, intoning, "Doan' ahsk vor nuh vor yuh frehn 'ere, 'cos theh ayun nah eksra."

This made no sense whatsoever to Flowers, but his British pal snapped, "I di'n't and I wou'n't. Come along, Tommy."

"Don't get in a stew," Tommy urged him as they strode away.

"No Maconochie's," David replied ruefully, shaking his head as he examined the tins. "There won't be any stew today."

"No, I mean, don't let yourself get bothered by him."

"'Oo's 'im? Oh." David was still studying his rations, as if by so doing he could turn them into something better. "You're right, mate. I shou'n't. But between 'im an' Poppert, seems like the 'ole King's army is going out of their way to be rude to you today."

"Your major was real nice. And you're the best friend a fellow could have."

David glanced briefly at him. "Go on with you."

"I mean it, Davey," Tommy said with the utmost sincerity as they sat down next to, and leaned against the wheel of, a caisson. "You know, I've never had a brother–" He had meant to say something from his heart, but he realized as soon as it was out how inappropriate it was in David's case. "Oh, God, David, I'm so sorry–"

"Don't be sorry, Tommy. It's true. You never 'ad a brother, and I don't 'ave none anymore."

Tommy gave him a sad smile. "Well. You've got me now."

David looked up with a much more cheerful smile. "So I do," he said, patting Tommy on the knee as he offered him a thick, whitish piece of… something or other.

"What is it?" Tommy asked, not entirely successful at hiding the apprehension in his voice.

"Why, it's a bit of biscuit, of course."

"Oh." The Yank made to bite into it, and thought at first he'd chipped his tooth.

"A little 'ard, isn't it?" David murmured sympathetically. "'Ere, try wetting it in some tea."

It made the biscuit just barely edible. Tea was not familiar to Tommy's palate, either, and he wasn't sure he liked the weakly warm, sugary brew. With foreboding he watched his friend open two more tins.

"Ticklers," David stated as he opened the first and offered Tommy some jam, which Tommy thought not half bad; but David muttered, "Plum and apple again. What a surprise! Just once I wisht it was strawberry."

"We get strawberry sometimes," Tommy said spontaneously.

"You do? Good for you." The second tin contained a strange red-and-white substance. "'Ere, mate," David said, extending it to Tommy. "You get bags on."

"What is it?" the Doughboy asked doubtfully.

"Bully beef, don't y'know. Never 'ad it?"

"No." It looked horrible – fatty and stringy. Tommy picked at a little piece of it, tasted it, and felt compelled to ask, "What do you get for dinner?"

"This *is* dinner, Tommy."

"No, I mean, your good meal–"

"This *is* the good meal, Tommy!" David cried angrily, snatching away the beef and biscuit. He sprang up as if ready to walk away. "Per'aps I'm not your brother after all. Per'aps I'm just a poor relation–"

"I'm sorry, David," Tommy, still sitting, said quickly. "I liked it, really. Can I have a little more?"

"All right for you and your patronizing, Sammy."

"David!" cried Tommy, now springing up, too. "I said I was sorry. I – omigosh!"

"What?" asked the still-cross David.

"I'm gonna be late getting back to Pierregot. I've got to run – and I mean run."

"Get a move on, then."

"Do you know a short-cut?"

"Di'n't you come by that road?" David asked, pointing back toward the *château.*

"No. I took the road you and I took, and–"

"You came the long way, then."

"I know."

"You know? Then why'd you do it?"

"I mean, I didn't know, but an Australian I met on the way told me."

"An Anzac? Hah! Best be careful of that lot."

"He was a little rough, David, but I liked him."

"Oh. I see. Your new best friend," said David, sitting back down. "Per'aps 'e's got better rations."

"*You're* my best pal, and you know it." David said nothing in reply, and Tommy added, "I'm not gonna leave here 'til you tell me you're not mad at me anymore." David looked up at him in surprise. "Then it'll be your fault when I'm late and the captain court-martials me."

That almost got David to laugh, but he held back at the last instant and said "You're daft," with a dismissive wave of his arm.

"So be it," said Tommy, folding his own arms and sitting back down. For a few seconds – precious seconds, in view of Tommy's tardiness – they said nothing and didn't look at each other.

Finally David said sharply, "Get a move on!" At length he looked over at the still-seated Tommy, locked eyes with him, and added, "...Mate."

As he leapt back to his feet, Tommy said, "Did I tell you – we go up the line this afternoon."

"No!" said David, himself jumping up and following the American as he headed toward the *château* and Pierregot. "Why would you do that?"

Tommy stopped. "What do you mean?"

"Keep walking. I'll walk with you a little ways." Tommy obeyed, and David went after him double-time. "What I mean is, why would you go up the line in the afternoon instead of after dark? It's much safer then."

"Your major said it was a quiet sector."

"I've known chaps kilt in quiet sectors, Tommy. Be careful. Please."

"I already told you, we're both gonna live through this war."

"But not if you're careless."

"I won't be. I can't be. After all, I've gotta have *you* come over to *our* camp for dinner when I get back," Tommy said with a grin and a finger pointed at David.

"If I'm 'ere."

"Stop talking that way."

"I only meant–"

"We're gonna fight side by side 'til the war is over. And that's that." Tommy looked again at the sun. "I've gotta start walking faster, Davey. Running, really."

"Do it, then," David replied, puffing a little bit. "I'll stop 'ere."

Tommy stopped again, too, and this time he was the one who didn't ask; he grabbed David and gave him another strong hug, right there in the middle of the road, at almost high noon. "Thanks for everything, David," he whispered in the Briton's ear. "The bath, the food – everything. You're a pal."

"You're still a funny one, mate."

The Yank was already off at a trot. Over his shoulder he hollered, "See you soon!"

"Kill some Jerries for me! And see you soon!" Pearson yelled in return, though he added to himself as he watched Flowers recede in the distance, "...God willing."

# Chapter VI

Thanks to the midday sun, Tommy was thoroughly soaked in perspiration by the time he made it back to Pierregot, thereby canceling the good effects of his bath. But he did make it back just in time, since the road that ran directly from Molliens proved to be about half as long as the way he had taken that morning. And when he reported to Dougherty, the frosty corporal was able to tell Willnor that the golden boy had come back all sweaty and winded, so the captain didn't even bother to see him again, simply assuming that his punishment had been a rousing success.

The British major had told Tommy the truth about the message he had carried; when Dougherty came back from seeing the captain, the corporal told the private, "Get your gear in order. You're moving out at 1400 hours."

"The whole company?"

"The whole brigade. And don't ask questions," Dougherty snapped in reply.

Tommy snapped a salute and a "Yes, sir!" in return, and raced back to the tent he shared with Carson. "Did you hear, Harry?"

"I heard, Flower. This is it. We're going up the line."

The deployment of the entire 66th Brigade to the Vaden line of trenches, a mere eight kilometers east of Pierregot, involved a much higher level of command than Captain Willnor – indeed, the order was signed by the 33rd's major general, George Bell – so the troops set off at a time reasonable for the distance they were marching, even taking into account the full kit each man carried on his back. The order had specified that routes should be taken which would minimize damage to growing crops, so at times Tommy and his compatriots found themselves marching two abreast down country lanes between rippling fields of grain. Tommy's marching partner was Andy Kopinski, a tall, stocky, redheaded Pole from the South Side of Chicago; everybody called him Ski.

"Does Iowa look like this, Flower?" Ski, an urban dweller through and through, asked as they tromped on under the still-fair sky.

"The land here rolls some like Iowa. But where I come from, it would all be covered with corn."

"Ain't this corn?"

Sweeping his eyes over the green fields, Tommy replied, "No. Could be wheat, but I'm not sure–"

"Oats. Oats and barley," a voice from behind piped up. It was Walt Sleziniak, another Doughboy whose parents had immigrated from eastern Europe, in his case to a farm in North Dakota. Like Tommy, Walt somehow had ended up in the Illinois Division.

"You think so, Sleaze?"

"I know oats when I see them. Don't you rotate crops in Iowa?"

"We rotate fields, not crops."

"All right!" came the sharp voice of Sergeant Eddie Maple, cutting short the agricultural discussion. With some difficulty he was squeezing down the line of his men, and therefore squashing the nearest oats, or barley, the general's instructions notwithstanding. "Shut yer yaps. This ain't no Sunday stroll." In an ongoing attempt to counter his tender age of twenty-three, Maple generally made strenuous efforts to exude authority.

His command came just as Tommy's company quit the country lane for a wider road already filled with other Doughboys from his division, some of whom, here and there, Tommy recognized. "Stay together!" Maple shouted. "Keep in line!"

A shadow passed over Tommy, and there was Vern Sanders at his side, towering over him. "This is really something, isn't it, Vern?" he said cheerfully.

"You said it, Tommy. I feel like I could kill a hundred Fritzes."

Their inclination to chatter further, or sing as they marched, was stifled by Maple as they approached the village of Contay. Just past it, they crossed the River Hallue (which was a narrow little stream to Flowers' eyes) and began to encounter hundreds of Tommies – the troops they would be spelling in the trenches, if only for the next twenty-four hours. "'Ullo, Yanks," one of them muttered to Flower of Iowa and his pals as he passed, noting their full kits. "'Ow do you think you're going to fight Jerry, carrying all that lot?" The Tommies all looked dirty (each man appeared as filthy as Muffett, David's friend who wouldn't bathe) and tired, and old, though from what David had said, some had to be no older than David and Tommy.

As they neared the trench system itself, the fine June countryside that Tommy had so enjoyed just this morning, when he had met Jamie on the road to Rainneville, slowly but surely gave way to something so different as to be almost unrecognizable as being on the same planet. The bright early summer green of the grass and crops receded, and mud, endless mud, brown and sticky, came to dominate the landscape. No undulating lilacs here; blackened stumps increasingly outnumbered living trees, and even those that were alive seemed stunted and deformed.

Tommy and his companions marched along an increasingly rutted road until they reached the edge of a chewed-up hillside that dipped slowly and raggedly away, to rise, fall again, then rise once more. They began to descend, not only down the hillside, but also into the ground.

★

His first real trench wasn't at all the way Tommy'd imagined it, not like the practice trenches at Eu after they'd first landed in France. It was narrower, allowing a view of only the slightest sliver of sky. It was shallower; the tops of the heads of some of the tallest Yanks seemed almost even with the edge of the parapet, a dangerous situation indeed if David had told the truth, and Tommy was sure David would always tell him the truth. The earthen walls were nothing like the neatly stacked sandbags he had seen heretofore. In places they appeared perilously ready to collapse inward on whatever unlucky soldier might be passing; at these points, two men had to turn sideways to let each other pass. Underfoot, the duckboards were a sometime thing, disappearing here and there into the muck. Even though it hadn't rained since last night, when he and David had taken shelter in the little stable, the trench was awash in mud that tugged insistently at Tommy's boots with every step.

When Tommy's company finally came to a halt, he had no idea where they were. They had simply stopped in a section of trench that didn't look appreciably different from what they'd been slogging through for the better part of an hour. The temptation to peek over the top, to get the lay of the land, was a powerful one; but even without David's story of his friend who "'ad 'is 'ead blowed off," Tommy knew better than to do that. He had the feeling they'd been heading down the hillside and back up the next one, but it was only a guess, and he couldn't swear to it. Though Tommy couldn't know from where he stood, it would take almost two more hours for the entire 66th to occupy the Vaden line, a respectable performance given their greenness and the condition of the trenches.

As the light began to fade, the order came down the line: evening stand-to. Tommy didn't quite understand; if it was so dangerous to stick one's head above trench level, why would a whole company, regiment, or even brigade all look over the top at once? From what he'd heard, the Germans did the same thing, too, twice a day. There must be some sort of understanding.

As the stand-to order reached the section occupied by Company E, he mounted the fire-step between Ski and Carson. In the fading dusk, the landscape that loomed before him resembled nothing he'd ever seen – pockmarked with holes, muddy, still sloping down and away, then up again. He could discern a large, shapeless mass just before the crest of the upward slope, which he had to assume was barbed wire. There were many other strange shapes at odd points in the wasteland that he couldn't quite make out. But he saw no sign of any Germans.

After the order to stand down had arrived, Ski whispered to him, "They've got all the high ground. That's not good, is it?"

"It probably doesn't matter, Ski. This British officer I met this afternoon said it was a quiet sector."

A few minutes later, Maple came along the line with orders: later that night, Carson, Sanders, and Ski would crawl out into no-man's-land as part of a wiring party; Flower and Sleaze were to move forward right away, to the outermost part of the Allied line in their sector, in order to staff a two-man listening post. There they were to stay all night, reporting back any unusual enemy activity as necessary.

Tommy and Walt made their way to the post, far in front of the line where everybody else remained, along the most crazy set of zigzag trenches Tommy had yet experienced. The passageways seemed to get narrower and narrower, and after a while they were definitely moving uphill; Tommy wished that David, with his "mem'ry for places," was with him, although Walt was a more-than-adequate companion. They couldn't talk, anyway, only whispered passwords with sentries as they made their way, as quietly as possible, to the farthest-flung edge of the Vaden line. Their assignment was strictly to listen – no looking over the top, not even with a periscope, which would call attention to itself and them. As the ground sloped ever more sharply upward, they at last reached their destination, a hole deeper than the trench from which they had come, and at least big enough so that two men could turn around comfortably. They weren't there very long before Sleaze broke the silence, whispering in the lowest of tones, "You know it's part of our job to keep each other awake?"

Although it hadn't occurred to him, Tommy silently nodded in assent. "'Cause I've heard," Walt went on, "that sometimes sentries fall asleep, and then they get killed. We're the furthest ones forward, and if the Jerries stage a raid, or even if there's a wiring party, we're the first ones they'll take prisoners… if they don't kill us."

Tommy could feel sweat flowing rapidly down his sides, a situation not aided by his nervousness over the mere fact of Sleaze's talking. But he had to make some kind of reply. "We've got our guns. Why wouldn't we kill them first?" Tommy wasn't as skillful as Sleaze at pitching his voice so whisper-quiet; though he was speaking as softly as he could, he felt his words echoing loudly through the little hole in the ground in which he and his friend were standing.

"Because there'd be more of them than us."

"We'd still fight. It's our job."

"Not if there's too many of them."

Tommy wondered what country Walt's parents had come from. Maybe he was German. Maybe Tommy was stuck in a forward listening post with a Boche spy.

*"Amerikaner!"*

The word came faintly but clearly through the night, and because of his train of thought, Tommy turned sharply to Sleaze and demanded, "Did you say that?" But he could see that now it was Walt who put a finger to his lips and demanded silence.

*"Tom-mee!"* came the same voice as before, and though it was a warm evening, Tommy suddenly went cold all through. The chill deepened when Sleaze smiled and silently pointed at him. How could the German – the one in the other trench – know his name?

The barest hint of a titter carried through the night air, and a correction wafted over to their post: *"Sam-mee!"*

Walt's face remained inches from Tommy's. Again he put his finger to his lips, this time adding a negative shake of his head. If there was no wind, and there had been none at stand-to, Tommy reckoned that the voice was coming from within a hundred feet, maybe fifty.

*"How iss Shee-cow-go, Sam-mee?"* Maybe they didn't really know his name, but the Boche's intelligence was mighty impressive, even so. Tommy's hand went to a grenade of English manufacture – a Mills bomb, the British called them. He meant the gesture only as a precaution, in case this voluble German suddenly advanced with his friends, but Sleaze saw him do it and grabbed Tommy's wrist, shaking his head yet again, in a gesture of his own that seemed to say, our mission is to listen, not to attack.

Then there was silence, no more from the enemy listening post. The whole intrusion had happened so suddenly upon their arrival that he and Walt had not yet gotten into proper position. There was a funkhole that served as a sort of alcove, a half-step up on the far side of their little hole where the prime listener could position himself, with the back-up man behind and slightly below him. The idea was to switch off during the night; too long in the alcove, and one started to hear things.

Several hours – or perhaps it was only about two – of boredom passed.

Tommy was in the prime listening post when suddenly their dark warren was illuminated in a brilliant shade of green. "What the hell?–" came Walt's voice in a sharp whisper behind him.

"It's Very lights," Tommy replied with self-assured accuracy. He had a wider and better view of the sky than he would have had in the main trench, and farther off, he saw a second of the silent shells burst into a gorgeous red. It was like the Fourth of July at the county fair in Montezuma, only with a lot less noise, and the noise had never been Tommy's favorite part of fireworks, anyway. A third, white light followed. Just as Tommy had nearly relaxed in his enjoyment of the show, there was a burst of noise – a Maxim, not more than fifty yards to their left

– then the louder report of a trench mortar, the much-feared weapon the Tommies called a Toc Emma, which although fired by hand had an effect more like a whizz-bang shell. As he and Walt instinctively ducked, Tommy remembered: if you can hear it, you've got a chance… though that was only the slightest of consolations in this suddenly too-small hole.

But in fact the TM was being aimed well to their left. After a second round of that and another short burst of machine-gun fire, Tommy heard a man's voice cry out sharply, very clear and near; he estimated thirty feet away at the most. Utterly chilling, the cry contained no recognizable words, so there was no way at all to determine if it had come from a German or an American.

Next, after a noiseless pause, came the sound – or so Tommy thought – of men in motion. It went on for a little while, possibly moving back in the direction of the Americans' main trench, but as intently as Tommy was listening, he couldn't be sure.

After that, there was only silence, and Walt ran down to the nearest sentry post to report what they'd heard. It made for a particularly tense few minutes for Tommy as he waited alone, but Sleaze was back very soon, shaking his head. Then there was silence again, silence which lasted for so many minutes, then maybe hours, that Tommy's head started to ache. Still later in the long night, he carefully changed places with Walt. The boredom was deeper the deeper in the hole you were. Given their self-imposed quiet, there was little for Tommy to do to keep alert but voicelessly sing to himself. Once Sleaze turned around and noticed Tommy doing this, and suppressed a chuckle, startling them both. Tommy's eyes had adjusted to the moonlit night, and his attention abruptly fixed on Sleaze's regular features and dark, straight hair; Sleziniak, it occurred to him for the first time, was a good-looking fellow.

That was the high point until dawn broke, when a whispered password from two Doughboys they'd never seen before announced they were relieved of their sentry duty, and should proceed back to the main trench. When they began to hit the somewhat wider trenches on their wild zigzag back, Walt finally spoke. Throwing his arm briefly around Tommy's neck and shoulders, he said with considerable self-satisfaction, "Well, Flower of Iowa, we made it." Somehow, hearing his familiar nickname after the long hours of silent boredom, punctuated by moments of high tension, made Tommy feel home and safe.

# Chapter VII

Tommy and Walt were more than ready to rest when they finally returned to the main trench, but Maple had other plans for them. One of the basic strategies of the 24-hour test was to keep the men of the 66th Brigade awake and occupied, since spells of that length and much longer were a staple of trench life. Accordingly, the two were sent to another section of the main trench, where what Tommy had previously envisioned actually had occurred: the walls had partially collapsed, rendering passage nearly impossible. Maple had warned them their next assignment would entail the use of their entrenching tools, but those basic implements seemed pretty pathetic compared to the mountain of rubble with which they would have to contend. Fortunately, they weren't the only ones assigned to the task; better yet, three of the others who were, were Carson, Sanders, and Ski. But though all of them were anxious to exchange stories of their first night in the trenches, they were under the command of an officious corporal who countenanced absolutely no talking as they went about their work.

It was hot labor, as the sun rose on another fair day. After an hour, perhaps two, the crew had made very little headway in clearing the trench, and the corporal, annoyed, sent word that more men would be needed. A half dozen more were duly dispatched and silently set to work, too. But orders also came back that the enlarged crew required a slightly higher level of command, so a sergeant was on his way.

Tommy was as close to a genuine ill humor as he ever got. He was tired, he was sweltering under a sun that was close to noonday, and his shoulder and upper arm muscles throbbed from the labor, which never seemed to yield any visible progress. Chatting or singing with his buddies would have helped take his mind off the ache and the tedium. He began to imagine bad things happening to the corporal, although he wouldn't allow any of those fantasies to involve fatal interaction with the Germans – that was something you shouldn't wish on anybody from your side, no matter how angry with them you were.

His bout of near surliness was interrupted just as he was digging into a particularly intractable chunk of Picardy chalk. "Why, if ain't Tommy!" came a voice strange yet familiar.

Unable to resist turning about and looking up, Tommy caught sight of his friend from the Rainneville road and injudiciously cried, "Jamie!" then colored a bit and saluted.

His recovery was not quick enough for the supervising corporal, who managed to salute Jamie and turn on Tommy all in the same instant: "Sir! – How *dare* you speak to an officer–"

"It's all right, Corp'ral," Jamie's easy voice cut in. "He has my permission."

"But, sir–" the corporal began to protest, and Jamie's tone changed completely: "That is *all*, Corp'ral. You are relieved."

"Yes, sir!" The corporal saluted, and then beat a hasty retreat.

"Hold up a minute, men," Jamie announced as the man he had replaced on the detail receded into the next section of trench. The diggers stopped where they were working, stood up straight, and stared at this odd newcomer in the strange hat. He strolled casually along the lot of them, just once, then said, "Your shirts are all soaked through, men. Do you like it that way?"

There was silence, then Tommy, confident of Jamie, piped up. "No, sir. Permission to take our shirts off, sir."

Colbeck gave him a big grin. "Granted."

"Sir?" It was Ski.

"Yes?"

"Is that an order – to take our shirts off, sir?"

Jamie frowned a little. "You can take yours off or not, as you like, Private. What's your name, anywise?"

"Private Andrew Kopinski, sir."

"They call you Andy?"

"They call me Ski, sir."

Jamie gave him a peculiar once-over. "I think you make a better Andy," he finally said.

"As you like, sir."

"My name ain't 'sir'," Jamie said evenly, addressing the whole crew. "I'm Sergeant Jamie Colbeck of the Australian Brigade, Australian Corps. Call me Sarge if you like, but Jamie's all right, too.

"Naow, I've got a little business to take care of up in the next section. I'll be back in a few minutes. You can work on your own 'til then, can't you?" There were nods all around. "Good. Any questions?"

Tommy held up his hand and said, "Jamie?"

"You're not in school, Flaowuhs," Jamie said drily. The whole group laughed, but Tommy didn't mind, because Jamie hadn't said it unkindly; and besides, it was sort of stupid to have raised his hand. It was the first time Jamie had called him by his last name, and he liked the way it sounded with that Aussie accent. "What is it?" Jamie added.

"Can we talk to each other?"

For the first time, Jamie looked ever so slightly nonplussed. "We're talkin' to each other naow, ain't we, Tommy?"

"No, sir – Jamie. I mean – I meant all of us." Tommy said this with a flourish of both arms that took in the whole crew.

"Well, I'd like to know haow you can work together if you don't talk to each other."

"Ask that corporal," Sanders cracked, and the group laughed again, but Jamie didn't.

"Don't get too fresh, soljuh," he said to the larger man, his tone equal parts friendly and serious, stopping the laughter in its tracks. His eyes swept over the whole group, then he added, "Of course you can talk to each other while you work." He paused, twisted his torso slightly, and spat in the direction away from the men, in an obvious comment on the leadership abilities of the lately departed corporal. "Naow I am goin'. I expect to see more progress on this work when I come back. Understood?"

Virtually the whole group replied in the affirmative. Colbeck surveyed the crowd one more time, and his eyes settled on one of the latest to join the digging, a dark, relatively short man Tommy had never seen before. "You, soljuh. What's your name?" Jamie asked him.

"Giannelli, Sarge."

A faint smile played across Jamie's face. "And your first name?"

"Vincent."

"They call you Vince, then?"

"Vinny."

"Vinny," Jamie repeated with a nod. "You're in charge while I'm gone. But don't let it go to your head."

"Yes, sir," Giannelli replied, with no particular crispness in his salute. Then he smiled and corrected himself: "Jamie."

Jamie smiled, cocked his head slightly, and then was off.

With the exception of Ski, the crew quickly stripped off their shirts. "What's the matter, Ski?" Carson said in a lilting, feminine-sounding voice. "Shy?"

"You," said Giannelli, who had never met Carson. "Shut up."

Carson glared at the upstart. "The sergeant told you not to let it go to your head, Dago."

Before Giannelli could respond, Tommy injected in a grave tone, "Hey, Harry, there's no call for that. Let it be. I'm sure Ski has his reasons."

"I'm a redhead," Ski volunteered with a mixture of defiance and defensiveness, "and I burn real easy."

"See?" Tommy said to Harry, who gave him, Ski, and Vinny all dirty looks. As they resumed their digging, Tommy felt a sense of triumph about his little intercession – but that only sharpened a keen sense of disappointment that Jamie hadn't left him in charge. That feeling lasted about a minute, until Giannelli stopped the men and suggested – not commanded – that they divide the labor of the detail in a different way. Despite the resistance of Carson and Sanders (Vern always tended to side with Harry), everyone complied, and it quickly became apparent that Vinny's suggestion was a good one. Tommy conceded to himself that maybe Jamie knew what he was doing, after all.

"How come you knew this Australian, Flower?" Carson asked, an edge to his voice, and Tommy explained why to all of them as they continued their work. When he was finished with his story, several of the men muttered comments to the effect that they wished the American Army had more sergeants like that.

"So, what happened to you last night?" Tommy asked Ski after they had worked for a while without conversation.

Ski stared at him and frowned, continuing to concentrate on the task at hand. "We went on a wiring party."

Tommy laughed. "I know that, Ski. But how did it go? What happened?"

Ski's jaw tightened, and he seemed to focus even more fiercely on what he was doing.

"Ski doesn't want to talk about it, Flower," Carson broke in. "He doesn't have much to brag about."

"Why? What did you do?" Tommy persisted, and Ski shot both Harry and him a cold look, but Carson wasn't about to let up:

"Got all scared is what he did. Didn't you, Ski?"

The redhead from Chicago angrily threw down his entrenching shovel, but rather than confront Carson, he strode over to Giannelli and asked his supervisor, "Can I work at something else?"

Vinny had not been paying any attention to the conversation. He gave Ski a brief look and a terse "No." When Ski then failed to budge, Vinny looked at him in surprise and told him, "I'm giving you the count of five to get back to work." Ski folded his arms. "One." No movement. "Two."

Tommy could see the look on Ski's face, and it was awful. His lips were trembling, and Tommy was afraid he might start crying in front of the whole crew. "Three," Giannelli continued, but Tommy cut in,

"Giannelli, can't–"

Vinny turned ferociously on him: "You stay out of this!"

But that was enough to break Kopinski's resolve. "I'll go back to work," he muttered quietly. "Don't pick on Flower."

"I'm sorry, Ski," Tommy said plaintively as the redhead walked past him.

"Drop it, Tommy."

"Why should Tommy drop it?" Vern Sanders, ever eager for conflict, began; but before he got any further, a loud voice behind them interrupted:

*"Tenn-hutt!"*

They all figured some lieutenant, or Captain Willnor, or maybe even someone higher ranking than that, must be passing through their section of the trench.

They were therefore surprised, after they stiffly came to attention and saluted, to see Colbeck, who was so unable to control his laughter he was almost doubled over. "Scared you," he finally managed to say. "At ease, men."

Sanders turned back to his digging, and Jamie added with a decided edge to his strange Aussie drawl, "I didn't say back to work, big boy." That caused Vern to snap to in a manner so insolent that he looked ready to strike the noncom, which might well have been the case. "What's your name, soljuh?" Jamie asked, looking him straight in the eye.

"Vernon Sanders."

"Vernon Sanders what?"

"Vernon Sanders… Jamie," the huge private answered, not only using the sergeant's first name when it clearly was not wanted, but also mimicking his accent.

Tommy expected Jamie would be one to give as good as he got, but just how he did so surprised Flowers: "And just what makes you so big for your britches, Vernon Sanders?" Colbeck asked, his voice turning into a crackling Midwestern twang as he pronounced the private's name.

Harry Carson, clearly worried that his friend was going too far, took the risk of stepping in: "Vern don't mean nothin', Sarge. He's just still all fired up 'cause of our wiring party last night."

Colbeck countenanced the interruption. "And what," he asked Carson, "happened at the party?"

"I shot at a German," Vern answered proudly.

A strange smile stole over Jamie's face as he gave the Yankee giant his full attention. "Oh. You shot at a German in the dark, eh? Naow, where did I put my list of medal recommendations–"

"Beg pardon, Sarge," Carson cut in again, this time sounding almost injured. "But that took real guts–"

"You shut your fuckin' maouth, you! You're pushin' your luck!" The verbal explosion from the heretofore genial Australian shocked them all, especially Carson, who literally backed off several steps without even realizing it.

Colbeck wasn't about to let Sanders off the hook. "Naow, why don't you tell all of us what you did last night that makes you so God-*damned* important?"

Sanders remained visibly sure of himself, but those who knew him better, like Tommy, were surprised to see him take the defiance and sarcasm down a notch or two as he began, "We were crawling forward on our bellies in no-man's-land when some Very lights went off." Tommy's attention, already well fixed on Vern, redoubled. "Then suddenly they started shooting at us, with machine guns and shells. We was all laying flat and still, but I picked up my rifle and fired back at them. I heard someone cry out, and I was sure I'd hit a Jerry." Sanders turned to Kopinski with a look of pure contempt. "That's when I realized the others were trying to shut up Ski. I was almost sure I'd shot a German, but who could tell with him screaming? Screaming like a scared girl."

"That's enough, Sanders," Jamie interjected in a quiet tone that brooked no argument. Everyone was staring at Ski, who was staring at the ground, his jaw working more furiously than ever.

Tommy felt terrible for him, so much so that he impulsively reached over and patted Ski's shoulder. It was a gesture everyone had to notice, but only Jamie acknowledged it, cocking a single eyebrow in Tommy's direction in a movement that came and went in a flash but was unmistakable. At last Colbeck broke the uncomfortable silence. "Is all that true, Andy?"

"Some of it. Well, I guess most of it, pretty much, sir."

Jamie walked over to Ski's side, as if to whisper in his ear. But he spoke in a calm, even tone loud enough for all to hear. "I'm not 'sir' – remember?"

"Yes, Sarge."

"You shouldn't've screamed, Andy. You could've given away you and your mates' position. You know that, don't you?"

"Yes – y-yes, sir, I mean S-Sarge," Ski stammered in total misery. With every fiber, Tommy was voicelessly aiming a plea at Jamie to stop, but the sergeant didn't even look his way. "I tr-tried not to," Ski stumbled on. "It's just – it was only when it all started again–"

"Started again?" Jamie asked with elaborate lack of interest, as if verifying the most insignificant detail.

"Yes – y-yes, Sarge. I was all right during the first round, but then the second–"

"There was only one round, you coward." That was Carson, re-emboldened by his friend's compelling tale.

Colbeck was ready to jump on Carson again, but before he had the chance, Tommy said plainly and clearly, "Sure sounded to me like two."

"What the hell do you know?" Sanders shouted at him. "You weren't even there!"

"Let Flaowuhs talk," Colbeck told Sanders, with a great deal of threat behind his tone. "What did you hear, Tommy?"

He was relieved to be talking directly to Jamie. "I was in the listening post. I saw three Very lights – one green, then one red, and finally a white. I heard – it sounded like a machine gun, and then a trench mortar. We ducked, then it stopped. But then there was another TM, and more machine guns. Then I heard someone cry out. I couldn't tell who it was – if it was one of ours or theirs."

"Did you hear two men cry aout?"

"No, just one."

"Aour friend Ski, then."

"You're a liar, Tommy," Vern insisted. "It all happened at once. You wouldn't know–"

*"Shut up, soljuh!"* No one had ever seen Sanders back down quite so quickly. Colbeck continued, "Who was in the listening post with you, Flaowuhs?"

"Private Sleziniak, Sarge," Tommy answered, gesturing at Walt.

"Sliz–?"

"You can call me Sleaze, Jamie," Walt said helpfully. "Everybody does."

A smile from Jamie inadvertently broke through. "Sleaze it is. Well?"

"I wasn't in the front listening position, Sarge. But from what I could hear tell, Flower of Iowa's got it right."

Jamie regarded them all, turned away, and stepped back a couple of paces, then turned about with studied drama. "Private Kopinski made a mistake aout there last night, men," he began. "A mistake that could have cost him his life – and the lives of his mates." Ski stared hard at the ground, as if hoping to dig a hole in which to hide. "Naow, we all get scared aout there," Jamie continued, "but you can't get so scared you do something to endanger your mates. Andy did, and no matter how sorry he is today" – here Jamie shot a look, not at Ski, but at Tommy – "he shouldn't have, and that's all there is to it."

Colbeck took another pregnant pause, and Tommy hoped Ski's torture was over. "But there's something else we should learn from this story," Jamie resumed. "Andy made a mistake that could have killed ev'ryone in his party, because the Jerries could've got a fix on their position.

"But he wasn't the first man who made a mistake last night. He wasn't even the first to make a mistake that jeopardized the lives of his mates."

Jamie started pacing rapidly among them, but his eyes stalked the biggest man there. "This first man did what he was supposed to do when the Very lights burst and the shells started to whiz: he hit the dirt. But then he made a big mistake. He had to show ev'ryone how *brave* he was, so he fired at the enemy.

"Naow, there's no way to be sure the Boche knew the wiring party was even there. Once in a while they'll send up Very lights in a quiet sector and fire a raound or two from their Maxims and Toc Emmas, just to remind us they're there."

Jamie stopped dead in front of Sanders. "But if some brave soljuh fires *back* at them, why, then they'll not only know someone's there, they'll have a fix on the whole bleedin' party's position. And then they'll know exactly where to send their next raound, won't they?" He shot a look at Ski. "Close enough to scare the living daylights aout of you, anywise – and only that, if you're lucky."

Jamie resumed pacing among them, then paused and concluded, "So, y'see, men, you might think the most dangerous man to have with you on a mission is a man who might get scared and make a noise. And he might be.

"But as for me, I would be even more scared to be on a mission with some soljuh who just *has* to prove he's a hero, and is willing to risk his life" – here Jamie stood again in front of Sanders, and very deliberately stretched out his words – "and – the lives – of his mates – just to prove how *brave* he is."

Colbeck pulled back one last time, so that his vision encompassed the whole crew, whose full attention he surely had. "If I was a hero like that – or his friend" – this look was for Carson – "I'd be careful abaout calling any of my mates a caoward or a liar. Wouldn't you?" No one dared say anything in reply, and the silence thickened as their sergeant seemed to look past them. Then he commented in a completely different, everyday tone, "I see you have made some progress. So, naow, why don't you boys get back to work?"

The hard feelings generated by their dispute ensured that the crew would work in silence, at least for a while. The interruption came when Tommy heard a sudden cry of "Oh, my God!" from one of the other soldiers he didn't know. The tone was one of such distress that everyone immediately gathered around the man to see what was wrong, even as Colbeck pushed his way through the assembled group.

The man, a big, hairy-chested blond who looked to be a farmboy, had been digging in the same glutinous mud as the rest of them. His attention was riveted to a blackened, roughly cylindrical object about two feet in length, which broadened at one end, with three slender projections. "What is it, Sarge?" he asked.

Jamie crossed over to him and looked closely at the thing. "What do you think it is, soljuh?"

"It looks like – like – an arm. Part of an arm, and a hand."

Jamie shook his head. "Can't pull the wool over your eyes, can we?"

Despite themselves, several of the Doughboys gasped audibly. "How'd it get here?" one of them asked.

Jamie stared momentarily at them, even as they were gawking at the rotting limb; then he reminded himself how new to all this the Americans were. Gravely, without sarcasm, he intoned, "The Boche have been fighting with the Tommies over this graound here for three years, and with the *poilus* before that." The men looked blankly at him, and Jamie smacked his hand with his fist. "This same graound. Don't you understand?" He glanced down at the arm. "This could belong to anybody, y'see." He laughed, catching his own unintentional joke: "Any… body." He looked back at these newcomers. "You'll have to get used to seeing things like this, men. Bodies, and parts of bodies. This is not like the war in your schoolbooks. I'm sorry, but that's just the way it is." Sensing the need for an appropriately theatrical gesture, he slid a glove over one hand, leaned down, and picked the thing up by the fingers. "You find something like this, you just throw it away."

Unfortunately, the arm was too far gone; as Jamie heaved it, most of the flesh slithered off the bone, landing with a revolting plop right next to Carson, who immediately turned a much uglier shade of green than that cast by the Very light Tommy had seen the night before. Both Harry and another soldier got sick, and Tommy felt his gullet fill, but he choked it back down, even as he noted with wonderment that the bone had flown a surprisingly long distance.

Jamie was regarding them with a look almost sheepish. "Sorry, men," he repeated, even casting a sympathetic eye at Carson, "but you will have to get used to it. And I know you will."

"Sergeant Colbeck?"

They all turned around to the unexpected sight of Eddie Maple.

"Yes, Sergeant?"

"I've come for the men from my squad. The orders have come through to start evacuating this trench."

Tommy and his friends never thought they would be so glad to see their pompous young NCO.

# Chapter VIII

Even a spell of rain on the march back to Pierregot couldn't discourage the tired Doughboys; Tommy and his friends were just happy to be out of the Vaden line. When he got back to his tent, Tommy, mindful of what David had told him, took advantage of the fact that he could change out of his wet clothes. He thought about saying something to Harry; he didn't hold any grudge, and hoped Carson didn't, either. But the bigger man had already collapsed into slumber.

A nap, at least, would have made sense for Tommy, too; he hadn't slept since that short time in the stable with David night before last. But he was overtired, edgy, and once he was in reasonably dry clothes, he felt compelled to roam outside. He wandered into the confusion of Pierregot village, with the vague intention of walking on to Molliens to try to find David, when he heard a beeping noise and a call of "Flaowuhs!" It was Jamie, pulling up alongside him, driving a vehicle much too small to call a lorry.

"Hello, Jamie," Tommy said with considerable tentativeness. His mind was still areel over the Australian's hideous gesture in the Vaden trench.

Colbeck seemed like the last man to state the obvious, but in the ensuing awkwardness, when Flowers said nothing more, he did: "I got a motorcar, Tommy."

"So I see. Good for you."

"Want to take a ride?"

"No. Thanks, anyway." Tommy turned and walked away. Why doesn't he just leave me alone, he thought.

But Jamie followed him in the motorcar. "Don't worry. I swear I washed my hands," he said, reminding Tommy of exactly what the latter was trying to forget. The Doughboy continued his evasive action. "What's both'rin' you, son?" Colbeck called after him.

Flowers turned back around and snapped, "I'm not your son." In the split second he delivered this retort, he was rewarded with an unexpected reaction on Jamie's face, which closed right up again; but Tommy was surprised and abashed by what he'd seen: a trace of injured feelings. "Look, Sarge, I'm sorry," he began, taking a single step back in Jamie's direction, "but–"

Colbeck cut him off with a piercing, leaden stare. "All right for you. I don't care. I can't be your Sarge and be concerned abaout your opinion of me."

"But you were. Just now."

Jamie gunned the motor, looking down as he did. "Talk like that's insubord'nation, soljuh," he said grimly. The motor purred and he added, still not looking at Tommy, "So. Where's the best place araound here to get a drink?"

They both knew Jamie had been in the area far more frequently, and for far longer a time. But the Yank simply replied, "The just-a-minute in Rainneville is the only place I know."

"Ah. *Chez* Mme. Lacroix."

"And Nicole."

"Nicole?"

"You know. Her niece?"

"No niece there last time I was in this area." Jamie, finally looking at Tommy, winked. "I'd remember."

"She's in the area now."

"So. Shall we go pay Nicole a visit?"

Tommy knew he shouldn't say no; it was unusual enough for a sergeant of another army to fraternize with a private, and here was Jamie offering him a highly prized ride in a motorcar to boot. But his previous notion already had solidified. "I was gonna go to Molliens to see if I could find a buddy of mine."

"Does your mate go to just-a-minutes?"

Tommy nodded. "Actually, that's where we met."

"We could all go, then."

"Molliens 's out of the way to Rainneville."

"Don't I know? I seem to recall teachin' you that." That got Tommy to smile, almost laugh, even as Jamie turned quite serious. "Last chance, lad. I don't beg anybody for their comp'ny."

Tommy opened his mouth to politely decline one last time, but then he closed it again, and instead got into the motorcar – why, he couldn't explain. They drove out of Pierregot in a brief silence, until Jamie said, "You want to clear the air here with me?"

"I don't argue with a sergeant about how he does his job, Jamie. Especially one as good as you."

"Tryin' to butter me up, are you?" He looked over at Tommy. "Go ahead. Argue with me. I can bear it."

Tommy looked away at the green, rolling landscape fading in the deepening dusk, then back to Jamie. "Ski's a good man, Jamie. You shouldn't've done that to him."

Jamie grinned. "That's what I like abaout you Yanks. You speak your minds."

"We're brought up to do that."

"I like it. Tommies never do that."

"Why are you with us, anyway?"

"Special orders. I've fought with the Tommies, the *poilus*, even the Eyetalians and the Russians–"

*"Russians!"*

"–and naow you Americans."

"Why don't you just fight with the Australian Corps?"

"I do, most of the time. But I always like to try new things." Jamie gestured at Tommy. "And you're what's new right naow."

"But how can you just move around like that?"

"Because I'm good at what I do, and they all know it. But they don't like me, so they're always happy to send me on to the next army. Here's Molliens. Do you know where to find your mate?"

"He's with the London Rangers, other side of town."

Jamie slowed the motorcar. "I remember naow. You thought I was with the Rangers."

"That's right."

"Your friend's a Tommy?"

"Uh-huh."

Colbeck stopped the vehicle. "Don't much like Tommies."

"They don't seem to like you Aussies, either. Why?"

"Ask them."

"But why don't you–?"

"They're no good movin' forward. I was with them on Gallipoli. They got no nerve and they don't think on their feet."

Tommy was indignant on David's behalf – and he didn't think Jamie should be talking like that, now that they were in the British encampment. Having gotten the sergeant onto the subject, he tried his best to move him off it: "You were at Gallipoli?"

"And Flanders. Naow, they were good in Flanders. You ask a Tommy to hold his graound, and they're the bravest men araound. But don't ask them to take inish'tive. They don't think for themselves."

Tommy counted it a moral victory that he'd at least gotten Jamie to say something nice about the British. He terminated the conversation by jumping out of the car and heading for where he recalled the Rangers' camp to be.

A lot of Tommies were milling about, a few of them eyeing him curiously, most ignoring him altogether. He couldn't find David, or Muffett, the only other man he was sure he would remember. The rest hadn't made a strong enough impression on him; furthermore, he'd have to recognize them in their khakis instead of their birthday suits. He was about to ask just any old stranger when he caught sight of a young man with a pink complexion, wavy blond hair, and penetrating blue eyes who was a little taller than the rest of the group with which he was standing, all of whom were puffing away on cigarettes. The blond private suddenly rang a bell with Flowers: he was the man whose rude remark in the showers had so embarrassed him, whom David had so soundly squelched. That was hardly an auspicious introduction; but as always, Tommy couldn't sustain a grudge, and he called out to the man, "Private Ardison?"

Startled, the entire circle of Tommies swiveled their heads to regard him. The British blond did a short take, blew a perfect smoke ring, then finally said, not without contempt, "It's *Hardison,*" hitting the "h" David had omitted. "You're Peahson's Sammy pal, aren't you?"

"That's right," Tommy agreed, all smiling friendliness. "How are you?"

A slight titter ran through the ranks as Hardison answered, "Why, we're all in the pink, of course. Decent of you to ask. You wouldn't be looking for Peahson now, would you?"

"Yes, I am, actually."

"We thought 'e was off to see you… actually." The laughter grew louder when Hardison repeated Tommy's last word.

"Do you know which way he went?"

"Nobody seen 'im go, but that's all we 'eard 'alf the day. 'Wonder 'ow Tommy did in the trenches?' – That's you, you're Tommy, right?"

"Right," Flowers said, ill concealing his delight that he had been in his friend's thoughts. "Thanks." He cut back over to Jamie and the motorcar; Colbeck had been at a distance that allowed him to see, but not hear, the exchange. "I need to go back to Pierregot," Tommy told him.

"What for? We were just there."

"They think he went there to look for me."

"They think?" Jamie shook his head. "We just came that way. You would have seen him."

"We might've missed him. But I'll walk back, if you wanna go ahead."

"Naw. Jump in."

As they headed back out of Molliens, Jamie went back to part of their previous conversation as if it never had been interrupted: "I know Andy's a good man, Tommy. From what I've seen, all your lot are good men – even that big swell-head Sanders, and his partner in crime Carson.

"But I want to tell you abaout something that happened when I was on Gallipoli. I was with my own army then. Some of the boys I served with there were boys I knew from Melb'n – that's where I come from."

"But Melbourne's a city, isn't it?"

"You are a bright one, lad. Haow'd you know that?"

"I had geography in school."

"They must have good schools in Ioway."

"Of course they do. It's America. Everyone gets a good education."

Jamie shook his head. "You Yanks sure are praoud o'your country."

"Australians aren't?"

"We're praoud. But not quite like your lot. Nobody is."

"You think that's bad?"

"No, Tommy. It's just somethin' t'see, that's all. Somethin' t'see."

There was a brief pause as they very quickly were back in Pierregot. "I'm sorry," Tommy said. "I interrupted your story."

"I'll finish it later. Go ahead naow and find your mate."

"All right. But I do wanna hear the rest of your story."

Jamie laughed. "You've made yourself clear. Do you write your mother, Flaowuhs?"

"What? Of course I do!"

"Tell her your sergeant from Daown Under says she did a good job raisin' you up. You got the best manners of any soljuh I ever met."

Back at the tent, Carson was still sound asleep – snoring loudly, as a matter of fact, which struck Flowers as odd, because he hadn't heard him snore at all before. Then again, Tommy realized, although he and Harry officially had been tentmates for three days, so far they'd actually only spent the first night sleeping in the same tent together. Maybe this was Harry's usual way of sleeping. He hoped not.

Understandably, most of Company E was at rest, but eventually Tommy found Eddie Maple – or rather, the sergeant found him. "Flower of Iowa!" he called after Tommy as the latter stalked the tents, trying to find someone who was awake.

"Sarge," Tommy responded, with a smart salute; but with no duties pressing him, Eddie was unusually easygoing.

"At ease, Private," he said as he ambled over to Flowers. "There was some limey here looking for you. Couldn't have been much more than five minutes ago that he gave up and left."

"Did he say where he was going?"

"He asked me to tell you if I saw you – strange message – I think it was 'Just a minute.'"

Tommy grinned at his regular sergeant and said, "Good."

"So that makes sense to you?"

"Yes, it does. Thanks, Sarge."

"So are you on some kind of mission with him?" Maple persisted. "How come I don't know about this? I'm your NCO." It didn't take long, Tommy thought, for Eddie to revert to his old officious self.

"We're friends, Sergeant. That's all."

"How come you're friends with a limey?"

Tommy shrugged, trying to control his rising annoyance. "We happened to meet, and we hit it off. He's a real nice fellow."

"Seems to me there are plenty of American boys for you to be friends with."

"There are, Sergeant. But my best buddy's a Tommy."

"Tommy's best buddy a Tommy. That's kind of funny."

"We've heard that one before," Tommy patiently acknowledged.

"Best buddy. You'd do better with an American," Eddie reiterated. "We won't fight with the Brits forever."

"Well, he's my pal, all the same."

"Then go find him, Private," Maple said, saluting. "Though if you were smart, you'd get some shut-eye."

"Guess I'm just not smart, Sergeant." Tommy saluted in reply. "Thanks again for the message." Maple shook his head and walked away as Flowers scampered back into town.

"Well?" Jamie asked as Tommy got back into the motorcar.

"We'll catch him on the road to Rainneville."

"Which road to Rainneville?"

Tommy just smiled and punched his superior officer's arm. "You were gonna tell me about Gallipoli."

"I will," Jamie promised, turning the engine. "But answer me a question first. Why did you say, 'But Melb'n's a city,' like you were so surprised?"

"I was, a little. I thought you were from the country."

"Why?"

"You always seem to know what you're doing. With the war and all."

"So? Why would that mean I'm from the aoutback?"

"Outback?"

"Country, like you say."

Tommy shrugged. "I wouldn't think someone from the city would know their way around as well as you."

"Why's that?"

"We're not exactly fighting in the city."

"It hardly caounts as country, either. It's–"

"No-man's-land?"

"To coin a phrase, yes."

"Are you from a rough part of Melbourne?"

"You really have a lot to learn, lad. You jump to too many conclusions."

"Sorry."

"Don't apologize. Just be more careful abaout doing that. As it happens, I come from a beautiful area of the prettiest city in all Australia."

"All right. I said I was sorry. Why does it matter so much I jumped to the wrong conclusion about something like that?"

"'Cause if you do it abaout one thing, you're like to do it abaout others." Jamie looked over at Tommy and could tell the American still didn't quite understand. "I can see maybe naow would be a good time to tell you abaout Gallipoli."

# Chapter IX

"What do you know abaout Gallipoli, Tommy? Did your schools teach you anything abaout it?"

"We didn't learn much about it, no. There was a little bit about it in the paper. Was it real bad?"

Jamie stared at the Yank for a second in astonishment. He had to remember that not everyone in the world lived under the British or Ottoman empires. "Yes, it was bad. Very bad.

"Y'see, Gallipoli's a part o'Turkey – a high, narrow, rocky bit o'land that sticks aout into the Mediterranean Sea. The Turks and their friends the Germans were there first, so they had all the high graound – they always do. And the stupid Pom brass landed us on the beaches right under all that high graound. By the time I got there, aour boys had already been there a few weeks. We were dug in partwise up those hills. I don't know what they thought we were doin' there, but for my money we were just there to be target practice for the enemy."

"Were you facing Turks or Germans?"

"Turks. Why?"

"They must not have been so tough, right?"

Jamie shook his head. "Lad, you *really* are bad at jumpin' to conclusions. Where'd you get that idea?"

Defensive, Tommy shrugged. "I wouldn't think Turks would be such good fighters, that's all."

"You're wrong again, Flaowuhs. They're as brave as any men I've fought against. And I've fought against a lot, as you know. It was their own country they were defendin', after all." Tommy had nothing to say in reply to that, and Jamie continued, "If you thought that trench yesterday was bad, imagine that with dust, and flies – the biggest, blackest, meanest bitin' flies this side of Australia – and a sun that makes you feel you're on fire from the moment it comes up in the mornin'. Imagine havin' no fresh water but a little sip twice a day. And other vermin besides the flies like you've never seen, and don't want to see, believe me.

"Like I said, I was there with a lot of aour boys from Melb'n. We all came over together, and there were a lot of us were pals. By the time we got there, they'd already wasted hundreds, maybe thaousands o'good men. They just kept throwin' 'em up over the top in broad daylight against Maxims. And we never got the artil'ry support we were supposed to have, shootin' from the water. The Royal Navy, huh! Sometimes their guns fell short and it all hit us, killin' and cuttin' up aour own boys.

"I was only a corp'ral then, but I always have been one to speak my mind. I says to my sergeant and leftenant, why don't we try a night raid? I reckon they were ready for that kind of suggestion, because word came back a few nights later for us to give it a try. Of course, they didn't give me the credit, and maybe I didn't deserve it anywise. Anybody could have seen we should try somethin' new. But I didn't care; anything was better than sittin' there under that sun day after day, waitin' for orders to go over the top to face those Maxims.

"My sergeant was a good man, name of Fritz Weller. Naow, I know what you're thinkin': what's a man named Fritz doin' in the Australian Army? Y'see, Fritz's parents came to New Saouth Wales from Germany when he was just a baby. But he fought for country and King as loyally as any man–"

Tommy was listening so intently to Jamie's story that he almost missed the small figure in brown briskly walking along the roadside. They were within sight of the point where the road forked back to Molliens. "David!" he cried impetuously, rudely interrupting Jamie, then quickly apologizing, eliciting a grunt from the Aussie.

The Englishman, still walking forward at a rapid pace, turned partway about with a big smile on his face, as if he'd been expecting his Doughboy pal. The smile faded to something else as he noticed the Yank was riding in a vehicle, then to something else again when he saw the driver and his distinctive headgear, which David immediately marked as belonging to a member of the Australian Corps. "Hey, pal!" Tommy said cheerfully as the two men slowed to a stop next to him. "How are you?"

"I'm in the pink, Tommy," Pearson said guardedly, echoing his unpleasant fellow Tommy, Hardison. "'Ow is it you're in this motorcar?"

"This is my friend, Sergeant Jamie Colbeck of the Australian Corps," Flowers said in explanation as Colbeck, though still irritated at the interruption, silently noted how correct and deferential the American was being. When Tommy went on to give him David's name and rank, Jamie made his own interruption:

"Don't tell me. I know. The London Rangers. Pleased to meet you, Peahson," he said without enthusiasm.

"Pleased to meet you, sir," David responded in a similar tone.

Tommy waited for Jamie to correct David, to urge the Briton to call him by his first name, or at least "Sarge." When that didn't happen, Tommy strove to break the ensuing awkwardness: "Ready to ride the rest of the way to Rainneville, David? To the just-a-minute?"

David gave him a curious look. "I don't know, Tommy. Maybe I'll just 'ead on back to me camp."

"But–" Tommy sputtered, "my sergeant said–"

Jamie cut Tommy off. "We've already been to Molliens and back to Pierregot, and naow to here, lookin' for you so you could join us, soljuh. I think you better come along with us."

It was effectively a direct order, something neither David nor Tommy wanted or liked. "As you wish, Sergeant," David said grimly, and he stepped onto the running board of the vehicle, on the passenger side.

Not satisfied, Jamie said, "Sit *daown,* Private. Flaowuhs here will make room for you."

As David squeezed Tommy into the middle of the seat – there was no back seat in the small vehicle – Flowers, flustered by the turn of events, told him, "Jamie was in the middle of a really interesting story about when he was on Gallipoli." At the mention of that battlefront, David's shoulders seemed to tighten up a little more. "Why don't you go on, Jamie?" Tommy prodded, turning back to the sergeant.

Jamie looked over at the two privates with the intention of saying no, then changed his mind: "Like I was sayin', Fritz was my sergeant. He led a few of us – it was six of us – aout of the trench and up the hill that night. The idea was to crawl forward and cut the enemy wire, raid the nearest trench, and take some prisoners. Cut and dried.

"One of the men with aour party was Kerry Saxton. Kerry was a good lad, but very young. I think he'd lied abaout his age to get in." Jamie didn't catch Tommy and David exchanging the briefest of glances at that information; he was concentrating on his story – as well as his driving, since south of the Molliens fork, as they were heading uphill, the Rainneville road was suddenly clogged with men and mules, most of them moving in the other direction, north toward the front. "It was a moonless night, and for once I think we caught the Turks when they weren't very alert. We were makin' good progress in the dark. We had even started cuttin' the enemy wire, when suddenly somebody, somewhere fired a Lewis gun–"

"'ow d'you know it was a Lewis gun?" David demanded, much to Tommy's surprise.

"I know a Lewis gun when I hear one," Jamie growled, "and I did then. It wasn't a Turk who fired, I'm sure of that. It was one of aour own. In fact, I'm sure it was one of the Poms in the next sector over. Some Tommy probably got spooked in the dark and fired his rifle."

Flowers' discomfort at sitting between his English and Australian friends was increasing geometrically, but Colbeck went on: "I can't say for sure why he did it, but it was the kind of mistake men in a war make all the time. Only sometimes it's costly, especially when there's a second mistake.

"Y'see, Kerry was aour lead man; he was already through the wire, while the rest of us were at it. I was bringin' up the rear on Fritz's orders, to keep aour group together. Kerry got scared when that shot rang aout, and he cried aout. Not real laoud, but laoud enough for the Turks to hear it. And he was real close to their trench, maybe closer than he knew.

"They fired, and Kerry was hit right away, and cried aout some more. Fritz was right next to him. Fritz was a good sergeant, and he knew he shouldn't, but he went to help Kerry. The second raound got him, I believe. The Turks had to know there was more of us, so they just started sweepin' the area with their Maxims and set off a couple of TMs. All the other men ahead of me – Billy Sampson from Melb'n, a Greek boy from Sydney, and another one I didn't know from the aoutback – got blasted away.

"I was just behind them and dug in at the first shots, right there under the wire. But I was in a hurry and I didn't calculate it right, and a piece o'that barbed wire dug into my back, deep – got stuck there. I couldn't cry aout, or they'd know there was still one alive. So I waited there for haours with that wire in my back, not makin' a saound. Towards dawn, I started digging myself in deeper, and finally I got free. I was partwise back when aour sentry hollered for the password. Just right then I couldn't remember it, and I thought he'd shoot me. But I recognized his voice, so I called aout his name. According to the rules, he still should have shot me. But they came aout and got me, and in the end I was lucky, got sent back to Alexandria, to the hospital. By the time I was ready to come back, it was too late. We were already creepin' off Gallipoli, with all those fine boys lost and nothin' won."

In the wake of such a tale, the American was quiet. But David promptly inquired, "D'you 'ave a scar, then?"

In an abrupt, blind fury, Jamie brought the vehicle to a jolting halt, right in the middle of the busy road on a sharp uphill slope. "I don't like your attitude, Tommy!" he snarled as he stood up, and he wasn't addressing Flowers.

"I was only–"

"You don't believe me, Pom? Here!" Jamie shouted as he turned around and ripped off his shirt and tunic in one motion. The two younger men stared at his back, cleft horizontally with a deep brown scar that looked to Tommy like the valley of the Mississippi River at Davenport. Jamie refastened his shirt, still in a rage, and yelled, "Maybe you *should* go back to your camp, Peahson!"

"Gladly," David muttered defiantly – though Tommy could tell he was actually shaken by Jamie's outburst – and he stood up to jump out of the motorcar.

But Tommy gripped his friend's arm with a "Don't go," then turned to his superior and said calmly, "He didn't mean it the way you heard it."

"Bloody hell he didn't–!"

"It was plain old curiosity. I was about to ask you the same thing myself," Tommy lied. He still had David by the arm, and Jamie was brought up short by his intercession, so he pressed his advantage. "And another thing. I don't like the way you two are acting towards each other. We're all supposed to be allies. The Huns are the enemy, remember?"

"Don't you go comparin' me to a Tommy private," Colbeck said, shaking an accusing finger at Flowers.

"And don't go pulling rank on me at this late date," Tommy rejoindered.

"That's insubord'nation, soljuh."

"We're off duty. But if you wanna report me, go ahead. I don't care. I'm right, and you know it."

There was a tense silence, which Jamie finally broke with a loud guffaw. Tommy wasn't surprised, but David was stunned. "I think I've und'restimated you, Tommy," the Australian said good-naturedly. "You got even more gumption than I thought." Turning his attention to the Briton, he added, "I don't know what you did to make such a good friend of this man, David, but you're sure lucky."

It was a comment that could have been taken any number of ways, but what Pearson and Flowers both noticed was that Colbeck had called David by his given name for the first time. *"Allez, allez!"* boomed a strange, loud voice behind them – an old French peasant with his horse and cart and a wide load thereon, unable to negotiate his way around the stopped motorcar.

Jamie's mood had changed entirely, and he smiled and shouted back with a mocking bow, *"Mais bien sûr, monsieur. Désolé."* He swiftly sat down and turned over the motor as Tommy, still gripping the arm of the dazed David, tugged at his English pal until the latter plopped back down hard in the seat. They roared off to a renewed start, and once again Jamie resumed a conversation as if no interruption had occurred: "So y'see, Tommy, maybe if I'm particularly hard on a boy like Andy, or even on a blowhard like Sanders, maybe some night, when they're in the same situation, they'll remember and not make the same kind of mistake. And maybe five good men, or more, won't have to die like that, hangin' on the wire." He looked over at both younger men, casually taking in the fact that the Doughboy had protectively thrown his arm around the shoulders of his little Tommy friend. Pearson said nothing, but under Colbeck's gaze, Flowers felt compelled to:

"So you've made your point, Jamie." Colbeck laughed, and Tommy continued, "Didn't I say to start with you were a good sergeant?"

"Flatt'rer."

"And Jamie?"

"What?"

"Thanks. For telling me – us – that story."

"Oh, don't encourage me, lad. I've got plenty of stories. Just you wait till we get to Mme. Lacroix's."

Tommy heard David very quietly sigh, and felt him shift uncomfortably beneath his arm, but nobody said anything more on the short hop to Rainneville.

# Chapter X

Nicole Lacroix had taken advantage of an inexplicable lull in the late afternoon to run upstairs to the small set of rooms over her aunt's *estaminet,* to her even smaller room, to brush out her shoulder-length hair. As she watched herself combing in the cracked piece of glass that passed for a mirror above her tiny dresser, she again fancied that in the summertime, her chestnut hair glistened with auburn streaks. But nobody else ever seemed to notice, least of all her Aunt Eglantine, her father's brother's widow, under whose all-too-watchful eye she spent her days and nights.

Though she and her auntie always, always needed money, Nicole found herself hoping that the current odd absence of customers would continue into the evening. She could remember that, when her father had first sent her away from Cumières, nearly three years earlier when she was but a girl of fourteen, she had wanted nothing more than to be allowed to work at the public house that her aunt, unable to live on her war widow's pension, had decided to open. But Papa and Tatie had insisted on sending her instead to study with the nuns in nearby Villers-Bocage, at least until she reached her sixteenth birthday.

By the time that event finally occurred, twin disasters had befallen the Allied war effort on the Western Front. One of them, Verdun, had wiped out so much of Nicole's previous life that she seldom allowed herself to think, much less speak, of it. The other, the Battle of the Somme, had brought *les Tommies* to Picardy en masse, and as a consequence prosperity to her aunt's establishment. The influx had persuaded Aunt Eglantine to at last put her niece to work, but in one sense it was too late; Nicole already had accumulated a resentment of the men in khaki, sharing in the general anger that the British had taken so long to launch their attack while France was being bled white at Verdun. That 60,000 sons of the Empire, most of them eager, inexperienced volunteers, had fallen on the very first day of the ill-fated offensive did not mitigate, in the opinion of the French (Nicole included), the larger fact that it all had come entirely too late.

Matters were not helped by the way the Tommies often seemed more like an occupying force in Picardy than allies who had come to help drive the Boche out of France. Nicole's spell in the *estaminet* these last twenty months had brought her a smattering of English, but it hadn't been calculated to improve her opinion of soldiers who spoke it... until three nights ago, that is, when *les Américains* arrived, speaking their own peculiar version of the language. She immediately liked them better; they were more generous with their money (how could she know they had more to spend?) and treated her in a more gentlemanly fashion (half the Tommies seemed to assume she was a *putain).* She had found herself actually enjoying her work again for the first couple of nights after the Americans showed up. Then, last night, there had been only Tommies again. Rumor – always easy to come by in Picardy – had the Americans up the line already.

"Nicole. Nicole!" came her aunt's harsh voice from downstairs. Pinning her hair back, she rushed down the hall to the top of the stairway, disappointed. *Zut!* Please, *mon Dieu,* not another night of serving drunken Englishmen. She halted at the top of the stairs, then descended slowly and with a great deal of self-conscious dignity.

*"Ces gentilshommes t'attendent!"* Tatie scolded as the *estaminet* came into Nicole's view. Her aunt stood behind a long oaken counter. Two long benches with a table between, all of the same material, faced it; and two smaller tables stood near to the fireplace. All else was standing room. Tatie was gesturing at three men who had come in and taken one of the always-prized smaller tables. As they had been surprised to find the *estaminet* empty, so she was surprised at the composition of the trio: yet another diminutive Tommy, with brown hair and eyes and the type of pleasing face she nonetheless dismissed as typically English-looking; an Australian (she could tell by the hat – they didn't get many Australians, but when they did, she found them more like the Americans, and consequently tended to like them better), a rather old man with wavy black hair; and an American.

And what an American! Hair like the wheat that used to grow west of her home village before the war; eyes the color of the lapis brooch she had inherited from her long-gone mother; and simply the most beautiful face Nicole thought she had ever seen (and as much as she disliked the Tommies, some very fine specimens of British manhood had made eyes at her).

*"B'jour, m'sieurs,"* she said effusively as they all looked up at her. She instantly recognized the looks on the faces of two of them: the beautiful American and, even more, the old Australian regarded her as countless soldiers had in the past two years – as if they hadn't seen a woman, let alone one her age and with her looks, in much too long a time. The Tommy, she noticed to her relief, regarded her with a less intense interest. *"Que voulez-vous?"*

The Australian, with far too big a grin on his face, responded, *"Biére."* Nicole knew the English word, and allowed to herself that at least he was trying to use the French pronunciation – especially in comparison to the Englishman, who ordered the same beverage with a flat "Beer," then added to the American, "but you might not like it. It's not very good." Nicole didn't understand all his words, but she knew the important ones, and his tone told her the rest.

There was no response from the American, who merely looked fetchingly puzzled. Turning her full attention to him, she cooed, *"Et vous, monsieur? Vous n'avez pas de soif?"*

The Australian burst into hearty laughter; obviously he had some genuine command of French. "What'd she say?" the American asked, his tone eager.

"She says, 'Aren't you thirsty?'" the Australian replied.

The American gave her a charming smile and a shrug and said, "I'm sorry. I don't speak French."

Nicole understood that one; she had heard it often enough, and before it always had irritated her; this was France, after all! But this time, she merely raised her finger partway to her lips and said in English, "You wait. Yes?" This caused general laughter at the men's table, but it was of the good-natured variety, so she didn't mind.

"Hey! *I* can speak French, y'know," the Australian called after her as she headed across the room to give her aunt the order for the two beers.

Nicole tossed her head back, and with her most beguiling smile repeated to the older man, "You. Wait."

She was very glad she had just brushed her hair.

"Looks like you've made a friend, Tommy," Jamie said as the three of them watched the French girl at the counter.

"Do you really think so?"

"'deed I do. And she is quite the looker. Good idear to come here."

"You're awfully quiet, David."

The Briton shrugged. "I told you before, she's pretty enough, but 'er auntie keeps a very close eye on 'er. I do think she fancies you, though."

"So what should I do?"

"Why are you askin' him? He wouldn't know." This caused not only David but also Tommy to flash a look at Jamie, who went on, "I mean, he's the same age as you. There's only one man o'the world at this table." Jamie saw the other two exchange a glance, and knew he'd blundered. How could these two be so tight? Sometimes in a war, he knew, it could happen almost instantly, but these boys couldn't have known each other more than two or three days, and they hadn't been under fire together, which always quickened friendships. "I'm not braggin'," he added apologetically, half hating himself for doing so. "It's just the way o'the world."

After a brief pause, it was David who, in an unexpectedly friendly manner, asked the Anzac, "So what d'you think 'e should do?"

Jamie looked over at the Doughboy and answered, "She's got boys all over her, all the time. Don't be too eager. Stand off a mite. She'll like that. Guarantee." Following this smooth dispensing of advice, he inadvertently vocalized a different thought: "But she sure is beautiful."

"You like her too, don't you?" Tommy said.

That brought Jamie up short, but not for long. "So what if I do? It's you she's got her eye on."

As if on cue, Nicole returned with a tray containing two mugs of beer and two very small glasses, one filled with a liquid that looked to Tommy for all the world like urine, the other holding a brownish-red concoction. She placed the tray on the table and the beers before Jamie and David, then picked up both the glasses and put them in front of Tommy. With each motion she repeated to the appropriate customer, *"M'sieur... m'sieur... m'sieur."*

Jamie wasted no time in quaffing half his beer. Tommy just stared at the two glasses in front of him, and David was watching Tommy.

Nicole gave Tommy her sweetest smile and thrust both her hands toward him in encouraging fashion. *"Pour vous. Essayez, s'il vous plaît."*

"Am I supposed to try them?" Tommy asked Jamie.

"You sure picked a bright one for a mate, Peahson," Jamie said wryly to David.

"What is it?" Tommy asked, also directing his attention to David.

David pointed in turn to each glass and said in his rough French, "Van blank. Van rooj."

*"Oui,"* Nicole said brightly, gesturing herself. *"Vin blanc, vin rouge."* She spared a smile for David, who gave her one in return; not so bad for a Tommy, after all.

Having gotten the message, the American picked up the glass with the darker liquid and drained it. It was sour as an underripe persimmon, harsh as the sun in the dog days of an Iowa August, and Tommy's reaction to the taste of it showed so clearly on his face that he evoked mirth from everyone else around the table. "I don't like that," he muttered needlessly; then he looked so apprehensively at the other glass that Jamie broke into a chortle.

"I know what you're thinkin', mate," the sergeant said, "but it ain't horse piss. I know it looks it, but I swear it ain't."

"Does it taste like the other one?" Tommy practically whispered to David.

"Not really. 'Ard to say 'ow it's different, but it tis. Per'aps a little sweeter."

Tommy lifted the glass to his lips to discover that David had it exactly right. But he still didn't like the stuff.

Nicole was about to ask him which he'd prefer when they all were distracted by a commotion at the door. Eight men came in at once (though not all together), six Tommies and – a relative rarity in this area – two *poilus.* "You can take care of them first," Tommy said to her with a smile and a gesture toward the newcomers. If Nicole didn't understand his words, she hid it well, flashing a brilliant smile and a nod before she headed off to take care of the new men.

"Never ever seen 'er do that," David commented when she was out of earshot, though that scarcely mattered.

"You seen her much?" Jamie asked.

"A few times, just. But she's usually a bit short with the soldier boys."

"Not with aour Tommy here. Not today."

"She just had some extra time," Tommy said. "We were the only ones here."

"But it was clever of you not to make up your mind right off," David teased.

Tommy smiled at his pal and retorted, "But I really meant it."

"So you really didn't fancy the wine?"

"Not at all."

"Try this, then."

Jamie watched as David, rather than shoving his still-untouched mug over to Tommy, lifted it toward the American's lips, and Tommy cupped his hands around David's to guide the drink home. "Uggh!" the Doughboy exclaimed as soon as he tasted the warm, weak French beer.

Jamie laughed again, as did David, who said as he glided the mug back to his own lips, "I warned you you might not fancy it."

"You were right, Davey."

"So I gather you really aren't thirsty," Jamie interjected, as much to fend off the feeling he was being excluded from a private discussion as to keep the conversation going.

"No, I am. I really am. Isn't there anything else to drink here?"

"'Fraid that's it," said Jamie.

"Sometimes, in a just-a-minute, they've got cider," David countered.

Finishing his beer, Jamie turned on the Briton. "Naow haow would you know that? You've hardly been here. And anywise, they only have cider in the fall."

"It's true I've only been 'ere a few weeks," David readily conceded. "But 'twas me brother told me you could sometimes get a cider in a just-a-minute."

"Your brother? Where's he naow?"

Tommy, anxious to impress upon Jamie that he should not get combative, rushed in with the information: "David's brother, Colin, was killed not far from here."

That had the desired effect. Jamie looked at David a little differently from before, and simply said, "Oh. Sorry, Peahson."

David cleared his throat. "What Tommy says is true, as far as it goes. But it wasn't me brother Colin told me about the cider. It was me brother Doug." Before any further misunderstanding could arise, he felt compelled to add, "He fell at Passchendaele."

Despite himself, Jamie sat up and repeated, "Passchendaele? That so? I was there, y'know."

"Did you know 'im, then?" David asked, abruptly eager to be talking with the Australian.

"Doug Peahson. Doesn't come right to mind. He wouldn't've been with the Rangers–?"

"Somerset Light Infantry."

"I–" Jamie began, but Tommy, feeling very much left behind, intruded with,

"Where's Passiondale?"

Instead of answering Tommy, Jamie addressed David. "Was Colin killed in the big push hereabaouts, two years ago?"

"That's right. July of '16."

"And Doug – that would have been late last year."

"October. Yes."

Now Jamie turned his attention to Tommy. "Passchendaele's in Belgium, north of here, near Ypres." He pronounced this last name "Eep."

"D'you mean Wipers?" David put in.

"Yes, Wipers, that's what the Tommies call it. Worst place on the whole Western Front, for my money, give or take Verdun."

"I've heard of Verdun," Tommy volunteered.

"Eh. Glad they taught you something in those Ioway schools."

*"M'sieur?"* They were all startled out of their grim talk of the war by the unexpected return of Nicole. Looking at Tommy, she repeated, *"Alors, que voulez-vous?"*

"Can you ask her about the cider?" Tommy pressed Jamie.

Relishing the opportunity, the sergeant turned to the girl with his biggest grin. *"Mam'selle. Un cidre, peut-être? Pour mon ami?"*

Nicole rewarded him with a sizable smile of her own. *"Peut-être. Je vais aller voir. Mais je crois que non."*

*"Mais c'est pour mon ami ici,"* Jamie emphasized, gesturing toward Tommy.

*"Oui. Je comprends."*

*"Pour mon beau ami, n'est-ce pas?"*

That did it; Nicole giggled and blushed. "What'd you say? What'd you say?" Tommy demanded, but Jamie muttered "Wait," as he simultaneously tried to figure how he could keep this delightful girl in conversation and avoid telling the Doughboy he'd called him "my handsome friend."

But Nicole had recovered and said to Jamie, saucily, *"Bel, m'sieur. Votre bel ami."*

*"Belle? Mais c'est vous qui est belle."*

A voiceless scoffing noise that sounded quite serious in its intent abruptly came from Nicole's throat; then she turned to go, to resume her other duties. But she turned partway back round and said in English to Tommy, "You. Wait."

The men all laughed, the more so when Tommy said, "We've got to teach her some more English."

As the laughter subsided, they were distracted by the sound of women arguing – the only two women in the place, of course, being Nicole and her aunt. The older woman seemed particularly exercised, and was gesticulating in the general direction of their table. But Nicole was giving as good as she was getting. Finally, with a defiant last gesture of her hand, Nicole whirled about and headed for them, carrying a bottle and a glass on a tray, as the dozen or so other men in the *estaminet* (for the crowd had grown some more) laughed at the whole scene, as if the argument had been staged solely for their entertainment.

Distracted and trying not to look it, Nicole put the tray in front of Tommy and announced triumphantly, *"Votre cidre, m'sieur."*

"How do I say thanks?" Tommy asked Jamie. The Australian supplied the word, and the American repeated, *"Merci."*

The French girl smiled and colored again, and gave the French expression for "You're welcome," which Jamie duly translated without being asked. The Aussie then added, *"Tout va bien?"*

*"Ah, ça va, m'sieur, mais–"*

*"L'addition?"* Nicole smiled warmly at the older man, grateful that he had guessed, as Jamie said to David, "We forgot to pay up for aour beers when she brought them. That's why she and the old woman were fightin'."

"We wou'n't cheat them–" David began, but Jamie had already asked Nicole, *"Combien?"* and she had responded, *"Deux francs en tout, m'sieur."*

Jamie went for his pocket while David quickly leaned forward to hand her a franc note. But as Nicole reached for it, Jamie batted David's hand away, and gave her three franc notes. *"C'est deux, m'sieur,"* Nicole repeated, and Jamie answered gravely, *"Je connais,"* then chanced a wink.

Beaming, the girl half curtsied, then archly corrected him – *"Vous savez"* – at which point her aunt very loudly called her name from across the room. Without another word, or even a change of expression, she turned about and was gone from the table. Jamie noted with satisfaction that she hadn't even stolen another glance at Tommy before leaving.

Everything had happened too fast for Tommy. "How much do I owe you for the cider?" he asked the sergeant.

"If I wouldn't let Peahson pay, why would I let you?"

Tommy recalled David's meager rations. "Because I owe my fair share."

"Some other time," Jamie responded lazily. "I'm pullin' rank." He had done so in a way designed to dampen any gratitude from the younger men, and no expressions of it were forthcoming. Unperturbed, he said to David, "Just haow much French do you know, anywise? I think you're holdin' aout on us."

"I know the words for 'two francs' when I 'ear them. But I 'ardly know French like you seem to."

"Seem to? You think I'm puttin' on airs?"

"That's not what I said, Sergeant."

"Mm." Jamie hadn't eaten or slept, and the beer was going straight to his head. "So, haow did your brothers die, Peahson?"

Tommy, aghast, looked daggers at Jamie, who ignored him. But David didn't seem to mind the question. "We got tellygrams, and with Colin also a letter from 'is leftenant. They said Colin was shot clean through the chest. Doug–" He faltered a little. "Doug was shot in the 'ead."

"Right," Jamie said in a tone that made both of his tablemates uneasy.

"What d'you mean, right?"

Jamie looked at the boys through a slight alcoholic haze. "Don't you know anything, you two?" When they gave him blank stares, he went on. "I mean, ain't it funny haow ev'rybody gets shot clean through the head or the heart in those wires." He directed his next observation to Tommy: "Somehaow nobody ever gets blown into a thaousand pieces like that poor fellow whose arm I tossed away today." Then he was back to David: "Naow, I do believe that your brother who was killed in the push araound here probably was shot clean through the chest… if you call what a Maxim does to a man clean. They sent those poor lads forward, over the top, in straight lines against machine guns. The Jerries chewed them up like they were gum. You could call what a Maxim does clean, but for my money it looks more like someone took sheep shears to a man's middle–"

"Stop it, Jamie!" Tommy said sharply. David didn't, or couldn't, speak; and Jamie wasn't finished.

"Naow, as for Passchendaele, maybe there's one chance in a thaousand your other brother was shot in the head, during a quiet time. But if it was a push; and it was a push, wasn't it?" – David nodded dumbly, even as Tommy implored him not to respond at all – "then there's a very good chance he wasn't shot at all.

"Y'see, the graound at Passchendaele was all chewed up, from shells on top o'shells on top o'shells. No grass or trees anywhere, just the mud and the shell holes. And it rained and rained ev'ry day, and still those mis'rable donkey gen'rals – that butcher, Haig – sent more men forward. It was the kind of mud you got stuck in, and sank in, and draownded. I know it; I sawr it; you can ask anyone who was there. I swear more of aour boys – more of all the boys, the Germans, too – draownded in that mud than ever got off so much as a shot."

David was ashen; Tommy was pale, too, but he was livid. A tense silence followed, then David stood up and said quietly, with great difficulty, "Thank – thank you – for telling me… the truth about that, Sergeant Colbeck…. I – I'm sorry, but I 'ave to be off now. Good-bye, Tommy," he added without looking at his American friend.

Tommy felt paralyzed as he watched his pal walk away. But when he looked across the table and saw Jamie staring smugly back at him, his tongue came untied in a hurry. "And what was the lesson you were teaching us there, Sergeant?"

"I was just tellin' the truth, Flaowuhs."

Dumbfounded, Tommy stammered, "I – I–" then shot up out of his seat. Making a considerable effort at self-control, he said with as much dignity as he could muster, "There was no excuse for that. *No reason* to do that." When Jamie didn't answer, he drew himself up a little taller yet and said, "I reckon I'll walk back to camp, Jamie. I really don't wanna ride back with you." As an afterthought, he added, "But thanks for the ride here, and the cider."

At that, Jamie laughed. "Didn't I tell you you've got good manners? So God-damned polite, even when I can tell you'd like to knock my head off. Come on, lad. Sit daown."

Tommy stood clenching his fists, and for a moment he actually seemed ready to use them. But he simply said "No," and headed for the door as Jamie called after him, "Come *on,* lad."

Tommy ignored the sergeant – but he couldn't ignore the young Frenchwoman who had paused ever so slightly in her busy routine when she noticed he was leaving. He cut over to her, even as she was standing serving the two *poilus,* and interrupted the proceedings with a brisk "Excuse me" in English, then made a slight dipping motion that passed for a bow and said in very bad French, *"Merci, mam'selle."* They exchanged shy smiles, and he ventured further, gesturing at her: "… Nicole." There was a gasp from her aunt, the two Frenchmen, and even a couple of the nearby Tommies at the particular, indiscreet way he had pronounced her first name. "Me… Tommy," he went on, thumping his chest with his open palm.

*"Tommy? Mais… vous n'êtes pas américain?"*

Tommy rolled his eyes, wanting to explain, defeated by the language barrier. But before he could, one of the *poilus* stood up and began speaking close to his face rapidly and threateningly, the smell of the Frenchman's breath temporarily blotting out everything else – until Nicole began to berate the man in their native language. Her aunt chattered hysterically from behind her counter. The whole *estaminet* was becoming caught up in a scene, which Tommy interrupted by leaning over and saying with great intensity to Nicole, "I'm sorry. *Merci.*" With that the trouble temporarily subsided, and he backed away from the crowd toward the door, his hands gesturing in front of him in wild, choppy motions. "I'm… sorry," he repeated.

Then he was out the door. He had to find his British buddy.

# Chapter XI

Jamie sat nursing the balance of David's beer and Tommy's cider; he had paid for the drinks, and he'd be damned if he'd let them go to waste. While he felt no particular emotion about the scene with the two boys – he had absolutely no sense that he'd done anything wrong in his harshly graphic speculations about the fate of the young Englishman's brothers – he still admired the American lad's brashness, which he saw as akin to his own. He thus was annoyed when he eavesdropped on Mme. Lacroix and the two *poilus,* as they roundly criticized the Yank's inappropriately forward behavior toward Nicole. As if the two French soldiers wouldn't gladly have had their way with such a girl in half a minute, given half a chance. That it put him on the same side of the argument as Nicole was merely an added bonus.

The *estaminet* was becoming more crowded by the minute, so it took a while for her to make her way back to his table, during which time he continued to command it in solitary splendor. By the time she did return, he could tell that her mood had turned truculent.

*"Encore de bière, m'sieur?"* she asked, her voice edging toward curtness.

*"Non, merci... cochons."*

She hadn't been looking at him when he spoke the delayed last word, and now she did so with surprise and disbelief, wondering if she'd been insulted. *"M'sieur?"*

*"Cochons,"* Jamie repeated, a little too loudly, inclining his head in the direction of the *poilus.*

Ordinarily Nicole would have been the last one to quietly accept such an insult to the gallant soldiers of France, least of all from a soldier of the British Empire; but just now, the comment shook loose a smile from her otherwise-dour countenance. *"Tous,"* she replied. *"Tous les hommes sont cochons."*

"Ah, that's not fair!" he cried defensively, in English.

*"Mais pas vous, m'sieur."*

Thanks to the vagaries of spoken French, just as Nicole had been initially unsure if he was calling *her* a pig, so Jamie wasn't certain whether she was including Tommy along with himself in the select company of men who were not pigs, though he suspected as much. He strove to conceal his sudden irritation – too successfully, perhaps, because she proceeded to make it quite clear: *"Votre ami, m'sieur... c'est vrai qu'il s'appelle 'Tommy'?"*

*"Oui, c'est vrai."*

*"Mais–"*

*"Il est américain, je sais. Ça, c'est son nom."*

She shook her head. *"Je ne comprends pas."* He had been clear enough about Tommy's name, but her confusion was too attractive to be annoying.

*"Et puis, il s'appelle 'Fleurs' aussi."* In his mind, Jamie was translating Tommy's last name for her; he had thought about telling her the nickname, but had decided "Iowa" was a term beyond his powers of explanation in French. Besides, he was still trying to change the subject.

But the same language problem as before caused Nicole to hear the name in the singular. *"C'est bon,"* she told the old Australian brightly. *"Vraiment, il est comme un fleur, n'est-ce pas?"*

Losing patience, Colbeck ignored her observation and hastily volunteered, *"Moi, je m'appelle Jacques,"* not really choosing the right French name for himself.

"Jack," Nicole repeated, assuming he had meant the English name, which she'd heard plenty. *"Merci,* Jack," she said graciously, her attempt at a hard English "j" confusing Jamie, who knew the name didn't sound right but couldn't quite place why. As she began to move away from him, to his disquiet, he was sure he heard her softly repeat to herself, *"Fleur."*

"'Scusin' me, Sergeant, but d'you s'pose our crew might able to share that table with you?"

It was a trio of Tommies, their leader a little better-spoken than your usual British private. But Jamie had had his fill of the Poms today, as he usually did any day circumstances forced him to spend time in their company. "You can have the whole bloody thing, mates. I was just abaout to leave, anywise."

As he headed outside for the motorcar, it occurred to him that he still could and would look for Flowers on the road back to Pierregot, although not too sharply in this hour of fading light. Jamie had other things on his mind. He needed sleep, and he knew there was a lot of work ahead. Judging from their twenty-four hours in the Vaden line, his Doughboy charges were indeed fine lads – he'd certainly told the truth about that. But they were a far sight from ready for a real spell in the trenches.

Tommy knew that by speaking his mind to Jamie and then stopping to take his leave of Nicole, he had spotted David a lead of several minutes, but he was confident his longer stride would allow him to make up the difference and catch up with his friend. As he headed out of Rainneville and down the hill into the countryside, he was struck by how much less traffic there was than at about the same time of dusk two nights before.

Only two nights ago? Tommy marveled at the compression of time, mentally surveying the past forty-eight hours to make sure he wasn't mistaken. It was ridiculous, he knew, but he felt as if he'd already known David, Jamie, even Nicole, for a very long time; that he'd been in Picardy for months, not days; that he was, after all, a veteran of the trenches, even if very little had been fired in his direction yet besides Very lights.

Several minutes of vigorous striding yielded no sign of his pal, and he wondered if Davey had gone off in some different direction rather than the obvious one of returning to Molliens. It was getting steadily darker, and in the almost-sultry air Tommy was perspiring some, not to mention feeling his lack of rest. Heading on back to the camp and sleeping would have been the smartest course, just as Maple had suggested. Then, too, there was the possibility that Eddie, or even Captain, might conduct a bed check; Tommy sure didn't want to get in trouble again.

But he had to find David. He couldn't leave things as they were. He was the one who had pressed the search for David before, which had resulted in Jamie ordering the Briton to join them, which had led to everything else. Tommy felt responsible for that.

As the long dusk deepened under a cover of clouds, the thought suddenly occurred to him: David's short-cut. Why hadn't that come to him immediately? Had he already passed it? Tommy had a fair sense of direction, but he would never claim David's "mem'ry for places." If David had taken that route, then there was a natural hiding place where he would have gone, to get away from Tommy, Jamie and his terrible tales, his other mates, the war. Flowers already had passed several side paths forking off the main road; now he stopped and pondered whether any of those might have been the one he'd failed to notice two nights ago, until Pearson had called it to his attention.

A passing vehicle, headed the same way, seemed to slow to a crawl next to him, even though he was off to the side of the road. From the lorry – no, it was a motorcar – there came a familiar voice: "Sure you don't want a ride, soljuh?"

An idea came to Tommy just as he was about to issue a pithy rejoinder. Without a word, he jumped into the passenger side and took a seat, next to the last man in the world he felt like talking to just now.

Jamie picked up speed again; the Aussie took it as a victory that the Yank was willing to accept a ride, and didn't press the private's silence at first. But after a quiet minute, during which time Flowers hadn't even bothered to look at him but kept his eyes fixed on the side of the road, Colbeck couldn't resist: "Nicole asked me abaout you after you left."

"Oh?" Tommy responded, with a surprising lack of interest in his voice for a man who had just risked a near riot to take his proper leave of the French girl.

"Yes. Wanted to know your name."

"I told her my name."

"So I gathered. But 'Tommy' confused her."

"I kinda reckoned it did. I wanted – I tried to explain. But I didn't have the words."

"I did. But I made it easier. I told her your last name. In French, y'see."

"What is my last name in French?"

*"Fleurs."* During this entire exchange, Tommy remained turned away from Jamie, still intent on scanning the roadside. With the conversation seemingly at a dead end, Jamie added, "She liked your name. Said it fit you."

That worked, at least for a moment. Tommy turned his head just enough to catch Jamie's eye and ask him, "Really?" before his attention shifted back to where it had been.

"Yes." More silence. The rudeness, the very sort of thing that never much bothered Jamie in anybody, was getting to him now. He knew full well what, or rather who, was causing Tommy's reconnaissance of the roadside. But there was something odd in the way the Doughboy was going about his business, as if he expected to find his Pom mate hiding behind a hedgerow rather than walking out on the road. Deliberately pretending the situation was otherwise, Jamie intoned, "I'm sure there ain't any Germans araound here. You can relax, Flaowuhs."

"Heh," Tommy said, a short, sharp little laugh with no follow-through. But a few moments later, as they reached the intersection of the Pierregot and Molliens roads, the American abruptly cried, "Wait! Stop!"

Jamie obligingly brought the motorcar to a sudden, screeching halt; it was fortunate that traffic was so light. To Colbeck's surprise, although no one else was in sight, Flowers jumped up and out of the vehicle, heading toward Molliens. Then he figured the private had understood the significance of the fork before he had. "We can turn here, Tommy," he said, recovering quickly. "I can take you to Molliens. No need for you to walk."

"I can't – It's not," the Yank began, then shook his head, still walking slowly toward Molliens, looking off to his right for – what? "Thanks for the ride, Jamie. I'll see you later."

"I'm sure he's gone back to Molliens by naow, Tommy. I'll drive you there. It's the least I can do."

That caused Tommy to stop, and Jamie likewise just sat there in the motorcar, both of them amazed by what the Australian had just said – tantamount to a confession of wrongdoing, even though in Colbeck's mind none had taken place.

"I told you, I–" Tommy began again, then faltered. "Let me go find him, Jamie. Go on back to Pierregot."

"But it's gettin' dark, lad."

"Please. This is something I need to do. By myself."

Jamie shook his head. "As you wish, mate," he said, revving the motor.

"Thanks again for your help," Tommy told him, flashing a smile.

"Ah, you and your manners," Jamie replied with a dismissive wave. But the agreeable undertone was unmistakable.

The last-second idea that had come to Tommy when Jamie had unexpectedly materialized had paid off. He never could have been sure which of the side paths off the road from Rainneville was the one he and David had taken, but he recalled clearly that the path had merged with the road to Molliens not far from where the latter began, off the Rainneville-Pierregot road. After leaving Jamie, he continued slowly toward Molliens, and when he came upon the first side path that led off to his right, he was confident he had the correct one. And the ride had probably allowed him to gain time on David, to boot.

Now that he was sure he was on the right track, he felt another surge of energy sweep away his weariness. He had heard his father use the expression "second wind," but this had to be his fifth, sixth, or seventh.

The clouds that had covered the sky since early that afternoon were beginning to part; it was an increasingly clear night, pleasantly warm but beginning to cool off some. The same sensations as he had felt on their walk along this path two nights ago came back to him, but more faintly without the smell of fresh rain. It was much earlier yet in the evening than then, with the sky just now a dark blue, and figures still distinguishable at a distance of a hundred yards – such as the small man coming toward him. Tommy was about to hail the fellow, on the assumption it was David; the height was certainly right. But as the man drew ever nearer, Tommy could see the walk was all wrong. This fellow moved like someone considerably older than his English pal. Closer still, and it became apparent that the man, a French civilian, was very old indeed, maybe as old as Tommy's grandfather.

*"B'soir, m'sieur,"* the old man said as they met, tipping his cap.

"Hello," Tommy replied, assuming he was giving the proper response, and unable to think of anything else to say anyway.

The man answered him with a lively stream of French that Tommy didn't comprehend at all, except he caught one word: *"Anglais."*

"American," the Doughboy corrected; then he remembered Nicole's pronunciation, and tried to mimic it: "Americ*ann.*"

*"Ah, oui, Américain,"* the old man repeated, and he jabbered on excitedly, patting the Yank on the back, as Flowers nodded from time to time, not knowing a thing that was being said. At one point the man seemed to be pointing upward at the sky, and then he poked Tommy's chest.

Finally he seemed to be finished, and the American carefully said, to ensure closure, *"Merci."* This caused another minute's worth of further verbiage from the

Frenchman, who eventually clapped the young man on the shoulder and headed off in the direction of the Molliens road.

Of a sudden, Tommy was acutely aware that he was in a country not his own, where the people spoke a language not his own. It seemed an absurd realization, since he'd already been in France almost a month; but he'd been surrounded by other Americans most of that time, and it had been an easy matter to forget. The young Doughboy had taken one of his instant likings to the old Frenchman, who reminded him of Grandad; even as he was failing to understand the man, he had wished for the power to speak with him. But now it was an opportunity lost, an incident that made him wonder about even trying to see Nicole again.

It occurred to him then that, absorbed in the brief encounter with the French civilian, he might have missed somebody else passing by. But surely he would have noticed Davey, or Davey him. The narrow path now seemed quite lonely and deserted, and he upped the tempo of his stride as he moved uphill, continually inspecting the passing landscape, trying to locate the rise with the copse that hid the stable. He was convinced more than ever that that was where he would find his friend.

The utter stillness of the area, with not even the sounds from the relatively nearby front intruding (it must be an awfully quiet night there, he thought), might have spooked a city boy, but it all felt quite familiar to Flower of Iowa. With the clouds parting further still, the moon and stars had begun to illuminate his way, and he slid into a relaxed rhythm, his alert scouting for his destination notwithstanding.

They appeared so suddenly that he scarcely had time to react. One moment the path ahead was empty; the next, accompanied by a chorus of thunderous howling, three, maybe four large dogs were virtually upon him, making fierce threatening noises, one of them snapping at his leg. He collected his wits just in time to register exactly what was going on, and was flooded with a sense of genuine peril; he was without his gun tonight, and he knew the pack could smell his fear – and it seemed capable of actually carrying out an attack. But Tommy was a farm boy, so he also knew that dogs were cowards at heart. With all the lung power he could muster, he yelled at the marauders, "No! Get away! Stop! Go away!"

The canines continued their angry cacophony, but stopped moving in his direction. He took a step forward, and their leader – not the biggest, but the meanest – began barking maniacally and took two steps toward him. He shouted again, full strength; it was as if they were in a screaming match, as if Tommy were having a violent, passionate argument with a dog on a lonely path somewhere in France. The pack was not backing off the way he had hoped or expected.

Abruptly the wild thought came to him that perhaps these dogs only understood French. Since he by no means felt out of danger, changing languages was worth a try; the only trouble was, as with Nicole and the old man, he didn't know many useful words in French, and none that were germane to his predicament. So, in his sternest cadences, he hollered the few he thought he did know at random: *"Merci! M'sieur!"* Still the pack snarled, permitting no passage. *"Nicole!"* They seemed to bark more furiously yet. *"Estaminet!"*

To his surprise and relief, the lead dog backed away a good half a foot. Tommy took another step forward, and the leader hesitated. *"Estaminet!"* he cried again, and the dogs all inched away a bit; at last he was able to maneuver past them, so that they now stood between him and where he had come from, not where he was headed.

But as soon as he attempted to walk away, they came after him again, forcing him to turn around, nipping at his heels, fangs glistening in the moonlight, eyes glowing and glaring – truly the hounds of Hell. *"Estaminet! Estaminet!"* he cried, this time to little effect. Frustrated and not a little frightened, he cursed them in English, employing language he never used with people: "God *damn* you! Go away! Leave me alone!" Again they backed away a little; again he turned around, and again they followed, still barking madly. "Shut up! No! Go!"

Holding his breath, he whirled around, placing his back to them once more, and strode quickly away. This time they just stood there, still barking their fool heads off. As he began increasing the distance between himself and the pack, Tommy was trying mightily to calm himself. He could feel his pulse still racing. The standoff had lasted only a few minutes, but he felt he had been there for hours with the raging beasts. He tried to control his shaking by reminding himself, humorously, that this might turn out to be the most harrowing action he would see in France. He had to remember to tell his mother and Susan all about it the next time he wrote them.

The droning noise crept up on him from behind and above; at first, it was off the surface of his mind, in the back of his consciousness; then, he became dimly aware that the drone was competing with the steadily receding barking of the pack. Still, he didn't bother to look for the source, assuming that the front, miles away, finally had become active and was making itself heard. But suddenly he realized the noise was drowning out the dogs – and everything else. Now he did turn round – and he saw a massive black shape heading straight down the path toward him, hovering over it at a heart-stoppingly low height.

He had seen an aeroplane before, once, when his father had taken him and his sisters to a big carnival in Newton. But that had been an exhibition, in the daylight – and in peacetime. It hadn't begun to prepare him for this wondrous sight. Since he was miles behind the front lines, he simply assumed it was an Allied plane, and as he stood in the middle of the path, lit by the stars and the moon, he began enthusiastically to wave at the craft's pilot.

He saw the flash from the middle of the dark mass and heard something whiz past his ear in what seemed to be the same instant. No more than a few eternal seconds later, he would find himself astonished by the harefooted speed of his reflexes; even as his mind had not yet registered the fact that he was being shot at, his body somehow got it, and was already taking appropriate evasive action. He dove into a pathside ditch and hit the ground all in one motion. It was an act that probably saved his life, he decided as he watched the rat-a-tat-tat stitching of gunshots tearing up the surface of the path, veering ever closer to where he lay… but then the aeroplane was past him (he could swear he heard laughter as it roared by), and he was safe for the time being.

He pondered whether he ever could move that fast again if he had to and, thinking of his foolish waving, remembered Jamie's lecture about making assumptions. He'd better listen more closely to the Australian sergeant in the future. Seconds passed; then, breathing heavily, he staggered up and out of the ditch, back into the middle of the path. He heard more shots fired down the way, and his first panicked thought was that the aeroplane might have picked out the old stable for target practice. He must hurry to help David, he thought, and he commenced running, looking frantically for the rise and the copse… at least for a few seconds, until his ears alerted him and he looked straight ahead: the infernal machine had wheeled about, and was coming toward him again!

Not about to make the same mistake twice, Tommy tore to the opposite side (yes, he found, he *could* run that fast again) and hid behind the biggest tree available, which turned out to be an enormous lilac bush, laden with blooms whose fragrance immediately, irrationally, took him back to the yard of his aunt's house in Belle Plaine. This time the aeroplane came buzzing lazily down the path, firing away sporadically; as it rumbled past the spot where Tommy crouched, concealed among the lilacs, he thought he caught sight of the iron cross insignia in the moonlight. Then there was an explosion, maybe twenty, thirty yards away – pretty close to the precise spot where he'd jumped into the ditch before – and dust, mud, a few lilac blossoms, and who-knew-what-else showered down on him. He wasn't hurt, but at that moment, the sheer insanity of it all got to him: this beautiful night, the heavenly scent of the lilacs, yet some man or men he didn't even know had come out of the sky and were trying to murder him – as ready to do him in as those dogs, maybe more. It was just crazy!

His train of thought was interrupted by more firing in the distance, accompanied, or so it seemed to Tommy, by a sickening yelp; but he was half convinced that that was just because he had been thinking again about the pack. Still he crouched beneath the lilac bush, still filthy with debris, for minutes on end, until he felt reasonably sure the aeroplane was not coming back yet again. He should return immediately to Pierregot and report what had happened, in case they hadn't heard it. Maybe the Boche were starting another big push.

That was what he should do, all right. It was his duty. But what if his pal had been hit just now? That was his duty, too – to help a friend, a buddy, an ally, in time of trouble. And he desperately needed to see David again right now, just to convince himself they both were all right.

Shaking himself off as best he could, Tommy returned to the middle of the now-pitted path and looked once more in the direction of Molliens, from where the flying terror had come, and where he had last seen it heading. Then he turned decisively around, again facing in the direction of Rainneville, and that little stable.

Not more than two or three minutes after he resumed his trek, the rise and the copse appeared on his left; as soon as he saw them, he was dead certain he had the right place. He began to gallop up the hill, eager and relieved because he was sure he would find his friend. But halfway up, he stopped in his tracks – not because he had the wrong hill after all, nor because the copse and stable weren't there.

His young heart had had plenty of strain tonight, but it seemed to him to be beating harder than ever as he stared at the place where he and David had slept a mere two nights ago. Without question, the abandoned building was intact; also without question, smoke was issuing from it. Indeed, the stable looked to Tommy as if it might well be on fire.

# Chapter XII

Breathless from his run the rest of the way up the hill, Tommy unceremoniously grabbed the stable door and threw it open with such force that, with a sharp report, it partially gave way. His action revealed not a building in flames, but a few wispy strands of smoke and a shadowy figure who shouted *"What?"* as he shot up from a crouching position. So very startled was this man that he lost his footing and fell over backward. Nearly black though the interior of the stable was, illuminated only by the light of the moon and stars streaming in the doorway, Tommy still had no trouble recognizing David by his voice in the single word he had uttered. The Doughboy charged into the building, finding by instinct the place where his pal had fallen, and attempted to scoop his smaller comrade in his arms, intent on rescuing them both from the smoldering stable, which might yet burst into flames at any second.

But Tommy was rewarded instead with a rude, powerful shove that sent him spilling backward himself. David, roused from his own initial shock, shouted, "What d'you want? Leave me alone!" as he scrambled to his feet with escape on his mind.

Again Tommy's instincts proved quick; he sprang up and caught the fleeing figure just at the stable door. The two grappled briefly as the realization finally struck Tommy that he had been assuming – for no good reason; there he was, assuming again – that David knew who he was. That awareness was immediately followed by another – that David was trying to reach for his knife, as he too had left camp without his gun. Tommy amazed himself by the quiet, calm way in which he announced to his still-struggling friend, "Davey, it's me. It's Tommy."

The matter-of-fact, conversational tone, as much as the information itself, caused Pearson to stop dead, and Flowers used the opportunity to drag them both out of the stable and into the moonlight, where he released his hold. The pair stared at each other, a couple of feet apart. Coming from dark to relative light, their eyes adjusted quickly, so they both could get visual confirmation of what their ears already had told them.

"Bloody 'ell!" David finally exclaimed between gulps of air. "It *tis* you."

"You shouldn't have called out to me in there if you didn't know," Tommy said in the same strangely calm voice. "What if I'd been a Hun, there in the dark? It would have helped me to find you, to kill you." His mind remained very much fixed on Colbeck's lessons, and without thinking, he added, "Remember Jamie's story."

David turned sharply away from him and said bitterly, "Like I could ever forget that bloody man's stories."

That wasn't what Tommy had intended at all. Chagrined by his misstep, he impulsively moved over and grasped his friend's shoulders from behind, muttering, "Dear God, Davey, I'm sorry–"

But the Briton broke free and turned fiercely on him. "Why don't you just leave me alone?"

The American, still acting on impulse, took a step forward and said in the same quiet manner as before, but with even more conviction, "Because I won't. Because you're my friend."

It touched David to the quick. His own tone changed entirely, becoming shaky and light. Though he didn't look at Tommy, he put his hand out in a halting motion. "Please, Tommy," he said. "Don't be doing this to me. Leave me in peace."

"I won't," Tommy repeated. "I'm your friend."

"Then you should leave me me pride."

"You don't have anything to be ashamed of."

"I – I will if you don't leave now," David said, his voice breaking. He whispered "Please" once more, but with no voice; too choked up. Tommy could see him mouthing the word.

Then David started to cry. Tommy grabbed him as he lost control, convulsed with loud sobs. Gently the Yank lowered them both to the ground, as his buddy wept for his lost brothers, and Tommy held him, sharing the heartbreak. They sat there that way for a long while, Doughboy and Tommy, until David broke free of Tommy's embrace and turned away again. This time Tommy didn't move. Presently David looked back at him and said, "My God, what you must think of me."

Looking his friend in the eye, Tommy said, "They were your brothers, Davey. I'm your best buddy. What else is there to think?"

David shook his head, reached back across the space between them, and put a hand on Tommy's upper arm. "You are me best chum. You really are." He removed his hand, looked over at the building with its broken door, and added, "Even though you've gone and ruint me favorite 'iding place."

They both laughed at that; then Tommy said earnestly, "I thought it was on fire. I was afraid the aeroplane had shot at it."

"The aeroplane di'n't shoot at it, but it almost was on fire, thanks to me and me own foolishness. I 'ad the lantern lit when I 'eard that bloody thing, and I was in such a 'urry to put it out, I knocked it over. Some of the straw caught fire, and then I 'ad to put that out, too. The 'plane could 'ave seen the smoke. I was lucky, I was."

"So was I. And I did something much more foolish than you." Tommy told David then about his own misadventures with the aeroplane. The Englishman agreed that he had been too careless, but dissented when Tommy added, "I should probably get right back to camp and report it. It might be the start of a big push by the Germans."

"Oh, Tommy," David said, a slight touch of scorn in his voice.

"What?"

"One aeroplane. You cou'n't even be sure it was one of Jerry's."

"I saw the iron cross!... At least, I think I did. And besides, we're behind the lines. They'd have to have known I was on our side. Why would our own boys shoot at me?"

"I've 'eard sometimes they get drunk and shoot at anyone they see, just for fun."

"That's a terrible thing to say, Davey."

"Well, I've 'eard it, all the same."

"I don't believe it." David just shrugged, and Tommy went on: "What if I'm right, and it was a Jerry plane? Shouldn't I report it right away?"

"What's one aeroplane? Even if it was the Boche, they do things like that all the time, too."

"So I shouldn't even report it?"

"Oh, you can. But I wou'n't go running back to me billets double-time just to do it. Someone else probably 'eard it anyways." There was a pause, then David added in a very different voice, "I'm glad you weren't 'it, Tommy. I'd 'ave felt terrible if you was 'it while you were looking for me. And you were looking for me, weren't you?"

They were still sitting apart, not touching; but now Tommy scooted back over next to David, and put his arm around his friend's shoulder as he said, "Do you have to ask?"

David smiled. "No, I s'pose I don't."

The American squeezed the British soldier's shoulder lightly and rocked him a bit. "I'm glad you weren't hurt, either."

David looked away. "Not by bullets, anyways." At that, Flowers tightened his grip slightly, and Pearson continued, "I can't stop thinking about it, Tommy. I can't stop thinking about Doug dying that way, drowning in that mud." David's eyes were dry now, and his voice was strong enough; still, Tommy pulled him closer, and David welcomed the contact. After a minute or more had passed, and David had relaxed more deeply in Tommy's hold, the Englishman murmured, "Never 'ad a friend like you."

"Me neither."

"D'you think we should go back soon?"

"It's still early. Unless they do a bed check."

"My lot won't."

"Mine might."

"We should go, then. I don't want you to get in trouble on my account again."

"I'll take my chances. It's a night for that. The plane, the dogs–"

"Dogs?"

Tommy told David about the pack attack, and it caused the Briton to stir uneasily. "I don't feel safe lying 'ere on the ground, then, if there's dogs about."

"They weren't wild dogs. They were farm dogs."

"Even so." David stood up and gazed down at his American chum. "Let's walk awhile. We don't 'ave to go all the way back to billets just yet. We'll find another place to stop. A better place." He stretched his hand out to Tommy, who grabbed it; and with a strength unexpected, David pulled him up.

As they trudged down the rise, and then back along the path, David requested, and Tommy gave, a full account of the American's adventures in the Vaden line. The Doughboy told his stories more or less chronologically, and so it was that after many minutes of talking and walking, negotiating the now-bullet-riddled path, he came to the final anecdote, the story about Jamie and the rotted arm.

Up to this point David had been an eager, interested listener, asking questions where appropriate without rendering judgments, but when Tommy was finished, he felt compelled to inquire, "What is it you see in the likes of 'im?"

"He's a good man, Davey. I know he has his faults, but he's a good man, and a good friend. And he may be the best sergeant there is."

"Lucky for me, 'e's assigned to your lot," David said drily.

"You could learn a lot from him, David. I know I have, and I aim to keep learning from him."

"What's this?"

Their discussion of Colbeck's pluses and minuses was interrupted as they reached a particularly shot-up section of path. The light from the stars and moon was quite bright by now, and it revealed, in stark outline, several large clumps in their way that didn't look like pieces of dirt. There was also a faint sound on the air, a distant wheeze, as well as a number of unfamiliar odors, some foul, some sickly sweet.

David struck his tinder lighter to get a better look, carefully covering the glow so it was cast only downward. "Would these be your dogs, then?" he said gravely to Tommy.

Stunned, Tommy took in the scene. The clumps were composed of fur and covered with blood and whatever else had leaked out. He recognized the leader – an animal he wasn't likely to have forgotten so soon – or rather his front half, because the other half of the dog had been blown clear away… or was that it, lying on the other side of the path? "My God," Tommy said dumbly. "My God."

"Over 'ere," David called, and Tommy picked his way carefully to a spot where one canine lay, barely breathing what was clearly his last.

"You know, we really should be carrying our guns be'ind the lines," David said, exasperated. "Now I'll 'ave to use me knife to put this poor dumb beast out of 'is suffering."

Tommy was near nausea as he remembered the yelp he'd thought he only imagined. "Can you do it clean?" he finally managed to say.

"Yes. Me dad 'ad a bake shop – we still do – but to make some extra shillings I worked for a time at the butcher's down our street. I mean, I think I can kill 'im with one cut. 'Twill probably make a mess on me, though."

"How could this have happened? How could they all have been hit? What bad luck."

"'Twasn't an accident, Tommy, can't you see that? 'Ooever it was was in the aeroplane decided they'd make good target practice."

"But they were just dogs. Just farm dogs."

"They almost got you, di'n't they?"

"But that's a farm dog's job. They were just doing their job."

"So was the poor bloke 'oose arm your friend Jamie throwed away today, most likely. No matter which side 'e was on."

The dying dog let out the faintest of whines, and Tommy put his hand over his eyes. David saw him do it. "Are you all right, Tommy?" He got no answer, and put his hand on the American's shoulder. "Why don't you walk on down a piece and let me do this? We don't both 'ave to see it."

"How can you do it?"

"'Ow can I not? 'E's in mortal pain and 'e can't 'elp 'imself. It wou'n't be right to leave 'im 'ere like this. Go along now."

Tommy took his hand from his eyes and said, "Now I wonder what you must think of me."

"I think you're still me best pal, and I said it before and I'll say it again: you've a large 'eart, Sammy. Nothing wrong with that. Now go on with you."

Dutifully, Tommy walked about twenty feet farther down the path and waited, feeling foolish for letting the dogs' fate affect him, but unable to help it. He braced himself, tensely awaiting some sort of blood-curdling howl that would haunt him for the rest of his days; but in a matter of seconds, David was by his side.

"You couldn't do it, could you?"

"Oh, I did it, all right."

"I didn't hear a sound."

"'E di'n't make any. I would like to clean me knife somewheres, though. I b'lieve there's a pond by a different path I've took, off of this one, per'aps a little further down."

"I don't remember seeing another path, David."

"It was dark, of course."

"But you saw it."

"Noticed it. Yes."

"Do you think it would be all right to use the pond like that? It might belong to some farmer – Oh, no!"

"What is it now?"

"The old man. The old man, Davey!"

"What old man? D'you mean Jamie?"

"No, a *really* old man." Tommy realized he had forgotten to tell David that part of his story, too. He had to do better; if he had been out on a scouting party and David had been his superior officer, he'd have missed telling him half or more of what he'd seen.

He began to relate the incident to Pearson now, prompting the latter to interrupt with the comment, "You've 'ad quite the evening, 'aven't you?"

When Tommy got to the part about trying to speak with the old Frenchman, he remembered something even as he was describing it, acting it out: "He – he pointed to the sky, then he touched my chest. Davey! – Do you think he was a spy?"

"Cor! What makes you think that?"

"What I just told you. He pointed to the sky. Maybe he knew the aeroplane was coming."

"Or 'e could 'ave been talking about the weather. There aren't many Frenchmen 'oo'd 'elp the Boche, you know. They 'ate them."

"But why would he do that?"

"I don't know. Why would 'e tell you about it if 'e was a spy? I'm sure 'e was on our side."

Tommy paused, and came back to his first thought, when he had first recollected the old civilian. "Do you think they shot at him?"

"Per'aps, if they sawr 'im. Dogs, you, an old man – what would they care?"

"We have to go look for him."

"But you said 'e was moving slow. We would 'ave caught up to 'im by now, if 'e'd still been out – or if 'e was 'it. 'E probably knew to get out of the way. Look anyways, 'ere's our new path. And beyond is our pond."

David's memory for places proved unerring once more. As Tommy watched him dip his bloodied knife in the water a short time later, the Yank was suddenly beset by a new surge of weariness. Funny how it came in waves. The old man was abruptly forgotten. "Can we stop and rest now?" he asked.

David didn't answer at first, but straightened up and scanned the landscape. At length he said "Follow me," and in a few minutes they had made half a circuit of the pond, to the shore farthest from their usual path, where a small, treeless hill sloped upward. Near its crest was a double dip: the ground sloped briefly downward, then up again to form an outcropping of Picardy chalk, but an old one, covered with moss. Then the hill sloped up again, a few yards farther, before it crested. "Lovely," David pronounced as he led the Doughboy to it. "'Igh ground, clear of chats I 'ope, a little 'ard but also a little soft." As they climbed and then doubled back onto the outcropping, he added, "And a view, too."

It was true. In the light of the night, if they looked carefully, they could make out the entire valley – the path they had been traversing, and even the main roads connecting Rainneville, Pierregot, and Molliens. "You've been here before, haven't you," said Tommy as they both surveyed the terrain. He was sure David was noticing all sorts of important features that he himself was missing.

"Never before, no."

"Truly?"

"You know I wou'n't lie, Tommy. Not to you."

"You're right. I do." Tossing aside their caps, they both lay down on their sides, faces turned toward each other while their bodies were turned toward the view, away from the crest of the hill. "It's spooky, you know, the way you can find things."

"D'you fancy I'm a ghost, then?"

That was all it took for Tommy to shift slightly behind his buddy and wrap one arm around David's chest as he continued to lean on the other. "You're no ghost, pal," he said, and David shifted in turn so that his head rested on Tommy's chest as he gripped Tommy's arm, lightly. Neither spoke for a time. Then Tommy, his heart full, said, "I was so afraid that I'd find you hurt or–"

"Ssh, ssh," David countered. "We're both in the pink now. That's all that matters." Tommy ever so slightly drew his arm closer around David; the Englishman ran his hand down the length of the American's arm, then cupped his hand over the top of Tommy's. Tommy lowered his chin so it touched the top of David's head. Completely at ease, David said, "There's so much I don't really know about you. Tell me about Susan. What's she like? Is she fair, like you?"

"Blond, you mean?" David nodded, the hair on the top of his head tickling the bristles of Tommy's chin, and vice versa. Tommy went on, "Yes, she's blond, blonder than me. And she's got blue, blue eyes."

"Very pretty, then."

"Yes, very pretty."

"D'you 'ave a picture of 'er?"

"No, I don't. I don't know why. I should write and ask her for one. I wish I did."

"Me, too. Wisht I could see a picture of your girl."

"And what about your girl?"

"Don't 'ave a girl. Never 'ad a girl."

"Why not?"

"Don't know. Just 'aven't. Colin 'ad a girl, and Doug 'ad a 'ole crew of girls. Will you marry Susan when you go back?"

"I reckon I will."

"You don't sound too excited for it."

Tommy paused, then: "It's just that that all seems so far away right now."

"Because 'tis, I s'pose. Is Susan as pretty as Nicole?"

"Even prettier," Tommy said loyally.

"D'you love 'er?"

"Susan, or Nicole?"

"Either. Both."

Tommy thought about it, sincerely, then answered, "I don't know. I reckon I could love either one, given half the chance."

"You met Susan at school?"

"No, she lives down the street–"

"Ah, yes, of course, that's right."

"–and we went to school together later on."

"D'you miss 'er?"

"Sometimes. Not right now." Stabbed by an immediate pang of guilt, Tommy added, "She's a very sweet girl. Very sweet to me."

They were quiet for a while, David's curiosity about Susan apparently quenched, then Tommy started another line of questioning: "You said your father was a baker?"

"That's right. Dunster's a small town, y'see, and there's farms all round it, but there's a mill to buy flour from, so 'e decided to make a go of it. We still own the shop. It's just me mum and me sis now. That was the 'ardest part for me, me leaving for France and only them to mind the shop."

"You didn't go to school?"

"Of course I did. I can read and write, and I used to keep accounts at our shop. Even when I was going to school, I always worked there, too."

"And at the butcher's."

"And at the butcher's. But I liked our shop better."

"Less blood?"

"That's part of it, I s'pose. Also, it was ours. It was going to be all of ours someday – me, Doug, and Colin. Now it'll be mine. Di'n't you work while you were at school?"

"Summers and holidays. My father works at the pharmacy in Brooklyn–"

"Pharmacy?"

"Medicines?"

"Ah. An apothecary."

"–but I worked at the hotel. I did odd jobs, helped carry luggage to the rooms, things like that."

"Fancy that – you, in a 'otel, like the inn on our 'igh street! Will you go back there, then? Or will you work with your dad at the apothecary?"

"I don't have to do either one. In America, you can do whatever you want. But I might like to learn about how to run a hotel, to be the manager. I liked working at the hotel."

"You wou'n't work outside, then – a big strong boy like you?"

"I grew up doing some outdoors work. Everybody in my part of Iowa does. But I'm no farmer."

"D'you think you'd like to move to a city, then?"

"I might. But I don't think Susan would cotton to it."

"You're more adventurous than she is."

There was a long pause, and then Tommy said, "I reckon this is my big adventure."

"Mine, too." There was more quiet, until David said, "I need to sit up for a bit."

"That's all right with me. My arm was getting tired."

David sat up. "So why di'n't you say something?"

"'Cause I… liked it fine the way it was."

"You're probably more tired than me. Why don't you lie down? Then you can use me for a pillow."

They more or less switched places, with Tommy lying full-length on his back, his head in the lap of the now-sitting David, whose legs were stretched out before him, one hand on the ground and the other on Tommy's chest. From his new vantage point, Tommy had a view straight up. "Look at the stars, Davey."

As David did so, he leaned forward slightly, took his hand off the ground, and began idly stroking the blond man's hair. Eyes still fixed on the heavens, he said, "They are beautiful, aren't they?"

"Did you ever just look up at the stars in Dunster?"

"Many times. I used to take country walks on warm nights with me brothers. We'd find a meadow and lie down and look up, and point out the constellations and such."

Excited by a recollection, Tommy suddenly stirred, causing David's hand to drop from his hair back to the ground. "Do you remember Halley's Comet?"

"'deed I do. Nineteen and ten. I was ten years old."

"Me, too. The papers wrote about it for months. We went to my Grandad's – he has a farm – and I got to stay up late to look for it."

"Did you see it?"

"Yes. Did you?"

David nodded. "I sawr it on a 'ill above town, with me 'ole family – me Dad was still alive then – and most of the other people from the village. It was like a fair, it was."

"There was a celebration at the farmhouse next to my Grandad's. And then another one at the bandshell in the park, in town. I got to go to both."

David considered, then said, "Di'n't look all that grand, really, did it? The comet."

Tommy laughed. "No, not after everything I read about it. But it was still something. I was glad I got to see it."

"I am, too.... Fancy it, Tommy, you and me, on two sides of the world, looking at the same sky for the same comet, and we di'n't even know each other then."

There was more quiet, then Tommy said, "Sing me a song, Davey."

"What, cor?"

"Sing me a song."

"You're the one what can sing. I 'eard you that time at Madame's, remember?" Tommy nodded. "Why don't you sing instead? You'd do much better."

"Will you sing something if I sing something?"

"Go on with you."

Tommy pondered a few seconds, then asked, "What are the words to 'Tipperary'? Do you know them?"

"Every Tommy knows those."

"This Tommy doesn't. Help me." Still lying on his back, his head in Pearson's lap, Flowers softly began to sing:

*"It's a long way to Tipperary,*
*It's a long way to go.*
*It's a long way to Tipperary...* What?"

"To the sweetest girl I know," David said plainly.

*"To the sweetest girl I know....* Right?" He meant the tune.

"That's right. You've got it."

"Sing me the next part. Don't just say it."

David looked bemused but, singing very low, complied:

"Goodbye, Piccadilly–"

*"Goodbye, Piccadilly,"* Tommy repeated.

*"Farewell, Leicester Square,"*

*"Farewell, Lester Square,"*

Then they both sang, *"It's a long, long way to Tipperary,"* and David finished, *"But my 'eart's right there,"* and Tommy echoed him again, though he put in the "h" in "heart."

"D'you know it now?"

"I think so." A little louder and stronger than before, Tommy sang the whole thing, missing neither a word nor a note.

David smiled when he was done and said, "I got a mem'ry for places and numbers, you got a mem'ry for music and words."

"What does that mean – Piccadilly and Lester Square?"

"Those are places in London."

"And Tipperary, too?"

"No, that's Ireland."

"So why do English boys sing it?"

"I don't know. Maybe the Piccadilly and Leicester Square parts. But that wou'n't explain why Scots and Welsh lads do, would it?"

"No."

Another pause, then David said, "You're very good, you know. At singing."

"I sing all right. But I liked your voice, too."

"I'm no singer, Tommy."

"I sang for you like you asked. Now sing for me."

David looked down. Tommy had sung "Tipperary," and well, flat on his back; his head still lay where it had been all along. "What is it you want me to sing?"

"Doesn't matter. Sing the first thing that comes into your head."

David took the suggestion seriously, and in a quiet, unsteady voice, began:

*"Roses are shining in Picardy,*
*In the 'ush of the silver dew.*
*Roses are flow'ring in Picardy,*
*But there's never a rose like you.*
*And the roses will die with the summertime–"*

He stopped, suddenly hearing the words quite differently from the way he had always heard them before. But just as quickly, he made a decision and hurried on:

*"And our paths may be far apart,*
*But there's one rose that dies not in Picardy:*
*'Tis the rose that I keep in my 'eart."*

"You rushed it."

"I know. I'm sorry."

"Don't be. It was nice." David could see Tommy smiling up at him in the moonlight, face upside down in his lap. With an odd glitter in his eye, Tommy reached up with his right arm and brought his hand to the back of David's head, applying a gentle downward pressure. At the same time, he gradually lifted his own head up. Halfway, their lips met, long and slow. Then Tommy released the pressure on David's head and slowly dropped his own back into David's lap.

"What was that?" David, breathing shallow, tried to keep any specific emotion out of his voice as he asked the question.

Tommy was still looking up and smiling at him, and he shrugged. "I don't know. I just wanted to."

David swallowed, then barely hesitated. "All right." But, not ready to leave it there, he added, "You're still such a funny one, Yank."

"I know. So are you." Then Tommy yawned, covering his mouth with the back of his hand.

"I think you're very tired, Tommy. Shall we try to sleep?"

"Mm-hm," Tommy responded, and he sat partway up. David came round, and they both lay back down again, facing each other full length on their sides. "I can't miss roll call," Tommy said.

"Not to worry. You won't."

They put their arms around each other, the way they had two nights before. Each of them thought about saying something more – "Good night," at least – but nothing came, and soon they were both sound asleep.

Despite his long period without rest, it was Tommy who awoke first this time, while all remained still and dark. He was wide-awake, too, as soon as it happened, although nothing in particular had roused him. He felt warm and safe there with David: the dogs, the aeroplane, the old Frenchman, Jamie and the rotten arm – everything seemed far away. But he felt pressure from his bladder, and he didn't want to foul the nest he and his buddy had made. A trip to the crest would satisfy that need, as well as his inevitable curiosity about what was on the other side; a song from his childhood, about the bear that went over the mountain, came back to him.

He carefully extricated himself and, with a few light-footed sprints, found himself at the top. But as he looked over the crest of the ridge, what he saw gave him a profound chill, and made him forget all about his mission: just below the top, on the opposite side of the hill from where they had been sleeping, were perhaps twelve makeshift wooden crosses. Tommy didn't need much in the way of war experience to know that this was a temporary military cemetery, not the regular churchyard kind, and although it was of course too dark to read anything, he had an immediate and deep conviction that it was a resting place for British soldiers. He and David had slept comfortably while dead Tommies lay in their graves just a few feet away. He wasn't superstitious, but there was something frightening and awful about it. What if this was where Colin lay?

Tommy made a twofold resolve: to get the two of them out of there as quickly as possible, and to not let David know what he had seen, or even that anything had bothered him. He trotted the few yards back to the outcropping and promptly shook his pal awake. "I think we need to get going" was all he said.

David blinked into consciousness and looked at the sky. "We're late," he said, equally businesslike.

A night sky looked like a night sky to Tommy, but he was glad for David's ability to differentiate, and for his friend's preoccupation. They were already moving down the rise and around the pond. Tommy was afraid to look back. Even though he knew better, he had the dreadful feeling that the ghosts of the dead buried on the other side of the ridge were standing on the crest, watching them go.

# Chapter XIII

By the time Tommy got to his tent, the sky was a pearly shade of gray, and growing lighter by the minute. He was convinced by now that Harry was a sound sleeper – indeed, he was counting on that – but as he entered, Carson stirred.

"Flower of Iowa! Boy, are you ever in trouble."

"Sorry, Harry. I tried not to wake you up."

"Oh, you're not in trouble with *me,* Tommy… although I do wish you would tell me about that mam'selle of yours. She's sure been keeping you out late–"

"So who am I in trouble with?" Tommy asked, cutting him off, feeling bad about the rudeness but too anxious to wait.

"Maple was here in the middle of the night, pulling bed check. He was none too pleased when you weren't here."

"I – I was with Sergeant Colbeck," Tommy managed to say, resorting to at least part of the truth.

"Colbeck? That digger bastard!"

"He's a good man, Harry."

"Huh! Maybe a good sarge, anyway," Carson grumbled in assent, much to Flowers' surprise; then he quickly added, "But don't tell Vern I said that."

Tommy smiled. "I won't. So what else did Eddie say?"

"Something about reporting you to Captain."

"Uh-oh. What do you think I should do?"

"I think you should find your Aussie friend and make sure the two of you have the same story," Carson replied with a yawn, a chuckle and a wink. "But you better hurry. We got roll call soon."

"Thanks, Harry. I'll be right back," Tommy said as he breathlessly ducked out of the tent. He searched the immediate area in the pre-dawn light as the others slept, taking the risk of having Maple see him. But he had no idea where Jamie's sleeping quarters were, no notion of how to find him.

Eventually, he did find a pail of half-clear water, and he splashed himself – and his boots – with the liquid, determined to be presentable at roll call this time. When dawn came, however, Maple, strutting back and forth as he inspected the company, was clearly in a poisonous frame of mind. When he got to Flowers' name and Tommy shouted out "Present!" Eddie departed from his business-as-usual tone and sneered, "Nice of you to join us this morning, Flowers."

Tommy stiffened, longing to say something snappy in reply, but he knew better. Maple continued on down the alphabet, and when he finished with Young, the married man from Watseka, Illinois, he barked out the order for the troops to fall out for their morning chow – all but Flowers, that is, of whom he said, right in front of everybody else, "Our Tommy doesn't get any breakfast this morning. He's been a bad boy. He's comin' with me to see the captain."

The others duly fell out, and Maple snarled, "Well, Flowers?"

"I can explain, Sergeant, sir!" Tommy said in his best soldierly voice, though he was deep red from the public upbraiding.

"Save it for the captain!" Maple took a step closer, his face in Flowers'. "He won't be happy seeing you again this soon, I can tell you. And I'm not happy about it either. Makes *me* look bad."

Tommy gauged that no reply was needed or wanted, so as Maple turned about and started walking, he fell in behind the sergeant. Neither spoke another word as they marched to the converted schoolhouse in Pierregot village.

Dougherty was at his desk, his smirk even more pronounced than usual. Tommy and Eddie were ushered directly into Willnor's office, where, with a quick salute, Maple announced he was there to report Private Flowers to the captain for misconduct.

"Another problem with Private Flowers?" the captain asked, his eyebrow cocked.

"Captain, sir, I can explain, sir."

Willnor frowned. "No one told you to speak, Private," he said severely. "Your sergeant hasn't even told me what the problem is yet. Sergeant Maple?"

"Sir, at 2 a.m., Private Flowers was not in his tent, sir!"

"I see," said the captain, the same eyebrow still up. "And you say you have an explanation for this, Flowers?"

"Yes sir, Captain, sir."

Willnor inclined his head slightly in Tommy's direction. "Proceed, Private."

"Sir, I was at the *estaminet* in Rainneville–"

"The what?"

"The *estaminet*. It's like a tavern, sir."

"Oh. Of course. I knew that. I couldn't hear you clearly. You should speak up." Tommy was unsure if he'd been given permission to continue, and he chose not to speak until the captain said in a tone of slight exasperation, "Well, go on."

"Sir, I was with Sergeant Colbeck, and" – Tommy almost said "an English friend of mine," then thought better of it – "and he was giving me a ride back to camp in a motorcar. We got as far as the road to Molliens–"

The Captain tried to nod sagely while making a mental note to ask Dougherty where "Rainville" was, and in relation to Molliens; at least he'd heard of the latter village, since HQ was there.

"–and then I realized I didn't have my hat, that I must have left it back at the *estaminet*."

"Your… hat?"

"Yes sir, my field cap. And I sure didn't want to show up again for inspection with my uniform not in order. So I got out and started to walk back towards Rainneville–"

"Why didn't this Sergeant Killbeck take you back in the motorcar?"

"Sergeant Colbeck offered to, sir," Flowers replied, daring to correct the captain's pronunciation in the process. "He wanted to, but I wouldn't let him."

"What do you mean, you wouldn't let him? He's a sergeant, and you're a private! You needed to go back to get your cap, to be in full uniform. As an NCO, it was his duty to make sure you were in full uniform in the first place."

"But he didn't know that was why I needed to go back, sir. I just told him I needed to. I wouldn't tell him why."

"He should have asked."

"He did. I'm afraid I was – I was being stubborn, and I didn't tell him the real reason."

"Why?"

"Because I was embarrassed that I forgot my cap, sir. Besides, it was my fault. It was my duty to go back and get it, not his."

After a brief pause, during which it became apparent Flowers had nothing further to add to his story, Willnor spoke testily to Maple: "I want you to find this Sergeant Cobeck and bring him here to me. Now."

"Yes, sir," Maple said with a salute.

"And you" – Willnor addressed Tommy directly – "wait outside, where Corporal Dougherty can keep an eye on you."

At first Dougherty wasn't there to keep an eye on him, but as Tommy stood patiently in the hallway, the steely-eyed corporal returned to his station. "So what did you do now, Private Flowers?" he asked as he re-seated himself with considerable ceremony.

Even Flower of Iowa was learning not to trust everybody. "I didn't do anything," Tommy replied tersely.

"Sure. You're here to see the captain on a social visit."

The sarcastic statement didn't seem to require a response, and the private offered none. But the corporal was in a voluble mood: "You went on those trench exercises yesterday, didn't you?"

"Day before yesterday, yes. I did sentry duty night before last, in the Vaden line."

"Was that where you got into trouble?"

"I told you, I'm not in trouble," Tommy stubbornly maintained.

"Oh, yes. I forgot." After a pause, Dougherty persisted, "See any Jerries?"

"Heard some."

"How do you know?"

Tommy's body language had been as evasive as his words, but now he looked directly at the corporal and spoke in a tone of pure insolence: "'Cause they were speakin' German."

The corporal frowned. "How did you know it wasn't French?"

"I can tell German from French. Can't you?" It wasn't in Tommy's nature to be insubordinate, but something in this snide man brought it out in him. He watched Dougherty's cold eyes flash, like a fire you lit outside in the dead of winter. The corporal exhaled hard, just once, then said, "I shouldn't be sitting at this desk, you know. I should be out there fighting at the front."

He said it with such unexpected conviction that Tommy immediately took him for sincere. "But there are plenty of fellows who would be glad to trade places with you–" he offered, tentative.

"Because it's a nice, soft, cushy job?" Dougherty demanded through clenched teeth, looking a little dangerous.

"No, because it's an honor and a privilege to work for the captain."

Dougherty stood, elevating his threatening tone. "I should be in the line. I should be an officer in the line. It's too bad I don't have you under my command. Then you'd learn how to behave like a proper soldier – or die trying."

"You talk mighty large for a corp'ral warming his arse at a desk." Both private and corporal swiveled about, startled. "Sergeant Colbeck reportin' as requested," Jamie said with a smart salute at Dougherty, even as Maple, who trailed him by several steps, caught up. Dougherty returned the salute in a high fury, but said nothing as he turned on his heel to inform the captain of the sergeants' arrival.

"What's goin' on here, Flaowuhs?" Jamie continued, but before Tommy could reply, Eddie interrupted:

"Beggin' your pardon, Sergeant Colbeck, but I don't think you should be talking to Private Flowers before Captain Willnor sees you."

Jamie regarded his fellow sergeant as one might a yapping dog one wanted to humor. "Ah, of course, you're right. Smart man, Sergeant Maple. Smart man."

"Just doing my job, Sergeant."

"Of course," Jamie repeated.

"Gentlemen," came a brusque interruption from Dougherty, "the captain will see you now."

Willnor was peremptory. "You're Sergeant Colpick? But you're not with the United States Army."

"I am naow, sir. I reported to you from the Australian Corps two days ago. Remember?"

A blank look passed across Willnor's face, then: "Oh. Yes. Of course. So. Tell me, Sergeant, do you know this enlisted man?"

Jamie shot the most cursory of glances in Tommy's direction, then smiled at Willnor. "Private Flaowuhs, sir? Sure I know him. He's a good man."

"Did you see this man at any time last night?"

"Certainly I did, sir. I had me the use of a motorcar, and Private Flaowuhs rode with me to Rainneville at my invitation, to the just-a-minute there."

"To the just?–"

"The tavern, sir," Tommy put in.

"You keep quiet, Private!" Willnor exploded, turning on Tommy with his voice rising out of all proportion to the situation. "You speak only when you're spoken to! Understood?"

Humiliated, Tommy merely nodded in reply. But he couldn't help noticing – nor could the captain and Maple – the open look of contempt Colbeck gave Willnor. So overt was it that the captain was forced to ask, "Was there something you wanted to say, Sergeant?"

"Just that there's no need for us to jump daown Flaowuhs' throat, sir. That was my fault, using a phrase unfamiliar to you, you bein' new to the area and all. The lad's right. I should've said tavern." He had boxed Willnor in, being respectful and apologetic – and including himself in the blame – while effectively reprimanding a superior officer for his treatment of a private.

Willnor spluttered, then managed nothing better than a weak "Very well. Were you at this – tavern – with the private all night?"

"No, sir. We left not long after sundaown. The sky was still light."

"And you drove the motorcar back here?"

"I did, sir. We were almost as far as the Molliens road when Flaowuhs suddenly says, 'I have to get aout.'"

"Did you ask him why?"

Jamie shot Tommy a look so fleeting that Willnor might not have caught it. "Of course. But he didn't seem any too eager to tell me."

"Did you order him to tell you, then?"

"No, sir." Another quick look. "Y'see, sir, I actually had a pretty good idear what it was, anywise."

"You did? And what was that?"

Jamie cut a longer look at Tommy, long enough to be obvious to both Willnor and Maple. Tommy felt almost sick from the tension of worrying how much Jamie's story might depart from his. "Well, sir, there's this little French girl workin' at that tavern, and I think she's sweet on Flaowuhs, and I thought he was on her, too. So I figured that was the real story, why he was in such a hurry. But I didn't want to embarrass him, sir, by makin' him tell me that in so many words. So I just let him go."

"Did he say anything to you at all about his uniform?"

"His uniform, sir?"

"Yes. Was his uniform in order?"

"Far as I could see, sir, yes."

"Including his hat?"

Another lightning look to Tommy; then Jamie said with great deliberation, "Maybe – maybe not, sir. Come to think, maybe he wasn't wearing his hat."

"And you didn't reprimand him?"

"We were off duty, sir. And it was very warm. Didn't seem strange to me that he wasn't wearing his hat."

"Do you remember what Private Flowers was drinking at this tavern, Sergeant?"

Colbeck's face burst into a broad grin. "'deed I do, sir. It was cider. Apple cider."

"He went to a tavern to drink apple cider?"

"Hard cider, yes. Of course, we had beer–"

"We? You mean there were others with you and Flowers?"

Tommy's anxiety soared further; but Jamie, who didn't even bother to look at him this time, was perfectly at ease. "No, sir," he said with a shake of his head. "That's just an expression us Australians use sometimes – sayin' 'We did that' when we mean 'I did that.' It was just Flaowuhs and myself. Well" – he grinned again – "the girl was there, of course, and then–"

"So, Flowers." Willnor cut Colbeck off, abruptly and decisively shifting his attention to Tommy. "Do you still maintain you forgot your hat?"

Tommy saw Jamie, no longer in the captain's field of vision, give a smirk worthy of Dougherty, and maybe a wink. "Yes, sir, I do–" he began.

"'Course, if he left it at the just-a-minute, that would have been convenient, eh?" Jamie said to Willnor in his most ingratiating voice. Tommy struggled not to shoot the Aussie a look; he wasn't as skillful at that kind of communication, and he knew it. But he did think Jamie was overdoing the business about Nicole, and he wished he could tell his friend so.

"Flowers, did you go back to see that girl?" the captain demanded.

"No, sir." Tommy decided a flat denial would sound too insincere, even though it was true, so he added, "I – it's true I liked this girl–"

"She liked him, too."

"Sergeant, do you mind?"

"Sorry, sir."

"–and I did get the field cap back from her – she was the one that found it. But I didn't leave it on purpose. And it was so late I started right back."

"Sergeant Maple?"

"Captain?"

"Approximately what time was Private Flowers missing from his tent?"

"About 0200 hours, sir."

Although he was again unsure of himself as he ventured onto the treacherous subject of the local geography, Willnor nevertheless decided to forge ahead: "It took you that long to get back?"

"Oh, no, sir. I mean, it shouldn't have. But I tried to take a short-cut because I was so late, and then I got lost. And – and then a pack of dogs came after me – and then a German plane shot at me–" At first Tommy was too caught up in weaving what really had happened to him into his hat alibi to realize that the other three men, Jamie included, had begun to regard him as if he were a lunatic. But then he did notice, so much so that he inadvertently added, "Well, it's true!"

"Dogs – and an aeroplane, you say?"

"Yes, sir. The aeroplane shot at me, and then it went and killed those poor dogs. I could take you right back to where it happened and show you."

Willnor merely shook his head in clear disbelief, but Colbeck spoke up again: "I know his story saounds strange, sir, but you know, I believe Flaowuhs. It's too strange for him to make up."

"Hm. Did you report this – aeroplane attack – when you finally did get back to camp?"

"Not right away, sir. Everyone was asleep, and it was long gone. Then, at morning roll call–"

"Enough, Flowers. Be quiet." Willnor paced about officiously for a minute or so, while the others waited in silence. Finally he stopped in front of Tommy. "Flowers, I have seen you twice too often this week. I don't know if I believe that you're truly serious about being a soldier." He raised his finger to head off a response from Tommy, then wagged it in the golden boy's face. "What I do know is that a young man like you should not be hanging about in taverns and chasing after French girls. I don't think your mother would be very proud of *that.* This is a war, not some kind of night on the town.

"Your friend the sergeant here says you were drinking apple cider, but it sounds to me as though you had something stronger. All this talk about dogs and aeroplanes–"

"It was only one aeroplane, sir."

"Silence! You also do not know how to behave in the presence of a superior officer. Though Lord knows, you're certainly not getting a good example by fraternizing with this man." Willnor gestured at Jamie, who clenched his jaw.

"Missing bed check is a serious offense, Flowers. And if you really were attacked by an aeroplane – though I've had no other reports of any such thing last night – failing to report that in a timely manner is a serious offense as well. You are hereby ordered to latrine duty for the next two days, and kitchen duty if there's not enough latrine work to fill up your time. And that tavern is hereby declared off-limits to you."

Willnor turned sharply to Jamie. "As for you, Sergeant, if the example you set is typical of the British Army, it's no wonder we had to come over here to clean up this mess for you. You could never win a war with an attitude like yours."

Tommy could see that Jamie was bristling, but the Aussie said in a steady voice, "Beg pardon, sir, but I would like to ask one question."

"What?"

"I just wondered how many battles it is you've fought in in this war?"

Willnor colored. "Why–"

"Because I just wanted you to know, sir, that I've already been in more battles in this war than I can caount. And I think I know good soljuhs when I see them. Naow, this private may have missed his nurs'ry check, but I know he'll be a good soljuh when we need him to be. And maybe I'm not your idear of the best kind of sergeant, but I guarantee you, when the shells start to fly, you'll have no complaints with me. And there's just one other thing, sir, beggin' your pardon–"

"That's quite enough, Colbeck!" Willnor shouted, finally getting the name right.

"I ain't British. I'm Australian. Just so you understand, sir. There *is* a diff'rence."

Willnor paced over to Jamie and shook his finger in the sergeant's face. "You are the most insubordinate NCO I've ever had the displeasure of dealing with. I don't know who placed you with the United States Army, but I'm going to see to it that you're sent back to where you came from."

"Then I suggest you take that up with Colonel Kelly, sir."

To Tommy, Willnor looked like a hot-air balloon at the Poweshiek County Fair with the air slowly leaking out of it. "Colonel… Kelly?"

"Yes, sir. It was Colonel Kelly who specially ordered my transfer."

Willnor stalked back to the safety of standing behind his little desk. He turned about and glared at all three men, Maple included. "You're all dismissed!" he pronounced.

Outside the schoolhouse, having walked past Dougherty without even acknowledging him, the three stopped, and Jamie said to Eddie, "Sergeant, I know you need to take this man to dig shit all day, but can I surrender him to your care in, say, ten minutes?"

Tommy was sure Maple would never consent to anything so irregular; but Eddie, a smile playing on his lips, looked at Jamie and said with a salute, "He's all yours, Sergeant." Then he was gone.

"I can't believe he did that," Tommy said impulsively.

"He liked the way I stood up to that bleedin' fool of a brass hat," Jamie said, brimming with confidence. "I could see that." Flowers had nothing more to say, and finally Colbeck said, "Well, Tommy?"

"I'm sorry I got you into trouble, Jamie."

The Aussie laughed. "Trouble always knows where to find me. It don't need your help. Let's walk while we talk, eh?"

It was a fine summer day, Tommy noticed, though they were walking amid the squalor of too many soldiers packed into too small a bivouac. "I can't believe you talked back to the captain like that."

"You're not believin' a lot of things this morning, are you? I always push the salient. Especially with an arse like him." Tommy was ready to defend the captain one last time, then didn't. "Don't you worry abaout me," Jamie continued. "I'm not angry for your usin' my name. You were with me last night, after all."

"Not when Maple did his bed check."

"Bed check. Bed check! Like you were little boys at school. They're askin' you to face bullets and shells, and they're treatin' you like – Oh, never mind."

"Thanks for getting me out of a jam, Jamie."

"You call pullin' two days' latrine duty gettin' you aout of a jam?"

"I deserved it. I was late."

"You were there for morning roll call. That's all that caounts. Are all your officers such bleedin' idiots? I thought Americans would be smarter than Poms. This Willnor bird makes me wonder." Tommy kept quiet; it occurred to him that he was beginning to enjoy the way Jamie thumbed his nose at authority. "Did you make that all up, abaout the dogs and the aeroplane?"

Tommy shook his head with vigor. "No. It all really happened. Don't you believe me?"

"I don't believe you'd ever lie on purpose, lad."

"But I just did. About my hat."

Jamie chuckled. "I still believe you about the other, anywise. Where did it happen?"

"On a short-cut that Davey showed me."

Jamie pulled out a cigarette, lit it, and began to smoke. "So we did find aour little Davey?"

Tommy didn't like the tone or phrasing one bit, but he answered, "Yes."

"And he was with you when this aeroplane – you say there was only one?–"

"Only one. Shooting at anything he could."

"–he was with you when it attacked?"

"No." Tommy was desperate for Jamie to have a better opinion of David. "But after, when we found the dogs, and one was still alive, he put it out of its suffering. I couldn't bring myself to do it."

"You would've if he wasn't there," Colbeck said dismissively, though he added, "But he did the right thing. You want one?" He indicated his cigarettes.

"Not right now."

"You say these dogs attacked you?"

"Yes."

"Guess that aeroplane took care of that problem for you."

"It was after I already got away. They were just farm dogs, Jamie, doing what farm dogs do. What the aeroplane did to them – it was cruel."

Jamie took a long puff, then: "You'll pard'n me if I'm not too concerned abaout what happened to some dogs in the middle of this war." Another puff. "Why didn't you report all this right away?"

"David said not to."

"Eh?"

"He said I could report it, but there was no rush."

Jamie stomped out the butt of his cigarette, pocketed it, and shook his head. "I'm afraid your friend will never make much of a soljuh."

"Both his brothers already died in the war, Jamie."

"Yes, we know that. Doesn't mean he'll be any good. Or that they were, for that matter."

This harsh assessment caused Tommy once again to literally pull away from Jamie, who noticed. "So, haow did my story work?" the Aussie coaxed.

"I told you, you helped me out of a jam. It worked pretty well with my story. But… I thought you went on too much about Nicole."

"I did it on purpose."

"You did? Why?"

"It's a much more believable story. Your hat. Really, Tommy, your *hat!* Couldn't you think of anything better? Nicole makes a lot more sense."

"But if I said it was Nicole, I'd've been in bigger trouble. So why–?"

Jamie gave him a hard look. "If he'da believed the hat story, you might've got off scot-free."

"Oh. And he'd've come down hard on you," Tommy said with absolutely no rancor. "You had to protect yourself. I understand. You did enough for me as it was."

Jamie stared at the Yank, then laughed lightly. "Sometimes you come aout with the most amazin' things, lad." He paused to consider his words. "I didn't give a fig abaout whether he'd come daown on me. I *was* worried about you getting away withaout any punishment at all.

"You were careless again, Tommy. It's not the stayin' aout, and I'm sorry you got the latrine duty. You didn't rate that. I would have declared the just-a-minute off-limits, and left it at that."

"I'll be OK. I've worked on farms. I've shoveled cow pies."

"Caow pies?" Jamie laughed heartily. "Naow, there's a phrase for you. Believe me, what men make ain't no pies."

"I'll be all right. You really did help me out."

Colbeck shook his head once more. "I was helpin' myself. I have good reason to believe somethin' big will be happ'nin' soon."

"A battle?" Tommy asked, wide-eyed.

"More like a skirmish, maybe. Wonder what that aeroplane was really up to last night. Anywise, I want you in my squad if somethin' does happen."

"What? What's gonna happen?"

"That's as much as I can say, and more than I should've. Don't tell your mates."

"Do you really know Colonel Kelly?"

"Colonel Kelly wouldn't know me if he fell into my trench. Not that a colonel'd ever get anywheres near a trench."

"So you don't know him! What if Captain–?"

"Your captain won't take the risk of findin' aout if Colonel Kelly knows me. He probably thinks Kelly's with the 33rd. But there is no Colonel Kelly with the 33rd, far as I know."

"He – he doesn't even exist?"

"He exists. His name was on the order sendin' me here – I told the truth abaout that. But we've never met. He works for Pershing."

"Pershing? You know *Pershing?*"

"No, lad. But Gen'ral Monash knows me, and Gen'ral Pershing asked Gen'ral Monash for some help with his new army. I'm part of that help."

"So you really don't have to worry about getting in trouble with Captain."

Jamie shrugged. "You never know who can cause you trouble daown the line." His aspect changed. "I've got to take you back to Maple naow. I wanted you to know why I did what I did. I wanted to help you, but I also wanted to remind you at the same time: you're still too careless, Tommy. You can't be so careless. Ev'rything that's happened to you up to naow is nothing. Nothing! What's comin' up – and soon – is very serious. Willnor was right abaout one thing, even if I could tell he wasn't speakin' from personal experience: war is serious, serious business. You haven't seen it yet. Don't think you have."

Tommy looked gravely at his friend. "You want me to be careful so I don't get killed."

Jamie smiled again a little, and looked slightly embarrassed. "You talk too much, Flaowuhs. Be more careful abaout that, too."

"Can you do me one more favor?"

"Naow what?"

"David will be at the just-a-minute waiting for me tonight if he can get away."

"If he didn't get in trouble himself, you mean."

"Were you going there anyway?"

"Probably I was."

"Could you tell him what happened – why I won't be there?" Flowers almost thanked Colbeck then again, specifically for leaving Pearson's name out of his account. But he decided to heed the Australian's just-proffered advice.

"All right. Anything you want me to tell Nicole?"

Tommy looked vacant, then shrugged. "Tell her I said hello."

"That's all?"

The Doughboy shrugged again. "Tell her I'm sorry I won't get to see her again, since I can't go there."

"You think you're banished f'rever?"

"I didn't hear Captain say when I could go back. Did you?"

"No, that's true. Does that bother you?"

Tommy took very little time to ponder his answer. "It's not the worst thing I could think of that could happen to me."

Jamie couldn't stop himself from shaking his head one last time. "Can't argue with that."

# Chapter XIV

Jamie was right, as he was wont to be about so many things: the smell of human waste, a whole day of it, no less, was much more difficult to endure than a week's worth of cow pies. And the chloride of lime used so liberally in the maintenance of the latrines actually seemed to combine with the waste to create a new odor that was still more foul – not to mention, after a day's work, all over Tommy. He feared he might drive Harry right out of their tent, but he was too exhausted to do anything but collapse into slumber. As he did so, he vowed yet again to avoid future trouble with Captain.

David drummed his fingers lightly on the countertop in the rapidly filling *estaminet* as Mme. Lacroix frowned at him from across the way. He knew that when the pub began crowding up, the old woman preferred that customers take their drinks and move away from the bar, to some other part of the small public area, so others could sidle up and place their orders. Coming from a family business himself, David understood; nonetheless, he had never seen anyone quite so intent on the pursuit of every last ha'penny, or in her case, *sou.*

Then again, maybe Madame was giving David the evil eye because her niece was being so especially nice to him tonight. Nicole, who had never paid any particular attention to the likes of him, had greeted him with a warm smile, and had given him another long, happy look when she'd brought him his beer. David knew Madame had noticed it, as he knew how much she disliked her niece paying special attention to any soldier, be he *poilu,* Tommy (a group that comprised a majority of the customers this evening), or Doughboy (a group that constituted the rest).

Nicole really was an extremely pretty girl, David mused after being graced with that second look. He really ought to have been more excited by her attentions, or flattered, at least. But he wasn't one to delude himself; he knew she would have regarded him no more or less than any other British soldier had he not been here yesterday with Tommy.

Even as he was thinking this, he heard a rustle of skirts next to him over the din, and caught a hint of the sweet scent of rose water on the sweat-and-smoke-tinged air; then he spied, out of the corner of his eye, a flash of chestnut hair. He wasn't imagining it; the lovely girl was back for a third time, stopping right next to him, her dark eyes sparkling. Quick and low, she said something to him in French. The only word David caught, or thought he did, was "*ami.*" He gave her a beguiling smile of his own and shook his head to indicate he didn't understand.

She then said two more words, even more quickly: "friend" and "*fleur.*" As her aunt shouted Nicole's name loud enough to cut through the noise, the realization sank in to David that the first of the two words had been in English, and that she was probably asking him exactly what he expected she would.

"Here, tonight," he said, stabbing his index finger toward the floor, then at himself. "Meeting me."

Though Nicole didn't know the meaning of his words, and probably couldn't have heard them even if she did, she nodded animatedly, even as Tatie repeated her name and several soldiers obnoxiously took up the chant. She flashed an evanescent smile at David, muttered something dark in French, and then was gone.

Left to his own thoughts once more, David found himself wondering if Tommy had had any difficulty returning to camp so late the night before. With Poppert – an NCO he had come to know rather well – in charge of his own company, David knew exactly how lax discipline would be; nobody had said a word about his creeping into billets at the break of dawn. But Flowers' situation, he knew, might be different.

He had one eye cocked toward the doorway in anticipation of Tommy's arrival; but instead he saw three chums from his company enter – not all chums, actually, since one of them was Hardison. Pearson got along well with most of his fellows, but Hardison was an exception; they seldom were in each other's proximity without an exchange of words. In an effort to avoid unwanted camaraderie, David edged away from the bar, deeper into the interior of the now-packed *estaminet.*

It was a decision he regretted almost instantly, as his evasion tactic abruptly brought him face-to-face with Tommy's detestable Australian pal, and without Flowers in tow. "Peahson!" came Colbeck's brassy greeting. "Just the man I was lookin' for!"

"Some'ow I doubt that, Sergeant."

"That so? You should have more faith." Without warning, Jamie lifted the smaller man by one shoulder, and quietly but firmly forced him up against the back wall of the *estaminet.* Had the place been less full, Jamie's move might have caused a major scene; as it was, the gesture seemed to catch the attention of no one – except, of course, David, who found himself pinned to the wall before he could react. "Naow, you listen, you," Jamie hissed at him, his beery breath uncomfortably close to David's face. "I don't like you and you don't like me. That's fair. But we have us a friend in common, and I told him I'd give you a message from him, and I mean to give it."

This interested Pearson sufficiently that, the rough treatment notwithstanding, he decided not to challenge the other man physically, a fight he was likely to lose at any rate. Instead he simply said, "I s'pose Tommy's not coming, then."

"That's right, you little Pom bastard, he's not. And it's all because of you."

"What d'you mean, because of me?"

"It was you kept him aout so late he wasn't there for bed check, wasn't it? And you that told him not to report that aeroplane–"

"I di'n't tell 'im not to. I said when 'e got back to 'is camp–"

"–but you didn't tell him to get back to his camp right away, did you? Did you?"

David backed down under Jamie's stare – and grip. "No. What would it matter? The aeroplane was long gone."

"You're a poor excuse for a soljuh," Jamie said disgustedly, but he loosened his hold on David.

"But don't you just cut a grand figure of a bully."

Still in control of the situation, Jamie stared in disbelief at the Englishman's impertinence. "I ought to slap your silly little face."

"Go a'ead. 'Tis the sort of thing bullies do, isn't it? But mind what the other Tommies 'ere think of an Anzac slapping about one of their own."

Unbeknownst to David, his show of defiance was actually increasing Jamie's respect for him. Still, the sergeant said, "Your mate had to shovel shit all day because of you, y'know. Tomorrow, too."

David hid his concern at this news, snapping back, "Sod off. Tommy's a big boy. 'E can take care of 'imself."

With that, Jamie let go of David entirely. "Well, he won't be coming back here anymore, I can tell you that."

"'E won't? Why not?"

"His captain's declared this place off-limits to him."

"Indefinitely?"

"Indefinitely?" Colbeck repeated in nasty mimicry. "Yes, indefinitely."

"Cor! What will we tell Nicole, then?" It was a spontaneous question, but even as he uttered it, David realized it was precisely the right thing to say to Jamie; by raising the subject, he caused the Aussie's attitude toward him to change completely.

"What abaout Nicole?" Jamie asked, with far less conviction than before.

"She thinks Tommy's coming 'ere to meet me. She was very excited for that, she was."

"Haow do you know?"

"We talked about it. After a fashion."

"Talked abaout it? I thought you said you didn't know any French."

"I don't. But I can point, and smile, and shake me 'ead, and so can she. You'd best be the one to tell 'er Tommy's not coming. Even if I 'ad the words, I wouldn't 'ave the 'eart."

Jamie looked away from David, down at the floor, then said, after a lingering pause, "Thanks for lettin' me know that, Peahson. I'll talk to Nicole."

"Likewise for giving me Tommy's message. I s'pose I shou'n't try to go see 'im at 'is camp, then?"

Colbeck looked up, toward the bar, then over at Pearson, shaking his head. "No, don't. Not tonight. Maybe tomorrow night, if you're free. I think his latrine duty ends at sundaown."

David wrinkled his nose, in a gesture Jamie could imagine some girl finding "cute." "Two days' latrine duty and 'e can't come 'ere, all for missing one bed check?"

For the first time, the Australian smiled at the Briton. "I know. His captain's a bleedin' dingo."

David smiled back, quizzical. "A dingo? And what would that be, Sergeant?"

"A no-good, mangy wild dog. Look, I'm goin' to try to talk to Nicole. I'm sure I'll be seein' you araound, Peahson, as long as Flaowuhs and me are in the same camp."

David wasn't sure whether Jamie meant anything cutting by putting it that way, but he decided not to challenge the sergeant on that, either, merely grunting and beginning to make his own move toward the door. If Tommy's not coming, he thought, it's time to go, anyways.

Nicole's annoyance at Tatie had reached some sort of zenith tonight; so rattled was she that the Doughboys in the crowd seemed virtually indistinguishable from the Tommies. Her one cause for optimism was her "conversation" with the good-looking little Tommy who was friends with Fleur.

Pushed about by the crowd as she made her way through, she caught sight of the American's other friend, the one who spoke some of her language, the old Australian with the dark, wavy hair. *"B'soir, m'sieur,"* she said with considerable buoyancy, even though she staggered under the weight of a tray filled with mugs of beer and glasses of wine.

*"Bonsoir,"* the Australian answered in sunny reply, and as she moved on, he tried to follow. *"C'est moi, Nicole,"* he called after her.

*"Oui, je sais,"* she responded with a distracted smile. *"C'est vous. M'sieur* Jack." He was pleased that she remembered what she thought was his name, wrong though it was.

As Nicole struggled further to place drinks before various customers sitting at the long table, she tried to keep at least part of her attention directed toward this Jack fellow, to see if he had news of her Fleur. But as Colbeck began to say something else to her, a blond man, tall for a Tommy, suddenly, drunkenly stood up between the sergeant and the French girl and shouted, "'Ey, Colonial! Wait your turn. Just because you know 'ow to talk like a Frog–"

"You better sit daown and shut your maouth, mate, while I'm still in a mood to forgive and forget."

"Oh," the Tommy said to his friends, "'E thinks 'e's the cock o' the walk, this one, just like all 'is kind." Turning to the Australian, he added, "Wasn't that you I sawr earlier, pushing around our Peahson? Only reason I dinna stop you then is sometimes 'e needs it. Still, I don't like to see some son of a convict pushing around a real Englishman–"

"I'm a better man than you, Pommy, and he is, too, I'm sure," Jamie said, his fists clenched. "Naow I'm warnin' you one last time: get aout of my way."

"Go a'ead. Make me."

A maleficent grin spread across Jamie's countenance. "Happy to oblige," he said, and before the last word was finished, Colbeck's fist connected with Hardison's jaw, sending the tall Tommy sprawling onto the table, spilling all the drinks Nicole had just served – many of them into the laps of the men who had ordered them – and breaking several glasses and mugs in the process.

There ensued the shocked silence that can precede an outbreak of complete chaos; and into this stepped Mme. Lacroix, spouting furious French at both Colbeck and Hardison. "I know, I know," Colbeck said to her in English, "I ought not a done that." This he repeated to her in French, adding something that he then repeated in English: "I'll pay for the damage. I'll pay." He was deliberately translating himself for the benefit of the surrounding Tommies and Doughboys, in an attempt to cool the situation. Ordinarily he would have relished a full-fledged fight that would have wrecked the place completely – but not here, not at this *estaminet.*

While Jamie and her aunt were having this brief exchange, Nicole slipped behind the bar to get a broom and dustpan. Returning to the long table, she proceeded to hand these to Jamie with great ceremony. As he accepted them, he spoke rapidly in French to her, the gist of which was a request that she provide him with the opportunity to talk to her aunt away from the crowd.

The young Frenchwoman then took charge of the situation with surprising authority: addressing the two fellow Tommies with whom he had arrived, she pointed contemptuously at the still mostly unconscious Hardison and said, "Him. Out." Next she escorted her still-babbling aunt to the bottom of the stairway leading to the living quarters they shared and shooed her upstairs; finally, even as the soldiers were catcalling at Jamie while he worked at his assigned task, and the potential for another, bigger outbreak of fisticuffs still hung in the air, she strode back to the long table and announced, quite loudly, "Gentlemen! *Tournée générale!*"

She looked imploringly at Jamie, who was still engrossed in his work but constantly keeping one eye on her. "She says the next raound of drinks are free!" he bellowed, "… And I'm payin' for them."

Something partway between a cheer and a roar greeted this pronouncement, and a startled Nicole looked to him for further explanation. He walked over to her, carrying a trayful of broken glass and shattered clay, and told her what he'd added to her offer. As she took him over to the stairway up which she had sent her aunt, Jamie scanned the crowd for the friendliest face he could find. In Tommy's absence, he lit upon Kopinski, the redheaded Pole from Chicago on whom he had come down so hard in the Vaden trench. "Ski!" he hollered, and the private, who like everyone else in the place was staring at the Australian and the French girl, pointed to himself with a dumb, questioning look. "Yes, Andy, you," Jamie said, beckoning. When Ski complied by drawing closer, Jamie said to him, "You ever work at a tavern in Chicago?"

"No, Sarge."

"You ever *been* in a tavern before this one?"

"Yes, sir."

"Jamie," the sergeant corrected automatically. "Think you could help this young lady at the bar while me and her aunt have a chat and settle up? She's got her hands full."

"I can try, Jamie."

"That's a good lad."

The smile Colbeck got from Kopinski told him he had picked the right man. The boy was basking in his approbation.

Five minutes or so later, Jamie descended the stairs looking appropriately grim. It wasn't all acting; Mme. Lacroix drove a hard bargain. Despite his impulsive extravagance in declaring he would pay for the damages and the drinks, and despite the fact that in more than three years he had managed to save up some, the pay of a sergeant in the Australian Corps wasn't all that much. His punch at Hardison was proving costly indeed. But the old woman had agreed ultimately to take some of his payment in the form of barter – if Colbeck could pull off the next part of his plan with that fool Willnor.

All seemed well downstairs; Ski had done a good job assisting Nicole, and business was back to its usual pace. Colbeck asked Kopinski for an extra minute's help as the old woman returned to her post behind the bar; then he took Nicole aside and apprised her of his deal with her aunt. She rewarded him with a melting smile and a *"Bon, M'sieur* Jack," when he was finished.

*"Jacques,"* he said, wanting to make whatever he could easier for her.

Then she asked, inevitably, *"Et votre ami, Fleur?"*

Jamie sighed. *"Impossible pour lui venir ici cette nuit. Demain, peut-être."*

She didn't ask why it was impossible for Tommy to be there tonight, but her visible disappointment was too much for Jamie. *"Il te dit 'Bonjour,'"* he added, bringing a smile back to her face. In her delight, she didn't seem to notice his erratic French, nor that he had used the familiar form of "you" in addressing her.

As Nicole went back to her business, there seemed nothing left for Jamie to do but leave the *estaminet,* return to camp, and get a good night's sleep. He would need to rise very early to successfully complete the deal he had struck with Madame. But as he turned to make for the door, he was waylaid by an unexpected figure – from the dim corner of the bar farthest from the door, Flowers' friend Pearson discreetly motioned to him. Curious, Colbeck duly edged in the Tommy's direction.

"Pretend you're not talking to me," David said, seemingly speaking to the wall to his right. "Don't look at me."

Jamie looked away, at Nicole and Madame, who were now down at the other end of the bar, and scratched his head. "What's this all abaout?"

"Some of me mates are waiting outside to jump you for what you did to 'Ardison."

Jamie exhaled hard. "Doesn't surprise me. But I can take care of myself."

"There's too many."

Jamie figured "too many" in David's book was probably two men, three at the most. "Haow many?"

"Ten or twelve, I'd say."

That gave even Colbeck pause. "You don't say.... I don't have much choice, though. The motorcar I came in is aout there."

"They don't know that. But they will if you go for it."

"I have to go aout that way."

"There's a back door I've noticed. Ask Nicole."

Colbeck wondered how Pearson had noticed a back door when he hadn't. "Can you drive the motorcar araound back?"

"Wou'n't know 'ow. What about one of the Yanks?"

Colbeck spied Sleziniak and Kopinski across the room. One of them probably would know how. "Don't like to leave anyplace with my tail between my legs."

"'Ave some sense. There's too many," David repeated.

"Why should I trust you? Haow do I know they ain't aout back?"

"You're Tommy's pal. I wou'n't do that to Tommy."

Jamie wished he could look David in the eye, but in keeping with the ground rules for their conversation, he refrained. "I was wrong abaout you, Peahson. You're all right."

He heard Pearson snicker; then the Englishman said, "I'm doing this for Tommy, not for you."

"All the same, I owe you my thanks."

"You best get out of 'ere in one piece before you thank me. Oh, and one more thing, Sergeant: if you need a witness that 'Ardison started it – a witness 'oo's a Tommy – you know where I am."

There was a silence, then Jamie said, "I really was wrong abaout you, David. You've got guts."

"Go on with you, now. We shou'n't talk any more."

"Sure you don't need a ride, too?"

"It would be worse for me if I did. I'll make me own way back."

"I'll pay you back for this someday."

"Go on with you, I said."

Elaborately casual, Colbeck ambled back across the room to Sleaze and Ski. Sure enough, Sleaze said he had driven a motor vehicle before. Jamie wrote a quick message in French and had Ski slip it to Nicole, who nodded, caught Jamie's eye, and motioned almost imperceptibly toward the stair he had ascended before. Sleaze and Ski left the *estaminet* shortly thereafter, and Jamie moved over near to the stairs. To his surprise, while Nicole attracted everyone's attention by being particularly playful with one of the Americans, it was Madame who walked over to the stairway and, looking around to make sure the rest of the men in her establishment were distracted, motioned him behind the stair. Then she unlocked a door that led into a wine cellar and, in the cellar, unlocked a storm door that led outside. She saw Jamie to it, then closed it behind him.

It was growing dark, and for a moment as he emerged outside, Colbeck had the sharp, sinking feeling he had walked into a trap. But then a motorcar suddenly swung around the side of the *estaminet,* and there were Sleaze and Ski. "Get between us quick, Sarge, and keep down and keep quiet!" Ski hissed.

Jamie obeyed, though he couldn't resist asking, "So there *were* Poms waitin' to jump me?"

"About twenty," Ski replied, still in a fierce whisper. "They were real suspicious. They almost didn't let us pass." So Pearson had told the truth. Colbeck hoped the little Tommy wouldn't end up on the wrong side of his mates for this. Sleaze gunned the engine, and after a few tense minutes, they were headed back to the relatively safe haven of Pierregot.

# Chapter XV

Corporal Daniel Dougherty prided himself on always being at his desk a good fifteen minutes before the captain's arrival each morning. Notwithstanding his conviction, so vehemently expressed the day before to Flowers, that his proper place was on the fighting line, he nonetheless made quite sure that his commanding officer would have no cause for complaints about him; indeed, that the captain would be thoroughly dependent on his adjutant. Despite his contempt for the physical surroundings in which he worked – namely, the old French schoolhouse where he was forced to sit behind a schoolboy's desk in a hallway – Dougherty did his best to make his "office" neat, clean, and important looking.

This morning, the only written communication on Dougherty's desk was an order whose gist the corporal already knew, thanks to the adjutants' grapevine: today the entire 33rd was to begin building a new trench, the "Daily Mail Line." Since Willnor had no appointments scheduled, there was little else for Dougherty to do while awaiting his captain's appearance but rearrange items on his desk that he had rearranged yesterday.

The sound of two sets of footsteps echoing down the hall several minutes in advance of Willnor's invariable arrival time was therefore unexpected. To his considerable annoyance, Dougherty saw the rude Australian sergeant approaching. Following behind him, inexplicably, was a civilian, an old French woman tottering along in a black frilled shawl.

"Mornin', Corp'ral," Colbeck called out in a hearty, warm greeting much at odds with his tone of the day before.

"What is the meaning of this, Sergeant?" came Dougherty's testy reply.

"This? Oh, us, you mean," the Australian said, gesturing to himself and the woman. Dougherty coldly nodded, and Colbeck adopted a conspiratorial tone: "Y'see, Corp'ral, it's very important that I talk to the captain first thing today."

"Why? And what is this old woman doing here?" the corporal added, waving his hand dismissively at her.

"Madame Lacroix is part of what I need to talk with Captain Willnor abaout," Colbeck answered evenly.

"You have no appointment."

"I'm makin' one naow."

"Why didn't you do it before?"

Patiently, as if he were speaking to someone not very bright, Colbeck replied, "Because this concerns matters that occurred last night, after you and the captain were long gone from here."

"What matters?"

"That's for me to discuss with the captain."

"He'll want to know."

"Then I'll tell him. When I see him." Dougherty shook his head, and Colbeck went on, "Might we have a chair for the lady here while we wait?"

Dougherty pointed down the hall whence sergeant and civilian had come. "Second door on the left," he said, still brusque. "There's some chairs there."

He expected the Australian to remove himself and the Frenchwoman to the indicated room, but instead Colbeck strode down the hallway alone and shortly returned with a single chair, which he placed with studied gallantry behind the old woman, who in turn gave him a curt nod and seated herself. Colbeck then leaned back against the far wall, folded his arms, and crossed his legs, standing at ease and staring at Dougherty in the most insolent of fashions. The corporal would have liked to tell the sergeant to move, but he was outranked and, just as importantly, intimidated.

Not wishing to sit and try to look busy under the visitors' gaze, Dougherty broke his usual routine and made for the schoolroom that served as his superior's office. Once in there, however, he couldn't find much to do, and then was seized with a sudden panic that Colbeck was rifling through his desk, or worse, that the captain would walk in and demand to know what his adjutant was doing in his private office. Anxiety rising, the corporal returned to his desk; as soon as he was back in their line of sight, he once again fell under the unnerving stares of the Australian (who hadn't moved) and the Frenchwoman.

What a relief, then, to hear the footfalls of Captain Willnor, who reacted with predictable disdain when he saw the two figures waiting in front of the corporal's desk. Dougherty noticed Colbeck offering a correct salute, but after returning the gesture, the captain focused on his adjutant, echoing him precisely, much to Jamie's amusement: "What's the meaning of this, Corporal? I don't recall having an appointment with this man."

"You didn't, sir. Sergeant Colbeck says it's important that he sees you first thing this morning, but he won't give me any explanation why."

"Is that right?" Willnor barely cast an eye toward the Australian and his strange companion. "I don't need to meet with a non-commissioned officer who hasn't made an appointment," he continued. "Find out what he wants and take care of it." Willnor was maximizing the contempt in his voice, referring to Jamie as if the sergeant weren't even there. "I'll be in my office, Corporal," he added, closing the schoolroom door behind him.

Dougherty lacked the artfulness to hide his triumphant smirk, and he compounded his gloating air by remaining seated as he said, "So, Sergeant? Are you willing to talk to me now?"

"If the captain wants to trust you with business as serious as this, then I'm sure we'll just have to go along with his judgment, Corp'ral. Y'see, it's abaout aour relations with the local civilian population."

"How's that?"

"To make it short, Corp'ral, I got involved in a bit of a row last night that made a right mess of this lady's tavern."

"Then that's your problem, Sergeant."

"And the army's."

Dougherty shrugged. "The Australian Army's, maybe."

"Well, naow, ordinarily I would agree with you, Corp'ral, only I'm in the American Army at the moment, as you know. And I wouldn't have got in the fight in the first place if I wasn't defendin' the honor of America."

"You don't say?"

"Yes, Corp'ral, I do. There was this Tommy who was talkin' daown 'the Colonials,' and I started arguin' with him, and, well, one thing led to another, I'm afraid. But he was the one started it all."

"The other man always seems to in these cases."

"There's at least two men from this division who'll tell you the same. And even a Tommy."

"I'm sure that's all very interesting, Sergeant, but even if what you say is true, I still don't see that it's in any way the American Army's problem."

"You don't?" Colbeck said, cocking his head as he asked, which seemed to naturally elicit a negative shake of the head from Dougherty as he replied, "No, Sergeant, I don't."

At that, the old woman, who had been quiet all this time, suddenly sprang to life; though Dougherty knew virtually nothing of French, it was clear to him that she was berating him ferociously. "Madame–" he began, alarmed, but that only seemed to make her more vociferous. Finally, the flustered corporal said to the sergeant, "Can't you get her to stop?"

Colbeck coolly muttered a few words of French to the old woman, whose imprecations abated in tone and volume but did not altogether cease. "What does she want?" Dougherty asked.

"She wants to get paid for the damage to her place."

"Well, then," Dougherty said with a snort, "we'll see to it that it's taken out of your pay."

Jamie was notching up his concentration on the task at hand, as he discerned that Dougherty was not so dull an adversary as he'd expected. "I already offered her that," he retorted.

Although it was the corporal's turn to be surprised by Jamie, he merely threw up his hands and said, "So, then, it's settled."

"Not quite. She wants her tavern cleaned up and repaired."

"So? She can do that when she gets the money from you."

"I ain't got that kind of money, and certainly not right away. And she wants her place repaired *naow*, before she opens for business today."

With an arrogant smile, Dougherty said, "Or else?"

"Or else she won't let any more American soljuhs in her tavern. And all of the ladies in the area who run taverns like hers will do the same, startin' tonight."

Dougherty, regarding the old woman carefully, was much less quick with his reply to that. At length he said, "I don't believe you. These people are in business to make money. Why would they turn away customers?"

"To make their point. No more soljuhs causin' a mess in their places."

"But that's your problem, as I said. You made the mess."

"And that's all you have to say abaout it?"

"That's all there is that needs to be said about it, Sergeant."

"Then I can refer the soljuhs to you when they can't get served at the taverns?"

"Yes, since I don't believe that will happen anyway."

"Don't be so sure." Getting no further response, Jamie added, "All right, then. It's your decision… as the captain said. Let me explain it to her."

"I'd rather–" Dougherty began, but Colbeck already was aiming a rapid stream of French at the old woman, who quickly turned red, stood up, and began to pound on Dougherty's desk, making an astounding amount of noise with her tiny fist – and her voice as well, as she screamed at him unintelligibly. The corporal stood up in return, towering over the tavern owner, but the gesture did not subdue her in the least. "Madame–" he began again, then, "Madame. Your interview is finished. *Fini.* Please leave at once."

The rant from the old woman continued full force; Colbeck said nothing. Then, from behind him, Dougherty heard Willnor calling his name. He turned sharply to the captain's door and opened it; in so doing, he could not see Jamie subtly signal to Mme. Lacroix, who decreased the volume of her tirade.

"Sir?" the corporal barked, standing in the now-open doorway of his superior's office.

"What's going on out there?" the captain shouted from his desk. "I thought I told you to take care of that situation."

"Some problems with the civilian population, Captain. I am taking care of the situation."

"It doesn't sound to me like you are, Corporal. We don't want any trouble with the local civilians. I suppose I'll have to come out there and take care of it myself after all."

Dougherty gritted his teeth. "That's not necessary, sir. I can handle it."

"Are you sure, Corporal Dougherty?"

"Yes, sir. I'm sure." The entire exchange, as Dougherty to his bitter humiliation was keenly aware, was perfectly audible to Colbeck, but when the corporal closed the captain's door and turned back to face his troublesome guests, the Australian betrayed no indication he'd heard anything at all.

Under pressure, Dougherty made a snap decision to reverse field, and he breathlessly asked Colbeck, "Sergeant, how many men would it take to make this woman's tavern ready for business today?"

More French followed between Colbeck and the woman. "She wants at least four," the Australian said, "but I think maybe I can talk her daown to two."

"I think one would be enough. And I suggest that one be you, Sergeant."

"Oh, I agree that I should be one of them. That's only fair. But it will still take at least one other man."

"Then let the British supply that man. You say they started the fight. Talk to them."

Colbeck was impressed by Dougherty's recovery of authority, but didn't show it. "I don't *parlez-vous* with any Poms," he snapped, in a savage tone that both surprised the corporal and was immediately understood by him.

"All right, then," Dougherty said, throwing up his hands once more. "If you can get her to agree to two, take someone else from the company."

"*Anyone* from the company?"

"Isn't that what I just said, Sergeant? Take whoever you think can help make the work go the fastest."

Colbeck talked to the woman again for a long time, until, to Dougherty's amazement, she turned to the American corporal, curtsied, and said, "*Merci, m'sieu le caporal.*"

Dougherty looked at Colbeck, who grinned back at him. "Good work, Corp'ral. Two men it is. I'll be back as soon as we're finished."

"I'm sure the captain expects nothing less."

"I'm sure," Jamie agreed with a salute, commencing a hasty exit with his unlikely companion even as he endeavored to make it look casual and unhurried. He didn't want the corporal to think too hard about his "good work."

Tommy, his muscles still unexpectedly sore from his day of latrine duty, had had a restless night. So worried was he about keeping Harry awake with his tossing and turning that he had quit their tent in the early pre-dawn and found the nearest available tree, against which he had propped himself while staring vacantly up at the sky, awaiting reveille. If Davey were with him, Tommy mused, his British pal probably could have told him exactly what time it was by the shade of the sky, but the American could only guess; it seemed to him that reveille was late today. He assumed that after morning roll call, Maple would send him back to the latrines, or maybe to the kitchens if he was lucky. But in the interim it was relaxing simply to lie against the tree and take in the sights, even the smells, of the camp – anything but what he had smelled yesterday. He could feel himself drifting off, but that was all right; he was confident the bugler would awaken him, along with the rest of his company.

He was walking hand in hand with Susan down the hill of Jackson Street in Brooklyn, toward the intersection with Front Street where the First National Bank and the Poweshiek County Savings & Loan stood guard over the two blocks of downtown, when a kick to the booted part of his leg abruptly returned him to France and the camp. As he blinked awake, the first thing he noticed was that the sky was now considerably brighter. Had he, after all, missed the bugler's call? This apprehension was compounded when a voice above him, not quite fixed in his mind thanks to his still-half-drowsing state, said something (Tommy thought) about his being in trouble again. Forcing himself awake, Flowers sprang to his feet, then tottered, a bit dizzy, until the person attached to the voice grabbed him by the shoulders and lightly shook him, saying, "Tommy? Hello? Are you there?"

The Doughboy looked dumbly into the eyes of his questioner, then said, startled, "Jamie!"

"So you are awake, after all."

"What's – Am I late for roll call? What are you doing here?"

"You're not late, lad. Roll call's late, I'm not sure why. But it doesn't matter. You're on special assignment today–"

"I know. I have to report to Eddie–"

"No, I already talked to Maple. You're under my charge this mornin', assigned to me."

"You're assigned to latrines?"

"Latrines? Me? Not on your life! No kitchens, neither. I told you, I'm takin' you on special assignment."

"And Maple said that was all right?"

"Actually, it was your good friend Corp'ral Dougherty who said it was all right," Jamie told the Yank with a laugh.

"You're making all of this up."

"No, I'm not. Naow come along smartly to the motorcar with me, and no more arguin'. You're under my orders."

Tommy finally remembered to salute. "Yes, sir, Jamie," he said; then, walking alongside his sergeant friend with an easy gait, he added, "Any chance of me getting some morning chow first?"

"Don't worry. When you see who's waitin' for us in the motorcar, you'll realize we won't have to worry abaout breakfast."

# Chapter XVI

Mme. Lacroix made a tasty omelette – even better than the way Tommy's mother made scrambled eggs, and considerably more flavorful than army chow. She continued to eye him suspiciously, though, as she had from the moment they had seen each other, when Jamie had led Tommy to the motorcar; this despite the fact that, to both men's disappointment, Nicole was nowhere in sight when they got to the *estaminet,* and she hadn't been seen since. Tommy thought with amusement that if Jamie had been extremely resourceful in turning his incident of last night into an opportunity for both of them to get away from their regular duties to see the girl, Madame had nonetheless outfoxed the Aussie, keeping her niece sequestered elsewhere while getting her tavern repaired for free.

It was going to be hard work, too, though less odious and more satisfying than latrine duty. If Jamie's lighthearted recounting of his story as they rode to the *estaminet* had given either man the impression they were escaping camp for a morning of easy tasks, one look at the place when they arrived disabused them of the notion. "I swear," Jamie muttered to Tommy as they surveyed the wreckage, including a great deal of shattered crockery and a split in the short bench, "she must have had a trench raid after I left here. I don't remember this much damage."

Indeed, the sergeant was so convinced there had been extra trouble that he argued with the old woman while he and Tommy were having breakfast. In between bites of egg – and sips of dark, bitter coffee, another new experience for him – Tommy tried to follow the progress of the heated discussion, despite his lack of French. When at last Jamie turned away from her in frustration, he addressed his American friend: "She sure wants her paound of flesh. Ord'rin' me to find her some new crock'ry."

"What?"

"You heard me. I'll have to… borrow… some mugs from the army."

"But Jamie, that's stealing."

"Don't concern yourself with it. I'll handle it."

"Just tell her you won't do it."

Jamie shot him a grin. "Naow, you know this lady is goin' to get her way."

Clearing up the broken clay and glass was simple enough, but fixing the splintered bench was more complicated. The few rusty tools Madame produced were inadequate to the project. There ensued another torrent of French between Madame and Jamie, who finally turned to Tommy and said, "I'm goin' in the motorcar to fetch some decent tools."

"Fetch? Or 'borrow'?"

Colbeck laughed. "Don't get fresh with me, lad. There's a pail over in the corner and a mop, and a well aout back. She wants the place all scrubbed daown. You can start that while I'm gone."

"Scrubbed down? She really is getting a good deal out of this."

"Didn't I say she would? She'll be upstairs if you need to talk to her – though haow you'll do that is beyond me. You'll just have to communicate the best you can withaout me."

"Thanks, Jamie," Tommy said with an ironic edge to his voice.

"Sure you'll be all right here?"

"You're talking to an Iowa boy. I've cleaned out whole barns."

"And shoveled caow pies. I remember."

The scrubbing was hot, wet work, and Tommy took off his tunic and rolled up his shirtsleeves as he went about the chore, thinking of Jamie's account of the events that had put the *estaminet* in such a condition. It had been very satisfying to hear his Australian friend concede, "That Peahson's a bit of all right, after all." Tommy was proud of his English buddy, and somehow he'd gotten the idea that maybe David was waiting for them at the *estaminet,* to help join in the clean-up – it sounded as if somebody from the British Army ought to be – so he was disappointed not to find Pearson there. Maybe tonight, after all of the day's work was over.

He was awash in perspiration, and after a slight hesitation, he removed his shirt, too. He supposed Madame would have apoplexy if she suddenly descended the stairs and saw him naked from the waist up, but that wasn't too likely, and anyway, if it did happen, what did he care? He was beginning to appreciate this assignment less and less – indeed, all the assignments he'd had since the Vaden trench. He was here in France to fight Germans. What was he doing cleaning out latrines and scrubbing down taverns?

He was vigorously attacking the back wall when he heard the front door open. Assuming it was his friend the sergeant, he said loudly, "I don't know if this was such a smart idea after all, Jamie. You said they were gonna start digging a new trench today? I think I'd rather be outside, myself."

He expected some kind of sassy reply from Colbeck, but instead there was a strange silence that made him uneasy. In the instant before he turned around, he caught an unexpected word from an unexpected voice on the air. *"Fleur?"* it asked, tiny and timorous.

He whirled about to see her standing in the still-open doorway, a basket of summer flowers in her hands, a white one – it wasn't a flower familiar to him – tucked behind each ear, a floppy straw hat bending low over her brow. He had long thought Susan beautiful, but he had never seen any girl as radiant as Nicole looked this morning, the sunlight streaming out on all sides from her like she was a saint in a painting.

Tommy was suddenly, acutely aware of his shirtless state, and although he was not the slightest bit chilled, he crossed his arms over his soaked chest as he smiled and said to her, *"Nicole. Bonjour."* Having no other words, he added in English as he made to reclaim his shirt, "I'm – cleaning up your aunt's tavern. Sh–she's upstairs right now."

But the girl rushed over to him, and before he could put the garment back on, she reached out with no hesitation and touched the side of his neck with her hand, then slowly, very slowly, ran it down his shoulder and arm. When he was too stunned to react, she placed her other hand on his chest and rubbed that wet spot in a circular motion, murmuring softly to him, *"Que tu es beau, mon fleur. Que tu es beau."*

Though he didn't know her words, her import was unmistakable. Seizing both her arms, he pulled her to him, and as they kissed, the contents of her flower basket went spilling on the freshly scrubbed floor.

*"Nicole?"* Mme. Lacroix's sudden, sharp inquiry startled them both.

Tommy's first instinct was to stoop to gather the flowers, but as he did so, Nicole reached down and cupped his chin in her hands, tilted his head upward, and said with decisive urgency, *"Allons, allons-nous en, vite!"*

He rose, dumping the flowers back into the basket, and she grabbed him by the forearm and tugged insistently. Of one mind now, they fled the interior of the *estaminet* even as they heard Madame shout *"Nicole!"* in an even louder voice, and the first sounds of her footfalls echoed down the upstairs hallway.

Tommy had never before ventured in the direction Nicole now led him, away from the road back to Pierregot and Molliens, and away too from the even busier route toward Amiens. A few startled civilians noticed the soldier and the girl running through Rainneville, he still struggling to get his shirt on, but in short order the two came upon an undamaged glade on the southeast edge of town, and beyond that a field, waving green in the early summer and looking prettier than any he had seen on the march to the Vaden trench. There she fell down laughing, pulling him with her.

He had almost managed to get back into his shirt, but she kissed him now while running her hands underneath it, her touch on his bare skin electric, delicious, dreamlike. From where they had dropped, the only thing he could see was the tall green grass (or was it wheat?) overhead, and then he made one last, half-hearted attempt to remain true to Susan and his upbringing, asking her, "Nicole? Do you think we should–?"

She silenced him by kissing him again, and then she started touching him in places where no one had ever touched him before. On fire, he rolled over so he was on top of her and, now knowing no hesitation himself, began touching her in kind. The way she sighed under his caresses urged him on further. Neither one of them had had the slightest schooling in what to do – just the off-color jokes Tommy had heard other boys tell in the army, and Nicole had giggled over with other girls at the convent – but it scarcely mattered. They were both sweaty and breathless and totally immersed in each other, and soon it was over, though it seemed at one and the same time to have been much too fast, and to have lasted forever.

Tommy was the first to revert to a plainer reality, suddenly sitting up, regarding the two of them in their disheveled state, and exclaiming, "Oh my God, what have I done! Nicole, I'm… I'm sorry."

It was her turn not to understand his words but to completely comprehend his meaning. She laughed, shook her head, grabbed him by the neck and pulled him back down to her, hugging him hard. The only words he understood were *"beau, beau, beau,"* repeated over and over. They kissed again and again, but Tommy was becoming ever more conscious of what they'd – he'd – done: he'd left his post of duty, and run off with this young girl, and…

"We have to go. Now," he said, fairly abrupt; but even as she grabbed his hand and let him pull her to her feet, her mood of elation clearly remained unchanged.

*"Ah, mon fleur,"* she said brightly, kissing him again as they stood out in the open field. *"Mon beau Fleur."* He held her to him, but he couldn't shake a feeling of foreboding about what they'd done.

Of course Jamie was there with Madame when they made their attempt at a nonchalant return to the *estaminet*. He was sitting at the bar conversing with her, his back turned to the door, when they walked in; Madame immediately turned pale, and Jamie swiveled round, his face darkening as he saw the two of them entering together. But the sergeant had only gotten as far as "Where the *hell* have you been?" when Nicole's aunt let out an unearthly shriek, rushed over to her niece, and began simultaneously berating and slapping her.

"Stop it! Stop it!" Tommy shouted, grabbing the old woman's arm; but then he felt his own arm being twisted behind his back.

"You just come aoutside with me and let these two ladies take care of themselves."

"No–!"

"I don't think you've got much choice, soljuh," Jamie said icily, "unless you want to be reported for insubord'nation."

At that, Tommy surrendered, letting the Australian drag him out of the *estaminet* even as a frightful howl came from within the tavern. Outside, Jamie loosened his grip and said through clenched teeth, "Naow, can I trust you to stay right here while I try to calm that old harpy daown? Not that I should trust you at all abaout anything ever again after this."

Tommy suddenly felt as if he were an aeroplane heading too quickly for earth. "I'm not going anywhere, Jamie."

"I'll say you're not." The sergeant turned on his heel and entered the public house. Tommy listened in anguish as Madame screamed, Nicole screamed in return, and Jamie shouted at them both, trying to calm them. Though none of their words was intelligible to him, for an excruciatingly long time he tried to follow what was going on anyway. First Madame was yelling at, perhaps threatening, Nicole. Next Jamie was trying to talk sense to Madame. Then Jamie and Nicole were having words…

The Doughboy felt like running away. He was still trying to comprehend what he'd done, to a poor foreign girl who couldn't even understand English. He attempted in his head to compose a letter to Susan, telling her that now he had to marry this French girl, because of what he'd done. But how could he even mention such things to Susan – or to his mother; what would she say when she found out?

After minutes on end, the noise from the women died down, and Jamie strode grimly from the building. "Get in the motorcar," he snapped, and that was all. Tommy obediently got in next to the sergeant, who turned over the engine, and the vehicle took off with a savage lunge.

Jamie's fury was so evident that it had Tommy cowed, but at length he could no longer stand the cold silence. "I'm sorry, Jamie," he finally said.

"Your sorries are worthless. You're a failure. You'll never make a soljuh."

"I just – when Nicole showed up, I took a break, and we lost track of the time–"

"You fucked her, didn't you?" Jamie rudely interrupted, his eyes flashing and now fixed on Tommy.

"I–" was all Tommy got out before Jamie demanded, "Didn't you? *Didn't you?*"

"You – you make it sound so crude–"

"Don't give me your innocent airs. I'm not the one who fucked her."

"But you would've if you could've."

Jamie brought the vehicle to a halt so violently abrupt that they both were thrown against the dashboard. Tommy had the wind knocked out of him, and Jamie turned on him: "You're damned lucky, you sorry excuse for a soljuh, that I'm a professional soljuh, unlike the likes of you. 'Cause if I wasn't, I'd beat you to the bloodiest little pulp ever, right here and naow. At the very least, I should make you walk the rest of the way back. But I was the one crazy enough to choose you for this aouting, and I'm the one who'll deliver you back to your friend Corp'ral Dougherty, safe and saound. He can give you your next orders. After that, soljuh, you're not to speak to me unless you're spoken to, and I guarantee you I won't be speakin' to you. Not that it matters much anywise, because you're goin' to be dead within weeks or maybe even days, as soon as you're really in this war. You won't survive, because like I said you're a failure as a soljuh."

Tommy could feel his eyes stinging, but the last thing he wanted was to let Jamie see him lose control under these circumstances. He stiffened, and saluted, and said in his best soldierly voice, "As you wish, sir!"

"That's more like it," Jamie said to the steering wheel as he gunned the motor again, not bothering to look at Tommy. At least, Tommy thought as he watched the countryside pass by, shivering in Jamie's silence, Davey's still my pal.

# Chapter XVII

Locked in her room by her aunt, Nicole lay on her little bed and watched the late-afternoon light streaming in through the tiny window. Rubbing her stomach, she recalled with pleasure her moments in the field with Fleur, the pain accompanying her first time quickly forgotten. She had been a woman possessed from the moment she had seen him there like that, a vision of beauty amid the broken clay and splintered wood. It seemed to her as if it had been some other girl who had been so bold with him, who had insisted on their impulsive run from the *estaminet,* through the village to the field. Others might blame it all on the young American soldier, but Nicole could see no blame for either him or herself, but rather this other girl who had so thoroughly, if temporarily, taken over her body and soul.

That girl had disappeared with her aunt's first slap. Only the kindness of the old Australian had saved her from a much worse fate at the hands of Tatie. She still marveled at how, despite his raised voice, he had been so understanding in trying to mediate, had been so solicitous of her, even though she could tell he was angry with her, and especially with Fleur. Because of his intercession, Tatie had ceased to strike her, and she hadn't resumed even after he'd left. Her aunt's bitter words, however, had continued to pour out – to the effect that Nicole was a reprehensible, wild, ungrateful child, and most of all to relentlessly remind her that the whole town knew, that all of Rainneville had witnessed her disgraceful behavior. That wasn't true, of course, strictly speaking; only a few people had seen Nicole with Fleur. But at least two of those villagers had been among Tatie's fellow business owners. With these women watching, it was the same as if the whole village had been.

Perhaps Tatie would send her away now, now that she was spoiled. She wished she could go back home to Papa, back to Cumières.

Cumières. It was Nicole's cry for her home village that ultimately had broken Jamie's anger with her. When she had begun repeating the name as she argued with her aunt, Jamie, who had been trying with great difficulty to follow their conversation (however much he impressed the likes of Flowers and Pearson, his French wasn't that good), at first did not recognize the name. He figured it for some French term he lacked, and asked her to repeat the word slowly. When she did, and he still didn't understand it, she explained, *"C'est mon village."*

With that came a chill, as he recognized the word she had been repeating: Cumières.

When Jamie had told Tommy and David that Verdun was as bad as Passchendaele, he was once again speaking from experience. In the fall of 1916, after taking part in the disaster on the Somme that was meant to relieve the French at Verdun, that took the lives of Colin Pearson and all those other British boys, Colbeck, already a veteran, briefly had been sent as an observer to the Verdun sector. The titanic slaughter there, the months-long collision of great armies that had taken the lives of hundreds of thousands of French and German boys alike, had long since crested. But the terrain around Verdun remained nightmarish, blasted to bits, devoid of vegetation and smelling of corpses (though he still would maintain Ypres was worse; at least around Verdun, even after the stupefying damage, there was some roll and dip to the terrain, not just a flat, muddy swamp).

The Aussie's mission there had been a brief one, but he keenly recalled a conversation with a Gallic officer whose English was better than Jamie's French. One night, in an underground room, the man had spread out a map of the area, one that did not resemble the others Colbeck had been using. "See here, my friend," the French lieutenant had said, "do you recognize this area?"

"I gather it's araound here," Jamie replied, "but I think the map is aout of date."

The Frenchman smiled with approval. "1913," he replied, "before the war." Then his smile evaporated. "See here." He proceeded to point and point at various places on the map. "You see these villages? Fleury. Douaumont. Louvemont. Tavannes. Bezonvaux. Souville. Cumières. Harcourt." He lapsed into French to make his point: *"Ces villages n'existent plus. Ils ont existé, mais maintenant...* "

Somehow all that Jamie had personally seen up to that point – at Gallipoli and the Somme; all the good soldiers he had watched die for nothing; his knowledge of all the others who had been lost in all the other sectors and on all the other fronts – none of these had brought home to him the nature of this war quite so devastatingly as this distraught lieutenant's list of villages that had simply vanished from the map in its wake. "But won't the people come back and rebuild them when it's over?" he had asked.

"I think not," the lieutenant responded with a shake of his head. "Not enough men. In some cases, no men at all, except for the very old. These villages are all dead – killed by the war just as surely as the men."

So strongly did the memory of that conversation persist that when at last Jamie understood the word Nicole had been repeating, she was struck by his immediate change of expression. "You don't know, do you?" he said to her in English, causing her to shrug in incomprehension. "My poor girl. You don't even know."

No, he couldn't stay angry with this beautiful young woman who had been through God knows what. And perhaps, in a few days, he might even apologize to Flowers. Not that he wasn't in the right from the point of view of a commanding officer whose charge had left his post without permission. But no matter how he felt about what Tommy and Nicole had done, Jamie knew he had unfairly pulled rank in being so rough on the lad. After all, it was his own damn fault for setting things up the way he had, trying to please Nicole by bringing her back her beloved Fleur. She was obviously interested in Tommy, not Jamie, and he should have seen that. It was natural for a girl like that to want someone more her own age.

But as Colbeck admitted that to himself, he realized it might in fact take longer than a few days for him to feel ready to apologize to the American.

Numbed by his experiences of the morning, Tommy was at least grateful that the sergeant had delivered him to Dougherty without telling the corporal about the private's scandalous behavior with the *estaminet* owner's niece. Tommy had thought that Jamie might, but the first thing Dougherty had done when they reported to him was to indicate to Colbeck his severe displeasure that Flowers had been chosen for the work detail. "You said I could choose whoever I thought could help get the job done fast," Jamie had answered sullenly, "so I did. I followed your orders, Corp'ral. To the letter."

Dougherty had given Colbeck, then Flowers, a hate-filled look, then snapped at the latter: "Report to Sergeant Maple at once. You're to spend the rest of the day entrenching with the rest of the 66th."

The assignment was fine with Tommy. Though digging a new trench was back-breaking work, it meant he was able to rejoin his friends from his company. Ski, Sleaze, Vern, Harry, and the others wanted to know where he'd been all morning, but Tommy was in no mood to brag. Disappointment came at the end of the day when Dougherty reappeared and reminded him his two-day punishment was not yet over; he was confined to quarters for the night. So much for the chance to see David.

The Americans were worked not only hard but also extra long on their first day of digging the new trench, so by the time Jamie got to the *estaminet,* it was late, near to closing time, and the place was overrun with Tommies, plus a few Aussies who were not familiar to him. He warily scanned the room for Hardison but didn't see him, didn't see Pearson either, and then he worked his way over to the bar, where an overwhelmed Madame was trying to cope with the entire crowd alone.

*"Où est Nicole?"* he stage-whispered to the old woman.

She frowned at him and replied, *"Dans sa chambre,"* while shaking her head to indicate that staying in her room was Nicole's choice.

*"Voudriez-vous que je dis avec elle?"*

The grammar was bad, but Madame got the gist of his offer to speak with her niece. She paused to think for a moment, then waved him away with *"Plus tard, plus tard."*

Jamie got a beer from her, then lingered inconspicuously in a corner of the tavern for about fifteen minutes, until Madame began to shoo everyone else out of the place. As the last group of five or six, including Jamie, was being shown the door, she touched the Australian sergeant's sleeve and murmured, *"Un moment, m'sieu."*

Jamie sat at the long table for minutes that stretched to nearly half an hour. Once or twice he heard Madame's voice upstairs, and footsteps, but other than that there was no sign of life in the whole place. Just as he was crossing over to the bottom of the stairs to shout to Madame that he was leaving, Nicole appeared at the top, still dressed as she'd been earlier in the day, but with her clothes wrinkled, her hair wild, and her face red from crying. *"M'sieur,"* she said gravely, nodding once, and slowly she descended the stairs, as Jamie unconsciously backed away from her, to the table.

She walked over and sat down, not across from him, but on the same bench, although not right next to him. Her expression was so tragic that Jamie abruptly found himself stifling a laugh. She seemed unable to say any more, so he finally asked, *"Et vous, mademoiselle. Tu ne va pas bien?"*

The mixture of formal and intimate language, deliberate or not, touched her, and she faltered: *"Non, m'sieur."* She hesitated further, blurted out, *"Ah, m'sieur,"* and began to sob.

Jamie could do no more than follow his impulse, and scoot down the bench and take her in his arms, although he was quite conscious of the possibility Madame was watching – he assumed as much, actually – so he made every effort to appear paternal, comforting her while maintaining a rather stiff posture. When Nicole finally began to speak again, gulping out the words, *"Fleur. Mon Fleur,"* there was no need for him to force the stiffness.

*"Oubliez lui,"* he commanded.

But she was not about to forget him: *"Non, non. C'est impossible. Il faut que je le revoie."*

*"Ça, c'est impossible,"* he replied coldly. Maybe it wasn't really impossible for her to see Flowers again, but he had decided he would do all he could to make it so.

She cried pitifully on his shoulder for a long while, then said softly, *"Cumières. Je voudrais retourner a Cumières."*

His heart sank. Now there was something truly impossible. He couldn't bring himself to tell her, so instead he asked, *"Qui est là? Votre famille?"*

She shook her head, almost scornfully. *"Ils sont tous partis."*

If she knew her family all had left Cumières, perhaps she knew about the fate of her village after all. *"Où?"* Jamie asked.

*"Ma mère est morte. Mon père et mon frère, ils combattent pour la France."*

He caught that there was but one brother fighting alongside her father for the glory of France, and he wanted to avoid an inevitable question. Instead he said, *"Vous n'avez pas de sœurs?"*

*"Non, M'sieur Jacques."* She held up her left index finger. *"Une soeur – moi."* Then she raised her right hand, fingers spread, thumb crossed over palm. *"Quatre frères."*

There was no point in avoiding the question now. *"Les trois autres frères–?"*

*"Lucien. Mort en quatorze. Richard. Mort en quatorze aussi. Philippe. Mort en seize."* The accounting brought back her tears.

*"Et votre frère qui combatte toujours?"*

A smile of pride shone through. *"Pierre. Et Papa aussi."*

Aunt be damned. He held her closer to him in a decidedly less fatherly manner, stroking her hair. *"Ah, Nicole, Nicole. Je suis désolé. Je suis si, si désolé."* He didn't care any longer what she'd done with Flowers. He wanted to kill the whole German Army for her. Three brothers dead, and the last one fighting with her father. He had meant to ask her why she wanted to return to Cumières if she knew none of them was there, but in case she didn't know, he now knew he could wait a great deal longer before telling her that her village, too, was no more.

Jamie spent about half an hour more comforting and speaking with Nicole. Eventually Madame did show up again, and politely but firmly made it clear that it was time for him to go. He was gratified to be leaving Nicole in better spirits, and aunt and niece on better terms.

It was quite dark when he left the *estaminet;* he had parked the motorcar a short distance away. He sprang into the seat and gunned the engine, and the vehicle lurched forward, but didn't get very far. There was a sound of hissing air, multiple hissings, in fact, and he turned the motorcar off and jumped back out to check the problem. To his annoyance and disgust, he could see the front right tire was flat. When he walked around to the other side, that front tire was flat, too. And when he walked to the back and saw a third tire down, he knew it couldn't have been an accident. Crouching low, he was examining the fourth tire, and had just discerned the slash in the rubber, when a blow came raining down on his head.

"Get up, you dirty dingo!" shouted an English voice, and as Jamie staggered to his feet, he thought how odd it was that a Pom should know the worst insult for an Aussie to receive. But he was no sooner up than a fist crashed into his jaw, and he knocked his head against the motorcar, and fell unconscious to the ground.

Hardison and his two buddies added a couple of swift kicks, but then they were interrupted by the *estaminet* door opening, and the woman who owned it shouting something at them in French. They weren't quite finished with Colbeck, but when they didn't move, Madame took out a firearm and shot it into the air.

That was enough to send them scurrying. Striding out to make certain they had fled, Madame found the prone and bleeding figure of the only foreign soldier she'd come to like in all of these months and years behind the bar. *"Nicole! Nicole!"* she shouted. *"Viens, viens!"*

More hard physical work coupled with his restriction to camp had led Tommy to an early sleep. He was slumbering in his tent when the trembling ground abruptly shook him awake. A not-so-distant noise, and then the ground shook again, and then it happened again, all in equal, measured spurts. By the time Tommy scrambled to his feet, the noise and the shaking had stopped. The camp was in loud disarray, many of the men shouting to each other to ask what had happened, others shouting at their fellows to be quiet so they could go back to sleep. Tommy went running in search of his sergeant and found Maple as confused as anyone else. "It came from that direction," Eddie told him, pointing east and south. "I think I'll head toward Molliens and see what's going on."

"Can I come with you?" Tommy asked.

Maple was not at his spit-and-polish best, and he answered more like an annoyed playground monitor: "Aw, Tommy, if I let you come, everyone'll want to. Besides, what time is it? What time is it? Someone?" he inquired of the chattering Doughboys nearby.

"Half past eleven, Sarge."

"You're still restricted to camp 'til midnight, Flowers," Maple said in a friendly, matter-of-fact manner. "I'm going by myself."

Off he disappeared into the dark, and Tommy found himself wandering the camp, awaiting word of what had happened. He found Giannelli with Sleaze, and they started to smoke cigarettes as they waited, until an agitated corporal came by and told them, "Put out those fags! You wanna make us all a target for another aeroplane?"

"Aeroplane?"

"Yes," said the strange corporal. "Didn't you hear the noise?"

"Of course we heard it," Vinny replied. "That was an aeroplane?"

"An aeroplane dropping bombs on Molliens," the corporal responded as he hurried on past.

"Molliens!" the privates all cried out at once. "Wait!" But their source of information had vanished into the night.

After several more minutes of nervous pacing by Tommy and his pals, Maple reappeared, on the trot. “Sarge, is it true?” Tommy blurted out. “They said an aeroplane bombed Molliens.”

“It’s true,” Maple confirmed breathlessly, and immediately the crowd around him swelled. “Three hits in the center of town. Thank God, looks like none of our boys were hurt. But I’m afraid some of those Tommies weren’t so lucky.”

Flowers froze at that comment, and then he couldn’t stop himself: “Please, Sarge, can I go see if my buddy is all right?”

Maple shook his head. “Sorry, Tommy, but you know you’re confined to camp.”

“Can I go, then, Sarge?” asked Ski, and then another soldier asked, and another.

“*Nobody* is going,” Eddie replied, his hands out in front of him, palms spread. “It’s night. There’s nothing to see, and there might be more Jerry planes around. Now go back to your tents, and go to sleep.”

Maple seemed unaware of the irony involved in the juxtaposition of his final two statements. No further aircraft appeared, but the men had a restless night, none more so than Flower of Iowa.

An hour before reveille, Tommy stole from his tent, eluding the one tired MP he saw between himself and the short road to Molliens, and then he was off and running. A few minutes’ trot brought him to the area where the London Rangers were camped. The man standing sentry duty, after a fashion, was none other than Muffett. “’Alt!” the fat soldier cried. “’Oo goes tha’yeh?”

“Muffett, it’s me, Flowers, Pearson’s Yank friend.”

“Ah. ’Ullo, Yank. Wha-ah yew ’ee-uh naow?”

“I heard about the aeroplane and the bombs.”

“Ahh, the aahplyne, yezz. Orf’l. Jis orf’l.”

“Any of your boys get hit?”

“Mos’ ahh boys waahn tha’yeh, tha parr town. Othuh boys gaa ’it, though. Some gaa ’urt, an’ some gaa kilt.”

“Oh, no....”

Muffett shrugged philosophically. “Iss wahhh, y’know.” He leaned closer to Tommy – uncomfortably so, given his personal hygiene. “I ’urrd th’ three chaps wha wuh kilt at the Kaffee doo Norrrd wuh on thah way home foh leave. K’n’you bea’ thah’?”

“That’s... that’s terrible. Did you know any of them?”

“Only knew Peah’z’n.”

It made no sense. Time stopped for Tommy; then he grabbed Muffett fiercely by his greasy lapels. "*Pearson?* Did you just say Pearson was killed?"

"Naaww, Peah'z'n waahn kilt, jis 'urrrt."

"Hur–hurt? Then why did you–"

"But iss awwr-rawight. 'E's gone Bligh'y."

"Gone Blighty?"

"Yezz. Big Bligh'y wooon."

Tommy was beginning to lose control. "Big – he was hurt? A big wound? Where is he now?"

"'E's gone, I tol' ya. 'E gaa a Bligh'y wooon. Theh sen' 'im to Cazh'ty Clin Staish."

"No, no!" Tommy shouted in a frenzy, starting to pound the fat private's chest. "Stop it! Stop it! You're not making sense! I don't understand what you're saying!" Now he couldn't help it; he began to cry. "Where's my friend? What are you saying? Where's my friend? Where's Davey?"

Muffett pushed him off. Under normal circumstances, the little fat man was no match for Flowers, but in his highly emotional state Tommy was not up for a fight. "Wha' yew crahh-yin?" Muffett asked with a scowl. "Doan' feel bahh foh Peah'z'n. I tol' ya, 'twas Bligh'y wooon. Daft Yank," he added, incongruously brushing himself off.

Tommy just stood there a minute, forlornly sobbing like he hadn't since he was a very young boy. Then he turned around and began to trudge back toward Pierregot. Davey was gone, Jamie wouldn't even speak to him, and he would probably never get to see Nicole again, either. Let's get on with this war, he said silently to himself. He couldn't wait to start fighting Germans.

# JULY 1918

# CHAPTER XVIII

As he caught his first real glimpse of what he reckoned was now the most famous river on earth, Tommy thought he'd made a mistake, that another, larger body of water must be just over the next ridge. He actually had crossed the Somme twice before, by train on his way to Abbéville his first week in France, and by bus (or perhaps it was a lorry, as David would have put it) on the ride to Pierregot. But that had been farther downstream; this was the Somme of legend. Just east of where Flowers and his company were standing, thousands upon thousands of brave men had died on its banks during the past two years – so many that, even two months after the latest "big push," the Germans' spring offensive, had petered out, it seemed to him that the river should still run red.

Actually, he thought, back home in Iowa this notorious stretch of water might not even qualify as a river. Here, south of the town of Bussy-les-Daours, it was little more than a creek – placid, hardly in motion at all, lined by the stumps of what had been, not so long ago, avenues of tall, elegant trees – a distinctly non-turbulent brook coursing through the most unimaginable man-made turbulence.

In the six days since Molliens had been bombed by the Boche aeroplane (he would wonder, always, if it was the same one that had chased him, that he had failed to report in a timely fashion), Tommy had come closer to his wish to be thrust directly into the full force of that turbulence. Three days ago, the men of Company E had left Pierregot with joyous whoops, flushed with the news that they were to join the 4th Australian Brigade for training preparatory to combat. The next day, as the Americans practiced well behind the lines, Tommy had seen tanks in action for the first time: weird, ungainly metal monsters that looked to him like some sort of motorized farm machinery run completely amok. But they were as deadly as they were awkward, and he was glad he was on the side that possessed the strange new weapons.

From the moment the Yanks joined the Australians' 43rd Battalion near Allonville, Tommy found himself surrounded by those distinctive Down Under accents, reminding him of the sergeant friend he'd made, then lost. He had neither seen nor heard from Jamie since that tense drive back to camp from the *estaminet*, and he felt the absence strongly. Then, this morning, as the Doughboys of Company E awaited orders that they expected would send them to a third day of training with the tanks, Eddie Maple had called his squad together and taken them to hear two lieutenants, an Australian and an American they didn't know. These officers informed the Yanks that in two days, on the Fourth of July, they would be taking part in an attack on a German strongpoint near a village called Le Hamel. As the meeting broke up, Tommy's excitement, indeed joy, matched that of his compatriots… until he caught sight of a gaunt, limping figure, with a face swollen almost – but not quite – beyond recognition.

Unable, as usual, to restrain his impulses, he rushed over to the Aussie sergeant and cried, "Jamie! What happened to you?"

But before Flowers could say anything further, Colbeck gave him a look of solid stone and said in a low, grim voice almost as unrecognizable as his face, "Didn't I say not to speak to me unless spoken to, soljuh?" then turned and walked away without looking back.

So the wounds from their falling-out remained as fresh for Tommy as David's wounds from the bombs falling out of the sky onto Molliens, which had sent the Briton back to Blighty. In the two days that had followed the bombing, before his company left camp, Tommy had made considerable efforts to track down his pal, so he could at least write to find out how Pearson was faring. He did manage to learn that the "Cazh'ty Clin Staish," that utterly unintelligible bit of information offered by Private Muffett in his horrendously garbled English, was in fact the Casualty Clearing Station, the first stop to which wounded Tommies – those fortunate enough to make it back from the battlefield – were brought for hurried examination by some harried, overworked doctor, who then either patched them up as best he was able, or sent them on to a station farther behind the lines meant to give attention to the most serious cases. With some luck, Tommy learned, a man with a Blighty might make it back to England within a day or so of being wounded. The American tried to picture Pearson resting comfortably in a hospital in Dunster, tended by a pretty young nurse. He wasn't sure how realistic that was – and he'd been told repeatedly by his squadmates not to think about Davey at all, that you couldn't do that in a war where you always stood to lose a buddy at any moment – but the image made him feel better nonetheless. He regretted the dispute with Jamie, and not getting the chance to see Nicole again. But above all, Tommy missed David.

"Hey, Flower!" The voice – and a splash of water that doused the bottom of his puttees – broke his reverie. He looked down to see a smiling Andy Kopinski standing in the stream, waist-deep and without clothes, flanked by others of their company.

"Thought you burned easy, Ski," Tommy said with a grin.

"Not on a day like today," Ski retorted, happily shaking droplets off his red hair. "Come on in for a swim."

Tommy recalled his own thoughts of a few moments before, about the river running red; God only knew what might be in this water, after all the killing upstream. But he'd already learned never to pass up a chance to bathe, and in moments he had joined them, splashing in the surprisingly cool Somme with his friends. As their horseplay escalated, so did their accompanying noise, until the voice of Eddie Maple broke through from overhead on the riverbank, shouting a familiar refrain: "Shut yer yaps, boys! Keep it down!"

They were so used to that kind of chiding from their sergeant that their initial response was laughter. But then a taller, darker man, unfamiliar to most of them except for Flowers, crouched down on the bank and said in a low, authoritative voice, "Sergeant Maple means what he says, gentlemen… even if he was saying it a little too loud himself. There's a lot of us moving into this sector, and what we need to do most of all is take Jerry by surprise. You might think your one voice wouldn't make a difference, but if every man here thinks the same thing, the Boche will hear us, and he'll know something's up. And there goes our element of surprise."

It was a convincing argument, reasonably delivered, and the men dropped the level of their chatter to a low buzz, most of it concerning exactly who this man might be. For his part, Tommy piped right up: "Corporal, sir. Congratulations! You're in the line. You got your wish."

Dougherty frowned at the familiarity. "I'm where I belong, Private," he said in a harsh tone; then he rose from his crouch to a standing position, to confer quietly with Maple, the sergeant whose authority he had just simultaneously reinforced and undermined.

"For a minute there, I thought he'd gotten better," Tommy murmured to Ski and Sleaze, who chorused – quietly – in return, "You know him?"

"Sure. That's Corporal Dougherty, Captain Willnor's adjutant. He always acts high and mighty. But you should've seen how Jamie put him in his place–"

With a swift movement, Dougherty returned to his crouching position, a few feet away from them; though he couldn't possibly have heard their words, he muttered fiercely to Flowers, "You got something to say to me, Private?"

The men were surprised and irritated by this intrusion into their private conversation by a mere corporal. Tommy's own voice hardened as he replied, "Nothing, Corporal. Nothing at all."

"Nothing," Dougherty repeated, very slowly rising again. "I should have known that. That's all you ever have to say, Private Flowers. Nothing."

As the corporal walked off with Maple, Sanders, who was a little farther away in the water but close enough to have caught everything, said in a voice loud enough for Dougherty to hear, "Hey, Flower of Iowa, what's his problem? Looks to me like he's got it in for you."

"I really don't know, Vern," Tommy replied with a shrug.

There was a pause, then Harry Carson declared, "The hell with him! Water fight!" He ripped a sheet of spray at the group of them, and they resumed their play. But, more conscious of the Germans now, they tried to keep their noise to a minimum.

Later that afternoon, after they ate their last hot meal until the fight was over, the Americans were moved in small groups into their trenches. Once settled in, they were told to keep quiet and out of sight. During the evening some of them, including Tommy, even had the opportunity to nap, a rarity in the upside-down world of the trenches, where night was generally the busiest time. But at about three in the morning, Flowers was awakened by artillery (he didn't know why, but this time he knew, authoritatively, that it was artillery, and that it belonged to his side). As the explosions continued to echo, he wrapped himself ever more tightly into the small funk hole where he'd been dozing. The barrage went on, and a slight figure tried to squeeze with him into his little shelter: Edwards, a young corporal with the Australian battalion to which Company E was attached. He was a cheerful, dark-skinned, curly-haired lad from the outback, of whom Sanders wondered aloud whether he had any Aborigine blood. Tommy doubted that; the colored troops in the American Army couldn't fight alongside white troops, so why would the Australians allow it?

"Don't be afraid, mate," Edwards said, jaunty and encouraging. "It's just the nightly show."

"I'm not afraid," Tommy said, with a little edge to his voice.

"Didn't say you were, ne'sarily. Just thinkin' it was your first night here and all."

Edwards sounded like Colbeck; since he was barely visible in the dark trench, it was all the more eerie. Tommy abruptly yearned for friendship, and his own tone grew more amiable: "What do you mean, 'the nightly show'?"

"Aour lot's been doin' this for the last several days naow. Light barrage, same haour, lastin' the same amaount of time. In fact, it's almost over. Any time naow, the Boche will give us a sally back." On cue, there was a burst much closer to their trench, clearly coming from the other direction, and Tommy shrank farther into the funk hole, or tried to. "Never you mind that, neither," said Edwards with a laugh. "Their aim ain't very good, and neither's aours. There ain't been any casualties for days. It's like it's one of those gennelmen's agreements, it is.

"But it'll be a right rude surprise for them tomorrow when they get more than they're ready for, won't it?" Edwards concluded, satisfaction in his voice. For a moment, though he knew he shouldn't, Tommy tried to imagine what it would be like on the other side, expecting the usual harmless barrage and suddenly facing something much deadlier. It was odd, this business of "gentlemen's agreements" that could be broken in fatal fashion at any time by either side.

The next afternoon was warm, and the command to keep quiet had become the supreme order of the day. Overwhelmed with boredom, Tommy sat and pondered how the Germans, who were so close, could possibly fail to hear the increased activity on his side; but, endeavoring to be a good soldier, he tried with limited success to concentrate on being absolutely still and silent.

A gangly Aussie private, so tall he had to stoop to avoid being seen over the parapet, came shambling down the trench and stopped before him. "You Flaowuhs?" he asked in a high-pitched, too-loud voice, and the surprised Yank nodded. "Come with me." Fending off the questioning looks of his sleepy-eyed squadmates, Tommy took off after the man. So long were the private's legs that Tommy, not exactly a runt himself, had to lope double-time to keep up; David, he mused, wouldn't have stood a chance. The discomfort of moving so fast while carrying a full kit began to bear down on him, and he found himself perspiring ever more heavily as he continued to trot after the man through the twisting, winding maze of trenches. Abruptly the ground seemed to rise and they came to a cul-de-sac. The tall Aussie stopped dead in front of Tommy, saluted someone, and announced, "Private Flaowuhs, as requested, sir," then cut to his right and vanished. Only then did Tommy see the recipient of the salute. He looked markedly better than he had yesterday morning, but his expression remained uncharacteristically blank.

"Private Flaowuhs," the man repeated with the curtest of nods.

"Sergeant Colbeck," Tommy replied stiffly, saluting, breathing a little heavily after the quick, unanticipated end to his long journey. There was a long, awkward silence as Jamie stared at him, a gaze that caused Flowers to cast his own eyes elsewhere.

Finally the Australian said, "There's somethin' I want to show you, soljuh," and brushed past Tommy without looking at him. With the barest of sighs – and even that was involuntary; he was determined to remain stolid in Jamie's presence – Tommy turned about, realizing he was to go on yet another walk. Fortunately, Jamie's legs weren't as long as those of the gangly private, and his still-battered state had slowed his step. It was an easy tromp behind the sergeant, or would have been had Tommy not already felt winded.

They were walking uphill, and soon they were aboveground, in a half-ruined village. "What town is this?" Tommy wondered, realizing too late he had done so out loud. Jamie would think he was trying to make conversation in defiance of the order to speak only when spoken to.

But although Colbeck didn't turn around to look at him, the Aussie answered matter-of-factly, "This is Vaire. Vaire-sous-Corbie, to be exact. '*Sous*' means under," he added helpfully.

"So the town of Vaire is under the town of Corbie?"

"Not really. Corbie's west of here. But it's on the north bank of the river, and Vaire's on the saouth bank. Keep your voice daown, naow." He led Tommy through the nave of a shelled-out church on the edge of the village. Sweeping his left arm to take in the panorama that hove into view near what would have been the altar, he whispered "See that?" and actually put his right hand on Tommy's shoulder. "That's where we'll be fightin'." One by one, he pointed out the sights: "See that ridge, and the taown partwise up to the top of it? That's Hamel." The village lay several hundred yards upward of the Allied trenches, on gently sloping land; beyond it, the slope was much steeper.

"It's all ruined, isn't it? No one's there."

"It's taken a lot o'shells, but believe me, I've seen worse," Jamie said, and Nicole's home village of Cumières fleetingly came to the Aussie's mind. At least there was enough left of Hamel for the inhabitants to come back someday – so far. "No one's left from the taown," he added, "but there's plenty of Boche. That's what a place looks like after the back-and-forth of four years."

Next Jamie directed Tommy's attention to also damaged, though still intact, woods on the village's right flank. "That's the Bois de Hamel and the Bois de Vaire," he said, pointing in turn. "The Bois de Hamel, especially, is as full of Maxims as an aoutback anthill is full of ants."

"If it's closer to Hamel than Vaire, why is it called the Bois de Vaire?"

Jamie looked directly at Tommy for the first time. "You always ask the strangest questions, Flaowuhs," he said; there was no smile on his face, but there was a hint of one in his voice. "Haow would I know?"

Tommy shrugged. "I thought you knew everything."

There was no sarcasm in the statement; embarrassed by the hero worship, Jamie guided Tommy's gaze back to the forthcoming field of battle. "See where those crops are growin'?" Tommy nodded. "That's no-man's-land."

"It's been like this for a while, then."

"Since their spring advance. That's when they claimed the high graound. Now they've gotten comf'tably dug in."

Tommy paused, said, "Even I can tell this whole arrangement works in their favor."

"You're right. There's been so much harassing fire that aour brass decided we had to do something abaout it."

"The American brass?"

Jamie gave him a sour look. "Australian brass."

"Oh, of course. I'm sorry."

Colbeck shook his head. "Still sayin' you're sorry." Then he turned his head quickly away, to cut off further conversation. Tommy was hoping that they were about to discuss their quarrel, but he understood he was being asked to focus on the task at hand.

He looked carefully at the village, the woods, then down to his right where the Allied trenches lay. The prospect of charging over the ground in between was daunting, but Tommy was reassured when he remembered the lieutenants' description of the planned attack: in the dead of night, with artillery and tank support. It sounded to him a much better idea than the way Jamie had described the launching of the disastrous big push just across the Somme two years ago: rows of Tommies marching in line uphill in the morning sunlight, falling before the systematic rattle of the German machine guns. What a way for Davey's brother to die. Tommy had half convinced himself he didn't mind dying – but not like that.

"Come on," Jamie said suddenly, and Tommy was again following the sergeant's back through Vaire-sous-Corbie.

"Will the other boys get to see this?"

Colbeck didn't turn around. "No. Remember what you've seen, and tell them abaout it. All the platoon leaders have been up here, and I'm one of the few sergeants. You're prob'ly the only private."

"Why?"

"Because I decided I wanted you to see it."

"Didn't you need some kind of permission–?"

"I got it. Haow do you think we got past the MPs? Use your head, Tommy."

It was the first time since their falling out that Jamie had called him by his Christian name. Tommy was emboldened to ask a risky question: "Why me?"

Still speaking over his shoulder, Colbeck replied, "I thought it would be good if one of the privates in aour lot saw the graound before the battle, in case somethin' comes up. Officers and NCOs have a way of not bein' araound at the wrong times."

"'Cause they stay back?"

"No, 'cause they get hurt or killed. So it pays to have a corp'ral, even a private, who knows what's what. As long as he's a bright one."

Heartened by the implicit compliment, Tommy could no longer contain himself. "Thanks, Jamie!"

Colbeck, heading downhill back into the trench system, didn't stop, nor did he look back around. He simply added over his shoulder, "I also thought you should see it in case this turns aout to be where you die. Naow get on back to your station, soljuh."

There was nothing remotely humorous about Jamie's tone. Tommy's gratitude died on his lips.

# CHAPTER XIX

In the midnight blackness of the trench, Tommy could hear someone making his way slowly down his sector, stopping to talk to each man, Doughboy or Aussie. Late that afternoon Company E had been divided up into platoons, each of which was assigned to a different Australian company; and as had already been done with their Down Under counterparts, some of the men from each of the Yank companies were put in reserve, to form the nucleus of a new company in the event the rest were wiped out. It was a practice the British Empire troops had learned to employ on the basis of hard experience. Though Tommy didn't know the reason for it, he was relieved when his platoon, his squad, were not among those put into the reserves.

In stark contrast to the previous evening, everything had been busyness since nightfall. As soon as dusk arrived, a few members of the Australian intelligence unit, including Edwards, had gone up over the top. The dark corporal had told Tommy his "lot" would be laying down the tape for the troops' jumping-off point. Colbeck's cautionary tales notwithstanding, Flowers realized he had always pictured himself part of a vast group charging over the parapet in broad daylight, breasting the Boche guns in a burst of bravery. Instead, the battle plan called for the Allies to steal silently over the top in small groups under cover of darkness, and then advance only as far as the jumping-off tape. Later, after the artillery barrage, would come the real charge.

In the meantime, as the hour for this exercise drew nerve-rackingly close, this someone continued to come down the trench. Tommy could see he was handing each man something – extra ammunition, perhaps? The gaunt figure, sporting an Aussie accent (perhaps it was the gangly private of this afternoon), finally stopped in front of Flowers and harshly whispered, "Cuppa?" Tommy already was carrying two days' rations and two full water bottles, but like all of his mates, he gratefully took the metal cup full of steaming liquid in hand; though it was a warm summer night, he was feeling a chill, and the hot drink calmed him. He remembered the tepid, weak beverage David offered him when they had shared the Tommy's "dinner." He hadn't liked tea much then, but this time it was different – warmer, tastier, with a buttery flavor that slid down his throat and heated his insides.

The tea man passed on, and Tommy resumed his stance of agitated silence. He knew his friends, Vern and Harry, Walt and Andy, were nearby, and he had glimpsed both Dougherty and Colbeck earlier. But it was not a time for unnecessary talk, and each man was alone with his thoughts. In the light of early evening, spurred by Jamie's off-the-cuff remark, he had written four short letters, each almost the same as the other: one to Susan, one to his mother and father, one to

David, one to Nicole. Each had said very little, except that he was about to go into battle, and if anything should happen to him they shouldn't be upset, because he was doing his duty for his country. Well, the one to David was a little different; in it, he asked his friend how his wounds were healing, and shared with him his sense of excitement, exhilaration in fact, that at last he would be going over the top. Only Davey among his correspondents would have truly understood that.

The letters were tucked in his tunic, close to his chest. There was no postman to pick them up before the battle. Besides, he didn't even have an address for Pearson, and not much of one for Nicole. But he hoped if he was killed, someone would find the missives and send them.

Now another figure was coming down the trench: Eddie Maple. Suddenly there was something reassuring about their overbearing young sergeant, still barking out orders (if you could bark and whisper at the same time) the same way he always did. He was two or three men away when Tommy heard him say to the squad, "All right, boys. Time to go over. You know what to do." Then, quite out of character, he added, "God be with us."

Tommy climbed onto the fire-step, his heart moving faster than at any time since the aeroplane had chosen him for a target. He was part of a silent, single-file line headed a hundred or so yards forward, to the jumping-off tape. Though everyone was perfectly orderly and quiet, he had to wonder how the German sentries could not have noticed. Then he recalled the crops growing in no-man's-land; tonight, they were the Allies' allies. And the brass had had the sense not to pick a moonlit night for the attack.

No one made a sound as they reached the white tape that Edwards and his companions had so efficiently laid out. The men, Tommy among them, hit the ground at intervals of five yards. He was dimly aware that on either side of him were Australian privates he didn't know, or at least couldn't remember – was the one on his right named Jackson? – and that Ski was on the other side of that man.

It wasn't even one o'clock yet, and zero hour was after three. Tommy nervously gripped his British Enfield rifle. The Yanks would have much preferred to use the American Springfield, but there weren't enough of those to go around; besides, they were fortunate compared to most other Doughboys, who had to use the notoriously less reliable French Chauchat, which at times was as apt to do damage to the soldier firing it as the soldier who was supposed to be on the receiving end. Having practiced with Springfields at Fort Dodge, Tommy couldn't understand why he and most of his mates (Harry Carson, jealously guarding his Springfield a few men down on the left, being a conspicuous exception) were stuck with the British rifles. The truth, beyond his knowing, was that there weren't enough American rifles available for the U.S. Army; in fact, there was very little in the way of American-made equipment of any kind. The Doughboys had to rely on the

British and especially the French to supply them, and the latter two Allies were only too happy to outfit America's men – and accept America's money.

Trying to relax, he let his senses drift a bit, and caught a powerful scent on the air – not death, not gunfire, not even too many men who had washed too little; no, the overpowering odor, quite suddenly, was clover. Up ahead in the crops, there must be bushels full of the blooming summer flowers, white and red, so profuse he couldn't understand why he hadn't noticed them, or at least the bees they should have attracted, when he was looking at this ground from Vaire with Jamie. They must have been hidden by the summer wheat.

The smell took him from where he was. He was back in Iowa, on a hot summer's day, under puffy clouds in a blue sky, chasing his grandmother's cat into a field of red clover, where he startled and angered a bumblebee, which extracted its revenge. He had run home scared and crying, seven years old he must have been, more frightened then than now. The white clover reminded him of cutting the broad lawns of Brooklyn, his own family's, Susan's, and those of anyone else who would pay him a penny, to make a little extra money, so he could take Susan down to the Rexall on a Saturday. He felt the letter to her, flat between him and the earth. Here he was in this French meadow, sniffing the clover like at home, about to kill some Germans. Good thing he wasn't like poor Henry Adamly, his classmate who always sneezed when he was around clover. Good thing Henry wasn't here!

Concentrating hard, he heard, to his surprise, crickets, not unlike the ones he'd hear sitting on the front porch swing at home on summer evenings with his sisters. It would be easy enough to pretend he was younger, still at home, just playing soldier. But then the insects reminded him of something else, and he began to itch fiercely. Being in the ground, lying on the ground, had given him cooties just like David had warned, just like everyone else. That had never happened to him in Iowa; the worst he could remember was a few chigger bites.

The time seemed to go by at a rate of about an hour per second. But at last, at a couple of minutes after three, the kind of "light" artillery barrage that had awakened Tommy the night before began again. This time it was accompanied by the buzz of aeroplanes, flying very low overhead. It was too dark to tell whose they were, but they weren't firing, and Tommy could only presume and hope they were on his side. Then an unearthly rumble emanated from behind him and he felt the ground shake – the tanks, moving into position. Even though he was tense, waiting to spring, the cleverness of the strategy did cross his mind: the barrage and the aeroplanes were drowning out the sound of the approaching tanks. These Australians were smart.

After a few minutes, the barrage began to get much heavier, so that Tommy's world was suddenly a swirl of dust and smoke, flashes of light, the odor of clover blasted from the night. He just had time enough to think briefly again about the men up the hill, how the leisurely nightly barrage was turning into something else for them, when Eddie Maple came running from his left in front of the tape, shouting, "All right, boys, let's go!" He was several strides past Tommy, who had just scrambled to his feet to head into the battle, when a shell came whistling down – from behind – igniting a stupendous storm of light and dirt that tore in all directions, just off to Flowers' right. He heard several agonized screams, cut short, and was sure one was the voice of Andy Kopinski. Instinctively he whirled in the direction of the explosion, but it was too dark in the aftermath to see what had happened. No more than two seconds passed before a star shell burst overhead, and he caught a quick glimpse of mangled mud and men, a horrific tableau that vanished again with the night.

"Come on, *move, move, move!*" yelled a voice off his left shoulder; it came from the blackened face of Daniel Dougherty. "Let's *go,* Flowers! Move ahead!"

Obediently, Tommy began to do so, but at the same time he tried to communicate what had happened to the corporal: "Our artillery, sir – I think it's falling short!"

"Keep *moving,* Private. That's not your problem. Now charge!" Tommy and the Americans nearest him started to do so with great gusto, as did the accompanying Australians, though they moved a tad less quickly. Within seconds, another huge explosive, again coming from behind, landed right in front of the Yanks, sending shrapnel all over creation. Tommy heard other men's howls, but somehow again he remained untouched.

"Slow *daown,* men, slow *daown!*" came an authoritative Aussie voice – Jamie's – out of the smoke and blackness. "Don't run ahead of your own barrage."

"Our own barrage is hitting us, Jamie!" Tommy yelled recklessly into the night, and Dougherty's voice rang out:

"Shut up, Private. Move ahead!"

"Slow *daown,* Tommy," Jamie repeated in direct contradiction. In the heat and dust, he and Dougherty both suddenly emerged visible. "There's no time to argue abaout this," the Australian said to the American, gesticulating wildly. "We're lucky no one's shot at us yet. Move ahead, men, but pace yourselves!"

"What's your authority here, Sergeant?" Dougherty demanded.

"Corp'ral," Jamie said in exasperation, "Sergeant Maple and Leftenant Cross" – Tommy recalled that as the name of the Australian leader of their platoon – "ain't here anymore to give orders, so naow it's up to you and me to get these men to aour objective."

"Jamie–" Tommy began in interruption.

"I *know* it's aour artil'ry, Tommy," the sergeant said, talking fast but with strained patience. "Sometimes that happens. You have to keep moving, but keep behind aour barrage. Just trust me."

Tommy did, and so did the other Aussies and Doughboys in the vicinity. Up the gentle slope the group ran in the darkness, advancing through the wheat and clover for one hundred, then two hundred yards with no opposition whatsoever. Every three minutes the barrage would lift so they could gain more yardage; it was like a deadly game of football, open-field running. This is easier than I thought, Tommy mused fleetingly, shutting from his memory the disaster he had just witnessed. Seconds later, he heard the fatal rattle of Maxims ahead, heard men cry out and fall heavily to the ground. The Germans must have been counting the lifts, awaiting the next one for an opportunity to hit their targets. Tommy was following Jamie's cues, and the machine-gunning hadn't slowed the sergeant's step, so it didn't slow his. Around his group he could hear the tanks roaring up front; overhead, the aeroplanes continued to drone and swoop, with no apparent opposition from airborne Boche. There was a tremendous, ghastly cry far off to their right, and Jamie said in a quick, dry aside, "Saounds like one of aour tanks caved in one of their trenches."

A scattering of bullets indicated that Aussie troops were cleaning out the machine-gun nest ahead; so intent was Tommy on following Jamie forward that he scarcely noticed stretcher bearers taking the Maxims' victims back toward the Allied lines. Overexcited, he fired his Enfield once or twice, with no sense of where he was shooting, and the ever-watchful Dougherty loudly scolded him, "Don't waste your fire, Flowers!"

The Germans were certainly audible if not visible by now; the dark rang out with cries of *"Kamerad! Kamerad!"* as the terrified enemy surrendered. With the tanks continuing to move ahead of the infantry and the aeroplanes in command of the skies, Tommy's confidence grew, and he found he was beginning to enjoy the show.

With little opposition, they soon were within sight of Hamel, many of its ruined buildings now aflame. Far to his right, out of the corner of his eye, Tommy saw a tank move into the village; shortly thereafter, for some reason, it moved back out – and then its turret turned crazily about. "No!" Flowers shouted, his voice useless in the din, and the tank fired a round that came shrieking in his direction, hitting its unintended targets – three Americans, including an officer he barely knew – no more than fifteen yards away.

"Oh, God, no!" Tommy repeated.

"Keep *moving*," Dougherty repeated, and Tommy did.

They were almost to the edge of the village. "All right, men," Jamie hollered. "Let's go!" Just ahead, for the first time, Tommy actually saw men in field gray, and he fired his rifle, but in the chaos he again had no idea whether he was hitting anything, though he heard Harry Carson's self-satisfied voice off to his left: "Got one!"

The Yanks and Aussies advanced into the village itself, where Tommy suddenly noticed dead bodies, mostly German, all about him. He'd scarcely seen a corpse before, but they held no curiosity for him right now; his mates were attacking a dugout at the edge of town whose occupants refused to surrender, and they needed his help. Shots were exchanged crazily in the night, and then he heard Jamie's voice cry, "Fix bayonets!" Like his compatriots, Tommy did so, and when Jamie yelled, "Charge, men!" he found himself running, bayonet thrust out in front of him, over the top of the Jerry dugout. Jumping down inside, he found himself face-to-face with a man old enough to be his father, a man with an enormous mustache who reminded him of his Uncle Larry. The Boche didn't immediately raise his hands in surrender, and Tommy lightly poked the man once with his bayonet. The man moved toward him a little, and from behind him Tommy heard Jamie's voice shout, "Don't be so shy, men! You've got your bayonets, naow use them!" He couldn't be sure the old German didn't have a gun, so the American blindly lunged forward with his bayonet, and felt it slice into his enemy's torso. The Boche's eyes turned huge and white, and then he threw up blood, all over himself and Tommy, collapsing at his feet.

All Tommy could think was how fast could he get his bayonet out, but at first it wouldn't budge. He tried twisting it, and the man – who still looked like Uncle Larry – groaned and then screamed. Finally the Doughboy pulled his weapon clear; more blood spurted, and the German shrieked in still greater anguish. "Stretcher!" Tommy called weakly, and suddenly Dougherty was by his side.

The corporal looked down and said nonchalantly, "No need for a stretcher, Private Flowers. You did a pretty good job here."

"But – he's not dead–"

In a single fluid motion, Dougherty pulled out a pistol and fired once at Uncle Larry's head, splattering them and the dugout with still more blood, as well as brain matter and who knew what else. "He is now," the corporal said laconically. "Let's go."

Numb, Tommy stumbled out of the dugout. Not twenty yards farther into town, an order rang out: "Dig in! Dig in!"

Vern Sanders abruptly appeared next to him. "Just when we were having fun! Got your shovel, Tommy?"

"I've got a pick. Right here."

"Let's start digging, then." Kneeling, they began to chop at the hard, unyielding Picardy chalk. "This is something, hey Flower?"

"It's something, all right, Vern."

"Didja get any Jerries?"

Tommy felt his stomach turn over. There was sound and fire all around them, but it seemed to be sweeping past the village, and there was something peaceful, if urgent, about their entrenching task. “One, I think,” he finally answered. “Me and Dougherty together got him. I… saw him die.”

“Really? I think I got one, too. You’re so lucky, Flower of Iowa. Maybe you’ll get a medal.”

“Yeah, maybe,” Tommy said stonily, stabbing the earth of France again and again.

# Chapter XX

The digging was hard work, though not hot work, since the sun had yet to make its appearance. Tommy and Vern had been scratching away for at least half an hour, and had achieved little more than a narrow, shallow ditch, when the ambient noise of the Allied barrage, which they had grown well used to, suddenly dwindled down. Sanders noticed it first, and commented uneasily, "What's happening?"

"God *damn!*" came the familiar voice in the pre-dawn; Jamie and some Australians, it turned out, were a mere ten to twenty yards away. "Those bloody buggers!" Colbeck continued to swear. "Get daown, men!" Flowers and Sanders obediently dove into their sort-of trench, then lay coughing as they inhaled the chalky dust.

Seconds passed, then minutes, and absolutely nothing happened. "This is stupid, Tommy," Sanders muttered, and Flowers replied, "Jamie knows what he's doing, Vern. He said to stay down. He hasn't given the all-clear."

"He doesn't know we're here. They're up and digging again. Can't you hear them?"

"No."

"Well, I'm sure they are." In the dimness, Tommy could see Sanders raise his huge forearm from its flattened position and point. "He was right over there, wasn't he?"

"Vern, I wouldn't–" Tommy began, but the big man was already on his feet and walking in the direction where he thought he'd heard Colbeck's voice.

"Hey, Sarge!" he shouted, and at almost the same instant, Tommy heard a burst of machine-gun fire, a cry of "Aaaaghh!" from Sanders, and the loud thud of the big man falling heavily to the ground.

Tommy suppressed his instinct to shout the way Sanders had, but he whispered as loud as he could to his fallen friend, calling his name, and was rewarded with an echoing groan which in turn elicited more machine-gun fire. A softer groan followed. Sanders was still alive, but even collapsed on the ground he would make a tempting target when it began to get light, which could happen at any time. Tommy had no interest in repeating his friend's mistake, but neither could he leave Vern lying there. Decisively he scrambled out of his ditch, keeping low to the ground, crawling as fast as he could on his belly. After a minute of this he took in too much dust and started coughing in spite of himself; Henry Adamly again came to mind, but moments later the sound of shots nearby drove the thought from his head and the cough back down his throat. He crouched, very still. The shots had been aimed somewhere between where he was and where he thought Sanders was.

Or was Vern there? It seemed to Tommy that he should have reached the big man by now. Again he threw his voice in a loud whisper – "Vern? You there?" – and he caught the very faintest of moans from *behind* him, seemingly from the same direction from which he'd just come. He'd really become disoriented. If only Davey was with him. Spinning 180 degrees in the dirt, Tommy started his crawl all over again. A minute later, or maybe two, he grabbed hold of a leg, or at least something that felt like a leg, in the darkness.

He whispered "Vern?" even as the leg kicked at him, very narrowly missing his face, and the body connected to it scurried about. Tommy heard a rifle cock, and he knew he had no chance of reaching his own in time; heart plummeting, he said faintly, "No!"

Scarcely more than a second elapsed, though it seemed much longer; then, instead of a fatal shot, what burst forth from the dark was a whispered "Tommy Flaowuhs, you're lucky you got a big maouth!"

The shock of encountering Jamie's voice instead of the business end of a rifle proved too much. Tommy began to shake uncontrollably where he lay on the ground.

"Tommy? Tommy!" Jamie whispered again but, try mightily though he did, Tommy couldn't speak, only continue to lie there shaking. Jamie scrambled over to him. "Naow, don't go gettin' all scared on me, Tommy," he said, his voice low and husky.

"I–" Tommy finally, tentatively, found his own voice. "I'm not–"

Colbeck put his arm around the Yank's shoulder and began rocking the boy lightly. "It's all right, Tommy," he said with a gentleness Flowers could not have imagined the Australian possessing, especially right now. "You're fine. You're doin' a good job. I was wrong; you are a good soljuh. But you can't freeze on us naow. We've got to help your buddy Sanders–"

"That's what I was out here for."

"Then let's do it," Colbeck said, letting go of him.

"Is – is Vern dead?"

"No," Jamie said briskly. "I don't waste my time on dead men. You'll learn not to, either. Naow, igaree."

"Huh?"

"That's a word we use for 'Hurry up.'"

"Oh. OK."

As it turned out, Vern was mere feet away. Tommy had grabbed Jamie's leg just as the latter had reached the fallen man. Colbeck felt for Sanders' wounds, then said, "He's hurt pretty bad. We better not pull him very hard. Just tug him, careful-like." Sanders was motionless, no longer groaning, and he was as heavy as he looked, maybe more so; as they started to move him, the expression "dead weight" came to Flowers' mind. Indeed, Tommy would have sworn Vern was dead but for Jamie's quiet urgings as the two of them grimly dragged the big man back toward the Aussies' hastily dug trench. After five minutes of this, they had managed to advance him only a couple of yards. It was slow, but it was progress, and Tommy's concentration was entirely given over to the task. He was therefore even more startled than he normally would have been when an aeroplane swooped out of the sky and began spraying bullets and bombs in their general area, much too close.

"God *damn,*" Jamie loudly repeated, then he added in a lower voice, "You all right, Flaowuhs?"

"I'm all right, Sarge. Was Vern hit?"

"I don't think so." As soon as these words were out, another fusillade crashed in even greater proximity, and the Boche aeroplane followed up by dropping breathtakingly close to earth, maybe no more than twenty feet above them. Hard upon that, though, they heard other firing in the air, coming from a different direction. "It's abaout time," Jamie said. "That should be one of aours. Where the hell's he been?" An exchange of *rat-a-tats* echoed overhead as they continued to lie still and flat on the ground. After a while, Colbeck said with great seriousness, "Flaowuhs, can I ask you a question?"

"Sure, Jamie," Tommy replied, although his tone was more guarded than his words.

"What is it abaout you that seems to attract aeroplanes?" At that, sergeant and private alike broke into huge fits of laughter, and simultaneously tried to stifle the impulse. Eventually Jamie was the first to recover; with as much sternness as he could muster, he ordered, "Stop laughin', Private, or you'll get us both killed." He then proceeded to break into another prolonged round of mirth himself, which was interrupted a minute or two later by a strange voice:

"Sir?"

"Aa-a-" Jamie said with a start, wheeling about for his gun, but he failed to complete the motion. In the pre-dawn that was steadily shading into a lighter and lighter gray, he and Tommy could see that they had been joined by an extremely young-looking Australian soldier. The boy had to be at least a couple of years Tommy's junior. "That you, Norman?" the sergeant said, recovering, his hands dropped to his sides.

"Yes, sir. I was sent 'round to help. Were you… were you laughing, Sarge?"

Jamie was suddenly all business: "I'll explain later, Norman." As he listened to Colbeck and Norman confer about the best strategy for moving Sanders, it occurred to Tommy that the boy didn't have the same accent as Jamie, Edwards, and all the other Aussies he'd encountered.

With three of them tugging, they ultimately managed to move Vern to the edge of the Australians' trench, a surprisingly deep affair compared to what Flowers and Sanders had achieved. There, six men – Colbeck, Flowers, Norman (Tommy still didn't know if that was his first or last name), and three others who had been waiting – lowered the big American inside. It was almost sunrise now, and in the waxing light, Vern looked very, very pale, except for a large, dark-red stain on his upper right leg and groin.

"He needs to be carried aout of here on a stretcher," Jamie muttered.

"I've done that kind of work before," said another of the Down Under boys, a ginger-haired lad maybe a year or two older than Tommy. "If we could make aour own stretcher, I'll help carry him back."

Tommy, who found the offer astounding (after all, these men didn't even know Sanders), interjected, "But they're still firing out there."

All of the Australians looked at him as if he were mad, except for Jamie, who patiently explained, "That's what stretcher bearers do, Tommy. They carry men aout under fire. Anybody could do it after the shooting stops." Turning to the man who had volunteered, he added, "Chris, do you think we can put a stretcher together?"

"Let's see, Sarge. We have blankets, and" – Chris spied the shovels they had been using to dig their trench, and gestured – "these." Within minutes they had taken two of the blankets and knotted them together tightly onto four of the shovels. Then they rolled Sanders onto this attempt at a stretcher. He made no sound, and Colbeck briefly placed his hand on Vern's wrist, then cocked his head to listen to the wounded man's chest.

"Better igaree," Jamie said, mostly to himself; then, to Chris, "Who'll go with you?"

"Anybody else here done this before?" Chris asked. Nobody had.

"I'll go," Tommy volunteered.

They all stared at him again, but again Jamie intervened. "That's a good idear," the sergeant said. To head off any dissent, he nodded toward Tommy and added, "He's a big, strong lad. Good for this job."

"All right," Chris acceded with a shrug. He directed his attention to Flowers. "But understand, the most important thing ain't strength; it's coordination. You've got to work together with your partner, or your wounded man will be the worse for it."

"Just tell me what to do," Tommy said. With Chris leading at Vern's head and Tommy following at his feet, they slowly lifted up Sanders who, seemingly even heavier than before, swayed wildly on the makeshift stretcher.

"Look," said young Norman, pointing at a rapidly spreading dampness on one blanket. "There goes my spare blanket." But he said it without rancor, almost cheerfully.

"Pretty precarious, ain't it?" Jamie asked Chris, but the latter responded, "I think we'll make it."

"All right, then. Off with you."

That was it. No "Godspeed" or "good luck." But then again, Tommy thought, Eddie had said "God be with us" and… No. He couldn't think about things like that when Sanders needed his help.

As he and Chris stumbled out of the trench with their charge, they emerged into a sunlit morning; Tommy, dazzled, had begun to believe it was a night without end. At a trot, the two men headed through the smoking ruins of Hamel. It was relatively quiet for the first ten seconds or so, and then the sound of artillery landing behind them, farther up the hill, overwhelmed the stillness, as did another cry of "It's abaout time!" from the trench they had quit.

Chris shook his head and flicked a smile back at Tommy. "Sarge was sure mad when they stopped aour barrage too soon. Naow we'll have some cover."

"I don't know," Tommy demurred. "From what I saw before, I think I'm more afraid of our own barrage." Their zigzag run down the slope, the same area he had surveyed with Jamie yesterday, revealed a completely altered landscape. Dead men were lying about in grotesque, twisted poses, causing Tommy to comment, "Do you think they're all Germans because we won the battle?"

"Maybe," Chris said laconically, "or maybe it's just because aour stretcher bearers've already been here for haours, and theirs can't get to them."

"What happens if they're lying there just wounded, but not killed?"

"Then aour bearers will pick them up, too. But they won't risk their lives to do it. They'll wait 'til the shootin's done."

Tommy thought about lying out there wounded and unattended, shuddered, and shifted his attention elsewhere. Not only men and buildings had been blasted apart. The wheat crop in the former no-man's-land was in tatters, and the clover smell had been banished completely from the air. Tommy wondered whether crickets were able to survive shelling, since lice obviously did.

They were most of the way through the chewed-up, bloodied clumps of wheat when the sound of rending fabric could be heard faintly above the din of the action farther back up the ridge. Tommy felt Vern shift dangerously and, feeling safely out of sniper range, yelled "Chris!" at the top of his lungs.

The Australian, still straining forward, looked back and immediately comprehended the situation. "Oh, ain't that bonzer," he said, his tone ironic; then he added, "We should stop, Tommy. But slowly." They glided to a halt, then gingerly lowered Vern to the ground even as one of the blankets tore some more.

"This'll never hold naow," Chris grumbled, inspecting what was left of their stretcher. He looked up at Tommy. "We're more than halfwise there. I could run the rest of the way to get help if you stay here with him."

"Sure, I can do that," Tommy replied, and without a word the Aussie took off, leaving the two Yanks together in the now-blasted grainfield.

Alone with Sanders, Tommy suddenly found himself more afraid than he had been during the entire battle. It wasn't fear of what might happen; he actually felt fairly secure here, well clear of whatever was taking place on the ridge. But Flowers shivered as he realized what already had occurred. It started when he looked down at his companion. Sanders – the biggest, toughest man in their outfit – was deathly still, and suddenly seemed fragile in the extreme. Maple and Ski – what had happened to them? And the boys he saw who were targeted by their own tank? He couldn't even begin to bring himself to think about the old German who looked like Uncle Larry. Instead he started to wonder if Muffett and the other Tommies had told him the truth, if David really had only gotten a Blighty. He didn't like waiting here in this field with Sanders, didn't like thinking about these things. He'd much rather still be in action. To give himself something to do, every once in a while Tommy would look down and say, "It's going to be all right, Vern. There's help coming. It'll be all right."

Eventually that help did arrive, when Chris returned with a real stretcher and another man, an American from Tommy's platoon who looked familiar. This man, somewhat older, in his mid-twenties perhaps, recognized Tommy, too: "Hey, aren't you the one they call 'Flower of Iowa'?"

"That's me," Tommy allowed as the three of them moved Sanders onto the new stretcher with considerable care. To Chris, he added, "Should I go with you?"

"The two of us can handle this. Why don't you take the banjos back to the Sarge?"

Tommy looked at Chris as if the Aussie had lost his mind. "Banjos? What banjos?"

"Right there," Chris retorted, gesturing at the shovels.

"Oh." Why can't these Australians talk normal, Tommy thought. Gesturing in turn at the bloody, discarded stretcher, he asked, "What about the blankets?"

Chris gave them an instant's survey. "The one's not so bad, but I'd leave the other. Peter was right abaout that."

"I thought his name was Norman."

Chris, already lifting Sanders with the other Yank, looked quizzically at Tommy. "That's his name. Peter Norman."

"How old is he, anyway?"

Chris gave Tommy a baleful look. "We don't ask. Do they ask abaout you?"

"Let's go," the Doughboy stretcher bearer told his new partner; then he said to Flowers, "You talk too much."

In other circumstances the words might have angered or wounded him, but Tommy didn't care now. "How come he doesn't talk like you and Jamie and the others?" he pressed Chris.

"We're Australian. He's from New Zealand. More Irish than anything, really. Look, Flaowuhs, I'd love to stay and chat at your tea party, but we've got a wounded man here."

"Then go," said Tommy, rankled by their hostility, and he turned his back to them and gathered up the shovels and the intact blanket.

"Hey, Tommy," came Chris' voice, and the American turned back around to face him. "You did a fine job for someone who never done this before. You're all right, y'know."

Tommy flushed. "Pleasure doing business with you, too, Chris."

"Let's *go!* Jeez!" shouted the other American, with whom Tommy already had developed a mutual dislike, and they set off in their separate directions.

After an uneventful run back up the hill, Tommy came upon Colbeck and his men, digging their trench still wider and deeper with the remaining implements at their disposal. For the next half hour, until they were satisfactorily dug in, Tommy silently worked alongside the Australians. Finally Jamie called out, "All right, men, rest. But keep your voices daown." The crew did so, Peter Norman and the three boys Tommy didn't know sitting and conversing quietly among themselves. Feeling not a part of the group, Tommy positioned himself several feet away, his back propped against the rear wall of the trench, known as the parados, and closed his eyes. Rather than falling asleep, though, he quickly became aware again of his itching, and of the sound of gunfire still farther up the hill, more distant than before.

This non-reverie was broken when he heard someone sit down beside him. Tommy kept his eyes closed, and after a while Jamie's voice intruded upon his darkness: "So, Flaowuhs?"

Tommy opened his eyes and looked over at his grimy leader and, maybe once more, friend. "So?" was all he could think to say in reply.

"That's all you have to say?"

Tommy thought about that, and finally ventured, "You all right?"

That brought a soft laugh from Jamie, and a brief pat on the Doughboy's shoulder. "That's aour Flaowuh of Iowa," he said, "Always thinkin' of the other fella. No wonder Nicole is so crazy for you."

It was the strangest thing, bringing up her name in such a way, and at a time and place like this. But Tommy had been waiting a long time for his chance to apologize to the sergeant: "I'm sorry about that, Jamie–"

"Leave it, Tommy." Jamie cut him off with a shake of his head. "Just leave it." They regarded each other, and a hint of a smile crept across Colbeck's face. "After all, it ain't exactly like she *hates* me."

"Oh?" Tommy said, cocking an eyebrow in a successful shot at humor.

Jamie laughed a little more, then turned solemn. "Her and her auntie took care o'me after the Poms beat me up."

Tommy shifted his body to face Jamie directly. "What Poms? What happened, Jamie?"

Without interruption for a change, the sergeant quickly told the private his whole story, including how Nicole and Madame had nursed him at the tavern for several days before returning him to the Australian Corps. When he had finished, Tommy said, "I'm really sorry, Jamie. Since I asked you to take that message to David, I feel kind of responsible–"

"You're always apologizin' for things you didn't do. Stop it!" Tommy shut up, too quickly and too completely, so Jamie, still curious about something very important to him, said, "Ain't you got anything else to say abaout my story? Besides that it's all your fault, which it ain't?"

"You know I do."

Aha. So he *was* jealous about Nicole. "So? Aout with it."

Tommy shifted where he was sitting. "If David had been there, maybe you'd've escaped again. And if he hadn't been there the night before, they'd've gotten you then."

Colbeck paused, reordering his thoughts. "Oh. Peahson. Well, you're prob'ly right abaout that."

"You know I am. Just admit it. You were wrong about him."

"Didn't I already say that before – that I thought he was all right?"

"I'm proud of him, the way he helped you."

"Praoud of him, eh? I still mean to thank him myself when I see him again–"

"You won't see him again," Tommy blurted in a voice loaded with emotion.

It took Jamie completely by surprise. "Do you mean–?" he began, and the Yank spilled out the story of the bombing raid on Molliens, which the Aussie had missed entirely during his convalescence at the *estaminet* in Rainneville.

"I'm sorry, Tommy," it was Jamie's turn to say when the story was complete. "I really didn't know. But at least it was a Blighty. He's really rather lucky, y'see."

"If it's true."

"Prob'ly it is. Officers will lie abaout things like that, but rankers don't." He chortled, half to himself. "Well, maybe Pom rankers do–"

"Will you stop blaming everything on the British?" Tommy heatedly demanded, and the other men in the trench looked over at their sergeant and the American with curiosity.

"I'll stop blamin' the bloody Poms when they start doin' things right," Jamie replied in a sharp, low tone. "We were the ones aout there on the graound, but who was it stopped the artil'ry too soon? Who was it made it fall short at the start?"

"I thought the artillery was Australian. How can you be so sure it was British?"

"It had to be Poms givin' the orders, makin' mistakes like that."

"You don't know that. That's not fair."

"Fair? You haven't learned yet not to think abaout fair?"

Tommy had been engaging Jamie eye to eye, but abruptly the younger man looked down and away, and a sad weariness, like nothing Jamie had ever heard from him, entered his voice: "All I know is I saw more boys I know get hit by our own fire than by the Jerries."

Jamie didn't argue. "Sometimes that happens."

"You can't tell me those were Poms in that tank."

"No, they weren't," Colbeck conceded further. "I sawr that, too."

"Those boys were killed, weren't they?"

"I'm sure they were." There was a thick silence between them, then Jamie said, "It's a war, Tommy. Mistakes happen in a war."

"Mistakes that kill our own soldiers."

"That's right. Haow do you think the boys in that tank felt when they realized? It just happens sometimes."

"Are?… "

"What?"

He finally looked back at the sergeant. "Are Eddie and Ski dead?"

"I'm sure Maple's dead. Quite sure. Andy, I don't know. Prob'ly. Or maybe he just got his legs blown off."

"'Just got his legs blown off.' By his own army, before he could even get into the battle."

"You've made your point, Tommy," Jamie said testily. "I suggest you move off it naow." Tommy looked away, didn't reply, and in an aside, Jamie added, "They won't tell their mothers that's haow it happened. And if Andy lives, even with no legs, he wouldn't tell her that either."

But Tommy, as requested, did move off the subject, and back onto the previous one. "Did you think our aeroplanes did a good job?"

"I did. Except when it took too long for one to show up to chase away that Jerry aeroplane. But mostly I did."

"So, were those Australian pilots or British pilots?"

"Christ, you're argumentative!" Jamie exploded, but it came out more good-natured than angry. He chuckled and added, "Guess that's what I like abaout you."

"Are we friends again, Jamie?" Tommy asked, looking the sergeant in the eye and offering him his hand.

Jamie looked over at his mates, who once again had grown interested in their conversation. "Stop that, Tommy," he said gruffly, batting away the Doughboy's hand. But as he had intended, Tommy took it for a yes. "That was a fine bit o' solj'rin,'" the Aussie added for good measure, "with that German you bayoneted."

Jamie could not miss the stricken look that crossed Tommy's face. Gamely the American said, "I think I'm prouder of what I did for Vern."

"Of course you are. But in a war, you can't have the one withaout the other, y'see." Tommy closed his eyes and leaned back again, signaling his desire to end the conversation, but now it was Jamie who was persistently chatty: "You goin' to see Nicole if they send us back to Pierregot? I'm sure Willnor's order will be lifted naow–"

"Probably," Flowers responded, not opening his eyes. "You?"

"No 'prob'ly' for me. It's the first thing I'll do when I get the chance." Leaning over toward the Doughboy, he added, "Her auntie likes me, y'know."

"I'm sure she does. Why shouldn't she?" There was a long quiet between them then, until Tommy broke it. "Know what I'll tell Nicole when I do see her, Jamie?"

"What?" Colbeck asked suspiciously.

Relaxing against the parados, eyes still shut, Flowers said, "I'll tell her whatever I did worthwhile in the battle was because I was following the best darned sergeant in the whole war."

Momentarily struck speechless, Jamie finally retorted, "Shut up!"

"I mean it."

"Shut *up!*" Jamie repeated, even as he watched a smile spread over the face of the supposedly sleeping Yank.

# Chapter XXI

Her face lined with worry, Mme. Lacroix tiptoed down the upstairs hallway in the cold, hard deep of a warm, soft July night. It was concern for her niece, rather than the all-too-usual distant rumble of artillery, that was keeping her awake. Gently she opened the door to the girl's room. A sliver of moon cast its light directly onto the bed where Nicole lay, her hair all askew on her pillow. Madame shuffled over to the edge of the bed, placed her leathery hand on her niece's forehead, noted its coolness, and silently withdrew.

Nicole wasn't sick, then. That was both a relief and a vexation, the former because the girl's listless lethargy of the past day had frightened her aunt, the latter because it left no reasonable explanation for her behavior, or rather none Madame would have cared to hear. She did have her suspicions, though. The night before this one, when Nicole had seemed fine, some of *les Américains* had come in with news that a few of their number had joined the Australians in a full-fledged battle south of the Somme. Gossip yesterday among the folk of Rainneville had confirmed the rumor; by all accounts, the battle really was a complete Allied success for a change, and the newcomers had fought well. But any battle meant casualties, as Eglantine, who was not nearly as old as the men thought, and whose beloved husband Marc had fallen on the Marne in *la patrie's* first great victory of this cursed conflict, had reason to know.

She was therefore inclined to believe that Nicole was sick with worry for her tall, blond American, the one with whom she had behaved so indecently. For her part Mme. Lacroix, who had managed to inure herself to caring about the fate of any individual soldier in the long, dark years since 1914 (a resolve made easier by the fact she was coming into contact with mostly foreigners), found herself filled with anxiety about the Australian they called Jacques, the man with the dark, wavy hair who obviously adored her niece.

She wondered again why young girls weren't more sensible. Jacques was much the better catch – a man of the world, better looking to Madame's eyes than the callow young Doughboy and, at least as important, much more likely to survive the war. But although she could tell Nicole had grown fond of *l'Australien,* the girl's affection for him paled beside her obsession with *le Sammy*. Madame smiled as she admitted to herself that it was reminiscent of when she, the young Eglantine, could have eyes only for her Marc. *Tant pis.*

★

Nicole knew from the information she had gathered – from villagers, the stray *poilu,* those Tommies and Doughboys who could speak a little French, and her own limited English – that only a few of *les Américains* had participated in the clash two days ago. But from the time Fleur had first appeared at the *estaminet,* she had watched him and his friends, and their friends, very closely. She had noted which of the Americans Jacques spoke to, and assumed them to be friends of Fleur's also, and probably from the same unit, for Nicole had observed that soldiers who were friends were likely to be from the same unit. What worried her, then, was that none of those soldiers had come by for days – not the man who looked to Nicole like a giant from her book of fairy tales, not the one with the strange hair the color of a poppy in bloom, not the Tommy who so clearly was Fleur's best *ami,* and most of all, not Jacques himself, who always told her everything he could about the American in his odd French. The Australian had still been unsteady when she and Tatie had finally led him back to his army. She couldn't fathom his absence from the *estaminet,* unless he had been in the battle. And that meant Fleur probably had been, too, a prospect that induced a shiver in the midsummer heat.

By the time Tommy, Jamie, and Walt Sleziniak arrived at the *estaminet,* fresh from the bathhouse, the tavern had reached capacity. A freckle-faced young Doughboy they'd never seen before stood outside the door, forming the nucleus of a line. As the three men queued up behind him, the boy in front caught a little of their conversation, turned around and asked, wide-eyed, "Were you in the battle?"

"We're just back from the battle," Sleaze told him, his attitude just short of gloating.

Without another word, the freckled Doughboy walked past all three of them and stood behind. "Then you should be at the front of the line," he said gravely, his voice brimming with respect.

"Naow there's a class act," Jamie said, loud enough for the boy to hear. Just then a boisterous group of Yanks burst forth from the *estaminet,* so all four of them began elbowing their way inside. Tommy thought the place had never felt so smoky and close – or more like a part of home.

Jamie, taking the lead as usual, shoved his way up ahead to the bar, where both women were frenetically busy. As it happened, he arrived at the older woman's end of the counter, so he shouted to the preoccupied Eglantine, *"Madame! Madame! C'est moi, Jacques! Je suis retourné!"*

His voice carried effectively, and the proprietress swiveled toward him. Both hands flew up to her cheeks, and she happily cried out the name by which she knew him, then turned about and called out to her niece the joyous news that Jacques had returned.

Striving to maintain a professional demeanor, Nicole completed the motion of serving the two Doughboys in front of her before twirling casually in Jamie's direction, an expression of calm and grace on her face. *"Vous êtes revenus, M'sieur Jacques,"* she called. *"C'est bien."*

She did seem genuinely happy he was back, but Colbeck also detected a note of fear beneath her restraint. Guessing the reason, he called reassuringly to her, *"Fleur est ici aussi. Avec moi."*

Containing herself with monumental effort, Nicole lightly said, "Ahh...," then looked away from Jamie, out into the room. With great deliberation, she moved out from behind the counter and crossed to a table where her practiced eye had espied a new crew of Doughboys replacing the batch who had just left the tavern. *"Messieurs, je suis désolée,"* she said in her most unctuous tone, *"mais cette table est réservée."*

Though none of them knew French, her import about the table being reserved was not lost on the Americans, who immediately raised objections. "Says who?" the boldest of them demanded.

Nicole looked to her aunt in appeal, and Madame confirmed the ruling less sweetly than her niece, waving her hand peremptorily and shouting, *"C'est vrai, messieurs. C'est réservée."*

"Why is it reserved?" the bold soldier persisted.

"'Cause we're just back from Hamel," came Colbeck's authoritative voice. "Are you?"

"No, Sarge," answered the crestfallen Doughboy in a mixture of shame and resentment, as he and his fellow soldiers quickly exited the table.

"C'mon boys," Jamie said to Tommy and Walt, who had just managed to catch up with him. Tommy in particular wasn't keen on the way they had been extended special treatment, but they all took advantage of it nonetheless. Noting the table had room for a fourth, Colbeck called to the other Yank who had stood in line with them, "You too, son."

"But... I wasn't at Hamel–"

"You're with us. That's what caounts."

Shyly the boy slipped into the extra seat. He was by no means oblivious to the glares of the just-evicted group, but was too in awe of the Australian sergeant to turn down the offer. Tommy was pleased by Jamie's generosity, but he could see the new man was uncomfortable, so he offered his hand and made introductions all around, by nickname. The boy had just started his own recitation in return – "Private Frank Gillis, 33rd Division" – when a feminine voice disrupted the proceedings:

*"Messieurs. Bienvenue, heureuse de vous revoir."*

"She says welcome back," Jamie translated automatically, but the object of his affections and his pal had already fixed eyes upon one another.

*"Fleur,"* Nicole said simply, almost in a whisper; more tentatively, he responded with her name, smiling broadly.

"Enough o'this," Jamie said brusquely. "We need some beer." He proceeded to repeat his demand in French.

Nicole nodded to him in amusement. *"Mais bien sûr, M'sieur Jacques."* She tossed her head and moved away.

*"Très bon,"* Jamie called after her with a mischievous grin. She shot him back a mirror image of his expression.

Frank, who had been watching the entire exchange closely, ventured, "She sure is pretty, isn't she?" then added to Tommy, "You sweet on her?"

"I, uh–" Tommy began, but Jamie interrupted in a savage tone that surprised both Frank and Walt, *"She's* sweet on *him."*

"And *he's* sw– ow!"

Tommy had started to make the observation for Frank's benefit, but a swift kick from Jamie put a stop to it. Gillis, chagrined at having stirred up controversy, anxiously searched for a safe subject as Flowers rubbed his aching leg. Turning to Walt, he asked, "Did you kill any Germans in the battle?"

"Flaowuhs here did," the Aussie interjected.

"You did?" Walt exclaimed, turning to Tommy with genuine interest.

"Not – not really," Flowers replied.

"What does that mean?"

"Dougherty was the one actually finished him off."

"I think he was a dead man anywise, after you were done with him," Colbeck volunteered, but that drew no further response from Tommy.

"What was it like?" Gillis pressed.

"I'm – I'm sorry, but I really don't wanna talk about it," Tommy said, a little irritably.

*"Qu'est-ce qui se passe?"* came a perky voice as Nicole returned, carrying a clay pitcher filled with beer and four mugs. She had marked the uneasy atmosphere at the table.

Jamie saw his chance and took it: *"Fleur a tué un Boche."*

Far from being repulsed at the news that Tommy had killed a man, Nicole turned to the Doughboy with excitement. *"C'est vrai? Mais, c'est fantastique, Fleur!"* She made a slight curtsy and said, *"La France vous dit 'Merci.'"*

"She says–"

"I think I can figure that one out, Jamie," Tommy said, his voice sharp in contrast to the warm smile he was giving the girl. "Tell her I thank France for being here. But France shouldn't thank me for what I did."

"Why not?" Frank asked, as Jamie said coolly, "I'll tell her the first part. But not the second." And so he did, eliciting a sigh of delight from Nicole. As she swept back to the bar, Flowers tossed a one-word question to Colbeck: "Why?"

"You got to learn not to speak your mind quite so much, Flaowuhs."

"Why? You always do."

That brought a chuckle from Colbeck, but he continued, "These people are your hosts. That was a nice compliment you paid them. But you don't follow it right after with an insult."

"I don't understand what's going on," Gillis confided to Sleziniak, who shook his head and shrugged in agreement.

"Haow long you been up here, Gillis?" Jamie abruptly asked him.

"Four days, sir," Frank replied. "I'm a replacement."

"You from Illinois?" Tommy asked.

"No, sir. Pennsylvania. Near Pittsburgh."

"Frank," Flowers admonished, "I'm not 'sir'." He pointed to Colbeck and added, "Even he's not 'sir.'"

"You're gettin' right big for your britches," Jamie said to Tommy, half in jest – but only half. "Two weeks ago you were exactly like him."

Tommy shot Jamie a look, said firmly, "It's been a long two weeks."

"*Touché,* Flower of Iowa," Walt said with admiration.

"What's Flower of Iowa?"

Sleaze rolled his eyes, flicked a thumb at Tommy, and told Frank, "Him."

"See, even though I'm 33rd, I'm not from Illinois, either," Tommy explained; then, looking around the table, he added, "Actually, no one here is."

"Can I ask you just one more thing about the battle?" Gillis aimed the query at all of them.

"Sure," said Jamie. "Just don't ask Flaowuhs abaout his dead Jerry."

"The newspapers said the Doughboys were crying 'Remember the *Lusitania!*' as they went over the top–"

All three reacted at once. Jamie smiled and snickered; Tommy said, "*What?*"; and Walt said dismissively, "That's the stupidest thing I ever heard."

"So it's not true?" said the disappointed Gillis.

"Did they really say we said that?" Tommy asked in return, and Frank nodded. Tommy turned to Jamie as Walt started to laugh out loud. "Maybe it happened. Maybe somebody did."

"Did you hear anybody say it?" Jamie retorted.

"Well, no–"

"Did you, Walt?"

"No, Sarge," Sleaze answered, still chuckling.

"Me neither. Ain't that peculiar?" He turned back to Flowers. "And you're sure you don't remember cryin' '*Lusitania!*' yourself as you jumped into that German trench?"

"You're making fun of me, Jamie."

Shaking a finger, Colbeck said, "Just understand this, Tommy – and you two, too. The papers *lie.* They've been lyin' since this war started, and they're goin' to keep on lyin'."

"That's a pretty serious thing to say, Jamie," Tommy countered. "Maybe they just made a mistake."

"They *lie!*" Jamie said fiercely, his voice now threatening to drown everyone else's in the *estaminet.* "They said the Somme was a vict'ry, they said Gallipoli was a vict'ry. They *knew* that wasn't true, but they said it anywise. Naow, I don't call that a mistake, I call it a *lie.*"

The sergeant's vehemence had completely silenced not only their table, but all of the soldiers within a radius of several feet. Having drained his mug, he added in a calmer tone, "Anybody ready for more beer?"

"I am," said Gillis.

"Me too," seconded Sleziniak. Tommy's mug was practically untouched. He didn't like French beer any better than he had before.

"Hey, Gillis, take off your cap for a second," Sleaze ordered of a sudden, and the docile Pennsylvanian complied. "What do you think, men?" Walt continued to the other two. "Is his hair as red as Ski's?"

"Not near," Colbeck replied, a bit bored; but Tommy's throat tightened too much for him to utter a response.

"Who's Skeeze?" Frank asked, self-consciously replacing his cap.

"He was a friend of ours," Sleziniak said flatly. "Fought with us at Hamel. Didn't make it back."

"He never even–" Tommy began, and Jamie shot him a deadly look.

"Never even what?" Gillis persisted.

Tommy looked over at Jamie and Walt, both of whom were eyeing him intently. "Never even… Andy never even complained after he was hit."

"Andy Skeeze?"

"Andy Kopinski," Tommy said, repeating the full name for the first time since he'd learned his friend's fate. "He died a hero."

"But you're all heroes. You were all in the battle."

Suddenly all three of them, but especially Tommy, were weary of Gillis' youthful enthusiasm. "Walt," Jamie said abruptly, "it's gettin' on closin' time. Why don't you make sure Frank here gets back to his billets all right? He prob'ly doesn't know his way araound yet."

There appeared to be plenty of time before the *estaminet* shut its doors – no one was yet being shooed out by Madame – but Sleaze caught the message that Jamie wanted to speak to Tommy alone, and said, "Sure, Sarge. Come on, Frank, let's go."

"Thanks," Gillis said to the other two, and Jamie turned to Tommy.

"Another polite one," the sergeant said. "You two should get along famously."

As soon as the other two were out of earshot, the Aussie turned to his young friend, put his hand on the Yank's shoulder, and said, "I know it's hard, Tommy, but you've really got to get over this. If you're lucky enough to live through this war yourself, you're goin' to see a lot of men die. You can't be so sad, lad."

"Sad lad," Tommy repeated with an ironic little laugh. "Guess that's me."

"Don't let it be," Jamie ordered, withdrawing his hand. "Look lively for her" – he indicated Nicole, who was headed their way – "if you won't do it for yourself."

*"Y a encore des bières, messieurs?"* she asked. *"Dernièr service!"*

Not about to miss last call, Jamie simply answered. *"Oui. Deux, s'il vous plaît."*

As Nicole smiled and nodded, Tommy said, "I don't want another beer. I haven't finished this one."

"You pickin' up French on us?" Jamie replied, and before Tommy could respond, he added, "Who said the second one was for you, anywise?"

That got Tommy to smile, which in turn put him in a mood to talk shop: "When do you think we'll be in another battle?"

Catching his changed tone, the Australian cocked an eye at him. "Saounds like you didn't mind it so much after all."

The American looked down and said in a low voice, "It was exciting. A lot of it was terrible, but it was still more exciting than anything else that's ever happened to me."

"Saounds right," Jamie replied. "That's the way it is for most." Then he answered Tommy's question: "It's hard to tell. That might turn out to your biggest excitement of the war."

"But you said–"

"I said I didn't believe you'd live through this war. I know. But there's many more ways to die in this war than in a battle, Tommy. It's queer that you were in a battle before you ever had a spell in the front line."

"What about that time in the Vaden line?"

"Come naow. I'm talkin' abaout a real spell."

"What happens then?"

"Nothin', mostly. But men keep on dyin' anywise. A sniper here, a Toc Emma there, a whizz-bang the next day. You know what the brass calls that?" Flowers shook his head, and Colbeck spat out the word: "Wastage. That's what those butchers call it when good men die for nothin', not even in a battle. Wastage."

Jamie was barely through the second beer from his last order when Madame began to clear everyone out in earnest.

"Think we can ask her to stay later?" Tommy asked.

Jamie knew why, but he concealed his anger as he responded, "Not on your life. Look what happened to me before, when I stayed after. It ain't safe." Colbeck laughed loudly, amused by himself. "Ain't safe. Listen to me. After what I just told you." Tommy was looking at him only half comprehending, so he added, "Most men go through this war and never see a battle like you did. Understand?"

"And some men, like you, see many battles."

Embarrassed once more by Tommy's tone, Jamie quickly said, "Yes, some. Not many." Eager to change the subject, he added as he rose, "No motorcar tonight. We've a long walk."

Tommy almost automatically answered with "I know a short-cut" – but just before it was out, a flood of memories caused him to not trust his words, and he merely shrugged in return.

# Chapter XXII

Dougherty's persuasiveness in convincing the captain to attach him to the Hamel operation had proved distinctly beneficial to both of them. The captain, who had come no closer to the battlefield than his desk in Molliens, was able to talk about the action with great authority thanks to his aide's eyewitness reports, while the corporal assumed that his exemplary performance had not only cinched his promotion to sergeant, but also freed him of the burden of being seen as a "desk soldier" who had no real intention of getting anywhere near the front line.

His own blooding actually had made Dougherty more tolerant of his duties with Willnor, and this morning, his first back as adjutant, he was bringing to them the same zeal he had carried up the ridge at Hamel. When Willnor came smartly down the hall at his usual time, both men allowed themselves a smile. The captain began with an officious "Welcome back, Corporal. What do we have this morning?"

Dougherty gestured to several piles of papers on his desk. "Reports on the action at Hamel, sir, including a digest of the English newspapers. An up-to-date list of our personnel, with vacancies noted where they've occurred and there's a need for them to be filled. And a request for more recommendations for officers and men to be sent to training courses." He had carefully buried the pile that mattered most to him in the middle of his explanation, and hid his disappointment when Willnor picked up only the first stack of papers.

With an "Excellent!" the captain disappeared into his office, closing the door behind him. The corporal remained at his desk, drumming his fingers, biding his time.

On Company E's first full day back at their encampment, Tommy enjoyed his longest and soundest sleep since he'd come to France. When he finally blinked awake, he could tell it was quite light outside the tent, mid-morning from the look of it. Thrusting his bleary head through the opening, he found his tentmate sitting just outside, on a bucket turned upside down. "Morning, Harry," he mumbled. "What's going on?"

"Oh. Hello, Flower. Don't know. There wasn't any reveille or roll call for us. I hear tell most of the brigade is still out on that terrain exercise."

"Are we too late for morning chow?"

Carson shrugged and repeated, "Beats me. I wasn't hungry anyway." Harry had been morose ever since he'd learned that Vern Sanders had been carried off the battlefield at Hamel on a makeshift stretcher, though he was grateful that Flowers had been one of the bearers.

"Does anyone know whether we really have the morning free?"

"Not without Maple around," Carson said with gloomy emphasis. It occurred to Tommy that Harry wasn't the ideal tentmate for him these days, at least in terms of keeping his own spirits up.

"Splendid. Splendid!" cried Henry Willnor as he burst through the door. "You didn't tell me the part about 'Remember the *Lusitania!*'"

With the captain safely behind him, Dougherty assumed his trademark smirk and said, "I must have forgotten, sir."

"I think the Redcoat press is half in love with the 33rd."

"So it would seem," agreed the corporal with a nod.

"I only wish they hadn't made it sound like we were all from Chicago. As you know, *I* grew up near St. Louis."

Diplomatically ignoring that the captain had not been part of the "we" whose actions were being praised in the press, Dougherty followed his superior officer's tangent: "I know what you mean, sir. I grew up on the train line to Chicago, but not in the city."

"Good job, soldier," Willnor declared as he placed the pile back on the corporal's desk, and Dougherty, growing irked with his patronizing, simply nodded again. He could not tell if he was being lauded for his conduct in battle or in organizing newspaper clippings. "What's next on the order of business?" the older man continued.

Dougherty handed him what had been his second stack and reminded him, "Personnel reports, sir. Vacancies and such?"

Willnor took them but regarded them with considerably less interest than the previous batch. "And the others?"

"Training courses?" The corporal was barely able to conceal his exasperation.

Willnor stood before Dougherty for a moment, then tossed the papers in his hand back onto the desk and smiled. "I'm going to report to the major about what I've read. He'll want to know. Why don't you look at these and make some recommendations for me to approve? I'll be back later."

"As you like, sir."

Flowers had failed to check for mail in the excitement of yesterday's return, so once he had filled his stomach with breakfast, he sought out Staff Sergeant Searles, who handled the post. Tommy had seen him only once or twice a week for the past month, but when the blond private approached, the slight, bespectacled older man gave him an effusive greeting: "Flower of Iowa! Congratulations."

"Thanks, Sergeant, but why? Did I win something?"

"Why, the Battle of Hamel, didn't you?"

"Nawww..."

"*And* you've got some mail since you've been away."

"I have? *Some* mail? That means more than one letter?"

"Five pieces, to be exact," the NCO said, thumbing through his stack and producing Flowers' packet with a grin.

Tommy took the packet with joy, strode over to a shady, quiet place under a tree, and began methodically to open his mail. The first piece, from Susan, was dated June 12:

> Dearest Tommy,
>
> I hope that you are quite well and are being very careful as you do your duty for our dear country. I was down at Bates & Godley yesterday and I found the sheet music for my favorite new song. I have copied down the words for you.

Tommy read the lyrics, about a girl who was staying true to her beau while he was overseas, with embarrassment, as thoughts of Nicole crowded his mind. The refrain, which Susan had painstakingly copied after each verse, struck him like the jab of a bayonet with its final lines,

*Every night I say a prayer*
*For the boy who's over there,*
*My sweetheart is somewhere in France.*

When it came to his morale, her second letter wasn't much better. A shorter missive penned five days later, it began,

> Dearest Tommy,
>
> I am very sad as I write you today.

This opening alarmed the young man reading it. Susan had at least two cousins serving in the Army. Had something happened to one of them? Both of them?

> When I woke up this morning, Pa was standing at my bedroom door waiting to talk to me. He told me that Brownie had passed away in the night.

Brownie was Susan's family's dog, a nice enough boxer; in his mind's eye, Tommy could see her stubby tail wagging when she got excited. But Brownie was very old, and after all just a dog, hardly meriting the fancy expression "passed away."

> I am very blue about it, as she was a part of our family for as long as I can remember. There was only one thing I could think of to do to make myself happier again, and that was to write to you. I hope that you are quite well and staying out of harm's way. Remember, we are all praying for you.

The thought of the farm dogs, shot to pieces in their prime by an aeroplane on a French country lane, fleetingly crossed his mind, and then he almost allowed himself to think about Maple, Ski, the German who looked like Uncle Larry, the others. But he stopped himself and gave in to a general anger at her. All the things he was going through, the things he'd seen, and Susan was writing him the words to foolish love songs and asking him to mourn for her dead dog. He was supposed to feel sorry for her over that?

Just as quickly, another emotion rushed in. He loved Susan, didn't he? And part of what made him love her all the more now was that she knew nothing of what he had seen. She thought the world was the good, kind place he had thought it, not so long ago. And she should never know otherwise. As he replaced her letters in the packet he was already mentally composing one of his own, in which he would mention the battle much as he might have described the baseball championship games played on the diamond near the South Brooklyn Bridge two years ago, when Jay Lavery had led Brooklyn High to the state championship. Yes, he would make it sound something like that.

And the same would be true of what he would tell his parents, who had written him within two days of each other, at about the same time Susan had posted her letters. His mother's letter seemed to him remarkably like his sweetheart's.

> Dear Tommy,
>
> It is a warm June this year. We all are missing you very much and hoping that you are staying warm and dry in France. Are you remembering to change your socks?

He had to smile at that, after all the lectures the Doughboys had gotten about trench foot.

> There has been some kind of flu going round and your Aunt Hortense was terrible sick, but she is getting better now. But two of their cattle took sick, too, and one, the Hereford, died

That was better than if Aunt Hortense and Uncle Elrod's Holstein had died; at least they'd still be getting milk. Tommy wondered if they'd been able to butcher the Hereford, or if the sickness had tainted the meat.

> There was a new Mary Pickford show at the Majestic and your papa and me went to see it Saturday night. The piano player was singing before the picture

show, and when she started to sing Laddie Boy I do believe every mother in the place, including yours truly, started to cry whether she had a boy away or not…

Tommy had heard this song before, one where boys like him were urged to go and "do their bit." As he recalled the words now, one line,

*And when you hear the shells begin to sing,*

struck him particularly wrong, after Hamel. He hoped nobody was singing the song at a picture show where Andy Kopinski's mother was in attendance.

… and I dare say maybe even a father or two did, too. But we know you are being very careful and we are all so very, very proud of you.

If "Laddie Boy" or anything else in the show at the Majestic had moved his father to tears, there was nary a mention of it in the old man's letter, which was, as usual, quite brief.

Dear Tommy,
There is some sickness going around that is keeping us real busy at the pharmacy. It is hot for June. I know the work you are doing is important, but please try to remember to write your mother and your sisters. They are anxious to hear from you.

The fifth letter was actually an official-looking brown postcard, addressed to "Pte. Thos. Flowers, 33rd U.S. Division, Pierregot, France," which was very strange, since nobody was supposed to know anything but that he was "somewhere in France." The mystery was solved when he turned it over to read a typed message.

Dear Tommy [his name was the only handwritten word],
I am at 1st London General Hospital, Camberwell. I have been slightly wounded but am now in the pink.
Yours truly,
Pte. David Pearson, London Rangers

The other underlined parts were typed in a different print from the rest. Though he'd never actually seen one before, Tommy recognized this as one of the British Army's famed field postcards, which Davey had described to him: formal communications to let the receiver know the sender was alive, at least at the time he had sent it. Even a Tommy with very serious wounds would be described as "in the pink." Flowers knew that Pearson would have written much more were it not for the rigid format.

Even so, the note excited Tommy more than all of his post from Iowa combined. It meant that his worst fears had been in error; David was alive and (Flowers hoped) on the mend, in London, and he hadn't forgotten about Tommy. Best of all was an aspect of the note that initially confused the Doughboy: the date printed in the upper right hand corner, which read "4.7.18." At first that made no sense to Flowers; he had still been at Camp Dodge in Iowa on April 7, and wouldn't even have met David, who by his own account was just arriving in France at about that time. Then it occurred to Tommy that a couple of times since landing in this country, he had seen what were obviously supposed to be dates written the wrong way; somewhere, he couldn't remember where, he had seen "14.6.18," which made absolutely no sense... unless Europeans wrote dates backwards. That must be it.

So David had sent this post just three days ago, on July 4 – the very day that Tommy, Jamie, and the others had been fighting at Hamel! The American began composing a different letter in his head, a long one to David, telling him everything the way it had really happened.

Captain Willnor had been gone more than an hour when Corporal Dougherty heard footsteps coming down the hallway, but the latter's keen ears told him it wasn't his superior officer returning. He looked up to see someone whose appearance generated a very different reaction from him than a few days ago. Saluting rather casually, he said, "Sergeant Colbeck."

"Corp'ral Dougherty," Jamie replied, his tone toward the other man also altered. "Is the captain in?"

Dougherty almost reverted to form, to remind the sergeant he didn't have an appointment, but instead he struck a conciliatory note: "I'm afraid not." To his surprise, the always-confident Australian appeared slightly at sea at this news. "Is there anything I can help you with?"

"There seems to be a bit of confusion abaout orders for the squads I'm workin' with."

"What confusion? Company E has the morning free. They fought at Hamel."

"Don't I know. But so did you, and so did I. We're workin' today."

"They'll be working this afternoon, Sergeant. Don't you worry about that."

"Who will give them their orders?"

"The usual chain of command."

"That's just it. Part of the usual chain of command don't exist anymore. That's aour problem."

"Don't I know," said Dougherty, relishing the irony, then: "If you'd like to take a seat, Sergeant, you might even be able to help me solve that problem."

"You?" Jamie took a chair next to the desk, facing Dougherty, but his eyes had narrowed with suspicion. "Haow's that?"

"This is the list that shows where we need to fill positions," the corporal explained, indicating the stack in his hand. "Captain asked me to make some recommendations for him." He paused and said with significance in his tone, "He'll probably do whatever I suggest." Despite Hamel, Dougherty had to swallow hard before then adding, "You're a hell of a soldier, Colbeck. You know the men better than me. Care to help?"

Colbeck cocked an eyebrow at that, then returned the compliment. "Where will you put yourself?"

"I… was wondering how… appropriate that would be."

Jamie shrugged. "You know your own army better than me. If showin' good leadership under fire is an 'appropriate' thing to caount, then I'd say put yourself on the list."

"I don't want to stay behind this desk. But Willnor won't want to let me go."

"He can't be that much of a jackass."

"I need someone else he respects to back me up on this."

"Well, don't look at me, lad. I'd be pleased to put in a word for you, but as you well know, he hates me."

"Not necessarily. I already told him you were the best NCO in the whole battle."

Coming from Dougherty, the compliment did not elicit an embarrassed reaction; Colbeck merely took it as his due. "You put in a word for me, then I do it for you? If I was him, I'd be suspicious."

"*You* would be." It was the closest thing to a disloyal remark about Willnor anyone had heard from his adjutant, and Colbeck marked it. "Besides," Dougherty continued, "now that you're going back to your own army, he won't hate you so much."

"I'm not goin' back."

That caught the corporal off guard. "You're not?"

"No. I don't want to."

"But – the Hamel action is over. Weren't you sent here specifically to help with that?–"

"Maybe I was. Maybe I wasn't. Maybe I like it here, with this army. I'm stayin'."

In an instant the old Dougherty smirk re-emerged. "I don't think that's for you to decide."

"You might be surprised," the Aussie said drily.

"What does that mean?"

"Aour side is caountin' on you Americans to tip the balance in this war."

Dougherty snorted. "So? Everybody knows that."

"So then, there's nothin' more important for anyone to do than to get you ready for the real battles ahead."

"You're saying Hamel wasn't a real battle?"

"Not in numbers. It was fierce, certainly, and a fine piece of solj'rin' as far as it went, present company included," Jamie said, flattering both Dougherty and himself. "But in sheer numbers, it was no more than a skirmish. I'm talkin' abaout somethin' on the scale of Verdun, the Somme, Chemin des Dames – or what the Boche did this spring."

Conceding that particular point, Dougherty went on, "And you will be our commanding general?"

"No. But if I'm havin' a good effect where I am – and you seem to agree that I have–"

"Still, it's not your decision."

"Gen'ral Monash will be very happy to keep me here. So will Rawly – and Pershing."

"You forgot Foch," the corporal said sardonically, but the sergeant didn't smile, and Dougherty was ever more unsure how much of what he was hearing was bluster and bluff. "So," he finally added, "if you'll be here, you'll be here. All the more reason for you to help me with this… little chore."

"Let's start with aourselves, then. I want to be put in perm'nent charge of Company E."

"*I* want Company E," Dougherty said. "There's only one spot for a sergeant there, and I fought with those men."

"So did I."

The corporal's mind, nimble in the ways of bureaucracy, moved fast. "You know, we also lost a lieutenant, in that tank attack."

"I could have been a leftenant years ago," the Aussie said with a sniff. "I like bein' an NCO."

Dougherty was determined to hold his ground. "The U.S. Army pays better than all the other Allied armies combined. Every adjutant knows that." It was an exaggeration, but the basic point was sound, and for once Colbeck was on Dougherty's turf. Exercising an instinct that would have been off the mark a week before, Dougherty pressed: "We're going to win this war, Sergeant. If you've got the influence you say you've got, combined with the recommendation of the captain, we could get you a temporary commission as a lieutenant in the United States Army. You'd be my commanding officer in Company E, and you'd be making the kind of money that could buy you a nice ranch in Australia after this war is over."

"Maybe that's not what I want," Jamie countered, but without his characteristic cockiness; he was wondering how much it would cost to buy an *estaminet* in France instead. If Nicole had learned anything from Eglantine, surely it would be an appreciation for money, and those who had it. "Is there room for a new corp'ral in that company, too?" he finally asked.

"I don't want to stay a corporal–"

"I was thinkin' of Flaowuhs."

"What? No!"

"He fought well. You know it's true."

"He's totally unfit for promotion."

"Why do you hate him so?"

"Why is he your pet?"

Far from being nonplussed or miffed, Jamie replied gruffly, "If I want to have a pet, I'll have a pet. At least you can caount on me choosin' good quality."

Dougherty was momentarily brought up short, but then he repeated, "No! First of all, there's no corporal position open in Company E. And if you think *I* hate that simpering idiot, Willnor despises him."

"Willnor despised me, but you say you changed his opinion." Colbeck gave Dougherty a hard look, then added, "You want to put me in for leftenant, and you for sergeant? Then put him in for corp'ral."

"I told you, there's nothing open."

"The lad deserves *something*."

Inspired by his own agenda, Dougherty seized the other, smaller stack of papers. "Let's send him away for training, then. A week's training is something most privates would give all their spare socks for."

"What kind of trainin'? Where?"

"Let's see." Dougherty shuffled the papers. "Infantry specialist training in Langres, infantry candidate training, also in Langres. There's some gas defense courses at Chaumont and Gondrecourt later this month, and – no, that one's entirely wrong."

"Which one?"

"Machine-gun training."

"Where?"

The corporal squinted. "Grantham, England, but–"

"That's perfect!"

Patiently Dougherty said, "You aren't listening, Sergeant Colbeck. It's all wrong. First of all, it's machine-gun training, and Flowers isn't even in our Machine Gun Battalion."

"Details. He certainly might have to face them again."

"More important," the corporal said, all fussiness, "it's for officers only. We sent several colonels there last month."

"So? Make a mistake. A clerical error."

"Why? If you really want to give him a training course as a reward – though God knows why – there are plenty of courses for privates right here in France."

"France isn't far enough away. He'll be in England longer than he'll be somewheres else in France."

"But why do you want him gone now all of a sudden? I thought he was your friend. You were just trying to make him a corporal–"

"He is my friend." Suddenly Colbeck's face lit up with a new thought. "And he can visit his buddy Peahson. He's in hospital in London. Tommy'll like that."

Dougherty blinked. "There's something going on here. You're not that soft-hearted."

"Sure I am," Jamie said with a puckish grin that in fact telegraphed to the corporal that he was right.

"It's impossible," Dougherty said at length.

"I daoubt it. If you could get Willnor to sign this, haow far could Tommy go before someone discovered the mistake?"

"Probably all the way to Grantham, if I handled the paperwork," Dougherty admitted, unable to contain his pride.

"So. Do it."

"No! Why do you want this?" Dougherty's gaze fixed on Colbeck, and Jamie thought again that he'd underestimated this man.

"All right. I want him away from here for just a little while. Long enough for my own purposes, that's all. And if he's aout of danger for a spell, and it makes him happy at the same time, why, so much the better."

"But what, exactly, are your 'own purposes'?"

"That's for me to know, and you to keep your maouth shut abaout. I'm loyal to the cause. Don't worry abaout that."

"I didn't."

"Do you want to be a sergeant in Company E, with me as your leftenant? You could learn a lot from me."

"I know that." Dougherty stared at Colbeck, then silently nodded. When that didn't seem to be sufficient, he added, "All *right*."

Colbeck stuck out his hand. "It's a deal, then… Sergeant."

# Chapter XXIII

Standing on the deck of the old troopship, Flowers inhaled the salty spray of the Channel as, almost imperceptibly, England hove into view in the misty light of an early dawn. He should have been tired after nearly twenty-four hours of continuous travel, but his excitement outweighed his fatigue. He now could confirm that it was true, that a wounded Tommy really might make it back from the front to his homeland within a day; at approximately this hour yesterday, he had been standing impatiently at a railhead west of Amiens, artillery clearly audible in the distance. The system the British had devised to transport their own back to England seemed to move at a much faster clip than the one used to bring the Doughboys to the front.

He could not quite understand why his wonder at finally seeing England was so much greater than what he'd felt upon catching his first glimpse of France. After all, Britain didn't even have the distinction of being Tommy's first foreign country. Still, he was seized with a strong sense of coming home for the first time to a land, and especially a city, that he'd never seen but nevertheless seemed to know well: London Bridge is falling down; do you know the muffin man who lives in Drury Lane; goodbye Piccadilly, hello Lester Square. He clutched his orders inside his greatcoat (it was surprisingly cool out on the water for a July day), having re-read them a hundred times or more already, ever since Dougherty had called him in to the captain's office in the late afternoon, day before yesterday. With barely a look in Flowers' direction, the corporal had astounded the private by announcing that he was hereby ordered to attend machine-gun school in Grantham, England, for a week, and was to leave camp that very night. Dougherty would offer nothing more than that, and Tommy barely had time to find Jamie and ask the sergeant what he knew about the arrangement.

"You fought well at Hamel, lad," Colbeck had told him by way of explanation.

"But machine-gun training? Does that mean they're transferring me to the MG Battalion?"

"I daoubt it," the Aussie replied with what seemed to Tommy undue vexation. "You had to face Maxims at Hamel, and there's ev'ry likelihood you'll have to face them again."

"But–"

"Aren't you glad to get away, Tommy?"

"Well, of course, but–"

"Leave it there, then, and enjoy yourself." When Flowers, lost in thought, said nothing in reply, Jamie prompted, "I'll tell Nicole where you went, if you're worried abaout that."

"Oh. Thanks. Yes, you should do that. But I was thinking about something else."

Jamie's look bespoke satisfaction. "Don't tell me. Peahson?"

"Do you think there's any way at all I could get to see him?"

"You'll prob'ly have to change trains in London. That would be your best chance."

"How far is that hospital from the station?"

"Naow, haow would I know? I've never been to London."

"You haven't? I thought you've been everywhere."

"Hardly. And naow you'll be somewheres I ain't been. So, y'see?"

Slapping his hands with his orders, Tommy mused aloud, "If there was only a way…"

"If I know you, lad, you'll find a way. Quit makin' ev'rything a problem."

Thinking again about their conversation as the boat neared Folkestone, Tommy wondered what he'd have done in this war without Jamie to advise him. The orders made it clear that when he got to Charing Cross Station, in London, he was to report to an American Army office there, presumably to facilitate his passage on to Grantham. Maybe it would be as simple as having enough time between trains.

It was a lovely, sunny day, and according to the comments Tommy overheard as the railroad car trundled through the Kentish countryside, it was coming as a relief from weeks of hot, steamy weather. He had never imagined England could be as warm as Iowa in the summertime. More of his jumping to conclusions, Jamie would say. So far he thought the land was pretty, green and rolling like home, though it seemed somehow to be on a smaller scale. He wasn't sure why, since the biggest hills were at least as high as any around Brooklyn. Maybe it was a look that came with land that had been tended for many hundreds of years – something he'd noticed also in France, before reaching the wreckage of the front. Watching the passing pastoral scene, it did not seem possible that a place like the front could be only a day away.

The people were another matter entirely. Of course the train was jammed with Tommies, almost all of whom appeared as tired as, and dirtier than, Flowers himself; since many were obviously fresh from the front, that came as no surprise. But the civilians, to a man and woman, had a gray, torpid, nearly lifeless air that was nothing like Tommy had anticipated. He'd managed to get a seat as the train departed, but two stops out, at Sandling, an older woman laden with packages had boarded, and he had immediately stood up for her. She accepted the courtesy with not so much as a nod in his direction, staring vacantly straight ahead as if focusing, transfixed, on some faraway disaster. Which, thought the American, might be the case.

Eventually the pleasing verdant undulation gave way to a dull flattening and a palette of browns, grays, and blacks. The sheer dinginess of the outskirts of London compared unfavorably with the bright energy of greater New York, which Tommy recalled from the train trip that had carried him from Camp Upton on Long Island to the docks where he boarded the *Leviathan.* Still, his pulse quickened as the locomotive wearily chugged its way across the Thames and he snatched a peek at the first sights familiar to him from picture postcards: Big Ben and the Houses of Parliament. It was like seeing the Woolworth Building and the Statue of Liberty as his ship left New York City – unbelievable that these famous things he had seen in newspapers and books and at the picture show would be there captured in his gaze, available for him to reach out and touch if only his arms could bridge the distance.

The look at world-renowned places was an exceedingly brief one, though, as in short order Tommy's train was swallowed up by the chiaroscuro of dark and light, noise and confusion that was Charing Cross Station. The Doughboy held back as the train slowed to a halt and its load of passengers, with a great surge of energy, gathered their things and burst onto the platform; truly not a city boy, as he'd sworn to Pearson, Flowers was somewhat intimidated by such mass movements on the part of civilians, all so very purposeful and each seemingly completely at odds with everyone else. When the train was nearly empty, a uniformed elderly man who looked senior to Tommy's Grandad stepped into the car, his well-accustomed eye scanning for luggage left behind until it lit upon the tall, golden-haired foreigner. Taking the American in at a glance, the conductor jerked his thumb with unexpected authority and said, "End o'the platform, me boy. Right, then left up the stairs."

Tommy asked as he stood to go, "How did you know–?"

"All the Yanks are goin' that way," the old man said, perhaps a little bored by the question. His rolling r's made for another strange accent to Tommy's ears, different from David's, Jamie's, even Muffett's or Hardison's, but still identifiably British, and so an improvement from the utter confusion of French.

The station hall seemed to him almost as chaotic as the battlefield at Hamel. Tommy followed the man's simple directions and immediately got lost. He obediently struggled to the end of the platform, took a right and then a left, and no stairs materialized. Searching in vain for another railway official, he was reluctant to stop any of the civilians, all of whom seemed to be in such a determined hurry. At length he settled on a young girl about his age, her hair wrapped in a scarf that would have been more appropriate on an older lady, and which seemed too warm for this day anyway.

"Excuse me–"

"Pahd'n?" The girl looked up with gray eyes that reflected both suspicion and the same tired look everyone else seemed to have.

"Would you – do you know where the American Army office is?"

She broke into a warm smile, marred only by the usual British dental work, or lack of it. "Wisht I did, soldier," she said brightly. "D'you know if it's s'posed to be in the station?"

This one sounded a little like Davey. "Up some stairs to the second floor, I think."

She appeared confused by that, then she pointed. "Don't know 'bout a second floor, but if you go that way, then 'round, there's a stairs, I b'lieve."

"You're not from Dunster, are you?" he blurted out.

"Cor! What's that?" she asked sweetly, evidently flattered that he was trying to continue their conversation.

"Just a town. A friend of mine's from there."

She shrugged. "Sorry, never 'eard of it. Meself, I'm born and raised in London."

"Oh. Thank you, anyway." She looked disappointed as he headed in the direction she'd shown him, but there was little left to say, and he was unsure whether he had minutes or hours to make his connection to Grantham.

This time there was indeed a flight of steps that ascended away from the public area of the station to a long main corridor, off of which were short hallways with doors that might lead to offices. Unfortunately, none of the doors was marked, and there was no one around to ask further directions. In frustration, Tommy knocked on the first door he came upon. A stout woman with short, dark, curly hair, wearing some kind of uniform as well as a look of surprise, opened the door to the similarly surprised Yank and said, "'Ullo! And 'oo would you be?"

After a moment's hesitation, Tommy saluted – she was in uniform, even if she was a woman, and for all he knew she outranked him – and began his standard "Private Thomas Flowers, 33rd U.S.–"

He was interrupted by a peal of laughter. "I ain't your leftenant, lovey! But you do do that right smart."

"Sorry," Tommy said, feeling foolish, his hand feebly gesturing at her clothing.

"I'm with the railroad, dearie," she explained. "Now tell me what I can do for the pretty likes of you."

Flushing more deeply, Flowers said, "I'm looking for the American Army office at Charing Cross Station."

"You're at Charing Cross. So that's a start."

"I think it's on the second floor."

An odd look. "Second floor? Don't know of no second floor 'ere."

It was Tommy's turn to be mystified. "Aren't we on the second floor?"

"No, love, we're on the first floor."

"But – I took a stairway up from the first floor to get here–"

"That warn't the first floor, dearie. That war the ground floor."

Maybe this wasn't going to be much easier than trying to get by in French, after all. "So, do you know where the office is?" he said with a sigh.

"No, dearie, I don't, but – *Minnie!?*" She turned and shouted this at great volume; both the abruptness of the gesture and the presence of an unseen other person came as a bit of a jolt to Tommy. "Do the Sammies 'ave some kind o'bureau 'round 'ere?" She pronounced the French word "byoo-*row*," hard on the second syllable.

"Out front, 'cross the street, first floor," the invisible Minnie screeched knowledgeably in return, presumably referring to the second floor of the building in question from Tommy's point of view. Her name inevitably reminded Flowers of moaning Minnies, the dreaded *Minenwerfer* with which the Boche shelled Allied soldiers.

"Thank you, love," shouted the other woman, who apparently called everyone by that endearment, for she turned back to him and asked in a more normal volume, "'dyou get that, love?"

"Yes, thanks–"

Not missing a beat, the woman swiveled back and yelled to Minnie, "Our 'andsome soldier lad says thank you."

"You're keepin' a 'andsome soldier lad to yusself?" came Minnie's bellowed, accusatory response, as Tommy hastily repeated his gratitude and backed away. He shook his head as he fled back down the stairway whence he'd come. The woman he'd seen, and probably Minnie too, was at least as old as his mother, and they had been flirting outrageously with him. No woman that age in Brooklyn would dare do such a thing, or even dream of it. Was it London? The war (the image of Nicole and himself in the field flashed through his mind)? Both?

Almost afraid to ask directions of anyone else, he somehow found his way to another set of stairs that led out from the front of the station, then up to a wide main street. There his awe of big cities overcame him completely – so many people! so much noise! so many motorcars and carriages! so many buses, and with passengers on two levels! He gaped dumbfounded across the street, where there were many, many buildings; who knew which of them, if any, housed the office he sought?

In despair, and by reflex, he looked left and right at the crowd packed on the curbside with him. He was growing frantic at the prospect of missing his next train. Glancing left again, he spied a figure that seemed to offer a last modicum of hope: a fellow Doughboy, even taller than Tommy, his back turned so that only his hair and his neck, both very dark, were visible. The man must have gotten a lot of sun in France. Fearful of missing this possible contact, Tommy yelled above the crowd the only thing he could think of: "Hey! American!"

The other Yank turned toward him all right, with mistrustful eyes, loudly replying "Yep?" but Tommy was quite unprepared for the sight of his face. The man was colored. Tommy had seen very few colored people in his life, and had never talked to any; even so, he pressed ahead with his question. "It's here on the Strand, across the street," the other Doughboy called back evenly; then the crowd around and between them suddenly charged as one in that direction, and Tommy closed the gap between himself and the colored soldier.

"Do you know which building?" Flowers asked, hope rising.

The dark man nodded. "I'm goin' there now myself." As he always did, Tommy offered his hand as he recited his name, rank, and division. The other man looked surprised at this display of courtesy, but shook Tommy's hand as he replied, "Private Ralph Manton, 93rd U.S. Division."

As Ralph said this, Tommy glanced to his left and noticed the street was still free of carriage and motorcar traffic, so he stepped off the curb as he continued their conversation – "Glad I ran into you, Private Manton" – only to feel the other man's strong right arm restrain him, just as a large lorry whooshed by from his right.

"You almost got ran into yourself, Private Flowers," Manton intoned drily. "You were looking the wrong way."

"Thanks," Tommy responded, a little short of breath. "Do people just take whatever side of the road they want in this country?"

"No, they take the left."

"But in America–"

"You ain't in America."

"–and France–"

"You ain't in France."

"You've been here before?"

"Once."

"Really? But how – why would–?"

"Why would a colored boy've been in London before?" Manton demanded, his tone not at all friendly.

"No. No, that's not what I meant. I just meant – where are you from, anyway?"

"New York City. Harlem."

"So why would a boy from New York City, Harlem, know his way around London?"

Manton looked right as the crowd did and said briskly, "Now let's cross." As they did, he added, "On our way through to France, we docked at Liverpool, and then we came through London."

"Where were you in France?"

It was the wrong question; Ralph's swarthy face seemed to darken further. "Le Havre. On the docks." He virtually spat out this information.

"The docks?"

"You heard me, farm boy. I didn't come over here to unload boats. I came to fight. But the U.S. Army won't let the colored soldiers fight."

"I knew that. I mean, that's what I heard." As he followed Manton into a musty old building and up yet one more flight of stairs, Tommy could see that Ralph was unhappy, maybe even furious, at not getting his chance to fight the Jerries. "I've done things myself like clean out latrines and sweep out taverns," he volunteered in an attempt to placate.

"They won't let you fight, either?"

"Oh, no, I fought," said Flowers, who could not conceal his pride. "At Hamel." Manton gave him a harsh look, and Tommy resumed his previous effort. "But supplies are important, too."

"And you wouldn't care if you was unloading cargo ships instead of fighting?"

Flowers shook his head and, without hesitation, deliberately committed a falsehood. "No, I wouldn't."

"Mm-hm," Ralph said skeptically. Just then, by some miracle, Tommy actually found himself at a door marked "U.S.A."

Lieutenant Johnny (never John) O'Malley was the sort of bureaucrat's bureaucrat who might have inspired devotion in Daniel Dougherty. Unmarried and in his thirties, he had worked before the war at a bank in Boston; as a man of good family ("lace curtain" Irish), he subsequently had wheedled a quick commission through connections that had carried him all the way to this assignment in London, a position with which he was more than content – glamorous enough to write to his mother about, but a fine, safe distance from France and its horrors. He told the folks back home he was working in intelligence, directing troop movements. Since what he mostly did was verify the papers of the wayward Doughboys who wandered into his little office on the Strand and send them on to their next destination, it was a true statement, if you were able to draw the kind of fine distinctions he had learned from some of his Jesuit teachers.

Today the relative quiet of O'Malley's afternoon was being broken by an odd pair of Doughboys striding into his office and up to his desk. (O'Malley didn't rate an aide; his was a one-man show.) The strangest thing about them was that one was colored; O'Malley couldn't recall a colored Doughboy ever coming into his office. On top of that, the white, indeed very blond Doughboy who accompanied the darkie, and acted like his friend, had about him one of those sweet-but-goofy farmer-boy airs that caused O'Malley to regard him with both annoyance and fondness all at once.

"Lieutenant, sir!" the two of them shouted at the same time, and they saluted, the blond much more crisply.

"State your names, gentlemen," O'Malley said with an answering salute, and when they both did so at once, he hid his amusement with feigned exasperation: "One at a time," adding in the farm boy's direction, "You first, Private." Once Flowers and Manton had identified themselves and O'Malley had done likewise, the lieutenant turned back to the fair-haired one. "State your business, Private Flowers."

"Ah… begging the lieutenant's pardon, sir, but Private Manton would've got here well before me if I hadn't stopped him, and he hadn't been nice enough to–"

"So? It was you I asked to state your business, soldier. Now state it."

Tommy could feel not only O'Malley but also Manton glowering at him, and he faltered. "I – my orders were to report to you, sir." Clumsily he thrust the papers in question at the lieutenant.

The orders consisted of a few pages, and O'Malley spent a quick minute riffling through them. Something was not right, said his veteran eye, although on the surface they looked perfectly in order. When he got to the final page, the lieutenant murmured aloud, "Grantham? Why would you be going to Grantham?" Even though he seemed to be addressing Flowers in his use of "you," he expected no reply.

Notwithstanding, Flowers piped up, "For a training course, sir." The blond boy's hand reached over the top of the page O'Malley was reading and helpfully pointed out. "See? Right there."

"Machine-gun training," O'Malley said dubiously to himself, then: "Private Flowers, perhaps I *will* take care of Private Manton's situation first. Yours could take a little time. Sit over there," he added, pointing to a bare bench next to the door.

"I won't miss my train, will I, sir?"

Johnny O'Malley was a far cry from regular army, but even he was growing irritated by this boy's impertinence, especially in front of the colored boy. "Just sit down and shut up," he growled, giving the lad a baleful stare.

Once more caught lacking in the military polish department, Tommy slinked over to the bench as directed, on edge because of the lieutenant's tone about his papers. Surely there was nothing wrong with them? He tried not to listen as

O'Malley quizzed Ralph, but that was hard to do when you were sitting so close you could have leaned over and touched the other private's sleeve.

The conversation was not a pleasant one. Like Flowers, Manton presented O'Malley with his written orders. Manton's papers caused an even quicker, even more negative reaction from the officer: "And just what is the meaning of this, Private?"

Ralph's reaction was much cooler than Tommy's had been. "Meaning, sir? I don't understand. As the papers say, we're havin' some problems with supply at Le Havre, and–"

"I know what the papers say, and I don't doubt there are problems with supply at Le Havre. I'd be surprised if there wasn't. But what I don't understand is what that has to do with you being here in London–"

"Major Harlan wanted some matters cleared up, and he decided to send me, sir–"

"You? Why you?"

"He told me that I knew the supply system and the problems with it better than anybody else, sir, so–"

"Why didn't he come himself?"

"He was too busy–"

"But not too busy to send you." O'Malley, face reddening, paused, then said, "You're asking me to believe a major in the Supply Service would send a *private* to England to straighten out some problems in France?"

"Yes, sir. That's the truth of it, sir–"

"A private and a *nigger?*"

Ralph flinched slightly at this last; and so, startled by the remark, did Tommy. He watched the colored private clench his fists, but the two words that came out of Manton's mouth were spoken in a mild if dogged tone: "Yes, sir."

From the lieutenant's point of view, an easygoing, relaxed afternoon had now been thoroughly disrupted because both of these men had presented suspicious papers; as a result, he was spiraling down into a foul mood. "Sit over there with Flowers," he snapped at Manton, and as the dark private silently did so, O'Malley stared at his orders, squinting as he tried to focus and find something that would expose the papers as fraudulent. Next he picked up Flowers' orders, stared at them for a while, then rubbed his eyes. "I can't concentrate," he complained at length, then he said in a more civil tone, "I need an hour to look over both of these. Leave me alone, and report back here in an hour."

"Yes, sir," the two privates chorused in unison as they stood up – with far too much eagerness, O'Malley thought. The lieutenant regarded them both with increased wariness, half convinced that the pair had been in cahoots long before they'd supposedly met while on their separate missions, en route to his office. "If you don't return promptly in one hour–" O'Malley began threateningly.

"We wouldn't do that, sir," chimed in the ever-insubordinate farm boy, and the lieutenant rejoindered, "*You* wouldn't."

Although O'Malley didn't notice the flare of Manton's nostrils, Flowers did. But Tommy wasn't quite ready to take his leave. "Beg pardon, Lieutenant, sir, but do you think I can make it to Camberwell and back in an hour–"

"Camberwell?" Unlike most officers of the American Army, O'Malley knew a great deal about London. Camberwell was an unlikely destination for a Doughboy with a free hour. "You'd probably have just enough time to get there and turn around. What's in Camberwell?"

"My best buddy, sir," the golden boy said with something that looked and sounded to the lieutenant like genuine emotion, "in the hospital there." O'Malley's eyes narrowed, and he looked from Flowers to Manton and back again. Maybe they weren't conspiring against him after all. At any rate, he didn't want them spending the hour together. "Manton," the lieutenant said, "You be back here in forty-five minutes – no, make that thirty." Shifting his gaze, he added, "Flowers, when you go out the front door of this building, walk to your right, down the Strand to Trafalgar Square. There are coaches that stop on the far side–"

"Coaches? You mean like stagecoaches?"

O'Malley smiled in spite of himself. "We'd call 'em buses. There's quite a few different bus lines. You want the one that stops on the far side of the square and says 'Westminster' and 'Elephant and Castle.' Ask the conductor where to get off for the hospital. Be back here in an hour and a half, sharp."

Tommy's eyes shone as if he'd been made privy to some magic incantation; and in fact, that was how "Elephant and Castle" sounded to him. "One last thing, beg your pardon, sir: I don't have any of the English money–"

"You're in uniform. You don't need money to ride the bus any more than you did the train. What else would you need it for?"

Flowers had the sense not to push things too far at this point, though he would have liked to buy something to take to Pearson; he simply said, "Thank you, sir," then O'Malley dismissed them both. As they headed back down the stairs, Tommy couldn't believe his luck. But Ralph Manton had no trouble believing his.

# CHAPTER XXIV

It was back to business as usual at 1st London General Hospital, Camberwell; Sister Jean Anderson was worried about her favorite patient. To be sure, on any given day Sister Jean was likely to have a favorite patient, and was likely to be worried about him; but for the past two weeks, ever since David Pearson's arrival, she had had a favorite who had caused her very little concern. True, when he'd first arrived the shrapnel lacerations to David's right leg had looked quite hideous, but after more than two years of nursing, Sister Jean had learned that, just as Tommies with injuries scarcely visible to the human eye might inexplicably and rapidly fade and die, so too did soldiers with the nastiest-looking wounds sometimes heal with unexpected ease and quickness. It was just so with David, who had suffered a classic Blighty wound. Jean suspected that the medical officer in the field had been inexperienced; otherwise, bad as his injuries appeared, Pearson might have stayed in France. All that was left of his trauma now were some fierce-looking scars that made his leg look like a barber's pole – and the pronounced limp, of course; that, he would probably carry with him for the rest of his life.

Nonetheless Sister Jean was anxious, because for the past two or three days, David had been as blue as the uniforms Tommies wore to signify they were wounded. While neither depression nor an unreasonably resolute cheeriness was uncommon to wounded Tommies, this was just not like Pearson, whose exceptional brand of good humor was what had caught her eye in the first place, had won her over from the day he had been carried in and confided to her with that irresistible smile, "At least I di'n't get 'it on a Friday."

She did not deceive herself as to why she liked him so much. There was something about him that immediately had reminded her of Arthur. And it was because of Arthur, mostly, that Jean Anderson was a nursing sister.

Growing up a stagestruck little girl in Hamilton, Ontario, Jean had always felt the odd child out, unable to share her dreams with her much older, practical-minded brothers or her sternly religious parents. The loneliness finally had been dispelled when, at the age of eight, she was sent for the summer to her aunt and uncle's farm in Saskatchewan. Their youngest son, her cousin Arthur, was the closest in age to Jean, being a mere eighteen months her junior; but more important, he immediately understood the workings of her imagination, the one that everyone else thought was too wild. Throughout that long first summer, and for many summers thereafter, Jean led her newfound friend in games only they could comprehend, creating magical worlds in the hayloft, behind the chicken coop, under the back porch. Her mother in particular was at first pleased that her difficult daughter at last had found a playmate in her sister's shy little boy. But as they grew into their teens and young adulthood, Jean and Arthur confounded everyone by remaining close, exchanging long letters and spending almost all of their school vacations in one another's company. Both families grew apprehensive about the depth of the tie – Jean and Arthur were first cousins, and there was no question of them getting married – but that only proved how little they understood the bond between the two. While it seemed the most natural thing in the world to Jean and Arthur, none of their kin could fathom two people of opposite sexes being each other's best friends in the whole world, without the complications of romance. When Jean, almost ready to graduate, dropped her nursing studies and defied her family to pursue a career on the stage (to her parents, an actress was barely distinguishable from a prostitute), only Arthur had given her his stalwart support, traveling all the way to Thunder Bay to applaud her debut. Likewise, when Arthur decided to eschew farming in order to become a reporter, Jean pored over every article he sent her, proclaiming him the best writer in all of Canada.

Their constancy was not shaken even when Jean met Maggie Callahan, an Irish actress who had come to Toronto with a touring company, and suddenly acquired a sort of second best friend. It was Maggie who persuaded Jean to take an even greater leap of faith than the one she'd made by leaving Hamilton and nursing; six years ago, Jean had returned with Maggie to London – London, England, not London, Ontario. Arthur's letters had kept coming faithfully as Jean struggled to find small parts and create a niche for herself on the West End stage.

And in 1915, it was Arthur himself who came to London – as a corporal in the Canadian Army, on his way through to Flanders and Picardy. Even then, with Britain full of rumors about Canadian soldiers being crucified by the Huns, life did not seem a grim matter; if anything, seeing her cousin in uniform aroused a rare jealousy in Jean, that the greatest of adventures were still reserved for men. But the demand for theater in wartime London was even greater than before, and both Jean and Maggie found themselves getting more and better parts. At the front, it was Arthur's good fortune to just miss the disastrous Battle of Loos; in Belgian trenches, he devoured the London papers, which arrived within two days' time, and wrote wonderful, enthusiastic letters when he noticed either of their names in the theater reviews. Later he managed to smuggle to them an occasional copy of *The Wipers Times,* the Tommies' own newspaper, generally forbidden to civilians because its dark humor was too realistic about life at the front. Sometimes the paper included articles written by Arthur. If some of the other soldiers' stories were more pessimistic than anything Jean was reading in London, she didn't let it bother her at the time. She knew there was a war going on, of course – it was unavoidable – but, improbably, life in wartime seemed almost to be a lark, and only getting better.

Then, within one week in April 1916, Jean's world changed forever. It began when a Zeppelin bombed the East End neighborhood close to the docks where she and Maggie shared a cheap flat. Jean was at a rehearsal, and their building wasn't hit – but Maggie, out for an evening stroll, was. Maggie lived through the attack, unlike many others that night, but when Jean finally found her in a hospital the next morning, she could not walk, and would not talk. Jean continued her rehearsals, rushing to and from the hospital in between, but six days later Maggie's father arrived from Ireland, come to take his crippled daughter home, and no amount of Jean's pleading could stop either one of them. Her vivacious friend was giving up the stage, returning to her homeland in a wheelchair.

The very next day, Jean received a telegram that her cousin had been severely wounded – gassed, in the Ypres Salient. She walked out of rehearsals and to the nearest hospital, told the head sister there that she had nearly achieved her degree in nursing, and then set out to prove it. Within three months Jean was a full-fledged nursing sister; within six, Arthur was living with her in her flat, continuing a slow and painful recuperation that the doctors had sworn was not possible. Days she worked at Camberwell – in fact, she was there in time to help deal with the terrible flood of wounded created by the Somme – and nights she took care of him.

She succeeded all too well. By early '17 Arthur was ready to go back to the front. He was last seen alive in May of that year, charging up Vimy Ridge.

Jean did not share the terrible uncertainty of so many whose loved ones had simply vanished in the conflict; she knew, to the depths of her soul, that Arthur was gone. She knew, too, that bringing cheer to doomed Tommies as an entertainer was an honorable thing to do, but for her it could never again be enough, not a tangible enough effort, not so long as this war that had already destroyed the two most important people in her life continued. Roaming the wards, she could forget about her own sorrows, because here there was pain and misery beyond imagining to attend to, and on good days to alleviate. The bright spots for her now were her favorites among the patients. One or two other Tommies had captured her heart like David Pearson; that they were all stand-ins for her lost best friend, and that she knew it, did not lessen the gladness they brought her. Anything she could do to help David out of his moroseness, she would.

As the bus marked "Elephant and Castle" slowed to yet another stop, the conductor – or maybe you were supposed to call her a conductress? – made a point of coming over to where Tommy stood, taking in the gray cityscape. "Your stop 'ere, love," the tall older woman said, reminding him of the stout lady at Charing Cross. For that matter, the driver was a woman, too, of about the same age and build as Flowers' mother, though he could never imagine his mother driving a bus. Women, it seemed, were running England these days, as their menfolk held the line at the front – and they seemed to be doing a pretty efficient job of it.

This sense only increased after Tommy ascended the grim gray steps of the cheerless-looking building where he hoped to find his friend; another woman, this one wearing a starched white headpiece, presided over the desk just inside the entrance. Her English sounded different yet – as starchy and clipped as the sister herself.

"Yes, soldier?" she asked as Tommy, having waited in line for several precious minutes, reached her desk.

"I'm looking for a friend of mine," Flowers began.

"And–?" the woman responded impatiently.

"He's with the London Rangers–"

"That isn't particularly helpful. What's his name?"

"Pearson. David Pearson."

"Do you know where he is?"

"Here."

With a show of exasperation, the woman asked him, "Do you know which ward?"

That hadn't occurred to Tommy, who was already beginning to worry about O'Malley's deadline. "No, I don't. I got this letter from him," he said, brandishing the field postcard.

The piece of mail did not interest her a whit. "What kind of wound does he have?" she persisted. "Gas? Nerves? Is he an amputee?"

"No, no. He's supposed to have just a Blighty wound."

The sister frowned more deeply at this expression. "This hospital is for serious cases. There are no 'Blighty wounds' here."

That alarmed Tommy, but he endeavored not to show it as he pressed his case: "I'm sure he's here. Don't you have a list?"

The woman sighed, still more annoyed. "Let me see." So she did have a list of the patients' names; why was she making things so difficult? "Pearson… Pearson," she muttered as she pored over it with excruciating slowness.

"*David* Pearson?" came a far friendlier feminine voice from behind Tommy. As the sour sister glanced up, the Doughboy turned to see a striking, dark-haired nurse who, passing by, had stopped upon hearing the name.

"Yes, Sister Anderson," the grumpy woman reluctantly acknowledged. "This Sammy is looking for him. Would you happen to know if he's on your ward?"

The nicer nurse ignored her colleague and instead broke into a smile as she took in the sight of the blond Yank. "Why, you're Tommy, aren't you!"

Amazed to hear this woman – who sounded American and reminded him of his oldest sister, Annie – calling him by name, he simply smiled and nodded in return. "I'll take him to Private Pearson, Sister," the younger woman said, and the receptionist abruptly shifted her attention to a woman standing behind Tommy in the line. "Come with me," Sister Anderson told him, throwing in her first name for good measure. Although she was a head shorter than Flowers, he had to quicken his stride to keep up with her. "Does David know you're coming?" she continued, talking right through Tommy's negative reply. "He'll be so pleased. He talks about you all the time! I can't believe you're really here. What a wonderful surprise! However did you get here?"

Having been allowed a word in edgewise, Tommy explained his presence at Camberwell as they hurried up two flights of stairs and down a series of halls filled with men clad in blue bathrobes or pajamas, some in bed, some sitting or standing around. Sister Jean Anderson seemed to know every last one of them, calling each by his name whether he responded cheerfully, sullenly, or not at all; all the while, she listened to Tommy's account. Some of the men were missing one or more limbs, some were slightly or terribly disfigured, and some stared vacantly into space, rather like the older lady on the train this morning. Still others seemed fine. Tommy would have found it difficult to look at the badly wounded men had Sister Jean not invariably done so in the most frank, matter-of-fact way. When he had finished telling her his story, concluding with O'Malley's timetable, she stepped up her pace even further. "We haven't much time, then," she told him. "What a shame. And you're his first visitor."

"You mean his mother and sister haven't even visited?"

"No, his mother writes, but Dunster is quite a ways from London, and it's only the two of them to run the shop."

Tommy found himself surprised, maybe even a little jealous, that she knew as much about David's family as he did. Recalling the receptionist's comment about Blighty wounds, he hesitated before gathering the nerve to ask, "Is he hurt bad, Sister?"

"Oh, no, not at all. Still, I'm sure seeing you will do him a world of good."

"What do you mean?"

"He's been a bit down in the dumps."

"David? That's not like him."

"I know."

"I reckon after the bus ride I have, what, maybe fifteen minutes?"

"Better make it ten. Here we are."

They had come upon a large solarium, albeit one whose windows, which could have used a good wash, looked out over a dingy courtyard. Scores of blue-robed Tommies were lounging about, but Sister Jean seemed to know exactly where she was heading, toward the window in the far corner.

"This his usual place?" Tommy asked.

"The last few days, yes," she answered. "He just sits and stares out the window."

"That's not like Davey, either."

"I agree," she said with a nod and a smile that made no sense to Tommy. She was remembering a conversation with Pearson about his American friend:

"'E calls me 'Davey,'" the private from Dunster had told her. "Nobody calls me that. But I don't 'alf mind it, coming from 'im."

"What do you think is wrong?" Tommy asked, snapping her back to the present.

"Sometimes it happens when a man is about to be discharged from hospital. I think they'll be letting him go tomorrow."

"But that should make him happy."

"It doesn't, always. And that seems to be the case whether they're going back home, or back to the front. Here we are," she repeated, and Tommy suddenly made out the familiar form of his friend, looking smaller than usual, seated in an old chair with his back to the two of them, quite still, either staring out the window or fast asleep.

Sister Jean came round Pearson's shoulder. "David?" she said, and from behind Flowers saw his head turn toward the nurse. Then she smiled broadly at his friend and simply pointed toward Tommy, whom she had left several steps behind her. Obediently, David swiveled about in the direction Sister Jean had pointed. He wore a half smile in deference to his favorite nurse, but it broke wide open when he caught sight of his pal. He cried out Tommy's name as he turned and stood. Meanwhile the Yank couldn't push from his mind's eye the sight of the other wounded men; as he watched Pearson stand, Flowers actually counted silently to himself (two arms, two legs, two eyes), so that by the time he closed the distance between himself and David, he was rapidly blinking his eyes, and just managed to pronounce David's nickname in return; then he threw his arms around his eagerly awaiting buddy.

The depth of this display of emotion caught the attention of most of the solarium. Even Sister Jean was surprised by the ferocity of it. But unlike many of the wounded Tommies, she did not look askance upon the outburst. Turning toward the other soldiers, she said in a fair imitation of a sergeant, "All right, men. Leave them be now." The other patients, who adored Sister Jean, sheepishly directed their various attentions elsewhere. Next she turned back to the two men who were still silently holding each other, oblivious to the stir they had created, and placed a hand on Tommy's shoulder. "You've only got a few minutes. David's bed is just down the hall. It will be quieter there this time of day." She led them out the other end of the solarium, down a short hall to a ward that was, indeed, largely unpopulated.

As they walked the short distance, Tommy noticed David's heavy limp with escalating dismay. "They can't really be thinking of letting you out tomorrow," he said spontaneously as Sister Jean's eyes flashed at him and David replied, "But I'm in the pink now, Tommy."

"Here's David's bed," the nurse announced, though her focus was on his visitor. "I'll be back in a few minutes to make sure you catch your coach in time." David really did seem fine but for the leg; nevertheless, he doffed his robe and, in his pajamas, allowed her to help him climb into his bed. As she fluffed the pillow, she gave Flowers one more look – one that seemed to say, don't spoil things by bringing up David's leg again – before she departed.

They were now as alone together as they could be in the hospital. For all the emotion they had demonstrated, they barely had said more to each other than their names. David shifted toward Tommy, who was sitting next to his bed, and without thought took his friend's hand, which squeezed his in return. "It's so good to see you, Tommy," Pearson said. "I can't believe you're really 'ere."

"I can't believe it, either," replied Flowers, but then a trace of resentment escaped from him: "And I can't believe your mother and sister haven't been here."

"Oh, don't be too 'ard on me mum and sis. They've been writing, and the shop is a 'andful, it tis."

"At least pretty soon they'll have you back to help them with it."

David gave him a perplexed look. "What are you talking about, Tommy? I'm going back to the front."

"You–? But, your leg…"

"It's just a small limp. I'll be all right."

"I don't think–"

"What?"

"Nothing. Never mind."

"They may give me a few days after I get out of 'ere, before they send me back. I 'ope so, anyways. I'll try to go to Dunster if I can. Wisht you could come with me."

"I wish I could, too. But I'm here in England because they're sending me to a training course, in Grantham."

"Cor! A training course in what?"

"Machine guns."

David's face fell. "You'll be changing battalions, then."

"Jamie says no. And I think he's the one that got me the course."

"'Im? 'Ow could 'e do that? 'E's only a sergeant."

"But he's the best there is, David. And now they all know it. I know you don't like him, but you should have seen him at Hamel."

"So you were at 'amel?" David exclaimed, immediately agog. "I read about it, and thought about you. You were under fire! What was it like?"

"Well, one thing I can tell you, nobody really said, 'Remember the *Lusitania!*'"

"They di'n't?"

"No. Honest. But it was exciting as all get-out – and really confusing, too."

"Were you frightened?"

"I was scared," Tommy admitted, surprising them both with the directness of his answer. "I was wishing you were there."

"Did you see Jerries?"

"Lots of 'em. Mostly dead."

David's eyes widened. "Did you kill any?"

As Tommy replied "One," his stricken look was so unmistakable that the Briton posed his next question with particular gentleness:

"What was it like, Tommy?"

Flowers paused, then finally said, "You remember when you said that comet wasn't all that great?"

"Something like that, yes."

"This was – it really wasn't – I don't know. I'm glad it wasn't him doing it to me, but–" Unable to go on, Tommy looked away.

David was still holding his hand; he now placed his other hand on the American's forearm. "It's all right, Tommy. It's our job, remember."

"I know." Tommy looked back at his friend. "I just wish you were there."

"I will be. Next time." Unthinking, David regarded his injured leg. "I won't miss it."

"How did it happen, Davey?" Tommy asked, gesturing at the limb.

Pearson shrugged. "I was walking along in Molliens, minding me own business. I 'eard the aeroplane and 'it the dirt like they say you should. I 'eard a terrible noise–"

"So you knew you had a chance," Flowers said in an attempt at humor, but his pal didn't catch it.

"–but it was bombs, not shells. I felt something 'it my leg, like nothing I ever felt."

Upset that his joke had misfired, Tommy asked solemnly, "Did it hurt?"

"Worst than anything. But I don't remember very much after that. 'Ardly remember coming 'ere, really. I thought–" He faltered. "I thought they might cut me leg off."

Tommy sucked in his breath and shivered. "That would have been terrible."

"There's other blokes 'ere 'oo 'ad it 'appen to them. They're getting on with their lives, most."

"Still..."

"I know. You're right."

They looked at each other, temporarily at a loss, and then a painful memory surfaced for Tommy. "Muffett – I couldn't understand what he was saying."

David didn't understand why Tommy had brought up the fat private, but he chuckled. "I can't meself, sometimes."

"But this was awful. I was trying to find out where you were – I thought he was telling me you'd been killed. I was so – I started to beat him up."

Out of sync with Tommy's mood, David laughed. "You and Muffett? That wou'n't be a fair fight."

That made Tommy laugh, too, but then he quickly grew serious again. "I hit him because – it was just that that scared me more than anything that happened later, in the battle."

"What?"

"That I thought you might – you know – that I might never see you again."

"Ah. But 'ere we are." They had never once let go of each other's hands, and now they held each other's gaze with an intensity that unnerved them both a bit; still, neither flinched.

They were all the more startled, then, when Sister Jean suddenly emerged out of nowhere and declared, "Tommy, you'd better get going now."

"But I'm feeling all right," David said plaintively.

"It's got nothing to do with that," said Tommy, instantly calm and businesslike. "If I'm not back in time, I'll be in a whole pack of trouble."

"But you just got 'ere."

"I'm sorry, David. I knew I wouldn't have much time, but I wanted so bad to come see you, I figured any time was better than nothing."

David visibly bucked himself up, then relaxed back into his bed. "Of course. You're right about that. I'll be back soon, anyways. Per'aps your training course will end at the right time, and we can take the boat together back to France."

"That would be great if it worked out that way." Suddenly, in front of Sister Jean, the two grew shy of each other, and Tommy finally released David's hand.

"Thank you for coming, Tommy," Pearson said, sounding almost formal.

"See you soon, Davey," Flowers replied with a heartiness he didn't really feel, and which sounded forced to Sister Jean. The Yank turned abruptly to the nurse and asked, "Which is the way out?"

"I'll show you," she said, and Tommy followed her out of the ward, not chancing so much as a backward glance.

# Chapter XXV

As Tommy and Sister Jean rushed back the way they'd come just a few minutes earlier, the soldier gave voice to what was uppermost in his mind: "They wouldn't really send him back to the front with his leg like that, would they?"

The nurse pursed her lips. "You haven't seen much of this war, have you? Of course, you wouldn't, being American."

"I fought at Hamel!" Flowers countered indignantly, then he added, "And anyway, aren't you American, too?"

"I'm from *Canada,* thank you very much," she said with quiet pride.

"Oh."

They were already nearly back to the main entrance where the sour sister presided over the reception desk. "England doesn't have the luxury of sending only her most able-bodied men to the front," said Sister Anderson, referring to her mother country the way a diplomat would. "She hasn't for a long time."

"I'd have to say I've noticed that," Tommy acknowledged, his mind on Muffett and the men at the bathhouse.

"So. You've probably already seen Tommies at the front who were in worse condition than David is. Let me walk with you out to the coach stop. I could use the air."

As they exited outdoors, where the day had turned even nicer, Tommy switched subjects. "Was I wrong to come, Sister?"

"Absolutely not."

"He seemed more blue than ever when I had to leave so soon."

"Still, for you to come at all… thank you for doing that, Tommy." She stuck out her hand for him to shake, in a straightforward gesture Flowers had never seen from a woman and wasn't sure was proper. But he took her hand all the same.

"David's lucky to have a nurse like you."

"And a friend like you. If you come through London again – ooh, here's your coach. Hurry!"

"I will," Tommy said in reply to both her suggestions, and she watched and waved as the young man from the small town in Iowa jumped on the back of the London bus as if he'd been doing it all his life.

★

Tommy was sure he'd met O'Malley's deadline with several minutes to spare, but as he re-entered the office, he was not encouraged by the lieutenant's expression. Forgetting himself and military discipline, he followed his first instinct and tried to cajole the officer with a familiar "So was everything all right with Private Manton, sir?"

The lieutenant stood, slowly drawing himself up, and said with a glacial demeanor, "Private Flowers, you are speaking to an officer of the United States Army!"

Instantly realizing his error, Flowers froze into a sharp salute. "Sir! Reporting as ordered, sir! Beg pardon, sir!"

O'Malley eyed this strange boy again and stifled an interior laugh. "Private Manton is none of your concern, soldier. You're in enough trouble yourself."

Tommy felt his heart nearly stop. "Trouble? But sir–"

O'Malley stepped out from around his desk and drew his face close to the farm boy's. "You will learn to speak only when spoken to!" Tommy nodded. "Don't even nod unless I tell you to." Enjoying this rare exercise of direct power, the lieutenant returned to his chair and said gravely to Flowers, who still stood stiffly at attention, "I've sent some wires, and I've gotten some of the answers I needed. I'm waiting for the others.

"The course you said you were going to take is for *officers only,* Private Flowers. You will not be going to Grantham to take any such course. The question is, where *will* you be going next?

"Somebody has made a mistake here," O'Malley continued. "Maybe it's some knuckleheaded corporal somewhere" – the now-terrified Tommy immediately thought of Dougherty; had Willnor's adjutant plotted this? – "in which case you're lucky – you got to see London for an afternoon, and you'll be on the first train headed back for the Channel and the front."

O'Malley paused for dramatic effect, then went on. "But if it's your mistake – if, as I suspect, you planned all of this so you could see your buddy... if there really is a buddy, which I doubt; if there is, I think your buddy is probably named Betty, or Lulu, or something like that – if that's what you've been up to, soldier, you've made the biggest mistake of your life, and I'll have to turn you over to some of our friendly MPs."

Having scored his points, O'Malley expected some sort of response from the boy. He waited, until it dawned on him that Flowers was obeying his injunction about not speaking. "Well, soldier? What do you have to say?"

The fear in the private's voice was palpable. "I don't understand this at all, sir. I'm sure when you get the rest of your wires, they'll explain it. I was told–"

"Enough!" the lieutenant said abruptly, cutting him off with cruel relish. "You can tell your side to the court-martial. I don't need to hear this. The only thing in your favor is that you came back to this office on time. But I can't figure out if that means you're innocent or just overconfident.

"Now," the officer continued, rising. "I've been waiting too long to use the loo."

O'Malley saw Tommy's look of incomprehension and crudely explained, "The crapper, Private. I didn't want to be out of the office when you got back, to give you any kind of excuse. But the way these limeys work things, I have to walk up two floors to shit. I'm of no mind to take you with me, so I'm going to have to trust you not to touch anything in my office while I'm gone. But I'm not going to trust you not to go AWOL–" Tommy shook his head to indicate he wouldn't think of such a thing, causing the lieutenant to shout, "I said *no nods!*" Then O'Malley added, "So I'm going to lock you in my office. I'll only be gone a few minutes. I expect you to conduct yourself like a soldier in the meantime. Is that understood?"

"Yes, sir," Tommy sighed, saluting, with a defeated air.

He meant to conduct himself as a soldier, he really did. But Tommy had a feeling he needed outside help in this situation, never mind that it was entirely not his fault. Locked in O'Malley's office, it seemed he was unlikely to find much in the way of assistance, but for a bit of temptation that lay quite literally within his reach.

There was a telephone on O'Malley's desk. It wasn't something they had at the Flowers household back in Brooklyn, but there was one at the hotel where Tommy worked, and also at his Dad's pharmacy. Tommy knew perfectly well how to use it, presuming there were no rules particularly different in another country. At least they spoke his language.

Surprising himself with his decisiveness – if he was going to do this, there wasn't much time – he grabbed the receiver and was rewarded with a woman's voice (another woman!) asking what number he was calling.

"Camberwell Hospital, please."

"Do you mean First London General, Camberwell?"

"Certainly," he said with bravado.

"Certainly," she echoed, and Tommy held his breath, heard several clicks, then yet another woman's voice came on the line.

"First London General, Camberwell."

"I need to talk to Sister Jean Anderson."

There was a pause, and then the voice, with a decided edge to it, asked, "And may I ask who would be calling her?"

"Private Flowers." He had the feeling "Tommy" would have ended the conversation.

"Private Flowers," the voice repeated with audibly strained patience, "Sister Anderson is on duty. She is not to be disturbed unless it's an emergency."

"It *is* an emergency," Tommy insisted, nervously eyeing the door.

There was a longer pause, then the hospital operator said coldly, "I'll page her, then. Once. That's all."

"Thank you," the Yank said effusively, already convinced this desperate ploy would not work.

The wait was agonizing, but in truth unexpectedly short. To his relief Sister Jean's voice, full of alarm, came on the line. "Tommy? What's wrong?"

"How did you know something was wrong?"

"Never mind. A woman just knows."

"I'm in a whole lot of trouble, Sister."

"Tell me about it."

He did, talking double-time. When he had finished, he added, "I'm sorry to bother you, but I didn't–"

She interrupted. "You were smart to call me." Then she asked, "Won't the other wires this Lieutenant O'Malley gets exonerate you?"

The mention of the officer's name caused another nervous glance at the door. "Exon–?"

"Prove that you're innocent."

"I sure hope so. But even if they do, they'll put me on the first train back to the front. I mean, I want to fight, of course, but–"

"–that would be a shame, now you're here. I know."

"I think I hear the lieutenant coming."

There was only the slightest hesitation, then he thought he heard her say, "Hmm. O'Malley." More clearly, she added, "I have an idea. It's worth a try. Where are you?"

"On the Strand, near Trafalgar Square, across from the Charing Cross station. It's the second floor. Or maybe they call it the first–"

"I'll find it. Hang up now. Try to stay there as long as you can." He obeyed the first of her orders just in time to replace the phone and scramble back to the bench, even as the lieutenant's key turned in the door. O'Malley entered, eyed Tommy suspiciously, then returned to his desk. "And now, Flowers," he announced grandly, "we wait."

A good half hour or more passed, with O'Malley giving all his concentration to papers on his desk and studiously ignoring Flowers who, still trying to cover his nervousness, was unsure where he should be looking. The lieutenant really did remind Tommy of Dougherty; maybe O'Malley and the corporal knew each other, and had conspired together to put him in this fix. Tommy was no longer likely to imagine the two were secretly German agents; he was now more inclined to believe they were both members of some clandestine club for rude, nasty American officers.

His tension was simultaneously broken and heightened by a knock at the door. A breathless dark Doughboy (though not so dark as Manton; he wasn't colored, but more resembled Giannelli) burst into the room and announced, "Some wires for you, Lieutenant O'Malley, sir." The lieutenant took the papers, curtly dismissed the private, and commenced reading.

Tommy allowed his eyes to drop, ever so briefly, to the papers in front of the lieutenant. He didn't have time to make out what they said, but there were only two sheets, and neither one had much printed on it. Why was O'Malley taking so long? The lietuenant glanced up and caught Flowers looking at him. He seemed about to say something, but the younger man succeeded in glancing away so quickly that it precluded any remark. More agonizing minutes passed before the officer finally, suddenly shouted, "Atten-*tion!*"

Tommy leapt to his feet and froze, not looking at the other man, whose voice eventually emanated from somewhere beneath his line of sight, which terminated upon an American flag. "Private Flowers, it appears that it was your captain who made the mistake. This wire from Lieutenant Colbeck appears to exonerate you completely." Tommy was glad he'd just learned the meaning of the word from Sister Jean, but relieved though he was, he feared Jamie had extended himself too far on his behalf, pretending to be a lieutenant. In a tired, deflated tone, O'Malley added, "And since the captain outranks us all, I suppose we'll have to put it all down to a clerical error." Then the lieutenant seemed to come back to life. "So, soldier, looks like you've gotten a free ride to London – and back. I want you on the first train to the first boat back to the front. Now let's just see when that would be."

As O'Malley picked up the telephone to verify that information, Tommy was trying to figure out how much time had elapsed since his call to Sister Jean. He was remembering her second command, to stay there as long as he could. Now that the bigger crisis was over, it did seem very wrong that he should have to turn right back around without seeing David again, as long as he was here. O'Malley was not speaking into the telephone, and no one seemed to be talking at the other end yet, so Tommy took the chance: "Sir?"

"What, Flowers?" O'Malley demanded irritably. "Can't you see I'm on the telephone?"

"Yes, sir, but about that bathroom, sir?"

He emphasized his request with a bit of body English, and a look of understanding dawned on the officer's face. "Oh, all right," the latter grumbled, fumbling in his desk drawer. "Here's the key. It's two floors up."

"Yes, sir. I remember. Thank you, sir."

As he closed the office door behind him, Flowers heard O'Malley shout, "Hello?" Tommy had just barely managed to buy a little more time.

He took the stairs in uncharacteristic fashion, one at a time, as slowly as if they were duckboards ankle-deep in trench mud. His deliberately leisurely pace gave him time once again to marvel at his situation – not only had he already fought in France, but here he was in London, England! At the very least, he should send his parents and Susan postcards before he had to board the train back.

Tommy's sluggish movements sped up as he reached the fourth (third?) floor and tried to locate the bathroom which, he realized, he honestly did need to utilize. The doors on this hall were not marked at all, except for one that said "WC," which struck him as unlikely to be the place he sought. Not thinking about the key he had borrowed from O'Malley, he twisted the knob of the nearest door and once again startled a woman in uniform, this one young and vivacious, in an outfit he didn't recognize as belonging to the railroad, a nursing sister, or the army. "Oh!" she cried as he bulled into the small room where she sat at a desk.

"I'm sorry," Tommy hastily offered. "I was looking for–" Suddenly he remembered he was asking for these particular directions from a woman, and he turned crimson, faltering, "... for..."

"The WC, perhaps?" she said brightly, kindly.

"No," he said quickly. "I need to use – uh..." His mind searched for O'Malley's expression. "... the loo?"

Her manner changed and she wrinkled her nose. "Don't get fresh, soldier. I asked if you were looking for the WC."

"Oh. Is that the same thing?"

"Be off with you," she insisted, not placated, and with a hurried "Sorry," he was. The key fit into the locked door marked "WC," and he could see he was in the right place. It would have been nice if O'Malley had warned him. But he no longer expected people like the lieutenant to do nice things.

He took his time in the WC, thinking of trench and camp latrines, and enjoying the civilized comforts of indoor plumbing and privacy. But eventually he couldn't dawdle any longer, so he returned with leaden tread down the stairs. Approaching O'Malley's office, he braced himself for a lecture from the lieutenant about his tardiness. At the threshold, though, a gust of feminine laughter swept over him from inside. Sister Jean had arrived! He congratulated himself on his stalling tactics.

But when he actually swung open the door, confusion reigned again: the woman standing in front of O'Malley's desk, who clearly had the lieutenant's full attention, was dressed in the black of a religious sister, not the white of a nursing sister. Before Tommy had a chance to say anything, this woman swirled about to reveal the face, but not the voice, of Sister Jean Anderson. In a melodious tone, this strange apparition cried, "Ah, Private Flowers! You wouldn't be forgettin' me now, would you?"

"No, Sister–" he began, and she cut him off:

"–Flaherty, that's right. It's good to be seein' you again." To his further astonishment, the "nun" winked at him; then she nodded back toward the officer. "I've been tellin' yore Lieutenant O'Malley, here, about how much yore little visit helped our Private Pearson."

Forgetting himself entirely, Tommy asked anxiously, "Is he all right? Did something happen?"

"Why, of course, he's all right, Private, just as fine as when you left him, like I was tellin' yore fine Lieutenant Johnny, here."

Johnny? Tommy's amazement was increasing, but so was his ability to think on his feet. "How – how is it you came here, Sister, uh, Flaherrty?"

The woman gave O'Malley no time to ponder Tommy's stumbling over her name. She tittered, said, "Ah, silly me," and produced a Doughboy's cap. "I was so shore it was you had left this at the hospital, and I remembered where you said you would be goin' next. Chased you down to here, and then it turns out it isn't even yores," she said with a full-throated laugh, gesturing at Tommy's capped head.

He couldn't believe she was using a hat as an excuse (and where had she gotten it, anyway?)! If only Jamie were here to see and hear this performance – and he had realized by now that this was indeed a performance, and quite a good one. Looking properly abashed, he replied to her, "No, ma'am, I'm afraid it isn't mine. I'm sorry for your trouble."

"You should have telephoned," O'Malley admonished her, finally breaking into their conversation.

"Ah, well, but the Lord works in mysterious ways, Lieutenant Johnny. Our Private Flowers wouldn't be just headin' on, then, now would he?" she asked.

"Of course. He's going back to the front," O'Malley declared.

"Right away?"

"Yes, Sister," he said flatly. "As I told you, he was sent to London by mistake." Sister "Flaherty" flashed Lieutenant O'Malley a look, and he stumbled. "Not – not that I'm saying it was his fault, you understand. And if, as you say, his visit helped his friend, then maybe some good came of it all. But he's needed back in France, where he belongs."

"Well, and of course he's needed there. But Lieutenant, can't you see it's an act of God's will that's brought him here?" As she said this, Sister Jean shifted her body so that she was almost bearing down on the lieutenant.

"Well – I–"

"Not that I don't agree entirely that He'd want those terrible Huns beaten. That's why there's thousands of good boys fightin' the good fight over there in France. But I just know that if our Private Flowers could be spendin' a little bit more time with our Private Pearson, now he's here, then they'll both be ready to face the Huns again."

O'Malley shifted uncomfortably in his seat. "What are you saying, Sister?"

"I'm sayin' I really think that's why God made the 'mistake' you mentioned, Lieutenant. Only, as you know, the good Lord doesn't make mistakes."

O'Malley flushed. "Sister, you don't understand. I have no authority to keep this man in England."

"Oh, I'm shore you're much too modest, Lieutenant Johnny. I'm shore yore a much more important man than that."

The hapless officer was now quite visibly flustered. Tommy had the good sense to let his ally do all the talking, but he couldn't conceal his surprise when O'Malley finally said, "But what would I say? This man came to England because of a clerical error. He's not entitled to any leave. There are men with many, many more months of service than him, who've had no leave at all."

It was Tommy's turn to flush – he had to agree with the logic of O'Malley's argument – but Sister Jean staunchly held her ground: "And I'm shore they're all very deservin' of a leave, too. But Private Flowers is already *here, now.* You know" – she leaned into the lieutenant – "sometimes a little fib isn't a sin if it furthers the work of the Lord."

"Sister!" Johnny O'Malley cried in a voice full of shock that also was not entirely free of delight. At length he added, "How long are we talking about?"

Tommy's disbelief was now total. She had the lieutenant negotiating with her to keep him in England!

"A week would be–" she began, but O'Malley interrupted.

"That's out of the question, Sister. Be reasonable."

Both men watched as the woman made quick calculations. "Would there be such a thing as a 72-hour pass?" she inquired sweetly. "For a family visit?" O'Malley gave her a quizzical look, and she struck home. "Private Pearson, you know, hasn't any brothers… any more." When the lieutenant didn't answer immediately after that, she pressed her advantage: "And I'll see to it that Private Flowers doesn't get into any trouble, if that's what yore worryin' about."

O'Malley threw up his hands, and one last barrier of resistance. "He's been here since noon. Seventy-two hours from noon."

"No, Lieutenant, from now. Don't be stingy when yore bein' generous. This is the will of God."

The lieutenant exhaled long and hard, then finally took a piece of paper from his desk and said, "This is highly irregular. But for you, Sister. Seventy-two hours in this country, to assist with Private Pearson's recovery, under your supervision. Bring Private Flowers back to me here at 1800 hours Sunday–"

"Sunday? The Lord's Day?"

"All *right.* 0800 hours Monday." In a single motion, O'Malley scribbled something on the paper, stamped it, and handed it to Jean, who closed her eyes in a gesture of supplication.

"Oh, bless you, Lieutenant Johnny. I'll remember you in my prayers."

"I'd like that, Sister," said O'Malley with a rueful grin. Tommy had kept silent during their exchange, not even daring a smile. "Private–"

Tommy stiffened and saluted. "Thank you, sir."

"Don't thank me," the lieutenant replied with a scowl. "Behave yourself and mind the sister." He turned back to Sister "Flaherty." "Now if you will excuse me, Sister, it's been a long day and–"

"Oh, shore, Lieutenant, we wouldn't be takin' up any more of yore time. You've been more than generous already."

"I know I have," O'Malley said ungraciously, even as Sister Jean grabbed Tommy by the arm as if he were her pupil, and deftly slipped the pass into his hand.

# Chapter XXVI

On the stair, safe from public view, they made a scandalous sight: a Doughboy and a nun in wild, gleeful embrace. "Jean, you were *wonderful!*" Tommy shouted, and she put her finger to his lips to quiet him. "How did you figure all that out?" he continued in a much lower register. "You're not really a nun, are you?"

"Of course I'm not a nun," she replied, happiness mixed with a slight trace of scorn. "But I *was* an actress."

"You still are! You had me fooled there."

"I'm glad to know I've still got it."

"You do. You sure do. And I can't thank you enough–"

"You don't need to thank me. I did it for David and you. But thanks to that stuffy leftenant, I also haven't had this much fun since – well, since I became a nursing sister. Here, now, we're about to go outside. Look serious."

Out on the Strand, Tommy asked, "Are we going to see David now? I can't wait 'til we tell him all about this–"

"You'll have to wait. The first thing we must do is go back to the West End, so I can get out of this costume and give it back. This, too," she said, indicating the Doughboy cap.

That caused Tommy to tell her about the time he'd used retrieving his hat as an excuse for being late, and had drawn latrine duty for his inventiveness. She laughed at the story and Tommy's imitations of both Willnor and Colbeck, then said, "And what were you really doing?"

"I was with Davey."

"At that hour of the morning? Doing what?" she asked, her tone racy and implying any number of things – alcohol, French girls.

Tommy trusted her at that moment almost as much as he did David or Jamie, and he simply answered, "Nothing in particular. We were just – out." Rather than pressing him further, she simply smiled and nodded, and he switched the subject: "I can't believe you pulled that off with the lieutenant. What made you think of it?"

"I just used my head, Tommy. You could've done the same thing."

"I don't think he would've believed me as a nun."

She laughed. "No, but the strategy you could've come up with. Maybe you could've been a priest instead."

"I'm not an actor. Really, how did you figure–?"

"Leftenants are notorious for obeying commands from higher authority. And you told me this one's name was O'Malley, so I figured he was an Irishman.

"I had – have – a friend who's Irish," she continued, but the break in her voice was abrupt. Then she recovered: "This is her costume, in fact. She always told me that Irishmen were in awe of nuns." Although she was trying to relate this lightly, Sister Jean's voice remained pensive. "When I went to get the habit, the Doughboy hat was there – a prop. It all just fell into place. The rest was easy."

"I'll have to thank your friend for loaning the costume."

Another pained pause. "She's – not here anymore. She's back in Ireland."

There was quiet between them, then Tommy said, "You really miss her, don't you?"

She turned suddenly to him at that, then smiled when she saw the sincerity in his look, and relaxed a little. "Yes. I do." Without changing tone, she went on: "We're almost there. Down that alley. Wait for me outside the stage door."

After an uneventful few minutes, she reappeared in her nurse's uniform. "On to Camberwell," Tommy said jovially, but she demurred.

"It's too late in the day for visitors." Seeing his reaction, she added, "Don't worry. They'll release him tomorrow, probably in the morning. Then you can go with him to Dunster for a day or two, maybe three if the train schedules work out."

"And you'll be coming with us?"

"I'll do no such thing. I have work to do at the hospital."

"But – I was supposed to stay with you–"

"That doesn't matter. You have the pass. As long as I bring you back to the leftenant on time–"

"But – he said–"

"Tommy, break some rules for once," Sister Jean said in a sudden, sharp burst of exasperation.

He was nonplussed, but only for a second. "I did. I called you for help."

Her mood shifted, and she laughed. "And that worked. So do it again. Leftenant O'Malley, or his spies, won't follow you to Dunster. He wouldn't dare doubt the word of a holy sister."

He wondered briefly if they should be toying with O'Malley's religious convictions, but said, "All right. I will," and smiled back at her, looking so much like Arthur she had to turn partly away from him.

"I have to go home now," she began, only to be interrupted by "Is there a place to stay at the hospital?"

"You can't stay there. You're in perfect health." Then it dawned on her. "You don't have anywhere to go, do you?"

"No. I thought I'd be at a camp in Grantham by now."

"Of course," she said with a nod, mostly to herself, and he added for good measure, "I don't have any English money, either." That was a detail neither one had thought to discuss with O'Malley.

She barely hesitated before her quick mind was off in another direction. "You can come home with me, then."

He couldn't prevent his own scandalized reaction: "Sister!"

"I don't mean to stay in my flat," she corrected patiently, betraying neither amusement nor annoyance. "There's a lovely couple I let from. They own the building. They lost their only boy in the war. I know they'll be glad to put you up for the night. Honored, in fact."

They were heading in some direction determined by Jean, but abruptly he broke stride. "Oh. I couldn't."

She turned back to him, ever so slightly irritable again. "Of course you can, Tommy. It'll make them happy."

"But," he said helplessly, "I can't… I can't… stay in their bed."

"Why not?" she asked, but even as she did, he involuntarily scratched himself. "Oh, I see. Of course. You've got cooties."

"Sister!" he cried in consternation; they were out in public, and this time he was the one who wanted to shush her.

"Every soldier who comes direct from the front has them," she said airily. "It's nothing to be ashamed of."

"Still, I wouldn't want to – you know, their sheets."

She didn't have to think long. "Tell you what. I'm sure there's some powder about. When we get there, I'll give you the powder, and we'll draw you a hot bath. It will be all right."

He hesitated a bit more. "Well… if you're sure…"

"Come, Tommy. Don't be a horse's behind. Let's go. I'm tired and I have to get up early."

Sister Jean lived south of the Thames, on the same side of the river as the hospital, in a tired-looking neighborhood of houses such as he'd never seen; whole blocks of them seemed to be glued together. As they walked down her street – which she referred to as a "gardens," and indeed there was a very small park, surrounded by an iron fence, directly across from her building – she explained that until shortly before the war, the area had been well-off, with one family apiece in each of the houses. Now they were divided into apartments, or as she called them, flats.

"Have you been here a long time?" he asked as she turned the key to her locked front door.

"No. Two years." Her voice tightened once more. "My Irish friend and I lived in the East End, near the docks. But a bomb from a Zeppelin hit near our building."

Incredulous, Tommy said, "Really?"

"Yes, really."

"That's terrible!"

The look she gave him wavered between friendliness and annoyance. "Of course it was terrible. This is a war. Many terrible things have happened, and still do. You know that."

"I'm sorry."

"For what?" she asked testily. "You didn't drop the bomb."

"But I said the wrong thing, and I upset you."

Her hostility abruptly vanished, and she touched his cheek. "My stars, you really are a nice boy. No wonder David likes you." He had no response to that, and she moved her hand to his chest and added, "Wait here. I want to talk to the Shipleys."

As he again stood and waited for Jean, an overwhelming weariness overtook him. He wasn't sure why. He'd been awake thirty-six hours or more, having catnapped at best on the voyage over, but at Hamel he'd stayed awake and alert a great deal longer than that. He remembered David and Jamie talking about being up for days at a time in the trenches. He must get himself in better condition.

"Tommy?" Someone awoke him by poking him between the ribs. It was Jean; he had been dozing on his feet. For half a second he reacted physically, almost grabbing at her; then he recoiled and apologized. "It's all right," she said matter-of-factly.

"You didn't even flinch."

"I've wakened lots of soldiers. I know to stand back."

"Oh… uh, so?"

"Everything is fine. I've got your towels, and I'll go get that powder we talked about." They entered the house, and she pointed up the stairs. "The bath is on the next floor, to the right."

"Where do you live?"

She did not take the question as fresh, though it came close to that. "I'm on the top floor. I'll be right down with the powder."

"And the – Shipleys, did you say?"

"Yes. Gordon and Marion. They live on the ground floor. The flat on the first floor is empty – their son lived there before he went away – but there's a bed in the front room. Marion will put some linen on it while you bathe."

"Everybody shares the same bath?"

"Of course." They were walking up the stairs.

"You said you had to get up early. Don't you want to use it first?"

"Such a gentleman. But no. I can wait. I believe you've had a longer day than me."

Fully dressed, Tommy ran the water in the bath for a long time before its temperature even began to reach tepid. There was a knock on the door and he hollered, "It's all right. I'm decent."

In came Jean, who handed him the lice powder, then tested the bathwater. "This needs to be much hotter for it to work. Let it run a while longer."

"I will. Thanks. For everything."

She turned back and gave him one more grin. "Happy to help."

Then he was alone again. He slowly stripped off his clothes and powdered himself, then waited the requisite few minutes for the stuff to begin to take effect. Once steam was rising off the bathwater, he turned off the taps and stepped gingerly in. He let out a sharp hiss at the shock of the initial contact, but then, much more quickly than he imagined he'd be able to, sank in up to his neck.

He realized one of the things he'd been missing most was the feeling of being clean. He'd been dirty so long, despite a couple of trips to those horrid English bathhouses, he'd almost forgotten how it felt. He could almost hear the lice dropping off him, succumbing to the combined effect of the powder and the heat. Relaxed, he mused that he should get dressed afterward and perhaps ask Sister Jean if she wanted to go out. Of course, he had no money. But she was an attractive woman and she had been very good to him. Asking her out seemed the decent thing to do.

The thought persisted as he toweled himself. He hadn't even noticed that a dressing gown was discreetly placed on a hook on the back of the door. He smiled to himself. First Susan, then Nicole, now Sister Jean. Maybe she really did want him to come upstairs. He was getting to be quite the ladies' man.

As he hurried down the hall from the bath to the front room, he noticed that the other chambers on the second floor, their doors open, were quite bare – no furniture, no lights, no drapes except for blackout curtains. But at the end of the hall was a room with a bay window flanked by flowered curtains and overlooking the little park. And the bed, all made up and turned out with a summer coverlet, looked irresistibly inviting in the light cast by a single standing lamp. He dropped his clothes, which suddenly seemed to him unutterably filthy and disgusting, on the floor. Sister Jean would probably use the bath next; maybe he should just take a little nap. There were nightclothes laid out, too, but he could tell at a glance they were several sizes too small for him. He shut the door, doffed his robe, slipped under the covers, and closed his eyes.

In his next conscious moment, he felt his arm being gently but firmly rocked back and forth. Coming to with less violence than before with Sister Jean, he awoke to a room filled with bright sunlight. An older man, a good ten to fifteen years senior to Tommy's own Dad, a man with kind eyes, was sitting on the edge of his bed. It was this gentleman who was shaking his arm.

"Who – who are you?" Tommy demanded blearily.

"I'm Gordon Shipley. I'm sorry to waken you, Private Flowers, but Sister Jean said–"

"Sister Jean? Where is she?" Tommy sat up in bed, and the sheet fell away, revealing his bare chest. He remembered then he was naked under the covers, and quickly clutched the bedding around him. The effect was comical, as Gordon Shipley quietly appreciated.

"She was up at dawn and gone to work," the old man said with a chuckle.

"At – what time is it?"

"Why, it's half past eight."

"In the morning?"

Gordon gave another small laugh and gestured at the window. "What do you think?"

Tommy fell back on his pillow. "I – must have slept–"

"–a long time, yes. You were tired," Shipley said with simplicity. He indicated a pile of neatly folded clothes, underthings. "My wife was up early, too. These are clean."

Remembering the nightclothes, Tommy began, "Thank you, but I really can't–"

"Oh, they're yours." Seeing Tommy's look, Gordon continued with a wink, "Don't worry. She used a very hot iron. On your uniform, too, though there wasn't time to give it a proper cleaning." As he offered this apology, Gordon pointed toward the door where the uniform hung. There might not have been time for a "proper cleaning," but it had been so thoroughly brushed and pressed that it looked almost new. Tommy's eyes stung, the more so when Gordon's voice intruded on his thoughts: "We would be so very pleased if you would join us for a spot of breakfast before you have to leave. If you like, of course."

"I wouldn't think of doing anything else, sir. The honor is all mine."

"Please," Shipley said. "Call me Gordon. And my wife is Marion." He patted Tommy's bare shoulder and rose. "We'll see you downstairs, then, in a few minutes."

Alone again in the room, Tommy slipped on his clean underclothes and moved to the window. Drawing back the curtains, he let the morning light hit his eyes, which began to fill up again, and not just from the brilliance. So many kindnesses in the last day, from people who didn't even know him. It overwhelmed him for the moment – especially this house and the people who owned it; he hadn't even met Marion yet, but already the Shipleys made him miss his parents more keenly than at any time since he'd left Brooklyn. He reminded himself one more time that the front was less than a day away from this pretty little garden with its few midsummer roses. Suddenly David's singing came back to him –

*Roses are shining in Picardy*

– and he had to stop himself. He broke away from the view and practically jumped into his uniform, stopping only at the WC and then the bathroom, to brush his hair. With the bath and the clean uniform, even he, not one to dwell on his own looks, could see that he looked better than he had in a long, long time.

When he walked through the open door of the room directly below where he'd slept, a small, plump woman turned to greet him, emitting the slightest of "Oh!"s at the sight of him. He wanted to hug her, to throw his arms around this sonless mother, especially when he saw, arrayed on the mantel behind her, photos of a man a few years older than himself, many taken in a Tommy's uniform. But instead he said self-consciously, "Good morning, ma'am. I'm Private Thomas Flowers, 33rd Division, United States Army–" He felt silly, suddenly, for giving his division, but it was second nature for him at this point.

"I'm Marion Shipley," she replied. "Please call me Marion," with such warmth that he could do no less than offer the short form of his own first name in return. He was not used to calling people the Shipleys' age by their Christian names. "Are you hungry, Tommy?" she asked.

It took just that question, asked that way, to remind him how long it had been since he'd eaten. He nodded enthusiastically, and she motioned for him to sit down at a table he couldn't help but notice was set with what was surely their best china – three place settings. He wondered how long it had been since they'd done that, or whether they had continued to do so since their son's death.

Famished though he was, the first thing she brought him was a small brown egg – the kind you might not have bothered taking out of the coop in Iowa – resting in a metal cup, and a pot of tea, accompanied by bread whose color, despite a toasting, could not be classified as anything but gray. Tommy remembered David's "biscuit" with a shudder; he hoped she wouldn't serve him bully beef.

Gordon came in reading a newspaper and sat down across from him. He finished his article and looked up. "Go ahead, lad. Don't wait for us. We had a mite earlier, anyway. The tea should be ready." Tommy tapped at the egg with his spoon as Gordon poured tea for all three of them. "Have you never eaten an egg that way before?" the older man asked.

"Well… no."

"Here, then. Let me." Shipley tapped the egg lightly and deftly cracked the shell, removing it from approximately the upper third of the egg. "Go ahead. Dig in."

Tommy did, and found the soft but solid white and yolk more than satisfactory. As he continued working on it, Marion arrived with more toasted gray bread and a tray with milk and sugar. "How d'you take your tea, Tommy?" she asked, and he shrugged, put the dark brew quickly to his lips, then even more quickly replaced the cup on the saucer.

"With milk, I think. And a little sugar."

As he consumed the rest of his breakfast, which also included a tomato that had been fried(!), they began to politely query him about his family and so forth. He eagerly offered them his own history, carefully avoiding questions about theirs, not wanting to bring up the subject of their son. He was so ravenous he even ate every available slice of the toasted gray bread, which was easily the least tasty part of the meal. The thoroughness of his appetite clearly pleased them both, and he was glad, because he so wanted to please these wonderful people. He resolved to send his parents that postcard as soon as possible.

"That was delicious, ma'am," he declared when it became apparent nothing else was forthcoming, although he could have eaten more. "And thank you, too, for cleaning my clothes. You didn't have to do that. I really appreciate everything."

"You're our guest," Gordon replied plainly, as Marion added, "I only wish some of Jeff's clothes would have fit you."

There. The subject had come up. He had to say something. He stood, strode over to the mantelpiece, looked at the photos and the medals, noticed that the name was in fact spelled "Geoffrey."

"I'm so sorry," he finally said. "You can tell he was a fine fellow."

The couple was still seated, and they each quietly nodded. At that moment it occurred to him that in fact, they wanted very much to talk to him about their Geoff. Moving back to the table and re-seating himself, he said, "What was he like, if you don't mind my asking?"

Tommy's insight proved correct; for the next half hour, he heard all about the Shipleys' only child, born late in their marriage, who had become a professional soldier several years before the war started. Rushed to the front with the British Expeditionary Force in August 1914 when hostilities broke out, he had been an officer, a second leftenant.

"He was at Mons," Gordon said solemnly. "Do you know about Mons?"

Tommy had to admit that he did not.

"There were angels at Mons," Marion intoned. "Angels saved our lads from the Huns." Tommy looked over to Gordon, who nodded in agreement. It sounded weird to the American, the more so as the elderly couple related the story of ghostly medieval horsemen blocking the path of the German Army, allowing the British to slip away. Clearly they believed this account as much as Flowers did not; though he had to admit from his own limited experience that hallucinations wouldn't be that hard to come by on a battlefield.

Angels or no, Geoff had survived the retreat from Mons, and had been part of the regrouping that September that had culminated with the French stopping the Germans just short of Paris, at the Marne – the same battle, although Tommy didn't know it, that had claimed the life of Marc, the beloved husband of Nicole's aunt.

Just when Tommy had managed to digest the story of the angels of Mons, Marion volunteered another tale that sounded equally preposterous. She got up and went to the mantelpiece and came back to him with a small cigarette case he had overlooked among the medals and photos. "D'you see that?" she asked. As he nodded, it occurred to him her accent sounded more like David's than Gordon's did.

"Geoff got that from a German lieutenant."

"Did he kill him in battle?"

"No!" Gordon broke in, emphatic almost to the point of indignation. "It was a Christmas present."

"A – *what?*"

"A Christmas present," Marion repeated. "Christmas 1914. They stopped the fighting for the day and had Christmas together, the Tommies and the Huns."

Tommy was struggling to conceal his complete disbelief at this one. "Do you really think that happened?"

"We know it did," Gordon replied, the slightest edge to his voice. "Our son wrote us about it, and sent us this. They didn't fire a shot that day. They even played a football game."

"Really?" Tommy repeated, then he shook his head. "I never heard."

"It happened, all the same," Gordon insisted.

"I wish it could happen again," Tommy said impulsively, partly out of diplomacy but partly expressing a genuine wish. He also had made the comment partly to himself, but when he looked up and focused, he saw that they were staring at him silently, with a gaze he interpreted as disapproval. "But it can't now," he added. "Not anymore. Now we have to teach the Jerries a lesson."

"Yes," said Gordon, nodding, "so it can never happen again." Tommy thought by "it" he meant the war, but "it" could maybe have meant the Christmas truce, too.

There was a prolonged pause that became awkward, then Flowers said, "Did Sister Jean mention a time I was supposed to meet her at the hospital?"

"You're to go to the station, not the hospital," Gordon said. "You're to meet your friend there."

"Oh… is that the Charing Cross Station?"

"No," Gordon said as Marion began to clear the dishes, "Paddington Station."

Tommy shook his head. "I don't know where that is."

"I'll go with you."

"It's not necessary, if you just want to give me directions. You've both already gone out of your way so much–"

"Nonsense. I'll go," Gordon said flatly, getting up. Following his wife into the kitchen, he added, "You'd best get ready."

As he collected his few things and stopped at the WC one last time, Tommy was nagged by the feeling he had somehow disappointed the Shipleys. He shouldn't have doubted their stories, and then said he wished there was peace with the Germans.

But when he returned to the top of the stairs, both of them were waiting patiently for him at the bottom, and Marion, who had packed him some more gray bread with a bit of yellow cheese, told him, "I won't be going with you to the station, Tommy, but I do want you to know, it's been such a joy to have a young man in the house again." This time he didn't hesitate, scooping her up in his arms and giving her a hug as fierce as the one she returned. "God watch over you," she whispered into his ear, and he, blinking, took his leave and headed out the door with her husband.

# Chapter XXVII

During the long journey to Paddington Station – first a five-minute walk, then a bus, and then another new experience for Tommy, an underground train ride – Gordon said practically nothing, save for the grunts and other small noises needed to guide the young American in the proper direction. Nevertheless, when they finally arrived at Paddington, Tommy was glad the older man was with him; the place was even more confusing than Charing Cross. Hordes of civilians trudged about purposefully; everyone but him seemed to know exactly where they were going. He noticed Tommies here and there, but overall the military presence was much less.

"Oh!" he heard his escort say suddenly, "Look at the Q." Tommy didn't know quite where to look, as he wasn't sure of the meaning of this mysterious letter. He figured "Q" must be an abbreviation for something, but he couldn't imagine what. Gordon's attention seemed to be directed toward a long line of people standing in front of a window marked "Train Information."

"There's nothing for it but to wait," Gordon added with a sigh. "I hope you won't miss your train." With that, the older man hurried toward the line, with Tommy scurrying in his wake to catch up. By the time Flowers joined Shipley, the latter was engaged in conference with a couple of women who were just in front of him in the line, in which Tommy counted twenty-six people.

"They've reduced the schedules again," Gordon said, turning suddenly back to him, pronouncing the key word "shedules." "That's why the queue is so long." Tommy finally recalled that David had used "Q" as an expression for "line."

"You've done so much for me already, Mr. Shipley, you and your wife. I can wait myself."

Shipley hesitated. "But you don't even know what to ask for–"

"The train to Dunster, right?"

"–and what if it's been canceled? I can't leave you alone here, all by yourself."

"Didn't you say my friend was meeting me here?" The older man nodded. "Then I'll be all right. He always takes good care of me."

Gordon looked at him quizzically, then said, "I do hate to leave Mrs. Shipley alone for too long…"

"Then go ahead. I'll be all right here."

"If you're quite sure–"

"I'm sure." Tommy stuck out his hand, and Gordon took it. "Thank you for everything, Mr. Shipley. Really."

"You're quite welcome. God be with you, Tommy."

Flowers watched as the bent figure disappeared into the crowd, then he shook his head and turned back to the line. There were now several people behind him, and the women with whom Shipley had been conversing had turned back to face front. Ten, fifteen, twenty minutes passed as the line moved slowly, fitfully forward. For Tommy, impatience alternated with the realization he didn't really know what time his train was, so there was no point in getting anxious; since David hadn't shown up yet, there must not be any rush.

Another five full minutes passed once he had achieved the number-two position in the line; whatever the woman in front of him wanted was taking a long time. He tried hard not to fidget, and exhaled with relief when at last he advanced to the window, facing a mousy woman who appeared tired beyond endurance despite her relative youth. "Excuse me, ma'am," Tommy inquired, "but could you tell me where I could catch the next train to Dunster?"

The woman wrinkled her nose as if he'd uttered a curse word. "Dunster? Don't know of no Dunster. What'd it be near?"

"Near?"

She gave him a withering look. "Yes, dearie, near. What town? It must be near to some bigger town, where you'd 'ave to change trains."

"But isn't that what you're supposed to know?"

"If I knew it, I wouldn't be asking you, now would I?"

"But I don't know what it's near. I don't know where it is. I just know I'm supposed to go there. I'm an American," he added by way of explanation.

"I can see that," she snapped; then she shrugged. "Sorry, love, if that's all you know, I can't 'elp you."

Tommy was now genuinely worried that his precious pass time with David was evaporating, so he dug in his heels: "But that's your job."

"Don't tell me what's me job," the woman replied caustically, as the people in line behind Flowers stirred restively. Already annoyed from the long wait, they weren't inclined to take his side.

"Can I talk to someone else?" Tommy persisted.

"There ain't no one else. I can't 'elp you. Now step aside."

"Please. I have to catch the train to Dunster."

"Step aside," she repeated, and the order was echoed by a couple of other people in the line.

Just when the situation had grown so uncomfortable that the Yank decided to back down, someone gripped his arm and demanded, "What's going on 'ere?" He turned to see David, looking considerably spruced up, in a neatly pressed, clean brown Tommy's uniform, with a blue armband.

As if his friend had just wandered away for a few minutes, Tommy explained in a conversational tone, "She can't tell me where to catch the train to Dunster.

Says we probably have to transfer somewhere bigger, but it's up to me to tell her where–"

"It's Taunton," David said fiercely to the woman behind the window. "You should know that, you stupid cow. It's Taunton."

The woman, so impervious to Tommy's pleas, shrank from David's glare and looked hurt, while a man behind them, one of those who had said "step aside," muttered, "There's no call for that kind of talk." Tommy himself stood a bit stunned and dismayed; he'd never heard David talk so harshly to anyone, even Hardison.

"And you," David continued, turning on the man, "you should be ashamed, the 'ole lot o' you. This man's been fighting for you at the front. 'E isn't even from our country." Pearson whirled back to Flowers, gripping his arm again. "Come on, Tommy. I know where our train is. That's where I was waiting, 'til it dawned on me you might be 'ere. Come along before we miss it. I'm sorry you 'ad to deal with this lot." He waved contemptuously at the line of civilians.

But another man didn't give up, and said loudly to the group, "'Ow's 'e come by that armband, I wonder? 'E looks all right to me."

The two soldiers already had started to move away, but now it was an incensed Flowers who wheeled about and shouted, "He didn't limp like this a month ago, Mister."

It effectively silenced their critic and everyone else in the line, but David looked at least as aghast as they did, and he stalked off, leaving Tommy to follow him. Again trying to catch up with his would-be guide – an easier task with the wounded Pearson than the elderly Shipley – Flowers called after his pal, "I'm sorry, David. It isn't that bad, really. That was just the first thing I could think of."

David turned to face him squarely. "Because it *tis* that bad. That's why you did think of it, y'see." Half to himself, he added, "I can't be cross about it. I'll just 'ave to get used to it." He paused again, then said, "Others 'ave 'ad much worse, after all."

Tommy regarded him with admiration. "That's true."

"So let's not let me leg cause us to miss our train."

"But–"

"It's soon, Tommy. No time to chat. Once we're on board."

"Maybe I should carry you."

Pearson gave Flowers an odd look, then burst out laughing as he began to stride forcefully away, limp and all. "You're still a funny one, Yank," he called over his shoulder.

The train to Taunton was crowded, but the civilians on it were a little more respectful than those in the line at the ticket window, and Tommy and David got to sit across from each other in a first-class compartment with two older women who were traveling as far as Bath. Once they were settled in, the American said to his friend in a low voice, "Those people – I can't believe what happened back there."

David looked over at their compartment mates, who were paying no attention to them, lost in their own thoughts, staring out the window. "Bloody civs," Pearson muttered quietly, again worrying Flowers. "They're all so mad to win the war, but they're sick of looking at the likes of us."

Tommy started to speak, stopped himself, thought about all the people he'd seen since coming to England, said, "Maybe they're just tired, Davey. I think they're just tired. They don't seem all excited about the war, not like the people back home."

David didn't reply right away, then said guardedly, "Your lot'll get tired, too, if they're in it long as this." Another pause, and he added angrily, "But that's no bloody excuse."

"No, of course not," Tommy readily agreed.

"They don't even try to know what it's like. Only us soldiers do, y'know. They 'ave no idear."

Flowers, afraid the older women were listening to this although they appeared not to be, chose to avoid replying, and both men remained silent all the way to Bath, where they helped the "bloody civs" get off the train. No one joined their compartment, so the two moved to face each other next to the window, then continued to ride in silence, until Pearson finally remarked, "You're being very quiet, Tommy."

The Doughboy regarded his pal, and thought about saying what was on his mind, asking David what was wrong; then he thought better of it. "There's so much I've been wanting to ask you," he said instead. "So many things have happened, and I wished you were there with me." This, Tommy noted to his pleasure, seemed to lighten David's mood a fraction.

"What sort of things?" the Briton asked.

"Well, for instance, at Hamel–"

David leaned forward. "Tell me what 'appened there, Tommy. You di'n't before, not really. Tell me about it, from the beginning."

So Tommy did, starting with the lying and waiting, and he found his memory for detail became unexpectedly vivid: "... then another fellow, an Australian, came by and said, I think it was 'Copper?' and he gave me something to drink–"

"'Cuppa.' A cuppa tea, y'see."

"That's it, then, that's what he gave me, some tea, and I drank it, but it didn't taste the same as the tea you gave me–"

"'Ow did it taste different?"

Tommy thought about that. "It tasted like – almost like it had butter in it?"

David nodded. "Rum, then. Those Aussies put it in their tea, give it to their boys before they go over the top."

"Oh."

"What else was there you wanted to ask me about?"

Tommy's thoughts strayed from Hamel as he pondered what else. "I stayed last night with these friends of Sister Jean's – the Shipleys? They lost their son at – uh – Plug – Plug–"

"Plug Street Wood," David put in.

"Yes, that's right. But before that, he fought at – Mons?"

David nodded. "Mons, yes."

"And they said – you won't believe this, but they said–"

"–there were angels."

"Yes!" Tommy shook his head. "It's like you always know what I'm going to say."

"And if it stopped being that way?"

David said this abruptly, aggressively, as a demand, which threw Tommy, but only momentarily. "It will never stop being that way, Davey," he replied. "You always know things I don't." Pearson didn't say anything in response to that, and Flowers went on: "Do you believe there were angels at Mons?"

David shrugged. "Wou'n't know. Wasn't there."

"Your brothers – Colin and Doug?–"

Now David shook his head, his jaw tighter. "No. Too early in the war for that."

There was yet more quiet; David certainly was not being talkative, but Tommy persisted. "They talked about something else that was even stranger."

"The crucified Canadian?"

"No."

"The Russians 'oo went to the front through England?"

"No."

"What, then?"

"They talked about – that first year – a – a truce, at Christmastime. Huns and Tommies playing games and giving each other presents."

"That 'appened," David said flatly. "Everybody knows that."

Now it was Tommy who shook his head. "But that would be the most fantastic thing of all."

"It *'appened,* just the same," David repeated with the same peculiar emphasis that Gordon and Marion had used regarding the same subject.

Tommy wasn't about to make the same mistake twice in one day. "All *right.* I *believe* you."

David turned away, and looked out the window. After a while, he said, "You rather skipped over the rest of 'amel, there." He looked over to Tommy. "What was it like – really?"

"Killing the Hun. That's what you mean, isn't it?" David nodded once more, and it was Tommy's turn to shrug. "It doesn't seem like it was anything anymore. I – at the time, and after, it bothered me, but now it doesn't. I thought he might kill me, so I killed him first. That's all there was to it."

"But what did it feel like?"

Tommy realized he had been leaning far forward, and he sat back. "Soft. Sticking a bayonet through a man – it's real soft. It was easier than cutting your turkey at Thanksgiving."

"Thanksgiving? What's that about?"

Tommy smiled at the opportunity to explain something to David. "Something we do in America. It's a special day when we thank the Lord for what we have–"

"That would be the Thanksgiving part, then."

"–and my mother cooks a turkey – it's a bird, like a chicken, but bigger–"

"I know what a turkey is. But we only eat them at Christmas, if we can afford more than a goose." A smile actually flickered briefly across David's face. "Fancy that."

More quiet, and then Tommy could hold back no longer: "What is it, Davey? Tell me what's wrong."

Pearson shifted uncomfortably, then directed his gaze out the window again. After a long while, he spoke: "When a bloke gets 'it like I did, and 'e's wounded, and 'e just lies there day after day, 'e's got a lot of time to think."

The pause that followed was extraordinarily long, so Tommy finally prompted, "And?"

David's eyes dropped, then refocused on the landscape. "And, for one, I know I'll never be much of a soldier, I can tell you that."

"Don't – don't say that."

"Why not? It's just what's true."

"That's what Jamie says about you. I want you to prove him wrong."

David glanced at Tommy – "But 'e's right, y'see" – then back away.

"You don't know that. He doesn't know that. You never know 'til you're actually in it. He thought I was no good as a soldier. But after Hamel, he changed his mind. He told me he was wrong."

Still looking out the window, David murmured, "You trust 'im a great deal, don't you?"

Tommy wasn't about to fall into that trap, either. "As a soldier, I'd trust him with my life. I *have,* and I would again… But as a friend, I'd trust you – not him."

David turned back and looked at Tommy in wonder. "Is that so?"

Impulsively, Tommy crossed over so that he now sat next to David. "You know it is. You're my best buddy. You'd never let me down. 'You wou'n't do that to me.'"

It was a fairly credible imitation of Pearson, and it could have offended him, but instead David gave Tommy a faint grin, though his tone was serious. "You're right. I wou'n't do that to you. Ever."

With peace restored between them, Tommy sensed he should again remain quiet, and so they both did, sitting side by side, staring out at the countryside the rest of the way to Taunton.

# Chapter XXVIII

Something about disembarking at Taunton to wait for their connecting train to Dunster elevated Pearson's spirits, and to Flowers' great relief he finally became talkative: "I can't wait for you to meet me sis. Per'aps you and Betty will fancy each other. Wou'n't that be something, if you married 'er and we were all there together in Dunster?"

"It sure would," Tommy replied with enthusiasm. He hadn't forgotten about Susan, or Nicole, or even Sister Jean, but it was obvious that the prospect pleased Pearson; so Flowers not only politely omitted mention of any other girls in his life, but also found himself hoping things would indeed turn out that way.

The crowd, Tommy couldn't help but notice, was growing larger by the minute, unexpectedly so for a train headed for a town he'd never heard of before meeting Davey, and one the woman at the Paddington ticket window hadn't recognized, either. He wondered aloud about it to David, who replied, "Think about it, Tommy. It's July, and it's a Friday. Everyone's wanting a 'oliday at the seaside."

"Seaside? I thought you said Dunster was on a hill."

"And so 'tis, a large one. But the stop after us – it's the last stop – is Mine'ead, and that's right on the beach, y'see."

"On the ocean?"

"No, the channel."

If geography wasn't Tommy's strongest subject, it wasn't his weakest, either. "You're on the English Channel? But we've gone west."

"Not a very good choice of words, that," David said, flashing a quick, ironic smile – "gone west" was an expression sometimes used at the front for someone who'd been killed – then he added, "It's the Bristol Channel, not the English Channel. We're 'crost from Wales."

"Can you see the water from Dunster?"

"From the north of town, yes. And Wales, when it's clear."

"I didn't know you lived by a seaport. You never told me that."

"It's not a seaport. We're a few miles up'ill from the beach, and that's all there is at Mine'ead, a beach, not a port. What's so important about being on the water, anyways?"

"I grew up a long way from the sea. I think it's exciting to be on the water." With Pearson fully engaged in their conversation, not detached like before, Flowers let his imagination take flight: "Maybe we could be sailors after the war, Davey. We could sail around the world together, you and me."

To Tommy's gratification, David responded with his broadest, easiest smile yet. "I'd like that," the Briton said. Then he quickly added, "But only in the merchants' navy. No more military after the war is over."

"Right."

"Look. 'Ere's our train."

It was much smaller and older than the one that had brought them from London to Taunton, even though the throng of passengers was almost as big. So great was the crush that Tommy and David did well just to stand together in the same car, in the same clogged aisle. Even so, almost an entire family – a mother and three children, with their things – sat in the aisle between the young men.

Notwithstanding, Tommy loved the ride. The sweeping green hills were as formidable and as beautiful as any he'd seen anywhere. He thought again of his first impressions of England from yesterday morning – could it really only have been yesterday morning? – that the countryside at times resembled Iowa's, but somehow felt cozier, less expansive, the rises slightly higher and closer together. The trackside blazed with white flowers, and the names of the stations once they left Taunton – Bishops Lydeard, Crowcombe Heathfield, Stogumber – simultaneously amused and charmed him, so different from the plainness of town names back home in America, save for the occasional Indian word.

An elderly conductor came struggling into the crowded car – Tommy realized that since coming to England, when he'd seen men in such positions, they'd all been quite old – and gave Flowers the once-over. "What brings you all the way out 'ere, Sammy?" he asked, not unkindly.

"My mate," said Tommy, deliberately using the British term and indicating David, who was watching the scene closely over the heads of the family seated in the aisle between them. He nodded and smiled when he heard Tommy put it that way.

The conductor took in the blue band on David's arm and grew more effusive. "Ah, bless you both, boys. Bless you both."

"Thank you, sir," Tommy responded.

"Are you on holiday to Minehead, then?"

"No, sir. My friend is from Dunster. I'm going home with him, to see his family."

"Ahh, that's lovely. Just lovely, isn't it?" The conductor addressed this to the people crowded around and between them, most of whom nodded approvingly; evidently they'd been listening to the whole exchange. It was embarrassing for both soldiers, but in a vaguely pleasurable sort of way.

As the conductor moved to the family sitting between them, the smallest of the children, a blond girl who was maybe six, fastened her gaze on Tommy, then mumbled to her mother, "Mummy, please."

"All right," the woman said gently, and as she handed the conductor their tickets, she asked Tommy, "Are you an American?"

"Yes, ma'am."

"You see, dear?" she said quietly to the little girl, who gave him a long, solemn look, then whispered something else in her mother's ear. "Winifred would like to give you something," the mother added.

Her tone somehow conveyed the message that it was an inconsequential gift, so Tommy didn't protest, just simply said, "I'd be honored." Shyly the little girl reached up and uncurled her tiny hand. In it was a slightly crumpled flower. Had he been in Iowa, Tommy would have been certain it was a daisy; here, he couldn't say for sure. "Thank you," he said with outsized gratitude as he took the offering and carefully placed it through the second buttonhole of his tunic. As he did so, his eyes strayed over to David, and suddenly he felt awkward: David, after all, was the British soldier, wearing the mark of the wounded, but she'd presented the gift to Tommy.

But as though he'd read Tommy's mind, David broke the slight tension of the moment by addressing the girl's mother: "'E's always got a way with the ladies, that one." The remark caused considerable merriment in their general vicinity, and Tommy added to the good will by leaning over and giving the girl a kiss on the forehead, causing her to snuggle, giggling, back into her mother's embrace. He looked over to his friend, eyes shining; the comment was so like the David he knew. Pearson just cocked an eyebrow in return, and that, too, seemed so in character that for a moment Flowers had to look away, fearing his elation of the moment would lead him to say or do something foolish. As he did, he caught a glimpse of coast and exclaimed with excitement.

"Yes," said David, "there's quite a lot of it 'round 'ere." This caused more laughter among the passengers. Tommy, the butt of the tease, just glanced once happily at David, then resumed scanning the horizon.

"Watchet!" the old conductor cried, and Tommy looked over to David and asked, "Watch what?"

This stirred still more laughter, but also a groan or two. "It's the name of the station. Rather an old joke in these parts," David said, explaining the reaction.

"New to me," Tommy said with only the slightest hint of defensiveness. The crowd did not seem to be lessening any with each stop. "How much longer?"

"'Alf an hour. Less." Still, that meant it would be late afternoon by the time they arrived. Tommy thought: two days ago, I was at the front. He stopped himself from projecting in the other direction, timewise.

The moment for conversation having passed, he and David contented themselves with riding quietly for the next twenty minutes or so, taking in the scenery and occasionally telegraphing looks to each other. When somebody, not the same conductor, called "Blue Anchor," the woman and her three children quickly got up to hustle off the train, and Tommy called good-bye to Winifred, causing the little girl to giggle once more and her somewhat harassed mother to offer a fleeting smile.

The two soldiers moved to stand alongside each other as they watched the woman and her children being greeted on the platform by a man older than themselves, but not any older, probably, than Colbeck. He was not wearing a uniform. As the train began to gather speed again, David was the first to comment: "I 'ope that's 'er 'usband."

The thought that it might not be had not even occurred to Tommy. At first he didn't say anything, reluctant to give credence to the idea that this nice woman could be taking her children with her to meet a man who wasn't her husband for a holiday at the beach. Finally, he ventured, "Even if it is her husband, why isn't he in the army?"

"Don't fool yourself. There's plenty 'oo didn't go in."

"But isn't it the law?"

"Even so," David replied, a statement he apparently saw as a final pronouncement on the subject, for he had no more to say.

Presently Pearson, peering out the window in the direction opposite the water which continually came and went in their field of vision, said, "Ah. 'Ome."

Tommy turned to see a tower crowning as tall a hill as he'd yet laid eyes on in England; and behind it, on a second hill, a fortification of unanticipated size. "Is that the castle?" he asked, his voice so filled with little-boy awe that David couldn't completely stifle a laugh before answering, "So 'tis."

Shaking off the image in favor of something else on his mind, Tommy said, "Maybe you should see your mother and sister by yourself first. It's been such a long time, and–"

"Cor, not. I'm not letting you out of me sight." After a brief pause, David added, "And anyways, they won't be at the station. It's too steep a climb back up for me mum, and the shop will still be open, this time of day."

This rather astounded Tommy; two sons gone, the third one coming home wounded, and they couldn't even close the shop early to meet his train? He recalled his resentment at their failure to visit David in London, but said nothing more than "What about your sister?"

"Betty won't be there," David said, with a renewed edginess that hinted at incipient irritation.

Tommy moved quickly to squelch it by changing the subject. "Is it a long walk?"

"Twenty minutes or so," David replied, then added with emphasis, "All up'ill."

"We can take it," Tommy said with a wry smile, then realized he was forgetting David's leg.

But before he could apologize, David said, "'deed we can. Though per'aps 'twill be a bit longer than twenty minutes. But don't even think of carrying me."

Pleased at his success at keeping his friend in a good humor, Tommy chanced something: "But I'm a little tired, myself. If somebody offered us a ride, I wouldn't say no."

"Well, if we see Jamie Colbeck in a taxi, I can tell you, I'm not getting in."

The quip caused them to arrive at Dunster station laughing, as David reached through the window, opened the door, and they disembarked. "You know," Tommy said as they walked through the small station, "sometimes it seems like you're reading my mind–"

David proceeded to prove his point: "She only 'ad the one flower."

The American simply regarded his pal in amazement, a reverie interrupted by a voice calling, "Hallo!" It was an old man – another old man – out front of the station in a motorcar, whose back seat contained the two other passengers who had detrained at Dunster. He was addressing David: "Aren't you the last of the Pearson boys?"

The phrase was of course accurate, but Tommy was appalled by the choice of words. David, though, didn't seem to notice or mind, simply nodding a friendly assent. "I've got me room for one more–" the taxi driver began.

"We 'aven't the bob," David retorted, and the old man said, "No charge for you, of course," looking directly at the blue armband.

David hesitated, and Tommy spoke up. "Why don't you go ahead? Tell me the way and I'll meet you there."

"You can't ride two more?" Pearson asked, and the driver surveyed Flowers with an eye not unfriendly, but clearly alarmed by the Yank's size.

"Sorry. No. Can't."

"The running board?" Tommy asked David – quietly enough, he thought, not to be heard by the others, but the driver answered, "'Tisn't permitted."

With a hint of brusqueness, David told the man, "Ah, well, then. Thanks, all the same."

"You shouldn't be so stubborn," said the driver, and before Tommy could chime in his agreement, David repeated, "Thanks, anyways," in a tone of rising annoyance.

"Suit yusself," said the driver. As his car sped off, David started walking, his limp, it seemed, less pronounced than at the station in the morning. He turned around to the still-standing Tommy and said,

"It gets better in the p.m.'s. It's worst when I first get up."

Tommy shook his head. There was no point in wonderment if David read his thoughts this consistently; he should just accept it as a fact.

"What?" David said in response to his look.

"You don't know? I thought you could read everything in my head."

"Don't mock me, Tommy." This was said with dead seriousness.

"Only when you need it." He walked up next to his friend. "I could carry you at least part of the way, you know."

"Try it, and you'll end up in the Bristol Channel."

Tommy laughed at that, then said, "But we will take it slow, right?"

"Probably the only way I *can* take it," David said in an abrupt admission of vulnerability.

Touched, Tommy added, "Promise you'll tell me if it starts to hurt."

"Yes, mumsy." But David's sarcasm didn't sound as harsh as it might have. "Can we start up this 'ill now?" he continued, not waiting for Tommy. "Standing 'ere isn't 'elping any."

"Fine," said Tommy, falling into step. "But if there's anything you need–"

David turned back around and almost shouted, "I know that!" Then his tone changed again. "Please don't treat me like a cripple. It will be bad enough with the others."

"Whatever you want, Davey," Tommy replied, taking his friend's arm, but David shook it off.

"Wait 'til I need it. When I need 'elp, you're the first I'll ask. I promise."

The hill was as steep to walk as it appeared, a much sharper slope than, say, at Hamel, and even though it was late in the afternoon, Tommy had broken a sweat by the time they finally approached the town. David, keeping pace surprisingly well, suddenly stopped and commanded, "Look 'round," and Tommy did, catching a full vista of hillside and channel, with what must be Wales visible in the distance, as promised.

After a while, the American asked, "What's it like to grow up somewhere as beautiful as this?"

"I s'pose one forgets it's so beautiful, until we get a visitor. Isn't Ioway beautiful?"

Flowers thought about that for a couple of seconds, then said, "Yes, it is beautiful. But not like this, not in the same way."

"Still, per'aps that's why we get on. If one of us came from someplace ugly…" David trailed off as Tommy laughed appreciatively. They hung back, quietly surveying the view, until the Doughboy asked,

"Are you lollygagging?"

"A bit, per'aps."

"Remember what I said about going to see them first, without me? That's still OK."

David shook his head. "'Tisn't what I want. I'm rested now. Let's move on."

Another "Oh!" escaped Tommy's lips as they ascended and rounded one more curve and, quite suddenly, the half-timbered buildings and cobbled street of the main square of the village of Dunster materialized. The castle, which had disappeared from their line of sight partway up the hill, abruptly reappeared, looming large over the town which, but for the occasional motorcar, looked very much like the illustrations of English villages from long ago in Tommy's schoolbooks back in Brooklyn. Tommy looked over at Davey, who seemed as entranced by the sight as he was, and said, "To think you actually live here."

"Not 'ere, actually. This is the 'igh street. We're on the west street, a little further on."

"Further uphill?" Tommy asked. David nodded. "Do you need to rest again?"

"No."

As they walked along the high street, Tommy alternated between gawking at the shops, which looked almost swank to him, and keeping a close eye on David. It seemed to him that if he were returning home, limping, to Brooklyn with the war still going on, people would come running out of stores like these to greet him, but there were not too many people about at this hour, and no one did so for David.

They made a right at the end of the high street, just below the castle, and began climbing a steep, narrow lane. An old woman came down the curb toward them, and her face reflected recognition. "David Pearson, isn't it?" she asked as she came closer.

"Yes, Mrs. Landis, it tis," David said in the kind of easy, cheerful voice Tommy was used to hearing from him, but hadn't heard much since coming to England.

"You're home from the war, then?" the woman persisted.

"Just a visit," David said stoutly. "This 'ere's me mate, Mrs. Landis. Private Flowers. 'E's American."

The old woman nodded, eyeing Tommy a little suspiciously, but she kept her attention on David. "I was at your shop earlier," she added.

"Oh? And 'ow's it going there?"

"You're sister's doing very well running it, you know. She has a good head for business."

"I'm pleased to 'ear it."

"Well, God watch over the both of you."

"And you too, Mrs. Landis."

"Oh, I don't need it so much. I'm an old lady." She inclined her head toward Tommy. "Do keep an eye on our Private Pearson for us, Private Flowers."

"Oh, I do, ma'am. And he watches out for me."

The old woman nodded again, grunting in approval, and tottered on.

"Neighbor?" Tommy asked as she moved out of earshot.

"Teacher," David replied. "She told me before I joined up she'd already lost eleven of 'er old pupils, and di'n't want to see me making it a dozen."

"Does she have children of her own?"

"Two generations in the fight. Last I 'eard, they were all all right, or as all right as a bloke can be in this war. Last I 'eard. 'Ere, 'ere's me street."

The lane they were traversing curved sharply left just past a churchyard on their right, turning into a rutted thoroughfare whose curbs were crowded with shops rather more modest than those on the high street. They began heading slightly downhill again, and shortly the odor of baking bread came wafting up the street. A small white shop with a large picture window appeared among the two- and three-story buildings on their left, and with no warning David took an abrupt turn into it. Tommy followed him through the doorway, and suddenly there they both were, standing in Pearson's Bake Shop.

The shop wasn't big at all, and there were no customers, only a smallish young woman with jet-black eyebrows and hair bustling behind the counter. A little bell sounded as they entered, and she looked up. With a lack of warmth or excitement so singular that it stunned Tommy, she called out, "Mum! He's 'ere!"

"Hello, Betty," David said with guarded formality, and she gave him a "Hello, David," in the exact same tone of voice.

Before anything else could be said, a gray-haired woman who looked old enough to Tommy to be his mother's mother emerged from the back, her arms covered with a light dusting of flour. In a pleasant voice, with more warmth but no more excitement than her daughter, Mrs. Pearson pronounced her youngest son's name and glided over and stopped just short of him, all the while toweling off her still-coated hands. "'Ow are you, then?" she said simply.

"I'm in the pink, Mum. I brought me mate, Tommy, with me. 'E's American."

"American, is it?" she said, nodding a little in Tommy's direction; then she returned her attention to her only remaining son. "'Ave you been traveling long?"

"A few hours. We started in London."

"You must be tired, then, the both of you. Why don't you and Thomas go upstairs and rest a while?"

David hesitated a fraction, then said, "Per'aps we will, Mum. Thanks."

"We'll 'ave a bit o'supper after we close the shop," she called after them.

More shocked than he'd been by most of what he'd seen and heard at the front, Tommy followed his friend behind the counter and up one, then two flights of stairs. The second flight, especially narrow, led to a small room with a dormer window facing the street and a similar window on the back wall, which overlooked a tiny garden blooming with summer roses and, beyond, a green hill sloping sharply upward. As this back window faced generally east, the late-afternoon sun was striking the hillside to dramatic effect; the front window's curtains were drawn.

Tommy could not help but be struck by the beauty and serenity of the scene; even so, he could not keep his concentration on it. He heard David say, half to himself, "I am tired, at that," and flop down on the bed behind him.

Tommy turned from the back window and said in his best even tone, "Did they know we were coming?"

David lay on the left side of the bed, closer to the front window, eyes closed. "Of course they did, Tommy. Sister Jean sent a wire this morning. You 'eard 'ow Betty said, ''E's 'ere.'"

"I sure did," Tommy replied meaningfully.

There was a long silence as Tommy looked down at his friend, then David sighed and said, "You're being 'ard on them again, aren't you? You think I should 'ave got a warmer welcome."

"You're right. I do."

David opened his eyes and regarded his pal. "'Tisn't easy for them, either, Tommy. Leave it be. But thank you for looking out for me." Tommy had no response, and David patted the empty side of the bed. "Why don't you 'ave a lie-down? Take off your boots. You must be tired, too." Tommy hesitated for just a second, then sat down on the edge of the bed, his back turned to David, and slowly removed his boots. When he swung his body up onto the bed, it felt comfortably soft, but also rather a tight fit for someone of his stature. If just about anybody else but Davey had been beside him, they would have been uncomfortably close.

David shifted onto his side and turned toward Tommy, his eyes closed again. At length Tommy said, "You don't look like you're comfortable."

"It's all right. You're bigger than Colin or Doug. But I knew that already. It's all right."

"You used to sleep in the same bed?"

"Yes, all three of us."

"In this bed?"

"Yes, in this bed."

Tommy tried to imagine three lads, even the size of David, all fitting in, and couldn't. "Where did everyone else sleep?"

"Me dad and me mum's room is below us. Now it's just me mum's. Betty's first floor in the back. The pantry and the loo are ground floor, be'ind the shop."

There was another pause. Tommy thought he should say something positive. "These are nice pillows."

"Best in the 'ouse. Mum's and Betty's, probably."

"What?"

"Mum wouldn't 'ave it any other way."

"Are you sure? How do you know?"

"Some things you don't 'ave to ask, Tommy. I just knew, the way she said we must be tired." David opened his eyes. "So, y'see, you shou'n't be so 'ard on them."

"Betty, too?"

Now the eyes looked down. "Ah, Betty."

Tommy spoke his mind. "I don't think I could go for a girl who treats you like that."

David looked back up. "She was engaged to a bloke, Tommy."

It was getting to be much too familiar a story for Flowers, who simply asked, "And where was he killed?"

Pearson closed his eyes again. "Somewhere in Flanders."

There was a protracted pause, then Tommy said, "I'm sorry, but it's still not a good enough excuse." Raising no response, the American added defensively, "It's just that I think you deserve better."

"I know you do," David murmured, "and I bless you for it."

The choice of words elicited a light laugh from Tommy, and a smile from David in turn. Focusing on him again, Tommy said, "You sure you're comfortable?"

"I told you, I'm all right." Then David opened his eyes once more. "Are you?"

"Why don't we–?" Instead of completing his sentence, Tommy simply stretched his right arm full length. David, understanding, lifted his head a bit, and Tommy wrapped his arm around David's shoulders, pulled his buddy a little closer, then relaxed. Then, remembering the Briton's earlier standoffish behavior, he asked, "Is this all right?"

Though apparently napping, David replied, "It's lovely."

With the smaller man's head comfortably cradled on his shoulder, Tommy followed a sudden impulse and brought his own head down 'til their noses lightly touched. David's eyes flew open. "What?" he said pleasantly.

Embarrassed, Tommy pulled away slightly. "Nothing. Why don't you try to take a nap?"

"I was. Will you, too?"

Tommy turned away to yawn, trying to cover his mouth with his free hand. "Sure," he replied, returning to David. "Me, too."

# Chapter XXIX

Tommy drifted off with David, all right, but when he woke, he realized that, quite the opposite of the previous night, he'd slept but a short time, maybe only an hour. Although the sun was noticeably lower, it was still light out. David continued to sleep soundly curled up next to him, a comfortable feeling for them both in an existence lately short on comfort, so it was awfully tempting just to lie there, awake or not.

But Tommy had something on his mind, and David's continuing to sleep made acting on it easier. He carefully disengaged himself and managed to put his boots back on without waking his pal. Once he had squeezed out of the little room – how could three growing boys have shared such a space? – and cleared the door, he declined to tiptoe down the narrow stairway, choosing a regular tread instead. Ordinarily he would have been concerned about disturbing the two women of this house where he was a stranger; but with this pair, he hoped he did.

As he tromped down the second set of stairs, he heard Betty in conversation with someone. Turning the corner into the public area of the bakery without hesitation, he elicited a reaction that looked to him like disapproval from the older woman on the customer's side of the counter. Betty turned sharply, saw him, said nothing, then redirected her attention to the customer: "David's just come home for a short spell, Mrs. Parkham. And he's brought a friend with him."

The frown began to transform into a smile, which grew wider when Tommy stepped forward with a "How do you do, ma'am?" and his usual recitation of name, rank, and division.

"You're an American," Mrs. Parkham said with evident approval, redundant though it seemed after Tommy's introduction.

"Yes, ma'am."

"How wonderful that David's made friends with an American!" Mrs. Parkham said to Betty, who responded with a pained smile. "How ever did you meet?"

"We're camped near each other in – somewhere in France," Tommy said, faltering as he remembered, in time, all the injunctions against revealing his location there to anyone. Then he quite deliberately added some more information: "That's where he was wounded."

"Wounded? Oh!" Mrs. Parkham cried, turning to Betty. "You didn't say he was wounded."

"He's all right," David's sister snapped, and Tommy feared he might snap himself.

"He's limping pretty bad," Flowers stressed to the older woman. "He was hit in the leg by shrapnel when a plane bombed–"

"Oh, my!"

"He's *all right,*" Betty peremptorily repeated, to Tommy's escalating annoyance.

"Yes, he's all right, other than the limp," Tommy said to the both of them, pointedly adding, "thank God."

"Thank God indeed," Mrs. Parkham echoed, with more feeling than Tommy had yet heard from either Mrs. Pearson or Betty. There was an awkward pause; then, in an entirely different tone, she asked him, "What part of America are you from, Private Flowers?"

"Iowa, ma'am."

"Iowa. I don't know that. One of my sons is in Baltimore. I went to visit him there once, you know."

"Is that so? I've never been there myself."

"Yes. Well, welcome to Dunster, Private Flowers." He realized that this was the first time he'd heard those words since arriving in this village, as she continued, "Good day to the both of you."

They responded in kind; but as soon as Mrs. Parkham had closed the door behind her, Tommy turned swiftly to address Betty, saying brusquely, "He was almost killed, you know."

She made a pishing sound that only caused him to be still more irate. "I've already 'ad *two* who were more than *almost* killed," she said, adding stubbornly, "'E looks all right to me."

The Yank struggled to maintain courtesy, nearly shouting, "Davey's your brother, too! I would think–"

But she cut him off and, to his added irritation, broke into a snicker. "Davey? I never heard nobody call him Davey."

"Well, now you have." Suddenly Tommy couldn't stand to be in the same room with Betty. He couldn't begin to picture any of his sisters behaving in this way. Without another word, he stalked out of the public area, down the first-floor – no, it must be the ground-floor – hallway, not knowing where he might be headed.

Just before he reached the end of the hall, where a door opened onto the garden, he passed a doorway on his right. He was well past it when a voice drifted out: "David?" Backing up to the doorway, he caught sight of David's mother sitting at a small wood table, peeling some kind of vegetables. "Oh, it's you, Thomas," she said. He couldn't read whether it was pleasantry or disappointment in her voice.

"Yes, ma'am. David's still sleeping. But please call me Tommy."

"Tommy, then. Would you like a cup o'tea, Tommy?"

He wished he could ask if she had some rum to put in it, but merely said politely, "That'd be nice, Mrs. Pearson."

"Come sit," she said, patting the chair next to her not unlike the way her son had patted the bed, then rising to put on some water for the brew. Returning to the table, she smiled once at him, then quietly resumed her peeling.

After a few seconds, he asked, "Can I help?"

She looked up at him in surprise. "This is women's work."

He thought about all the women he'd seen in this country doing men's work, and said, "Where I come from, I used to husk corn. This ain't so different."

She hesitated, then got up, fetched a second knife, and handed it to him along with one of the vegetables. "What is it?" Tommy asked.

She again regarded him dubiously, said, "Why, it's a turnip, of course. They don't 'ave turnips in America?"

"Yes, but they don't look like this." Recalling how defensive David had been about his food, he added hastily, "I mean, there's nothing wrong with these–"

"Of course there's nothing wrong with them. I don't serve bad turnips."

"Of course you don't." He began to peel the thing, and she carefully noted the expertise with which he did so. She rose and poured the water into a teapot. "I read somewhere this was all there was to eat in Germany last winter," Tommy said of the turnips.

"And that's too much for the likes o'them," she said flatly.

"Hm."

She poured two cups of tea, and put one in front of him. She hadn't asked him about milk. At least this tea tasted like there was already sugar in it. "What's your family name, Tommy? David di'n't say."

Because you barely bothered to have a conversation with him, Tommy thought. "Flowers," he answered, and she replied, "What a pretty name. Too pretty for a boy."

"Well, it's my name, all the same. Would you like to give me another one of those?"

She picked up another turnip and handed it over. "You're quick," she observed.

"At some things. Your son's a lot quicker at some others."

She started. "My son? – Oh, yes."

It seemed obvious to Tommy she had automatically responded to "my son" by thinking of Colin, Doug, or both, but certainly not David. When she said no more, he couldn't hold back. "Mrs. Pearson, can I ask you something?"

"I s'po–"

He didn't wait. "Do you – do you *care* about David??"

She stared at him, then put down her knife. "Why, what a completely peculiar question! A mum cares for all of her children, of course. What d'you mean by asking me such a question?"

Tommy was defiant. "I – I just wanted to point out to you that you still have a son who's very much alive, right here."

She looked at him in something like horror, then retorted angrily, "I know that!" Then she turned away and added in a different tone, "But sometimes it seems 'e's already gone."

"But he's *not!*" Tommy said emphatically.

She turned back to him. "I b'lieve I understand your meaning now, Private Flowers. You think I'm 'orrible."

"I don't think you're horrible. I just don't understand – David's *here!* Why aren't you happy about that?"

She looked at him with eyes that suddenly seemed to him incredibly sad. "'E's ere, and I *am* 'appy for it. But 'e's going back, limp and all, ain't 'e?"

"Yes."

She looked down, then back over at him, and said with great difficulty, "Colin and Doug – each one of them came back 'ere, oncet, after it started, and I was so 'appy. And each time, I never sawr them again… D'you understand what I'm saying?"

"Yes, ma'am." Abruptly his anger didn't seem so righteous. He cleared his throat. "I'm sorry," he finally managed to add. "I had no right."

Thoroughly abashed now by the results of his outburst, Tommy withdrew into his task, silently peeling until he heard Mrs. Pearson say, "There'll be nothing left o'that if you don't stop." He put it down, and put his hand over his eyes, like he'd done on the country lane in France, when David had put the dying dog out of its misery; in the same way, he couldn't bear to look at her. He heard her get up, and felt her walk over and position herself directly in front of him. He wondered for a moment if she intended to slap him for his impudence. But instead her voice came down clearly from above: "You're a good boy. Your mother should be proud of you."

There was no hint of sarcasm, and he uncovered his eyes and looked up at her, saying doggedly, "He's a good boy, too."

She had looked quite serious, but now the slightest smile began to form. "I like 'ow you always come to 'is defense. Are you two truly good friends?"

"We're best mates," he replied in the English style, and she smiled a little more, showing – he noticed – good teeth.

"Good," she said. "That's very good. 'E's never 'ad a friend like you."

The similarity to David's phraseology sent a little chill through Tommy. "That's what he says, too. I don't understand it. A fine fellow like David – he should have lots of friends. And girls, too."

At that, David's mother's manner instantly became opaque, in precisely the same way her son's could. "Why don't you go upstairs now and wake up your best mate? It'll be time for supper soon."

"Sure, ma'am." As he rose, he couldn't help adding one more time, "I'm sorry about–"

She had picked up a wooden spoon for some task or other, and she shook it at him: "I don't want to 'ear that from you again in my 'ouse. You just be as good a mate to me David as you are, and you'll 'ave nothing to be sorry about. Now upstairs with you."

★

When Tommy reascended to the top room, David was awake, lying calmly on the bed, his hands folded behind his head, in the fading light of the day. "What 'ave you been up to?" he asked lazily when he caught sight of his Yank chum.

"You always read my mind," Tommy replied, sitting again on the far edge of the bed. "You tell me."

David sat partway up, leaning on his elbow, and said, "'Ave you been giving me family a 'ard time?"

Tommy pursed his lips and made a noise, and threw up his hands. "You see?" He turned his gaze to the hill opposite the house, which was changing colors rapidly in the late dusk of summer.

"Will it be safe to go to supper, then?" David finally addressed his back.

"Yes," Tommy said, adding with more emotion in his voice than he'd intended, "since your mother forgave me for being such a rude American."

"You're not rude, Tommy. You're never rude."

"I was to your mother," he said, swiftly turning about and looking at David to emphasize the point.

But David, who had returned to his original position, wasn't looking at Tommy just then, and he smugly said, "I don't believe it." Then he caught Tommy's gaze, paused, said "Oh," and eventually added, "And Betty?"

"I can't see that I owe her any apology."

David understood his meaning there, and he marked his friend a little longer, then said, "You do form your opinions in a 'urry, don't you?"

Misreading the comment entirely, Tommy said, "I can go back to London early, by myself, if you want me to."

That caused David to sit up completely. "What's this? 'Oo said anything of the kind?" Tommy turned away from him again. "Why are you being so tetchy?"

Flowers looked back. "Tetchy?"

"You know – taking offense so easy."

"Oh, touchy!" Tommy deliberately paused a moment, then said to his friend, "Why don't you people learn to speak English?"

The Yank was still on the right side of the bed, his feet planted on the floor, his torso twisted toward Pearson as they conversed. At this last wisecrack, David made a playful lunge in a mock effort at strangling his pal, causing Tommy to shift his weight full force back onto the bed and grab for David. Within seconds they were engaging in that boyish sport called "rassling" back in Iowa, something Tommy had seen other fellows do with their brothers, or maybe their friends, but had not participated in himself; clearly, though, it was a familiar game to David. They grappled and tumbled and giggled on the bed like a couple of schoolboys, their hilarity growing by the moment.

After a minute or two of this tomfoolery, David made to break free, but Tommy was quicker, enveloping his friend and throwing him back down on the bed, then climbing on top of David, pinning the latter's hands on either side of his head, although the Briton had ceased to offer much resistance. They both were still laughing, a little out of breath and full of fun.

Suddenly Tommy felt suffused with a particular kind of warmth, lying there on top of his yielding buddy and gasping for breath. He looked down at David, who appeared totally happy and carefree as he gulped for air in the same way, and some urge from nowhere seized him. Much quicker than the one other time he'd done so, Tommy bent down his head and kissed David full on the lips, letting himself linger once he was there.

But unlike the previous time, it wasn't a single, isolated action, and David didn't question it; this time he brought his hand 'round the back of Tommy's head and kissed him in return, and now Tommy felt that warmth rushing along the length of both their bodies. It was just like what had happened with Nicole – but how could that be? The fleeting thought was obliterated by David's insistent mouth and hands, as they began to respond to each other, first slowly and gently, then fiercely, frantically, almost furiously, until there was a sheer need to come up for air.

Tommy pulled his head, which was now swimming, back up slightly from David's, and as had happened with Nicole in the field, there was a sudden recognition of what they'd been doing – only this time it was different, because they both seemed to come to at once; David looked up into his face, still swallowing air, and said plainly, once, "Oh!"

And there was something else different for Tommy: he wasn't overwhelmed with guilt; he wanted to do more, take it further. They hadn't progressed beyond kissing and touching, and were both still fully clothed; he wanted, needed to find out what came next.

"David! Tommy!" came a voice from two stories below, and rather than startling them, or causing either one to tense, they started laughing with each other. "It's time for supper!"

"We'll be right down, Mum," Pearson eventually called from his position on the bed beneath Flowers, more confidence in his voice than there'd been in weeks, maybe ever. His eyes never left Tommy's face. Then he whispered, "You'll 'ave to let me up, Tommy."

"Never," the American said with a sly smile, to the pure delight of both.

But then David said "Come along, now," and although his voice remained cheery, he was beginning to push at Tommy for real. Fear came flooding into Flowers' head and heart – fear that now this had happened between them, if they went down to dinner, nothing like it would ever happen again. But he could tell David really meant it about getting up, and he couldn't fight that.

He sprang up and off the bed and turned again to the back window, where the deepening blue of sky colored the garden and the hillside. He straightened himself, his uniform, brushed his hands through his hair as he heard David doing likewise behind him. Something about the peaceful view – probably the shade of the early-evening summer light – perversely made him feel he was back at the front, and with the advent of that feeling, he tried to blot out of his mind everything that had just happened between him and his pal. That in turn was interrupted by the feeling of David's arms – those strong, small arms he'd noticed that first night in the stable – wrapping themselves firmly around him, the head resting on his upper back. "C'm'ere, you" came David's voice, in a low, guttural growl Tommy'd never heard from him, but liked. The Doughboy swiveled about and, standing this time, they were right back at each other again.

After what seemed like too few moments, again it was David who broke it off. Neither one said a thing; David just nodded slowly at Tommy, raising his eyebrows once or twice, smiling and exhaling long as he straightened the Yank's tie. Tommy grinned wide in return, and he descended the stairways behind David fully confident they were thinking and feeling the same way, without another word exchanged.

The hard part would be sitting still through dinner.

# Chapter XXX

Mercifully, Mrs. Pearson had placed David and Tommy opposite each other, and the four of them proceeded to have a pleasant supper comprising the turnips, some potatoes, carrots, and peas, all stewed with a very little bit of mutton, something Tommy'd never tasted. The bread, he couldn't help noticing, was of the same gray variety as he'd had at the Shipleys'; he'd hoped for better at a bakery but, back on his best behavior, didn't dream of mentioning it.

On the other hand, Betty, who sat like a smoldering dark cloud at her end of the table, had no such compunctions. They were well through the meal, with Tommy relating the composition of his family back in America to Mrs. Pearson, when the daughter of the household said, apropos of nothing, "I'm sick of this rotten potato bread."

Breaking the awkward silence that followed this outburst, Mrs. Pearson said, "We're all sick of many things, dear. 'Tis a sacrifice we all 'ave to make. 'Tisn't much compared with what your brothers and Mr. Flowers, 'ere, 'ave 'ad to put up with."

Not cowed, Betty turned a resentful face to Tommy and said, "You don't eat gray bread made from potatoes in America, do you?"

"Why – no, our bread's made from wheat–"

"Ours used to be wheat, too, before the war. Now we can't afford it. Only rich Americans can–"

"I'm – not a rich American, Miss Pearson."

"All Americans are rich – or they're getting rich, off o'the likes of us!"

"Betty, you're being rude." It was David, sternly cutting through the conversation. She grew silent, evidently intimidated by this comment from her brother. But then he tried to add a little levity: "When the war's over and I come 'ome, we shan't 'ave any more potato bread 'ere at the bakery. It'll be only wheat bread, I promise."

Betty made a brief, angry, inchoate "ohh" sound and stood up, saying, "Excuse me, Mum," then stormed out. They all listened as she marched up the stairs and down the hall to her bedroom.

Had any of Tommy's sisters behaved so in front of company, his mother would have been mortified for a minimum of one week, and his father would have soundly spanked her. But Mrs. Pearson remained relatively untroubled. While acknowledging with a nod her daughter's inappropriate behavior, she said with a shrug, "She's just become impossible."

"Why?" Tommy asked from genuine interest, and he felt David give him a swift, if not particularly hard, kick under the table with his good leg. Rather than being annoyed by this, Tommy found himself enjoying the renewed physical contact, and he telegraphed that with a quick smile to David, who had to turn away because of the grin it aroused in him, even though he'd meant the kick.

"It's all the deaths, y'see," David's mother, oblivious, began, and now Tommy could see David's point.

"Per'aps I'll go up and try to talk with 'er," David interrupted brightly, in an obvious attempt to derail his mother's train of thought. As he rose, he added, "Tommy, you 'aven't told Mum about Susan."

It struck Tommy as especially out of place. His mind and heart were fixed wholly on David, and he didn't feel like discussing a girl thousands of miles away. But when Mrs. Pearson naturally, politely asked who this Susan was, he found himself rattling on about his girl in Iowa.

"You're engaged to be married, then," she said.

"Oh – no, ma'am, we're not, not exactly."

"Oh?"

"Well, I've always thought – I mean, everyone's always expected–"

Mrs. Pearson reached over to pat his hand. "When you get back 'ome. I understand."

He wondered if Colin or Doug had been engaged. He knew Betty had, but he didn't want to bring her up. That reticence proved unnecessary when raised voices – Betty's and David's – drifted down from upstairs. Mrs. Pearson sighed and shook her head. "I knew that wou'n't work. Those two 'ave never got along, not really."

"How come?"

"You said you 'ad sisters – three, wasn't it?" Tommy nodded, and she continued, "Do they all get on with each other, and with you?"

"Absolutely."

David and Betty's mother suddenly got that look of staring off into space, like the lady on the train yesterday morning. "They're the two youngest, y'see. She always looked up to 'er older brothers–"

"So did he. He still does."

She seemed pleased that Tommy knew this. "But she doesn't look up to 'im. She's older than 'im."

It seemed a weak explanation, so Tommy felt prompted to ask, "Is there anything else?"

"Oh… I don't know… David di'n't approve of Hugh."

She had dropped the "H" in pronouncing the name, and Tommy was momentarily taken completely aback. "What do you mean, he didn't approve of me?"

"Not you. Hugh. Hugh Collins, Betty's beau."

"Oh. Sorry."

"But Doug di'n't approve of 'im, neither. Colin di'n't mind. Anyways, now they're all gone – Colin, Doug, Hugh – all except David. Sometimes I think she resents David coming 'round and playing the boss with 'er." She related all this in a voice remarkably steady, considering she was discussing two dead sons and one potential son-in-law who was also lost. Then she seemed to snap out of her far-away trance, cutting a different look at Tommy. "Understand, if anything 'appened to 'im, she'd go wild. It would be – She can't take one more, she can't. And neither can I. But we're not the sort to show it."

In Tommy's opinion, David had a damaged leg to prove something had "'appened" to him already. But he knew she meant something much more final, and his sympathies were shifting back to David's family: they did love their youngest after all, he realized, and David knew it even if he, Tommy, had failed to recognize it. But he had no sooner completed this thought than David's mother said, "They were such unusual boys, Tommy – Colin and Doug."

Once again straining to remain cordial, he noted, "David said Doug always had a lot of girls."

"'E did. Colin was our oldest, and Doug – Doug was so special–"

"I happen to think David's special, too," Tommy blurted out.

"–so 'andsome. That's why there were so many girls." She paused long enough for the novel thought to surface in Tommy's mind that *he* thought *David* was handsome. At least he knew better than to say that. But Mrs. Pearson had returned to the subject of her youngest, after a fashion: "You're always speaking up for David. It's so nice. 'E's needed that."

Obviously, Tommy thought, but he said, "Everybody needs that."

As they finished this exchange, the object of their discussion came trudging back down the stairs and sullenly rejoined them at their table. "No luck?" Tommy inquired cheerfully, and David scowled and shook his head. Alarmed that the spirit between the two of them might have been spoiled, Tommy pressed, "Should I speak to her?"

David looked at him as though he thought the Yank had thoroughly lost his mind; but on second consideration, he said, "Tomorrow, per'aps. Not tonight."

Reading into that what he wanted to hear, Tommy replied, "Of course. Not tonight." The slightest spark in David's eye told Tommy the former had caught his meaning; to confirm it, Pearson half smiled and shook his head, looking away.

"Time to clear this away," Mrs. Pearson announced, breaking the ensuing quiet.

"Do you need help?" Tommy asked.

"Betty usually does," David interjected, and Tommy reminded him, "But she's not tonight."

"That's true," David said, largely to himself; then he asked his mother, "Shall we 'elp, Mum?"

She looked dumbfounded, then, nodding at Tommy, told her son, "You should stick with 'im. 'E's got good manners, that one, and it's rubbing off on the likes o'you.

"But no" – now she addressed Tommy – "you've done enough women's work for one day." To the both of them, she added, "I can manage these"; then, to David again, "You'll be wanting to take Tommy to the pub now, anyways."

"I don't know, Mum. We're both tired–"

"Word's 'round the village. They'll be expecting you at the Stag's 'Ead."

David looked over at Tommy. Neither one wanted to go out, and they both sensed it, but… .

"Just a little while, then," David said.

As they stepped out of the bakery onto the now-dark West Street, David turned to Tommy and said, "Should I show you 'round the town?"

"I'd like that… *tomorrow*." The extra emphasis made them both titter, but nervously; the ease they'd felt earlier had evaporated. They were stuck with talking about anything but what was uppermost in their minds. "So," Tommy finally said, "where's this pub?"

"Right up the street 'ere, on the other side."

"So, let's go have a drink. Pretend we're at Madame's. But I hope there's something better than French beer, or van rooj, or van blank."

"Yes, there's bitters. But I'm afraid there's no Nicole."

They were walking, but now Tommy stopped and gave David a look pregnant with meaning. "That's all right with me."

David rolled his eyes heavenward and smiled broadly. "You're incorrigible. Come along, then."

All was fairly quiet at the Stag's Head, but the instant they entered, Tommy liked its comfortable, homey feeling. It was just as smoky as Madame's *estaminet,* but with more and softer chairs, and a smaller crowd. An old man stood behind the counter, and Tommy had the feeling he was there not because some younger man had gone off to war, but because he'd been there for many a year.

"David Pearson," the old man called expansively as they approached the bar, and David introduced Tommy and ordered two bitters. Tommy remembered again he had no English money; when the drinks were served, he tried to give his friend francs, but David pushed the French money away. Tommy took the mug and lifted it to his lips – as warm and as bad as French beer. He made an elaborate show of liking the stuff to the old man, but he could see David, amused, wasn't fooled one bit.

There was a fireplace, but since it was July and the night was fairly warm, he and David sat down across from each other and stared at where the fire would have been. "Say," came a voice from behind both of them. They both turned to see a rather large man with a trim little mustache and a Tommy's uniform swaying somewhat uncertainly over them. He was clearly on his third or fourth bitters, at least. Addressing David, he said, "You're Colin Pearson's brother, aren't you?"

"Yes, I am."

"Good man, Colin."

"Yes, 'e was."

"You're – Doug?"

"No, Doug's–" David hesitated, then went on: "Doug's gone west, too. I'm David."

"Oh, right, of course, the little one. And who's this Yank chap?"

"Me best pal. Come 'ome with me on leave."

The large Tommy looked doubtfully at Flowers. "An American on leave? Your lot just got here." Though they were in England, the "here" clearly meant France.

"Spot o'luck," David said quickly, heading off any comment from Tommy.

"Can I buy you a drink?" the large man asked, and he offered Flowers a matching paw. "Name's Williburton. Evelyn Williburton."

As they reluctantly followed Williburton to the bar, Tommy whispered to Davey, "Eve-lynn? That sounds like two girls' names to me."

"It's a bloke's name 'ere. But only if you're" – David tilted his chin upward and rapped the underside of it a couple of times with the back of his hand, indicating "upper class" as clearly as if he'd said the words – "y'see."

"Well, then, we should get along," Tommy said quietly, "seeing as I'm such a rich American and all." This caused them both to snicker until Williburton wheeled about:

"So, gentlemen. What will it be?"

Two hours later, Tommy and David were staggering a little as they finally broke free of the very drunk Williburton and headed outside into the night air. So much had happened since the morning that Tommy felt as though he'd been awake for days. They were both trying to keep their balance, keep their voices down, keep from laughing in the manner of the slightly inebriated. They had stumbled the few houses back to Pearson's family bake shop when Flowers looked up and, just like that, sobered up. "Davey," he said solemnly.

"What?" Pearson responded with a half-drunken laugh; then he felt Tommy's arms grip him and turn him bodily so he was facing the heavens.

"Look at the stars" was all the Yank said, and doing so had the exact same effect on the Briton, who simply said, "Cor."

"Do you remember when you told me about how you went out in the country to see the comet?"

Recalling that entire evening, David replied, "'Ow could I forget that?"

"Do you think you could take me there, where you said you all went? Is it far?"

Tommy's eyes were aglitter in the moonlight, partly with alcohol but mostly with other things. Seeing this, David said, "'Tisn't far at all. We could go there right now."

"Then let's."

"Follow me," David said, both of them suddenly as businesslike as if they'd been ordered out on a night raid.

They returned back up West Street with David in the lead, then cut through the churchyard, then down a lane under a stone arch. Intoxicated with drink, the night, the village, David and himself, Tommy said with loud cheeriness, "You always know the way," but his pal shushed him.

The giddiness was superseded by a seriousness of purpose as they traversed around a circular stone building – "The dovecote," David informed him in a whisper – then under a second stone arch and past several houses with thatched roofs. At the end of the lane, they took a path that ran alongside a field, which sloped sharply upward to a wood. David hopped a stile in a fence, showing Tommy how to do it, and they began walking through neat rows of crops. The ground swelled ever higher, and just at the edge of the woods, David turned about.

"'Ere we are," he said, coming to a standing halt so unexpected that Tommy bumped into him; then, as Tommy turned round, the reason became clear: a 180-degree vista, breathtaking even in the nighttime, taking in Dunster and the hills surrounding it. With the ground now moist with evening dew, neither one was inclined to sit or lie down, and Tommy came around back of David and naturally slipped his arms around his friend, reversing what they'd done back at the house – a different fit, equally comfortable. "D'you know we're facing south and east?" David said as Tommy nuzzled the top of his head; the observation caused the American to look up and out. "I used to fancy, when I was little, that I could see all the way to France, 'cause if you go far enough south and east from 'ere, that's where you would land."

Tommy tightened his hold on David, finally said, "Can we not talk about France for the next couple of days?"

David stirred, looked back at him. "I wasn't thinking of it that ways. But it's 'ard not to, isn't it? I mean, the sky 'ere is no more magnificent than that night we were out in France, you and me. But the 'ole countryside's so different."

Tommy was trying to push the parts of that night he didn't care to remember – the dogs, the aeroplane, and above all the makeshift cemetery – from his mind. "What's different is here everything's at peace," he said.

"'Ow can you say that, Tommy?" David cried, breaking free of his embrace and turning completely back around to face him. "You can see 'ow the war's changed everything 'ere, even if you've never been 'ere before. You're much too bright not to 'ave noticed."

Concentrating, picking his words carefully, since David was so insistent on having this discussion right now, Tommy answered, "Sure, the war's changed things here, even more than it's changed things back home in Brooklyn – and it's even changed some things there. But no one's fighting *here.* There's no danger right here, right now. That's the difference. And that makes all the difference in the world."

They were both cold sober now. After a pause, it was David who reached out, entwining his arms around Tommy's waist and leaning his head against the Yank's chest. "I s'pose you're right. You remember that night, though, don't you?"

"All of it. As clear as yesterday. But I don't want to talk about it right now, either."

"No? What d'you want to do, then?" David asked, looking up at him not a little flirtatiously.

"I think I know what I want to do," Tommy replied in a husky voice, "but I don't want to talk about *that,* either."

More tentatively than before, David reached up, brushed Tommy's hair and then his cheek. Once that happened, they both lost their hesitation, and started romancing in the moonlight like many a couple who no doubt had stood here before them, but unlike them, too. They had just relaxed into each other's hold when there was a sudden, faint rustling noise in the woods up above them. Unlike the sound of David's mother calling them for supper, it caused them both to jump. Tommy grabbed David's hand, an urgent grip, and motioned with his head.

"Let's go back," he said with an imperative tone David couldn't deny and had no desire to, anyway.

Hand in hand, they walked back into town in agitated silence, then let go of each other as they crept through the deserted streets, across the churchyard, down West Street, and back into the dark bakery. As they ascended the double flight of stairs again, David whispered, "I've got to use the loo – and brush me teeth, of course."

"Of course," Tommy said, and they both tried to cover their laughter, remembering their previous discussion of toothbrushes. Then each recalled to himself that they'd had the talk while lying naked on the grass in the French sunshine, and their anxiousness increased.

Tommy waited upstairs, then descended to the loo himself after David returned; now he did tiptoe. When he reascended, the curtains to both windows in the upstairs room had been drawn – although they could easily have been left open on such a warm night – and a soft light was glowing within. David sat on the edge of the bed in his underclothes, much as he'd been dressed the first night in the stable. Tommy quickly shed his own outer clothes and sat down on the bed next to him. They'd said very little since standing on the hillside, and each still felt just a tad insecure about what would happen next.

"So," David finally asked, "what d'you think, mate?"

Tommy looked at David, looked at himself, cleared his throat, looked back to David, and took the final risk: "I think it's much too warm in here to wear underwear to bed. What do you think?"

David responded by standing up and peeling off his underwear. As he watched Tommy do the same, he whispered, "I think we must try to be very quiet, what with me mum and sis right below us." Both thoroughly aroused, they made an initial exploration of each other's bodies standing, running the flats of their palms over one another. It was the first time Tommy had seen David's leg, the skin of which was a frightening collection of stripes and zigzags. When he knelt to examine it more closely, David tried halfheartedly to break away and douse the light.

"No," Tommy declared in a whisper, and he began to massage the injured limb, first with his hands, then with his mouth. David shivered, ran his fingers through Tommy's hair, called his name questioningly.

"What?"

"Can we get into bed now? I don't want it all to go too fast."

Tommy rose and kissed him, and now he was the one who turned to put out the light, saying, "Me neither."

# Chapter XXXI

In the morning, Tommy woke to sunlight filling the room – and, to his keen disappointment, an empty spot next to him in the bed. He thought perhaps David had just gone down to the loo, but after enough time passed that it seemed clear he wasn't coming back immediately, Tommy reluctantly stirred. In the light of dawn, all of yesterday seemed like some particularly vivid storybook he had read; but no, there was the garden and the hillside out the back window, and out front there was the picturesque village and the quaint street, surprisingly full with people, considering it looked to be very early indeed.

Last night, too, might have passed for a dream, a feeling accentuated by David's absence, but there was plenty of evidence to the contrary, from Tommy's own unclad state (his stay at the Shipleys' notwithstanding, he seldom slept in the raw) to a slight stickiness on his skin and a few faint scents about the room, all reminding him it had been quite real. Under the circumstances, had he awakened first, he would have waited for David. But perhaps his beloved Davey was gifted with the same practicality that allowed his mum to send them upstairs before finishing the working day and shifting her attention to her sole surviving son, back home for such a short, precious visit. It was the kind of pragmatism Flowers was beginning to wish he could cultivate.

He dressed and ventured down the stairs, and noticed the bake shop was not yet open. Wandering down the hallway, he heard no sounds indicating the presence of other people, but passing the kitchen he discovered, to his dismay, Betty, who confounded expectations by pleasantly smiling and saying, "Good morning, Private Flowers. Did you get a good night's rest?"

Too thrown off by her changed manner to ponder the irony of his being asked this particular question this particular morning, Tommy gave an automatic, polite reply, true as far as it went: "I slept very well, Miss Pearson, thank you. I hope you did the same."

"I did," she said with a slight lilt to her voice. "That's good, that you slept well. It's early yet, so I thought per'aps you hadn't."

"Is it really that early? I seem to be the last one up," he pointed out.

"We're country people," she replied with an amiable shrug, "up before the sunrise."

"I'm country people, too."

"Really?" She paused, then: "Oh! Where's my manners? Would you like a cup of tea?"

Somewhat emboldened, Tommy responded, "You wouldn't have any coffee, would you?"

She hesitated a fraction, then smiled again. "Yes, we have a little, for special company. And I s'pose that would be you, wou'n't it?"

Having been made aware he'd requested special treatment, Tommy started to tell her to forget it, then decided that would only compound the awkwardness. As she made to prepare the brew, he changed the subject, and tested her good humor: "Where's Davey and your mother?"

She didn't smirk this time at her brother's nickname, and he had to wonder if some other girl had secretly replaced the unfriendly sister of yesterday. "They're at the market on the high street," she answered. "It opens at dawn, and there's so little there these days, you have to get there at first light or there's nothing to buy. It's something David always did with Mum."

Her sudden volubility opened up a wealth of possibilities for conversation, and Tommy thought about his offer to speak with her about her quarrel with David. She was pretty, he finally realized, even if she couldn't compare to her brother in his eyes. Gingerly Flowers said, "The war has changed everything here, hasn't it?"

"More or less," she agreed calmly, with a nod. "Would you like something to eat, too?"

"Did they already have breakfast?" he asked in return, and she shook her head.

"Don't think so. They usually wait 'til they get back."

"I'll just have the coffee for now, then."

"Suit yourself," Betty said lightly, "but I believe I'll have a little myself, if you don't mind. I'll have to open the shop soon."

Taking another chance, Tommy asked her, "Gray bread?"

She didn't look especially chastened by this allusion to her outburst of yesterday, instead admitting, "Mum was right. We have to make do. But I miss real bread, I won't deny it."

"Can't you put something on it to improve the taste?"

She again shook her head but said, "A bit o'jam, per'aps."

"Ticklers?"

She smiled at him once more. "Now, how would you know that? Do they have that same brand in America?"

"No, it was in David's kit. But I think the Tommies are all sick of it, at least the plum and apple."

"Well, they're not the only ones."

"I reckon you can't wait 'til the war ends."

To his surprise, she looked mildly troubled by the comment. At length she replied, "I s'pose I can't. I'd like having things like real bread again. And of course I want David to come back safe."

It was an acknowledgment he wouldn't have thought her capable of the day before; on the other hand, her order of priorities did not escape his notice. She continued, "But not everything about the peace – if we ever see a peace – might be all that wonderful."

"How's that?"

She decided the coffee was ready, and she brought him his cup, then came over and sat down next to him with her own cup and her toasted gray bread. Concentrating on the task at hand, she initially ignored his question, telling him, "We're out of milk. They should be back with some soon. I'm afraid I forgot to mention it. There is sugar, though."

"I'll just try it that way," Tommy said, spooning it in. The coffee tasted all right with the sugar, though milk would have improved it from his point of view.

Before he could say anything else, she picked up on his previous question. "The war has been horrible for me, Private Flowers. I wisht it never happened. But there are things I have learnt from it, things I might not have known but for the war. One is that I like running the shop."

Tommy was quick to catch her meaning. "So, when the war ends, and Davey comes back–"

"–it'll be his shop." A trace, and then some, of yesterday's tone crept back into her voice. "I'm the one's put the most work into it since Dad died, even before they all left. But it'll be his shop."

Tommy noted, without their names ever being mentioned, that her resentment extended to Colin and Doug. If she hadn't proclaimed the situation an injustice in so many words, clearly she felt that way. "Well, of course, he's a man," he said. "He needs a trade."

"Any man that's still standing will be able to choose his trade once this war's over," she retorted, "especially a young man what's fit. But what am I s'posed to do?"

"Why – you'll get married, of cour–"

"To *who,* Private Flowers?" she interrupted. "To who? 'Ow many young men 'ave you seen 'round 'ere?" She was now as angry as ever, and it occurred to him that when her emotions were aroused, she sounded more like Davey and her mother, dropping her h's as they did.

He stated the obvious. "Not many, of course. They're all at the front."

"Even more's *dead,*" she said emphatically. "There's not many are coming back, and certainly not in one piece. Not near enough for all the girls like me to marry. And the best are already gone."

He found room to resent this last remark, but after all the politeness, her bitterness was bracing. "Still, a girl like you–"

"A girl like me stands no better chance than any other, Private Flowers. I 'ave to be a realist. If I've learnt anything, it's that."

Endeavoring yet again for something to keep a conversation civil, Tommy recalled, "Mrs. Landis said you had a good head for business."

He could see that, momentarily at least, he had hit the mark. "'Ow do you know Mrs. Landis?" Betty asked.

"We met her yesterday, on the walk in."

"And she said that?"

"About you? Yes, she did."

Betty could not hide being pleased; but then her expression darkened, and she declared, "All the same, there I'll be, working for 'im, at 'is pleasure."

Tommy could think of no response; then, to his astonishment, her voice took on a pleading tone: "You're 'is best mate. I can tell 'e listens to you. Can't you talk to 'im about it? You understand, don't you? You're an American. You're not stuck on old-fashioned notions like an Englishman."

"Next you'll be telling me women should vote, Miss Pearson."

"And why not?"

That brought him up short. He had mentioned the issue carelessly, had tossed it out because he'd assumed everyone in the world felt about it the way those back home who ventured an opinion did. There was something in his pride at being an American that prevented him from telling her outright that he believed as strongly as David in the "old-fashioned notion" that the shop was her brother's by right. Whether or not she sensed this, she played on it expertly. Having elicited no response from him on women's suffrage, she pressed him on the matter closest to her heart. "Am I wrong about Americans, then? Per'aps you're not any more modern than fussy old Englishmen, after all."

Feeling he was being compared to the likes of Williburton rather than David, Tommy inevitably replied, "Of course we're more modern–"

"Then you'll talk to 'im about it?"

Reluctantly he said, "I'll talk to him, if that's what you want. But I'm not promising anything."

She gave him her largest, most sincere smile yet. "Oh, thank you, Private Flowers. Thank you." As they continued a few minutes more, sliding into the smallest of small talk, Tommy had trouble shaking off the feeling he'd been led into an ambush.

Presently they both stirred at the sound of the bell and the banging of the front door to the shop. "That'll be them," Betty said, and as they rose, abruptly Tommy was on edge about seeing David again, in the light of day, with others around.

They all converged behind the bake shop counter. David was loaded down with several packages, and Mrs. Pearson was carrying a few of her own. Davey's limp seemed especially pronounced this morning, and Tommy made to relieve him of some of his load. "'Ere," said David with a gruffness that was not unfriendly, but which stung Tommy nonetheless. "It's me mum needs the 'elp, not me."

Tommy turned to David's mother, but Betty already had gathered up half or more of her burden. "Y'see, there's milk for your coffee now, Private Flowers," David's sister sang out, and David said, "Raided the coffee, did we?" wounding Tommy further. The Yank thoroughly regretted not taking tea; how was he to know coffee was such a scarce commodity?

"Did you 'ave a bit o'breakfast, Tommy?" Mrs. Pearson asked as all four of them bustled into the pantry, everyone but Flowers busily putting items in their proper places.

"No, ma'am. I thought I'd wait for you and Davey."

"Oh?" It was the first time David's mother had heard Tommy's nickname for her son. "You di'n't 'ave to, y'know. You could've et with Betty."

"He did keep me company, Mum. We had a nice chat."

"That's good," Mrs. Pearson said to Flowers, who stood in deep confusion; it seemed the only person coming to his defense today was the one who'd been implacably hostile yesterday.

David, who didn't seem even to want to look at him, addressed his mother: "Were you planning on making us some breakfast, then, Mum?"

"Yes, David, I was, soon's Betty and I open the shop and all."

"Can we help you with that?" Tommy offered.

"No, Tommy," David's mother replied kindly. "We do it every day, so we 'ave our own way that works for us. Besides, I think our David's keen to take you 'round and show you the village while it's still early. It's very pretty at this hour."

Tommy thought Dunster was pretty at any hour, but by now he was eager to be alone with David again, and he readily agreed. However, the eagerness turned to something else after they took a right out the shop's front door and David announced in a brisk, businesslike tone: "So, 'ere's West Street in the daylight. That's the Stag's 'Ead over there."

"I think I can figure that out," Tommy said, more sarcasm in his voice than he intended. "I may not have your sense of direction, but I can tell that."

David looked at him without looking at him. "I s'pose you're right. It's not much diff'rent from the nighttime. Shall we go see the 'igh street, then?"

"We saw the high street yesterday," Tommy reminded him impatiently.

"But it's full o'people now. A bit more interesting."

Tommy couldn't believe they were having this ridiculous, trivial conversation, as if he were a tourist and David some stranger acting as his guide. Too upset to speak, he turned away from the Briton, facing the downhill slope of West Street. "All right, then," came David's voice from behind, sounding exasperated, "let's 'ave a look at the countryside." In a manner bordering on brusque, Pearson brushed past Flowers and led him down the street until they took a lane off to their left.

"What's this street called?" Tommy asked the back of David's head in temporary resignation, more to have something to say than out of genuine interest.

"Park Street. The one before it's Mill Lane. There's a water mill where we get our flour," David called back over his shoulder.

With his buddy so unresponsive, Tommy's attention roamed to take in his surroundings. It was, in fact, a lovely day. The early-morning sunlight was clear and brilliant, giving a light golden cast to the neat little houses washed in shades of pink and yellow as well as white, many with thatched roofs. They tramped down a narrow lane, then strode across a short stone bridge that spanned a shallow, sparkling stream. Tommy had just thought to himself that they would probably call it a "river" here when David confirmed it by informing him it was "the River Avill."

They passed one last set of thatched-roof white cottages, all pressed together into one long row, then reached a place at the village's edge where David jumped a weathered wooden turnstile. Tommy, truly not as good at directions, said tentatively, "This isn't the way we went last night?" and David, sounding testy, responded, "Of course not."

Tommy fell silent once more as he followed David up a steepening slope crisscrossed with muddy footpaths. As they climbed, he began to see, off to his left, the flat green plain and marshland surrounding the Avill, and on the other side of it Dunster rising on steadily sharper slopes, with the castle dominating all from its perch, hiding West Street and the Pearsons' place. Beyond that he recognized the hill they had climbed last night, crowned with woods and, he realized, the tower he had spotted from the train.

As they reached the crest of the hill they were now walking, they were suddenly surrounded by placid, slow-moving cattle, black and white. The glorious vista to the west, basking in the rays of the still-early sun, was now complemented by a sweeping view northward, back down the other side of the rise and out to the water, to the Bristol Channel. David, in front, stopped short, and Tommy pulled up behind, but did not gather the smaller man in his arms as he had the previous night.

"One of my favorite spots," David finally said, and Tommy commented guardedly,

"I can see why."

They stood there in silence for a while; then Tommy, suddenly feeling the lack of breakfast, took notice of a large, old, felled tree which, though damp with dew, appeared dry enough to be inviting. Without a word, the Doughboy plodded over to it and seated himself, gazing west, back toward the village and its castle, and away from Pearson. He looked down and, incongruously, fixed on his muddy boots. Good thing there was no roll call today; Maple would have marched him right back to the captain, yet again – no, wait, it wouldn't be Maple anymore. He wondered who his new sergeant would be when he got back to France.

The reverie was broken by a second pair of muddy boots materializing just to the left of his – David, seating himself next to Tommy, very close. Flowers said nothing, and Pearson's voice, full of the sort of gentleness Tommy'd missed all morning, floated to the Yank's ears. "So, 'ow are you, Tommy. All right, I 'ope?"

The American regarded the Briton full face and said, "Nice of you to finally ask."

A stricken look, though not a surprised one, swiftly made its appearance on Pearson's face. "You're cross with me, aren't you?"

"I reckon I am, some."

The stricken look deepened. "I'm sorry," David whispered quickly. With some difficulty, he added, "It's all me own fault, Tommy. I know it was wicked and evil–"

Tommy gave David a look of perfect perplexity, and interrupted: "What?"

David stared at him, then sighed. "Tommy," he finally said, "d'you 'ave any idea what they call… what we did last night?"

David's tone frightened Tommy. "No. I didn't know there was a word for it. I didn't even know it was possible 'til last night."

"It's called – the sin of Sodom," David said solemnly. After a pause, he added, "Surely you've 'eard of that."

"S-Sodom?" Tommy laughed nervously. Of course he'd heard of Sodom before, in Bible school, but nobody had explained what the city's sin was, only that it was so terrible God had destroyed it. "You must be mistaken, David. That was a long time ago. And this just happened, last night."

David looked at him in renewed amazement. "'Twasn't the first time in 'istory it's ever 'appened between two blokes, y'know."

"How – how do you know that?"

David rolled his eyes. "'Ow d'you think?"

Realizing the import of David's statement, Tommy felt a stab of pain so intense it might as well have been a bayonet. "David!" he cried, rising up distraught. "You mean there's others? Other fellows?"

"Was, Tommy. And only one, really," David answered truthfully. Seeing the agony on Tommy's face, he gripped the latter's hand. "'Twasn't anything like with you. Please don't think that. 'Twasn't the same at all–"

But Flowers could not let go of the thought, and he shook Pearson off. "But another fellow? Davey!"

Suddenly defensive, Pearson came back with "And what about you and Susan? Or your Nicole?"

There wasn't much to say about Susan, really, but Tommy realized at that moment he'd never had the chance to tell David about Nicole, about what had happened between him and the French girl in the field. "Nicole? She's a girl!" he shouted. "What happened with her and me – it's not the same!"

Instantly, Tommy could see his outburst had inflicted a wound on David as grievous as the one he'd just suffered. To comfort them both, he sat back down and added honestly, "I don't understand what you mean about wicked and evil."

David shook his head. "Tommy, 'ave you never 'eard of Oscar Wilde?"

"Who's that? What's he got to do with us?"

Trying another tack, David began, "They say–"

"They? Who's 'they'? The same 'they' that say it's bad luck to get killed on a Friday?" His anxiety overflowing, Tommy asked, "Is this why you wouldn't talk to me all morning? You wouldn't even look at me."

"I was afraid you wou'n't want to talk to me," David said plainly.

Thoroughly agitated, Tommy responded, "Why – why would I want that, today of all days?" Now it was his face that reflected pain. "Are you–?" He stopped, then he voiced his worst fears: "Are you – sorry? I was so *happy* last night, Davey. I thought you were, too–"

"I was. Am. So 'appy it frightens me. But I was afraid of just this – afraid it would upset you."

"If I'm upset, it's 'cause you wouldn't talk to me this morning – and you weren't there when I woke up."

Tommy let that sink in, and now it was David's turn for disbelief. His eyes widened. "And not – you're saying not because of the other…? You don't think it's wrong, what 'appened?"

"Davey, I *loved* what happened last night! I don't understand it, but I want it to happen again, and again."

The straightforward declaration hit Pearson with such force that from sheer relief, he began to laugh. "What?" Flowers demanded. "What's so funny?"

"N-nothing," David stammered through his mirth.

"What is it, then?"

"It's – it's not…" David waved his hands and looked away, and Tommy said, "You're turning red."

"I – I don't know I could ever get used to the way you Americans – just *say* things, sometimes." As he said this, David swung his head back toward Tommy, who replied, "Well, I hope you'll try to get used to *this* American." David smiled and looked away again. "Look at me," Tommy commanded, and David obeyed. "You're still red," he said, his voice softening by the second. "It looks so – it looks – it looks wonderful on you."

"Good God, Tommy!" David said, laughing and blushing more deeply.

"You're laughing 'cause you're embarrassed."

"Aren't I just?" Pearson concurred, surveying the ground. "Nobody's ever talked to me like that before. Certainly not a bloke."

There was a pause, then Tommy said, "But you want me to, don't you?"

After a pause, David slowly looked up, no longer laughing or blushing, and his voice didn't waver, either. "Yes. Yes, I s'pose I do. And I want to talk to you that way, too."

"Good. 'Cause I want you to."

"Honestly?"

"More than anything else in the world, Davey."

They leaned solidly into each other, even though they were very much out in the open. Bigger though he was, it was Tommy who put his head on David's shoulder. His voice suddenly close to a whisper, David said, "Whatever are we going to about this, Tommy?"

"Just say it's all right with you. Say it's all right."

"What about your Susan? What about Nicole?"

"This is different. I don't know why. It just is."

David looked down at him and said, some tension still in his voice, "It really is all right with you, then, is it?"

"Yes," Flowers replied unequivocally.

David caressed Tommy's flaxen hair, took a deep breath, and said, "It's all right with me, too."

Tommy pulled up so they faced each other. "Do you love me, Davey?"

Though still amused at the Yank's directness, the Englishman responded in kind. "Cor, but I do. That's the easy part, loving you. The 'ard part is" – though his tone was serious, David couldn't help grinning – "I *fancy* you."

Flowers smiled, so fetchingly his pal's eyes watered, and happily proclaimed, "I fancy you, too!" Unmindful of where they were, assuming only the cows were witnesses, they started responding to each other as they had the previous night.

Finally David pulled away, though only partway. "We cou'n't do this when we're back in France, you know."

To David's surprise, Tommy thought about that for only a moment, then agreed. "No, you're right. We can't."

"We could get in such terrible trouble. Besides, we're soldiers. We've a duty to do."

"You're right. So we won't. But we'll know, Davey. We'll *know*."

David looked down. "Anyways, they might not send me back to me old unit. Sometimes they don't."

Tommy's heart skipped. "They've got to." Resolutely he added, "They will. I already told you, we're gonna fight side by side 'til the war is over. Just like we said I'd see Dunster, and here I am."

David smiled up easily at Tommy, gestured at the magnificent view. "Yes, 'tis true. 'Ere you are."

Looking back at him, Tommy said, "I wanted so much to wake up this morning with you there beside me."

"I was afraid you'd wake up 'ating me. I cou'n't bear that."

"I don't hate you. Quite the opposite."

"I know." David swung his good leg forward, then back. "Fools in love, we are." His tone turned serious again, and he added, "I'm sorry, Tommy. I would never, ever do anything deliberate to 'urt you."

"I know." The American bent down his head so that their noses touched, the way he had done that first hour they were in the bedroom, then so quickly backed off. But not this time. Throatily he began, "Davey…?"

"No, love, not 'ere," David cautioned, relishing the chance to use the endearment as much as Tommy did hearing it. "We've taken chance enough just being out 'ere as 'tis. Anyways, we should get back soon. Mum's breakfast will get cold."

Tommy stood up and offered his hand. "Can we go back to bed after breakfast?"

"You're incorrigible," David replied in delight as his friend pulled him to his feet and, briefly, into his arms. "No, we can't. But I promise, when you wake up tomorrow morning, and the morning after that, I'll be right there."

# Chapter XXXII

In the early afternoon the sky began to cloud up, and David's mother and sister both expressed apprehension about the need to get some marketing done before the rain arrived. "Don't you usually 'ave it all done by now, Mum?" David asked, and his mother replied, "Yes, but today I've 'ad a couple of growing boys to mind." Clearly she was coming to enjoy the presence, once again, of young men in her house.

"We could run the store while you go out," Tommy volunteered, and David said, "Gorblimey! What d'you know about it?"

"Helping a customer is pretty much helping a customer whether it's at a hotel or a bake shop. You can teach me the rest."

"I like your attitude, Tommy," Mrs. Pearson told him. "Is there anything you boys need while we're at market?"

"Do they have postcards anywhere in Dunster?" Flowers asked.

"Postal cards? The stationers on the 'igh street might 'ave some," David's mother allowed. "'Ow many would you want, and what kind?"

"Two picture postcards, if they've got them. With pictures of England." Tommy turned to David, pressing francs into his hand. "Can you give your mom some English money to pay for them?"

David started to refuse the French money, then changed his mind. "'Ere, Mum," he told his mother, handing her a few pence. "That should do it." As the two women departed, Betty darted a significant look at Tommy, an apparent reminder of his promise to her earlier that morning.

Learning the ropes from David proved to be not all that easy; Tommy found the English money – shillings, pounds, guineas, pence – difficult to figure out. The two stood at a wooden counter behind the front area where the baked goods sat in a glass case, available for the customers' inspection – a recent innovation, David told Tommy, although the Yank had seen it before in America. Old-fashioned, too, was the wooden tray David used for the money, with compartments for the different denominations; Tommy already had used a cash register at the hotel in Brooklyn.

"No, you got it wrong again," David said when Tommy had counted change one more time.

"How come you don't make your money easy to figure out, like we do?"

"What is it makes your money so easy?"

"Everything comes in fives and tens. It's simple."

"So? I told you, twelvepence to a shilling, that's two sixpence to a shilling."

"How many to a crown?"

"Five. There, you've got your five. What's so 'ard about that?" Tommy shook his head, and David added, "I can't 'ave you 'andling the till 'til you get it right. We can't afford a mistake."

"Yes, sir!" They'd behaved since returning from their walk this morning, but now Tommy leaned into his friend with extra emphasis, until David abruptly called his name.

"Stop that! Someone could come in."

"Sorry," Tommy said sheepishly, pulling back.

Just then they were startled by the tinkling of the shop door's bell. Two older women, one of whom Tommy recognized as the teacher Mrs. Landis from yesterday, came shuffling in, loaded down with packages from their marketing. "'Ere, what's this?" the unfamiliar woman said as she approached the counter. "If we'd knowed there was two 'andsome soldier lads mindin' the shop, we'd 'ave got 'ere sooner, eh, Mrs. Landis?" Before her companion could answer, the woman addressed Pearson – "'Oo's your mate, David?" – and before he could answer, Mrs. Landis pronounced knowledgeably, "This is Private Flowers, Mrs. Dinsley," adding with great importance, "He's American."

"Ooh" was Mrs. Dinsley's response to this information – that and a theatrical roll of the eyes, as if Mrs. Landis had said he was a great lover. Tommy doffed his cap and gave his full name and division, causing the Dinsley woman to giggle.

In the meantime, Mrs. Landis was asking the young man in the charge of the shop, "What's fresh today, David?"

"Everything's always fresh at Pearson's, Mrs. Landis. You know that."

"Especially the soldier boys," Mrs. Dinsley put in with a laugh.

Ignoring her, David told her friend, "There's some specially good biscuits."

"Oh, that would be lovely. I'll take two of whatever you've got." To Tommy's mystification, although there did appear to be biscuits in the case, David reached for a couple of cookies, as Mrs. Landis turned to the American and said, "I read in the newspapers they're expecting another big push by the Huns any day."

Despite his discussions with the various Pearsons about how the war had changed life in Dunster, the actual fighting had been receding further and further from Tommy's consciousness, to the point that it was almost a jolt to hear it now mentioned. "Is that right?" he replied. "Did they say where?" Once the question was out, he realized again he should be careful in discussing the matter, lest he accidentally reveal their whereabouts in France.

"Could come anywhere along the front, they say," she answered.

"Well, wherever they try it, we'll be ready," he said. "Tommies, Doughboys, the French – we're all ready for them."

She regarded him with pleasure, as if he were one of her pupils who'd come up with the right answer to a question in class. Mrs. Dinsley added, "Thank 'eaven you Yanks are 'ere now."

"We're glad to be here," he said, then asked her, "Did you want anything today, ma'am?"

"Ohh." She seemed to be deciding on the spot. "Per'aps I will. Your mate is such a good salesman, David."

David gave Tommy a Dougherty-esque smirk and told Mrs. Dinsley, "I know."

"I b'lieve I'll 'ave two scones, Private Flowers."

Tommy looked over to David, and there was an awkward pause. "Well, go on, Tommy," Pearson said. "'Elp the lady with 'er scones."

Determined not to show his ignorance, Tommy carefully surveyed the contents of the case, then said, "Sorry. Looks like we're all out of them."

"But they're right there," Mrs. Dinsley protested, pointing at what he'd thought were biscuits.

"Oh, of course," Tommy said. "How could I have missed them?"

David turned away sharply and sneezed, or at least that was what he wanted the two customers to think; as they offered their God-bless-yous, Tommy could see his pal actually was laughing. "Go a'ead and take the money," David added, switching to a cough. "I'm going to get me a sip of water in the pantry."

"'Ow much is it?" Mrs. Dinsley demanded as David disappeared down the hallway.

"Uhh–" Tommy looked at the case and saw the notation "2d." "Two dollars?"

"Two dollars?" David interjected. "You're in England, Tommy."

"Oh, of course I meant two pounds."

"Two pounds!" both women shouted, in a mix of disbelief and glee, and Mrs. Dinsley asked, "Are you sure you don't mean tuppence, dearie?"

"Oh… uh, of course. That's what I meant. Two pence."

"Pearson's scones are good," Mrs. Landis commented, "but they're not *that* good."

"Of course not," Tommy agreed with a laugh. Having completed their purchases, the two women took their leave of him and the bake shop with considerable effusiveness, calling to David to mind his cold, and invoking God's protection when he and Tommy should have to return to France. The moment he was satisfied they were out of sight and there was no danger of any other customers appearing in the immediate future, Tommy ran down the hall and into the pantry, there finding David, who was doubled over with laughter. "You scamp!" Tommy shouted, catching the smaller man and beginning to tickle him.

"No! No!" David protested. "Stop. 'Elp!"

"I'll shut you up," Tommy declared, and so he did, mouth to mouth.

Panting again when they broke off, David said, not unpleasantly, "Blimey, you are full of surprises." As Tommy smiled in return, he added, "And by the way, you looked a perfect fool out there," laughed, then dashed down the hallway, with Flowers in hot pursuit. Just before they reached the public area, Tommy caught David again, and lightly twisted the Briton's arm behind his back.

"Who you calling foolish?" Tommy demanded.

"You – putting on airs, pretending like you knew what you were doing. You wou'n't know a scone from a stone."

"Reckon I had a bad teacher, then."

"And all that making eyes with that 'orrible old Mrs. Dinsley."

"Women customers buy more when you do that. You must know that."

"Let go of me, Tommy."

"Not until you say you're sorry for calling me a fool."

"But you were – oww!"

Tommy had twisted David's arm a little farther; but at this sound, he immediately released the smaller man and in the same motion turned him around to face him anxiously. "I'm sorry. Did I hurt you?" David stared up at him, then began to laugh once more. "What?"

Pulling himself together, David replied, "Sorry looks so wonderful on you. Foolish looks wonderful on you, too. *Everything* looks wonderful on you."

Flowers colored. "Stop it."

"I'm not teasing you, Tommy, I mean it. Di'n't you say you wanted me to talk to you like that?"

"I did. I do. And I know you mean it. But it's getting me all – all–"

"Me, too. But we can't do anything about it now, so we really must stop," David said decisively. He broke away from Tommy and moved out into the public area, to the far right end of the counter. "Let's keep at least a foot apart from each other until Mum and Betty are back – no, until tonight."

Tommy also moved into the public area, but took up a position at the far left end of the counter. "All right. Until tonight." There was a pause, then he declared with a grin, "Boy, tonight can't come too soon."

"Tommy!" David responded with a laugh, "will you stop it?"

Flowers scratched his head and conceded, "Okay. We better talk about something else. So. What is it about your English women?"

"*My* English women, is it?"

"You know what I mean."

Genuinely curious, David regarded Tommy from across the room. "'Fraid I don't, love."

"You thought *I* was making eyes–?"

"Oh… well… Mrs. Dinsley."

"But it's not just Mrs. Dinsley. It's just about every girl – and every grown woman – since I got here, to England. I've heard things about French girls, and I know some of the foreign fellows think American girls are fresh, but these English girls – and even the old ladies!–"

"It's the war. Too many men away for too long. I s'pose it's made the women a little – odd."

"Odd?" A troubled look passed over Flowers' face. "Do you think – do you think the war's made *us*… odd?"

Pearson flicked a significant look down the counter. "Per'aps. Or per'aps it would have been the same for us anyways." David turned to rearrange the contents of the baked-goods case in the wake of the most recent purchases. But after a few moments he turned back around, because he could feel Tommy watching him. "What?" David asked.

"I just think maybe you're right. That it would have been the same for us. War or no war."

"Don't see 'ow we'd 'ave met without the war, though."

"That's true. There's that much in the war's favor, anyway."

"Does it bother you, Tommy?"

"That we wouldn't have met without the war? That's just the way life is sometimes."

"No, love, I meant, does it bother you it might 'ave been the same for us, even without the war?"

Tommy didn't hesitate. "No. I can't imagine it any other way, now."

Pearson returned his attention to the case, only saying "Hm."

Tommy saw an opening, and took it. "David?"

"What?"

"What will you do when the war's over?"

Pearson turned swiftly back to Flowers with alarm. "I thought we agreed on that. I thought we were going to sail around the world together, you 'n' me."

"Well, yes, we are. But after that."

"Whart d'you mean, after that? I was thinking we would just keep doing that."

"We can't do it forever."

"I was rather 'oping we would."

"Well, maybe," Tommy said, trying to mollify David and wipe the injured look from his buddy's face, "but just saying we couldn't, what would you want to do? Come back here?"

"I'd rather be wherever you were, if it was quite all right with you."

David's visible anguish seemed to be getting worse, and as Tommy moved toward him with the aim of comforting him, the American stressed, "Of course it's all right with me."

"Stay there," David ordered, and Tommy halted, but continued the discussion:

"What if we came back to Dunster, together?"

"That's a long way from your family, isn't it?"

Tommy shrugged. "Brooklyn's a long way from yours."

"You like it 'ere that much?"

"I like being here with you that much, yes. And you do already own a business here."

David's relief was mixed with surprise at Tommy's practical streak. "Oh, well, yes, that." He thought about that, and expressed the first reservation that came into his mind: "Betty thinks it should be 'ers, y'know. Talk about women with odd notions."

"It's yours, of course. But maybe we could all run it together."

"She doesn't want just to run it, Tommy. She wants to own it." David paused, then added, "I can't see giving up what's rightly mine to the likes of 'er." There was a much longer pause, which seemed to indicate the subject was closed. But suddenly David said, "Of course, I'd share it with you, if that was what you really wanted."

To his surprise, Tommy found himself saying, "I'd feel strange about that. I mean, it doesn't seem fair to Betty–"

"Betty di'n't fight," David snapped. "You and I did. Are." David paused again, and Tommy actually could see an idea dawning on his friend's face. "But if you married Betty, I could own 'alf, and you and 'er together could own the other 'alf." Looking straight at Tommy, David said, "That's not such a bad notion, y'know."

Tommy, thunderstruck, was sorry he'd ever raised the subject. "But… I don't want to marry Betty," he finally stammered. "I want – I want to – I want to… be with you."

"But you would be with me, Tommy, don't y'see? We'd be partners–"

"I don't want to be just your business partner!" Flowers exploded; then, with far less assurance, he added, "I thought you wanted more than that."

Now it was Pearson who took a step forward on impulse, aiming to comfort; then he caught himself. "Tommy, love, you're missing me point," he said gently. "If you're me brother-in-law and me business partner, you can be 'ere and live 'ere and we can be *together*, and no one will think twice about it."

David had hit the word "together" with such meaning that Tommy couldn't help but understand; still, he was so dumbfounded by the implications that he had to verify them: "You mean – you and me – upstairs – even though Betty's my wife?"

"Of course that's what I mean. It wou'n't work any other way, now would it?"

Tommy thought about that, but not for long. "It wouldn't work that way, either! You say nobody would think twice? What would Betty think about it? She doesn't love me and I don't love her."

"That's why it might work."

"But why would she agree to such a thing?"

"Betty wants the shop now more than anything. If she marries you, she gets the shop – 'alf, anyways – and you 'eard Mrs. Landis, she 'as a good 'ead for the business–"

"But what if she meets some fellow?"

"She 'ad her fellow. 'Oo's she going to meet now?"

Temporarily stymied, Tommy switched tactics. "There's someone else, too. What about your mother? She'd be bound to notice–"

"She'd notice as both of the children she 'as left were 'appy. And she likes you."

Tommy stared straight ahead, not seeing, trying to picture this incredible arrangement. Finally he concluded, "I don't think it's a good idea, David. It just seems so… wrong."

David, not looking particularly worried, shrugged in his turn. "Then we'll sail around the world forever. Or think of something else."

Tommy regarded his beloved buddy dubiously. "Are you sure this is what you really want?"

Irritated, David replied, "I told you, Tommy, I want to be with you. Whatever keeps us together, that's what I want. I thought you'd want that, too."

"I do."

"Well, there you 'ave it. We may not solve all this today. And I'm getting a 'eadache."

"Can I–?" Tommy began, taking a step toward him, and David quickly replied, "No. Mum and Betty will be back any time." He cast a longer look at Tommy, then added, "But thank you, love. Thank you."

"Think nothing of it," Tommy responded, turning away to his side of the shop, suddenly eager for customers.

# Chapter XXXIII

They passed a rather formal afternoon together, waiting on customers until Mrs. Pearson and Betty returned, by which time the skies had opened. As the two women entered the shop, Tommy looked at the drenched younger one and tried to picture her as his wife. She was pretty, yes, but she did nothing for him, not even like Nicole, let alone David. Although he'd been practical – and proud of it – in pointing out David's ownership of the bake shop as a more realistic alternative to indefinite sailing, he'd been unprepared for what he saw as David's cold-blooded calculation involving his sister. Tommy didn't think he could ever be that pragmatic. He tried to push the proposal from his head even as Betty gave him a questioning look. He rolled his eyes in response, as if to say to her, I tried, but your brother's too stubborn. Let David mention his preposterous idea to her, if he dared.

That settled, Tommy concentrated on putting himself in a better frame of mind. He was still in Dunster with David, and there was such a short amount of time left, he couldn't allow it to be spoiled. Mrs. Pearson had brought him back the two requested postal cards, and before the evening meal, he excused himself to finally write those missives he'd been vowing to send. The easier to write, he decided, would be the one to his parents; for them he picked the card with the green, pastoral scene, somewhat like the view he and David had surveyed his morning, and wrote:

Dear Mom, Dad, Annie, Lidey and Peg:

You'll never guess where I'm writing from – England!

To his dismay, he had to stop right there. Explaining the turn of events that had brought him to this country would consume the rest of the card. He decided not to explain it at all, instead getting right to the main details:

I got to come here for a couple days with my best friend, David, who's English. This country is really beautiful!

He stopped again; having summed up so much that mattered so succinctly, he wasn't quite sure what else to say. Finally he wrote,

We'll go back to France in a few days, but the change sure has been nice.

After only a short pause, he added,

How are you? I hope you are all quite well. I am fine and very safe here. Don't worry about me.

Love,
Tommy

Having finished, he re-read his handiwork and frowned; it hardly captured how important the last few days had been to him. And this was supposed to be the easy one.

Though purchased in Dunster, the second postcard had a picture of London on it, and he had saved that one for the girl he'd always assumed he'd marry. She barely seemed like a real person to him anymore, but he dutifully wrote her,

Dear Susan,
Remember how we used to play London Bridge is falling down? Well, now I've been to London! It is a big, beautiful city, although everyone there is very tired of the war.

He stopped once more; it seemed a pretty glum thing to put on a postcard, no matter how true it might be. The censor wouldn't like it, Tommy thought; and then it occurred to him he was freer to speak his mind on this picture postcard than he ever could be writing from France. But still he should be cheerful in writing Susan. He wished he could erase the comment about everyone being tired and start over, but there he was, stuck with the phrase, unless he made a complete mess of the card. Determined to strike an uplifting note, he wrote:

Don't get me wrong. The English are very brave people. They've been fighting this war a long, long time. I only hope now that we're here, we can help them finish off the Huns.

He stopped yet again, frustrated. What kind of thing was that to write on a postcard to your girl? Susan would think he was losing nerve and faith, writing "I hope" instead of saying right out that the Americans would beat the Germans. Switching subjects entirely, he added,

How are you? I hope you are quite well.

He had almost written "I've been thinking about you," but he couldn't bring himself to do it, since it wasn't true. Instead he concluded with,

I will be back in France soon, and will write you again.

Sincerely,
Tommy

And once again, he re-read what he'd written with dissatisfaction, unsure now whether he should even mail it. But it was the only postcard he had to send her from England. He'd have to ask David for the stamps.

★

As the afternoon began to fade into evening, the rain continued, and grew in force. Although there was no way of knowing the weather in France, he now thought as David had when the two of them had first met; now Tommy, too, wondered about the men shivering in the trenches under these conditions.

It was the kind of wet summer's evening that would have driven him to restlessness back in Iowa, with the feeling of being trapped indoors. Here and now, spending an evening with David and his family, safe and dry, seemed the ultimate in cozy luxury. The Pearsons set a simple meal – soup, cheese, and that ever-present gray bread – but Tommy no longer speculated, as he might have twenty-four hours earlier, that the modest fare meant a lack of caring on the part of David's mother and sister. Talk at the table was of trifles, forgotten as soon as they were said, and that was comforting; even Betty, who presumably was disappointed at David's supposed intransigence about the shop, managed to be charming. After supper, as they all lingered around the table, she prompted Tommy, "You haven't said all that much, really, about your life in America, Private Flowers. Please, do tell us about it."

Tommy realized that, at least until he had written his postcards, he hadn't been thinking much about home lately. Betty's urging suddenly threw it back into vivid focus. In the meantime, Mrs. Pearson narrowed the initial inquiry to "'Ow big is your village?"

"It's about the size of Dunster. Maybe a little bigger. Not much. But there's no castle, and not much of a hill, at least not compared to yours. It's pretty different from here."

"'Ow else so?" David put in.

Tommy thought about that, and it came to him: "The country's so much bigger, and there's so much more space. I made it from the front to London in a day, but I traveled two days to get from Iowa to Texas, and even then I was still in America." Warming to the subject, he added, "And your houses here in England all seem to be right on the street. In Iowa, there's grass between the street and the house."

"You mean it's like our garden out back?" Betty asked.

"Well, I notice your garden has a lot of flowers," Tommy replied. "My mom and my sisters keep a few flowers out back of the house, and a few vegetables, too. But mostly we have grass, and a few trees – big trees, with lots of shade."

"In the front?" Mrs. Pearson asked, trying to follow him.

"In the front and the back," Tommy corrected.

"Front and back gardens?" Betty wondered aloud.

"Actually, we call them lawns, not gardens."

"Lawns!" Betty exclaimed. "It all sounds so grand. Is your lot rich, then?"

"Betty!" Mrs. Pearson scolded, and David threw in a dirty look for good measure, but Tommy answered cheerfully, "No, we're not rich and we're not grand. We're just Americans."

"And if it was a summer night like this one, what would you be doing in Brooklyn?" This question came from David.

Recalling his earlier rumination, Tommy said, "I'd probably be stuck in the house, going stir crazy."

"But if it wasn't raining?" David pressed.

"If it wasn't raining, I might walk downtown with Susan or one of my sisters."

"Downtown?" said Betty.

"Well, it's really not much further than it is from your place to the high street. And not a whole lot bigger. But it's down the hill, and we call it downtown."

"And when you were little?" David asked.

"How little?" the Yank asked.

"Oh, I don't know. Six?"

"There's a wooden swing hanging from the elm out front. I'd go out and swing on that for hours." David smiled with pleasure, evidently at the mental picture, and Tommy asked him in return, "What did you do when you were that age?"

"What, me? I'd be all over the town, I would."

"'Tis true," David's mother added. "'E was always one to be underfoot."

"With other boys?" Tommy asked David.

"Taggin' after me brothers, or by meself," David answered, and again his mother put in her piece:

"Our David was never as sociable as our Colin and Doug. 'E never 'ad a friend like you when 'e was little."

"So I've heard," said Tommy, smiling at David.

Later in the evening, after everyone had retired early, Tommy and David lay happily entwined in the third-floor bedroom, wide-awake, David's back to Tommy's front. At length, David grew very quiet, and Tommy asked him, "What is it?"

"Tomorrow night we'll be in London. And night after that, you'll be back in Pierregot."

"… And you'll be right down the road, in Molliens." The American squeezed his smaller friend tighter. "Don't even tell me they might send you somewhere else."

David drew Tommy's arms closer around him, but said, "Per'aps it would be better for us that way."

"Davey!"

"It's not I don't want to be with you, Tommy. It's that I want to be with you all the time now. If I can't, per'aps it's better to be apart 'til it's over." David paused to let Tommy say something, but Flowers' emotions were too mixed for him to speak, and Pearson continued, "I cou'n't wait to get into the war, y'know. Now I can't wait for it to be over."

It sounded vaguely unpatriotic to Tommy, who finally said, "I'm not done with the war yet." Having said that, he quickly kissed the back of David's neck. "I want to be with you all the time, too, but we've got a job to do first. I want to help win the war."

"Well, don't worry. You'll get your chance."

Tommy gently turned David around so they faced each other. "And after that, we'll be together the rest of our lives. I promise."

"What a thing to say, Tommy. No one can promise such a thing."

"I can. And I just did."

Despite himself, David laughed. "You Americans. Always so sure anything is possible."

"That's 'cause anything is. You and the French started this job; now we'll finish it. Then you and I will sail around the world, and then–"

David cut Tommy off by pressing his index finger to the Yank's lips; saying "Ssh"; then kissing him on the lips, once; then replacing his finger. "You can make anything 'appen?" he asked. Tommy, silenced, nodded. "Then make this night last a year. Ten years, even."

David removed his finger, and Tommy kissed him in return. "Forever," he said. "Why stop at ten years? Forever."

When Tommy awoke the next morning, there was no sunlight streaming through the windows, as the rain seemed to have continued all night. But true to his word, David – who clearly had been awake for a while – lay next to Tommy in the bed, leaning on his elbow, his head propped on his hand, gazing serenely down.

When he saw Tommy's eyes flutter open, David leaned down, and they touched noses. There was a long pause as they regarded each other, then David, eyes shining, said, "I was foolish not to wait for you yesterday. I've never been so 'appy in me life."

"Me neither," Tommy agreed, and he pulled David down to him, where they nuzzled in silence for a good long while.

"Shall we go on, then?" David finally said as he felt Tommy smooth his disheveled hair, felt the beating of Flowers' heart against his cheek, through the smooth skin of the American's chest.

"Go on to what?"

"To church, of course. It's Sunday morning."

"If that's what your family always does."

"Doesn't yours?"

"Of course."

"Well, then."

Tommy continued to slowly stroke David's hair; the latter said, "Our train's early in the afternoon. We'll be back to London by nightfall."

"What will we do then?"

"Sister Jean will meet our train, or send someone. We'll find out where we're to stay for the night, and in the morning she'll take you back to your Leftenant O'Malley."

It occurred then to Tommy that David and Sister Jean had gotten all of these logistics figured out ahead of time, and he hadn't even bothered to ask about them until now. What he owed that Canadian nurse! His face nestled in David's hair, he asked, "And what will you do?"

Tommy felt a small sigh escape from David as the latter replied, "I must go down to Aldershot, to get me orders."

Tommy didn't need to ask what Aldershot was, because he'd heard of it: an enormous military base south of London that served as headquarters for the British Army. After a pause, he said, "What do you think they'll do?"

"They'll send me back, of course. To me old unit, unless they need men more somewheres else."

Seizing the smaller man with some force, Tommy simply said, "No."

David submitted to the treatment, laughing. "'Tisn't your decision, nor mine. Are you ready to get up, then?"

"And leave this room?"

Still laughing, David said, "Of course, and leave this room."

"I never want to leave this room."

"But life moves on, Tommy. And we can't be afraid of that."

Lifting them both so they were now sitting, Tommy replied, "And I'm not. So let's go."

A short time later, their uniforms brushed, the two young men accompanied David's mother and sister, who were dressed in their Sunday finest, up the hill of West Street to St. George's Church. The church, far older than anything Tommy had seen in America, was quite full with parishioners, but Tommy noticed he and David were the only soldiers sitting there under the semicircular wooden beams of the church's ceiling; or at least, they were the only ones in town who had bothered to get up to attend services. And although the Pearsons and their guest were nowhere near the front of the church – their social station in Dunster hardly qualified them for that – the rector must have noticed the relatively tall Doughboy when he climbed up to the pulpit to deliver his sermon, because he departed from his text and said, "As we wait for the enemy to strike another blow at our young men and the young men of our allies, let us pray for just retaliation and a swift victory. We are strengthened by the new friends at our side, and together with God's help we will carry this through. Amen."

Tommy looked over to David, wanting to be certain he had heard correctly; his friend was flushed, so the Yank leaned in and whispered low, "Are you all right?"

"I can't but take so much o'the likes of preachers, acting like they're running the war. God's 'elp, indeed."

"I reckon he means well enough," said Tommy, a little dismayed by this quiet outburst.

"I'm not so sure o'that," David responded tartly, and on instinct, Tommy momentarily, surreptitiously took his hand, which seemed to work; the scowl at the clergymen vanished. The last hymn – "Praise God from Whom All Blessings Flow" – was a familiar one to Flower of Iowa, and he sang along lustily. As people began to leave their pews, David whispered to him, "I still like the way you sing," and Tommy kicked him, ever so lightly.

Mrs. Pearson led their small group through the receiving line where Tommy was introduced to the minister, who of course blessed him all over again in the name of the Lord; then suddenly David and his mother were ahead of him, walking down the street together arm in arm, involved in some private conversation of their own. The rain had stopped and it looked to be a warm, sunny July day, and abruptly, despite what he'd said to David, Tommy didn't want to go back to the war, didn't want to leave Dunster at all. He turned and there was Betty, looking smart in her Sunday clothes. In proper gentlemanly fashion, he offered her his arm, which she gracefully took with a smile, to all appearances enjoying the looks she was getting from the other girls because of the gesture.

"I could make a lot of girls jealous with you, I could."

Tommy nearly stumbled over the nearest gravestone in the churchyard when he heard her say this, but he knew he hadn't misunderstood. Recovering quickly, he half asked, half said, "You've been talking with your brother."

"Does that surprise you?" she said, looking up at him so sweetly that bystanders would have had no idea what they were truly discussing, and adding another question that was equally rhetorical – "Shall we promenade a bit?" – since they already were meandering slowly through the churchyard. He nodded, and she took him through yet another stone archway, to a flower-filled garden enclosed by four stone walls.

"You like the idea?" Tommy said at length, guardedly; much as he trusted

David, he wanted to be sure the proposed scenario hadn't become garbled in the translation.

"I do," she said with what seemed to him undue gaiety. "I want what's mine, and there's worse ways to get it. I don't see what's in it for you, or for him. But that's not my concern. You're more than presentable."

It was about as unromantic a comment as Tommy could imagine. He liked the whole idea even less than before, and he decided to let her know: "It's not – this isn't a sure thing, you know."

"Of course it's not. For one, you're going back to the front."

The brutality of her frankness astonished him, and provoked him to respond in kind. Indicating with his hand the churchyard they'd just left, he said, "Is there a stone for your brothers here?"

"Not yet," she replied, seemingly unaffected by the question. "When it's all over, there's talk there'll be one for all the boys from ere 'oo didn't come back – Colin, Doug–"

"Hugh?"

She stared at him and said, "Yes, Hugh, too," then added defiantly, "David, too, if 'e doesn't return."

A spasm ran through Tommy, who let go of her arm and leaned against the garden wall, his face a violent shade of red. "How in God's name can you say something like that about your own brother?"

"It's just the reality, Private Flowers. You could be on it yusself, but you're not from 'ere." Only her lapsing into the accent of her mother and brother betrayed Betty's true emotional state.

"I could never marry you," Tommy said decisively, turning to leave her there, but she called softly after him, "David says you'll come 'round."

He turned back, and now it was Tommy staring at Betty, who went on, "And since I really do believe you'll both be coming back, I'll ignore that you said that." She walked up to him. "Aren't you going to take my arm again?" He stood ramrod straight, his arms at his side, as if waiting for Captain Willnor. "For David's sake," she added, extending her arm as, making his reluctance plain to her, he took it without a word.

"We'll get used to each other," she said as they exited the garden and headed down West Street. "We don't 'ave to like each other, y'know. Though 'twould be nice if we did." Tommy merely exhaled, eager to get back to his beloved Davey, the only reason he would even tolerate the company of this, his prospective wife.

★

Leave-taking was predictably difficult; as on Friday, neither woman accompanied them to the train station, but before the two young men departed the bake shop,

David's mother clung to Flowers, imploring him, "Take care of my boy," to which he replied, "You know I will, Mrs. Pearson."

Tommy waited outside while David said his good-byes; then they walked down Dunster's steep hill in a summer heat that had become downright uncomfortable. Flowers decided not to look back, figuring that might somehow ensure his return; but when the train arrived, he leaned out the window to view the castle as he had two days earlier, which now seemed a lifetime ago. David stood next to him, silently taking leave of his hometown; then he suggested they take seats on the left-hand side of the less-crowded train, to catch any cooling channel breeze that might be available. They claimed facing seats, Tommy riding backward.

David, who had been limping again, was tired and napped much of the way to Taunton; while it was still a beautiful ride, Tommy didn't enjoy it as much. When Pearson ultimately wakened and became alert enough to talk, Flowers had to speak his mind. From across the way, he hissed, "David!"

"What?"

"I want to talk to you. About Betty."

"What, cor! Why now, Tommy? It's 'ot and I'm tired."

"I – can I sit next to you?"

"What a silly question. Come over 'ere."

Tommy gladly took the forward-facing seat next to David, who added irritably, "Why were you sitting acrost, anyways?"

"It's not a full train. People might have thought it was strange–"

"'Oo cares what people think? Bloody civs," David said, and with that he leaned his head on Tommy's shoulder, using the latter as a pillow.

"You're warm," Tommy said.

"Of course I'm warm," David growled. "I told you, it's 'ot. Like you cou'n't tell that yourself."

"But you're warm."

"Don't start, Tommy. I'm in the pink. Now what is it about Betty?"

"I can't marry her."

"Then don't. You don't 'ave to. I just thought it was a good idear."

Tommy couldn't let go of it. "I don't. You should've heard some of the things she said."

"Betty says lots o'things."

"This was something about you."

David shrugged. "If it was something not nice, it wou'n't be the first time."

Tommy couldn't bring himself to repeat the entire conversation. "She talked about you – and me – said we might not make it back–"

David barely stirred. "So? 'Tis true, isn't it? We might not."

Tommy pulled away. "Davey, it's bad luck to talk that way! You said so."

Pearson shrugged again. "I wou'n't talk that way at the front, or want another soldier to. But bloody civs – let 'em say what they want. They don't understand a thing about it, anyways."

Tommy leaned back in his seat, folding his arms. "I don't understand you sometimes."

"Well, I don't understand you sometimes. So, that's not so terrible, now is it?" David said, looking puckishly at him.

Tommy grinned despite himself. "I reckon not."

"I don't s'pose so, either. Now can I 'ave your shoulder back, if you please?"

"Sure, pal." Tommy put his arm around his buddy for good measure, and with David dozing, they rode like that the rest of the way to Taunton, and most of the way to London.

# Chapter XXXIV

By late afternoon, Tommy had fallen asleep, too, but as they neared the outskirts of London he came to, awakened by a peculiar feeling he initially couldn't place; then he identified it as a wetness on his left shoulder. He was, he slowly realized, thoroughly soaked there, and the cause was David, who was still lying asleep against him, and was totally bathed in sweat. Since it was a hot day, ordinarily Tommy wouldn't have been concerned; but the sun was well past its zenith and, most significantly, he himself was wearing an equally warm uniform, but had been perspiring very little. He was reluctant, nonetheless, to waken David, who only stirred when the train pulled into Paddington.

"Are we there, then?" Pearson asked groggily as he finally reached consciousness.

"Yes, we're back in London," Tommy replied, then he added worriedly, "Davey?"

"Hmm?"

"You're all wet."

"What?… Oh. Sorry. 'Ot day, y'know. Di'n't mean to get me all over you."

"That's all right," Tommy assured David, but it wasn't; the Briton had brushed off the phenomenon just as the Yank had feared he would.

As the train pulled abreast of the arrival platform, Sister Jean miraculously materialized right alongside their car, appearing in equal parts tired and elated at spotting them. But as the two young men reached through and opened the door, then stepped out, Tommy could see her good cheer recede, even as she cried "Welcome back to London!" and rushed to embrace them both.

Most uncharacteristically, David backed off from her, running his hands down his saturated tunic and mumbling, "I'm a bit of a mess. I need to find the loo right aways."

"Do you need me to go with you?" Flowers called after Pearson, who already had moved several steps past the other two, and responded crossly, "I'm not a little boy," then hurried on in search of the WC.

Turning back to the woman who had made his whole journey to Dunster possible, Tommy moved to complete the interrupted embrace, but now she, too, was suddenly all business. "How long has he been like this?" she asked him.

"Just since this afternoon, Sister. He was fine before that. We had such a wonderful time–"

"I don't like how he looks," Sister Jean said, cutting off his account of their weekend. "I don't like it one bit."

Since she was a nurse, the comment caused Tommy's anxiety to soar. "What?–"

he began, and again she interrupted: "I just hope it's not the 'flu. Oh, it can't be. Not David." She looked at Tommy, her face a portrait of apprehension. "You do know what I'm talking about, don't you?"

Tommy shrugged. "I reckon everyone's had the 'flu at least once in their life–"

"You don't know, then. This isn't like the 'flu you got over when you were a little boy. This is influenza. The Spanish 'flu. The Plague of the Spanish Lady, they call it. You haven't heard about it at all?" There was incredulity in her face and voice.

He asked a needless question: "Is it bad?"

"Tommy, it's killing people everywhere."

Trying to keep his own alarm in check, Tommy racked his brain, and could only come up with "My dad works at a pharmacy back in Iowa. He did write something about something bad going around–"

"He was right about that. I'm sure that's what it was."

"And you think Davey has it?"

Again she smiled at a moment that made no sense for Tommy, upon hearing the American use his nickname for Pearson. Rather than answering his question, without asking she put her hand on Flowers' forehead. "Do you feel all right?"

"I feel fine, Sister, honest. I'm just worried about Davey. Look, he's coming back."

David evidently had splashed water on himself and combed his hair, somewhat improving his aspect. If he noticed the worried looks from his two friends, he ignored them, instead cheerily announcing, "So, Sister, now I'm decent, I can give you a proper greeting. Tommy and I 'ad the most wonderful time–"

Sister Jean cut short the pleasantries and, as she had with Tommy, placed her hand on David's forehead. "You're burning up," she declared.

"Am I?" David looked at them both uncertainly. "Well, 'tis a 'ot day, y'know."

"We're taking you to hospital," Sister Jean said flatly.

"Cor, not," David replied. Less defiantly, he added, "I don't want to go back there. I've 'ad me fill of 'ospitals. I'm not sick."

"I think you are," Sister Jean said, as Tommy pleaded, "David, it's for your own good."

Pearson clenched his fists and stood his ground. "I'm not going, I tell you." To Sister Jean he said, "Tommy and I will find somewheres for the night if we 'ave to" – then, to Tommy: "or I'll find something meself." To the both of them, he concluded, "But I ain't goin' to no bloody 'ospital!"

Flowers was appalled by Pearson's rudeness to the nurse, but Sister Jean seemed to take it in stride, holding firm herself. "David, you could be very sick," she said patiently.

"I am not sick!" he repeated. "And if I am, I don't care."

Ignoring that, she proceeded to cross-examine the stubborn little Tommy: "Have you been coughing?"

"No."

"Coughing up blood?"

"No, I tell you."

"Any trouble with breathing?"

"No. I'm just tired, and it's been a little warm today."

Sister Jean turned pleading eyes to the Doughboy, but he felt compelled to admit, "It's true, Sister. He hasn't done any of those other things."

"Are you quite sure, Tommy? He might have, when you weren't around–"

"We've pretty much been together the whole time," he said, and as he added, "day and night," he was unconscious of how scarlet he was turning.

That caused the nurse to pause. "Well," she eventually said, regarding David but addressing them both, "I suppose it could be something else." To Pearson she said, "You really won't come back to Camberwell?"

"Sorry, Sister, but no, I won't." Then David added, "Can I sit down somewheres? I need to sit down."

Visibly making a decision, Sister Jean told him, "Why don't you do that? I need to talk to Tommy." David wandered off a short distance and found a space on a bench, where he sat, staring dazedly ahead. They both watched him until he was settled, then she turned to the American. "I have to go back to the hospital now–" she began, and this time he interrupted: "Back? Didn't you just come from there?"

"Yes."

"So you already worked there today?"

"Yes. So what? It's a double shift."

"You worked all day, and now–?"

"You soldiers do it all the time," she snapped.

"Yes, but–"

"Tommy, we're wasting time," she said impatiently. She pressed a key, a piece of paper, and some unfamiliar coins into his hand. "Pay attention, now. A friend of mine has a flat in the West End. I came here to give you the directions and the key, so you and David would have a place to stay tonight–"

"Is she there?"

"She who?"

"Your friend."

"It's a he. No, he's in America." Her tone grew sharper. "Tommy, I haven't much time. You must stop asking all these questions!" He nodded mutely, as if he'd been upbraided by Jamie or Captain, and she went on, "If he's really sick – if it is the Spanish 'flu – this is a terrible risk for you. Are you sure you want to take it?"

"You nurses do it all the time," he echoed to her; then he said stoutly, "I'm not leaving him alone. What is it you want me to do?"

For the first time, he sounded to her like a soldier. "I want you to take David to my friend's flat and make him rest."

"How do we get there?"

"By tube. You're to take the Circle Line from here to Baker Street, and change for the Bakerloo Line in the direction of Elephant and Castle–"

"Near you, then," Tommy said knowledgeably, but she said impatiently, "Nowheres near. Take the Bakerloo to Leicester Square, then follow the written directions I've given you. The money's to get something to eat. Can you do all that?"

"Of course I can… uh, but what was that about a tube?"

She rolled her eyes. "Sorry. It's what we call the underground train. I really must go now. I'll be 'round in the morning to take you to your stuffy leftenant. But ring me at the hospital if he gets worse."

"Will do, Sister." As she turned to go, he added with great feeling, "I don't know how to thank you–"

She turned back to him and gave him a smile both weary and radiant. "You two did have a wonderful time, didn't you?"

He smiled back. "Oh, Sister, you have no idea–"

"Then that's all the thanks I need." She disappeared into the crowd before Tommy could even begin to explain what he meant.

As he walked over to the bench where Pearson had been sitting all this time, Flowers felt a surge of anger. "Where are we going?" David asked dully when he saw Tommy.

"Lester Square," the Yank said curtly.

"Leicester Square? Tommy, I don't know if I could sit through a show right now–"

"We're not going to a show. We're going to get some rest. Or you are. Though you could have gotten a better rest at the hospital. Why are you being so stubborn?"

Although David's voice was not strong, he responded with conviction. "Don't y'see, Tommy? They'd never let you stay with me at the 'ospital."

Tommy, who had still been flushed with anger, paled. "Is that – is that what this is all about?"

"I promised, remember? This morning and tomorrow morning, when you woke up, I'd be there. And I will be."

"Oh, Davey." It took all Tommy's strength not to gather David in his arms right there in the station. "But what if you're really sick?"

"I'm not that sick. D'you think if I was, I'd put you in danger? I wou'n't do that to you." He paused. "But I do feel tired again."

"Then let's go. Right now," Tommy commanded, as he helped his ailing friend to his feet.

Finding Sister Jean's friend's place proved difficult, since David was barely alert and Tommy was left to navigate the London Underground pretty much on his own. After an interminable ninety minutes or so that Tommy could tell should have taken half that time, they finally found the building, an old one, on a noisy side street in London's West End.

The "flat," as Jean had called it, was little more than three rooms – a kitchen, a sitting room, and a bedroom, with the WC on the hall. In a serious obstacle to David's tenaciously held promise, there was but a single narrow bed in the small bedroom, and a settee in the sitting room. David collapsed onto the bed – it was nothing but a cot, really – as soon as they arrived; once Tommy had examined the situation, he decided to carry the cot, David and all, to the sitting room so that he, on the settee, could be next to Pearson.

It was now dark, or almost so. Flowers was hungry, but afraid to leave his buddy to use the money Sister Jean had given them, so he quietly meted out his share of the food David's mother had packed for them and ate it as he watched Pearson's labored breathing and renewed sweating. There wasn't a lot of air in the flat, but opening a window would make the noise worse. Imitating Sister Jean, Tommy placed his palm on David's forehead, which was as hot as before. To his surprise, David reached up and grasped his hand, hoarsely asking, "Tommy?"

"I'm here."

Gulping for air, David simply said, "Good," then released Tommy's hand.

Slowly, his breathing became a little more regular, and he drifted off to sleep. Tommy, beside himself with worry, was also keenly aware he would have to get up early to leave for France, but he kept his vigil, with the lamp on low, until his own eyelids began to grow heavy. Lying down on the ottoman, against which he had pushed Pearson's cot, he threw his arm around David, who was still giving off a tremendous amount of heat. For a moment, Flowers felt a flash of fear for himself – what if it *was* this 'flu that caused Sister Jean to speak with such dread in her voice? – but then he looked down at his sleeping pal, and drew him closer. It was a better reason to die than most these days.

In the middle of the night, Tommy woke with a start, unable at the instant of waking to recall whether he had been dreaming he was in France or Iowa; he only knew he hadn't been in England. The lamp was out, and that confused him, as he was fairly certain he had fallen asleep with it on. David still lay next to him, on the cot, and Tommy again reached out tentatively to touch his forehead. To Flowers' surprise and relief, Pearson, who was breathing evenly, felt cool and dry to the touch. Wartime blackout precautions notwithstanding, there was a little light from the city spilling into the room, and as Tommy's eyes adjusted, he could make out the features of his friend's face. Unable to resist, he carefully placed his entire body against David's, wanting to verify the coolness a second time. His gratitude over this development, as unexpected as the onslaught of the fever itself, was so profound that his eyes instantly watered, tears emerging and rolling down his cheeks onto David's.

"'Ere, what's this?" came a soft voice out of the darkness. Flowers felt Pearson's cool hand touch his wet cheek as the latter added, "What's the trouble, love?"

"No trouble," Tommy managed, seizing the hand and holding it against his cheek.

"I told you I wasn't sick," David said, ruffling Tommy's hair. "Well, per'aps I was a little unwell there, but not dreadful sick." David put his arms around Tommy, who was still too full of emotion to say much, and drew him to him. "There, there, it's all right. I would've woke you to tell you the fever broke, but I di'n't want your sleep to be ruint."

"You were up?"

"Yes, I got up and got me some water. 'Ad a bad taste in me mouth, I did, and I wanted rid of it."

Tommy lifted his face to David's and kissed him. "It's gone now," he confirmed, with a glint in his eye.

"Oh!" Tommy's sleep was punctured by a feminine voice saying this one word, loudly and sharply, followed by a sharp elbow – David's – to his bare stomach. In fact, as he came blearily to wakefulness, he remembered that neither he nor David, who had been sleeping intertwined, was wearing anything. And the next thing that dawned on him was that the woman's voice had been Sister Jean's – a realization that brought him to pellucid alertness.

He looked over at an equally awake David, whose eyes reflected Tommy's own terror. Sister Jean was nowhere in sight, and it was Tommy who broke the silence with a loud "My God!"

A calm, controlled voice emerged from the kitchen. "I'm – sorry, boys. I had another key, but… I should have thought to knock." Tommy and David continued to look at each other in helpless, speechless embarrassment, and when she got no response, Sister Jean added, "I'm a nurse, fellas. I didn't mean for it to happen, but – well, I do see men out of uniform all the time." That seemed to satisfy David, who just made a shrugging notion at Tommy. But still neither he nor Tommy said anything, so Sister Jean said, "I'll wait in the hall. You'll want to say goodbye to each other. Tommy, you best get a move on. David, you wait here and I'll come back for you."

David, finding his voice, called out, "All right, Sister. Thank you," as they heard the door from the kitchen to the hall close. David looked over at the still-speechless Tommy and repeated his shrugging motion. "It's true, y'know. 'Eaven knows, she's already seen me as God made me. 'Tis nothing to be ashamed of–"

"But David… we were… *with* each other."

"Bloody 'ell!" David said, suddenly angry. "We weren't doing anything when she walked in, just sleeping."

"But I – I don't know if I can face her–"

"Well, you'll 'ave to, 'cause she's the one's got to take you back to your leftenant."

It was Pearson's practicality kicking back in with a vengeance. He got up, and made to get dressed, but Flowers was breathless at the sight of him in the morning light, and said, "Don't."

"What?" David asked, but he knew; he let his clothing drop to the floor.

Rising, Tommy said, "I want to say good-bye just like this."

"I'll see you in France, then, Tommy," David said as their bodies met one more time. "Don't you worry."

Minutes later, his uniform on and his courage up, Tommy emerged from the flat into the hall where, to his surprise, Sister Jean, in her nun outfit (he had forgotten about "Sister Flaherty") was leaning against the wall, dozing. He gently touched her shoulder, and she cried "Oh!" with a start, reminding him all over again of her discovery of them. "Tommy," she said with an apologetic gesture of her hand. "I'm sorry. I must have fallen asleep."

"*I'm* sorry," he replied pointedly, but she simply said, "We must get going. We can't be late."

"Are we catching a train?" he hollered after her as she fled down the stairs in front of him; he was certain she didn't want to look him in the face, due to embarrassment, disgust, or both.

"We'll walk. It's not far," she called over her shoulder.

Not until they were out on the street did he catch up with her. To his surprise, she turned an untroubled face to him as he pulled abreast. "It looks like it's going to be a beautiful day, isn't it?" she asked brightly.

"It does feel cooler," he allowed. "Look, Sister, about–"

"Now, Tommy," she said almost coquettishly, "I said I was sorry. Can't we just leave it be?"

"But I–" He stared at her, mystified by her behavior after what she'd witnessed, and as he did so, the extraordinary weariness in her face, indeed her whole body, became evident to him. "How long has it been since you've slept, Sister?"

"Oh" – now she did turn from him, although they continued to walk along together at a brisk pace – "since this time yesterday, more or less."

"You will go home to the Shipleys' after you take me to the lieutenant, won't you?"

"There's still David to take care of, remember?" she said, returning his gaze again. "Even if he doesn't have the 'flu–"

It hit him then. "You never asked, this morning. How did you know?"

"I – saw enough to tell." He colored deeply, but she pushed on. "His color was too good. It must have been something trifling. I'm so glad."

"So am I," Tommy murmured.

She seemed about to ask him something, then to think better of it. "Look, here we are. On the Strand. I chose the flat 'cause it was so close. We're almost there."

"Sister? When do you have to work again?"

"Four in the p.m.'s."

"Please promise me you'll get some sleep before then."

They were already in the stairway of Lieutenant O'Malley's building. She turned to him and touched his face, as she had before his trip to Dunster. "You are such a kind, caring boy. It's really no wonder David likes you so much."

It passed through his mind at that moment that she could report what she'd seen to Lieutenant O'Malley, and he could be court-martialed. The lack of any kind of judgment, except positive judgment, in her voice overwhelmed him. "Is this good-bye?" he finally asked.

"Sister Flaherty is about to go into action," she said, slipping into the accent. "Then I'll have to be leavin' you with yore Leftenant Johnny."

Impulsive again, he hugged her even more strongly than when they had done the same thing in the same place a few days ago. "God bless you, Sister. Thanks for everything."

"No, God bless you, Tommy. It's you who's going back to the front."

Things went smoothly this time with O'Malley, and later that morning, Flowers boarded the troop train for Dover. He was acutely aware of being outnumbered – nothing as far as the eye could see but Tommies, who made him feel awkward as he towered over them, sticking out like the proverbial sore thumb. Were there no tall Englishmen save Hardison?, he wondered; but of course by now he could answer his own question: the best physical specimens had long since been swallowed up by the war. The train pulled out of Charing Cross, and he glimpsed Big Ben with longing, wondering when he'd see London again.

As he gazed out the window at the receding Thames, he noticed the Britons in his car had joined together in song. Eager to learn something new so he could sing it for Pearson when they saw each other again, Flower of Iowa became attuned to their ditty, whose refrain went:

*"Goodbye-ee, goodbye-ee,*
*Wipe the tear, baby dear, from your eye-ee.*
*Though it's hard to part, I know,*
*I'll be tickled to death to go..."*

As Tommy listened, the soldiers proceeded to a verse that somehow reminded him of Davey. He spoke up then, requesting they reprise this part, which they obligingly did; it recounted the adventures of a "little Private Patrick Shaw," who "was a prisoner of war." The lyrics had Shaw punching his German captor and escaping; Tommy marked both the words and the tune, memorizing and saving them for later. When the Tommies had finished serenading him, the American thanked them, and one of their number, a dark-haired, very young man (indeed they all seemed, if possible, younger than Flowers) with a mustache that appeared hesitantly penciled in, responded, "We're the ones what should be thankin' ye, Yank. It's up to ye boys now to stop Jerry."

"It's up to all of us," Tommy demurred.

"We'll all do our best," the mustachioed British boy, possibly Scottish judging by his accent, agreed, though he added, "but we're counting on yer lot to make the difference."

"And we won't let you down," Tommy said gamely.

# Chapter XXXV

The peculiar feeling of arriving home that had come over Tommy on his first glimpse of England was as nothing compared to the sensation that overwhelmed him as the crowded lorry lurched through Rainneville in the light of early morning. Flowers would have liked to ask the driver to stop, so he could get off and say *"Bonjour"* to Nicole and Madame, but of course at this hour the *estaminet* was closed, and the Frenchwomen might even be asleep; besides, he had been fortunate enough not to have to walk from the railhead near Amiens, instead hitching a ride on this lorry filled with friendly British and Australian soldiers, none of whom seemed to have the sort of difficulty with each other that he'd witnessed between David and Jamie.

As the lumbering vehicle began to roll down the green hillside in the direction of Pierregot, he again wished Davey were with him, here and now. His time with Pearson in England already seemed some kind of dream, much as Tommy's life with Susan in Iowa now seemed fantastic to him – and even though the times he'd had here in France with David seemed vividly, vitally real.

At the bottom of the hill, the lorry came to a slow, rather than a complete halt, and a large, ebullient sergeant bellowed, "Your station, Yank!" igniting good-natured laughter among Flowers' fellow travelers. Tommy disembarked with barely time to wave good-bye, as the vehicle picked up speed, kicking up a cloud of dust as it made toward Molliens.

Turning to face the familiar hill, he was hit by another wave of homesickness for the encampment at the top, as well as a surge of weariness. The ride from Amiens notwithstanding, it had taken him twice as long to return as it had to reach England from here. He was feeling the effects of two nights of sleeping in stations, as well as the heat, as he trudged up the slope carrying his greatcoat. It wasn't nearly as steep as the hill in Dunster, but even so, by the time he reached the top he was soaked inside his uniform. The village seemed strangely quiet, and so did the encampment. He was eager to find his buddies, especially Jamie, but went dutifully to report to the captain first.

Shuffling down the second-floor hallway of the old schoolhouse, he smartened his step in anticipation of facing Dougherty. He was therefore unprepared when he turned the corner to find no corporal, but an unfamiliar lieutenant, a young man with slicked-back blond hair, sitting at Dougherty's desk. Lest he appear insubordinate in his surprise, Tommy consciously snapped to and said, "Sir! Private Thomas Flowers reporting for duty, sir!"

The lieutenant, who had about him an air of slight officiousness but lacked Dougherty's aura of menace, regarded Tommy dubiously, then said, "At ease, Private." When Tommy struck the appropriate stance, he added, "Where have you come from, Private Flowers? I don't recall seeing you before."

"I'm with the 131st Regiment, 2nd Battalion, Company E, sir. I've been away for a week."

The lieutenant's eyebrows went up. "For a week? Where were you gone for a week?"

"To England, sir."

The officer's skepticism became still more evident: "England? Why would you have been in England?"

"Captain Willnor sent me there for a training course, sir." Newly acquired instincts told Tommy to stop his story there.

"He sent a *private* to England for training?"

"Yes, sir. The captain can tell you–"

The lieutenant scratched his ear, cleared his throat, and said, "Captain Willnor isn't here anymore, Private–"

"Was he killed, sir?" Tommy interrupted breathlessly, and the irritated lieutenant replied, "Don't interrupt an officer when he's speaking, soldier." Scornfully he added, "No, Captain Willnor wasn't killed. But it's convenient for you that he's not here, isn't it?"

"Begging your pardon, sir?"

"I'm suggesting you might have gone AWOL, soldier."

"Oh, no, sir! I'm no deserter," Tommy said with surprising calm; this was beginning to seem a familiar scene to him. "Is Corporal Dougherty still here?" he added. "He handled the paperwork. And Sergeant Colbeck knew about it, too."

The man seemed to flinch at the mention of both names, but responded, "Don't you mean *Sergeant* Dougherty and *Lieutenant* Colbeck, Private Flowers?"

This news shocked Tommy, but he recalled then the telegram O'Malley had received, and replied coolly, "Do I, sir? It was Corporal Dougherty and Sergeant Colbeck when I left here last week."

The lieutenant frowned, folded his arms, then commanded, "Sit down, Private." He began shuffling through papers the way Dougherty did, more or less ignoring Flowers. Tommy wanted to ask him what the problem was, but he had learned a few lessons, and so kept still until, at length, the officer looked up from his desk and said, apropos of nothing, "My name is Sand, Private Flowers. Lieutenant William Sand. I'm your new commanding officer."

"I see," Tommy said with a nod, venturing, "Are congratulations in order, then, sir?"

It was Sand's turn to be surprised, and he gave Flowers what the latter read as a friendly look and said, "Not quite yet. I'm being promoted to captain soon."

"Is that why you don't have an adjutant yet, sir?"

Sand stared at him, then said, "You have an awfully familiar manner with officers, soldier."

Tommy stiffened. "I'm sorry, sir."

"That's more like it." Then Sand himself relaxed a bit and added, "But you're right; I don't have an adjutant yet. It was queer that Captain Willnor only had a corporal to serve in that post."

Tommy found himself in the odd position of defending his old nemesis: "I think Corporal Dougherty was very good at it, sir."

"Not so good that he didn't botch the paperwork so a private went to England, apparently." Tommy said nothing in reply, but he thought, This Lieutenant Sand is smart; I never said one word about the orders being a mistake. Sand, looking at him, added, "Is that what you want, Tommy?" The use of his nickname, again something he had not mentioned, startled Flowers. "Do you want to be an adjutant?"

"No, sir. With all due respect, sir, I want to kill Germans."

That seemed to be the right answer, as Sand laughed appreciatively and said, "Good boy," as though Tommy were some sort of dog. "We're waiting for Lieutenant Colbeck," he added helpfully. "He's due to report to me soon anyway." The officer began twiddling with a pen, but carefully; he wasn't likely to accidentally stain anything or anyone with ink. Looking at the instrument rather than the Doughboy, he continued, "Do you... *like* Lieutenant Colbeck, Private Flowers?"

Tommy answered with guileless enthusiasm. "Yes, sir! Very much."

Sand's tone grew colder as, continuing to stare at his pen, he muttered, "All the men seem to."

"Yes, sir," Tommy agreed, oblivious to how much his assent was unwanted. "He's very well liked by the men."

"Yes," Sand repeated, almost frosty now; and then, without a word, he returned to his paperwork.

The wait proved to be not long at all. Tommy was situated so that someone coming down the opposite hallway might see Sand before spotting him; and so, before he ever caught sight of his friend, he heard Jamie's voice calling, "Mornin', Billy!"

Hearing the Australian's ever-insolent tone completed Tommy's sense of being happily back home again, but Colbeck's effect on Sand was altogether different. The lieutenant flushed slightly and, just before Tommy came into Jamie's field of vision, said to his fellow officer, "I'd appreciate it, Lieutenant Colbeck, if you showed a little more respect in front of an enlisted man."

"Oh, certainly, Billy," Jamie said as he turned the last corner, "I didn't know you had company"; then he cried "Flaowuh of Iowa! Where have you been?" throwing his arms open wide as he advanced on Tommy, looking for all the world as though he meant to give the Yankee private a welcome-back hug. Instead, he stopped just short of Flowers as the latter rose, gave his laziest salute, and said in a low voice, "Nice bars there, Lieutenant."

"Naow, don't you start with me," Jamie began, shaking a finger at him, all conviviality.

Sand rose at his ridiculous little desk, gesturing at Tommy. "Lieutenant Colbeck, did you have any knowledge of this man's whereabouts?"

"He's right here, obviously," Jamie said with a full measure of impudence. Before Sand could counter, he added, to Tommy's relief, "And he's been to England for trainin', of course."

"Then why did you ask him where he'd been?"

"It was what you call rhetorical, Billy. You *have* heard of that–?"

"What kind of training does a private need to go to England for a week for?"

Jamie looked with elaborate disinterest toward Tommy. "Machine guns, wasn't it?"

"You aren't in the Machine Gun Battalion," Sand said to Flowers, who thought again, He's sharp; he remembers things.

"No, sir, I'm not–"

"So why would you go to England for machine-gun training?"

Tommy started to shrug until it occurred to him that it was too un-military a gesture when being questioned like this by an officer. "Because those were my orders, sir."

"Who would have signed such orders?"

"Captain Willnor, sir."

Sand rolled his eyes. "Willnor again." He turned to Colbeck. "I think this private's been on a lark in Limey-Land, courtesy of the United States Army. And I think you were in on it."

Jamie did not hesitate to shrug. "I knew abaout it, Billy. But of course I didn't question the captain's orders."

"Huh!" Sand shifted his attention back to Flowers. "Well, I hope you enjoyed your little jaunt, Private, because you won't be getting another one for a good long while."

"Like I said, sir, I'm here to fight Germans."

"Good." Sand turned back to Colbeck. "And speaking of that, we have new orders to–"

"–march to the Baizieux line tonight and hold it for twenty-four haours. I know."

Sand sat down, a picture of frustration. "Since you seem to know everything–"

"I hear things, Billy. You know that. Permission to take this man back to his unit?"

Wearily, Sand replied, "I don't outrank you yet, Jamie."

Flowers was surprised to hear him use Colbeck's first name. The blond lieutenant added, "Take – what was it you called him?"

"Tommy Flaowuhs?"

"No, something about Iowa."

"Flower of Iowa," Tommy cut in. "It's my nickname, sir. My name is Flowers, and I'm from Iowa–"

"I think I figured that out, Private," Billy Sand said, flashing a peculiar, unexpected grin. "Dismissed."

Safely out the schoolhouse door, Tommy asked Jamie, "Why do you go out of your way to turn people against you?"

"I wouldn't want to turn Billy against me. He's a good man."

"He's sure a lot smarter than Captain was."

"You noticed that. I always forget haow smart *you* really are, because you do such a good job of hidin' it sometimes."

"So, when did you get promoted? And why did you take it? And what happened to Captain? And what's this about Dougherty? And why were you giving Lieutenant Sand such a hard time, if you think–"

"Stand daown, stand daown," Colbeck said with a laugh. "One question at a time." Flowers grew quiet, and the Aussie said, "Let's stop and have us a chat. We should do that before I take you to your unit, anywise." They found an old linden tree, one of the few still standing in Pierregot, and sat down under its shade. "I'm testin' Billy naow," Jamie continued, responding to Tommy's last question, "so that when he is my superior, he'll listen to me if I think he's makin' a mistake. He's very young, and he's scared abaout havin' this big a command. I want him to know he can trust me, and not expect me to say 'Yes, sir' to ev'rything."

Tommy nodded. "So that's Lieutenant Sand. What about Lieutenant Colbeck? The man who said he didn't 'give a fig for anyone but rankers?'"

At the recollection of his exact words, Jamie frowned. "You remember entirely too much too well, lad. You should be careful abaout that fresh maouth of yours."

"You have a fresh mouth, too."

"I only use it after I've decided to use it. It may look like I'm talkin' off the top o'my head, but I never do."

Tommy smiled at him. "I think you have one set of rules for Jamie and one set for everyone else."

Jamie nodded agreeably. "Maybe. Rank does have its privileges."

"Never thought I'd hear you say that."

"Y'see? I told you never to make assumptions." Tommy, more annoyed than amused, grew quiet again, and Jamie noted it and asked, "Haow was England?"

On impulse, Tommy turned to him and answered truthfully, "It was the best thing that ever happened to me in my whole life."

The spontaneity and depth of the response took Jamie somewhat aback. It made him wonder if Tommy had met some girl in England, but he was reluctant to ask about that just then, so instead he inquired, "Did you see Peahson?"

For his part, Tommy was realizing the possibilities for questioning his sudden declaration had created, and he backed off with a simple, clipped "Yes." Jamie, he thought, would never understand what had happened between him and Davey. Nobody would.

"Is he mendin' all right?"

"Yes. He should be back soon. Thanks for asking."

Jamie chuckled. "I've missed you. You and your manners." Now ready to venture into more dangerous territory, he added, "Nicole's been askin' abaout you."

To Jamie's dismay, this rekindled Tommy's enthusiasm. "About me? When?"

"Ev'ry day," Colbeck replied ruefully.

"How is she? How's Madame? Think we can go there tonight?"

"You weren't listenin' to Sand. Tonight we march to the Baizieux trenches."

"Oh. I heard. For twenty-four hours, like at Vaden."

"I'm not sure if it will be like Vaden. It might be more – active. Not like what's happ'nin' at Château-Thierry, mind you, but active."

Flower of Iowa nodded; it was not the first time he'd heard the latter place name in the past two days. "Wish we were there," Tommy said idly.

But Jamie, preoccupied, barely noticed the comment. He sucked in a deep breath and said, "Tommy, there's somethin' I need to warn you abaout. I think I made a mistake."

The way Colbeck said this was so unlike him, it aroused instant apprehension in Flowers. "What do you mean?"

Jamie exhaled and said, "I may have made a deal with the devil. Y'see, I decided it was time for me to be a leftenant, after all, as long as I could stay with the American Army. To do that, I had to make a deal with Dougherty. Part of it got you to England–"

"I thought you had something to do with it! So I do have you to thank–"

"I'm glad you enjoyed yourself, lad," Colbeck said, waving his hands, "but I'm not finished. Y'see, it wasn't all my doin'. Part of it was Dougherty's. Another part of the deal was to promote him to sergeant."

He gave the American a meaningful look that the latter missed. Instead, Tommy paused, then said, "Well, I reckon he deserves it. He was very good at Hamel."

"You're so fair," Jamie said, shaking his head. "Yes, he was. But that ain't the end of it. Willnor approved the promotions for Dougherty and all the rest, but when he faound aout Dougherty wanted to fight and didn't want to work for him anymore, he put his foot daown and said no."

"Oh. So?"

"So, the very next day some sort of ruckus kicked up over some orders Willnor signed. Two days after that, Sand was here, Willnor was gone – and Dougherty got his promotion and his squad. Do you see what I'm sayin', lad?"

Tommy didn't hesitate. "I think so. You're saying you think Dougherty sabotaged Willnor to get his way?"

"I knew you were smart. And Dougherty, he's so smart, he did it so it couldn't be traced to him. I can't prove it, but I'm convinced of it."

There was a moment's silence, then Tommy said, "He tried to do me in, too."

"What?"

"In London," Tommy said. "They found out my papers were wrong, and the lieutenant there was ready to have me court-martialed. The only thing that saved me was" – Tommy stopped himself, still determined to avoid any detailed discussion of his time in England – "was you, your telegram." Flowers laughed. "I was afraid you lied for me, saying you were a lieutenant." Then his good cheer disappeared. "But if Dougherty had his way, I'd be behind bars. I knew he was behind it–"

"Except he wasn't," Jamie said with another shake of his head. "He helped me write that tellygram, so the wordin' was exactly right, to save your skin."

Tommy was dumbfounded. At length, the best he could come up with in reply was "So maybe he's not so bad. I mean, even if what you're saying about him and Captain is true, it's hard to feel sorry for the captain."

"I agree with you there. But remember, he was totally loyal to Willnor. His most trusted aide. Or so we all thought. I don't trust him, Tommy, and you shouldn't, either. He was good at Hamel, but he's not very good when there's no fightin'."

"Maybe he'll get better."

"Let's hope so. For your sake."

Tommy froze. "You mean–?"

Jamie nodded. "He's your sergeant naow. Company E."

Back to reacting on impulse, Tommy cried, "Jamie, no! He *hates* me!"

"Two seconds ago, he was a fine fellow who came to your rescue."

"But – but–"

"I know, Tommy, I know. Your first instinct is prob'ly right this time. That's why I'm tellin' you all this. You should watch your back. You can't be careless with him as your sergeant."

"Can't you get me transferred?"

Jamie's aspect hardened. "Naow, don't go askin' me to wet-nurse you, like you're some schoolboy who's afraid of a strict teacher." Then his voice softened some. "Anywise, I'll be your leftenant – and his."

"But we hardly ever saw our old lieutenant. It was always Eddie."

"It'll be diff'rent with me. But I'm tellin' you, just so you know, don't come to me if you have trouble with Dougherty unless you've tried ev'rything else."

Looking and sounding every bit the schoolboy Jamie had accused him of being, Tommy replied, "Yes, Jamie."

Colbeck regarded Flowers with apparent affection. "You're a good lad, Tommy. I hate to put you through havin' that arse as a sergeant. But compared to the war, it's nothin'. It'll be all right. Oh, and one last thing, then we better get you back to your unit: don't say a thing more than you have to abaout England… which I notice is what you're doin' anywise."

# Chapter XXXVI

In light of the clear, hot weather of the day just completed, the condition of the Baizieux trenches came as a complete surprise to Tommy, at least until Young, the married private, informed him laconically, "You missed a lot of rain, Flower of Iowa."

Evidently he had. The Baizieux system was a slimy, muddy mess, complete with miniature torrents and freshets in the most unexpected places. As the 131st Regiment plodded in, the sticky earth of Picardy made loud, sucking noises with each tromp of every Doughboy's boot, a sound so obscene that it immediately generated jokes among the men, who in turn were repeatedly quieted, most of all by the cocksure new sergeant, Daniel Dougherty, who was hissing at his charges to maintain absolute silence, which Tommy thought a little foolish; the noise their marching through the muck was unavoidably creating could probably be heard in Berlin, easily drowning out any of their chatter. The only consolation was that surely the Huns were having to deal with the same conditions, although maybe not as bad, since as usual the enemy held the high ground.

Tommy and his squadmates – Carson, Sleaze, Giannelli, Young, and some unfamiliar faces – had been mutually standoffish for much of the day. The week's absence, with all the intervening changes, had put Flowers behind on regimental news, making him a bit of a stranger even to his old compatriots. He had anticipated trouble from Dougherty, but the latter had barely said a word about the private's trip to England – probably, Flowers guessed, because he was largely responsible for its coming about; and true to both Jamie's advice and his own druthers, Tommy kept quiet about his journey.

As his squad maneuvered into position, his mind focused on the misery of it all. A week ago, he thought – no, less – I was in London, in Dunster, and now this. He caught himself wishing the order would come down to foreshorten the twenty-four hours in these trenches; then he inwardly chided himself for taking such an unsoldierly attitude. Even so, as he felt the wet, glutinous French clay pull at his ankles, and heard it do the same with his comrades, he recalled Jamie's lurid descriptions of Passchendaele, and that made him all the more uneasy. Surely the Doughboys fighting at Château-Thierry were not having to deal with this. He imagined them charging over open fields as he had at Hamel, not sitting muddy and miserable in some rathole.

Tommy wasn't just being poetic, for even as he thought this, he felt one of the rodents crawling over his foot in the dark, and kicked violently at the thing, causing a commotion with two new squadmates next to him. Unfortunately, this occurred just as Dougherty came back down the line. "What's going on here,

Flowers?" he demanded, even though the other two men had made just as much noise in reaction.

"Just a rat, sir." There was no question of calling Dougherty "Dan," let alone "Danny" – the very thought was absurd – or even "Sarge."

"Rats are a part of trench life, soldier."

Tommy felt like saying, "I should know better than you," but instead he simply concurred, "Yes, sir. I'm sorry, sir. It's just that it took me by surprise–"

"See that it doesn't happen again."

"Yes, sir," Tommy replied, thinking what an asinine order that was; who was going to tell the rats they weren't supposed to sneak up on the soldiers? But he held his tongue, and Dougherty had more to say, moving on to another subject and addressing all of his squad, which was now gathered around him:

"Well, men, we finally have a clear night. In fact, now that the weather is in our favor, I'd say it's a perfect night. A perfect night for a trench raid."

This apparently was supposed to prompt enthusiasm from the men, but nobody spoke up, so their NCO continued, "So I've volunteered us for just that. We'll be jumping off in about ten minutes." Tommy could feel Dougherty looking at him as the sergeant added, "Flowers, you'll be on point. Carson and Sleziniak will back you up. I'll be behind you with the rest of the men."

"What's the objective, sir?" Tommy asked in a tone so dispassionate, he surprised himself.

"The German listening post. Other side of the wire. Now make sure your equipment is ready, all of you."

As Dougherty moved on, and the men fell to checking their gear as ordered, Harry Carson, carefully surveying his Springfield, muttered, "Damn fool."

"Who?" Tommy asked.

"That one." Harry, clearly visible in the moonlight, nodded in the general direction where Dougherty had gone. "Sergeant *Schwein,* we all call him." Although Carson mangled the German pronunciation, his meaning came across.

"What's he done to make everyone talk like that after one week?"

"Tells us we're all sorry excuses for soldiers. Says he's gonna make *real* soldiers out of us. Huh!"

"Well, maybe we can learn something from him, Harry. He was good at Hamel."

"Huh!" Carson repeated. "He really hates *you,* Flower."

"I know," Tommy replied, philosophical; then he switched the subject: "Heard anything from Vern?"

"No," Carson said with a shake of his head; there still had been no word as to whether Sanders was even alive. "How about your English buddy? You get to see him?"

The question annoyed Flower of Iowa, who hadn't assumed his whereabouts were general knowledge. Obliged to respond, he simply said, "Yes, I did. He'll be back soon, I reckon."

"That's good." Tommy wondered at the ornate courtesy they were showing each other even as they were preparing to crawl through mud, cut wire, and maybe kill a Hun together. "You worried about being point?" Carson asked in a voice so low that at first Tommy thought he'd imagined it, until Harry prompted, "Tommy?"

"Somebody has to be point. It might as well be me as anybody."

"I'll be right behind you."

"I know. You and Sleaze. So I don't reckon I have much to worry about."

"Keep it down!" It was Dougherty, suddenly very close, shushing both of them with the loud, whispered command. As the sergeant again moved on, Carson again muttered, "Sergeant *Schwein*."

The NCO whirled on Tommy. "*What* did you say, Private?"

"Nothing, sir." Tommy could make out the man's face in the darkness, staring at him with what he perceived to be a mixture of anger and pure hatred. Dougherty held his gaze for a few seconds, in a way that chilled Flowers, then moved on to the next couple of men down the line.

When the sergeant was safely out of earshot, Carson said, "See, Flower? I told you he has it in for you."

"So I notice," Tommy said, with a stab at irony.

When, a few minutes later, the call came down the line for the squad to stand to, Tommy had no explanation for his preternatural calm. As he scaled the fire-step at the signal to jump off, the muddy parapet proved slippery, and for half a second he found himself sliding backward, until a shove from someone – Harry, perhaps – propelled him over the top. For the second time in his life, Tommy was breaching the supposed safety of a trench for open ground, this time without the cover of an artillery barrage or aeroplanes.

He hadn't scurried, belly on the ground, more than two feet before he was thoroughly coated with mud. Worse, he and the men behind him were causing the morass they were crawling through to make the same sucking noises as when they had entered the trench earlier. What was a matter of mirth in the protection of the trench was no joke out here in the open; Tommy continued ahead on pure fear, waiting for the sound of gunfire or the dreaded whistling of incoming shells. So considerable was the Doughboys' racket that after a while the lack of a German response was unnerving; as wretched as he felt with the ooze soaking through to his chest, Tommy was mystified that they were proceeding unchallenged over the pitted landscape.

Just as the wire loomed ahead in his line of sight, the ground sloped slightly upward. As lead man, Tommy began to scale this low rise, only to find it so slick that he started to tumble backward, faster, louder, and more decisively than at the parapet. As he landed on his side a few feet back with a sharp splat, a sulfurous green star shell burst overhead. Solidly anchored in the muck, Flowers couldn't turn around to see his squadmates behind him who, he assumed, were now frozen flat to the ground, too. But when the light from the Hun shell died away, he distinctly heard the mud-sucking noises again… heading away from him, in the direction of the American trenches.

Torn between terror at being abandoned and his sense of duty, he opted in favor of silence as he struggled to disengage himself from the mud with an absolute minimum of sound; despite the cacophony coming from his fellows, he worried that his own noise, so close to the German lines, might give the enemy a focus to direct their fire. Mindful of Jamie's Gallipoli story, he was determined not to repeat the mistakes of the unfortunate Kerry Saxton.

Abruptly the darkness was split by another star shell, a red one that cast a bloody color over the mud and wire immediately in front of him; then the Maxims unloaded in a fierce fusillade. Unable to think of a better stratagem, Tommy flattened himself against the thick, disgusting mud from which he'd been trying to extricate himself only moments before. Only the sound of his own breathing and the sour smell of his own fearful breath blowing back in his face reminded him he was alive as shells exploded with a deafening roar all around him. He heard a cry, as he had that first night in the Vaden listening post with Sleaze; no, more like the cries at Hamel when Maple and Ski were hit; a shell had found its mark somewhere. As the tumult went on, and on and on, at the worst moments he allowed himself a soft whimper, easily drowned out by the chaos all about him. His right ear was stuck to the moist ground, but suddenly he felt something alive seeking to crawl inside it, and raw instinct overruled everything else; with a violent thrust he succeeded where he had failed before, tearing himself from the gooey earth that had imprisoned him.

No sooner had he broken free than he re-flattened himself, as the whizz-bangs and machine-gun bullets continued to explode from every direction. But he had managed to give himself a slightly better vantage point – though what he saw initially was scarcely encouraging. Looking back toward his trenches, he could see none of his comrades, only, perhaps, pieces of one or two. Turning away, he caught a strong, sickening odor, and then noticed off to his left, perhaps fifteen feet away, the shape of a corpse, one his nose told him was anything but fresh.

On the edge of nausea, Tommy turned away again, to face up the small rise leading to the wire. There his spirits lifted a bit when, after a few minutes, during which the exchange of shots and shells never abated, let alone ceased, he was able to discern that although he was enfiladed, the little slope of ground also seemed to be effectively screening him from the enemy fire, at least as long as it remained dark. Again recalling Colbeck's stories, Flowers settled upon a strategy: he would lie flat and still until the cross-bombardment came to an end, and then, before it grew too light, try to make it back to his lines.

That being resolved, Tommy needed to concentrate on something else, to take his mind off his immediate predicament. As had happened in the clover at Hamel, his first thoughts turned to home. The star shells again made him think of fireworks, this time from a traveling carnival that had passed through when he was, oh, ten years old, maybe the same summer as the comet he'd recalled with Davey. A large crowd had assembled to view the pyrotechnics on the carnival's last night, and Tommy had asked his Dad to lift him up on his shoulders to see, something his father had done many times before. This time Tommy was rebuffed, his father declining, saying his son was too big for that now. Anxiously Tommy had craned his head in an attempt to see the fiery display between the figures of the taller adults, and as a result he missed it when one of the colorful projectiles misfired, injuring one of the carnival workers and sending the crowd scattering. It had been a scary but thrilling moment, being surrounded by all those big people, stuck in their midst as they stampeded in all directions.

He was stuck in the middle of something scary but thrilling now, too, he thought, maybe for the last time in his life – but then, he had thought that the night of the fireworks accident. What, he wondered, would be the memory he would carry with him to the grave if he were killed tonight? The first that came to his mind, to his amazement, was the cool feeling of his mother's hand on his forehead as he lay in bed with a fever at the age of, it must have been seven. It was a hot summer and he wanted to be outside, but they feared it was scarlet fever, and he had been forced to stay in bed a week or more. Toward the end, as he clearly began to recover, the experience had changed from frustrating to almost deliciously sweet. He could see the delicate white lace of the curtains as a breeze finally blew through the open upstairs windows, and the blue-and-white-striped wallpaper in the room where he lay recuperating, different from his own bedroom.

The recollection of it all had a calming effect on him – which lasted until a small shell landed perilously near, splattering him with mud. Gingerly he touched himself all over, to see if he had been struck by any shrapnel without feeling the pain, but no, only rancid earth.

All he could do now was wait.

The exchange of artillery and ammunition went on for two more hours – or maybe it was only twenty more minutes; Tommy couldn't tell, losing all track of time as he attempted to silently sing to himself every song he knew. When he got to "Tipperary" and "Good-bye-ee," his thoughts inevitably turned to Pearson. He now hoped that David would stay in England until the war was safely over; at the same time, the thought of Davey made Flower of Iowa all the more determined to get out of his situation alive.

He was some time deep in these musings when it occurred to him the noise had stopped, and all was quiet again. Either his eyes had adjusted extremely well to the dark, or it was already growing lighter. He would have liked to shift his position again, but was suddenly superstitiously afraid of seeing, or for that matter smelling, the corpse he was sure lay off to his left, as well as the ones he was pretty sure lay between him and the American trenches. Reluctant to make a move too soon, he lingered there until his alertness began to dull; the sky was definitely getting lighter now, but he was growing weary, getting sleepy....

It happened so fast, Tommy had no time to think about it. Half-awake, he was seized by a strong pair of arms, one hand clamping over his mouth to stifle any cries. For a split second he expected to feel a knife at his throat, or in his side. By the time the thought was complete, his captor had spun him around, and although the man's hand still covered his mouth, Tommy could see in the faint light he was face-to-face with Jamie Colbeck.

Flowers' relief seemed matched only by Colbeck's tension and anger; Tommy could see no happiness on Jamie's part over finding him. The lieutenant sternly put his finger to his own lips, then finally removed his hand from Tommy's mouth, saying only in the softest of whispers, "Can you move?"

Tommy nodded, and Jamie asked in a like tone, "Are you fit?" Flower of Iowa nodded once more, and the Australian nodded back. Then, to Tommy's astonishment, Jamie glanced once at the sky and motioned Flowers to follow him... as he began crawling toward the wire and the German lines. There was no confusion about direction this time; Tommy was as sure as David would have been: the American trenches were behind them, the wire ahead.

Jamie was making his way around the right-hand side of the rise that had both caused Tommy to slide backward, and later protected him from the enemy. When Tommy obediently followed, he saw at least part of the reason for Jamie's decision – some of the wire on the far side of the rise had been blown open, probably in the shelling. He watched Jamie's body rise dangerously high in terms of being a target, then drop again. As Tommy scuttled to the same spot (the earth seemed a little more dry now, after the better part of a day and night without rain), Jamie turned abruptly and motioned him to stop. The American was just short of a place where the wire appeared to be gone – but on second glance, a vicious-looking string of it protruded low from the earth. Jamie was looking maybe twenty feet off to his own left, around the other side of the rise where Tommy couldn't see, and drawing his pistol. He again silently motioned to Tommy, indicating the Yank should stay where he was and draw his own pistol. Then the Aussie was off again, mostly crawling on his stomach, 'til he was concealed from Flowers' sight.

In the dead quiet, in the dead middle of no-man's-land, Tommy's nerves finally were nearing the breaking point. Hunching down as the bullets and shells had whistled and roared overhead was easy compared to the long, tense moments of waiting out here alone, gun drawn. After what seemed to be hours, but was perhaps less than a minute, he heard a rustling and saw two men at once come hurriedly around the corner of the rise, crouching in a run. Tommy's gun was cocked before he could finally tell that one of them was Jamie – Jamie holding his gun on a German!

Taking in the sight, Flowers was utterly disbelieving. Of course he had seen Germans at Hamel, but with the exception of the man he still thought of as Uncle Larry, none of them up close, and certainly none of them alive and up close, near enough to look like just another person who happened to be in a gray uniform. This German was a thin, wiry, dark man with a scrawny mustache much like the young Scotsman's on the train from London, somewhere between Tommy and Jamie in age, but much closer to Tommy. He was limping badly, and in the predawn light, a second glance revealed why: his upper left thigh was soaked red.

By the time Tommy had comprehended all this, Jamie and the German were over the wicked piece of wire and alongside him. Tommy had the presence of mind to hold his gun on the enemy soldier, too, but even so, Jamie still looked none too pleased with his American friend. "Follow me," he whispered harshly to Tommy; then he made his prisoner lead, with Flowers and Colbeck bringing up the rear. They alternately crawled and ran in a crouch back to where Tommy had sheltered during the firefight, but Jamie didn't stop there; a few feet farther on toward the American trenches, he yelled in the loudest possible whisper, "Come on!" and all three men took off running.

They were within sight of their goal when the firing began, first from the German lines and then from the American side. Jamie dove to the muddy ground in an instant, and Tommy was almost as fast; the prisoner, slower, was struck again in a flash of red on his already bloodied thigh, and crumpled down in a heap, loudly crying out.

"Damn it!" Jamie swore in the same kind of loud whisper, cocking his pistol, and before a cry of "No!" could even escape Tommy's lips, Colbeck aimed a perfect shot at the prisoner's head and silenced him forever in a shower of gore.

Shots ranged back and forth over their heads, and then Jamie's extraordinary sense of timing came into play; when he made his decision and motioned "Let's go," neither he nor Tommy hesitated, but took off in a full-fledged sprint that ended with both of them leaping over the American parapet as more shots rang out. Jamie landed on top of some (ultimately unhurt) private, whose bitter complaints were drowned out by the cheers of the other men in this section of trench, which was not manned by any of Tommy's squad. Tommy landed more cleanly, but as he stood up, the entire evening flashed past him, ending with the German prisoner's head exploding from Jamie's bullet, and he promptly threw up.

# Chapter XXXVII

Tommy was swinging on the wooden swing hanging from the elm in his front yard in Iowa. It was the first really beautiful day of spring; violets carpeted the yellow-green lawn, and the trees were all in leaf, in that ephemeral shade of light green that darkens even more quickly than the leaves of autumn turn brown. It had rained the night before, but the morning sun had been sufficiently strong that the grass was dry, and only the fresh scent of the whole world growing lingered on the air as a reminder of the shower.

It might have been Easter; as he looked down to survey himself, he saw the bow tie, neatly pressed short-sleeve shirt, and short pants of a well-dressed child. The sound of an opening door turned his attention to the front porch, and there was his family: Dad in a straw boater and dark suspenders; Mama in her best Sunday dress, the one with the high collar; his sisters, and Susan, too, looking like a collection of Gibson girls. Following them through the door – and this did not surprise Tommy – were David and Nicole, the French girl in the same sundress and carrying the same basket of wildflowers as the day she and Tommy'd fled to the field, and the British lad looking dapper and handsome in a spanking-clean brown uniform, his hair neatly slicked back.

Another noise, off to his other side, caused Tommy to turn in that direction, where he saw a thin German soldier with a thin, dark mustache limping on an injured leg, clad in his gray uniform but sporting an expression of friendliness. As he came nearer to Tommy, the Boche's face split into a smile, but it did not stop there; the smile crept past the edges of the man's lips, parting the flesh, revealing the blood and sinew beneath, and continued until the skin split clear around the Hun's skull, the flesh flapping off to expose the brain and the eyes in their sockets, the lower part of the face still grinning, even as the top part burst in a thousand directions.

Tommy awoke with a soul-deep shudder and, he thought, a scream. But a glance at his soundly sleeping tentmate told him his cry couldn't have been too loud, if indeed he'd made a sound at all. Harry Carson, he had learned over the past few weeks, did not sleep all that deeply.

Wide-awake now, Flowers made a swift transit from dream back to reality. He wasn't swinging clean and carefree in Iowa in his little-boy shorts, but lying filthy and foul in France in his mud-caked uniform which, a torturous itching reminded him, was thoroughly infested with lice, or as David would say, "chats." It was growing light outside, and he lay deliberating with himself whether to get up, a question ultimately decided by the chats; he had to get his shirt off and, at least, decrease its lousy population. Thus resolved, he gathered himself together and, successful in not disturbing Harry, quietly stole from the tent – only to find himself, once again, face-to-face with Jamie Colbeck.

Tommy blinked, both at the dawn light and the possibility he was dreaming again, but the Australian said, "Well naow, that was convenient. I just came lookin' for you. My luck."

"It's Harry Carson's luck, Jamie. If you'da come into our tent, you'da woken him up."

Colbeck gave him an odd look, then added, "I'm here to take you to see Sand."

Still smarting from his lieutenant's anger in the Baizieux line, Tommy said, "What did I do wrong, Jamie? I'm sorry. I did my best. I don't understand what I did wrong."

The Aussie's expression went from blank, to amazement, to concern, and he placed his hand on the young American's shoulder, gripping it firmly. "Is that what you're thinkin', lad? That you done something wrong?"

"Well… yes…"

Colbeck shook his head. "I'm sorry, Tommy." He laughed a little. "Naow you got me doin' that, sayin' I'm sorry. But mark me: you're the only one who did what he was supposed to be doin'. That's why we're going to see Sand."

"Oh.… Can I – can I get the chats out of my shirt first? I feel so dirty."

The look of concern grew on Jamie's face. "Not right naow, Tommy. We can try to get you to the bathhouse after." Impulsively, the Australian threw his arm around Tommy's shoulder, and said with a gentleness that could have matched the Iowan's mother's during that fever, "You'll be all right, lad," and brushed Tommy's sticky hair back from his forehead.

"You should be careful, Jamie. I've got chats." Tommy saw Jamie's face darken at this comment, and in his confusion wondered if he'd offended the officer.

Once they reached the schoolhouse, the stroll down the familiar hallway revealed yet another stranger at what Tommy still thought of as Dougherty's desk: a lieutenant who, but for his red hair, could have been Billy Sand's brother. This man snapped to but did not salute, pronouncing "Lieutenant Colbeck" mostly as a statement, but also partly as a question. Jamie merely nodded, and the other man said, "I'll see if the captain's ready for you," disappearing into what Flowers persisted in thinking of as Willnor's office.

"Did they replace Lieutenant Sand already, too?" Tommy whispered.

Jamie, regarding him now with undisguised worry, replied, "No, Tommy. Billy's double bars came through."

"Oh. Reckon he outranks you now."

Jamie looked pleased, even relieved, that Tommy was capable of drawing this conclusion. But before anything else could be said, the redheaded lieutenant returned to his desk, saying, "The captain will see you now."

As Tommy followed Jamie into Sand's more spacious new quarters, Colbeck greeted his superior with "Mornin', Captain," instead of calling Sand by his first name; but that was followed by an "...and congratulations" that couldn't have sounded less formal.

On the other hand, the fourth man in the room, Sergeant Daniel Dougherty, strove to remain correct as he also turned to now-Captain Billy Sand and demanded fiercely, "Begging the captain's pardon, but I thought we were here to report on the Baizieux exercise. What is Private Flowers doing here?"

"I assume Lieutenant Colbeck is going to explain that to us," Sand said to Dougherty in a mild tone; then he returned both of the newcomers' salutes and added, "At ease, men. Be seated."

Tommy sat somewhat stiffly on a too-small chair, probably once a French schoolchild's, directly in front of Sand. Dougherty, still bristling, was seated to Flowers' left, while Colbeck seized a chair to Tommy's right, turning it back to front so he could lean his arms on the seat back as he spoke, a gesture, no doubt deliberate, that tested the outer limits of Sand's tolerance – and even in his dulled state, Tommy could tell Sand was more tolerant than Willnor; the captain hadn't said one word about the condition of his uniform.

"So, Lieutenant Colbeck," Sand began, once more picking up a pen and idly toying with it, "what's this all about? As Sergeant Dougherty mentioned, this was supposed to be a report on the Baizieux exercise."

"'Exercise' is an int'restin' term for it, Captain. But yes, that's why we're here."

"So, as a lieutenant, you're the one responsible for reporting to me. Perhaps you could explain why the presence of Private Flowers – or, for that matter, Sergeant Dougherty – is necessary."

"It concerns certain actions taken at Baizieux, sir, that pertain to both of them." Tommy could feel Dougherty stiffen next to him.

"And those were?"

"Just to start, a decision to stage a trench raid... on a moonlit night... when the graound was still so muddy you could barely move over it."

"Indeed," Sand continued. "Who would have made such a decision?"

"Sergeant Dougherty, sir."

Tommy couldn't resist shifting his eyes left to catch Dougherty's expression; to his consternation, the old trademark smirk was spreading across the sergeant's face. The next instant he found out why, as Captain Sand quietly told Lieutenant Colbeck, "You're wrong about that one, Jamie. It was my decision."

The familiar use of the Australian's first name seemed particularly well calculated, turning the nickname back on Colbeck to put him in his place. Tommy had never seen Jamie so taken by surprise, and it scared him.

But Jamie didn't hesitate long; he quickly countered, "With all respect, sir, it wasn't a good decision. I expect you were given bad advice."

"Who are you to question the captain–?" Dougherty angrily demanded of Colbeck, but Sand cut him off:

"I'm perfectly content to listen to Lieutenant Colbeck's opinion, Sergeant – especially after the fact. I respect his combat experience. You should, too."

Not that he was suddenly alert, but the whole exchange was beginning to ease Tommy from his torpid mental state; for Sand to catch Jamie off-guard one moment, and put Dougherty in his place the next, gave Flowers increased respect for his new captain. He observed with fascination as Sand turned back to Colbeck with an airy "Go on. I gather you don't think things went well."

"No, sir. It was a complete failure. The men made so much noise crawlin' through the mud that Flaowuhs, here, who was on point, got pinned daown before he reached the wire. The sergeant and his squad all turned tail for the trenches at the first Very light. It was an unnecessary risk of men's lives."

"'Turned tail' doesn't seem necessary to me, Lieutenant," Sand chided Colbeck; then he turned to Dougherty: "Is this true, Sergeant?"

Coldly, evenly, Dougherty replied, "I used my best judgment in following your orders, sir, and that includes what happened once we were discovered. I'm not sure I understand the lieutenant's logic. He says I took an unnecessary risk with men's lives, and then he criticizes me for saving the squad's lives by taking quick action and bringing them back in sooner than he'd've liked–"

"He has a point, Lieutenant," Sand said calmly, and now it was the Australian, turning to the sergeant, who could not contain his anger:

"You risked ev'ryone's lives by goin' aout there in the first place! And you sure as hell risked this man's life" – he pointed to Tommy – "and he's here and alive because of his own brav'ry, no thanks to you."

Dougherty's nostrils flared as he responded, "I admire Private Flowers' courage" – a statement that came as such a shock to Tommy, he turned to confront his sergeant, full face – "but someone has to be on point, and since he did it so well, it seems to me I made the right choice. Besides, the man had just come back from a week in England, while the others–"

"You delib'rately tried to get him killed!" Jamie shouted, causing Sand to raise his voice for the first time:

*"Lieutenant Colbeck!"* That proved effective; the room descended into silence, and the captain proceeded. "That is an extremely serious charge, Lieutenant. Unless you can provide me with any evidence, I'm going to forget you said it."

"What more evidence do you want, Billy?" Jamie retorted, adding with an angry gesture at Dougherty, "He plans a moonlight raid in the mud with Flaowuhs on point. That's a *recipe* for gettin' killed–"

"Then why didn't you state your objections beforehand, Lieutenant?"

"I didn't know abaout it beforehand, Captain. They were all over the top before I knew what was happ'nin'. I was in a diff'rent part of the trenches when Sergeant Dougherty gave the order."

Sand frowned, turned to Dougherty. "Is that true, Sergeant?"

"Yes, sir, as it happened. The time was right, and I knew I had your approval, so we struck. It happened that Lieutenant Colbeck was not there."

With an annoyed aspect, Sand began, "Sergeant Dougherty, when I approved your plan–"

"–you never said anything about clearing it with Lieutenant Colbeck, sir. With all due respect." Tommy counted that exchange as a double victory for Jamie: Sand had admitted the idea for the raid originated with Dougherty, and Dougherty had found it necessary to interrupt Sand, which the captain could not possibly have liked.

Meanwhile, the young commander was not giving up on his point so easily. "Yes, Sergeant, but did you deliberately conceal the plan from Lieutenant Colbeck?"

Dougherty looked straight at Sand and said, "Of course not, sir. Why would I do that? As I said before, the time was right and I had your approval. Lieutenant Colbeck's absence was a coincidence."

Tommy could feel Jamie fidgeting on his right, restraining himself from making a response. That proved a wise move. Sand swept his eyes over the three of them, and then returned to Dougherty. "How much notice for the raid did you give the men, Sergeant?"

"I think it was half an hour, sir."

That was such a bald-faced lie that Tommy flinched… and Sand noticed it. Turning his attention at last to Flowers, the captain said, "You've been quiet all this time, Private. Why don't you tell me what happened?"

Tommy hesitated, trying to concentrate. "Well, sir, when I started up the parapet I fell back, 'cause it was so slippery, but then–"

"That's very interesting, Private," Captain Sand interrupted, "but I meant before. When Sergeant Dougherty told you about the raid. How much time did he give the squad to prepare?"

That particular memory came back to Tommy clear as a bell. "Ten minutes, sir."

In a voice as near to kindly as Flowers had ever heard from him, Dougherty said, "I think you're a little confused, Tommy."

Flowers was too dumbfounded at hearing Dougherty call him by his first name to say anything more, and Jamie used the opportunity. "I don't think he's just 'a little confused,'" the lieutenant told his sergeant. "I think he's got a mild case of shell shock. And you made him stay there the rest of yesterday and last night, until he came back to camp with the rest."

"Is this true?" Sand asked Dougherty.

"He's not shell-shocked, and the lieutenant's not a doctor," Dougherty snapped.

"I agree that that is a matter for a doctor. But you yourself just said he was a little confused," Sand reminded Dougherty, "and he doesn't look well to me." He turned to Colbeck. "Weren't you there when Flowers got back to our trenches?"

"He came out and got me," Tommy interjected helpfully, gratefully.

The captain spared him a smile and a nod, then refocused on Jamie. "You? A lieutenant? Why didn't you order someone else out there?"

"That was my decision to make, Captain," Jamie said stonily, "and I made it."

Sand nodded again. "All right, then. When you came back with Private Flowers, why didn't you overrule Sergeant Dougherty here and send Flowers back to base camp so a doctor could see him?"

"Because I went lookin' for you, Billy, first thing. In my judgment, the raid was handled so poorly, I needed to report to you right away. I spent haours tryin' to find you. I thought you were with aour troops, but I couldn't find you anywhere–"

"I was there early in the night, but if you must know, I was called back here–" Sand explained.

But Colbeck was completing his thought, shaking his finger at Dougherty: "–and it never occurred to me this man would make Tommy work all day and night after what happened – but it should have."

"Begging your pardon, Captain, sir?" "this man" put in.

"Yes, Sergeant?"

"I really have to question the appropriateness of Private Flowers being here while we discuss all of this."

Tommy was actually inclined to agree with Dougherty on this point, but the one person whose opinion counted thought otherwise. "I'm not ready to dismiss him yet, Sergeant," the captain said curtly. "I will decide when, and if, that is appropriate." Turning to Flowers, Sand's voice grew calming and gentle. "Tell me what happened, Tommy."

As Flower of Iowa proceeded to do just that, recounting the crawl forward, the slide back down the rise, and being pinned down, his mental numbness, already apparent to the other men in the room, returned with a vengeance. Just before he reached the point in his story where Jamie showed up, the captain quietly interrupted: "How long were you out there like that, son?"

It seemed peculiar to Tommy for this man, who must have been six or seven years older at the most, to call him that. "I really don't know, sir. Twenty minutes? Two hours? After a while I couldn't tell."

"It was more like five haours," Jamie volunteered. "We used up a lot of shells and bullets on this 'exercise.'"

Sand ignored Jamie's last caustic comment, instead exclaiming, "Five hours!" He looked over to Dougherty who, apparently figuring this was a detail too easily verified, simply nodded in reluctant assent. *"Five hours!"* Sand repeated, with a baleful glare at both lieutenant and sergeant. "You left him out there all that time?"

"I thought he was dead," Dougherty said flatly.

"Once he was aout there, it was foolish to send anyone else aout 'til there was a fightin' chance of everyone gettin' back," Jamie said, equally toneless. "When I sawr it, I went."

Sand returned to Flowers. "What did you do all that time, Tommy?"

"I sang to myself, sir – not out loud. And I thought about home, and… people I know."

"I'm sure you did."

"He also captured a German."

The long exchange among the four of them already had Tommy dizzy; this outright fabrication from Colbeck left him speechless, which was evidently what his friend wanted, because Jamie went on, "When I went aout there, near to dawn, Flaowuhs was just comin' back araound that rise he mentioned. He'd noticed some of the wire was torn, and he went through it and surprised a German in a listening post."

"I don't remember receiving any reports of prisoners from the raid," Sand said.

"The German didn't quite make it back, sir. The three of us were runnin' back in the last of the darkness and he was hit."

"You killed him," Tommy blurted out, quite plainly.

His eyes staying on Sand, Jamie said smoothly, "I had to, Billy. He was cryin' aout and drawin' their fire. It was either him or us. But it was a shame, after all of Tommy's good work. We might have got some good information from him."

Sand pondered for a bit, then said, "How did you catch him, Tommy?"

Flowers was torn between telling the truth and staying loyal to the friend who had saved his life but was insisting on giving him credit he, Tommy, didn't want. At length he said, "I really don't have any memory of it, sir."

"I think your report on the raid should include some kind of commendation for Private Flaowuhs, sir. To survive being pinned daown like that and then capture a German–"

"Enough, Lieutenant," Sand said abruptly, flinging both his palms up. "Enough. This has all been very interesting, but I think I've heard enough."

The young captain brought his hands together, pressed both index fingers against his lips, and looked pensive for a minute, maybe two – a long time for the other three men in the room. Then he began to speak: "Lieutenant Colbeck, I admire your bravery in going out yourself to get Private Flowers, although I think it's rather reckless to risk a good officer's life on such a task. And I also admire your concern for your men. I don't want to waste lives, either. But I do think you're a little too conservative."

Tommy couldn't believe that one – Jamie, conservative! But his friend stayed silent, and the captain went on, "You say the idea for the raid was a bad one, and the raid itself was a total failure. Yet the point man did capture a German prisoner, and almost made it back to our trenches with him. That's not my idea of a total failure. Sometimes you have to do the unexpected – like crawling through the mud in the moonlight – and you have to be more daring than the other side. If the British had been more like that these last few years, perhaps we wouldn't need to be here at all."

Tommy wondered how Jamie could just sit there and take this from the captain. And after all he had learned from Colbeck, Pearson, and others about the British war effort, Flowers was appalled by Sand's last comment, forgetting he had been just as ignorant a mere month ago. He looked over at the Aussie, who continued to remain quiet, but the captain noticed the look and said, "Yes, Private? What is it?"

Thinking on his feet, Tommy said, "Begging the captain's pardon, sir, but Lieutenant Colbeck isn't British. He's Australian." That answer caused all three of the others, especially Jamie, to laugh, easing the tension in the room. Tommy just hoped his remark wasn't a betrayal of David and his countrymen.

Sand was nodding, smiling at Tommy's observation; then he grew serious again, and continued speaking to Jamie. "It's clear, Lieutenant Colbeck, that you're concerned for the welfare of Private Flowers – enough to risk your own life for him. That makes it all the more curious to me that you didn't make certain he was well taken care of once you both made it back. It seems to me you let your anger at Sergeant Dougherty get the better of you."

Sand pivoted to his right. "As for you, Sergeant, I admire your initiative. I stand by my decision approving the raid; it showed daring. And I probably also would have put Private Flowers on point, seeing as he'd just had a week's lark in England, while the other men were in hard training.

"But I am at a loss to understand why you would organize the action on such short notice, and why you would, it seems to me, deliberately avoid seeking out your immediate commanding officer, who has so much more experience of this war than you. I'm also concerned that I have heard very little – nothing, really – about you and your men attempting to help Private Flowers once you retreated back to our trenches. That was first of all your responsibility, Sergeant, not Lieutenant Colbeck's. And for the life of me, I cannot understand why you would force a private who's just been pinned down by shellfire for five hours, and who's brought back a prisoner, to do another twelve hours or more of hard duty."

"As you said, sir, he'd just had a week's lark in England, and–"

"For you to say that after what Private Flowers went through makes Lieutenant Colbeck's charge seem more plausible," Sand said crisply. Dougherty shrank back, visibly, and the captain seemed finished at last; but abruptly he turned to Flowers. "Well, Private?"

"Sir?"

"What do you have to say for yourself?"

"I – I'm still not sure what I did wrong, Captain, sir."

Sand stared at Tommy. "Wrong?"

"Yes, sir. Maybe you should tell me, so I don't make the same mistake again."

The captain continued staring at Flowers, then recovered. "Well, now, let's see. You stood up under all that fire–"

"I was actually lying flat, sir."

Sand kindly ignored the interruption, rolled his eyes, and continued, "–and you took a German prisoner. I can't see that you made a mistake in any of that, Flowers."

"Sir, I told you, I have no memory of taking that prisoner. I remember seeing him fall and I remember Jamie shooting him, but I don't–"

"He wasn't a deserter," Jamie broke in. "He didn't get in front of aour trenches on his own accord."

Sand's eyes shifted to Colbeck, back to Flowers, again to Colbeck, and finally to Flowers again. Then he called "McAdams!" and the redheaded lieutenant entered the room, paper and pencil in hand.

"Take this down," the captain ordered. "The official report of the trench raid staged at Baizieux on 17–18 July is as follows: Sergeant Dougherty, showing considerable initiative, led his squad on a raid of opposing trenches. Conditions..." He paused, thought, then continued, "Conditions were less favorable than anticipated. Private Flowers, on point, was pinned down under heavy shellfire. Under Sergeant Dougherty's direction, the rest of the squad managed to return to our trenches without casualties. After a... protracted exchange of artillery and other weapons, Lieutenant Colbeck, demonstrating commendable courage, determined that he would set out alone in an attempt to retrieve Private Flowers, who, in the meantime, exhibiting great daring, captured an enemy soldier. As they returned safely to our trenches, the prisoner was killed by fire from his own lines."

Tommy heard this last with bewilderment: the captain had been told quite clearly how the prisoner had died. "All who participated in this action are to be commended," Sand continued, "with the caveat that future actions of this nature be scrutinized closely, as they may prove too costly in terms of materiel and, potentially, men." Sand paused to think once more, then concluded, "Private

Flowers' contribution to this action should be recognized at some point in a manner appropriate. End."

As Lieutenant McAdams departed to type up the report, the captain added, "Private Flowers, you are to report at once to the medical officer for an examination. Even if you are pronounced fit, you are to spend the rest of this day and tomorrow in rest, until your company is scheduled to go back into the Baizieux line, tomorrow night. That's an order."

The captain looked at all three, and said to the other two, "I appreciate your frank reports. As for the disagreements that have been aired here, I expect you to put them behind you and behave like soldiers.

"Sergeant Dougherty, Lieutenant Colbeck is your commanding officer. You are to follow his orders. If you have a countermanding order from me or anyone else, you are to let Lieutenant Colbeck know. Do you understand?"

"Yes, sir."

"Lieutenant Colbeck, I continue to find your methods unorthodox. I can tolerate that as long as they produce results. When they do not – as when you prosecute some vendetta against a junior officer – you are not helping the war effort. And helping with the war effort is why you are here with the American Army. You know that yourself; I am just reminding you." Sand looked at Colbeck, got no response, and prompted, "Lieutenant?"

"I understand, sir."

Sand again surveyed them all. "Thank you, gentlemen. Lieutenant, if you will escort Private Flowers to the medical officer–"

"Sir?" Tommy piped up.

"Yes, Private?" the captain answered, countenancing another interruption with exaggerated patience.

"Is there any chance I can wash?"

He had brought them all to laughter again. "Yes, Tommy," Billy Sand said with an easy grin. "Once you see the doctor, you can have your bath."

The walk back down the schoolhouse hallway and the stairs following the long interview with the captain took place in icy, strained silence. Flowers was pretty much still in a daze. But when the three men exited the front door and Dougherty made to go in his separate direction, Colbeck came round him and flattened him bodily against the outside wall of the schoolhouse, much as he had done with David at the *estaminet*.

"Naow you listen to me, Sergeant," Jamie told him through gritted teeth. "Here's your first order from your commanding officer. From naow on you're personally responsible for this man's safety. Either you both make it through this man's war, or neither one of you does. I'll see to that. Do I make myself clear?"

Dougherty, who seemed to Tommy commendably calm under the circumstances, said simply, "You're wrong about me."

Colbeck let up, backed away, and took Tommy by the arm, barking over his shoulder to the sergeant, "Prove it."

# Chapter XXXVIII

Poked and prodded by an overworked British medical officer, Tommy was indeed pronounced fit, though the man murmured approvingly when he heard of Sand's order, and urged Jamie in a very low voice to watch his charge for any more symptoms of incipient shell shock, noting that their onset was sometimes delayed.

Jamie then marched Tommy to the British bathhouse, where the Aussie lieutenant had some kind of "discussion" with the bath sergeant that resulted in Flowers being allowed the extraordinary privilege of two rounds under the water pipes. That didn't make the water any warmer, but it did give Tommy the chance to thoroughly soap and wash himself. Afterward he grabbed clean underwear and lay out in the meadow sunning himself with other naked soldiers, just as he and David had, only this time his companion was Jamie, who had taken his turn after Tommy. "Since we jumped the line, we either get to wear Tommy uniforms, or wait 'til they bring some more clean Doughboy uniforms," Colbeck said as he sat down.

"That's all right with me," said Flowers, lying on his back in the grass. "This feels fine. If we get cool, at least we can put on our shirts and pants."

Jamie was scratching his chest, and Tommy said matter-of-factly, "You've got a lot of hair."

"Be glad you don't. Chats are particularly fond o'fellas with a lot of hair."

Tommy's hands were behind his head, forming a pillow. Closing his eyes, he asked, "Does it ever get this warm in Australia, Jamie?"

"Hah! Warmer than this. Much warmer." He was still sitting up. "Especially in January."

Tommy's eyes flew open, catching sight of a perfect French blue sky. "January?"

"Yes. Aour seasons are opposite yours. You went to school; you should know that. It's winter back home naow."

"Will you go back to Melbourne when the war's over?"

Jamie cracked a chat and paused, looked over to Flowers. "I've thought about stayin' on here."

Tommy sat partway up. "In France?"

"That's where we are, ain't it? You're gettin' goose bumps."

"I know. I reckon I should put on my shirt and pants. I'm dry now."

They both proceeded to pull on their underclothes, which were reasonably clean and fit reasonably well, then sat back down on the ground, still awaiting their American uniforms. As if their conversation hadn't stopped, Tommy said, "It's Nicole, isn't it?"

Jamie's eyes narrowed, and he said warily, "What?"

"That's why you want to stay in France after the war."

"These people are gonna need a lot of help puttin' their country back together." Jamie took a deep breath and added, "As for Nicole, I'm sure she'd much rather go back with you to Iowa."

Tommy laughed a little, hugging his knees. "I'm not sure what Susan would think of that," he said brightly; then his tone darkened and he added, "It doesn't matter, anyway."

"Don't be so solemn, lad. You just might live through this war yet."

"I didn't mean that. I'm just not sure I want to go back to Iowa."

"Flaowuh of Iowa not go back to Iowa? To a big city, then? New York? Chicago?"

Tommy shook his head. "I was thinking of England." As an afterthought, he added, "They'll need help there, too."

"True, though there ain't been no battles there. I'll grant you that. But I am surprised. You're so praoud of America."

"I'll always be proud to be an American, no matter where I am. I just think I might want to live in England, that's all. If I was in America, I'd go back to Iowa, not to New York or Chicago."

Jamie couldn't help but notice how Tommy kept skating away from the subject of England, even when he was the one who brought it up. The Australian was intensely curious to find out what had happened there, who Tommy's mystery girl was, and why the Yank didn't want to talk about her – a married lady, perhaps? But Colbeck decided the subject could wait for another day, when Flowers was more ready to talk, so he used Tommy's last comment to change the subject: "Billy Sand is from Chicago, you know."

"Really? No, I didn't."

Jamie nodded. "Grew up there and went to school there. University. It shows."

"I think he's a good captain."

The Aussie looked at his Yank friend with irritation. "Of course he is. Did I say he wasn't?"

"Well, the way you were just saying the university shows–"

"That was no insult, Tommy. You're makin' assumptions again. Naow it's true, some fellows in the army with a fancy education are arses. But you get a good man, a smart man, and you give him an education like that, and he only comes aout better."

"And Billy's a good man. A smart man," Flowers said, somewhat tentatively.

"Wouldn't you say so?"

"I just did… but he's not always right. What he said about the British–"

"He doesn't know any better. He ain't been here."

"I know better. I haven't been here. And by the way, did I just hear you say the British didn't fight so bad?"

Jamie grinned. "You and your fresh maouth." He paused, looked away, then added, "Don't expect your leaders to be right all the time, lad, or you won't think any o'them are any good."

"You're always right."

Jamie turned to look directly at Tommy. "No, I'm not. What Billy said – part of it was true. I got so set on smokin' aout that dingo Dougherty that I let you daown."

"You didn't let me down. You saved my life. And you're taking care of me now."

Jamie, embarrassed, turned away again, and Tommy called his name. "What?" the lieutenant asked, his back still to the private.

"Why did you make up that story about me and the German?"

Jamie looked back at Tommy. "Five haours under shellfire doesn't impress them. Five haours and a German prisoner does. We already agreed Billy's a good captain. A good captain can make your life a lot easier. And naow you've impressed him. That's good. It'll make Dougherty think twice."

"He wasn't my prisoner," Tommy said doggedly.

Jamie smiled and, even though he knew it would offend Tommy, said, "By the time it was over, he was nobody's prisoner."

Tommy looked predictably askance, was quiet for a few moments, then asked, "Did you have to do it, Jamie? It was a horrible way for him to die."

The volume of Jamie's voice increased as he grew defensive. "Do you think I brought him all that ways just to kill him? I could've done that at the listening post. What would you have me do different, Tommy – what would you've done? It would've been more horrible for you to die like that, aout in front of aour own trenches. Or me, for that matter. I'd rather it happened to him."

"I'd rather it didn't happen."

"You saound like your President. Maybe once the war is over, you can help Mister Wilson fix matters so it doesn't happen again."

"You're making fun of me and my country."

"No. He's just an odd bird for a leader, that's all. College professor, ain't he?"

"I think he's a good leader. Most of the boys don't like him. They like Roosevelt."

"Ol' Teddy's more my cuppa tea, too." There was another, longer silence, then Jamie stood up and said jovially, "Well, Flaowuhs, we've discussed politics, the weather, home, aour captain, and the war. Nothin' much left to talk abaout. I've got work to do, and you need to take that rest Billy ordered. I'm tired of waitin'; let's go find us some Doughboy uniforms."

"Are you going to Madame's tonight?"

Jamie had been both cheered and annoyed by Tommy's seeming dismissal of Nicole from his post-war plans. Now Tommy's oblique raising of the subject of the French girl aggravated his annoyance. "Prob'ly. Don't tell your buddies, 'cause no one's supposed to know abaout it yet, but there's supposed to be a show at sundaown–"

"A battle?"

"No, an honest-to-God show. With a singer. Some American girl. We'll have to steal a motorcar to get to Madame's early, 'cause after the show it'll be craowded."

"But if there's a show, I'd like to see it. I want to see Nicole and Madame, too, but–"

"I'll try to save you a seat, then," Jamie said, as Tommy stood up at last.

"You really wanna see Nicole, don't you?"

Jamie's tone became harsher than it had been all day. "Don't mock me abaout her, boy. I don't like it." Tommy turned ashen, and Jamie remembered he was dealing with a potential shell-shock case. Before the American could pronounce his inevitable apology, his lieutenant cut him off with a wave of his hand and said in a completely different tone, "Ah, don't tell me you're sorry. I already know. Come on, lad, let's get you your rest."

Tommy drifted upward from his deep, dreamless sleep on the pleasantest of sensations: it felt as if someone were smoothing his brow, holding his hand, stroking his hair. As his eyes opened slowly, he thought, I'm still dreaming after all, because he found himself looking into the beaming face of David Pearson, as clean and neatly dressed as he had been in Tommy's earlier dream about Iowa, the one that had ended so horribly with the German soldier. But when David bent over to touch his lips to Tommy's forehead, it felt real, as though he were right there in the tent with the Yank.

Tommy blinked once or twice; and then he realized he *was* awake – and David was in his tent. "Davey," he said softly, the back of his hand brushing Pearson's cheek, "what are you doing…?"

Pearson's expression clouded, and he replied, "I'm sorry, Tommy. I know we made a promise about 'ere in France, but I cou'n't stop meself–"

Tommy's response was to take David's hand and squeeze it. "That wasn't what I meant. I meant, what are you doing here?"

David answered with a sunny smile. "What d'you mean, what am I doing 'ere? I'm a soldier. I'm back. With the Rangers. Just like you said I'd be."

"Oh."

The sunny face clouded again. "You aren't 'appy to see me, then?"

"More than anything!... It – it's just that–"

"What?"

"I want you to be safe." Tommy paused, collecting his thoughts. "I – I went on a trench raid the other night, and–"

"I know," David interrupted. "You don't 'ave to talk about that, if you don't want. Jamie told me all about it."

"Jamie?"

"Yes. 'E's the one what fetched me up to come over 'ere."

"Jamie Colbeck?"

"Is there another? If there is, don't tell me. I'm only finally beginning to like the first one."

At the old familiar joking tone, Tommy sat up and reached over, pulling David to him. "I've missed you," he said.

"And I've missed you. Wisht I was with you on that stunt."

Tommy shivered. "No, you don't. I told you, I want you to be safe."

"You weren't safe. We're never safe, none of us. And it's all our job, winning this war, together." Smiling, Pearson added, "But you must still love me, then."

"'Cor, but I do,'" Flowers answered, making them both laugh so hard they broke off their embrace, in what turned out to be the nick of time, as the tent flap opened and Harry Carson stuck his head in.

"What–?" Carson began at seeing anyone else in his and Flowers' tent, and then he recognized Pearson's uniform and said in a friendly tone, "Oh, are you Flower of Iowa's British buddy?"

"I am," David replied, then Tommy repeated both his and Harry's full names by way of introduction. "We've met, after a fashion," Pearson reminded them both as he shook hands with Carson. "It's 'ow Tommy and me met, actually. You were calling 'im 'Tommy' at the just-a-minute in Rainneville, and I thought you were calling after me."

"Really?" Harry said with a blank look. "I don't remember. Say, weren't you wounded when they bombed Molliens?"

"I was, but I'm in the pink now, so I'm back."

"That's good," Carson said, nodding vigorously, "and I'm sure Flower here's glad of it." Without a break, he added, "Hey, Tommy, I came back to see if you were awake, because you won't believe what's going on behind the château at Molliens tonight–"

"A show?" Tommy asked innocently, and Harry's face reflected disappointment.

"How didja know?"

"Jamie told me."

"Huh! But didja hear who it is?"

"No, who?"

"Elsie Janis!"

"*The* Elsie Janis?"

"Yes. Think of that! An American girl – a Broadway star – singing for us right here in France."

"She's famous, then?" David put in.

"Sure," Carson replied. "Everyone's heard of Elsie Janis. Isn't that right, Flower?"

"Reckon so."

"So are you gonna come?" Carson persisted.

Flowers turned to Pearson. "Do you wanna go?"

"It's partly why Jamie told me to come wake you."

Tommy thought, then said, "We'll be right along, Harry."

Carson looked at them both, eyes shifting between the two, then said, "OK. See you there," and exited the tent.

When he was gone, David turned to Tommy and said, "We could 'ave gone with 'Arry right aways, Tommy. It might have seemed more social."

"We can see him there. Did Jamie say he'd be at the show?"

"'E's already at the just-a-minute."

"That figures."

"Why?"

"That girl, Nicole?"

David instantly and unexpectedly bristled with indignation. "What d'you mean, 'That girl, Nicole'?"

"Well… you know…"

"Like I wasn't the first to ever point 'er out to you. Like anyone cou'n't see 'ow much Colbeck fancies 'er – and 'ow much she fancies you. Like I don't remember what you and 'er did, too–"

"But you remember who I fancy, don't you?" Tommy said, cajoling, reaching again for David, but the Englishman pulled away.

"We must be more careful, Tommy," he said, his voice hard. "Carson almost sawr us, and it would 'ave been a 'ard thing to explain. We could 'ave been in terrible trouble."

Flowers looked wanly at Pearson and agreed. "You're right, Davey. It's just–"

David's tone softened considerably. "I know, love. I know." Shifting tone again, the Englishman added, "We should start making our way over to the château. There'll be quite the crowd."

Pearson half stood – grimacing slightly in the process, enough for Flowers to notice – then pulled the American to his feet. Gripping David's hand, Tommy pulled the Briton back to him and gave him a quick kiss that brooked no argument, then said, "OK."

★

Tommy realized he'd slept longer than he thought as he and David stumbled from his tent and began following the stream of soldiers headed down the back road to Molliens. The sun was still up, but it clearly had no more than an hour of life left to it this day; and since it was July in Picardy, that meant it was going on nine in the evening.

Out back of the château, a large crowd, primarily Doughboys but with a sprinkling of Tommies and Aussies, had gathered around two large flatbed trucks with planks extending outward from the back of each to form a small stage. But the throng wasn't yet so numerous that they weren't able to find Carson, standing toward the front alongside Sleaze. The Dakotan clamped a hand on Flowers' shoulder and asked, "How're you doin', Tommy?" with genuine concern, and not a little guilt, etched on his face; he'd been no more help than anybody else when Tommy had been pinned down. "You remember Frank Gillis, don't you?" Walt added, and Flowers nodded at the redhead from Pennsylvania, who responded in a tone scarcely less hero-worshiping than the first time they'd met, "I heard about the trench raid. They said you captured a German."

"'They' talk too much," Tommy told him, his tone more gruff than he'd planned. Indeed, so stern did he sound that it elicited a chuckle from David.

"I think it was really brave of you," the Pennsylvanian persisted, and Flowers prepared to make another sharp remark, but Sleaze caught his eye, with a look that told him Walt and Frank had become good buddies since the night Sleaze had escorted Gillis back to camp from Madame's. So Tommy simply said in a mild tone, "I'm just an ordinary soldier who was doing his job. I didn't get hurt, not like my friend here. He got wounded when they bombed Molliens."

"Oh, so you're the famous Private Pearson," Walt said to David, much to Tommy's annoyance. Flowers couldn't recall ever mentioning Pearson to Sleaze, much less his name; why were soldiers such a bunch of gossips?

The exchange was interrupted by an approving roar from the international military crowd, as with no particular advance fanfare, a beautiful, willowy brunette woman, in a silver fur wrap, a smart hat, and a blue serge suit whose skirt fell well below her knees but stopped well short of her ankles, revealing black silk stockings, bounded onto the stage and, arms uplifted, sang out in a voice that soared over the men and caught each and every one's attention:

*"Are we downhearted–?"*

The line came from a song usually sung at a brisk, martial clip, but Elsie Janis sang it slow and drawn-out, giving the men time to chorus back the response line: *"NO!"*

Bouncing about the stage, the actress rolled into the tune's refrain,

*"Here we are, here we are, here we are again..."*

and the men roared their approval once more. Undaunted by their noise, which threatened at times to drown her out completely, the star proceeded to march around the makeshift stage, belting out the song and turning a cartwheel at its conclusion. Once the wild applause died down, she told a joke about the Kaiser, then allowed as to how honored she was to be there at the front lines with a white pass issued by the "British high command"; as she came to these last three words, she stiffened her posture and her voice turned into a perfect intonation of an upper-class Englishman. The men roared in delight, though Flowers glanced sideways at Pearson, wondering if the Tommies in the audience would be offended; but they were laughing even harder than the Doughboys, it seemed.

"I hear a lot of you boys are from Chicago," Elsie Janis called out, drawing a huge assent from the men; then she launched into a story and a song about that city. Partway through the number, the air came alive with the whistling sounds of shrapnel in the distance, and the actress paused, then said, her voice a mixture of little-girl innocence and slight perturbation, "Am I to be killed? I really don't want that, you know. I have *work* to do tomorrow."

Shouts of "No!", "Keep on!" and "You'll be all right!" encouraged her to continue and, tilting her head and batting her eyes, she did so without hesitation. The applause when she finished easily drowned out the shelling, which was abating at any rate; then she implored those in the audience who were from places other than Chicago to call out where. Walt and Frank, among many others, called out their home states, but Tommy remained silent, though David nudged him to speak up.

By then, though, someone had volunteered "Ohio," leading the actress to reveal she had been born in Columbus, in turn resulting in a brief ditty about the Buckeye State. At its conclusion she asked once more, "Anywhere else?"

Again there was a chorus of states, and some Australian and English place names as well. Just as this response died down, David, acting on behalf of the still tongue-tied Tommy, clearly called out "Ioway!"

It was loud enough to ignite laughter in the half of the audience closest to the stage, and Elsie Janis, a bemused smile on her pretty face, looked right in Pearson and Flowers' direction and called back in another perfect imitation, this time in the coarser accent of a lower-class Englishman, "Now, 'ow can that be, Tommy? D'you come from I-Oh-Way-*Shire?*"

The crowd erupted in full-fledged laughter, and David turned to Tommy and said admiringly, "She's a cheeky girl."

Thinking of David's sister who wanted her own business, and especially of Sister Jean who had once been an actress, Tommy replied, "Of course. Us Americans like our girls cheeky."

"It suits 'er," said David, his rapt attention already redirected to the stage, and Tommy felt a stab of jealousy, though he wasn't sure from which direction: he himself had been half thinking he might be willing to throw over Susan, Nicole, Sister Jean, *and* David for the likes of Miss Elsie Janis; that David might be contemplating something similar came as an unpleasant surprise. But in the very next moment, David reached over and wrapped his arm around Tommy's shoulder; and Tommy, responding in kind, suddenly felt as though he'd never been happier in his whole life, watching and listening to this wonderful girl with his beloved buddy beside him. What a great experience this war had turned out to be!

The star – who at this point could have led every last man unarmed into no-man's-land, with no dissension – was well into another song, this one slightly off-color and in French, when more shrapnel came whistling overhead, much closer this time. Drawing herself up in a parody of indignation, Elsie Janis expanded her already considerable repertoire of accomplished mimicry and began imitating the sounds of the shrapnel, then swept right into the refrain of the next song she had planned to sing anyway,

*"Oh, you dirty Germans, we wish the same to you!"*

In short order she had the whole laughing crowd singing this refrain, as she careened through verses conjuring up various miseries and misfortunes for the enemy, seemingly making it all up as she went along. The shrapnel died away again, this time for good. Tommy and David, as one with their fellow soldiers, would have been pleased for the show never to end.

# Chapter XXXIX

Not more than a couple of miles from where Elsie Janis held a throng of men in thrall, a lone woman had the equally devoted attention of a lone man. As sure as Jamie was about nearly everything else in this war, he was that uncertain about the young woman who was bustling around the otherwise customer-free *estaminet,* acting as though any business she had was more important than being sociable with Colbeck, now that she had provided him with his *vin.*

This mystified the Aussie lieutenant, since the French girl had been, as he had hoped, increasingly warm in her demeanor toward him with each day of Tommy's absence. He didn't think the reason for her distance tonight was her famously protective aunt; every time he and Nicole were together, that estimable woman smiled and nodded with almost embarrassingly evident approval.

Nicole briefly disappeared down the cellar stair, and Jamie's mind wandered to his conversation earlier that afternoon with David Pearson. Feeling guilty about his sharp words with Flowers, and still concerned about the American boy, Colbeck had acted on one of those hunches that had served him so well throughout the war and gone several miles past Molliens to Round Wood, where the Rangers were now camped, to see if he could learn any news about when Pearson might return – only to find that Tommy's Tommy friend had arrived back that very afternoon, less than two hours prior to Jamie showing up. With the English lad not yet back into his routine with the Rangers, it was easy for the Australian to find him. The look in Pearson's eyes when Colbeck materialized in his camp was familiar to the lieutenant, who quickly said, "Don't worry, David, Tommy's all right."

Visibly bucking himself up, the Briton replied, "But is 'e 'urt?" That prompted Colbeck into a full account, delivered sooner than he might have liked, of the abortive trench raid. David listened quietly, and when Jamie's account, which minimized the Australian's own heroics, was finished, he simply said, "You saved 'is life, then. Thanks ever so for that."

Deflecting his discomfort, Jamie immediately switched the subject: "You sawr Tommy while he was in England?"

"I did, yes."

"What happened, Peahson? Somethin' happened to him there."

David's manner instantly turned opaque. "What d'you mean?"

"Did Tommy meet some girl over there?"

David looked Jamie in the eye and said, "No, Leftenant. There was no girl."

"You're sure abaout that?"

"Absolutely," Pearson replied, again with such conviction that Colbeck could only assume he was telling the truth.

"David?"

"Yes, sir?"

"There's no need to call me 'sir' or 'Leftenant.' My name's Jamie."

David smiled and said, "As you wish, Jamie."

Mulling over the exchange now, Colbeck was still nagged by some feeling he couldn't quite place. Jamie had a keen sense for when men were lying, and unless David was a far better actor than he'd ever encountered, which seemed particularly unlikely, the Australian was convinced the young Englishman had told him the truth about Tommy not meeting a new girl in his homeland. But he was equally certain something *had* happened to Tommy there, something that most assuredly read to Jamie like a romance. It all made the lieutenant irritable; he didn't like mysteries, and between Nicole and Tommy, he now had two too many.

His restless reverie was broken by the French girl herself, who re-emerged from the cellar and, to his surprise, made a beeline for his table. *"Vous allez bien, M'sieur Jacques?"* she began, to his further bewilderment; she'd already served him, and that would have been the logical time for pleasantries about the state of his health.

*"Oui, très bien,"* he replied, *"et vous, mam'selle?"*

"Ah," she responded with a sigh as she sat down across from him, adding a shake of her head sufficiently negative for Colbeck to react with alarm.

*"Votre frère?"* he began, and she shook her head with more vigor.

*"Non, c'est pas mon frère. Mon père non plus."*

*"Ah, c'est bon,"* he said with emphatic relief, glad to hear there had been no bad news of her brother or father. *"Alors, qu'est-ce que c'est?"*

Nicole glanced tentatively over to where her aunt stood at the bar. Madame was engaged in some task that was occupying her complete attention; and this seemed to be what her niece had hoped for. Turning her gaze back to the Australian lieutenant, the French girl said rapidly, *"Je ne sais pas, mais j'ai mal, très mal."*

*"Mal? Maintenant?"*

*"Oui, mais hier aussi, et mercredi aussi."*

The news she had been feeling sick for three days came as a shock to Jamie, who hadn't even considered that as a factor in her ill humor. *"C'est mauvais?"* he asked in an attempt to gauge the seriousness of the ailment.

*"Parfois très, très mal."*

*"Où?"*

At that, Nicole colored and looked away from him, and Jamie understood in an instant; she was reluctant to tell him where it hurt so much, because she was hurting in a place women didn't mention to men. *"Je comprends,"* Jamie said to her quietly, daring to touch her on her forearm. *"Ne vous en faîtes pas."*

At his admonition not to worry, the young woman smiled at him, more genuinely than she had all evening; and at the same time, her aunt called to her, as the first soldiers arriving from the Elsie Janis show came through the *estaminet* door. But as Nicole rose to return to her duties, she whispered a heartfelt *"Merci"* to Jamie.

The *estaminet* filled rapidly and noisily within a quarter of an hour; in no time Nicole and Madame were overwhelmed, and the place was crammed to capacity... with one exception: Jamie refused to release – or even share – the smaller table he had commandeered. This act of defiance came close to causing several fights, but Jamie held his ground, and after nearly a month at this camp, the lieutenant was so well-known and so well respected by the local soldiers of all nationalities that no one pressed his case too strongly. Nicole or Madame, of course, could have ordered him to relinquish the table, or at least the three extra seats thereat; but the younger woman was inclined to indulge him in the hope her Fleur might appear, and the older woman was inclined to indulge him, period.

Jamie was sure there was now a line outside the place, probably a long one, and he knew Flowers was far too polite to jump it. Calculating quickly, he picked from the crowd a soldier sporting the khaki of His Majesty's Army he had spotted earlier in the day at the Rangers' camp. "Hey, Corp'ral!" he called out.

The young man in question, blue eyed and brown haired, leaned forward toward Colbeck amid the press of bodies and said in a lilting Welsh accent, "Was that me you were calling, Leftenant?"

"It was, lad. What's your name?"

"Glennon, sir."

Patiently, Colbeck said, "And your first name, Corp'ral Glennon?"

"That would be Michael, sir."

"They call you Mick or Mike?"

"Mike, sir."

"Mike, haow'd you like a seat at this table?"

"Oh, that's – very kind of you, sir," the Weelshman said with surprise and delight, beginning to squeeze through.

"My name's Jamie Colbeck. You can call me Jamie," the Aussie continued, offering his hand. "And you're welcome to a seat here if you do me a favor. But it'll require a man with nerve."

Less suspiciously than he probably should have, Mike Glennon answered, "I'm a man with plenty o'nerve, sir. I mean, Jamie."

"Good. You're with the London Rangers, ain't you?" Glennon nodded, and Colbeck went on, "You know David Peahson?"

"Gone Blighty, hasn't he?"

"Was. He's back. And unless I'm mistaken, he's probably aoutside in the queue, with an American. Tall, fair-haired fella, young like Peahson."

"So you want me to fetch him?"

"Both o'them. I've been savin' these places for them, but they may not know it."

Somewhat belatedly, Corporal Glennon did grow wary. "This wouldn't be some kind of trick?"

"No. I give you my word as an officer, it's not."

Glennon cocked his head. "But what if they're not at the head of the queue?"

Colbeck shook his head; maybe he'd overestimated this boy's intelligence. "They're prob'ly not."

"Then I could lose my place in here. They'd send me to the back of the queue."

"Never mind. I warned you this would take nerve. I'll ask someone else, thanks all the same–"

"Wait, Jamie."

"I'm waitin'."

"Would you buy me a drink, too?"

Colbeck stared at the Welsh corporal, and said in wonderment, "You'd cheat the devil himself if you could, wouldn't you?"

Far from being flattered, Mike Glennon looked worried, as if he feared he'd overreached himself. "No, Jamie, I–" he began, but the Aussie, producing a franc note, interrupted:

"Haow do I know you won't just leave here with this and keep walkin'?" he asked, waving the money in front of Glennon.

"Because you have my word as a… corporal."

"Hm," Jamie grunted, briefly pulling the note closer to himself, looking down as if to examine it, then offering it cleanly. "Here."

"I'll be back, toot sweet," Glennon said crisply, taking the franc and adding, "with Pearson and his mate." He pocketed the note in his tunic and vanished quickly into the crowd.

Jamie figured he'd likely wasted a franc, at least until he squeezed it back out of the insolent corporal at his earliest convenience; but to be fair, he decided to allow ten minutes before hatching some other plan. In less than five, all three men appeared, pushing their way through the crowd toward his table, Flowers and Pearson appearing predictably uneasy about their privileged status; the triumph on Glennon's face reminded Colbeck of Dougherty, minus the mean streak. The look grew even more pronounced as they all sat down and the Welshman handed the franc note back to the Australian, saying, "Here's your change, then."

"Change? What happened to your brew?"

"I took the money in case I would need it, to persuade someone in the queue. But the first man was a Yank, and when I told him about Pearson just being back, he and his friend seemed to know who Flowers, here, was. They didn't even put up an argument – or let the rest of the boys argue."

Jamie looked quizzically at Tommy, who simply said, "Sleaze."

"I believe I still owe you that drink, Mike," the Aussie said. "You're very enterprisin' for a soljuh of the British Army."

"Thank you, Jamie. I think."

"You know this man?" Jamie asked David.

"A little," replied David with no particular emotion, so Colbeck went on, directing his next query to Flowers:

"So, haow was the famous Miss Elsie Janis?"

"What a wonderful girl!" Tommy bubbled. "You should've seen her, Jamie."

"I've seen shows like that before. Even sawr Sir Harry Lauder once."

"'E's not exactly a beautiful lady like Miss Janis," David countered.

"No, but he lost his only boy in the war," Jamie retorted, effectively killing conversation at their table until, easing through the crowd, Nicole arrived.

As she caught sight of Tommy, her downcast look immediately evaporated, much to Jamie's disgust. Restraining herself, she simply said, *"Bienvenue, Fleur,"* then nodded and added *"Bienvenue, messieurs"* to David and Mike; she recognized the little Englishman, but couldn't recall his name, if indeed she knew it.

"What'd she say?" Tommy asked Jamie with animation, and on impulse, the older man responded, "I ain't tellin'," even though he knew it made him sound childish.

"She said, 'Welcome, Flowers,'" Michael Glennon helpfully told Tommy, drawing a daggers look from Colbeck.

"Actually, she said, 'Welcome, Flaowuh,'" Jamie corrected. "She don't understand it's 'Flaowuhs.'"

"If you say so, Jamie," Glennon said agreeably, and Colbeck replied sharply, "'deed I do."

*"M'sieur Jacques!"* came a feminine voice with its own edge to it, and Jamie turned to face Nicole and responded, *"Oui?"*

*"Pourquoi faites-vous le difficile, hein?"* Called on the carpet by the French girl's tone and choice of words, Jamie gave her a wordless, uncharacteristically meek shrug. Before any of the others could react, Nicole continued expansively, *"Alors, messieurs, que voulez-vous?"* addressing the entire table; then she added to Tommy, *"Un cidre, peut-être?"*

Catching her meaning, Tommy eagerly ordered his cider by replying in his best French, "*Oui.* Uh cedar."

"*Et vous, messieurs?*" Nicole asked the others.

Glennon replied, "*Bière,*" and Pearson chimed in, "*Deux.*"

Nicole nodded and shifted her full attention to Colbeck, who gave her a baleful look and said, "*Rien.*"

"Pfff!" the young woman said, pursing her lips and thereby making herself look exceptionally pretty and pouty; adding to the effect, she tossed her hair as she slipped back into the crowd.

"Well–" Mike Glennon began, turning to Jamie; that was quickly followed by an "Ow!" and he whirled on David and demanded, "Watch what you're doing, you little runt."

"Watch what you're calling my friend," Tommy warned in a low, dead-serious voice.

"What did you do? Kick him?" That was Jamie, addressing David, who simply gave a cat's smile.

"'Oo, me?"

"You're quite the scamp," Jamie told him, not without a tone of approval, and Glennon started to rise. "Where are you goin'?" the Australian asked him.

"The whole lot of you are crazy. I'd ruther stand."

"Sit daown, Corp'ral."

"Don't go pulling your rank on me now, Leftenant," said Michael Glennon, his blue eyes flashing.

"You tell him," Tommy put in encouragingly, and in the next moment, with amazing alacrity, their drinks arrived, served not by Nicole but Madame who, sniffing trouble, virtually slammed the tray onto the table and shook her finger at the lot of them, letting loose a stream of rapid-fire French.

"What's she saying?" Tommy anxiously asked the Welshman, who shook his head.

"I wouldn't know. She's talking too fast."

"She's tellin' us all to behave aourselves and mind aour manners, or we're aout," Colbeck said with a sudden surge of conviviality, happy to once more be the only one to understand the natives. To the woman he added, "*Un vin blanc, s'il vous plaît.*"

At Jamie's change of order from nothing to white wine, Madame Eglantine made a "Pfff!" noise remarkably similar to that voiced so recently by her niece; but she followed it up with a smile and a wag of her finger at her favorite, who smiled back at her. Shaking her head, the *estaminet* owner slipped away.

Jamie leaned smugly against the wall, his hands behind his head. Before he could say anything more, Flowers said to the still-standing Glennon, "Why don't you stay? You earned your seat at this table."

Looking not at the American private but the Australian lieutenant, the Welsh corporal replied, "You're right. I believe I will."

# AUGUST 1918

# Chapter XL

At the end of another warm, damp early August afternoon, Tommy was slogging back to camp, tired of the rain, and tired of the war. More than two weeks had passed since the Elsie Janis show, a fortnight of terrain exercises, inspections in trenches, and some quiet – genuinely quiet – time in the front lines, although a few nights ago the sky toward Amiens had flickered with searchlights trying unsuccessfully to find a German aeroplane that droned overhead. The news from the British newspapers was encouraging: The Americans and the French had turned back the Germans at Château-Thierry, and there was considerable anticipation of an Allied counteroffensive. If it was already happening, it was happening somewhere else; Flowers' life lately had settled into a tedium of routine and rain, rain, rain – the kind that meant your socks were never dry, and turned the simple act of walking through the mud into a continuous struggle.

Tommy's other constant companion (besides his chats, which kept coming right back despite his periodic visits to the bathhouse) was something he was reluctant to acknowledge to himself, let alone others: anxiety about David. He hadn't seen Davey in more than a week. First Tommy's own unit had had its spell in the front lines, while the Rangers were moved behind the lines to Round Wood, a short ways past Molliens; then, by the time he returned to reserve, the Rangers were at the front. Flowers had tried to steel himself, telling himself (as he knew Pearson was doing likewise) that he couldn't obsess about his buddy's safety in the midst of a war. It did give Tommy a dollop of sympathy for his parents and Susan (whom he could no longer think about without guilt) and their worries about him. But it did seem maybe worse, knowing that David, if he was still alive and unhurt, was probably no more than a day's march away and in constant danger.

Still, Tommy kept his anxiety hidden, mostly, the only overt indication being his nightly walks from Pierregot to Molliens in search of news, any news, about the London Rangers – of which, for the past several nights, there had been none at all. But the secret concern had had other effects, most notably at Madame's *estaminet,* where Nicole, who seemed increasingly peeved at his distractedness, was compensating, to the point even he had noticed, by paying elaborate attention to Jamie.

Reaching his tent, Tommy unhesitatingly threw himself down on the wet earth that served as his mattress these days, in an attempt to gain a little sleep. The unanswered letters from home would have to wait.

But later that afternoon, Tommy abruptly and mysteriously found himself summoned to the headquarters in Pierregot. The wait in the hallway of the old schoolhouse was mercifully brief. Billy was crisp and businesslike in returning Tommy's salute and ordering him at ease, and then he added with a kind weariness, "Sit down, Private."

"Thank you, sir," Tommy replied, taking up the offer.

"No need to thank me," Sand parried, and Tommy noticed the captain once again picked up his pen and began toying with it. Flowers kept quiet, and at length Billy broke the uncomfortable silence with: "Tell me, Flowers: how would you characterize the relationship between Lieutenant Colbeck and Sergeant Dougherty?"

Cautiously Tommy said, "Sir?"

That seemed to anger Billy Sand no end. "I asked you a question, soldier."

"Yes, sir. Of course, sir. They – really can't stand each other. At least, that's my opinion."

"Would you suppose that's only your opinion?"

"No, sir, I wouldn't."

"Who else's might it be?"

Tommy shrugged. "Everyone's, sir. It's not much of a secret."

"Apparently not" came the dry response from Sand, whose total attention was now on Flowers, not his pen. "Would you say this gets in the way of the army's business?"

"Oh, no sir, not really. They're both very professional."

"If they're so professional, how come you and everyone else are so sure they can't stand each other?"

Momentarily stymied, Flowers eventually said, "Well… by the way they talk and act with each other, sir."

"If you can tell from that, then they can't be talking or acting very professionally, can they?"

Tommy hesitated. "I – don't know, sir."

"Oh, come now, Tommy," Sand said with sudden, unexpected exasperation. "I didn't expect deviousness from you."

"Deviousness, sir?" Tommy asked, making it plain he didn't quite catch the meaning of the word.

The captain gave a dispirited sigh. "You should have had a better education, soldier. A bright boy like you."

"My education was just fine, sir," Tommy said defensively, with not a little edge. "Maybe it wasn't college, but it was still a good education."

That came close to insubordination, and for a long moment Billy Sand seemed to waver on the verge of an explosion; but then he visibly pulled back, suddenly laughed and said, "I knew you were the right one to talk to."

"Sir?"

"You're honest even when it doesn't serve you to be." Sand leaned back, fingers intertwined. "Sergeant Dougherty has complained to me that Lieutenant Colbeck is undermining him, and has requested a transfer–"

"That might make everyone happy, sir."

"I'm not in the business of making the men happy, Flowers," Sand snapped. "This is the army." He paused, then added, "In fact, both Lieutenant Colbeck and Sergeant Dougherty have complained to me about each other. How does that affect the men?"

Tommy looked down at his feet, squirmed in his chair, sighed, and looked wanly at his captain. He knew he couldn't get away with saying nothing. "It – it can get… embarrassing, Captain."

Sand drew back with a satisfied look. "Of course it can. You all have a right to be embarrassed, your leaders behaving so unprofessionally–"

Mindful of the outcome of Sand's previous "investigation" involving him, Flowers demurred. "I never said that, sir. I never said that." Defiantly he added, "Lieutenant Colbeck is a very good lieutenant."

"He's certainly an excellent soldier," Sand said pointedly, "one of the very best. Beyond that remains to be seen, I think." He paused once more, then said, "You see, I'm thinking of demoting both Lieutenant Colbeck and Sergeant Dougherty for their unsoldierly conduct."

The color drained from Tommy's face. "What?"

"You heard me, Tommy."

"But – sir, if I may say so, demoting Lieutenant Colbeck would make you very unpopular with the men."

Sand shot one of his particular smiles at Flowers. "As I told you, Tommy, that's why I picked you to talk to. You're honest to a fault." Then his aspect hardened. "I'm not here to be popular with the men. Sergeant Colbeck is popular with the men because he's all flash and bravado."

The way the captain said "Sergeant Colbeck," as if Jamie's demotion had already happened, chilled Tommy. Billy noticed, and asked, "What's the matter, Flowers? You look like you've lost your last friend."

"Maybe I have, sir. Jamie's been real good to me, and–"

Suddenly Sand was back to full intensity: "Tommy, you have *not* betrayed your friend! If I decide to demote him, it will be for the good of the U.S. Army first and foremost, but it will also be for his own good–"

"I should mention, Captain, he has friends. He knows–"

"General Monash, I know. I'm not impressed. I know I couldn't send Lieutenant Colbeck away – and I wouldn't want to. But he asked for his promotion, and I can take that away. I'm not afraid of him, Flowers. Most people are, I notice."

"Please don't demote Jamie, Captain Sand, sir," Tommy blurted in desperation. "It's true he said he never wanted to be a lieutenant, but he's real proud of it now."

Billy briefly looked agape at the private, then said drily, "Anyone can see that." Then his tone changed once more: "Tommy, listen to me. You can't not understand this. You're too bright. Don't you realize that if your lieutenant and sergeant can't work together, it could cost you your life–?"

"I'm tired of all this, sir! I thought we were here to fight Germans–"

"You really would try the patience of anybody, soldier! I *am* talking about the war. I'm talking about your safety and your well-being, and the safety and well-being of your squad. Honestly, why has Lieutenant Colbeck got all the men convinced he's the only one out here who cares if you live or die!?!"

Stunned by such an impassioned declaration from his cool, clever captain, Tommy finally said, "I – never thought of it that way, sir.... You're the captain, and I know you'll do your best for us. I – I just wish you wouldn't do this to Jamie, that's all. And if you are going to, I sure wish you hadn't talked to me–"

"I told you why I talked to you."

"But I tell lies sometimes."

"You haven't lied to me, though, have you?"

Tommy slowly shook his head. "No, sir, I haven't."

"I thought not." There was an awkward silence, then Sand made another candid comment: "I wish you were my adjutant, Tommy. I'd much rather work with an honest lad like you than that paper shuffler McAdams."

Completely overwhelmed, Tommy said, "Thank – thank you, sir. I know it's a great honor, and if I ever wanted to be anybody's adjutant, Captain, I'd want to be yours, or Lieutenant Colbeck's. But, beg pardon, sir, I don't *want* to be anybody's adjutant. I want to fight Germans."

Sand stood. "If you were my adjutant, you'd understand that you still would be fighting the Germans." He smiled again. "Thank you, Tommy. I'm sure you'll come to see you've done the right thing."

Tommy stood in return and gave his most halfhearted salute. "I hope so, Captain, sir. It sure doesn't feel that way right now."

The rain still hadn't stopped. Trudging back, Flowers was running the interview with Sand over in his mind when, abruptly, Colbeck sidled up next to him in a motorcar and announced, "I have some good news, Tommy, but I'm almost afraid to tell you."

The Doughboy lifted his wet head. "What?"

"The Rangers are back from the front. Peahson came lookin' for you."

As Colbeck had anticipated, Flowers straightened up and brightened considerably at this news. "He's not hurt?" Tommy asked, seeking reassurance.

"He's fine, lad."

"He's back at camp, then?"

"Yes, but he said you could meet him at the usual place. Is that near Nicole's? We can ride there."

Tommy duly got in, though he made it clear he wanted to be dropped off at the Molliens fork of the road to Rainneville. Although Jamie honored the American's determination to keep his exact meeting place with his British buddy secret, he said as Flowers alighted from the vehicle, "I'll probably be at Madame's for abaout an haour. Why don't you meet me back here? I'll wait for you."

Tommy hesitated; his mind was already focused on the climb he was facing, partway up the Rainneville slope to the little abandoned stable. Jamie's offer would save him still more walking later, but it also wouldn't leave him much time with David. "No thanks, Jamie."

"Have some sense, lad," said Colbeck, more cajoling than demanding.

Tommy pondered, said, "Can't you make it two hours?"

"*Estaminet* closes before that."

"Madame'll let you stay."

"Smart maouth." Jamie paused, then added, "All right. Two haours. I'll *force* myself to keep Nicole company, if Madame'll let me. So, don't go gettin' impatient and start back yourself."

"Yes, sir," Flowers replied, saluting with a grin.

"And don't 'sir' me," Jamie said, gunning the motor. "You know I don't like it."

Tommy needed the extra time; though he wasn't waylaid by any dogs, old Frenchmen, or aeroplanes tonight as he picked his way up the slope, the rain was complicating his hike, which took half an hour or more. But at last the stable was in sight, glowing in the fading gray light with the faint orange of an interior fire, its flicker visible through the still-broken door. Flowers picked up his pace, eager to rejoin his friend; then, at the last moment, he could practically hear Jamie chiding him about making assumptions. Stealthily, he came around the blind side of the building, rifle drawn (for this time he hadn't left camp unarmed); and to his amazement, a gray-clad German soldier stepped tentatively out of the doorway, testing the rain. The American clicked his weapon, and all in the same motion the German turned to him, calmly asked "Tommy?" and Flowers blinked… and the Boche dissolved into the most familiar of Tommies.

Lowering his rifle, Flowers called Pearson's first name in return, then staggered over and threw his arms around him, the Briton no less glad to see his mate. They limped inside and, facing each other, dropped down onto the stable floor which, mercifully, was dry.

Tommy told David the entire story of his interview with Sand, and then everything else that had happened since they last had seen each other also came spilling out. It was many minutes before he wound down, and belatedly realized they'd already been there quite a while, and he hadn't asked Pearson the first thing about himself: "Davey! Why didn't you shut me up? I didn't even ask how you are, and I've been so worried about you–"

"I di'n't want you to shut up, Tommy. 'Tis a joy just to listen to you after all this time."

Tommy gave him a look, then said throatily, "Come here."

They were still sitting cross-legged on the ground, still facing each other; but now Pearson moved over sideways into Flowers' arms, though he warned, "I'm all mucky."

"I don't care. So am I. God, I've missed you."

Filthy though he was, David looked up and gave Tommy that almost-flirtatious look. "Why?"

"Well, for one thing, no one listens to me like you do. Reckon that's why I went on so long, 'cause you're so easy to talk to."

"Go on," Pearson said, settling into Flowers' hold, and they sat together quietly until Tommy broke the silence:

"What did happen at the front, Davey?"

The Englishman looked at the ground. "Nothing… a bit of everything."

"What does that mean?"

David looked back up at him. "We di'n't go over the top, not even for a stunt. But we were 'it by shells and mortars more than oncet. 'It bad."

Flowers circled his arms more tightly around Pearson, said softly, "Anybody I'd know?"

"Stephens. 'E was with us at the bath'ouse that one time, d'you remember?"

Tommy shook his head. "I only remember Hardison – and Muffett."

They both laughed at the mere mention of the fat private, and David said, "That one wasn't anywheres near a bath'ouse."

"That's for sure," agreed Tommy who, with no thought for the irony, nuzzled David's grimy head. Then he added, "I remember Sergeant Poppert, too."

"Poppert got it," Pearson said in a peculiar flat voice.

Tommy was pretty sure what David meant, but said, "Got hit?"

"Kilt. 'It by a trench mortar. At least that was fairly clean, that was."

Dreading the answer, Tommy asked, "And Stephens?"

"Shrapnel right cut 'im in two," David said, with a chopping motion of his arms, his body steady but his voice thick, and he added needlessly, "It was orful."

"I'm sorry, Davey."

"Nothing for you to be sorry about."

"No. You're right. Since it wasn't you."

David looked back up at him once more, genuinely aghast. "Tommy! That's a 'orrible thing to say!"

Standing his ground, Tommy looked down at his friend, shrugged and said, "Still."

Rather than saying anything else in reply, David shifted a little more deeply into Tommy's hold, signifying his acceptance of the answer. Finally he said, "Bloody war."

"Jamie says there'll be a big battle soon."

"Someone's always saying there'll be a show," David noted wearily. He pulled himself up then and they switched positions, Flowers lying down against Pearson, who proceeded to ask, "'Ow much time 'ave you got, love?"

Having just gotten comfortable, Tommy shifted uncomfortably. "I'll probably have to leave soon. Jamie's giving me a ride from the bottom of the hill back to camp."

"'E knows you were meeting me?"

"Yes," Tommy responded, and went on to explain the arrangements with Colbeck.

"Cor!" David exclaimed. "Does 'e know about us, then?"

"Nobody *knows* about us, Davey. I wouldn't tell anyone."

"I wou'n't either.... But then, I wou'n't mind so much if somebody like Jamie knew, as long as 'e di'n't care."

"David, how can you say that?"

Now Pearson shrugged. "I just did, di'n't I? Anyways, 'e's been orful good to you."

Stabbed by guilt, Flowers said, "I know. But the captain has, too."

"That's quite the change from your old captain, isn't it?"

Tommy squeezed David's arm, his thoughts off on a different tangent. "I almost shot you just now. For a second there, when you stepped outside, you looked like a German to me."

Unexpectedly, David smiled. "But that's good, don't y'see? You're learning to be a proper soldier."

Tommy stared back at David, a little incredulous, still imagining himself pulling the trigger. He took a long, deep breath, then said, "If something happened to you, Davey, there'd be nothing left for me to fight for."

David continued to be both discomfited and pleased by Tommy's directness. "That's silly," he replied. "You di'n't even know me when you got 'ere. You weren't fighting for me then."

Tommy gave David a long look and repeated his earlier position: "Still."

Intimidated into being equally candid, David pulled Tommy back up to him, in the process turning the bigger man about to face him, and said, "I feel the same way, you know. King, country – it's just you I fight for now. You and me mates, but most of all you."

They said nothing for a bit, until Tommy ventured, "That's – not good, is it?"

David slowly shook his head. "Don't know, Tommy. 'Oo knows anything, with this war? I only know what is."

Impulsively, Tommy grabbed him again, holding on tight. "I don't know if it's worse having you here or not."

"Me neither. But that's also a part of what is, don't y'see? For now, anyways."

"I want it all to end. Soon. Now."

"And so it may, someday soon. And then we'll go sailing, you and me, like we said." They remained holding each other until at last the Englishman reluctantly said, "Come along, love, we must get you back. 'Ow long ago did Jamie leave you?"

"I don't want to go back. I want to stay with you."

David gripped Tommy's arms and gently but firmly tugged at them. "Don't talk that way. Not now. It'll do us neither no good. Now answer me question: 'ow long?"

Surrendering, Tommy relaxed his grip, though his hands remained on David's shoulders. "I don't think it was quite two hours."

"Then I'll walk you back the other way, and Jamie can catch you driving out of Rainneville."

"But that's more going uphill, and in the rain," Tommy protested.

"Yes, but it's shorter, y'see, and that's what matters most."

Tommy looked at his buddy as if by staring hard enough he could keep him at his side indefinitely. "Davey–" he began.

"I know, love, I know. But we must do now what we must do now. I wou'n't leave you, not really. You must know that."

Tommy smiled. "'Cor, but I do. You wou'n't do that to me.'"

David laughed as they both rose to their feet. "I don't know why I put up with you mocking me. I really don't."

"Because you fancy me as much as I fancy you," Tommy said confidently.

"Per'aps that's it," Pearson conceded with a smile, kicking the dust with his good leg to douse the fire.

As he departed the *estaminet,* Jamie thought he had never felt so discouraged, not even in the darkest of days on Gallipoli or at Passchendaele. But his despair had nothing to do with the progress of the war.

Arriving nearly two hours before, he had found the place oppressively crowded, as full as it had ever been; he suspected that Madame Eglantine was cheating on her own usual rules for how many soldiers were allowed in the place at once. There was a short line outside, and Jamie waited patiently in the rain until about fifteen minutes before closing time, when he finally gained admittance and squeezed his way to the bar, only to find Madame being assisted by some strange girl, a pale young woman with blond hair and dark circles around her eyes. Nicole was nowhere in sight. Attempting to hide his anxiety, Jamie ordered his beer from this new girl in his smoothest, chattiest French, concluding with, *"Et comment vous appellez-vous, mademoiselle?"*

"Odile," she responded glumly.

*"Ah, Odile. Et Nicole… ?"*

*"Je ne sais pas,"* she answered with the same gloominess, and a little brusqueness for good measure. Gaining no clue from Odile as to Nicole's whereabouts, he looked down the bar, where he saw that Madame was completely mobbed. Pulling away from the bar a bit and observing, he quickly saw why; Odile appeared to understand not even the simplest of English words, so that those soldiers who were similarly ill equipped when it came to French, and that was a good many of them, had to rely totally on Madame to get them their drinks.

In the face of such a chaotic scene, Colbeck retired against the far wall of the place, biding his time. Madame cheated on her closing hour, too; it was twenty minutes past the usual by the Australian's reckoning when she began to shoo the men out of her humid, crowded establishment and back into the rain. Only as the last dozen or so were being escorted out the door did she catch sight of her favorite, and then she did not grant him her usual response, instead pursing her lips and looking worriedly back to the bar. Recovering, she smiled and nodded, saying *"M'sieu Jacques,"* then grandly extended her arm, showing him the door, too.

Irritated that he had to request what lately had been offered without question, Jamie asked, *"Est-il possible que je reste ici un peu?"*

With a harried glance back toward Odile and the bar, she seemed about to refuse him, then relented: *"Oui, pour quelques temps."*

*"Merci,"* said a mystified Jamie, and as the door closed behind the last of the other soldiers, Madame hurriedly brought him another beer and gestured for him to sit at the long table, then went back to the bar to clean up silently with Odile. It was awkward, so Jamie volunteered to help; she turned him down.

Next Madame went upstairs with Odile, and was gone so long it bordered on rudeness. He heard the two women talking, though Odile's French was so strange he couldn't make out the conversation; then there was more silence. It occurred to him Madame was waiting for him to let himself out, but he wasn't about to leave without talking to her; he hadn't forgotten his arrangement with Tommy, but the Doughboy could wait.

At last, visibly reluctant, with a nervous smile, Madame Eglantine descended the stairs, came over to his table, and sat down across from him. *"Vous allez bien, M'sieu Jacques?"* she asked.

*"Oui, Madame. Mais vous–"*

*"Moi, je vais bien, très bien,"* she assured him with too much dispatch and too little real conviction.

Now that they had both agreed they were well, Colbeck longed to get to what he really wanted to know. But he calculated that being indirect might bring him greater success, so he asked her about Odile, and was rewarded with the girl's life story: a Belgian, she had lost both parents in the first days of the war, when the Boche had crushed her tiny country as it resisted being a pathway into France. One of the most heinous things the German Army had done was to summarily execute suspected *franc-tireurs*, civilian terrorists, and Odile's parents had been caught up in this slaughter. The glum girl had been in the care of an aunt who was a friend of a friend of Madame Eglantine's, and that woman had passed word that if ever Madame needed help at the *estaminet*...

Aha. Jamie saw his opening and took it: why, he wanted to know, would Madame need help at the *estaminet?* Before he could even utter Nicole's name, her aunt was off on an odd explanation: she didn't really need the help, because everyone knew there was a big push coming soon, so big it could mean both *les Anglais* and *les Américains* might be leaving the area. Because of that, she was trying to get as many customers as she could, right now, because who knew when–

*"Assez, Madame,"* Jamie said, abruptly losing patience. *"Où est Nicole? Est-elle partie?"*

Madame paused; then her eyes grew moist and she said softly, *"Oui, M'sieu Jacques. Elle est partie."*

He couldn't believe she was really gone, and pressed, *"Où?"*

*"Chez elle."*

*"Cumières?"*

She seemed startled that he knew the name of her niece's home village, then said, *"Oui."*

He had caught her in a lie. *"Ce n'est pas possible. Cumières, c'est un village qui n'existe plus."*

Floundering, she threw her arms out beseechingly and said, *"Mais s'il vous plaît, M'sieu Jacques–"*

*"Non!"* he cried, far more sharply and loudly than he'd intended. *"Il faut que je la vois!"*

At his demand to see Nicole, her aunt had a most peculiar response: *"Je ne crois pas que vous voudriez la voir, m'sieu."*

Her insistence that he would not want to see Nicole only increased his anxiety about what had actually happened, but angry as he was, he was reluctant to be that direct with Madame Eglantine. If he suggested outright that her niece was *enceinte,* he might lose forever the chance to see Nicole again, to tell her what he should have told her a long time ago. So he said, *"Villers-Bocage"* with some caution.

*"Comment?"* said Madame, looking at him with fright and worry.

*"Villers-Bocage,"* he repeated. *"Elle est avec les soeurs, n'est-ce pas?"*

Madame regarded him in horror, and he hurried on: *"Elle a été malade, et elle a fait une visite aux bonnes soeurs, n'est-ce pas?"*

She looked at him long after that; he had suggested that Nicole, not feeling well, had gone to visit the holy sisters in Villers-Bocage, with whom she had stayed before coming to work for her aunt. That was all he had said; much more could have been inferred from it, but he had been careful to imply nothing by tone or look, only to offer the explanation at face value. Finally, Madame said, *"Peut-être. Vraiment, je ne suis pas sûre,"* and rose, indicating their interview was at an end.

"Tell her I want to see her," he said impulsively in English as he too rose, and to her *"Comment?"* he repeated the phrase in French, causing her to repeat, *"Peut-être. Bonne nuit, M'sieu Jacques."*

*"Bonne nuit, Madame,"* he replied with a resigned politeness as she showed him to the door.

Although he was late for his rendezvous with Flowers, Colbeck sat in the motorcar for a long time, watching the *estaminet,* knowing full well he was being watched in return. Eventually he was satisfied that Nicole was not hiding upstairs; he hadn't really thought that anyway, but Madame had given him so little to hope for. *Peut-être.* Maybe. Could be. Maybe he had been right that Nicole was with the sisters at Villers-Bocage, and maybe she would let her niece know he must see her… could be, or not.

There was another reason Jamie wasn't in a hurry to meet the American private. If what Colbeck believed had happened to Nicole was right, he, Jamie, ought to kill Flowers, plain and simple. But eventually, he gunned the motor and headed out of Rainneville.… Rainneville; it seemed a good name tonight, with the heavens opening up like they had at – No, this was nothing like Passchendaele, not really.

He had barely started down the hill when he spied two figures waving frantically on the side of the road. Colbeck's hand went to his gun, though he figured it was only a couple of sodden stragglers from the *estaminet,* men he didn't have room for in addition to Flowers. But as his vehicle drew alongside, he saw it was the American, along with his British buddy Pearson, the two of them leaning on each other, both grinning happily like a pair of silly schoolboys.

With emotions more mixed than he might have thought, Jamie slowed down to admit both passengers. To his immense irritation, the man he was angriest with took the place next to him and immediately perceived his mood. "Thanks, Jamie," Flower of Iowa said, adding shortly thereafter, "What's wrong?"

"Nothing," Colbeck said tightly.

"But–"

"I said, *nothing!*" he repeated fiercely, and he noticed Flowers' reaction was to throw a protective arm around Pearson, as if it was the Pom who was the target of his ire.

The Yank, too dumb in Colbeck's estimation to let anything be, persisted with "Is everything all right with Nicole?"

"Yes."

That came out before Jamie could even think about his answer. He stared straight ahead in the rain and darkness. This would have been his opportunity to tell Tommy, cleanly and in honest response to the American's own question, the likely price of his one afternoon's dalliance – and without thought, Jamie had let it slip away, an action reversible now only by an admission on the Aussie's part that he had lied.

Out of the darkness on the other side of Flowers came Pearson's cheery voice, carrying the conversation beyond the subject of Nicole: "Tommy says you think there'll be a show soon, Leftenant."

"Jamie," the Aussie replied automatically, reminding Pearson of the privilege he routinely gave to everyone, but had until recently withheld from the little Tommy. "I'm sure of it," Colbeck added, repeating his previous response to Flowers. "The only question is whether they'll do it right this time."

"But that's always the question, isn't it?" David countered.

"Yes, but maybe the answer'll be diff'rent this time."

They were approaching the point where the road to Pierregot forked to Molliens, and even before it appeared, Colbeck noticed, Pearson made to stand up and began to thank him for the ride.

"Sit daown, David. I'm not goin' to make you walk all the way to Raound Wood from here on a night like this. We can at least go by way of Molliens."

"Thanks ever so, but 'tisn't necessary."

"Common decency is always necessary. Sit daown." With that, Jamie turned onto the Molliens fork. Neither he nor David seemed to notice that Tommy was keeping out of their conversation, and the Aussie and the Brit talked on.

As they reached Molliens in the darkness, Jamie, his concentration on driving, couldn't see David squeeze Tommy's hand, hard. "Thank you, Jamie," the young Englishman said. "Tommy, I'll be seeing you."

With the vehicle barely slowed to a stop, David leapt out, landing cleanly but limping away. Without a salutation from Jamie, with whom he'd been chatting so effortlessly, and with a barely audible "'Bye, Davey" from his American mate, Pearson watched as the motorcar picked up speed again, swerving in the direction of Pierregot.

Jamie seemed content to drive back to camp in silence, but of course Tommy wasn't. Hoping the topic was a safe one, the Doughboy ventured, "Thanks for giving Davey the extra ride."

Shaking his head and not looking at the Yank, Colbeck replied, "David's a fine lad, Tommy, even if he is a Pom. You picked a good one for a mate."

Flowers stared out at the darkness, unable to think of something else to say. Finally, fearing it had to do with what he'd told Billy, he turned and asked, "What is it, Jamie? Something's wrong, isn't it?"

Slamming on the brakes in the muck, Colbeck turned sharply and exploded at Flowers, "God damn it, I've had it with you! Get aout!"

"But–"

"Just get *aout,* I said!"

Tommy gave Jamie a long, injured look, then jumped out of the car, landing so hard that he grimaced and gritted his teeth as he turned to his lieutenant with a stony face… which immediately got splattered with mud, as the Australian, unmoved, gunned the motor again and tore away, leaving the American to trudge back to Pierregot in the downpour.

# Chapter XLI

Two days later, the August sun came out, clear and strong, and began an unexpectedly rapid drying out of the saturated ground of Picardy. Jamie had been nowhere to be seen since leaving Tommy on the Molliens-Pierregot road, and Dougherty was grim as he led the squad on exercises, pressing them all until they worked up a hard sweat. Flowers noticed the sergeant still sported all of his stripes, so Sand either hadn't made up his mind yet or had decided not to order the demotions after all.

The next morning, reveille came early, as Tommy and Harry were roused out of their tent and to attention well before dawn. This time roll call was conducted not by Dougherty, but by Colbeck – who, to Flowers' consternation, was wearing a uniform without any insignia.

"Men," the Australian announced, "I want you to fall aout and reassemble back here in ten minutes… in full gear." Jamie swiveled about and smiled. "We're goin' for a little walk."

Across roads that had, improbably, turned dusty, Tommy and his friends marched for much of the day and into the evening, heading toward the front. Along their way, they could hear artillery – a tremendous amount of it – booming up ahead, to the east and south. Eventually, as last light faded, they reached the village of Franvillers, where they just stopped and stood – at attention for a while, and of course Dougherty kept Tommy's squad that way long after others had been allowed at ease, until finally Jamie came down the line and peremptorily cried, "Fall aout, men!" casting a withering look at the sergeant; the chain of command appeared intact, at any rate. By that time, naturally, all of the good resting places already had been taken. But as Flowers and his friends milled vainly about, Colbeck abruptly took the Iowan by the arm anyway, with a quick "C'mere, lad."

Hoping this meant the sharp words between them were forgotten, but again fearful it had to do with his conversation with Billy, Tommy obediently followed, only to find "here" was a matter of a few steps, just far enough for them to pause in the midst of a group of totally unfamiliar soldiers – which seemed to be precisely what Jamie wanted, to be out of earshot of the rest of Tommy's squad. "What's going on, Jamie?" Tommy asked tentatively, and he found the Australian in a chatty mood:

"First of all, from what I hear, this show is *big*. There's activity all up and daown the front."

"Really? Then why are we just sitting here, missing it?"

"I wouldn't worry abaout missin' it, Tommy. If this is as big as they're sayin', we could sit here for days – which we probably won't – and still not miss it. We were supposed to move saouth of here for an attack tonight, but the Pom general in charge changed his mind."

For a change, it was Tommy who spat on the ground to register his disgust. "Maybe you're right about British brass, then."

"Actually, this one made the right choice. We've marched all day and night, and aour supplies ain't caught up with us. I've had a bellyful of that kind of fightin', and believe me, if you can avoid it, you should."

Flower of Iowa paused, taking in this information, rare enough to be in the possession of a lieutenant, let alone a private. He didn't bother to ask Colbeck how he had come by it all; Tommy trusted that Jamie had his ways. "So, how much longer do you reckon we'll stay here?" he finally asked.

"Not long, I'll wager. Hard to say. They're movin' so many men so fast." The lieutenant darted a look at the private, and added, "I'm trustin' you to keep your maouth shut abaout all this–"

"Of course."

Jamie nodded. "There's one other bit of intelligence I ain't told you yet. Guess who was right here in Franvillers, earlier today?"

Not focusing, Tommy simply ventured, "The Germans?"

Now the Aussie grinned. "No, you silly bugger. The London Rangers."

That had the desired effect, with Tommy temporarily agape, until he managed to say, "But – but they got sent behind the lines, aren't they?"

Jamie shook his head. "Not what I hear. They're at the front. I heard they moved on from here a few haours ago."

"How–?"

"I got word from Mike Glennon, through a mutual acquaintance. He's a sergeant naow, y'know – David's sergeant, in fact." Catching Tommy's expression, Jamie added, "What is it, lad?"

"I thought they were behind the lines," Tommy repeated, adding impulsively, "I don't want Davey to be at the front."

The Aussie looked perplexed. "It's the big push, Tommy. We're all in it. You wouldn't want to deny David his part. It's what we all signed up for."

Tommy thought long about that, said, "No, you're right. I reckon I wouldn't. Thanks for letting me know, Jamie."

Tommy expected another joke about his manners, but instead Jamie regarded him closely, then warned, "Don't spend any of your time worryin' about David, Tommy. You both got enough to worry abaout for yourselves."

"Like staying alive?"

"Like stayin' alive," Colbeck agreed.

Out of nowhere, Flowers said, "Don't you worry about Nicole?"

Jamie failed to catch the parallel Tommy was making; nor did he exhibit his usual anger when the American brought up the subject of the French girl. Noncommittally he said, "At least she's behind the lines."

Exactly, thought Tommy, but he didn't say it, only nodded, because he was afraid of how much he'd revealed in his previous question.

"I've got to report back to Billy naow," Jamie concluded. "Keep this all under your hat – if you didn't leave it again at Madame's."

The joke reminded Tommy how glad he was to have his friend back. "See you soon?" he asked, the hope in his voice palpable.

"I guarantee it," Jamie replied, almost jovial. "I ain't goin' to let you boys go up against Jerry all by yourselves."

As it turned out, mere minutes passed before Dougherty, agitated, came charging through the area where his squad was still milling about, and shouted, "Fall in! Let's go let's go *let's go!*" In short order the entire 131st Infantry Regiment was once more in motion, though in the darkness neither Flowers nor his compatriots could get any sense of where they were headed – that is, until they marched over a narrow stream they figured was the Somme.

But that was the grander scheme of things; what preoccupied the Americans a great deal more was the fact they were tired, having marched for many miles and hours, and were now on the move yet again – and their field kitchens still hadn't caught up with them. The grumbling of the soldiers matched the grumbling of their stomachs, at least where more permissive NCOs were allowing conversations. But eventually even the men in those units fell silent as they began to pass between two trench systems, and through the greatest concentration of British troops the Yanks had yet seen.

It was at about this point, in the depth of the night, that not only Jamie but also Billy rejoined Tommy's squad, marching at the head of it as Dougherty fell to the back. The sound of the artillery, closer than ever, was omnipresent; but the Tommies who surrounded them on both sides, though clearly on alert, were not actually fighting... yet. The Doughboys' steady movement through the British lines was interrupted when a voice softly called "Jamie Colbeck!" out of the darkness to their left.

Jamie and Billy, both marching directly ahead of Tommy and Private Young, looked sideways in the direction of the caller, and though the Australian couldn't possibly have seen the man, he called in return, equally softly, "Mike! Is that you?"

"So it is, Jamie, so it is" came the reply, and the lieutenant turned to his captain and said in his best professional tone, "Permission to speak with Sergeant Glennon, sir."

Sand didn't break stride or hesitate, saying only, "Be quick about it."

Tommy's anxiousness at hearing this exchange was so acute that Jamie could feel it, never mind that his back was turned to the private. Colbeck's tone toward Sand turned cajoling as he added, "Permission to take Private Flaowuhs with me?"

"Be double-quick, then," Billy snapped. "I expect you both to catch up with me in five minutes."

"Yes, sir," Jamie replied, with as smart a salute as Flowers had ever seen from him; then he unceremoniously grabbed the Yank by the arm as they hightailed it back to where they'd heard Glennon's voice, already quite a few yards behind them.

As they approached this particular British trench system, another voice familiar to Tommy cried out, "'A-a-l-l-t! 'Oo goes thay-ehh?"

Forgoing all military formality, Tommy answered enthusiastically, "Muffett, it's me, Flowers. Pearson's American friend."

Muffett hadn't forgotten his last set-to with Flowers; the fat private spat on the ground and muttered, "Daft Yank," but meanwhile his authority was superseded as Mike Glennon's voice materialized out of the darkness:

"If it tis Flower of Iowa, he must have Jamie Colbeck with him."

"Right you are, *Sergeant,*" Jamie responded with emphasis, since it was the first time they had seen the Welshman since the latter's promotion. "I ain't got much time, Mike," Colbeck added, "and you know what Flaowuhs here wants."

Glennon, his features now visible, cocked his head, thought for only a second, then gestured: "Down that trench to the right, Tommy, then take the first bend to the left."

Before Flowers could utter thanks to either of them, Colbeck said, "Start caountin' to a hundred naow, Tommy, and be back here by the time you reach a hundred. We're not foolin' araound with Billy's orders."

"So I noticed," Tommy retorted over his shoulder as he trotted off in the indicated direction, already counting.

"Smart maouth," he heard Jamie say agreeably, and the American headed down the trench in question, making his way with surprising ease until he neared the bend, where he turned and bumped headlong into a tall Tommy – Hardison.

"Hey! Watch what – It's you!"

"Sorry," Tommy said, determinedly trying to push past him, but the tall blond pivoted and blocked his way.

"That wasn't a proper apology," the Brit said, as Tommy's count reached twenty-two; he'd have to turn back at fifty.

"I said I was sorry," Tommy said coldly. "Now get out of my way. I'm on orders from Sergeant Glennon."

Hardison pondered that for a fraction – worth two more counts – then stood aside, though he added, "Bloody Yank."

"You're nothing but a great big idiot," Tommy, trying to think of the worst epithet he could, whispered in return as he shoved past.

Various Empire troops were resting, or trying to, in tiny funk holes along both walls of this section of trench. Tommy peered at one, then another, then one more; on the fourth try – and the count of thirty-four – he found who he was looking for, curled up in a shallow depression right under the parapet. Pearson was dozing lightly, and it seemed a selfish thing to waken him; but Flowers hesitated for only one more precious count before he leaned in right next to Davey's ear and whispered loudly – though not loud enough to carry to the next funk hole – "I love you, David Pearson."

David snapped to, disoriented, but only for a couple of counts before saying in a hushed voice, "What a thing to wake up to out 'ere! Is it really you, then?"

Tommy nodded vigorously. "Yes, but I have to go right back. Can you walk with me, back down the trench?"

As he popped out of the funk hole in a single easy motion, David said "Yes," adding in a whisper into Tommy's ear, "…love"; then he asked in a somewhat louder voice, "Which way?"

Tommy, his count at forty-six, indicated, and they took off, David hustling to keep pace until Tommy slowed down a bit; the Englishman's limp was still noticeable. "Did you fight today?" Flowers asked.

"We started to follow the 9th Londons into battle," David replied matter-of-factly, "but since then they've 'ad us waiting in reserve." That plain account given, he added with enthusiasm, "'Tis exciting, isn't it?" reminding Tommy of Jamie's comment about denying David the experience they'd all signed up for.

But Flowers, ever curious about details, chose to ask, "Aren't *you* the 9th Londons?"

"No, we're the 12th Londons," Pearson replied patiently.

"Oh. So, we're south of the Somme, right?"

"No, Tommy, north. Between the Ancre and the Somme."

"Oh. Did you see any Jerries?"

"Not in the fighting, but a 'uge lot of prisoners after. I b'lieve we're winning this one, I really do. But 'oo knows?"

They had just made the bend in the other direction, down the last line of trench to where Tommy had left Jamie and Mike, when again the way was blocked by Private Hardison – this time with a couple of cohorts in tow. Catching sight of them, Tommy, now on a count of sixty-five, clenched his fists, but it was David who immediately assessed the situation and said calmly, "Stand aside, 'Ardison."

"Your Yank mate needs to learn some manners, Peahson."

"And you need to learn 'ow to be a soldier. I'm taking this man back to Sergeant Glennon."

Once more Hardison hesitated, and this time the consequences for him were worse, as a voice from behind growled, "What is it's going on here?"

"Sergeant!" Hardison shouted, turning and saluting, as did all the others. Then the tall private belatedly added, "Nothing, Sergeant."

Glennon – with Colbeck in tow – passed a steely look over the situation and then said, "We were coming to fetch you, Private Flowers."

"Beg pardon, Sergeant, but my count is at seventy-eight. I thought I was on time."

"You were," said Jamie, advancing on the man whom he had last seen from the point of view of the ground, when the Englishman was kicking the Aussie in the stomach. Pulling even with him, Colbeck stuck his face directly into Hardison's. "You are the biggest horse's arse I've encaountered in seven armies," he hissed. "What I don't understand is why you're not dead yet." It caused everyone else, including those with no fondness for Hardison, to flinch; but Jamie was the ranking officer present, and no one challenged him.

"Better be gettin' going, Jamie," Mike Glennon said quietly, and Colbeck, his face still in Hardison's, answered, "I suppose you're right, Mike," then pulled away and added, "Let's go, Tommy."

Flowers gave Pearson a moment's look – only that, and got a similar one in return – then thanked Mike as he followed his lieutenant up and out of the trench, double-time, both of them racing to catch up with their captain by the appointed deadline. Not even a scowling Dougherty, still bringing up the rear of the squad, could distract them; they were in a full run by the time they caught up with Billy Sand.

Flowers made to fall back so that lieutenant and captain could converse, but Sand said crisply, "Stay here, Tommy." Billy was striding along at an easy gait, paying no attention to the fact that the two men next to him were now a little winded; they'd been granted a special privilege in falling out for five minutes, so they could damn well keep up. "So, gentlemen," the captain said, "did you learn anything?"

"Yes, sir," Colbeck and Flowers answered in unison, eliciting one of Sand's bemused smiles. In a moment of contrariness, Sand commanded, "You first, Flowers."

"Me?"

"You, Tommy."

"Oh… uh, all right, Captain, sir. We're between – the Anchor and the Somme? And those were the 12th Londons. The Rangers? And they followed the 9th Londons into battle today, but then they were kept in reserve, so they really didn't fight."

Sand looked vaguely pleased. "I see. Is that it?"

"Uh – they said they took a lot of German prisoners, sir."

"The 12th Londons?"

"The 9th Londons, I reckon. The 12th Londons said we were winning the battle." Tommy wondered whether the captain would cross-examine him and discover "the 12th Londons" was one person, but Sand simply said, "Thank you, Tommy," and the private unthinkingly replied, "You're welcome, Billy," then, realizing his breach, stammered, "I – I mean, I'm sorry, Captain, sir–"

"Never mind," Billy said with an indulgent smile, and then he shifted his attention to the man whose report, by protocol, he should have requested first: "Well, Jamie? Does Tommy's report square with yours?"

"As far as it goes, sir, yes it does," Jamie replied, betraying no surprise that Billy was behaving as casually with an enlisted man as he himself usually did. "Seems the 12th Londons were at Vignacourt yesterday, aout of the line, on rest. But they were only there a few haours when they were put back on a bus to Franvillers, and then they marched to the Bois d'Escardonneuse last night. They were in reserve there, and then this afternoon – well, the rest of what I heard is more or less as Private Flaowuhs reported, Captain."

"I see. Including the prisoners?"

"Yes, Billy, including the prisoners," Jamie said, adding helpfully, "Those are the Ballarat trenches they're in naow."

They strode along briefly in silence, until Billy abruptly said, "Jamie, didn't you tell me back in Franvillers that the London Rangers were there earlier in the day?"

"Yes, sir."

"But if what you just told me is accurate, they were there the night before."

While Tommy reeled again at his captain's sharpness – nothing seemed to get past Billy – Jamie ran over the timing in his mind, then admitted, "You're right, Captain."

"Of course I am. Either your sources have got to improve, or your interpretation of them does."

Tommy was amazed to see Jamie once again take a dressing down from Billy without complaint. "You're right, sir," the Aussie repeated, and Billy repeated, "Of course I am."

They marched farther along, and Tommy thought about asking if he should fall back, but before he could, Jamie asked, "Where do you suppose we're headed, Billy?"

"I have to suppose we're passing south through their lines, and we'll eventually turn east, to the front." The captain looked over to the man who had by far the more direct experience of the war. "Do you agree, Lieutenant?"

"Makes sense to me," Colbeck concurred.

"And do you think our side did as well today as the London Rangers told you and Flowers?"

Jamie mused for only a fraction. "I honestly believe we did, sir..."

"That's good. But?"

"... but I've seen good first days turn into nightmares before."

In the dimness – the sky was beginning to lighten – Tommy could see his captain nod at his lieutenant's note of caution.

# Chapter XLII

The sun was high overhead, beating down with no relief in sight, and to make matters worse, Tommy, like all his comrades, was terribly thirsty. Although it was still only the day after they had left their camps, it seemed as though they had been marching forever – and their rations (and even more important at the moment, their water) still hadn't caught up with them. A few long, painful miles back, they had finally passed through another village, Vaux-sur-Somme, where Davey's geography had again proved unerring; they were still, after all, on the north bank of that river, which was now tantalizingly, indeed maddeningly, close at hand; but there was no question of getting a drink from the Somme, or anywhere in Vaux, so on they marched. The men would have been unlikely to appreciate the irony that the next town up ahead was Sailly-le-Sec, its surname being French for "the dry."

They continued along in march formation; the sounding of the artillery had never ceased, night or day. None of their leaders – that is, Sand and Colbeck; the omnipresent, self-important Dougherty didn't count – had been seen for a couple of hours. But then the tedium and irritation, exacerbated by biting black flies, was abruptly relieved by a ripple through the ranks; something was going on just up ahead: the men in front of Tommy were breaking into a full trot. From out of nowhere Jamie suddenly materialized, shouting, "Double-time, men, double-time!" with urgency in his voice.

Dougherty, not to be left out when orders were being given, added his triple trademark "Let's go let's go *let's go!*" and with no word of explanation, the men of Tommy's squad, along with the rest of the regiment, were off at a steady canter, their full packs and the hot sun notwithstanding. Given the abruptness of this move, Flowers could only assume there was fighting somewhere dead ahead, and that any minute they would be greeted by a fusillade of bullets and shells when they encountered, at last, the Germans. But instead they continued in their semi-run, as the sweat streamed down their sides, soaking their shirts, their underwear, faces wet with sweat dribbling down from underneath their helmets.

As they continued, passing through the villages of, first, Sailly-le-Sec and then Sailly-Laurette, Tommy, like his comrades, found himself adjusting somewhat, feeling the heat less – no one fainted; no one had the time to – but his pack grew and grew in weight, until Flower of Iowa felt he was toting a load of bricks down this dusty French road under the August sun. It was minutes and minutes on end of this – the quick gait, the summer heat, the ever-heavier pack – until suddenly Captain Sand himself came along at something closer to a full run, crying,

"*Double*-double-time, men! Double-double-time!" Surely the Jerries were right up ahead now. Everyone broke into a flat-out run.

It was at this point that Tommy noticed how the ground to their left, leading away from the Somme, was sloping sharply upward, and he had a momentary seizure of fear that the Boche were instead overhead, that they'd been led into a trap and might be fired down upon at any moment. But that proved not to be the case, either.

For several minutes more they sped along at a full clip, remaining surprisingly organized, as the terrain grew more wooded (or marked by what was left of those woods) and cleft with ravines. The ground on their right began to rise above, and a little away from, the river. Suddenly Tommy saw men up ahead slowing down and fanning off to the right, and he prepared to do likewise, but with equal abruptness there was Jamie again, directly in front of him and shouting, "To the *left*, men! Fall aout to the *left!*"

As he obeyed, temporarily assuming the head of the column veering off in that direction, Tommy saw Colbeck swiftly whisper something to Dougherty, who nodded sharply once, then charged past Tommy with the simple cry, "Come on, men, follow me!" Immediately their dislike of the sergeant was irrelevant; Dougherty apparently knew what he was doing and where he was going, and that was all that mattered.

Trusting, the men of the 2nd Battalion (for the 2nd was being deployed left, the 1st right, and the 3rd behind, in reserve) followed their leader of the moment. Tommy was right behind his sergeant as they made their way up a wooded ravine, heading rapidly away from the river. Once or twice he glanced fearfully off to his right, where the shattered woods and rising ground surely, surely, held German soldiers; but all was strangely quiet. How could the enemy not be noticing so much commotion?

As they crested their own rise and started heading downhill, for the first time they saw other soldiers, and both Dougherty and Flowers made for their rifles; but the men up ahead were in khaki, not gray, and sergeant and private relaxed a bit as they ran onward. The other Americans – no, wait, they were British – stood or knelt where they were; none came forward to greet them until the Americans were very close, and then a man on the end turned and advanced a few steps. "Sergeant!" cried Dougherty, saluting, and the other man saluted in return and repeated, "Sergeant." It was not until then that Tommy put the face and voice together in this place; and his face must have shown it, for the British sergeant added matter-of-factly, "Hello, Tommy."

"Sergeant Glennon," Flowers replied, saluting smartly, as his own NCO turned to him in annoyance and bewilderment, but Mike Glennon smoothed things over:

"That's a good job of it, Yanks. We've been waiting for you to start the show, and they said you'd never get here on time… but here y'are."

"I told you I picked the right army to be with" came a voice from behind Flowers; Jamie, of course, though how he'd managed to catch up Tommy couldn't figure if he took all afternoon. Without breaking stride or catching his breath, Colbeck turned to his least favorite sergeant and said, "Good work, Dougherty. Naow help get the men in place, startin' with Flaowuhs, here. This is aour jumping-off point."

"Do we hit the dirt, Jamie?" Tommy asked eagerly, and the Aussie answered testily, "Use your head, Tommy. Do you see any of these Tommies lyin' on the graound?"

Coloring, Flower of Iowa admitted, "No, sir, I just thought, when our barrage started–"

"There ain't gonna be no barrage – from aour side, anywise."

One of the stronger impressions Tommy had carried away from Hamel, despite seeing so many of his own comrades killed by their own barrage, was how the shelling from his own lines had indeed provided some curtain of security as they advanced. Accordingly, this was not welcome news, and he couldn't stop from exclaiming, "None?"

"It's a surprise attack," Mike Glennon kindly informed him, but Jamie cut off further clarification for Tommy with a gruff "You'll be the one surprised if you don't pay attention to your job. The signal's comin' daown anytime. Get ready."

Checking his rifle, Tommy dared a look off to his left, past Jamie and Mike, wondering if he would catch a glimpse of David, but all he saw were long ranks of British soldiers; to his right there was a similar lineup of Americans, though still falling into place; Walt was to his immediate right, and Frank right next to him. Glancing left again, he was suddenly distracted by the sound of gunfire up ahead, up the ridge. Jamie caught his look and simply commented, "Skirmishers." Some patrols had been sent ahead to draw the enemy's attention.

Before Tommy had time to think about anything else, the signal came along the line, and once again he was over the top into battle, only this time it was in broad daylight, and as part of a much larger contingent of men. But though they were at a full run again, they were feet, not even yards, into their advance when the air was rent with the screams of shells and the rattle of machine-gun bullets, all coming from the opposite direction. "Keep *movin'!*" Jamie, who had crossed in front of him and was now running to Tommy's right, exhorted his men as they progressed up a slope and into a thicket of mostly blackened trees. Every shattered stump looked to Tommy as if it might hold a German, but none materialized, unless you counted a clump of dead ones just off to his right where a machine-gun nest, apparently, had been silenced by the skirmishers.

The bright day had been blotted out in the hail of the enemy barrage, and the swirl of dirt, smoke, and heat was every bit as disorienting as at Hamel. Tommy felt the ground sloping downward, decided he must have gotten turned around, and started heading up the slope again. "Here, here," came a familiar voice, and Mike Glennon's face emerged from the smoke so suddenly Tommy almost shot at him. "You're going the wrong way, soldier," Glennon said sternly.

"I am? I'm sorry–"

"You weren't running away, were you, Tommy?" Mike asked, dead serious, and Flowers answered with full indignation,

*"No!* I – I mean, no sir, I just got turned around."

"I believe you," Glennon said quickly, moving on and sharply motioning him to follow. "You Yanks've got the right spirit, but you're looking a little disorganized. You better stay with us, now you've lost your unit." Nobody could see Tommy's face flush on the battlefield; he followed Mike, but felt angry and ashamed for letting his country down.

That mood didn't last long, though, because suddenly a tremendous *THWACK!* landed very near them, off to their left, and debris – earth, stones, and wood splinters – sprayed everywhere. Tommy felt a small piece of wood lodge sharply into his upper left arm, but he didn't even turn to examine the damage; Glennon had fiercely whispered "Come on!" and was leading him in a run over to where the shell had hit.

By the time they got there, the smoke had lifted; but as soon as Tommy stumbled onto the scene, he found himself wishing it hadn't. Pieces of Tommies lay all about – a leg here, an arm there, and other, less distinguishable parts he wouldn't have cared to catalogue – and off to the side, his chest blown wide open, screaming in agony, was the funny, fat little mess private, Muffett. Flowers followed Glennon over to the man, who from shoulders to waist was a mass of loosely hanging white flesh and red gore. He was screeching, bleeding from the mouth; more terrible still, his usually unintelligible speech was perfectly clear to the American: "Mum! Mum! I wahnn me mum!"

Glennon looked about hopelessly as another report, this from a trench mortar, landed dangerously near; acting decisively, he took the nearest handy piece of torn clothing – who knew who it was from – and gagged the dying little man to muffle his cries, which the sergeant had decided were still drawing fire from somewhere. Tommy crouched near, feeling useless and helpless, trying not to think about who had been blown apart in the nearby pit, when to his terror – the worst he'd had in the whole war – out of thin air there appeared a man crouching in front of him – but he didn't look like a man, more like a giant fly; he was wearing his gas equipment. From out of this monster came a voice that very nearly caused the Yank to break: "Tommy, d'you 'ave a gas mask? Put it on!" Without waiting for a reaction from the American, David Pearson turned to Michael Glennon and added with the same urgency, "You, too, Sergeant! There's gas coming."

Wiping his eyes, Mike snapped his on in a single easy motion; Tommy had a little more difficulty, but he felt David's hands helping him fit the thing snugly. From inside the weird apparatus, he heard Mike tell David, "Help me with him."

"You'll 'ave to take that out of 'is mouth, Mike." David's words of advice came faintly to Tommy as the sergeant removed the makeshift gag and Muffett's renewed howls split the air so strongly, the fat private seemed to be inside Flowers' head.

Tommy had no idea where the instinct came from, but in the split second that followed, with Pearson and Glennon still having no luck in getting the gas mask on Muffett and the latter still screaming at the top of his shattered lungs, somehow the Doughboy *knew* there was a machine gun training its sights on all of them. Before the first bullets sounded, he lunged over and scooped up both Pearson and Glennon, and literally threw the both of them several feet away, then followed that up by springing on top of them. As Mike's curses and David's cries of confusion began, so did a murderous rain of machine-gun bullets. Muffett, hit and hit again, screamed even worse than before, screams combined with choking noises as the gas got to him, screams none of the other three was lucky enough to escape hearing despite their gas masks. They were all lying flat, Tommy on top of the other two, all of them shaking. It went on for at least a minute before Muffett's screams, and the machine gun's deadly hail, finally stopped.

There followed a deathly silence, until Flowers heard Pearson mutter softly but plainly, "Tommy, let up. You're 'urting me."

Tommy did let up, slightly, still covering them, not daring to stand or even crouch. Having heard nothing from Glennon, he grew fearful, and asked, tentatively, "Mike?"

"I can't see" came the chilling, despairing reply.

Tommy moved off a little bit more, and David came out from under him, staying low but swinging round so the two privates flanked the sergeant. Pearson gently turned Glennon's head from the ground, and although his own hand was muddy, he wiped the slime and grime off the Welshman's mask. "There," he said in a voice so low Tommy barely heard him, "Can you see now?"

"No," Mike said in the same tone. "There's something in my eyes. They sting."

David's fly face looked up and over at Flower of Iowa, and he said, "We should stand up, Tommy."

So they both did, leaving Mike on the ground, and then to Tommy's astonishment, after a second's hesitation, David ripped off his gas mask. "It's all right now, I b'lieve," he said; and, always one to trust Pearson, Flowers did likewise, returning to a world where sights were clearer and sounds less muffled, as the smoke was beginning to lift. There was much firing off in the distance, but none now in their immediate vicinity. Pearson addressed Glennon: "Can you stand, Mike?"

"Just leave me here" came the reply, muffled by the gas mask.

"No!" Tommy said automatically, and David told the Doughboy, "If there's gas left, it stays close to the ground. We 'ave to get 'im up."

Tommy nodded, and as he and David lifted the unresisting Glennon to his feet, he wondered how the Welshman could be so heavy now when he had managed to toss both the sergeant and Pearson a distance of several feet just a couple of minutes ago. Pearson ripped off Glennon's mask, and Mike gasped, expecting, perhaps, to choke, then gulped in the air. Around his eyes – his blue eyes which, it occurred to Flowers in a stray thought, were the sergeant's best feature – all was puffy and watery. "Leave me," Mike repeated, causing Tommy to repeat, "No."

Dejectedly, the sergeant added, "I have no idea where we are."

As Tommy expected, and to his relief, David said, "I 'ave a fair notion."

"We should go back," Tommy suggested, as he watched David take a piece of cheesecloth from his kit.

"We should go forward," Pearson corrected. "There's no one be'ind us. I b'lieve the Jerries are on the run, actually. D'you 'ave anything like this in your kit, Tommy?"

"I reckon I might."

"Good. We may need more." David looked down at the cloth, which he was forming into a blindfold. "We should wet this. But there's no clean water 'ere. So." He started to spit repeatedly on the cloth, stopping to urge, "'Elp me, Tommy."

Flowers' throat was so dry, he didn't think he'd be able to muster the saliva, but he did; together they at least got the cloth damp. "Sorry, Mike," David said as he fixed the blindfold around his sergeant's head. "'Tis the best we can do."

"You should just leave me here."

"I get tired of training new sergeants, don't you know," David said jocularly; then he seemed to look at Tommy for the first time, and the term escaped him involuntarily: "You've something in your arm, love."

Glennon started in confusion and Tommy hastily responded, "It's nothing to worry about now. Can you lead us somewhere?"

"I can try. Mike, if Tommy 'olds your arm–?"

"Just make sure I don't walk into any trees – or Germans," said the man behind the blindfold, showing some sign of liveliness for the first time since losing his sight, and ignoring Pearson's odd form of address to Flowers.

"What about Muffett and–" Tommy began, and Mike, reassuming authority, interrupted him:

"Leave him, and the others. There's cross-wallahs for that, and we've tarried too long as it tis."

As Tommy took Mike's arm and they began to obey David's keen sense of direction, the American gave his English friend a look. Taking it as a request for interpretation, David explained, "The cross-wallahs are the blokes what make crosses for the graves."

# Chapter XLIII

So good were Pearson's instincts that they were soon out of the first set of woods, climbing through what was briefly fairly open country, toward another larger, higher wood that echoed, even at a distance, with the sounds of combat. Tommy wondered about the advisability of venturing into these second woods with a blinded man, but David fearlessly led them onward, and luck, or perhaps a sense on Pearson's part even more uncanny than usual, took them right into an American mop-up patrol – some men only vaguely familiar to Tommy, except for the lieutenant leading them. Sometimes Flowers had to wonder if there really was more than one Colbeck.

The Aussie's greeting was anything but gracious. "Where the hell have you been?" was aimed at Tommy; "And where's the rest of your men? You're the first Tommies I've seen in ages" was snapped at David and Mike, though it seemed to die in Jamie's throat as he caught sight of Glennon's condition.

Trying to make light, the Welsh sergeant replied, "I haven't *seen* any of my men for a while, either."

But Jamie was not amused. Turning on Pearson and Flowers, he demanded, "Why did you bring him here? We don't need a blind man here."

Unable to contain himself, Tommy simply said reproachfully "Jamie!" but before the target of the rebuke, visibly more angry still, could fire back, Pearson said in fine professional form, "Leftenant Colbeck, sir, Sergeant Glennon ordered us to leave 'im be'ind. I'm afraid we disobeyed 'is direct orders and brought 'im 'ere with us."

That took the wind right out of Colbeck, who paused heavily and regarded Pearson with blatant admiration: "Lad, you've got guts."

"Beg pardon, Leftenant, but neither Sergeant Glennon nor meself would 'ave any guts left if Private Flowers 'adn't covered us with 'is own body when the Maxim fired."

Jamie actually smiled at that, then said in a serious tone, "Haow many did you lose?"

Mike spoke up: "Twelve, I think, Leftenant, sir. From a shell."

As Tommy's mind whirled at the thought that all those body parts could have added up to eleven men plus Muffett, Jamie glanced at the ground, almost shame-faced; but then he looked up and said to David, "What I want to know is haow you managed to reach us, with a blind man no less, when we ain't seen hide nor hair of the rest of the whole 175th Brigade."

Since that was the brigade to which the London Rangers belonged, this comment did cause Pearson's eyes to widen. "'Aven't a notion, sir," he said, and Mike interjected again, "Are you saying your flank is totally uncovered, Jamie?"

"Both aour flanks," the lieutenant replied acidly. "I'm not completely surprised abaout aour right; they had to take the highest part of the ridge, with the most Maxims on it. But here, after abaout the first five hundred yards, the Boche broke and ran. We got through their barrage, and now we're chasin' after them. So, what happened to you?"

The blinded sergeant hung his head a bit. "I don't know."

"Well, I don't either. All I know is I can hardly keep these American boys back, while–"

"You started off completely disorganized," Glennon charged. "That's why I found Private Flowers. He lost his way."

"That's for Private Flaowuhs to answer to me abaout–" Jamie began, and Tommy had to interrupt:

"I wasn't running away!"

"Shut up!" Jamie shouted; then he added unconcernedly, "Who said you were?" In still another voice, he continued, "Anywise, we ain't got time for this. I'm stuck here with this man who can't see–""

"Leave me–" Mike insisted once more.

But that was all he got out before Jamie repeated, "Shut up, Sergeant. I'm pullin' rank here. Private Peahson, you're hereby drafted into the service of the American Army until the rest of your army decides to make an appearance, which I'll believe when I see it. Private Flaowuhs, take your little buddy here and find Captain Sand. He's somewheres up ahead, but since David here seems to be able to find his way araound even when he's never seen the territ'ry before, I'll wager you find him. You know what he looks like, and he's even easier to spot naow – he's got a wound just like yours."

Tommy looked down, finally, at his left arm, with the piece of wood lodged in it; the limb was bleeding copiously. Even as he did so, Jamie was producing some kind of tourniquet out of who knew where, which he proceeded to apply to Tommy's arm just below the shoulder, although not too tightly, lest he cut off circulation to the rest of the young American's arm. "Don't have enough sense to take care of yourself," the Australian muttered loud enough for all to hear, then he resumed giving orders: "When you find Captain Sand, tell him I said Private Peahson has a better sense of direction than the rest of the British Army put together, and if there's any scaoutin' to be done tonight, he's aour man." Tommy gave Jamie a killer look, and the latter added, "And tell him I said if it's two-man patrols, you two would make a good pair." Putting the finishing touches on the tourniquet, Jamie stepped back. "Is all that clear?"

"Yes, sir," Tommy answered, deliberately using the form of address Jamie didn't like. Ever curious, he added, "Did you say Captain Sand was hit by a piece of wood, too, sir?"

"No, Tommy, a bullet. But he was still moving forward when I left him. Naow I hereby order you to shut your maouth, and I order you and Peahson to get aout of here and find the captain."

Tommy and David silently saluted and headed off, David in the lead. As he followed his mate, Flowers noticed for the first time that day, although it had to have been there all along, Pearson's ever-present limp. They were still in the battle zone, to be sure, and therefore picking their way forward with caution through this new woods, which even had a few trees bravely leafing out in defiance of the war's destruction. But it was clear enough that this particular battle, at least in this sector, had been a rout. The dead Germans strewn about among the stumps and downed branches were outnumbered only by the Boche prisoners being marched to the back of the Allied lines, sometimes by only one or two armed Doughboys. Neither Flowers nor Pearson said much for a while, until finally, as it was clear they were proceeding in relative safety, the American said, "Jamie can be a great big idiot, can't he?"

His English pal laughed a little, said, "You need some stronger language, Tommy," then added, "Yes. He can be quite unfair. But per'aps he's right. All I've seen since we left the first woods are Americans. Where are the rest of me mates, I wonder?"

Incredulous, Tommy blurted out, "They're all lying in pieces in a shellhole."

Flowers felt bad as soon as he said it, but Pearson didn't flinch, simply observing, "That was 'ardly the 'ole brigade, love."

The use of the endearment again caused a cracking within Tommy. "God, Davey, I was so afraid–" he began, but David cut him right off:

"Don't let's talk about it 'ere, Tommy. Not while we're still in the battle."

Bucking himself up, Tommy asked, "Was that – all of your squad but you and Mike?"

"Can't be certain. We got scattered at the start, as you did." This reminder, inadvertent though it was, of Jamie's harsh comment stung Tommy; seeing his reaction, David tried to cajole him with "I b'lieve, as luck would 'ave it, 'Ardison was somewheres else, too."

"Too bad," Tommy said automatically, then caught himself and looked over at his friend in horror. "Sorry. I should never say anything like that, or even think it."

"And yet we all do," David acknowledged with a shrug.

Stumbling into a clearing, the two were greeted by a grisly sight: two German soldiers, no weapons anywhere near them, dead but otherwise very much intact, blood still seeping from their wounds. The older one had been shot in the head; the younger one, who appeared notably younger than Tommy and David, had been shot in the back. It seemed quite clear that whatever had happened to them had happened only minutes before at the most, though neither the Doughboy nor the Tommy had noted any shots in the continuing dull din of battle. The two live men paused only long enough for the Briton to observe, "Poor sods. Nothing we can do for them now," and then they continued on their way.

But over the next low rise, they spied a Doughboy striding briskly up ahead, in the same direction David had them heading. Despite David's limp, they slowly gained ground on this man, and as they grew closer, Tommy recognized his tent-mate; in another fine display of incaution, he called out, "Harry!"

Carson turned sharply about with the look of a trapped animal, then broke into a grin of… it wasn't relief, not quite. "Flower!" he replied, as David said with an uncharacteristic officiousness, "D'you know where your captain would be, Private Carson?"

"Pearson! How come you're both here? You don't have to be right next to Tommy even during a battle, do you?" David ignored this, but Tommy, already apprehensive about another matter, frowned deeply as Harry continued with a peculiar sort of nervousness in his voice: "Yeah, I'm going back to the captain right now. He's not far from here. You're going in the right direction. We reached our objective, you know. I heard the captain tell Jamie that. Isn't it great, Flower? Hasn't it been a great day?"

The shattered remnants of most of David's unit – and Muffett's last moments – flashed through Tommy's mind, followed by what he'd just witnessed. "Where were you coming from just now, Harry?" he asked, in a tone not at all friendly.

Carson's aspect darkened; then he tried, unsuccessfully, to appear opaque. "What do you mean, Tommy?"

"I'm asking where you were, just now, before we ran into you," Flowers repeated with exaggerated patience.

Indignant, Carson replied, "What business is it of yours? You don't outrank me–"

"What have you *done*, Harry?"

"Tommy. Leave it." That was David, trying to get his mate to move on, but Tommy said emphatically, in as sharp a voice as he'd ever used with David, "No!" Then he maximized the irony in his tone as he asked Carson, "Kill any Germans today, Harry?"

Carson looked at him with uncertainty at first, and then defiance. "Two," he answered. "Two no-good Krauts."

"An old one and a young one?"

"It was them or me, Tommy."

"Really? Where were their guns? You got them with you? 'Cause we sure didn't see–"

"It was for Vern, Tommy," Carson said imploringly. Seeing the lack of impact that had on Flowers, he added, "and for Ski, and Maple, and everyone that got it today. Goddammit, they're the *enemy,* Tommy–!"

"They threw down their guns, didn't they? Once they–"

"They're still the enemy," Carson repeated in a fury, and Flowers' voice descended into a near-hiss:

"Didn't you tell me you had two kid brothers, Harry? That could have been your kid brother–"

"He was a *German*–"

Pearson grabbed Flowers' arm in a motion swift and certain. "Come along, Tommy. We're soldiers, and our orders are to find the captain. No good can come of this."

"No good already has," Flowers spat out at Carson, but he allowed Pearson to lead him away.

The pair was silent as they made their way farther forward until, near the crest of a ridge still within the woods, along a trench far more elaborate than any Tommy had yet seen – a trench that as recently as this afternoon had been in German hands – they found much of the 131st Regiment. Once that happened, they had no trouble locating Billy Sand, now ensconced in a handsomely appointed underground room, complete with table and chairs, which had previously belonged to a Boche of similar rank. Tommy, his mind still reeling over the exchange with Carson, was somehow cheered by the very sight of his commanding officer, whose arm was in a neat cloth sling. He went into a stiff military salute when brought before the captain: "Private Flowers reporting for Lieutenant Colbeck, Captain, sir! And this is Private Pearson of the British Army."

For his part, Sand remained in a decidedly casual frame of mind, nodding toward David with a simple "Private," then pronouncing Tommy's first name and extending his good arm in greeting, if not a handshake, as if he were hosting some sort of soirée. "We thought we'd lost you," he added matter-of-factly to Flowers. "Where've you been?"

That prompted a rapid recital of Tommy's movements since the jumping-off signal, concluding with Colbeck's instructions regarding Pearson, stopping short of their encounter with Carson. Sand, who had seated himself at the table, listened with his usual patience and intensity, then addressed David: "Well, Private Pearson, welcome to the American Army, at least for now, and thank you for your service today."

"Thank you, Captain, sir. You're welcome, sir."

"Now, if you'll go outside and turn right," Billy continued, "you'll come to another bay with another underground room like this one. There's a medical officer there, Captain Block. Tell him I sent you, and I'd like to have him check out your leg. When he's finished with you, tell him I want him to take a look at Private Flowers' arm." Regarding the latter, he added to the both of them, "I'm no doctor, but I have a feeling that shrapnel needs to come out."

"Beg pardon, Captain, sir," Tommy corrected, "but it's only a piece of wood."

"Shrapnel's shrapnel," Sand said curtly to Flowers, as Pearson put in his two cents:

"I agree about Tommy's arm, Captain, sir, but beg pardon, there's really nothing can be done about me leg. It 'appened last month, when the aeroplane bombed Molliens."

Billy gave David a brief, blank look, then recovered. "All the same, Private, let's let the medical officer decide that. That's an order."

"Yes, sir, Captain," David said with a proper salute, and then he was gone.

Alone now with Billy, Tommy braced himself for a cross-examination as to why and how he'd gotten separated from his unit. But instead, Sand said genially, "Sit down, Tommy. We've all had quite a day, haven't we?"

"Sir?" Tommy replied, seating himself.

"We captured our objective, and gave Jerry a bloody nose. It's been a very successful day."

"Yes, sir, for you, sir – congratulations. If you don't mind my asking, sir, how did you catch the bullet?"

With a slight frown, Billy rose and began circling Tommy. "By getting shot," he replied. "Now what do you mean, 'For you, sir'?"

"I meant no disrespect, sir. I just meant I wasn't any help. I got lost, and–"

"If I've heard correctly, you were just about the last American before the British lines started. I don't call getting mixed in with the nearest unit during a barrage 'getting lost'–"

"I–"

Sand lifted his good arm, index finger pointing upward, to indicate he still had the floor. "Furthermore, I would call saving the lives of two Allied soldiers, then finding your way back to our lines with a blind man, reporting to your lieutenant, and then finding your way to your captain and reporting to me, a pretty good day's work. Wouldn't you, Corporal?"

Flowers did a double-take to see if someone else was in the room, as Sand pivoted about and re-seated himself. "Sir?"

"You heard what I said, Flowers. You're promoted to corporal, effective immediately."

Tommy felt dizzy. "But–"

"But what?"

"Well, sir, when Captain Willnor promoted somebody, it took–"

"I am not Captain Willnor, Tommy."

"Oh, don't I know, sir," Flowers said, his tone just short of gushy. "Captain Willnor would never even come near the battlefield–"

"Stop it, Tommy," Sand said good-naturedly. "You're embarrassing me."

"Sorry, Billy," Tommy dared, and he saw his captain didn't mind the familiarity at all, at least right now. Pressing his good fortune, he swallowed hard and said, "Uh, Captain, can I ask you something?"

"Ask away, Corporal."

"Is – Does a corporal sleep in a two-man tent?"

Billy gave a sigh, sounding mildly disgusted. "I should have known. Sometimes I forget what matters to the men most, although I thought you–"

"Oh, I don't mind sleeping in a tent on the ground, sir. Not at all. It's just – I was wondering if I could have a different tentmate than Carson."

Sand narrowed his eyes. "Why? I haven't noticed any problem between you two. And I can't believe you're bringing this up at a time like this."

Tommy took a deep breath, then said, "I believe – I have reason to believe he killed two prisoners today, sir."

Billy's eyebrows rose, ever so slowly. "What are you saying, Flowers?"

"Unarmed prisoners, sir. One of them couldn't have been more than sixteen years old."

Sand stared at Flowers until the enlisted man was most uncomfortable. At length he said, in a plain, calm voice, "You never saw that, Corporal. And I never heard from you about it, either–"

"But sir, it's wrong–"

Sand's tone took on that cold aspect that had become all too familiar to Flowers. "This is a war, Tommy. Many, many things go wrong in a war. We're in the middle of a successful offensive, and you want me to worry about two more dead Germans? My concern is to keep winning – and to keep the rest of you alive. That is all. The matter is closed. Is that understood?"

Tommy looked at the floor in despair. "Yes, sir."

His voice turning extremely gentle, Billy added, "I admire your convictions, son, and your courage in expressing them. But you're going to have to learn to let go of some of them in this war." He paused, added, "I'll see that you get a new tent assignment – if we all make it back to camp. Now, is there anything else?"

"Yes, sir. A couple of things."

Billy rolled his eyes. "I should've known better than to ask. What?"

"What about Lieutenant Colbeck? And Sergeant Dougherty?"

"If you're asking me what I think you're asking, they both served their countries and this army well today. I'm canceling my plan to demote them for their prior behavior."

"Then they'll be promoted, too?"

"That is their promotion," Sand said drily, and only a little impatiently. "Now, what's the second matter?"

"It's about Private Pearson, sir."

"Well, he's British; I have no say in whether he gets promoted or not. He obviously comes from a class that doesn't move up easily in their army. But he apparently possesses a remarkable sense of the landscape. His own people have been very foolish if they haven't been taking advantage of it." It was as if Sand were musing privately, assessing this new man he'd just met; then he seemed to remember Flowers was there, glancing over at the Doughboy. "He a friend of yours, Tommy? Before today, I mean."

Deliberately choosing his words, Flower of Iowa replied, "My very best friend in the whole world, sir."

The captain's eyebrows arched quickly and sharply this time. "I see. How interesting, then, that you ended up saving Sergeant Glennon together. So, what is it you're asking me?"

"It's – about those recommendations by Lieutenant Colbeck, sir. About sending out patrols tonight."

Billy seemed to ponder the import of what Tommy was saying. "I'm of two minds on that," he said eventually, trying to fold his hands in front of him, though it was awkward with the wounded arm. "Our flanks are uncovered on both sides, but we need to press our advantage. We need to send out patrols, and we need to use the best men at our disposal – and as we've all agreed, Private Pearson seems to possess an instinct for the land that's invaluable for such a mission. At the same time, I don't like the look of his limp–"

"Neither do I, sir–"

"–which is why I sent him to the medical officer. And on the other hand, I question the wisdom of sending two, how did you put it, 'very best friends in the whole wide world' out on a two-man patrol together." Sand paused, then added, "There's one thing, though, that I'm not of two minds about: I never, ever would honor any man's request that another man be exempted from dangerous duty because they're friends. Never. Is that understood?"

"Y-yes, sir. I didn't mean any–"

"–disrespect, yes, Tommy, I know, you never do." At that moment, Tommy but not Billy was startled by ringing; the captain picked up a field telephone in excellent working order, and said into it, "Yes? Yes. Yes." Replacing the receiver, he went on, "That was Captain Block. He's finished examining Private Pearson. He's ready to take that splinter out of your arm."

"And then, sir?" Tommy asked, rising.

"And then we'll see who goes out on patrol tonight. Do you remember which way it was to the medical bay?"

"Yes, sir," said Tommy, saluting. "Thank you, sir, for everything – as always."

Sand, already returning to paperwork, looked back up at the newly promoted corporal with his characteristic bemused expression and said, “Not at all, Tommy. It’s always interesting for me, talking to you. Good day.”

# Chapter XLIV

Captain Block, not the warmest of medical officers, gave Tommy's arm the most cursory of examinations, yanked out the piece of wood with very little ceremony, then stanched the bleeding and wrapped the upper arm in some clean cloth. Just as this task was being completed, a rather disheveled officer appeared in the doorway of the medical bay – Jamie was back on the front line.

"Haow is he, Captain?" the lieutenant immediately asked, and the medical officer replied sourly, "There's nothing wrong with him."

"Then he's fit to go aout on patrol tonight?"

Sounding bored by the question, Block answered, "I see no reason why not."

At that, Colbeck, who seemed to have no fondness for Block, motioned to Flowers, and the Iowan, his arm feeling stiff, followed the Aussie back outside, to the main trench, where he was surprised to see it was still light out. Feeling a little resentful of the medical officer's treatment coupled with the apparent order to head out again on patrol, Tommy remained silent, glumly plodding behind his lieutenant, until Jamie turned around and pulled even with him as they walked, saying, "So, I hear you're a corp'ral naow."

"You've been talking to Billy. Do you know where David is?"

"He was takin' a bit of a rest while the doctor was takin' care of your little splinter."

"A rest before he goes out on patrol?"

"Before he goes aout on patrol, yes – with you."

This news did not mollify Tommy, who said, almost sullenly, "So what's the objective this time?"

For his part, Jamie suddenly snapped in return, "Don't be so impatient," and moved ahead of Tommy again. Once more Flowers followed in gloomy silence, until they were back to the bay with the underground room occupied by Captain Sand. When Tommy followed Jamie into the chamber, he got a shock: The table where he and the captain had sat earlier now had a real tablecloth over it. More amazing still, the table was set with real dishes and real silver, and real food – and wine. Furthermore, Billy was sitting in one chair, David in another, and there were two additional chairs, both empty.

At the sight of the captain, Tommy made to salute, but Jamie knocked his arm down; the Doughboy was glad his sore left wasn't his saluting arm. Colbeck went on, "Ain't none of us eaten since day before yesterday. There's time for you to chaow daown before you go back aout."

"Is this like a last meal?" Tommy retorted, and Jamie said in an even voice, "Not if you're careful," but David was more reproachful, saying, "Tommy!"

"What?" the Doughboy shot back, defiant.

Although Pearson's discomfort at having an exchange with Flowers in front of two officers was palpable – with Tommy's promotion, he was now the lowest-ranking man there – he forged ahead: "You're being rude. Captain Sand 'ere got 'old of some rations from the Germans, and 'e's sharing them with you and me and Jamie."

Brought up short again, Tommy's response was to redden, with no thought of what to say; but Billy, who had the most cause to be offended, smoothed things over with an affable "Sit down, both of you. It's been a long couple of days, and I'm sure everybody's tired and hungry."

"Thank you, sir," Tommy mumbled as he took the seat farthest away from the captain. As he did, he felt a leg – David's – nudge him under the table; whether in reprimand or encouragement, he couldn't tell.

"No 'sirs' around this table tonight, Tommy. That's an order." Sand grabbed the bottle of liberated *vin rouge* and began pouring it around like a good host, though he put only a very little in his and Jamie's glasses, and even less in David's and Tommy's. Glancing over at the man he knew least well, Billy added, "A penny for your thoughts, Pearson."

"His Christian name's David," Jamie put in helpfully. "Coming from his army, he'd never volunteer that to you."

"David, then," Billy said agreeably, with a nod at the Englishman.

"I'm – a little at sea, Captain," David admitted, and Sand immediately interrupted:

"Billy."

"B–Billy," the Briton stammered, then he continued, "Y'see, I wou'n't ever call an officer by 'is Christian name like that in me own army – and I wou'n't ever sit down to dinner with a captain and a leftenant. And even if I ever did, the captain wou'n't pour the wine 'imself. 'E'd 'ave a batman to do that."

Tommy wasn't quite clear what a batman was, but everyone else seemed to know, so he continued to keep quiet as Billy said, "Well, David, welcome to the American Army, at least for now. We don't have batmen for the officers in this army. I hope our democratic ways aren't too strange for you."

This was said quite genially, and Pearson responded in kind: "Actually, Billy, I rather fancy them."

This prompted laughter among all of them but Tommy; but as it died down, David's tone turned serious: "But since you asked me me thoughts–"

"Go ahead, David," Billy encouraged.

Pearson turned to Colbeck, who hadn't waited to start eating. "'Ow's Mike doing, Jamie?"

Jamie glanced over at Billy and started to explain, "Mike is Sergeant Glennon, the man who–"

"I know who Mike is, Jamie," Sand said peremptorily. "I was right there when you called to each other last night."

He just doesn't miss a thing, thought the still-silent Flowers, who also marveled once again at the stretching of time – could that really have been only last night? In the meantime, David was persisting: "So, 'ow is 'e? Will 'e be all right? Will 'e ever" – Pearson's voice caught, then he pushed on – "will 'e ever see again?"

It was Colbeck's turn to flash an unexpected smile. "I stayed with him 'til a medical officer came along – a better one than that bird Block." Sand seem to flinch ever so slightly at Colbeck's criticism of a superior officer, but said nothing. "He told me there was a good chance Mike might get his sight back, and he said if he did, it would be because of your quick thinkin', with the wet blindfold and all."

Now Pearson was speechless with embarrassment, but Flowers, so wordless 'til now, turned on Colbeck in a demanding tone: "You didn't tell me–"

"You didn't ask," the Australian reminded him. "You were too busy paoutin'."

That caused Tommy to look down stonily at his plate, but he felt another kick, a harder one; that was clearly David telling him to snap out of his blue funk. At the same time, Billy raised a glass and said simply, "To Mike's eyesight."

All three of the others had the good sense to clink; but Jamie and David both watched Tommy to see if he'd actually drink. Downing his own, David quickly turned to his Doughboy pal and said, "You should try it, Tommy. It's really good!"

As Tommy forced himself to drink the stuff – it was better than before, but still pretty sour, in his opinion – Jamie explained to Billy, "Aour Flaowuhs here doesn't care much for *vin rouge*."

"Can't say as I blame you, Tommy," Billy said heartily, "if all you ever had was that rotgut in the just-a-minutes. This is a different grade entirely."

"Madame wouldn't serve rotgut," Tommy said automatically, and Jamie laughed.

"I warned you, Billy. This boy's nothing but argumentative."

"I knew that already," said Billy between bites, regarding Flowers. "I don't know who Madame is, but I do know all the *estaminet* owners are alike. I wouldn't care to take a bet on the quality of her wines."

Now it was Tommy's turn to voice his surprise, as he finally tasted what was on his plate. "This meat is really good, sir – Billy. What is it?"

"*Weisswurst,* I think. Veal sausage. We used to get it in Chicago. There are a lot of Germans there."

"Germans?"

Sand shrugged. "Most of them signed up to fight for Uncle Sam faster than the rest of us."

"But they keep telling us the Germans are so 'ard off," said David, indicating the food, and Tommy, swallowing a mouthful, nodded in agreement.

"That's their people," Jamie informed them. "Their army is another story, and their officers are another story from that."

"I thought their men looked pretty healthy today, didn't you, Jamie?" That was Billy.

"Yes," the Aussie said, with a nod of his own, "though there were more old ones and young ones than I've seen before."

The two Germans killed by Carson flashed through Flowers' mind, and he put down his fork. He stared straight ahead, then caught sight of Sand looking at him, perhaps reading his mind; so he turned to Pearson, only to tell, at a glance, that David definitely was reading his mind. "So, Tommy," Davey said in his best cheerful voice, "I 'ear you're a corp'ral. Congratulations. I'm so proud of you."

If they thought this last was an odd thing to say, neither Billy nor Jamie betrayed as much, but it made Tommy a little nervous, so he said hastily, "You're the one who should be promoted, Davey." He stumbled, not having intended to use the nickname, but then went on, "You're a hero, really. They ought to give you a medal."

"Go on," David said, pleased but philosophical. "I'm other ranks. That wou'n't 'appen to the likes o'me."

"That's too bad," Billy put in, to Tommy's surprise.

"It's just 'ow it is," David demurred. "You can't change it." Then he added boldly, "Would there be any more o'that wine, Billy?"

Billy took a beat, then said, "Yes. But you and Tommy can only have a bit more. You're going out on patrol."

Determined to make up for his prior behavior, Tommy asked, "What's the objective, sir? Do we know where we are?" as his captain made good on his offer, pouring the wine but again giving himself and Jamie a little more, though only a little.

Billy didn't chide Tommy about calling him "sir"; the dinner was nearly over, and they were getting back to business. "We're in the Gressaire Wood," he informed them. "The Gressaire Wood and Chipilly Ridge, which is on our right, are the highest points in this area. After we won at Hamel, we captured the ground across the river from here. They've been firing at us from here ever since."

It was an explanation of the place's strategic importance clear enough for an enlisted man to understand, and these two did. "But now they're not," Tommy said with satisfaction.

"Don't be so sure," Sand cautioned, without rancor. "We've captured some of the woods, but not all of it. And the 1st Battalion got held up on the ridge. As for the 175th British, who were supposed to be on our left, with all due respect,

Private Pearson, you seem to be it so far." Before David could complete looking downcast over this, Billy said, "And I might add, we're mighty grateful for that."

"Per'aps they'll be along soon," said David, not sounding terribly convinced himself.

"They better be," said Jamie. "In the meantime, lads, I take it you get the picture the captain's drawrin'. Right naow we're aout here on aour own. We don't know who's up ahead or on either side of us. It looks like Jerry broke and ran – but he has this way of coming back."

David and Tommy looked at each other uneasily, and finally Pearson spoke: "D'you want us to try to find the Boche without engaging them, then?"

The question was aimed, properly, at Billy Sand, but it was Jamie Colbeck who answered. "You are a bright one, lad. Billy and Tommy are right. They're fools not to move you up."

"Thank you for the dinner, Captain," Tommy said, pushing himself away from the table. "It was real nice of you, and I'm sorry–"

Sand cut him off with a wave of his hand. "You both earned it, Tommy, ten times over. I wish I could do this for all my men."

David chimed in his own thanks as he stood, and as Sand acknowledged that, the captain glanced at the doorway and added, "It's still a bit too light for you to start. Why don't you two take a few minutes, then report back out front of here to Lieutenant Colbeck? He'll give you your orders, and send you over the top."

After the enlisted men departed, Colbeck turned to Sand and remarked, "You see what I said, Billy? I can't remember when I've seen two soljuhs who are so tight. It's like the one knows what the other one is thinkin' abaout all the time."

Talking mostly to himself, Sand mused, "Pearson always knows what Flowers is thinking, but that's not too difficult, he's so transparent. I'm not sure how much it runs the other way." Seeming to recall Colbeck's presence, the captain added, "Yes, they're obviously very close. That could make them ideal for this assignment. But I'm afraid if we lose one, we'll automatically lose the other."

# Chapter XLV

Leaving Sand's temporary quarters and taking a few strides beyond it, Tommy turned to Davey and said, "This isn't a good idea, is it?"

David knew exactly what he meant, but simply replied, "Sometimes I wonder if the 'ole war is such a good idear." Looking up at Flowers, Pearson could see his answer wasn't satisfactory, so he added, "We're soldiers, Tommy. It's our job. 'Ave you lost your fight?"

"No, I haven't lost my fight. I just don't see why they're sending us out again, after everything else we did today."

"I can't believe I'm 'earing this from you. You 'oo always says 'e wants to kill Germans–"

"I do want to kill Germans!"

"Then where's the problem?" Tommy fell silent and looked away from David, but the Briton wasn't about to let go of the conversation; after a pause, he continued, "I b'lieve I know the problem. You don't mind so much they're sending you out again. I think you're cross because they're sending me out again."

Tommy turned back to David, stared at him in the fading light, then said, "Well, what if I am? Like Billy and Jamie said, in our army you'd be promoted for what you did. Maybe get a medal. Isn't that enough for one day?"

"'Twasn't me point, love."

Tommy looked fleetingly about, saw no one, then answered, his voice full, "Davey, I thought I'd lost you when that shell hit your unit. And then there was everything else we went through today. To go out now, on this unnecessary patrol–"

"'Oo says it's not necessary? Your captain – and 'e's a very good captain, you know that – says 'tis, and that we're the best men for it." David leaned in to his Doughboy mate and added, "When you thought that shell kilt me, you put it out o'your mind so you could 'elp Mike with Muffett, di'n't you? Don't tell me different. I sawr you."

Backing away as if he were being accused of something, Tommy shook his head vigorously. "David, I never –"

"Of course you did, love. And even if I 'ad been 'it by that shell, it's what I'd want you to do. 'Elp them what's still alive. Your sorrow for me could wait, if I was dead. Wou'n't matter to me, not at that point."

Staring at him again, Tommy said at length, "You turned out to be a better soldier than all of us."

Looking down, David countered, "Per'aps not."

"Why? Everything you did today you did right."

David looked back up. "But I never said I di'n't agree with you that this was a bad idear."

Tommy's gaze didn't waver from David's as he said, "Oh."

"If they kill you, even if it's a shell, I know just what I'll do. I'll just use me sense of direction that everyone talks about so, and run and run until I find them, so they can kill me."

Tommy was struck speechless; when he regained his breath, he said, "You wouldn't even try to kill them?"

"Of course. I'd kill as many's I could, for King and country. But I wou'n't stop until they kilt me."

"What if you killed them all?"

"Then I'd find some more." As if his point was not getting across, David stressed, "I'd 'ave no reason to live, Tommy."

"Now you sound like me," Flowers retorted.

"Cor, but I do," Pearson responded, repeating softly for emphasis, "Cor, but I do."

Again looking away from him, Tommy said in a voice barely audible, "I know you do."

What was now the Allies' main firing trench had been until today the Germans' main reserve trench. As Jamie led them left of the bay that contained Sand's "office," then left, then right and right again, they came to what seemed to be a dead end. The wall facing the direction Tommy and David were to take was distinguished by very few funk holes and no fire-steps; it was now their parapet, but for years it had been the parados, with no expectation of an enemy coming from that direction, and little need to look that way. Jamie found the best funkhole he could and struggled into it, using it as a precarious foothold to look over the top; then, clambering down, he ordered David to do likewise.

Pearson tried, but he couldn't see over the edge; nearly falling backward, he said to the lieutenant, "I'm afraid I'm too short. D'you 'ave a periscope? Or per'aps Tommy can–"

"It's you I want to see this, David," Jamie retorted. "I've got a better idear. Tommy can lift you up on his shoulders."

Taking that as a direct order, the Doughboy turned his back on his British mate, who proceeded to climb on his shoulders, legs dangling on either side of the American's neck. As a physical act, lifting David like this was rather pleasurable for Tommy, despite the Briton's being a little heavier than expected; but Flowers was trembling slightly – if he had been unhappy about this mission from the beginning, he was terrified at the prospect of helping David to stick his head out over the parapet. But the corporal's apprehension was of no interest to his lieutenant, who shouted much too loudly (in Tommy's opinion) up at David, "Can you see naow?"

"Yes, Leftenant, very well," Pearson replied in spite of the darkness.

"What do you see on your left?"

There was a pause, then David's voice drifted down. "There's a woods. A different woods from this one, I b'lieve."

"That's right. It's called the Bois de Tailles, the Tailles Woods." It sounded to Tommy like Jamie was saying "Tie Woods." "That's where we think the Boche went," the Australian continued. "That's aour next target. That's where we want you to explore."

"Right-oh," David said cheerfully; but he had barely said this when Tommy heard a sudden, sharp report from somewhere and jerked backward with a small cry, losing his balance, then falling to the ground – but not before catching David, breaking his fall.

It all happened so rapidly; there he was, standing with Pearson on his shoulders, then there they both were, lying in the dirt, looking up at a glowering Colbeck, who gazed back down at them disdainfully and said, "Where's your nerve, Tommy? You're actin' like a scared rabbit."

"Sorry, Jamie," Flowers said as he scrambled to his feet, turning back to offer Pearson a hand, which David refused as he got up without assistance.

Declining to make any more of the incident at that moment, as he could have, Jamie simply said, "Naow, as soon as you catch your breath, it's over the top with the both of you." Changing his mind, he addressed Tommy after all: "Your reactions are gonna have to be better than that, Flaowuhs, if you want to bring yourself and your buddy back alive."

"Yes, sir."

Colbeck regarded Pearson and said with exaggerated weariness, "David, tell your mate I don't like to be called 'sir.' He obviously don't listen to me." The attempt at humor coaxed a smile from both enlisted men, visible to Jamie even in the darkness; then he said in a different tone, "Naow off with you."

The scramble over the top was a quick one, giving the two little time to think. With his longer legs and lack of a limp, Tommy could have moved faster than David, but since he hadn't the slightest idea where they were going, he held back, letting Pearson take the lead.

Despite the dark and his deficient sense of the terrain, even Flowers could tell that on what was now the front side of the Allies' trench, the trees were thicker, or rather there were a lot more real trees, instead of the shattered stumps and splinters he had come to expect whenever someone spoke of a "woods" or "forest" here in France. The war smells – cordite, blood, unwashed men, the dead – faded a bit, to be replaced by scents he once had considered more natural – earth and vegetation, mostly.

After about ten minutes, maybe less, of following Pearson's lead through dense underbrush, the Doughboy was suddenly brought up short when his Tommy pal pulled up sharply ahead of him, his hand raised in apparent warning. Flower of Iowa gripped his rifle and whispered, "What is it?"

Rather than replying, David motioned him into a crouch, even as he did the same. Only then did the Englishman whisper in his ear, "Tommy."

"What?" Flowers whispered back in agitation.

"I b'lieve I'm lost."

That of course was the last thing Tommy expected or wanted to hear. "That's impossible, Davey," he said automatically. "You can't be lost."

"I can be and I am."

Tommy paused as they continued crouching there together. "Do you think you could find your way back?"

"If I could, I wou'n't be lost, now would I?"

Tommy hesitated again, then: "What do you think we should do?"

"Proceed very carefully," David replied, straight-faced, and although the answer was perfectly good, serious advice, it caused them both to get a fit of the giggles. Tommy clapped a hand on David's shoulder in an attempt to steady them both; and as he did, there was the sharp sound of rustling in the nearby bushes, and they both froze and clicked their rifles, remaining in their crouched positions, tensed and waiting. There was silence and then the rustling happened again, very near. More tense seconds followed, and then suddenly something burst through the vegetation right at them, colliding with Pearson's leg and making an unearthly noise – something small and furry.

"It's a cat!" David exclaimed, then he dropped his voice back to a whisper as he picked up the struggling animal. "A bleedin' cat! What's 'e doing out 'ere?"

Tommy, who had collapsed to a sitting position, was shaking his head with relief. "Maybe he belonged to a German officer."

"Per'aps so," David agreed, stroking the animal and soothing it with a "There, there. Poor thing."

"I'm surprised one of us didn't shoot him. I reckon we're still not very good soldiers, after all."

"Or we're such good soldiers, we knew better than to waste ammunition on a poor little animal." David paused, then added, "A shame we'll 'ave to kill 'im." As he said this, he began to withdraw his knife from his kit.

"You can't be serious!"

"We 'ave to, Tommy. 'E's making too much noise. There could be Boche anywheres about."

"Let's just leave him here, Davey."

"D'you think that would really be such a mercy? Leaving 'im out 'ere in no-man's-land?"

"Yes. At least then he has a fighting chance."

"Like the rest of us, eh?"

"Yes, like the rest of us."

"All right, Tommy." David replaced his knife with one hand and with the other put the cat, which was actually barely more than a kitten, down on the ground. The animal, true to its nature, began to rub up against Pearson's leg, hooking its claws into his trousers even as he and Flowers both rose to a standing position. To discourage this, Pearson flung his foot in a rough kick. The cat held on tenaciously while protesting loudly – and it was at that point that the shots rang out. Tommy and David, standing no more than a foot apart, both hit the ground; the troublesome feline ceased being affectionate, instead streaking away in terror.

Down on the ground, Tommy was shaking again, certain he was all right but not at all sure about David, or what he could do if David was wounded or worse. He called Pearson's name softly even as he heard more rustling in the undergrowth – twin rustlings actually, two separate sounds made by beings much larger than that cat. He reached over and felt a wetness where he had reckoned David's face should be, and for a moment in the darkness, everything stopped – David's face was half shot away; he could feel the blood and…

Rising sharply back up, Tommy screamed, "You bastards! You *bastards!*" and let loose with a wild volley of shots in the direction of the twin rustlings. He heard a thud as one bullet hit its mark, then a cry of "King's army! We're King's army!"

Tommy was in such a blind fury that he wouldn't even have heard the man's plea had a low groan from below not broken his concentration. If the other two soldiers were really British and had heard him shout in English, then it was safe for him to crouch back down and see if David was, after all, still alive.

Swiftly back down, he whispered David's name and got a faint "Tommy?" in reply.

"It's me. I'm here," Tommy whispered, and before he could say anything else, David called out, in the kind of strong voice that seemed to indicate something besides half his face being shot away,

"12th Londons."

"And we're 9th Londons, damn you" came the reply, close by, though not at full voice. "Help us."

"Help *us,*" Tommy began, but David cut him off by half sitting up. "You're all right," said the American with wonder and joy.

"Right enough," the Englishman agreed, then allowed, "But me face, it's burning."

Tommy could make out the shape of David's face now, so close, and he gently placed a hand, first on Pearson's left cheek, which caused David to clasp his hand over Tommy's; but then Tommy placed his other hand on David's right cheek, and that elicited a loud whisper-cry of "Owww!"

"I'm sorry," said Tommy, quickly withdrawing the second hand. Mike Glennon came rushing into his head. "Can you see?"

"Yes, Tommy. Something stings in me cheek, that's all." Quickly Pearson added, "We must go 'elp the others," and Flowers automatically answered, "Right"; but then he hesitated. "But what if it's a Jerry trick?"

"That's why I said '12th Londons.' The way they said '9th Londons' right 'ways cou'n't be a Jerry trick."

"If you say so. But I'm not sure where they are."

"I am," said David, whose full faculties, including his sense of direction, seemed to have returned. Turning from Tommy with assurance, he pitched a loud whisper: "'Elp is coming!" and the same voice from before called back in a similar tone,

"Hurry."

In the darkness, Pearson grabbed Flowers' hand and, at a run, guided him through what seemed to be impenetrable underbrush. In less than a minute they broke into a small clearing where they could see, in the dimness, a man kneeling, cradling a man lying on the ground.

"Took you long enough," grumbled the kneeling man in a fierce whisper.

Rather than respond to that, David simply replied, "I'm Private David Pearson, 12th Londons, 175th Division. And this is me mate, Corporal Thomas Flowers, 33rd Division, U.S." Flowers was surprised that in the heat of the moment, Pearson remembered his new rank.

"Damned trigger-happy Yank," hissed the kneeling man. "You shot Jock."

"Jock shot at us first, or you did," Flowers retorted as he and Pearson both knelt down. "One inch to the side and my friend here would be dead."

"'Ere, 'ere, it's no time to quarrel," said Pearson, cursorily examining the wounded man. "Jock 'ere needs our 'elp. 'E's 'it in the stomach, isn't 'e?" David looked up at the other stranger and added, a little impatiently, "And 'oo would you be?"

"You're a cheeky little monkey, Private. Remember your place in the King's army. I'm Corporal O'Brien, 9th Londons, and this is Private MacLachlan that your mate's shot."

"What kind of great big idiot are you, O'Brien?" Tommy demanded. "Here we come to help you and–"

"Sod off, you bloody Yank–"

"Corporal–" David began patiently.

"Keep quiet, Private, before I have you writ up and–" O'Brien's order was cut short as Tommy let loose again, this time with a roundhouse punch to the jaw that knocked the British corporal flat.

There was a brief, shocked silence, then David exclaimed, "Tommy! Why'd you do that?"

"Davey," Tommy replied in his lowest tones, "nobody talks to you like that while I'm around."

"'Tis 'is right, Tommy. 'E's a corporal–"

"You're still with the American Army. I'm your corporal, and I say he can't." Tommy paused, then added, "Besides, don't you realize while we're sitting here arguing, the Germans could hear us? They could creep up on us, and we'd all be dead."

David emitted a loud sigh, then shook his head. "As if I di'n't know. We've all been very bad soldiers, Tommy. If any Jerries were about, we'd all be long dead. Now, 'ere we are with a wounded man–"

"Two, counting you."

"Two, counting me," David concurred without argument, "and another man you've knocked flat–"

"There's another reason I did it, Davey. With him out cold, I'm the ranking man. I'm in charge. I give the orders."

"So what d'we do?"

Tommy had expected David to argue; he'd underestimated the British soldier's habit of obedience to authority. "I say we should turn back," the American said.

"What?"

"Turn back. We're lost; we can't find our objective, even with you leading. Three of the four of us have been wounded–"

"Oh, Tommy!"

"–so I say it makes sense to turn around. What are we doing here, anyway?"

"We're on patrol, Tommy. We've a mission–"

"It's a ridiculous mission."

"I don't know about you, Tommy, but I 'ave no intention of being shot for a coward."

Though they were still barely visible in the dimness, the two friends stared at each other in heavy silence. Slowly, Tommy said, "Are you – calling me a coward, David?"

"Of course not, love. But that's 'ow it might look to Captain Sand and Leftenant Colbeck if we turn back now."

At that, Tommy hesitated much more. Finally he said, "So what do you think we should do?"

David pondered, then said, "Well, you're right there's no sense trying to move forward, now we must look after these two. We should find a safer place – away from a clearing like this – and wait until there's more light."

It made sense to Tommy. "And where would we find such a safe place?"

David hesitated only a fraction, then said, "Let me 'ave a bit of a look-'round."

Tommy wasn't enthusiastic about being left alone with a man he'd shot and a man he'd knocked out, even if they were supposed to be on the same side as him. "But there might be Germans."

"Tommy, we've already agreed, if there were any Germans 'ereabouts, we'd be kilt already. I won't go far, I promise."

Tommy considered that, then conceded, "All right." Ruefully he added, "I'm not much of a leader, am I?"

"You're a very good leader. You've been learning from your Captain Billy."

"But you're the one with all the ideas."

"A good leader listens to good idears."

"I didn't say they were *good* ideas."

They both laughed again, then both cut their laughter short, each recalling that a moment of inattentive hilarity had led them to their current predicament. "Don't you worry, love," David whispered. "I'll be back in no time."

Then he was gone, and Tommy was alone – alone again, he realized, as he'd been at Hamel with Vernon Sanders. Where was Vern now, he wondered – six feet under? Dead, like the two Germans who had been murdered (could you say anyone was murdered in a war?) by Carson, in Sanders' name?

Flowers heard another low groan, and was concerned that O'Brien was stirring, ready to fight; but it was MacLachlan, regaining consciousness. Maybe Tommy had done the Scotsman a favor and given him a Blighty. At any rate, he found himself comforting the man he had shot, slowly rocking him as he tried to suppress his own fear. As MacLachlan quieted again, Tommy realized he had no idea what either of these men looked like; if he were to leave them now in the darkness, and then encounter them tomorrow in the daylight, he'd never know who they were.

In the meantime, the country around him also quieted, and all he could hear were the night sounds of the summer insects – noises different from, but also the same as, the katydids and cicadas and crickets back in Iowa. Moments, or maybe minutes later, an approaching shadow told Flowers that Pearson was back from his reconnaissance. Casually slinging his rifle to his side as he rose to his feet, Tommy said, "So did you find anything, Davey?" – and the still-approaching figure suddenly froze, then threw his hands in the air and shouted, "*Kamerad!*"

Tommy froze in his turn; if his heart had seemed to skip several times today, this was the ultimate. He swung his rifle back up and pointed it at the man, who repeated much too loudly, in a voice that conveyed sheer terror, "*Kamerad!*"

It could be a trick, Tommy thought. What if he isn't alone? But he, Flowers, had just today taken a stand against what Carson had done. Pointing with his gun – though they were still barely visible to each other – Tommy made his wishes known, and the Jerry soldier scuttled over and obediently sat down on the ground, his hands behind his head. Tommy had the presence of mind to take the man's rifle, and toss it toward his unconscious Allies. But then, his gun still trained, he wasn't sure what to do next. Finally he asked the German, "Do you speak English?"

"*Kamerad!*" the German said yet again, and Tommy shook his head and kept his rifle on the prisoner. Long minutes passed in silence. Four sets of breathing punctuated the night – Tommy's own, which he was trying to keep steady; MacLachlan's shallow draughts, reflecting his shock at being wounded; the deep slumber of O'Brien, still out cold; and the prisoner's light breaths, betraying his conviction that this giant American might decide at any moment to kill him.

Tommy listened to this respiratory cacophony until he felt his mind was playing a trick on him, that there was somehow a fifth set of lungs at work; then the hair stood on the back of his neck, for he had the prickly, eerie sensation that someone *had* silently joined their foursome. Caught between hope and fear, he managed to choke out, "David?"

"I'm 'ere, love" came the reassuring voice, followed by a familiar touch on the arm as Tommy sighed, releasing all the cumulative tension. "That was very good," David added.

"What was?"

"I've just got back. I was quiet as I could, but you noticed me right 'ways."

"Only your breathing."

"But that's good, don't y'see?"

"Why did you do that?"

"Me eyes get better at night. I saw you 'ad a fourth man with you. I came in quiet as I could, so I could puzzle out the situation. Even oncet I sawr you 'ad the gun on 'im, I still 'ad to take care, so you wou'n't shoot me by accident."

"Then that was good soldiering on your part, too."

"Not good enough, since you 'eard me breathe. Did you take 'is gun?"

"Yes."

"And 'is bayonet?"

"His – oh."

Tommy's rifle had never wavered. Now David turned to the prisoner and said, "Bayonet, please." The German looked blankly back at the Englishman, unresponsive.

"Do you know any German?" Tommy asked.

"No," said David, eyes not leaving the confused prisoner as he threw his own hands up to indicate what he wanted. The German responded by lifting his hands high above his head. David then patted down the Jerry's tunic, finding and relieving him of his bayonet and several other implements. All through this procedure, Tommy's rifle remained trained on the prisoner.

"What now?" the Doughboy asked.

"What d'you think?" David was throwing the question back.

"Now I think we really should go back."

"So do I. But I b'lieve we should wait 'til there's more light."

"Did you find a better place for us to wait?"

"Can't say that I did. And 'ow we'd get two unconscious men and a prisoner there anyways, I don't know. I do 'ate being out in the open like this, though."

They were silent a minute, then Tommy said, "Do you think you know the way back now?"

"I might. I'm not certain, mind you, but me 'ead feels clearer, so I might."

"I think MacLachlan needs to see a medical officer. And now we've got a prisoner they could interrogate. Maybe you should try to get help."

"What, and leave you 'ere alone with all three?"

"I'll be all right, Davey. I won't like it, but I'll be all right."

Now David hesitated. "You wou'n't fall asleep, love?"

"No." But David's concerns were having their effect on Tommy, so he asked, his eyes still fixed on the prisoner, "Maybe you could take him with you–?"

"I'm not that sure where I'm going. And 'e'd be in me way. Slow me down."

"That's true." Making up his mind, Tommy added, "All right, then."

"Would that be an order, then, sir?"

Tommy smiled. "Do you think it should be?"

"I just 'ope O'Brien doesn't come to and do anything foolish. Bloody silly to 'ave to worry about such a thing, but–"

"So, are you going?"

"I'm going, love, I'm going."

And before Tommy knew it, David was indeed gone again. Keeping his gun trained on the prisoner, the Doughboy shifted position, trying to relax. Shortly after he did so, yet another voice startled him from behind. "Who are ye?" it clearly asked, and Tommy dared the quickest of glances away from the prisoner; it was the wounded MacLachlan, stirring again, perhaps a little delirious now.

His gaze returning to the German, Tommy responded, "I'm Private Tommy Flowers. I'm an American." It was so automatic, Tommy forgot about his new rank.

"Was it ye shot me?"

"Keep your voice down, Private MacLachlan. We're trying to save you."

"Save me? Who? You and that Englishman?"

"Yes. Private Pearson." Flowers hadn't answered MacLachlan's question; but for good measure he added, "The man you almost shot."

"I dinna do that. 'Twas Timmy shot at him. And then ye shot me."

"I – I'm sorry, Jock. I thought you killed Davey."

"Davey, is it?"

"That's right."

There was a brief pause, then Jock asked, "Why does he call you 'love'?"

Tommy still regarded the German. He didn't think long before answering, "Because we love each other."

"Oh."

After that, MacLachlan fell silent again, perhaps slipping back into unconsciousness. As the long minutes passed, Tommy noticed once more that the only sounds were four sets of breathing and the night insects.

# Chapter XLVI

As he had that awful night when he was pinned down under fire, Tommy lost all track of time. Somewhere in the night it began to grow a little bit lighter, and he watched his prisoner grow more and more tired. Though he once again feared a trick, Flowers found the German's drowsiness sufficiently convincing that ultimately he allowed the prisoner to take his hands from behind his head. But Tommy continued to regard the man with apprehension, waiting for him to spring from his feigned fatigue and attack. Instead, the Boche collapsed into slumber, in a disorderly heap. Obviously he hadn't slept for quite a while – and obviously neither had O'Brien. Tommy hadn't hit the British corporal *that* hard; it was as if O'Brien's body was using the knockout punch as an excuse to get the rest it needed.

But then, of course, Tommy himself hadn't slept since… when? He couldn't remember, and he kept himself awake a little longer by trying to figure it out. The battle had been… yesterday, yesterday morning and afternoon. And the night before that they had… marched all night. And the day before that they had… marched all day.

Well, it had been an interesting exercise, but when Tommy realized he was heading into his third day in a row without sleep, it made him tired, and that was dangerous, so he tried to force himself to think about something else. Not Davey; he was too close at hand, and besides, if Flowers allowed himself to think about Pearson, he'd inevitably start worrying about the Englishman's safety. As for home, it seemed to be getting harder and harder to conjure up Iowa, which increasingly seemed to him like a completely different and separate life he had once lived and left behind; difficult to conceive, now, of going back there.

He wondered what his parents and sisters, and Susan, were doing right now – sleeping, probably (the time difference didn't occur to him) – but yesterday, when he was lying on top of David and the blinded Mike, and the machine guns were cutting poor Muffett to ribbons, what had they been doing? It was August, he recalled dully, high summer back in Brooklyn. If it was a mean, hot summer, then that white-hot haze he had thought about earlier had probably settled over the corn and everything else; but if it was a nice summer, then there would be exhilarating crystalline days beneath blue, blue skies filled with white cotton clouds. The fields would be bursting green, and the white clapboard houses in town would be standing cool in the shade of a tall green canopy of elms. There were few feelings as delicious as that of taking a stroll downtown, down the hill of Jackson Street to the stores on Front Street, as a summer sunset transformed a warm day into a cool evening – especially if it was a Saturday. (What day of the week was it? He'd lost track of that, too.) Maybe that's what his family had been doing while he and Davey were sharing a German officer's dinner with Jamie and Billy. He'd like to think so.

"Tommy!" It came out of the dark in a sharp whisper, that voice he liked to hear above all others, all the more so right here and now.

"I'm here!" he whispered back, noticing at the same time that this failed to stir the three unconscious men – as did the sudden sound of multiple rustlings in the underbrush. Given his previous experience, he tensed slightly, Davey's voice notwithstanding; but then his buddy, clearly recognizable in the pre-dawn light, burst into the clearing, followed by three other soldiers, including Tommy's lieutenant.

Flowers started to rise at the sight of them, but Colbeck motioned him back down, crouching to his level instead. Glancing over at the still-sleeping prisoner, the Australian commented, "So, Flaowuhs, looks like you and Peahson made a good night of it."

"I don't know, Jamie," the American demurred, pointing at MacLachlan. "I'm afraid I shot this Tommy, when I thought he'd killed Davey."

"He almost did," Jamie said drily. "Show him your face, David." Pearson obediently crouched down, too, close to Flowers, who for the first time since his mate's return caught sight of his face; the right cheek had been bandaged. "Paowder burn," Jamie helpfully explained. "Can't get any closer than that to bein' shot, unless you are shot." Tommy tried but failed to suppress an involuntary shudder, and Colbeck went on: "As for your shootin' this Pom private, Captain Sand has already decided that the Jerry shot him." The lieutenant gestured at the prisoner as Pearson rose to help the other two new men – stretcher-bearers – with MacLachlan.

"Billy really likes to rewrite history, doesn't he?" Flowers said caustically to Colbeck.

"Don't you think he's earned your respect by naow?" Colbeck snapped.

"Sure he has. But that doesn't make this – habit of his – right."

Colbeck stared at him, but then the Aussie smiled. "You're always full of surprises, Tommy. But you are your own man, I'll give you that.... Naow, if you'll excuse me, I've got another impertinent corp'ral to attend to."

With that, Jamie got up and went over to the seemingly comatose O'Brien, and rather roughly jerked the man's head up and stuck something under his nose, which promptly brought the Briton back to consciousness. "Hope you had a nice nap, Corp'ral," the Aussie lieutenant told him. "While you were sleepin', aour Corp'ral Flaowuhs and Private Peahson, here – the men you were tryin' so hard to interfere with – captured a Boche and got help for your pal."

"Who the hell are you?" O'Brien demanded.

"I the hell am Lieutenant Jamie Colbeck of the Australian Corps, temporarily assigned to the American Army. So I suggest you mind your maouth, Pom."

"Your men shot Jock," O'Brien countered with reckless anger.

Jamie stuck his face inches from O'Brien's. "Naow you listen here, whatever-your-name-is: the *German* shot Jock. Just you remember that. You should be grateful I don't recommend you for writin' up on accaount of your unsoljuhly conduct."

"But he hit me!" O'Brien protested, pointing at Flowers. His tone, however, was changing from feisty to whiny; Colbeck was taking the fight out of him, and the lieutenant sealed it with a curt "Shut up," as he strode over to rouse the prisoner.

"Jamie!" Tommy called out in a sharp whisper.

"What?" Colbeck said irritably, turning back to Flowers. "And why are you whisp'rin'?"

"There might be Germans."

"Only German in the area is this one. All aour patrols say the rest are further ahead." A thought crossed Colbeck's mind, and he turned back to O'Brien. "What are you doin' here, anywise? Does this mean the British are finally showin' their faces?"

"We're on our objective," O'Brien retorted, begrudgingly adding, "sir. Jock and me were sent forward."

"Abaout time." Jamie turned back to the Doughboy and added, "Naow, Flaowuhs, just what was it you wanted that was so important?"

"It's just… he's been real cooperative," Tommy said, nodding toward the prisoner. "You're not going to hurt him–?"

"What kind of monster do you think I am?" Colbeck thundered, too loudly even if he was confident there were no enemy soldiers in the area; indeed, his outburst caused the one who was to stir. "This man's a prisoner of war, entitled to be treated properly. I ain't your buddy Carson."

"Carson ain't my buddy," Tommy snapped back at Jamie.

"And anywise," Jamie replied, ignoring Flowers' tone, "he's too valuable to hurt." To everyone's astonishment, perhaps Tommy's most of all, the Australian then turned and spoke harshly in German, telling the prisoner, *"Aufstehen!"* The man – well, hardly a man; he was, it was evident in the growing light, probably a year or more younger than Tommy and David – snapped to, springing to his feet, still clearly frightened.

"How many languages do you know, Jamie?" Tommy asked conversationally as the whole group made ready to depart for the Allies' main trench.

"I ain't tellin'," Jamie said good-naturedly. Noting the British corporal's reaction, he added to O'Brien, "What's on your mind?"

"Nothing, Leftenant."

"You liar. Aout with it."

"It's just that – you're so familiar with the men."

"So I am. And why shouldn't I be? They're good lads."

"I'll bet Billy wasn't happy when he heard you were coming out here yourself," Tommy put in.

"Who says he knew?" Jamie replied, sounding as carefree as if they were all on a Sunday outing. "The captain's gettin' some well-earned rest, and what he don't know won't hurt him. Naow, David, if you'll kindly lead us home."

Home, of course, was a relative term, but Tommy was still glad to see once again the trench he'd never laid eyes upon until a few hours ago. He was surprised that David was able to lead them back there in less than fifteen minutes; that meant they'd been in such peril only a short distance from what seemed to be such impregnable security – but then again, perhaps the Germans who had occupied the trench up until yesterday had felt the same way.

The main trench was thoroughly astir, far more so than when they had left it. Once past the sentries, the stretcher-bearers peeled off from their group with MacLachlan, presumably to take him to the cold ministrations of Captain Block; in the meantime, Tommy, Jamie, Davey, O'Brien, and the prisoner reported to a very much awake, and as it turned out annoyed, Billy Sand.

"Lieutenant Colbeck," the captain began, even before all the others had finished saluting, "while I was pleased to hear that Corporal Flowers and Private Pearson had captured this prisoner" – Billy directed a curt nod at the frightened young German – "I fail to understand why you deemed it necessary to personally lead the party which went out to retrieve him."

Jamie coolly regarded Billy and replied, "With all due respect, sir, I have far more experience of no-man's-land than anyone else here. I knew this prisoner might be valuable – and so are these two men, who've gone above and beyond the call of duty more than once these past two days–"

"I'm well aware of how valuable both these men and the prisoner are," Billy interrupted impatiently, working his jaw and reddening. Tommy could tell how angry his captain was, and he thought, Jamie's doing this on purpose; he knows how much Captain resents it when he acts like he's the only one who cares about the men's lives. "What I'm questioning," Sand added, "is your decision to go out there yourself. That is something we have discussed before."

"I'm sorry, Captain, sir, if I made the wrong decision. But we're all back, safe and saound. And you *were* asleep."

At that, Sand only looked still more furious; but with apparent effort he turned away from Colbeck, and toward the Allied soldier new to him. "Soldier, state your name and rank," he ordered.

O'Brien did so, then added, "Permission to speak, Captain."

"Granted," Sand said automatically.

"Sir, I regret to report that this corporal called Flowers shot Private MacLachlan, of the King's Army."

Everyone froze at this bald charge – everyone, that is, except Sand, who appeared perplexed, then slowly smiled and shook his head as he said, "I'm sorry, Corporal O'Brien, I didn't quite hear you."

Like some sort of repeating machinery, the British corporal re-stated his accusation, word for word. Sand ceased smiling and said, "I still don't hear you, Corporal." When O'Brien began again, the American captain savagely cut him off. "You're not a very *bright* soldier, are you, Corporal O'Brien? I don't understand your army – that you're a corporal, while Private Pearson here, who's an exemplary soldier, is still a private." Billy turned about and went over to his makeshift desk, briefly searched through a few papers, found what he wanted, and walked back over to the man he had just humiliated. "Here, Corporal," he said crisply, "see if you can handle *this* assignment. Your units are on position now. Finally. Return to your unit, and take Private Pearson with you. Report to your commanding officer, and tell him Private MacLachlan was shot by the *Germans,* and is being tended to by American doctors. Then give him this." Sand thrust an envelope at O'Brien, who took it with a soldierly "Yes, sir!"

"Do you think you can do that, Corporal O'Brien?"

"Yes, sir… if you can point me in the right direction."

Billy flashed another of his odd smiles. "No need for that, Corporal," he said. "You've got Private Pearson," to whom the captain turned and added, "Private, I'd like to thank you for all the service you've rendered the American Army."

"It was me pleasure, Captain, sir," David responded with a smart salute and a slight smile.

"You two are dismissed," Sand told the Britons. "God be with you." Billy might not have noticed Tommy's reaction when he announced he was sending David back to his own army – although Jamie had – but he did mark the Doughboy's quite physical reaction to his uttering of this phrase, and asked, "What is it, Tommy?"

"Nothing, sir," Flowers answered, having exchanged the most fleeting of glances with Pearson right before the private and O'Brien exited. "It's just that that phrase sometimes seems to be bad luck."

"Nonsense, Corporal. There can be no bad luck in invoking the Lord. Now, I'd like you to repeat for me: who shot Private MacLachlan?"

"This – this German did, sir."

Billy wheeled swiftly about to face the prisoner as he said, "And we all know what the penalty is for shooting an Allied soldier, don't we? A sentence of… death."

Sand turned sharply about again, in time to catch both the American corporal and the Australian lieutenant flinching in shock. Both thought about speaking, but neither did; and their captain continued, "Lieutenant Colbeck, did you ask this man if he spoke English?"

"Uhh… no, sir, I didn't–"

"I did," Tommy volunteered helpfully, and Sand cast him a withering glance.

"I wasn't speaking to you, Corporal Flowers. But since you mention it, how did he respond?"

"He – he didn't, sir."

"He didn't. That's odd. Because, you see, just now, when I made that preposterous statement, you flinched, and" – he added to Jamie – "so did you." Then he turned back to the prisoner and concluded, "…and so did you."

The American captain held the German private's gaze in the thick, tense silence that settled over the underground room. "Well, Private?" he said at length, and the prisoner looked back at him blankly, trembling with fear, totally speechless. Seeming to make a decision, Sand strode resolutely back over to his desk and picked up his field telephone. "Send up Sergeant Schultz," he ordered, then replaced the instrument. He had barely come out from behind his desk when a very large, burly man strutted into the room and saluted. Not bothering to return the gesture, Sand said to the new man, "Sergeant Schultz, I understand you speak German. Is that true?"

"Yes sir, Captain!"

"Where did you learn German, Sergeant?"

"From… from my parents, sir," said Schultz, eyes cast down, looking ashamed.

"And where was that? In Germany?"

"No, sir. Chicago."

Another Sand smile. "That's good enough for me. Sergeant Schultz, our friend in gray, here, pretends he doesn't know English, though I say he does. Since he won't answer me, maybe you can talk some sense to him."

"I'll do my best to get him to talk, sir," Schultz said with an enthusiasm that made Tommy uneasy.

"He's all yours, Sergeant," said Sand, dismissing both the German American and the German. Schultz rattled a couple of sentences in German at the prisoner, who looked as if he might die of fright on the spot. "Last chance, Private," Billy said to the prisoner. "Do you want to talk to the sergeant, or to me?" The boy whimpered – audibly, to all four of them; but that was all, so the captain snapped, "Take him away," and Schultz did so, grabbing the prisoner by the arm with extraordinary roughness.

Sand switched his attention to the remaining two men in his underground office. His eyes fixed on Tommy, then shifted to Jamie. "Our Corporal Flowers is just itching to tell me how wrong I am, Lieutenant."

"He'd be right this time, sir. That's just a scared kid."

Tommy could scarcely believe his ears, that Jamie would share his opinion on something like this. He was equally incredulous at Billy's response. "I see," the captain said mildly, addressing them both. "I'm facing an insurrection. Well, perhaps you're both right, and I'm wrong. But if I'm right, he might have some information that will save some lives – maybe even yours – in a few hours. Because we're attacking again at dawn. Every shred of intelligence we can get could save more lives. And if I'm wrong, all I've done is frighten what is already, as you've observed, a frightened child. Under the circumstances… I can live with that."

Sand arched his eyebrows, and focused his attention on Tommy. "You've done exemplary work, Corporal Flowers. There isn't much time before the attack, but I think you should get some rest."

"Yes, sir!" Tommy said, saluting; he hesitated, then added, "Permission to speak freely, sir?"

Sand sighed heavily, ready for more argument, then said, "Granted, Corporal."

"Sir, I hope you don't think I'm being–"

"Get to the point, Flowers," the captain snapped, seeming very near the end of his patience.

"Um… ah, I just wanted to say, sir, that I think I'm very lucky to have you as my captain. And so are the other men." Tommy's eyes darted over to see Jamie smirking – a little – and Billy somewhat stunned. "I – I really do mean that, sir."

"Shut up!" declared Sand, finding his voice, then adding much less loudly, "I know you do. Now let's quit congratulating each other and get ready for the next battle. Lieutenant," he told Colbeck, "Stay here. I need to speak with you."

"Sir!" Flowers said with a salute, turning about to leave.

"Tommy?"

The corporal turned around again to face his captain. "Yes, sir?"

"For what it's worth, that envelope I gave that fool O'Brien was for David's captain, telling him just how much he helped the American Army today."

Despite himself, Tommy broke into a huge smile. "Thank you, sir. That was very good of you."

Sand revealed a somewhat smaller smile. "No, it wasn't. It was simply the proper thing to do. Now go try to get some rest, soldier."

# Chapter XLVII

Tommy didn't know how long he slumbered, only that he did. He was jarred awake by the walls of his funk hole shaking to the booming of artillery, very close by. As he rapidly came to, he watched great globs of clay falling off the opposite wall of the trench. He could hear the sounds of many men scurrying along duckboards, but there seemed to be no one in his little section of trench. Jumping partway out of the funk hole, he saw why: huge chunks of earth now blocked the way he'd come. And when he turned completely about, the view in the other direction was scarcely more encouraging; about ten feet beyond, both walls of the trench had caved in on each other. He was trapped in a perfect little cul-de-sac, and thoroughly unsure what to do about it.

A small whizz-bang, landing perilously close and sending shrapnel in all directions, made his mind up for him. He felt the earth spatter all over his body and looked down, reflexively checking himself for pieces of metal. He couldn't feel any, nor see any blood, so even though he couldn't quite believe it, he had to accept that he was uninjured – for the moment. Following pure instinct, he dived back into his shelter. Minutes passed, and the walls of his funk hole shook with repeated concussions. Though the opposite wall of the trench crumbled further, on his side it held… until a large piece came crashing down, narrowing the area of his shelter. Tommy instantly reversed field, deciding he'd better get out of there before it became a prison – or a tomb.

As he emerged, it was clear there was nothing to do but climb one of the two mountains of earth blocking the trench at either end. Assessing both directions, Flowers initially decided the caved-in walls to his right might be steadier; but then again, he knew there was – or at least there had been – a communications trench leading back to the main one just the other side of the rubble to his left, and that seemed to outweigh the uncertainty of not knowing what lay on the other side, to his right. Once he made his decision, though, his first attempt to scale the mess resulted in his falling face down in the dirt (at least it wasn't mud, he thought), as the mound, too loosely packed, crumbled beneath him. Subsequent attempts to gain a footing proved impossible, so Tommy changed his mind yet again, even as he was sprayed with still more dust from an explosion much farther off.

Scrambling with relative ease up the pile of earth to his right, he turned in the direction from where the artillery was coming – and was awestruck by a view few foot soldiers were ever granted. He could see the main trench, a deep gash in the earth, no more than twenty yards ahead of him; beyond it, hundreds of khaki-clad Doughboys were advancing through splintered and intact trees, firing their weapons as they moved forward. Artillery was firing back at them from beyond a belt of land past the trees, open country he and David hadn't even reached last night. Not only were shells being fired from that direction, but so were machine guns.

Machine guns! There was a reason so few soldiers had witnessed such a scene, and fewer still had lived to tell about it. The idea that he might be making an ideal target of himself crossed Tommy's mind just as the sweep of a Maxim started to make visible traces across the ground between the main trench and where he stood, the way he might skip a stone on the creek south of town back home – only the gun was kicking up a deadly trail of dust, not water.

Again relying on instinct, Tommy lunged a couple of feet forward before diving to the ground, thinking: if I'd still been standing, I'd be dead; if I don't keep moving, I'll still be dead. Thank heaven the ground was hard and dry, something he wouldn't have imagined possible a couple of days ago. That allowed him to move faster than he might have expected.

The tumult continued as he crawled rapidly along, and though he noticed no more machine-gun bullets cutting up the ground in his direct vicinity, he had no idea otherwise whether it was his side doing all the firing, the Boche, or both. If he had to guess how much time elapsed, he'd say it took him between a quarter and a half hour to cover the distance to what had been the parapet, and was now the parados, of the main trench. Having gotten that far, he encountered a small mound of earth right before the very edge. It occurred to him then that if he stuck his head out from an unexpected side of the trench, any passing Doughboys might assume he was a Boche making a surprise attack. Then again, if the Germans had retaken the trench… and then a new fear seized Tommy: that he might be abandoned, left behind and alone by his advancing army.

Finally reaching the crest of the parados, he looked over and down to see a section of trench devoid of soldiers, save for one startled, youthful Doughboy he didn't recognize. As Flowers had feared, this young man swung his gun around and upward in his direction, causing Tommy to quickly cry out, "No! American!" But the effort of doing this carried him farther forward, and he lost his balance, tumbling head over heels down into the trench. Tommy tried his best to protect himself from the fall, but as he crashed onto the duckboards, everything went black.

Coming to at the scent of something sharp under his nose – maybe the same thing Jamie had used on O'Brien – Tommy found himself in an underground room with several other Doughboys, each of whom appeared to have some kind of wound. Captain Block, who was tending one of these other soldiers, saw him awaken and coldly ordered, "Get up, Flowers."

Tommy snapped to, rising into a sitting position and then swinging his legs out and standing – at which point a bolt of pain shot from his left foot and clear up his leg. Seeing this reaction, the exasperated doctor came over and motioned to Flowers to sit back down, then experimentally twisted the corporal's foot, causing him to yelp in pain. "Am I wounded?" Tommy asked. "Was I shot?"

"You're not wounded, Private," Block said stonily. "You were brought in unconscious. I'll admit from the look of your uniform, you probably had to crawl some distance during the shelling" – a comment that confused Tommy, who could only recall machine guns; how long had he been out? – "and your ankle is severely sprained. Other than that, I believe you may have fainted."

"Corporal," Tommy corrected, "and I did not."

"Well, at any rate, ordinarily you should probably stay off the foot for a while, but in an emergency, you're fit to fight, and this is an emergency. So, go report to your Captain. They've all moved forward."

Moving forward to his squad's position proved less than easy for the painfully limping Tommy, as the Germans now were definitely sending both machine-gun fire and shells in the direction of the Americans' new trench. That none of it seemed to be particularly aimed at him, a lone runner slowly making his way over open ground to the new line, wasn't much consolation, as that state of affairs seemed changeable at a moment's notice, as did the relatively low volume of fire, which was just recurrent enough to make the Doughboy apprehensive.

He had no sooner reached the comparative safety of the American trench than a gas shell came whistling over, and there was nothing to do but quickly don his mask and crouch there with similarly attired soldiers (whom he might or might not know, for all he could see of them) for minutes on end, as the increasingly warm sun beat down into their shelter. When the all-clear was signaled, he ripped off his mask to see a crowd of unfamiliar faces doing the same, so he headed down the trench in search of his commanding officer. But the first soldier he recognized was his sergeant, sitting lethargically, soaked with perspiration, his back to the parapet. Saluting, Tommy said, "Sir! Would you know where I could find Captain Sand, sir?"

Dougherty regarded him dully and said, "They carried him back to the main trench – if he isn't dead yet."

It came as a complete shock to Tommy. "What – what happened?"

Dougherty seemed bored, or maybe in shock himself. "What do you mean, what happened? We got shelled, you ass, and some of our men got hit. Where've *you* been?"

Ignoring the implied attack on himself, and trying very hard to keep in check his mounting distress at the uncertain fate of Billy Sand and who knew who else, Flowers curtly replied, "Beg pardon, sir, but if Captain Sand is injured, could you tell me who the commanding officer would be here now? Because I was told to report to my commanding officer."

The smirk faded, and Dougherty slumped back against the trench wall and looked away with an ostentatious lack of interest. "Who else?" he said with disgust. "Bastard'll probably outlive us all."

"I reckon he will," Tommy agreed, too enthusiastically, he knew, for Dougherty's taste; saluting once more, he turned his back to the sergeant with a correct "Thank you, sir."

"Someday, Flowers," he heard the NCO say behind him, though the man sounded more weary than anything else. "Someday."

Two more bends in the newly dug trench and there was Jamie, surrounded by several of the men of Tommy's unit, all of them busily repairing a shattered section. "Oh!" the Aussie said when he caught sight of the corporal, "Tommy."

"Jamie," he responded, beginning a salute, but the lieutenant, looking uneasy, motioned Tommy's arm back down, using both his own hands. "What happened?" Tommy repeated, trying to keep his voice low and steady. "I hear you're in charge now."

Colbeck gave the other men a glance that Tommy read as worried; then the lieutenant simply said, "Come with me, Flaowuhs," and led the corporal back one bend, to a short section of trench with no one else there.

His anxiety soaring, Tommy asked point-blank, "Is Captain all right?"

"I don't know, Tommy," Jamie replied, seeming distracted. "He didn't take the direct hit. Most of that was..." Notching up his concentration, Colbeck focused on Flowers, and told him plainly, "Tommy, Frank's dead."

"Frank... Gillis? But... but we were just talking – it couldn't have been yesterday–"

"Steady, lad, steady. I know. It happened so fast, the way it does. I think he may've saved Billy's life – by chance, but still, I think maybe he did."

"But... Frank?" Tommy repeated, his voice beginning to thicken. "This was his first–"

"*Steady,* lad," Jamie re-emphasized. "I know it's hard, but I need you to keep your wits abaout you."

Flowers drew himself up with tremendous effort, even as a runner suddenly appeared with an envelope, and handed it to Colbeck. Jamie snatched it and tore it open; as he read it, Tommy saw the color rise to his face. Crumpling the piece of paper and tossing it like a Mills bomb, Jamie completed his motion by slamming his fist as hard as he could into the side of the parados, punctuating the act with a furious "God *damn!*" Turning to Tommy but not focusing, he continued, "Those

Poms are just *sittin'* back there, and their boys up here are *too far over!* God *damn!* It's Gallipoli all over again! They're sittin' back there on their bleedin' arses, and here we are with ev'ry last man at the end of his tether – that's still standin', anywise–"

Abruptly Jamie looked up, saw Tommy's frightened face, and broke off; Flowers, for his part, had never seen Colbeck so close to losing control, except for matters involving Nicole. Colbeck thrust both his hands in front of himself, palms out and down, in an exact replica of the gesture he'd used moments before, when he had curtailed Tommy's salute. "It's all right, lad. It's all right. *I'm* all right."

"Are – are you sure, Jamie? I couldn't blame you–"

"Of course I'm sure," the Australian replied with a laugh that contained not a little anger. "I *have* to be all right. And we will be." Seeming to catch his breath, he added, "I've got a job for you, Tommy. I want you to go back to aour first trench with a message. Find Billy and give it to him, if he's still there and still alive. Tell them we *need some relief.* We're aout here and we're all very tired, and men make mistakes when they're tired. It's not like there ain't plenty of other men araound who could come forward, 'cos I know there are – this message proves it. Tell 'em we're takin' fire on aour left flank… where the Poms are supposed to be. Of course, Captain Sand already knows that part. Can you remember all that, Tommy?"

"Sure I can, Jamie… but I wanna stay here, with you and the other boys."

"Well, you're not goin' to. I've decided you're goin' back, and that's that. But we may have to wait 'til there's a break in the shellin', or maybe even 'til it gets dark. I don't want you runnin' araound aout there in their sights on that foot."

"Maybe someone else should go."

"I told you, Tommy," Jamie replied irritably, "you're *goin'*. And you stay back there, too, and have them look at that leg again. That's an order."

Seeing how crestfallen the corporal had become, the lieutenant changed his tone as he added, "I know you want to stay with your mates, lad. But you're not desertin' us. We'll be all right. You take care of your business, and I'll take care of things here." Patting the young American on the shoulder, Jamie said, a little absently, "That's a good boy," then turned back toward where he'd left.

"Jamie?"

Colbeck turned back around. "Eh?"

"Was anybody else killed?"

He shook his head. "No, Tommy. It was just one of those things that happen in this war."

"Wounded, besides Captain?"

"No… well, not exactly–"

"Who?"

Colbeck locked eyes with Flowers. "Think abaout it. Can't you figure it aout?"

Tommy thought for a moment; then it dawned on him: "Walt?"

Jamie nodded. "I always said you were a bright one. Sleaze went clear to pieces. We had to send him back with Billy – maybe in worse shape, though there wasn't a scratch on him."

Flowers swallowed, passed his hand over his eyes, then looked up and said stoutly, "Can I help repair the trench 'til it's time for me to go back?"

"Certainly," Jamie assented with another nod, "but stay on this side of it. Don't try goin' araound to the next bend."

"You mean there could be Germans in the trench?"

"Germans! No, lad… I'm afraid there's still some" – Jamie bit his lip – "some of Gillis on the other side. I want some boys who didn't know him to handle that."

Tommy tried forcing himself to think about it. "But – wouldn't it actually be better if some fellows who *did* know him–?"

"Tommy." Colbeck's tone halted Flowers' reluctant, tentative offer in mid-sentence. "I don't mind your back talk. You know that. Sometimes it's even what I like abaout you. But I can't take any more of it right naow."

Jamie held Tommy's eyes; he was asking for help as he almost never did. "OK, Jamie. I understand."

Tommy kept his promise, and kept quiet throughout the long afternoon, silently digging with Giannelli, Young, and Carson – the last of whom he didn't want to speak with, anyway – during those times it was deemed reasonably safe to work. More often, though, they all remained huddled miserably in the trench, as machine-gun bullets, whizz-bangs and the occasional gas shell sailed overhead. Because none of the shells hit home the way the one he'd missed so obviously had, the gas was the worst, forcing the Doughboys to put on their equipment and swelter inside it in the afternoon heat until the next all-clear, and then the next gas shell, when the whole process started all over again.

Toward midafternoon, some of the battalion fanned out to their left, to help close the gap with the 9th Londons. Jamie pointedly kept Tommy's unit in the same place, but went out himself to reconnoiter and make sure the maneuver was properly completed. He came back mumbling that at last the British had done *something*; and in an aside, he said to Flowers, "Guess who finally came up in support of the 9th Londons?"

"The 12th Londons?"

Jamie nodded, adding, "Though they're still too far back, for my money."

"Did you see David?"

"No. But it's quiet there naow. They should be all right – as all right as men can be in the front lines."

After a pause, Tommy said, "Should I be going soon?"

Seized with an apparent fit of conservatism, Jamie replied, "No. I don't want you to risk it yet. Let's wait until dark."

But just before dark, after the sun had set, waves of strange troops in khaki – Australians – began coming up from behind to join the Americans in their trench. Jamie conferred at length with his opposite numbers among his countrymen, then finally sauntered back to his charges. "Are we going back, Lieutenant?" asked a youngster Tommy vaguely recognized, then he recalled from where: it was the Doughboy he had startled that morning, when he'd fallen into the trench.

"No, son, we're stayin'," Colbeck answered. "But these boys are goin' aout ahead of us. They'll be the new first line, and we'll be the reserve." He tried to make this sound like good news for the Yanks – and indeed, to a certain extent it was – but something in his tone disturbed Flowers, who said, "So, if we've got relief, I don't need to go back."

"Wrong, Flaowuhs. In fact, it's high time you started."

"But your message – wouldn't it–"

"If Captain Sand's there, I want you to give him the same message. Exactly the same. Naow get aout of here."

Tommy's foot felt worse again, but the journey over what was no longer no-man's-land, back to what was no longer the Allies' main trench, was the easiest he'd made in days. Once he was past the sentries at the main trench and on his way to the medical bay, his heart was suddenly in his throat: he wasn't ready to actually hear that he'd lost his young captain. Captain Block was not particularly busy with any patient, so Flowers strode right up to him, saluted, and asked the whereabouts of his commanding officer. The phlegmatic medical officer simply indicated a chamber on the side of the medical bay, an area the corporal approached apprehensively.

Turning the corner, he saw his captain lying on the ground on a stretcher, his tunic torn away, the entire left side of his face and body heavily bandaged. Tommy knelt to Sand's right and looked closely, not sure if he was seeing Billy or just his body; the Doughboy couldn't quite tell, so still was the officer. There was something shocking about the sight of his captain's pale, exposed torso; Billy looked unexpectedly vulnerable, and much younger, lying there like that. And lifeless.

All of a sudden it all just got to Tommy, the whole last three days, and he broke. His sobs came in great heaves, though he tried to cry as quietly as he could. Stopping wasn't possible, not when he was so unable to control the images racing through his mind: Frank's eager, youthful face and voice, filled with hero worship for Tommy; Billy, always so smart, generously sharing his prized booty with Tommy, Davey and Jamie; funny, fat little Muffett; even O'Brien's angry defiance on behalf of his pal MacLachlan, wounded by Tommy; all these and more kept his hot tears flowing. After a time he felt someone's fingertips lightly brush his sleeve. It was more compassion than he'd have expected from Captain Block.

Only it wasn't Block. A familiar voice, in an unfamiliar rasp, spoke to him: "Tommy. Calm yourself. I'm not dead yet."

Blurred though his vision now was, Flowers could see his captain was awake and alive. He would have thought he might react with relief, or joy, perhaps throwing his arms around his wounded commander in gratitude; but instead he recoiled in embarrassment and shame, managing a salute to his superior and mumbling, "Sor – sorry, sir. I don't know what came over me."

"I think I do," Sand replied, his breathing labored. "And it's no reason to be ashamed."

"Yes, sir," Tommy replied; then, eager to be appear professional, he added, "Is there anything I can do for you, Captain? Anything at all?"

Though every word was clearly an effort, Sand responded promptly: "Once… you said… you didn't want to be anybody's adjutant… but I could use one right now. Someone I trust."

Tommy's eyes filled again, and with no regard for protocol, he answered, "Billy, I'd be honored to be your adjutant. From now until the end of the war. And after."

A smile slowly crept across the half of Sand's face that was visible. "I doubt that will be necessary. But thank you, Tommy…. Now, pull yourself together, and ask Captain Block what he has planned for me." Obediently, Tommy stood. "Wipe your eyes," Billy ordered, and Tommy did that, too. "It won't do to let Block see you like that." Tommy nodded, and left the chamber.

Block was now tending to a soldier Tommy didn't know, so the corporal stood nearby, patiently waiting for the medical officer to finish. But the captain felt his presence, whirled about, and asked with an irritation that was abundantly clear, "What is it, Private?"

"Sir, do you know what is to be done with Captain Sand?"

A baleful stare told Flowers the captain found the question impertinent, even before Block said, "Who wants to know?"

"The captain does, Captain, sir."

Without the slightest hint of courtesy, Block shouldered past Flowers, heading for the little chamber where Sand lay. Tommy followed the medical officer, hoping Billy was still conscious; otherwise he could envision himself being court-martialed. To the surprise of them both, and to Tommy's great relief, the young captain was still awake and, if anything, even more alert, and breathing somewhat more evenly than before.

"Hello, Ollie," Billy Sand addressed the medical officer, dispensing with protocol; for the first time, Tommy knew Captain Block's first name. "What's going on? I'd appreciate a report on the patient."

Block ticked his head toward Flowers and said, in a voice full of portent, "Captain Sand, if you wish to discuss your condition, I suggest we talk alone."

"I suggest otherwise, Ollie," Sand replied firmly. "Corporal Flowers is my adjutant. I've designated him to carry out my orders."

Manifestly uncomfortable, Block glanced back, once, at Tommy, then dropped the formality and said, with unexpected concern in his voice, "I trust you're comfortable, Billy–"

"As comfortable as a man filled with shrapnel can be when he's lying on the ground on a stretcher," Sand interrupted. "You seem to be avoiding telling me something. What is it? Am I done for?"

Block's hands fell to his side in a gesture of helplessness. "I did what I could for you, Billy. Patched you up and stopped the bleeding – on the outside, at least. I don't know if I stopped the bleeding on the inside."

There was complete silence as Billy considered this, and its grim implications, for but a very short time. "Thank you, Ollie, for everything you've done," he said. "You're saying, then, that there's nothing more you can do."

"Not here."

There was more silence; then Tommy, unable to contain himself, asked Block, "But what if we got him to a hospital?"

The medical officer looked as if he wished he could amputate all of Tommy's limbs, without anesthetic. Coldly he replied, "Obviously we've thought about that, Private–"

"Corporal," Tommy dared, and Block turned to Sand and said icily, "Billy, I will not continue to talk with this man!"

"Oh yes, you will, Ollie," Sand replied smoothly. "He's speaking for me." For good measure, he added, "I've been here for hours. Why haven't you moved me?"

Block shot an infuriated look at Tommy, then another at Billy. "I have been treating quite a few wounded men here over the last–"

"We're not questioning your motives," the young captain cut in. "We're just requesting an explanation."

"All right," Block said at length, composing himself. "All right. By the time I was finished working on you, the Germans were shelling again, and we only had a skeleton crew here. No stretcher-bearers. I had to make a choice, the way I always have to make choices–"

"–so since I'll probably die, you did the best you could and put me to the side. I understand, Ollie. That's all I wanted to know."

"But, sir–" Flowers interrupted.

"Yes, Tommy?" said Sand.

"You're *not* dead, and now we can get you to a hospital. There's all these Australian troops passing through. I could ask one of them to help me carry you–"

"You really are a fool, Flowers," Block snapped in a rage, and Sand just as quickly interrupted him: "Why?"

"Why? You're full of shrapnel, Billy. Do you understand what that means? The bleeding's apparently stopped, but if we move you, something could shift and pierce an organ. And you'd be dead in an instant."

There was another extended silence in the little chamber; then Sand said, "So my choices are to lie here useless, and maybe bleed to death internally, or take my chances of getting back to a hospital, and maybe die on the way, trying. Am I right?"

"It's not that simple," Block protested. "You'd have to be carried by stretcher to where we could put you in an ambulance."

"The Aussies are passing through," Tommy repeated. "I think it would be safe now to try–"

"You are such an idiot, soldier!" Block thundered. "I've just told you it's not safe for Captain Sand. And there are no stretcher-bearers at any rate. We can't stop soldiers of another army on their way to the front lines in order to help just one man."

"He's right about that, Tommy," Billy concurred.

But Tommy seized the initiative, addressing Billy: "Supposing I found another man to be a stretcher-bearer, Captain. Would you wanna try it?"

"You'd have to find two," Block countered. "With that leg, you're exactly the wrong kind of stretcher-bearer for Captain Sand."

"All right then, I'll find two men," Tommy said stubbornly, conceding Block his point: but his eyes never left his wounded commander, who finally put in, "Yes, Tommy, I would try it."

"And where would you rendezvous with an ambulance?" Block persisted. "It's a long way back to the road we came up."

His mind amazingly clear, Sand moved to take his fate in his own hands, noting, "The road between Corbie and Bray is closer."

"And how would you find your way to it?" Block insisted. "You'd all be stumbling around in the dark–"

Further inspiration hit Tommy from out of nowhere. "The 12th Londons aren't far from here," he said, "and I know someone from there who could find us and lead us back to that road."

Flowers was still looking at Sand, and he could see his captain knew who he meant. Addressing his fellow captain, Billy said, "Do we have telephone contact with the British?"

"I believe we do now," Block said with reluctance.

"All right, then," Billy Sand said without hesitation. "Tommy, find the signalman and see if we can get your friend to come over here to guide us. Then see if you can find two stretcher-bearers – but don't bother the Australians who are moving up, and don't go back forward. If you can do all that, I'm ready to go." Sand gave Block a look. "Ollie, I trust you'll offer all the help you can if we manage to do this."

The other captain threw up his hands. "It's totally against my advice, Billy. But it's your life… literally. Now if you'll excuse me." The medical officer gave Flowers one more hate-filled look, and left the chamber. Tommy started to follow, but then he heard Billy call his name, in a far weaker voice than before. Turning about, he saw his captain faintly beckoning to him, and he knelt back down next to Sand.

"That took a lot out of me," his commander admitted hoarsely, his breathing heavy again. "You'll have to do the rest. You have my full authority in this."

"Yes, sir," said Flowers, more alert and energetic than he'd been in hours. He started to rise again, but Sand gestured him back down. Though he obeyed, Tommy stressed, "There's no time to lose, Billy."

The captain shook his head slightly and said, "Don't look for bearers 'til you know Pearson's coming. There's no point otherwise. And Tommy?"

"Yes, sir?"

"You do read and write, don't you?"

"Well, of course I do, sir! Iowa has good schools–"

"Don't be offended, Tommy. Not all of my men can. I just want you to promise me, if I die, that you'll write Gillis' parents. It's my job, I know, and I wouldn't ask, but if I die before–"

Violating protocol in the extreme, Tommy placed his right hand – the back of it, since it seemed a little less dirty – over his captain's mouth, to quiet him. "You rest now, sir. Please? I give you my word. But I won't need to, 'cause we're gonna get you back alive. Let me take care of it. OK?"

"OK," said Billy Sand with a faraway smile.

# Chapter XLVIII

Tommy sped down the trench like a man who'd been hit by a flamethrower, until he found the bay containing the makeshift signal room, which was under the command of a Lieutenant Porter, a man somewhere between Billy and Jamie in age. As he and Porter waited to achieve contact with the British, Tommy fudged on his promise to Billy, and asked the lieutenant if he knew of any men who might be available for stretcher-bearer duty. Porter's initial reaction was to frown and remind Tommy that everyone was restricted to working with essential crew while the rest of the men were up front; but then an idea came to the officer: "Prisoners do that kind of work. And we do have a prisoner."

"Would that be the one I helped bring in, sir?"

"I don't know. What did he look like?"

"A German, sir. Pretty young. He was taken away by a sergeant – a sergeant with a German-sounding name."

"Sergeant Schultz," Porter suggested, and Tommy nodded. "It's the same man, then. Schultz has been interrogating him."

All this time? Tommy thought; but he had learned to hold his tongue on occasion. He remembered now how big and burly Schultz was, and asked Porter, "Could Sergeant Schultz be a stretcher-bearer, too, Lieutenant?"

Porter frowned again. "What's wrong with *you*, Corporal?"

"Captain Block says I can't do it because of my leg–" Tommy began to explain, but he had no sooner said this than a signalman cut in:

"Sir, Lieutenant Albertson says he wants to know the condition of a Private MacLachlan, who he says was left here–"

"Then we've got the London Rangers!" Tommy cried.

"–and whether he should send stretcher-bearers for him."

"That's it!" Flowers said jubilantly. "They can send four."

"They can send two," Porter corrected. "We do not ask our allies to take men out of the front line to carry one of our men to the rear. It's bad enough we're asking one of them to be our guide."

Though the lieutenant was taking a stand essentially no different from Billy Sand's, for the moment Tommy hated him for ranking protocol above their captain's life. "But – they're willing to send over stretcher-bearers for MacLachlan. And he's only a private."

"He's *their* private, Corporal. Do we even know if this MacLachlan is still here, or alive?"

That was a jarring reminder for Flowers, who had been contemplating the irony of enough stretcher-bearers being available for MacLachlan but not for

Sand. He was tempted to say MacLachlan was ready for transport, just to lure the British into sending a couple of men along with David. But what if the Scottish private was dead? They might refuse to send anyone at all – not to mention he would be responsible for MacLachlan's death… and then, indirectly, for Sand's.

"I'll send for the prisoner," Porter told Flowers. "Go back to the medical bay and find out MacLachlan's condition. And I suggest you look and see if there's someone whose wounds are light enough that they can carry a stretcher to Captain Block's satisfaction."

Block wasn't there when Tommy returned to the medical bay, so the corporal went to Billy's little chamber. Sand seemed to be sleeping peacefully, but to reassure himself, Flowers briefly placed his hand under his captain's nose, to verify the man was breathing. Satisfied, he returned to the main room of the medical bay and looked about him, at an assortment of Doughboys on stretchers and make-shift beds. Arm wounds, leg wounds, and much worse – none of them looked fit to carry a stretcher, certainly not if he wasn't.

"What are you doing back here?" The voice was singularly unfriendly, but Tommy turned to face Oliver Block with a determinedly positive expression.

"The British want to know about Private MacLachlan, sir. They asked if they should send over stretcher-bearers for him, along with the guide."

"Who's Private MacLachlan?" the medical officer asked with a scowl, and abruptly Tommy focused on Block's face, which was a pale gray even in the glow of the lanterns that illuminated the medical bay now that it was – what? Was it midnight yet? How much time were they losing? Tommy had been so busy disliking this man it hadn't occurred to him that Block might have been awake longer than Flowers himself, with all those sleepless hours spent trying to save men's lives.

"I'm sorry, sir. The Scottish soldier, this morning?"

To Flowers' consternation, Block continued to look at him, blank and uncomprehending. "He was shot in the stomach, sir?" Near exasperation, Flowers added, "He had on a kilt, sir. You can't've worked on too many men wearing a kilt."

It finally dawned on the medical officer. "Oh, him. They took him away hours ago."

Shaken, Tommy asked, "Alive, sir?"

"At the time. But I thought he might develop peritonitis. So I sent him to the back." Block regarded Tommy suspiciously and added, "I know what you're thinking, Corporal. But your Private MacLachlan was here – and gone – before dawn, before the regiment moved forward. Captain Sand came in at midday, with all of us under shellfire."

"I understand, sir. Thank you for everything you've done."

The captain gave Tommy a dubious look, as if he thought he was being patronized by a corporal. With a similar skepticism in his voice, he asked, "Did you find your stretcher-bearers?"

"One, sir, I think. I still need a second. Are you sure I won't do?"

"Quite sure, Corporal Flowers, quite sure. What about the guide the limeys are sending over? Can't he carry a stretcher and lead the way at the same time?"

"He's – the other Tommy you examined, Captain. Yesterday? The one whose leg looks like a barber pole?"

The metaphor was effective. "Ah. Yes. Him. No, he wouldn't do at all."

Tommy was seized with the sudden, irrational notion that Captain Block would ask him why he had such intimate knowledge of David's leg; so, as a diversionary tactic, he asked, "Do you reckon there's anybody in the wounded men here who could carry a stretcher?"

"You're just full of questions, aren't you, Flowers?… There's one man who *could.* There's nothing wrong with him – physically. But–"

It dawned then on Tommy. "Do you mean Private Sleziniak, sir?"

"You know him?"

"Yes, sir. We're friends."

"Hm.… Tell you what, Corporal. I'll go let the British know about Private MacLachlan – for Captain Sand's sake. In the meantime, I suggest you talk to your *friend,* if you want to."

"Thank you, Captain, sir. Where is he?"

Block's eyebrows shot up. "You're such good friends, and you haven't seen him? He's right over there." The medical officer pointed to what seemed to be a bundle of clothing in the farthest, darkest corner of the main room. "You try to talk some sense into him," he added. "I don't have the time – or the patience."

No, you sure don't, Tommy thought as the captain left for the signal room. With a shudder, Flowers recalled Sand's warning not to let Block see that he'd been crying. Billy was so smart. They couldn't afford to lose him.

Not until Tommy drew very near was it apparent that the mass of clothes in the corner in fact concealed a man. Flowers tapped Sleziniak on the shoulder once, twice, then called his nickname; but when the Dakotan finally turned his face to the Iowan, Tommy was unsure he'd been directed to the right soldier. The man who stared back at him out of vacant, haunted eyes looked twice Sleaze's age, and his haggard, drawn countenance in no way resembled the fine features Tommy had taken note of as they'd crouched in the listening post in the Vaden line.

It was a relief, therefore, when Sleaze spoke first and recognized him, hoarsely whispering, "Flower?" The feeling dissipated, though, when after a pause Walt added, more as a statement than a question, "You're dead, aren't you."

"No, Sleaze, I'm not dead. And neither are you." There was no response, and Tommy pressed, "Walt, I need your help."

Walt seemed not to have heard anything Tommy said; instead he fixed his eyes on the corporal and told him, "Flower, Frank's dead."

"I know that, Sleaze."

"They blew him to pieces," Sleziniak continued tonelessly. "There was blood all over the place–"

Not quite believing he was saying it, Tommy heard himself interrupt: "There's nothing we can do to help Frank now, Walt. It's too late. But we can help Captain."

"Captain? Captain's dead, too."

"No, he's not," Tommy retorted, straining to keep the impatience from his voice. "But he could be if we don't help him. If *you* don't help, Sleaze."

"Me?" Walt said in confusion, then he repeated, "Me?"

"Yes, you. You can help save the captain's life."

Sleziniak shook his head and turned away. "Can't save a dead man, Flower."

Maybe Block's lack of patience wasn't so reprehensible after all, thought Tommy; he was starting to lose his. "Captain's *not dead!*" he shouted, startling some of the other wounded men in the medical bay. "Why can't you understand that?" Sleaze stared back at him with those same empty eyes, and Tommy forced himself to stare hard in return, though to do so was frightening. "Please, Walt," he said, the pitch of his voice rising to a child's, to his chagrin. "Frank would want you to do it."

There was a pause so long, Tommy finally had to give up hope that this "conversation" would ever lead anywhere; and then, abruptly, Walt said, "Do what?"

Tommy exhaled deeply and said, "Carry the stretcher."

"What stretcher?"

Hope restored Flowers' patience. "The captain's stretcher."

Tommy was certain Walt would insist again the captain was dead; but after another long pause the private asked, "With you?"

"I'll be right there with you, but they won't let me carry the stretcher." More inspiration hit him. "They say I'm not strong enough. But you, you're strong enough."

Sleaze didn't question who "they" were; instead he demurred, "Can't carry a stretcher by myself, Tommy."

"You won't have to. There'll be a second man."

"Who?"

It was the quickest response Sleziniak had yet made, which encouraged Flowers… until he realized what answer he'd have to give: "A – a German."

"A *German!*" Walt drew himself up, and a welcome flash of fire showed in his eyes. "The Germans killed Frank."

Still thinking quickly, Tommy responded, "This German didn't. He's a prisoner. I captured him myself, this morning, before–"

"You captured a German?" Sleaze asked, as if they were conducting a casual conversation.

"Yes, Sleaze, I did–"

"And this... German... is gonna help me carry the captain?" Having slowly and carefully formed this sentence, Walt shook his head and said in the tone of a disbelieving child, "Tom-mee."

Desperate to get through to him, Flowers replied in frustration, "Well, at least he's willing to try to help. Why aren't you?"

Walt's aspect changed again; to Tommy's alarm and dismay, he screwed up his face, and then he started to cry. "I c-can't, Tommy."

"Yes, you can!" But these words of encouragement only seemed to make Sleziniak cry harder, and Flowers, unable to think of anything else, demanded, "Stop it, Sleaze! Act like a man!"

Through heartbroken sobs, Walt managed to say, "You d-don't understand, Flower."

Being tough with him wasn't working, so Tommy switched tactics again, crouching down lower and throwing his arms around his shattered friend. In a husky voice he said, "I think I do, Sleaze. Twice today I thought I'd lost my best buddy. And I'm scared to death about the captain." Holding the unresponsive Sleziniak, he noticed, was like holding a pile of sandbags; his own voice close to cracking, Flower of Iowa added, "I'll miss Frank, too, Walt."

Slowly, ever so slowly, Sleaze's arms came around Flowers, and it felt like Tommy was holding a human being in his arms. Walt sobbed quietly on his shoulder for another, very long minute; then his display of grief seemed to ebb slowly away. Eventually he let go of Tommy, looked up at him, and asked in a weak voice, "Do you really think I can help?"

It came so suddenly Tommy wasn't ready, but he wiped his own eyes and replied in his best hearty voice, "I'm sure you can, Sleaze. But you'll have to be very, very careful. If Captain moves around too much on the stretcher, he'll die."

"Oh." Sleaze looked down at the ground for eternal seconds, then finally said, "All right, Tommy. I'll try."

"Attaboy, Walt!" Flowers stood up, recharged. "I have to go back and get the German," he told his still-sitting comrade. "I won't be long." Without even waiting for Walt to answer, he turned his back on his friend, thinking, Please, please don't change your mind. Or lose it.

★

Tommy was barely out of the medical bay and into the main trench when he ran into Captain Block – and behind him, the silent prisoner. Fearful that his latest display of emotion still showed, the darkness notwithstanding, Flowers managed to wipe his face again and salute, all in a single motion. "Private Sleziniak has agreed to help carry Captain Sand's stretcher, sir," Tommy said, not entirely succeeding in keeping the satisfaction out of his voice as he delivered this news.

Block cleared his throat, paused, then said, "Very well. Maybe your limey friend won't be coming for nothing after all."

"Oh, he won't, sir, now that we've got our two stretcher-bearers."

"One, Flowers. You've still only got one for certain."

In confusion, Flowers corrected, "Beg pardon, Captain, sir, but with Private Sleziniak and this man–"

Tommy had gestured toward the German, and Block did likewise as he replied, "This man? *This* man?" The captain paused again, then added, "Lead us back into the medical bay, Corporal."

"Yes, sir." Thoroughly addled but obedient, Tommy did as he was told. When he saw the German, who was last to enter the soft glow of the medical bay from the darkness of the trench, Tommy let out a low gasp: the boy he'd left this morning frightened but whole had a deep bruise on his face and was bleeding from the lip, and moving with evident pain. Swiftly turning to Block, Tommy asked, "What happened, sir?"

Staring grimly back, the medical officer responded, "I don't know, Corporal. Ask him yourself. Apparently he does speak English. Sergeant Schultz says he got that much out of him."

Tommy's attention remained on Block. Clenching his jaw, he asked, "Yes, sir, but how?"

"That's an impertinent question, Corporal Flowers," the captain replied angrily. "My job is to see whether this man is fit to carry Captain Sand's stretcher. Yours is to find someone else if he can't. That is all."

Tommy burned to point out he'd already found two men under nearly impossible conditions, but he curbed his tongue once more, simply saying "Yes, sir," as Block turned his full attention to the prisoner, roughly telling the German, "Sit down here, Private. And don't pretend you don't understand me."

With the medical officer's attention elsewhere, Flowers stalked back to Sleziniak's corner to find the Dakotan had actually stood up and straightened himself somewhat. "Are we ready to go, Flower?" Walt asked in a voice nearly normal.

"Not yet, Sleaze," Tommy replied, unself-consciously reaching out to straighten Walt's tunic; he didn't want to give Block any further excuses to call off his mission, like Sleaze being too crazy to carry a stretcher. "But hold on. It won't be long."

Again Flowers left Sleaze in his corner. This time he headed for his commanding officer's chamber. To his immense relief, Sand was awake and alert; Tommy had been considering whether or not to disobey all rules and waken his captain.

"Hello, Tommy," Billy said in a voice that made up in cheer what it lacked in strength. "What's happening?"

Crouching next to his prone leader, Tommy said in a voice equally low and free of protocol, "David's on his way, Billy. And I've got Walt Sleziniak to carry the stretcher."

"And the other man?" Sand asked, clearly indicating his mind was sharp enough.

Tommy shifted uncomfortably on his haunches. "There's that prisoner, sir."

"Ah, yes," said Captain Sand, actually smiling. "So we're on our way. Good work, Corporal. I knew you could do it."

"Uh... there may be a problem, sir," Flowers said, avoiding Sand's eyes. "They – they beat the prisoner. Captain Block's looking at him now, to see if he's still fit to carry a stretcher."

Tommy got this information out quickly, before Billy could give him the anticipated order to forget anything he heard or knew about a prisoner being beaten. He heard Sand say in a dark tone, "Corporal, look at me," and he obeyed, waiting for the rest. But then Billy said, "Who beat the prisoner?"

"Sir?"

"You said, 'They beat the prisoner.' Who's 'they'?" Tommy looked away nervously and his captain said with astonishing quickness, "Tommy, *look* at me," then repeated, "Who's 'they'?"

"Well, Captain, you remember it was – uh – you had a Sergeant Schultz take him away... and I reckon he reports to – um – Lieutenant Porter? But they're all being rough with him, Captain Block, too–"

"Enough, Tommy. That's more than I need to know." Sand slowly looked away from Flowers and thought out loud: "Maybe you and Jamie were right." Looking back to Flowers, he added, "When Captain Block is finished with the German, tell him I'd like to speak with him."

"Uh – the captain, sir, or the German?"

Almost scornfully, Billy replied, "Now, what would the German and I have to say to each other, Corporal?"

"Maybe a lot, sir. Maybe you were right, after all. They say he speaks English. They say."

There was a familiar lift to Sand's eyebrow. "You are always full of interesting information, Flowers." He paused, added, "The German, then." After he said this, a peculiar, quite visible shudder ran through the captain's body, striking fear into Tommy.

"You're doing too much, Captain. You should rest."

"I'll decide that, soldier," Sand replied in a steady voice that perfectly blended sternness and warmth. "Now go check on Captain Block and the prisoner for me."

Momentarily relieved, Tommy smiled at his captain and lazily saluted. "Yes, sir."

# Chapter XLIX

Block, already checking another patient, refused to be diverted by Tommy, who once again stood restlessly behind him. Eventually the medical officer growled, over his shoulder, the information that Tommy wanted concerning the prisoner: "There's nothing broken, and no sign of internal injuries. I think he's play-acting. He could probably carry a stretcher – if you can get him to cooperate."

"Then with your permission, sir, I'd like to try."

"He wouldn't say a word to me," Block, still focused on his patient, pointed out with a shake of his head – apparently a sign of disgust rather than a denial of Tommy's request.

"Please let me see what I can do, sir. Maybe there's a better way than Sergeant Schultz's."

Block turned sharply about and glanced up at Tommy. "You mind your tongue, soldier."

"Yes, sir," Tommy replied. "I meant no disrespect, sir." After a pause, he added, "Oh – and Captain Sand said he would like to talk to the prisoner, sir."

Captain Block held Flowers' gaze. "That's a good idea – even if it probably did come from you. Go ahead; take him to Captain Sand. I want the captain to understand the risk he's taking."

"Yes, sir," Tommy repeated, saluting; then he turned about without waiting for Block to dismiss him. Between his impatience to save Billy's life and his dislike of the medical officer, he was straining – and at times failing – to keep within the bounds of military protocol. But Block had other concerns, and he let it go, let Tommy go, back over to where the prisoner sat absorbing the hostile stares of some of the more alert wounded Doughboys.

In his best friendly fashion, Tommy asked the German, "What happened to you?" The prisoner looked up, startled, and Tommy could see his first impression was still correct: the boy was unquestionably and noticeably younger than David or himself, probably of an age with Susan's kid brother Sam, who was – sixteen? But it wasn't at all clear to Flowers that the German really did understand English, whether he was responding to the American's words, or his tone. Billy or Jamie would have done this better, smarter, Tommy thought, but he gamely went on, even though he was acutely conscious of the other Doughboys watching them: "I want you to talk to my captain. He's a very good man. He can help you. But he needs your help first. Come with me."

The boy regarded him blankly, then looked about nervously. Though Flowers found his incomprehension fairly persuasive, the Doughboy once again turned his back and walked away from a man he'd been addressing. But Tommy neither heard nor felt the prisoner follow him, so after a few steps he turned back around. The German was still staring at him, not moving. "Come on," Tommy said – with an accompanying appropriate gesture of the hand, he realized too late; when the prisoner finally stood up, he again couldn't tell if it was the words or the gesture that had prompted the German, who proceeded to salute and stand at attention.

"Use your gun," suggested a strange wounded Doughboy who'd been watching. The man didn't understand that Tommy was after something more than simple cooperation. But in desperation, Flowers did gesture with his weapon, and the prisoner, apparently petrified, or perhaps just stiff from being beaten, promptly moved over to him. Another sweep of the air with the gun and the German stumbled ahead of Tommy, glancing back to make sure he was headed in the direction his captor desired.

As they entered Sand's chamber, Tommy noted with concern that Billy looked paler and less energetic than minutes before. From out of nowhere, the word *"Achtung!"* escaped Flowers' lips. He had no memory of where he'd learned it, only recalled somehow that it was the German word for "attention"; but it had the desired effect, as the prisoner snapped to and saluted the prone officer, who in turn carefully surveyed the German, then spoke… in French:

*"Parlez-vous français?"*

The German boy looked nervously about once more, but of course there was no one else in the chamber save Flowers and Sand. After a moment's more hesitation, he said, softly but clearly, *"Oui, Capitaine."*

Intent on the prisoner, Billy ignored Tommy's reaction as he continued, *"Et anglais aussi, je crois. N'est-ce pas?"*

Caught off guard, the German looked down at the ground for a second, then back to the American officer, and barely whispered, *"Oui, Capitaine."*

"Then do it," Sand said in English; not missing a beat, he asked in a tone almost conversational, "Where were you going to school? Heidelberg?"

Though the lad had finally admitted he spoke English, his answer came slowly, as if it took him a while to understand the captain and then form a response: "Stuttgart, *Capitaine.*"

"Ah. And your name, Private?"

Again the slow digestion of the question, but eventually: "Mueller, *Capitaine.* Hans Mueller."

Sand nodded slowly, then said abruptly, "Someone hit you, Private Mueller. Who did that?"

Mueller seemed to freeze at the question. After a quick, fearful glance at Tommy – a gesture the captain very visibly noted – the prisoner simply said, *"Capitaine?"*

*"Vous préférez que nous parlons en français?"*

*"Oui, Capitaine."*

Tommy was mystified by this exchange. Sand just lay there apparently lost in thought, then, with same abruptness he'd used with the German, told Flowers, "Tommy, wait in the other room."

It was Tommy's turn for a slow reply. "But – but sir, I'm your adjutant–"

"I know that," Sand said irritably.

"–and it's not – it might not be safe."

"I'm your commanding officer, Corporal," Billy snapped. "I'll be the judge of that. Now I gave you an order."

Tommy flushed and saluted a quick "Yes, sir," then quickly quit the chamber, feeling as humiliated as if he'd had an encounter with Captain Willnor or Dougherty. He didn't have too much time to think about it, though, for as soon as he was back in the main area of the medical bay, Sleziniak, who clearly had been pacing about restlessly, strode up to him and demanded, too loudly, "When are we going, Tommy?"

"Soon, Walt, soon. The captain is talking to the German."

The Dakotan's eyes narrowed. "Talking to the German? How can he do that?"

"The German speaks English." Flowers didn't bother to mention the French.

"Oh. So the captain's – interrogating him, right?" Tommy figured it was a good sign Sleaze could remember such a big word and use it correctly, but then Walt added "That's a good idea" with an excessive amount of satisfaction in his voice. The man's behavior still wasn't right, and that worried Flowers.

Just then there was a stirring at the entrance to the medical bay, followed by a welcome sight, as David Pearson entered and with great correctness reported to Captain Block who, distractedly indicating the direction, gruffly told him to go talk to Captain Sand. It was all Tommy could do to keep from embracing his pal in front of everybody as he intercepted the Briton: "You shouldn't go in there yet, David. Captain's interrogating the prisoner."

"What sort of 'ello is that, Tommy?" Pearson replied with his usual good cheer; then he noticed Sleziniak still hovering next to Flowers, and added, "'Ello there, Private Sleaze."

"Frank's dead, Pearson," Walt blurted out, the way a child might, and David's aspect turned solemn as he responded, "That's terrible news. I'm orfully sorry to 'ear it. 'E was your mate, wasn't 'e?"

"We were best friends," Sleaze answered, his voice beginning to shake.

Tommy's annoyance over David's getting Walt agitated was interrupted by the prisoner suddenly emerging from Billy's chamber, and his captain's voice calling his name. With a quick, sharp "Stay there" aimed at Mueller, Flowers sped into the chamber and asked Sand, "Is everything all right, sir?"

The captain seemed to think carefully before answering. "Yes, Tommy. We should get ready now, so that when Pearson arrives, we can leave–""

"He's here, sir."

Sand flashed another evanescent smile. "Good work, Corporal. Good work all around."

"Yes, sir," Tommy said with a return smile and a salute, again turning his back on an officer in his eagerness to keep his mission going.

But this time he didn't get away with it. Sand's cry of "Tommy!" came swift and sharp, and Flowers did a hasty turnabout.

"Sorry, sir," he said, executing another, crisper salute.

"At ease, soldier," Billy said, then he added in a more intimate tone, "Come here." Awkwardly Tommy walked over so he was next to Billy's stretcher, and stood there. "Sit down, Tommy," Billy ordered, his voice still soft, and Tommy crouched down. "I said sit," Billy stressed, and though he felt like a trained dog, Tommy obeyed further. An enormous wave of physical fatigue swept over him as soon as he hit the ground and his weight shifted from his legs to his backside; but at the same time he was enervated, and also most uneasy at his captain's tone. After an uncomfortable pause, Sand went on, "Tommy, sometimes, in a war like this, men do things they wouldn't ordinarily do–"

It struck Flowers then, and so did panic: the German knew English. He'd been there when MacLachlan had asked Tommy about David calling him "love," and he'd heard Flowers' answer. My God, thought Tommy, he told Captain! What am I going to do now? He forced himself to focus, and to hear the last part of what Sand was saying: "–do things they didn't mean to do – like beating a helpless prisoner. I don't condone it, but I do understand it. Do you understand what I'm saying?"

Flowers endeavored to keep his enormous relief from stifling a quick response. "I – think so, sir. You're saying I should forget about what Sergeant Schultz did to the prisoner."

Billy's countenance darkened. "I wasn't talking about Sergeant Schultz, Corporal. I was talking about you."

Alarm, if not panic, returned. "Me? – How – how could you say that, sir? I treated the prisoner *right,* sir, from the moment we captured him." The captain appeared unmoved, and Tommy lost all sense of protocol. "My God, Billy, he's just a kid. I wouldn't – did he say I hit him?"

Sand didn't reply at first, but continued looking intently at Flowers. "No," he finally replied, "No, he didn't. But I was wondering if you did. He seems particularly scared of you–"

"I don't know why, Captain," Tommy said, hating the way his voice was beginning to sound like a whine. "I swear I didn't hurt him. I wouldn't do that."

Sand held up his good hand. "All right, Tommy, all right. I believe you." There was a longer pause, and then Billy added, "Do you know this is the second time he's been taken prisoner?"

"The second time, sir? But – he's so young–"

"I know. But he already fought in a completely different sector. He was captured by the French. French Colonials. They – they did something to him – I'm not quite sure what, but it was something so terrible he didn't seem to mind being hit by Sergeant Schultz so much."

"So Sergeant Schultz did hit him?"

"Well, I think we both know that," said Sand with a nod.

"But what could the French have done to him that would be worse than that?"

The captain regarded the corporal for a couple of seconds, then said in a tone of enormous disgust, "He didn't say, exactly. But I have an idea or two. There's no need for you to know. Just treat Private Mueller well. I think he can help us."

"I *have* treated him well, Captain," Tommy reiterated. "I don't know why he's so afraid of me."

"Hmm. Who knows?" Sand mused aloud to himself. "After all he's been through..." Looking over to Flowers, he said plainly, "I think I hurt your feelings, Tommy, even thinking you might have hit him. I'm sorry. But I had to know, if we're going to do this. And it is possible for any man to lose control."

"You didn't hurt my feelings, Captain," Tommy said sturdily, but Billy's return look said they both knew it wasn't true, and he faltered: "And anyway, even if you did, what does it matter, with everything else that's going on?"

"It matters a great deal," Billy countered. "It's what keeps us from sinking to the same level as the beasts, even in the midst of all this."

His eyes threatening to fill again, Tommy gazed back at Billy and, slowly shaking his head, said baldly, "God, Captain, I don't want you to die."

"And I don't want to die," Sand said calmly. "So, Corporal, let's get this show on the road. The hardest part will come first."

"What's that, sir?"

Sand flashed another of those unexpected smiles. "You're going to have to stand up again."

They set off less than an hour later, after Block had supervised the careful strapping down of Billy on the best stretcher available. With David leading and Sleaze and Mueller carrying, it suddenly seemed Tommy was extraneous to the mission, a situation the medical officer was quick to point out, drawing a sharp reaction from his fellow captain: "This man is my adjutant, Ollie. I *need* him with me." Block lifted his eyebrow at that, then shook his head and said no more. "Tommy, you bring up the rear," Billy added, thus helping to set their order as they made their way through the trench system – at least, until Tommy noticed that putting

Sleziniak at the head of the stretcher and Mueller behind wasn't working. Consistent with their behavior as they were being given their instructions, the Dakotan was edgy, overeager, while the German remained slow on the uptake… and still particularly skittish around Tommy. As a result, Flowers observed, Walt kept tugging the stretcher forward, and the chief reason Mueller was able to keep up at all was his determination to steer clear of the American behind him. This caused their rhythm to be jerky, and despite the dark, Tommy was sure he saw Billy grimacing because of it. The corporal hollered "Halt!" just as they neared the edge of the trench system, and his English and American friends turned around and looked at him perplexed; but the German boy almost dropped the stretcher in fright.

Billy, who might have been drifting off despite Tommy's perception, drowsily asked, "What is it?"

There was a short silence as Flowers collected his wits; even Sleaze was staring at him as if he, Tommy, were the crazy one. Finally he turned to the prisoner and said, in a tone that strove to imitate his captain's, "Hans, you should carry in front." Following through, he added, "Walt, you bring up the rear."

The German seemed taken aback by Tommy's use of his first name; but he obeyed with greater alacrity than before, and Sleaze also responded promptly. When the two had exchanged places, it was David who looked to Tommy and said, "All right, then?"

"All right," the Doughboy replied, and they were off again, past the sentries and clear of the protective cover of the trenches.

After the shattered forest of the last day and night, a new landscape of rolling hills with a few intact trees, visible in the dim light (was it already growing lighter, Tommy wondered), made for quite a change. Indeed, the whole area appeared, improbably, almost pristine. They were perhaps five minutes out of the trenches, making slow but steady progress over the sloping ground, with Tommy regarding Billy apprehensively, ready for any sway of the stretcher to end his captain's life, when a terrific explosion accompanied by a brilliant flash erupted behind them, from where they'd just come. The German froze in place while Walt pushed forward, and Tommy watched in horror as, with an unreal slowness, his commanding officer began to topple out of the stretcher. Making a dive he couldn't possibly have repeated, he caught Billy, simultaneously pushing Sand gingerly back onto the stretcher while swearing *"Damn you!"* at the German and *"Stop!"* at Walt; then, in a different tone, he turned back to Sand, asking breathlessly, "You all right, Captain?"

"It appears I am," came Billy's surprised, airy voice, barely audible amid the ongoing barrage, which had only increased in intensity.

*"Damn* you!" Tommy repeated to Mueller in a voice mixing hot anger and relief. "You almost killed the captain!"

"'E cou'n't 'elp it, Tommy," David interjected, placating, and then he added with some urgency, "There's a scrape up a'ead. Per'aps we should be seeking shelter."

Flowers wasn't quite sure what a "scrape" meant in this context, but if Pearson thought it a good place to take cover, that was good enough for him. "No 'perhaps' about it," he said, then barked, "Let's go – but *careful*." So they did, even as the barrage, continuing at tremendous force and volume, seemed to creep ever closer to them. In between his anxious oversight of the stretcher bearing, Tommy found a moment to wonder how David had managed to locate the scrape – which turned out to be a shallow depression on a downhill slope – in the darkness and confusion; and once the two carriers had gently brought Sand to ground, in a smooth motion neither Tommy nor anybody else could fault, he asked his pal as much.

"While you were giving 'Ans such a 'ard time, I was using the light to get a good look at the land," David explained.

Tommy shook his head. "You are such a good soldier, Davey."

"Am I?" The four Allied soldiers were huddled together, with the German conspicuously crouching a few steps apart. Pearson looked over at Mueller, whose trembling could be clearly seen in the light cast by the bombardment; that it was coming from the Germans' side was evidently no consolation. "Get over 'ere, 'Ans," the Englishman said, though his tone was cajoling.

"Good idea," Walt chimed in. "He might try to run away."

"Oh, as if," David sniffed, and he returned his attention to the prisoner: "Per'aps you're right, you know. If we all get 'it at oncet, you're a free man. But it must be a bit lonely out there."

Hans hesitated, looked at David and then Tommy; then there was a closer explosion and flash, and he suddenly scuttled around them. Both they and Walt drew their weapons at the abrupt movement, in anticipation of Mueller attacking them or trying to flee; but instead the German boy scrambled behind Sleaze and yelled *"Kamerad!"* in near panic.

On an impulse that seemed to come from nowhere, Sleziniak turned to his comrades and cried, "Wait!" Turning back to Mueller, he said in a soothing voice, "It's all right. We won't hurt you." Back to Tommy and David, Walt added, "He's just a kid," as if this were the first time he'd noticed their prisoner's extreme youth. And then he turned back again to Hans and repeated softly, "It'll be all right," as the noise of the shelling kept up unabated.

With Sleaze thus preoccupied, the captain evidently asleep, and the barrage seemingly right over the next hill, Tommy followed an impulse of his own and encircled his arms around David, pulling his buddy closer. "'E's right, you know," said the Briton, his mouth close to the Doughboy's ear. "'Twill be all right."

"Don't see how either you or him can know that," muttered Tommy, who proceeded to ask, "Did you ever get some sleep?"

"Don't remember what that is," David said jovially.

Pulling him a little closer yet, Tommy continued, "How do you do it, Davey?"

"'Ow could I do otherwise?"

After that, with the noise so great, they didn't say anything more for a while, but took a simple comfort from huddling together closely for the duration of the bombardment, which finally began to move slowly away from them, back toward the Americans' trenches. On the opposite side of Sand's stretcher, Sleaze and Mueller were deriving a similar sense of security from each other, though they were not huddling quite so closely. In between the two pairs of soldiers, the captain appeared to be sleeping. Tommy thought this a good thing at first, but at length, given the din, he began to worry: how was it possible Billy was slumbering through all this? He placed his hand on Sand's chest to reassure himself.

"Yes?" came Billy's voice, drifting out of the dimness (it definitely was growing lighter, Tommy decided).

"Uhh – nothing, Captain," Tommy said, jerking away his hand.

After a pause, Sand said, "I know what you were doing, Corporal."

"Sorry, sir."

"Makes perfect sense to me. No point in going forward if I was dead." A thought seemed to come to him. "Though there wouldn't be much point in going backward, either, since they've obviously found their range on our main trench… which isn't too surprising, since it used to be theirs. Still, you'd need a good sense of direction if you left it in a hurry… which reminds me, Private Pearson, do you think we have far to go?"

They had all been listening rather mesmerized to Sand's ruminations, but David readily replied, "I should think about a mile, Captain, to where the two roads meet."

"What two roads?" Sand asked.

"The one from Corbie to Bray, and the one from Morlancourt to Chipilly."

Billy Sand listened with interest; though the English private's French pronunciation left a little to be desired, he couldn't help but be impressed. "How do you know all this, David?"

"'Twasn't 'ard to figure out, sir. This morning me unit was on the road from Corbie to Bray – the leftenants were calling it that. Then I was sent back to fetch some rations, at the other road. I read the sign there at the crossroads. It was still standing."

"You know how to read French?" That was Walt.

"No, but I can read the letters."

Now Sleaze seemed fascinated, too. "You been over this ground before, Pearson?"

"Not this in particular, no," David said, remaining patient and cheerful under the Americans' impromptu interrogation.

"So how do we know we're going the right way?" That was Tommy.

"'Cos I know the crossroads is west, and it's also north, away from the river, y'see. So I just led us away from the trenches where we came from, because they lead the other way, to the river, and also away from the light, 'cos the sun rises in the east–"

"Not in the middle of the night," Tommy pointed out.

"No, but there was enough light to tell the difference."

"There was?" said Tommy and Walt, both at once.

"Yes," David said plainly. "You cou'n't see it?"

"No, David," Billy piped up, then he added on all their behalf, "But we're glad you could."

Pearson shrugged. "'Tis just something I can do, that's all."

There was a brief silence as the others contemplated the value of the little Tommy's inner compass; then, ignoring rank protocol, Flowers asked him, "Reckon we should move out?"

David again seemed almost to sniff the air. "Meself, I would wait a little longer. The barrage is near to done, and the light will get that much better."

"Not that it matters to you," Tommy said with palpable affection, drawing a grin from Davey. They all grew quiet again, the Americans tacitly accepting the advice of a private from another army. At length, in yet another stab at friendliness, Tommy addressed the German: "So, Hans, the French took you prisoner, too?"

Mueller flinched at the very question, and it was all Flowers could do not to yell at him, "I've treated you fair and right! Why are you so scared of me?"

The young German looked at the ground, and Tommy thought he was refusing to answer; but after a painfully long pause, Hans simply said, "French... Colonials."

"From where, exactly?" This came from Billy, whose interest in Hans' story was obviously renewed.

But Hans' visible upset renewed the unexpected protective streak in Walt, who said unthinkingly, "Can't we just leave him alone?"

"*Private* Sleziniak!"

A look of horror crossed Sleaze's countenance as he realized how insubordinate he'd just been. Tommy feared his friend might go back to acting crazy, but the Dakotan froze and saluted the man lying on the ground and said tightly, "Sorry, Captain."

"You should be," Sand said severely. Turning his head back toward the German, he repeated, "French Colonials from where, Private Mueller?"

In a near whisper, the boy replied, "From – Morocco, *Capitaine.*"

"I thought so," Billy said in the suddenly dead-silent air; the bombardment had died away completely. Abruptly the American captain ordered, "Take off your helmet and turn your head, soldier." Trembling once more, Hans did as he was told, swiveling his head so the captain could see the left side of his face. "The other way," Sand ordered, and again Mueller obeyed, completely exposing the right side of his face. "You still have both ears," said Sand; it seemed to Tommy an extraordinarily peculiar thing for his captain to say.

"Yes, sir," Hans said in the same near whisper.

In the growing light, they all could see Billy, despite the condition of his left side, bite his lip on the right side. "All right, Hans," he said in a total change of tone. "I won't ask you any more. And neither will these men."

"But, Captain–?" Tommy began.

"What?" Billy snapped. "I gave you all an order!"

"Yes – yes, sir. I wasn't being disrespectful. I – I just wondered what that was, about the ears."

From his stretcher, Billy, still consumed with a sudden anger none of the other Allied soldiers could understand, looked at each of them in turn, seemed to consider something, then said, "The German soldiers fear the Moroccans more than any others on the Western Front. And with good reason. They're barbarians. They've been known to cut the ears off of prisoners and wear them around their necks as trophies."

As Sand spat out these words in disgust, all three – Flowers, Pearson, and Sleziniak – gasped in reaction. Even in the middle of this war, they hadn't heard of something quite like that. "That's terrible," Sleaze finally said, first to the others, then he repeated to the German, "That's terrible."

"Enough, Private Sleziniak," said Captain Sand, who seemed rather winded at having revealed this information.

"But Hans was lucky, sir," Tommy continued. "He didn't get his ears cut off."

*"Enough,* Private Flowers!" Billy said with more force and volume than Tommy had thought was possible right then from the captain, or good for his health. The corporal didn't know if he'd been busted, or if the captain had forgotten about his promotion in his outburst, but he wasn't about to find out, because Billy tersely announced, "Let's get this show back on the road."

# Chapter L

With that brusque order from Billy, the mission resumed. As the light continued to steadily increase, Tommy could see that Hans and Walt were now carrying the stretcher in fine coordination with each other, moving somewhat more slowly but, as more than adequate compensation, ever so much more surely. David's guidance, too, was even more self-assured than usual; and Tommy wondered whether, having heard Pearson's formula, he could have led them with a similar confidence if his pal weren't there.

They seemed to have entered some kind of magical kingdom as they moved up and down sloping green hills in the relative cool of the pre-dawn. Although it seemed to Flower of Iowa that this ground had to be part of that zone Colbeck had so vividly described as changing hands ceaselessly over the past four years, there was really no sign – or noise, now – of the war here at all, save for their little party.

The gentle rolling of the verdant downlands abruptly made Tommy homesick, causing him to suffer a wave of unexpected heartache as they continued on their way. Suddenly he saw himself back home in Iowa, maybe with three friends carrying another friend back to Doc Saunders, with nothing more serious to treat than a baseball injury…

"Tommy?"

He blinked and saw David standing directly in front of him, face a mixture of anxiety and bemusement; and, quite a ways down the slope, Walt and Hans standing patient and still, looking back up at the two of them. "What is it?" Tommy asked. "Why did we stop?"

"That's what I walked back up 'ere to ask you. We took a look back and you were just standing 'ere, and usselves going further and further aways. Did you 'ear something?"

"Hear something? No." Tommy looked into David's eyes, trying his utmost to concentrate. "Did I really do that?"

They were far enough away from the others that Pearson was able to answer, quite seriously, "'deed you did, love."

Tommy was more than a little unnerved by this inability to account for the last minute or so. "Maybe I better walk with you," he finally said.

"D'you think?" David responded cautiously. "It's usually much better with one man in front of the stretcher and the other one be'ind."

"You're right. It is." Fighting harder still to focus, Flowers asked, "What do you reckon happened, Davey?"

Pearson looked about him, a tad uneasy. "I b'lieve you fell asleep standing on your feet, Tommy. It 'appens."

Flowers blanched a little at this hypothesis. "I've heard sentries get shot for that," he said, thinking aloud.

"Well, I'm not about to shoot you," David said with a weary grin. "And the captain wou'n't either, so I b'lieve you're safe there." The Briton paused, added, "You're just tired, is all. You need a rest."

"*I* need a rest?"

Brushing off Tommy's concern for him, David said, "I'm sure we're only a little ways off now. I promise, in fact."

Feeling yet another surge of energy at this, Tommy declared, "Then let's get going."

They ambled back down the slope together, to where Sleziniak and the German stood. Billy, the corporal noted, was again fast asleep on the stretcher; at least he hoped that's what it was. The little party took off once more, but not before Tommy noticed Hans twisting his body slightly one more time, in what seemed a reflexive effort to avoid contact with him. Frustrated, the American almost said something about it, then decided to let it go.

Tommy fully expected David's senses of time and direction to be unerring, and so they were: after a long, slow climb up another hill, they reached a crest screened by a windbreak of trees; then there was another, shorter dip through open country, leading to a similar wooded hilltop; from there the view downslope revealed both the heavily trafficked major road from Corbie to Bray, and the lesser thoroughfare from Morlancourt to Chipilly that bisected it.

Flowers was surprised the group encountered no sentries at this last crest, but as they came down out of the windscreen, several Tommies came running up the steep grade to challenge them. With Sand still sleeping, or worse, Flowers counted as the ranking soldier in their party, but these new men directed their challenges to Pearson, who for all his fatigue responded with his wits about him: "Private David Pearson, of the London Rangers, reporting. The man on the stretcher is Captain Sand, of the American Army. I was sent at the request of Captain Block of the American Army, to 'elp guide the stretcher-bearers 'ere."

Having received such a thorough report, the biggest of this new crop of Tommies, a tall, mustachioed man who looked as if he could be Pearson's or Flowers' father even though he evidently was only a private, regarded the German and the Americans with suspicion, then eventually spoke, his burred r's betraying his Scottish roots: "Aye, then, Private Pearson. We'll lead ye to the crossroads. There's motor ambulances come there – whenever the Fritzes decide to stop dropping crumps on us."

Apparently they had had the good fortune to shelter in an area of relative calm while the German artillery had targeted both the crossroads that was their destination and the trench system that had been their point of departure. Continuing to trail the stretcher down the hill and into an area which, despite its recent shelling, was bustling with military personnel, mostly British and Australian, Tommy felt a pang of jealousy as he watched David chat effortlessly with his countrymen. The British soldiers led them to a small makeshift structure, and with Billy still not conscious, it fell to Tommy to report to the officer inside, a tall, thin Australian captain with a waxed mustache, and explain their presence at the crossroads.

But he didn't have to. The strange new officer interrupted Tommy's account almost before it began, introduced himself as "Captain Watson," and added, "We knew you were coming, Corp'ral Flaowuhs. Captain Block telephoned us."

Far from used to such efficiency, and still lacking a fondness for the American medical officer, Tommy again lost his soldierly bearing, replying, "Really?"

Clearly more amused than annoyed, Watson answered, "Yes, Corp'ral, 'really.' You've done a good job of it, bringing your captain in alive." He talked mostly like Jamie, but also a little like an English officer, Tommy thought.

"I just hope he stays that way, sir."

"We'll get him to hospital as soon as we can. You and the bearers, too. Captain Block said they were both to go back with you and Captain Sand – if you all made it here."

Tommy couldn't stop himself. "And Private Pearson, sir?"

A look of mystification shot across Watson's face. "He'll be returning to his unit, of course."

"Beg pardon, sir, but the only reason we did the good job you talked about is because Private Pearson led us. And I happen to know he's been awake for three days in a row." Watson was speechless, with shock at his insubordination or what, Flowers did not know, but having come that far, he hastily continued, "And – and he helped me catch that prisoner, and he helped Sergeant Glennon of the British Army when he was blinded, and–"

"Corp'ral!"

Tommy stiffened. "Yes, sir."

Without a break Watson, rubbing his chin, said, "Would you happen to know a Sergeant Jamie Colbeck, of the Australian Corps?"

"Why – yes sir, I would, sir. He's my lieutenant."

"Leftenant?" Watson smiled and said disarmingly, "That old dingo! Y'don't say?"

"Oh, I do, sir." Remembering Jamie's description of a "dingo," Tommy added, "But Lieutenant Colbeck is a good man, sir–"

Watson laughed. "I'm not sure abaout that. But he is a good soljuh."

"Yes, sir, he sure is."

There was a brief pause as the Aussie captain regarded Tommy, then said, "You remind me a little of him, Corp'ral."

"Me, sir? But – we're nothing alike."

"Maybe more than you know, son. Jamie has that effect on soljuhs."

"That's true, sir. Jamie does."

Watson chuckled appreciatively, apparently at Flowers' familiar use of Colbeck's first name. "So, what is it abaout this Private Peahson, Flaowuhs? Have you become best mates?"

"We always have been, sir." Thinking fast, Tommy added, "But even if he wasn't, Captain, I'd say he deserves a rest, and he – he'll serve the King better if he gets some sleep."

"Don't see haow he could serve the King any better than what you already told me," Watson pointed out drily.

"Well, that's true, too, sir," Tommy conceded, looking dejectedly down to the ground, assuming he'd lost the argument, until he heard Watson's hearty laughter.

"I don't care if your mate goes back with you, Corp'ral," Captain Watson said good-naturedly. "Saounds like he's earned it. But he needs an officer's permission, or he'll get in trouble. What would I tell his leftenant?"

"That – that Captain Sand requested it, sir. Captain's asleep, but I'm his adjutant–"

"You, an adjutant?"

"–I am for now sir, yes sir, and Captain Sand has authorized me to act in his place."

Watson let out a low whistle. "Well, then, soljuh, if you want to give that order, go ahead."

"With your permission, sir."

"Oh, no," the Aussie captain said, shaking his head. "It's on your head."

"Then I will."

Watson smiled again. "I like that. You didn't hesitate at all. That's being a good friend to your mate, and a good officer in charge."

Tommy smiled back. "I try to be both, sir."

Watson laughed, then nodded, rubbing his chin again. "Go on aoutside naow, Corp'ral, and get your group – your whole group, including Peahson – together so you can take the next motor ambulance out of here. And lad – ?"

"Yes, sir?"

"If you see Jamie again, give him my regards."

It occurred then to Tommy that Jamie was still back there on the front lines. Who knew if he'd ever see his lieutenant again? But if anybody would make it back…

★

A medical officer was looking at the still-unconscious Billy when Tommy returned to his group, the rest of whom were merely standing about, dog-tired. The new man wore a British uniform but sounded American; Canadian, Tommy guessed. Flowers saluted as he approached him, asking, "Can you tell me how the captain's doing, sir?"

The doctor failed to return Tommy's salute, instead holding up his right hand, which was covered with a sticky, foul-smelling greenish liquid. "This came from a wound in his side," he said gravely.

Tommy's heart sank at the appalling sight, and stench. "My God! Does it – Sir, does it mean he's–?"

"Calm down, Corporal. He's still alive. But there's truly no time to lose. We need him in an ambulance, out of here, now. You wait here while I see to it."

"Yes, sir." The medical man began to walk briskly away, and Tommy shouted after him, "Was it something we did, sir? I mean, did we do something wrong?"

The man snapped his head back around, looking as though he might reprimand the American corporal for his impertinence, but in fact he replied quite civilly, "I should say not. Quite the contrary. How you ever got him here alive, I'll never know."

"I see. Thank you, sir."

The officer grunted, saluted, then disappeared; and Tommy, who realized he had never learned the man's name, didn't see him again. But within five minutes' time, just as the "crumps" the old Scottish private had mentioned began to fall again, the promised motor ambulance, field green with red crosses painted on white squares on it sides and roof, swung into view and came to a halt in front of them. Unexpectedly, the driver who emerged from the vehicle was a Doughboy, a swarthy sergeant who gruffly introduced himself as "Stone," from another part of the 33rd Division, and from across the river from St. Louis.

Sergeant Stone opened the heavy canvas flaps at the back of the ambulance to reveal an unusually small interior: there was room for only one man stretched out on the floor, and one more each could lie on the benches lining either side, or three small men could sit, though there was scarcely room for their feet. As all five men lifted Captain Sand's stretcher onto the floor of the vehicle (for this task, even Tommy and David deemed it safe to join in), it was apparent from his jerky movements that Stone hadn't been briefed on the condition of the patient he would be carrying, and Tommy cautioned him about it. The others began to climb into the ambulance, and Stone suddenly snarled at Tommy, "I came out here to bring back Americans, not a limey and a Boche."

"We're all part of Captain Sand's escort, Sergeant," an embarrassed and incensed Flowers retorted. "The captain wants all of us to go back with him."

"The hell you say. How do I know that? There's no officer here except this one, and he's practically dead."

"Because I say so. I'm the captain's acting adjutant."

"You? You're just a private," Stone sneered, reminding Tommy that he'd never actually gotten a corporal's stripe, though it seemed to Flowers his promotion had happened a long time ago.

"I'm a corporal," Tommy said stubbornly, "and he's authorized me to act for him."

"This is a waste of an ambulance – and my time," the sergeant complained.

At that very moment, a whizz-bang burst not more than twenty yards away, and everyone took what cover they could, most diving under the ambulance. When the dust cleared, Flowers could see fear in Stone's eyes; the sergeant apparently lacked his close-range experience of shells. Taking advantage of that, Tommy icily told the recalcitrant NCO, "You can take this up with Captain Watson of the Australian Corps, Sergeant, if you insist on talking to an officer. But I say we get Captain Sand out of here before we all get blown to pieces."

Stone stared back at him with hatred, clenched his jaw, then said, "I'm not taking the German."

"You're taking *all* of us," Flowers countered. "And you got to drive very carefully, or the captain'll die."

To Flowers' annoyance, Stone began to laugh, in a most unfriendly fashion. "I just drove up this road," he eventually said. "Do you know what it's like? Full of holes and ruts."

"Then steer clear of them," Tommy said tartly. "That's your job. We've done our job. Now you do yours."

Stone gave him another daggers look. "Soldier, you better be acting for your captain, or–"

"I told you, I am. Now let's *go*."

Losing ground, the sergeant had a final parting shot: "Who's gonna ride up front with me?"

"Nobody. We came through this together, and we'll stay with Captain 'til it's finished."

Flowers and Stone locked eyes, until the latter blinked, saluted and said with obvious sarcasm, "Aye aye, Captain."

As Stone strode to the front of the ambulance, Tommy climbed into the back, sliding carefully past David to take the seat next to him on the right-hand bench, facing Walt and Hans, with Billy, who now seemed deathly still, lying between them. He had barely settled in when the vehicle was rocked by a terrific explosion, very close by. In unison the four of them reached over and down to steady the captain, while the ambulance rocked so violently that for the first few seconds it seemed as if it might tip over. Once the shuddering stopped, there was a moment of silence, then Flowers rapped on the frame of the divider separating them from the driver and hollered, "Sergeant Stone?"

"We're getting outta here!" the driver called back, and the ambulance came to life with a mighty jerk, causing Tommy to cry, *"Careful!"*

He got no reply but a loud grunt, apparently of assent, for the vehicle began rolling rather more smoothly. David and Hans reached over to close the back flaps, engulfing all of them in darkness. Before Tommy's eyes could adjust, they were shaken by another explosion, one that seemed a lesser burst only because of the force of the previous one. Stone's response was to accelerate, and they were well and truly off, bumping precariously along the severely rutted road. Tommy almost yelled at the driver again, but thought better of it; perhaps the man was doing his best.

At length, able to make out shapes in the dim light of the ambulance's interior, Flowers sat back, marginally more relaxed. A fleeting thought struck him: in these cramped confines, it became abundantly clear they all could use a trip to the bathhouse. The notion came and went as he watched Hans and Walt nodding off across the way, increasingly leaning into one another.

"Shou'n't 'ave let us sit down," murmured David, and Tommy once again drew his arm around the little Briton.

"Should've happened a lot earlier," he replied. Still regarding the German and the Dakotan, both already falling asleep, he asked Pearson, "What do you think the French did to him, Davey?"

Flowers felt Pearson's shrug. "Wou'n't know. Wou'n't care to know, actually."

"It must have been something awful."

"Well, 'e's alive, isn't 'e? Even 'as 'is ears. So it cou'n't 'ave been that orful."

Tommy sighed. "I reckon." His eyes hadn't left the pair across from them. "How can they just go to sleep like that? I'm so worried about the captain."

When no answer was forthcoming, Tommy asked, "Davey?" and looked down to see that his beloved buddy, too, had dozed off, on his shoulder. Flowers snuggled closer to Pearson but thought, well, someone's got to stay awake to watch over Captain. But after a few more seconds of the ambulance's rocking, he felt his own eyes growing heavy.

Tommy awoke to the dark of the inside of the ambulance, a more gentle rocking rhythm, and a peculiarly pleasurable sense of warmth, distantly familiar. Coming round, he remembered where he was, and realized that David was touching him in places that would have been off-limits to anyone else. Far from being disturbed by this, Flowers began to respond in kind, though he reminded Pearson in the lowest of whispers, "We said we wouldn't do this in France."

As soon as he said it, he regretted it, for he felt Davey tense up and pull away from him. In an equally soft whisper, the Englishman said, "You're right, love. I'm sorry. I cou'n't 'elp meself, what with the rocking, you right 'ere, and me moving up against you. It's just–"

Moving decisively, Flowers stopped Pearson's apology by covering David's mouth with his own. When, after some time, they broke off, it was David who cut through the ensuing silence, even as his hands returned to Tommy's body and Flowers' hands began to roam over him: "What if they wake up?"

"I don't care," Tommy lied, his voice thick with passion; he very much did care, but the danger of getting caught was somehow raising his level of excitement. Sealing the decision for the both of them, he whispered into his friend's ear, "I love you, Davey. And I *want* you."

They moved furiously against each other, aided and abetted by the motions of the ambulance; and as it had been for Tommy and Nicole in the field, this time it was over very quickly. Similarly to that other time, it was Tommy who spoke first when they were done, whispering as he began to pull his uniform back into order, "I'm a sticky mess."

David replied with an explosion of muffled giggles, even as he hurried to do likewise. "We were already a sticky mess before, all of us. 'Oo could tell the difference?"

Tommy started giggling, too, a little too loudly, for the Briton put his hand over the American's mouth to quiet him; and they collapsed laughing against each other. Their giggling eventually subsided and, against all Tommy's expectations, both of them promptly fell asleep again.

The second time Tommy awoke, it was with a sharp start, as the back flaps of the ambulance were pulled aside to admit the bright sunlight of mid-afternoon. Gathering his wits, Tommy first looked down at his own incriminating pants, then over at David, who was more calmly straightening himself, even as a couple of hefty Doughboy medics were beginning to tug at the captain's stretcher. "Careful!" came out of Tommy automatically, and one of the stretcher-bearers scowled at him and said, "We're always careful."

Once Sand's stretcher had been removed, Tommy again took the lead, jumping out and blinking in the fullness of the light, then once more regarding himself a little guiltily, until more sensible thoughts intervened: of course Davey was right; who could tell one stain from another on his filthy uniform? He finally looked down at his captain, who was too, too pale, and gasped at the sight: "Oh, God! He's dead, isn't he?"

"Give him a chance," chided the medic who had scowled at him. "He's in a bad way, but he's still breathing."

The man hadn't seemed to look at Billy any more closely than Tommy, but perhaps he was better trained to notice such things, thought Flowers, who then turned to face his recent adversary, Sergeant Stone, and stuck out his hand. "Thank you, Sergeant," Tommy said, "You did a great job."

Stone cocked his head oddly in return, but took the corporal's hand. "I hope he lives," Stone said with a nod toward Sand, and Flowers replied, "If he does, part of the credit's yours." Letting go of the sergeant's hand and changing tone, Tommy asked, "Where are we, anyway?"

"Vadencourt," Stone answered. "This is the main American hospital."

At the hospital – the village *château,* a two-story white building with black turrets, lower and smaller than the one at Molliens – Billy was whisked away, while a medical corporal informed the rest they would be checked out by a doctor whenever one had time: "Shouldn't take too long. Hasn't been a bad day for casualties, especially compared to the last couple." Looking at Hans, he asked the group, "Does he speak English?"

"Yes," they all responded at once, Hans included.

"Come with me, then," the medic said crisply to the German.

"Where are you taking him?" Sleziniak demanded, much too aggressively.

The medical corporal countenanced the interruption and said patiently, "Prisoners are treated separate. He'll be looked after, then he'll probably be put on a work detail." To Hans, he added, "You're lucky. Your war is over."

Hans nodded in evident agreement, but Walt demanded, "Why can't he–?"

"Walt," Tommy said, quickly cutting Sleaze off, "you know the rules. And you know they'll treat Hans right. We're Americans, after all."

"Hans?" the medical corporal asked.

"He's been a model prisoner," Tommy volunteered in reply, "And he's very young."

"I can see that. As you said, Corporal, we're all Americans. He'll be treated well."

David's muttered comment of "Di'n't know you Yanks cornered the market on decency" was pretty much lost as Hans turned to them all, the two Doughboys and the Tommy he had helped carry the American captain so many miles, and said with a stiff, formal bow, "Thank you, gentlemen."

"Hans!" That was Walt, still agitated. Looking around frantically, he asked, "Anybody got something to write with? And on?"

The others shook their heads, but the medical corporal said, "I'm sure we can find something later, Private. All of the patients write letters, if they can."

"I want something now."

"We can't do that now," the medic continued, still patient.

"Then can you see that he gets my address?" Sleziniak pleaded. That was highly irregular, and they all knew it, but the medical corporal nodded, almost imperceptibly, and Sleaze addressed the young German: "Write me when the war is over, Hans. Maybe you could come visit me in America." Tommy was reminded of David's invitation to come to Dunster, the one he'd already, improbably, honored.

"I vould like that, Valt," the German teenager replied with a smile that revealed all of his youth. Then he turned and saluted the medical corporal, who led him wordlessly away.

The medic's guess had not been wrong, for only about ten more minutes passed before he reappeared and announced, "There's a doctor ready to see one of you."

"Sleaze, you go first," Flowers ordered Sleziniak; Walt was staring ahead with a blank look that had Tommy worried about him all over again. The Dakotan quietly obeyed.

Tommy was in the midst of discussing his concerns over Sleaze with a patiently listening David when they were interrupted by a familiar but quite unexpected voice calling "Private Pearson! Private Flowers!" in a tone that could only be described as joyous. They both looked up to see Mike Glennon approaching them, appearing quite neat and smart, but for a red puffiness around his shining blue eyes. David automatically stood up and saluted, and Tommy lazily started to follow suit; but rather than return the gesture, the Welsh sergeant took the English private in a big hug, happily proclaiming, "You're alive!"

"And you can see," Tommy said, a little cautiously, not absolutely certain that was true; but then Mike turned and embraced the American as well, nodding and saying, "Thanks to you two."

Pearson, tongue-tied until now, finally spluttered, "It's – it's so good to see you, Sergeant."

"And it's wonderful to *see* you, Private," Glennon responded, and all three laughed.

"What brings you 'ere?" Pearson asked him.

"You, David. I'm taking you back."

"To the front?" Flowers interjected anxiously.

"No, Tommy, to camp. He's earned a spell of rest."

"That's what I've been trying to tell anybody who would listen to me for days," the Doughboy said. "But he hasn't seen the doctor yet."

"One of ours will look after him," said Glennon, who then ordered Pearson, "Come along now. There's a lorry waiting."

As Mike led him away, David turned to Tommy and said casually, "See you soon, Tommy." Tommy merely nodded in reply; but as soon as his mate and the sergeant whose eyesight they had saved disappeared from view, he was seized with a nameless anxiety. He felt suddenly abandoned there in the hospital hallway, with the tight little band of five who had made the trek of the last day and night now totally dispersed. He should, he thought, go see how the captain was doing, but his orders were to wait until he saw a doctor himself, so he decided he'd better stay put.

Another medic, a private, eventually appeared and took him to a room that looked and smelled horrific, with blood all over the several tables in it, and on the walls as well. "Sorry," the doctor there said, without conviction. "We've been using this for surgery for several days running." This man examined Tommy briefly, then sent him back to the hallway.

Unable to sleep again, Flowers sat there for some time, on edge, until the first medical corporal, the one who had been so kind to Walt and Hans, reappeared. "The doctor's orders are for you to get cleaned up and then catch the next vehicle to Pierregot," the man told Tommy. "I'll show you where to do both. Oh, and he wants you to stay off that leg as much as possible for the next couple days."

Tommy supposed he should have expressed his gratitude that the doctor hadn't ordered him immediately back to the front; but instead he asked, "What about Private Sleziniak?"

"The doctor's ordered him held here for observation." The medic turned, motioning for Flowers to follow him.

"And Captain Sand?" Tommy persisted. "How's he doing?"

"Don't know nothing about Captain Sand."

# Chapter LI

The medic might have become as brusque as he had been kind earlier, but he was as good as his word: within an hour, Tommy had bathed more thoroughly then he ever could hope to at a British bathhouse, and was issued a new, clean corporal's uniform. He was amazed they seemed to have taken his word about his promotion, since he'd never seen any paperwork; and although he tried not to be inordinately proud of this first tangible symbol of his new rank, he found himself occasionally glancing at the single stripe to remind himself it was real.

Once Flowers' clean-up was complete, the medical corporal was equally efficient in directing him to his transportation to Pierregot – surprisingly for this sector, a French Army vehicle, waiting out front of the *château*. Turning to the medic, Tommy pleaded, "Before I go, can't I just find out about Captain Sand?–"

"Last bus is leaving, Corporal. These fellas are headed for Amiens and the coast, but they said they could drop you off. I don't know when the next one'll be headed out in your direction. As it is, this one's so crowded, you'll have to sit up front with the driver."

"But, Captain Sand – I'm his adjutant–"

"Your captain is in good hands, Corporal," the medic said firmly. "Now, you've got to take this truck. And remember: the doctor's orders are for you to keep yourself clean and off your feet for the next couple days."

Tommy had run out of ideas – and fight. He didn't want his mission to save Billy to end like this, with such uncertainty, but there seemed to be no other avenue of appeal. Dejected, he gave the medical corporal – yet one more man whose name he'd never learned – a proper salute and a "Thank you for everything." Then he paced around the back of the French vehicle, which seemed strangely quiet for being so full, opened the passenger-side door and climbed into the front, wondering how he'd communicate with the *poilu* behind the wheel – only to come face-to-face with a most unexpected driver, whose name he did know, and cried out on impulse: "Ralph!"

Manton scowled, his eyes seeming to adjust to the intruder, and Flowers went on, "It's me. Tommy Flowers. From London?"

The colored Doughboy peered at him more closely, then a hint of a smile formed. "Oh, yeah," he said slowly, "I remember you, farm boy." With that, he looked away, back to his business, and started the engine; the vehicle took off much more smoothly than the last one Tommy'd ridden, with Stone at the wheel.

"So, how did you get here?" Tommy gabbled excitedly in the meantime. "How about that, us meeting again, here! What are you doing driving a French Army truck?"

"You haven't changed, have you, farm boy? Still just full of questions."

This comment shut Tommy up, and Ralph, now expertly guiding the vehicle through and then past the village of Contay, relaxed his tone as he continued, "I'm on special assignment here. Driving a bunch of Frenchies to the coast."

"I know. I mean, they told me that was where you were headed. But what happened to you after the last time I saw you, in London?"

Manton's jaw set as he seemed to remember. "Oh, you mean with that Mick-boy lieutenant? Major Harlan set him straight, finally. Took a while." He looked over at Flowers and asked, "What about you?"

"Oh, he got set straight in my case, too. But not by a major. By a nun." Ralph actually laughed at that, shaking his head, and Tommy added, "Actually, an actress playing a nun."

"You're pullin' my leg," Manton said, still chuckling, and when Tommy shook his head no, he added, "You're full of stories, too, farm boy. What else you been up to?"

Mindful not to boast about his combat experience, least of all to this man, Tommy simply said, "Oh, not much. But things must be better for you. You're a long way from working the docks here."

Flower of Iowa immediately wondered if he'd said the wrong thing, but the New Yorker's tone remained good-natured as he said, "After I cleared up that supply problem in London, the major said he owed me one, asked me what I wanted. I said I didn't want to go back to the docks, I wanted in the war." Now his voice grew chillier. "American Army won't let the colored fight side by side with the white. But the French don't care."

The thought of the Moroccans, the French Colonial troops who had mistreated Hans, flashed through Tommy's mind, but he didn't mention it. Instead he asked with interest, "Do you parlay French?"

"'Bout as much as you do, I 'spect," Ralph replied. "It don't matter. I get along. I turn right here, don't I?"

The sudden question threw Tommy off, but he fended for himself well enough; they had just passed Beaucourt, and there was a sign that pointed toward Molliens, so he responded, "I reckon so."

"You reckon?"

"Molliens will be fine. Once you get there, I can walk home."

"To America?"

"No, to Pierregot." There was an agreeable silence of a minute or so, then Tommy asked, "Have you been to the front, then, Ralph?"

"Not yet, Tommy," Manton answered, using Flowers' Christian name for the first time in either of their two encounters, "but once I'm done with this ride..."

Manton let it hang there, and didn't ask Flowers whether he'd been at the front. Although he thought he'd be itching to talk about it, Tommy was just as glad. A few more minutes and the familiar sight of Molliens loomed in the dusk, for the light was finally fading. "Pierregot's just up that ridge, about a mile past the *château,*" Tommy said, pointing with a renewed sureness. "I can walk it from here. If you go straight ahead, you can turn left at the big crossroads at the bottom of the hill, and that road'll take you right to Amiens."

Ralph whistled at this confidently delivered set of directions, even as he slowed the vehicle to a smooth halt. He looked over and, to Tommy's gratification, this time stuck his hand out first. "You're all right, farm boy. Good luck."

Tommy took the dark hand and, as they shook, said, "Good luck to you, too, Ralph. Kill a few Germans for me."

Manton smiled again as Flowers dismounted the vehicle and closed the door behind him. Only as Ralph's vehicle sped away did Tommy recall his orders to stay off his feet as much as possible. He was on the side of town where the Rangers had always camped, but he now found that familiar area nearly devoid of life, save for a very few Tommies he didn't recognize. It hit him then: most of the Tommies with whom he was familiar, whose faces if not names he had come to know through Davey, wouldn't be coming back, to here or anyplace else. He felt his stomach turn over at the notion. With the sour taste in his throat and his leg aching anew, he cursed his lack of judgment at passing up a ride for the last mile or so to Pierregot. Straight ahead lay the *château* of Molliens; he should, he figured, report to his army's headquarters. But once past the MPs, he thought of previous meetings with strange brass and grew anxious, wondering if, despite the papers he'd been provided at the hospital, they would think he was AWOL from the front.

A tall, thin lieutenant who looked for all the world like a younger version of President Wilson staffed the desk to which Flowers was directed. Tommy saluted the officer, and gave him his name and the papers. The other man, who curtly introduced himself as "Collins," glanced at them, then regarded the enlisted man with surprise. "Corporal," he said, "why is it you're reporting here instead of Pierregot?"

"Sorry, sir. I told the men who gave me a lift from Vadencourt not to bother. They were going past Molliens, and they were on their way to Amiens."

Collins pursed his lips. "So then, you disobeyed the doctor's instructions?"

Uh-oh. "Well – yes sir, I reckon you could say I did. I'm sorry, sir."

Tommy expected a lecture at the least, but the lieutenant gave a tight smile and said, "It's of no great significance in this case. But you shouldn't have done it. I take it you're capable of walking the rest of the way to Pierregot?"

"I – could, sir. Though my leg does hurt some."

"You should've thought of that when you turned down the ride. We have no spare vehicles to take you. And at any rate, I'm not sure that's where you'd stay once you got there."

"Sir?"

"Where did you think you were going to sleep tonight, Corporal?"

It seemed a surpassingly odd question, but Tommy answered, "My – my tent is on the north side of Pierregot, sir–"

Collins shook his head. "Not anymore, soldier. Those tents are all gone. There's hardly anyone left in Pierregot. That's why it's just as well you came here."

The two of them remained there in silence for an uncomfortable period, until Tommy finally said, "So – beg pardon, sir, but I'm not clear what my orders are."

The lieutenant gave a frown as tight and small as his smile had been, then said, as if reading something by rote, "You know your orders. You are to rest and recuperate for two days." Collins seemed to get an idea, and added, "But you are to report back here tomorrow at 1000 hours."

That certainly seemed to contradict rest and recuperation, but Tommy knew better than to point it out. "So," he responded at length, careful to keep any sarcasm from his voice, "begging the lieutenant's pardon, but where am I supposed to go to rest?"

"That's not my problem, Corporal. It's yours. Report back here to me at 1000 hours."

"Full gear?" Flowers asked.

"No," Collins snapped back, unsmiling. "You and your gun will do. Clean."

"Absolutely, sir," Tommy said, saluting, and wondering about all this sudden emphasis on cleanliness, although he wasn't sure if Collins had meant him, his gun, or both.

Tommy wandered bewildered back down the tree-lined lane (at least most of the trees were still standing) that led from the front of the *château.* Why on earth had the army been in such a hurry to send him back here, to a virtual ghost town? He was feeling even more abandoned than before… but he was also experiencing a rising sense of elation. Those moments with David in the ambulance had given him ideas he knew he shouldn't be having; but if he didn't have to account for his whereabouts, and he could find Pearson, maybe he and Davey could spend the night together, depending on the Briton's orders. So Flowers limped back into the village of Molliens, stopping the few stray Tommies he encountered to ask if they'd happened to see Private Pearson, just back from the front. Each man regarded him as if he were a German spy, and one with three heads at that.

Discouraged and sore, he sat down on the steps of the church as the sky grew dark; now that it was later in the summer, the sun was setting earlier. He pondered briefly what it would be like to soldier on through the winter, then shoved the thought from his mind. Tired again, he fell into a sort of restless doze until he felt a nudge and heard someone calling his name. His eyes and mind sputtered awake; it wasn't Davey, but even in the darkness he was able to place the man: Michael Glennon. "I've been looking all over for you," said the Welshman.

"I was looking for David," the Doughboy countered, prompting Mike to inform him, "They've sent him to Querrieu."

At this intelligence, Flowers snapped wide awake, and reproached Glennon: "Mike! You said they weren't sending him back to the front–"

"–and so they didn't. Querrieu's not the front. It's, oh, five miles from here, perhaps. They moved most of our lot there – what's not at the front, anyways."

"Then why are you here? And can we go there?"

"Now? No. It's too late, and too far, and too crowded. And as for your first question, I'm here because I let David take my place in Querrieu, and I promised him I'd find you."

"What do you mean, you let him take your place?"

"I got wind there's to be some big ceremony tomorrow. They wanted me in it, since I was blinded and all. I went to the major, and I told him, 'Give the honor to the man who saved my sight instead.'"

"So Davey's getting a medal?" Tommy asked, excited.

"Oh, nothing like that, I don't think. They won't talk about what it is; they're being so careful about it, even Jamie probably couldn't find out if he was here. So it must be important, but I don't think it's a medal. Anyhow, it's David deserves the honor, whatever it is."

Swallowing his disappointment over his aborted evening with his mate, Tommy said, "It's about time"; then, with sincerity, he echoed Ralph Manton's phrasing: "You're all right, Sergeant Glennon."

Mike shrugged. "'Twas the least I could do."

Despite the darkness, Flower of Iowa could see the Welshman was grinning with satisfaction, his blue eyes so full of life that Tommy had to remind himself they'd recently nearly given him up for dead, or at least blind. "So, Davey sent you looking for me?"

"That's right. You weren't hard to find; I talked to a bloke who said you were going 'round asking everyone about Pearson. David said you'd come looking for him. He told me to take care of you."

The choice of words sent a chill, or rather something like it but warm, through Tommy. There was a pause, then he asked Mike once more, "You're sure we can't just go to Querrieu? I'm at liberty 'til 10 o'clock tomorrow."

"I told you, Tommy, no. Besides, David's already asleep by now. But I came here in this motorcar, so I can take you to your billets."

For the first time Tommy noticed, behind Mike, a vehicle, very much like the one Jamie had borrowed. He must have been more asleep when Glennon had first tapped his shoulder than he thought. "I don't have a billet," he told the sergeant. "But I could use a lift somewhere, 'cause my leg–"

"You don't have a billet?"

"No. They left me high and dry for tonight. That's why I thought, maybe in Querrieu–"

"Out of the question, Tommy." An idea seemed to come then to Glennon. "But, wait… why don't you come with me? Yes, you should come with me."

"Where to?"

Mike's teeth shone in the moonlight as he smiled again, and Tommy idly wondered if he came from a seaport and so brushed his, too. "You remember where we all first met?"

Tommy didn't even have to think. "Sure. Where everybody meets. Madame's just-a-minute in Rainneville."

"Right. That's going to be my billet tonight. Our billet."

*"What???"*

Mike jumped into the driver's side of the car and said, "Don't argue, Tommy. Let's go."

He gunned the motor, and Tommy, suddenly desperate not to be left there on the church steps for the night, reluctantly got in on the passenger side and said, "Tell you what. If you can drop me off in Pierregot before you go there–"

"Not a chance, Corporal," Sergeant Glennon said breezily as the vehicle took off and they headed in the other direction, away from Pierregot.

"You must be pulling my leg, Mike. Madame doesn't take in borders."

"Oh, but she does now. Business is so bad, with most of us at the front, that she sent her niece away – which is too bad, but that's why she's got the room –"

Stunned at the news of Nicole's absence, Tommy also found himself wondering about the official explanation for it. Everything was coming back to Flowers at once – everything he'd left behind when he'd marched off to the front. He'd last been to the *estaminet* the first night he'd met Glennon, and although Mme. Lacroix was courteous enough when Tommy was there with Jamie, he knew she had never forgiven him for what he had done with Nicole. He grew panicky as Glennon made the turn for Rainneville. "I don't have any money," he blurted out.

"It's on me, mate. My way of saying thank you. As if I ever could, enough."

Putting it like that made it pretty well impossible for Tommy to say no. "Madame's probably asleep by now," he suggested.

"Oh, you know that one. She'd get up in the dead of night if it meant making an extra *sou.*"

"Maybe it's already rented out."

"'Twasn't earlier, and there aren't that many others about. I stopped and asked before I came to get you. I was looking to do this for myself anyways."

The little motorcar roared up the crest of the hill, and as Mike pulled it smartly to a stop in front of the *estaminet,* Tommy found himself wondering how the Welshman, a mere sergeant, had managed to requisition the vehicle. No wonder Glennon and Colbeck were friends – two peas in a pod, as they said back in Iowa.

Iowa seemed even farther away than usual as Tommy slowly followed Mike, who was already rapping at the establishment's door. He should, he thought, warn Glennon about the complications of including him in this little party; but he was too ashamed to do so. There was a prolonged wait, and Flowers harbored one last hope that Madame would simply yell out at them to go away; but then a faint glow appeared from within, accompanied by the sound of some muffled French. Glennon called something in return, and after a bit, Madame's voice could clearly be heard on the other side of the door, a hard edge of suspicion in it that was discernible even to one who did not speak her language. Mike glibly said something back to her, then turned and winked at Tommy, who in turn held his breath as the old woman opened the door a crack and then beckoned them inside.

As soon as the candlelight caught Flowers' face, there was, as he had feared, a sharp hiss from Madame, and a harsh, involuntary whisper of *"Fleur!"*

"She remembers you, Tommy!" Mike said. "I'm surprised."

"I'm not," Flowers retorted glumly, flushing under the old woman's glare.

Madame spoke rapidly to Mike, although her eyes never left Tommy. The Welshman, oblivious, translated easily: "She says since Nicole is away, we can share her room for the night. There's only one bed, and it's small for the two of us. But it's all she's got."

"I reckon we should look somewhere else, then."

"Too late for that," Mike said peremptorily, and he and Madame chattered on.

Tommy, recalling the last time he had shared a bed with a man, was momentarily dumbfounded by Mike's casual attitude, but then he caught himself; out here it was the height of luxury for an enlisted man, or even an NCO like Mike, to sleep in a real bed with real sheets and a real pillow. Glennon was genuinely grateful to Tommy, but he wasn't about to pay the no-doubt exorbitant price Madame would charge without sharing the bed. "How much is she asking?" Flowers persisted.

"I told you, Tommy, it's on me. We'll talk about that upstairs, her and me. She's going to show me the room now. You wait here."

Exhausted, his mind spinning, Tommy sat down at one of the short tables and watched the two ascend. The entire scenario couldn't have seemed more wrong to Flower of Iowa: sharing a bed with Mike rather than David, and letting him pay for it; and above all, sleeping in Nicole's room, in Nicole's bed, while she was squirreled away somewhere, probably, he couldn't help feeling, because of what he'd done to her, because he'd failed to do right by her. The very prospect struck Tommy as more uncomfortable than sharing a funk hole with a dead man. Why didn't Madame scratch and claw his face and throw him out for ruining her niece, and then not doing the honorable thing? He wished she would.

This unhappy reverie was interrupted by the sound of Mike's and Madame's voices, no doubt debating the price of the room, drifting down from upstairs. It occurred to Tommy, though he wasn't sure how he knew, that Mike's French was better than Jamie's, almost as smooth as Billy's. Time was he'd thought nobody did anything as well as Colbeck.

This train of thought caused Tommy an extra start when Mike suddenly yelled down, "Hey, Tommy! You got a friend named Jack? She keeps asking me about some fellow named Jack."

With a quickness of mind he wouldn't have anticipated, Tommy called back, "That's Jamie. Her and Nicole call him Jacques."

He had done his best to use the French pronunciation; in return he caught Mike's "Jamie! I should have known," and an increased animation to the sergeant's discussion with the old Frenchwoman.

The fluent French again brought Billy to mind, causing Tommy to wonder how his captain was doing right now, or even if he was still alive. For that matter, was Jamie still alive, or even David, in the supposed safety of Querrieu? If someone wasn't right in front of your face and breathing, you could never be sure in this war. He looked around the empty *estaminet* and thought of sharing this table, or one of the others, with Frank Gillis, and Andy Kopinski before him, and who knew who else who'd gone west, and suddenly he felt a chill that was cold and deep; the place was haunted, on top of everything else. More frightening still was the sudden cessation of conversation upstairs, and thus the possibility that Mike would remain in the room while Madame came down to get him, meaning he'd have to face her all by himself. He'd rather be alone in a trench with a dozen Germans.

But it was Glennon who presently appeared at the top of the stairs, giving a quick motion to indicate that Flowers was now being invited up into a part of the *estaminet* he'd never seen, despite his many visits here. Tommy trudged up the steps wearily, and was relieved when he reached the second-floor landing to find Madame already retired to her room. "C'mon," Mike told him, his smile oversized in the dim light coming from, presumably, "their" room. "It's real nice."

Tommy obediently followed the Welshman the few steps down the hall and into the chamber. A powerful sensation that Nicole was there swept over him the moment he entered, and grew as he surveyed the room while Mike quietly shut the heavy wooden door behind them. Certainly there was every indication that the real occupant might return at any moment: her hairbrush even sat patiently beneath the tiny piece of glass that doubtless served as her mirror. Where had they sent her? Would they not even let her brush that beautiful hair there, wherever it was? Had they made her cut it off in shame? The sick feeling at the pit of his stomach returned, even as he heard Mike enthuse, "Just think of it, Tommy! A real room, with a real bed. A sight better than a trench, isn't it?"

Not in this case, Tommy thought, but he politely said, "Sure is." He turned and looked at the beaming sergeant. "But you must have had a real bed in the hospital."

"That's just it. It was a hospital bed." Glennon's jovial expression faded a little, and he asked, "What is it, Tommy? Something wrong?"

So Mike wasn't so oblivious after all. Tommy weighed what to say; on top of all the other bad feelings he was having, it felt wrong to be spoiling Mike's treat. "It's just strange," he finally said. "This room is so much Nicole's."

Mike's grin returned. "Don't I know. That makes it all the better. Only wish she were here, too."

Tommy found the comment either alarming or infuriating, probably the latter, since it seemed to imply Nicole's services were available to any soldier willing to pay. To hide his reaction, he glanced the other way, at the bed, which looked impossibly small. He couldn't imagine fitting into it with Davey, and Mike was bigger than David, though smaller than Tommy. The only way to get through this suddenly excruciating evening, Flowers resolved, was to try to get to sleep as soon as possible, so he yawned extravagantly. It had the desired effect, as Glennon yawned in return and said, "You, too? I'm knackered."

Tommy didn't understand the word, and thought for a second Mike had said, "I'm naked," which he clearly wasn't; but even as Flowers thought this, Glennon began shedding his tunic, cheerily remarking, "It's warm in here."

Tommy said the first thing that came to his mind: "Maybe I should sleep on the floor."

"Nonsense," replied Mike, who with amazing dispatch was already halfway out of his shirt as his trousers slid down his legs. "It'll be a tight fit, but not compared to a funk hole."

Tommy thought about announcing that he'd sleep in his clothes, but then he remembered Collins' order; he couldn't show up at 1000 hours looking as though he'd slept in his uniform. Besides, it *was* warm in the room. His back to Mike, he quickly pulled off his boots and puttees – a painful thing to do standing, given his foot, but he did it anyway, gritting his teeth – and with equal swiftness shed his tunic and trousers, carefully folding them and putting them on top of the boots. Only then did he turn to face Glennon in the soft light of the lamp – and that in turn caused him to catch his breath. Just when Tommy thought it couldn't get any worse, it did: the Welshman wore only his undershorts, and with a jolt Tommy realized the sight sent a bolt of desire through him. "I'll put out the light," he said quickly, hoping he was keeping the panic out of his voice.

"All right," Mike, still standing by the bed, said softly. "Do you want the outside or the inside?"

Ordinarily Tommy would have had no opinion, but as he slipped hurriedly past Mike in his agitated state, the choice was obvious: "Inside," he said, virtually jumping into the bed and rolling over so that he faced the wall, then scrunching himself up further to allow maximum room for Glennon. Still, it wasn't enough; when Mike got into the bed, lying on his back, his body was jammed up along the length of Tommy's, making the American all the more uneasy.

There must be a God, Flowers thought, very seriously, and He must be punishing me for all the bad things I've done, with Nicole, with David, maybe even for killing that old German. If Madame had rented this bed out to anyone else, you sure couldn't tell; he was overwhelmed by Nicole's scent; after all this time and all he'd been through, he clearly recalled it. If he was a decent man at all, he'd be married to the French girl now, sleeping with her in this bed.

But he wasn't a decent person. Any doubt about that was being swept away here and now. He'd always believed what had happened between him and David was something special, something so beyond the usual order of things which happened between people, that that excused it. Though he'd meant it when he'd told Davey he thought things might have been the same for them had there been no war, in his heart he hadn't remained so certain. Now he was sure: it wasn't Davey's fault; his reaction to Mike lying next to him proved that it was all his, Tommy's, fault.

At this precise moment, with Flowers so absorbed in self-loathing, Glennon, who himself had been lying stiff and obviously uncomfortable, shifted in the bed, turning onto his right side – the side facing Tommy. Gently he placed his bare arm around Tommy's chest. There was a brief pause, then Mike whispered, with an uncharacteristic timidity, "Is that all right?"

Everything in Tommy cried out "No!" – everything except the fact that it felt good, coupled with his lingering determination not to hurt Mike's feelings. What had Billy said – that was what separated men from the animals? So at length he cautiously replied, "Are you more comfortable this way?"

"Are you?"

"I'm all right. Just a mite warm."

Another pause. "You could take your shirt off."

Unlike Mike, Tommy had kept his undershirt on up to this point. Deciding blindly, the Doughboy said, "All right," wriggled out from under the other man's arm, peeled off his shirt, and tossed it on the floor. He was now virtually pasted to the wall, and there was no choice but to settle back into Mike, who easily draped his arm around Tommy once more.

Tommy lay there waiting for the tension to drain from him, or at least from Mike, but it didn't. After a couple of minutes, he found out why, when Mike shifted slightly against him – enough for Tommy to realize the sergeant was, unmistakably, as aroused as he was. Paradoxically, this realization finally allowed Tommy to relax a little: maybe David was right; maybe they weren't "the first time in 'istory it's ever 'appened between two blokes." Breathing easier, he hesitated only a few seconds, then took a chance, and pulled Mike's arm around his torso somewhat more snugly... and also drew the Welshman's hand lower, onto his stomach.

It seemed to be all the encouragement Glennon needed; his hand dropped lower yet, and he ground his groin into Tommy's hips. The dead silence that followed was finally broken by Mike saying, "Wish Nicole was here."

Tommy realized he did too and, no particular surprise, he wished even more that Davey was; but now he was the one more sure of himself. "But she's not," he replied tentatively.

There was another long pause, and Tommy felt Mike's hairy chest – quite different from David's smooth one – tickle his back. That made him even harder – that and Mike's restless hand. He wasn't inclined to do any more of Glennon's work for him, so he kept silent. After an interminable minute or more, the sergeant said, "I can't stop thinking about her. Can you?"

"No," said Tommy truthfully, taking his cue, but again stopping there.

Mike's heavy breathing on Tommy's neck was coming nearly in gulps now. In the faintest of whispers, he added, "Shall we help each other out, then?"

Turning to face him, Tommy said with a casual assurance that was not feigned, "Sure." To himself he added, I'm probably going to Hell anyway.

# Chapter LII

It was light – long since, from the look of things – when Tommy awoke, but he immediately recalled where he was and why. Mike stood looking out the window, fully dressed. Though he probably heard Tommy as soon as the American stirred, not until Flowers had pulled on his undershirt and shorts did Glennon turn around to say, "A good thing you woke up. I was going to rouse you if you didn't soon."

This was said both in a tone, and with an expression, of studied, pleasant neutrality. Glennon didn't need to say anything more; it was clear he preferred to pretend the night before had never happened, though not because he was upset about it. Mike's attitude toward their whole encounter had become obvious even as it was happening, when Tommy had moved to kiss him, as he always did David: "There now, no need for that," the Welshman had said with a smile, his voice friendly but firm. He seemed to regard the whole thing in almost businesslike fashion, so much so that now Tommy had to rein in his own habitual courteousness; if he thanked Mike this morning for sharing the room with him, he'd feel… well, he couldn't quite believe it, but he sure knew what it would make him feel like.

He therefore pulled his clothes on as rapidly as possible, and the most he ventured was, in a conversational tone, "Sleep good?"

"Yes. And you did too, didn't you?"

"Yes." This was not a polite lie; once they had achieved some level of physical comfort with each other, the soft bed and their fatigue had become more significant factors than the close quarters.

"You said you have to be back by 1000?" Mike asked, though Tommy suspected the sergeant already remembered that, and was just filling the empty air between them.

"Yes," Flowers repeated, brushing his hair and neatening his uniform in Nicole's tiny mirror. Satisfied he would pass muster, he turned to the other man and added, "Mike?"

"What?" Glennon asked warily in return, evidently concerned that Tommy was about to make more of last night than he wished.

"Can you help me talk to Madame?"

"To Madame? What for?"

"About Nicole."

Glennon remained in the same state of high alert. "And what about her?"

"Mike, don't you wonder what happened to her? Where she went?"

Glennon shrugged. "What should I care? All I know is she's not here. And she wasn't here last night, and that was too bad."

Tommy was taken aback by the strength of his own reaction to Mike's words; he actually felt insulted. He was tempted to say something like "You didn't seem to mind it last night" but held his tongue, not only because of his innate civility, but because there was something he wanted from Glennon more than the satisfaction of seeing him embarrassed. So instead he pressed his case: "Will you do it, Mike?"

"Since you're so keen for it," Glennon said with undisguised irritation. "Though I doubt she'll tell you anything."

I doubt it, too, thought Tommy, but for me to set my life right, she's just got to.

Flowers turned then to make up the bed, and he heard the first note of affection creep into Glennon's voice, albeit mixed with exasperation: "Tommy, what are you doing? We paid for the room! I thought David told me you worked in the hotel business."

Tommy laughed a little, at himself, stopped what he was doing and said, "That's right. *You're* right. I did." He felt the tension between the two of them abate. But he wished Mike hadn't mentioned Davey; he was having enough trouble trying to keep Pearson out of his thoughts this morning without being reminded of him by others.

Mme. Lacroix was sweeping the *estaminet* floor as they descended, which recalled all too easily for Flowers the day he had cleaned her place, and then run off to the field with her niece. Like Mike, the old woman appeared eager to finish their business with as little ceremony as possible. A look of annoyance crossed her face when the Welshman began to speak to her, and when he went on at some length, presumably making the inquiry Flowers had requested, she first looked blankly at Tommy, then seemed almost flustered… until a smile spread ever so slowly across her face. She eventually said something to Glennon, with great emphasis, and despite Flowers' lack of French, he was sure he caught the word "Jacques." This was subsequently confirmed when Mike turned and addressed him: "You said Jamie was Jacques, did you not?" Tommy nodded. "Then she says to tell you Jamie was right."

"About what?"

When Mike communicated that question to Madame, even Tommy could hear that her answer was the exact same phrase as before. "I don't understand what she means," the Doughboy complained.

"She's not going to tell us more than that," said Mike, shaking his head.

"Then I reckon I'm just going to have to ask Jamie," Tommy said with a sigh. Bowing slightly, he addressed Mme. Lacroix in his best French: *"Merci, madame."*

In return he got a sniff and a "Hm!" as the old Frenchwoman returned to her chores.

"I told you not to ask her," Mike admonished. "Now she has it in for you."

"Let's just go," Tommy countered, unable to hide his frustration.

They headed out of the *estaminet* and into a clear summer morning of striking beauty – warm air, puffy white clouds, and a fine blue sky. As their motorcar headed down the hill from Rainneville, Tommy sat silent in the passenger seat, thinking wryly to himself, another beautiful day at the front. He wondered what this area would be like after the war, and how long it would take for the war to end. It mattered more this morning than before, because he had resolved to ask Nicole Lacroix to forgive him, and to marry him.

As Tommy and Mike neared the outskirts of Molliens, they saw that the same village that had been a near-ghost town the night before was now bustling with American and British troops. And as they reached the edge of the old Rangers' encampment, and the lane that led up to the *château,* they encountered a new sentry post. Since it was manned by an American, Tommy, his lower rank notwithstanding, took the lead in informing the Doughboy sergeant who stood guard, a tall, friendly type, about his appointment with Lieutenant Collins.

"You can proceed," the American MP told Flowers after hearing him out, "but your escort here will have to turn around."

Mike was not pleased at what he perceived to be uppity behavior by this Yank. "He's got a bleedin' hurt leg," Glennon barked, and Tommy could see the Doughboy NCO, misunderstanding, actually check his countryman's leg for blood. "Are you going to make him walk all that way up to the *château?*"

The American sergeant, detecting no blood, hesitated, then replied apologetically, "I'm afraid so, Sergeant."

Tommy had barely dismounted from the motorcar and turned about to say a clipped "Thanks, Mike" when his bedmate of the previous night jerked his vehicle about and sped off in a cloud of dust. Flowers took a couple of involuntary steps in Glennon's direction, and only then did the American sergeant notice his limp.

"Sorry," the man said sheepishly. "Sorry."

His eyes still fixed on Glennon's rapidly disappearing motorcar, Tommy replied, "It doesn't matter." The long walk up the lane, though, did. Knowing he was somewhat ahead of schedule, Tommy took it slowly, until the last few paces, when he was suddenly seized with the feeling he'd lost track of the time.

As he headed past two more MPs and down the same hallway as yesterday, he saw that Collins was already talking with another man, a dark-haired officer, apparently English. But as Tommy drew closer, the figure suddenly looked familiar – as familiar as any lieutenant could possibly be. He checked himself from calling out Jamie's name, instead striding directly over to Collins' desk, saluting and announcing he was reporting for duty as ordered. Collins, who Tommy would have thought a stickler for all formalities, didn't return his salute, instead saying, "Corporal Flowers, I believe you know this man?"

Regarding Jamie, he answered with a smile, "Yes, sir, I sure do."

"Good. He will give you your orders for the morning. I have enough other matters to take care of." Then Collins did salute Jamie, and said, "Lieutenant."

But as both Colbeck and Flowers made to leave, he suddenly asked, "Corporal, did you find a place to sleep?"

You couldn't have cared less last night, Tommy thought, but he answered, with a dart of the eyes to Jamie, "Yes, sir. In Rainneville."

"Good," said Collins, but the thin lieutenant wasn't looking at them; he was already focused on his paperwork, which somehow reinforced his resemblance to the president in Tommy's mind.

Flowers didn't have much time to contemplate Collins, however, because Colbeck, his voice stiffer than usual, said, "Let's go, Corp'ral," and Tommy found himself following Jamie not back the way he'd come, but deeper into the *château.*

He was concerned his mention of Rainneville had angered Jamie, and even as he hastened with some difficulty to keep up with his lieutenant, he hastened to explain, "I was with Mike Glennon last night." Having said it, and knowing what had passed between him and Glennon, he didn't like the sound of it.

But it scarcely mattered to Jamie, who sarcastically responded, "Well, I hope you both had sweet dreams, lad. Because while you were sleepin', we were clearin' Jerry aout of Étinehem."

Tommy recognized the name of the village on the river near where his company had been. "You moved forward?"

Colbeck, not looking back, nodded. "While you were in the land o'nod, your company was straight'nin' aout the front line."

"So how did you get here?" Tommy called after Jamie, who had increased the distance between them; he was moving too fast for Tommy and his game leg to keep up.

Jamie caught the fading voice, glanced back, and stopped dead. Flowers kept advancing, and Colbeck, spotting a bench off to the side between them, ordered him, "Sit daown."

"I can keep up," Tommy said, drawing even.

Without warning, Colbeck grabbed him by the shoulders and forced him onto the bench, saying through gritted teeth, "I told you to sit daown. Naow *sit daown!*" He got gritted teeth in return, because he had pushed Tommy down in a way that shot a sharp pain through the American's bad leg. "God damn it!" Jamie cursed, and Tommy automatically said, "I'm sorry," causing Colbeck to shout, "Shut up!"

Silence fell in the *château* hallway, with Flowers sitting painfully, awkwardly on the bench and Colbeck standing in front of him, evidently about to explode. Instead, the Aussie lieutenant drew in a deep breath, and his voice went completely different: "What is it abaout you that keeps makin' me take things aout on you?"

For Colbeck, that was pretty close to a straightforward apology. Flowers responded by asking, "What's wrong, Jamie?"

The Aussie lieutenant shook his head. "You heard me. Eight haours ago I was gettin' aour troops – your comp'ny – into position in their new line. We took Étinehem, though God knows if we'll keep it. Maybe." To Tommy, that last sounded unusually optimistic, coming from Jamie, who went on, "Naow I'm here, and I ain't had no sleep, and I can't even sit daown on this bench with you, because if I do, I'll fall asleep on the spot."

"But you stay awake for days in the trenches."

"But this ain't the trenches, naow is it?"

"No." Though he didn't understand any better what was going on, Tommy felt he should do something to make himself useful, so he offered, "I'll cover for you, Jamie, if you want to sleep."

At that Jamie did explode, with laughter. Tommy laughed too, but only a little, because he wasn't sure how much of Jamie's reaction was aimed at him. Eventually Colbeck regained some control, and said, "I've missed you, Tommy. There ain't nobody like you. They're really ain't."

Still uncertain as to his lieutenant's true attitude, Flowers returned to his first question: "Why are you here, Jamie?"

Still chuckling to himself, Jamie replied, "Why, indeed. I could blame Billy Sand, but if I did, I'd have to blame Gen'ral Monash, too."

"Jamie, you're not making sense! What did you say about Billy? Is he – is he alive? Is he all right?" Abruptly Tommy feared he had it all figured out: Billy had died, and Jamie had been called back to be made their captain.

Jamie could read this, or something very like it, on Tommy's face, and it momentarily sobered him. "Billy's alive, lad. Thanks to you. He's alive and awake. I sawr him not two haours ago." As he watched the relief flood over Flowers, Colbeck continued, "We're here right naow because of him. Well, you are. I'm here because of him and Gen'ral Monash."

Trying hard to contain his elation at the news Billy had survived, Tommy said, "I still don't understand what General Monash has to do with it. And, what is 'it,' anyway?"

Jamie put one foot on the bench where Tommy sat. "We're havin' a very important visitor today – the 33rd Division… and also some of the Pom divisions… and also the Australian Corps. Gen'ral Monash wanted me back for the Australian part of it, and Billy wanted you here for the 33rd part. When he learned the gen'ral was ord'rin' me back anywise, Billy ordered me here, too."

"But who's the important visitor, Jamie?" He brightened. "General Pershing?"

Jamie nodded. "Pershing's here, naow." But then he added, "But I didn't mean Pershing. Think higher."

To Tommy's thinking, that could only leave, in the Allied chain of command, the man who gave orders to both Haig and Pershing. "Foch?" he whispered.

Jamie leaned in closer. "Tommy," he said gravely. "It's the King."

This didn't sink in at all, not at first. Then: "The King? The King of England? We're going to meet the King of England?"

Tommy was swept by a visible excitement he couldn't contain, and Jamie was quick to calm him down: "We won't exactly be shakin' hands with him. But he's comin' to give some medals to some of your – aour – 33rd troops who fought at Hamel. Naow, you're not on the list to get a medal, and neither am I. But they've got abaout three hundred men who will be the honor guard for the ceremony, and you'll be one of them. Billy knew abaout this before we ever went to Chipilly Ridge, and he fought to have you in that honor guard."

This news caused Tommy's throat to tighten, but he choked back his emotion and said, "And you?"

"I'll be right next to you. Thanks to Billy, and Gen'ral Monash."

"This is incredible! Aren't you excited, Jamie?"

"No, lad, I'm not. But I'm glad you are, and Billy will be, too–"

"Wait 'til I tell Davey!–" Then it hit Tommy: "But… wait – Davey's gonna see the King, too!"

Seeking to spare Tommy disappointment, Jamie said gently, "I – I wouldn't caount on that, Tommy. David deserves it, but the Poms handle these things different–"

"But Mike – Mike said he gave up his place in some big ceremony today so Davey could be in it! That would have to be the King!–"

"Well… maybe," Colbeck conceded.

"Mike's all right after all," Tommy said to himself, but aloud.

"Who ever said Mike wasn't?"

"Nobody," Tommy said, his attention back to his lieutenant. "Jamie, this is the best day of my life! You and me and Davey are all going to see the King of England! How can you not be excited?"

Jamie looked briefly away. "You don't really want me to answer that, Tommy. I don't want to spoil your happy day."

"You couldn't. So tell me."

The Australian sighed, looked back at the American. "I would've rather stayed at the front with my men. I don't want to see this man – and that's all he is, a man

– after seein' so many good men die in his name. I suppose it ain't his fault – not like it's Haig's – but still…" Jamie could see he was in fact dimming Tommy's excitement, so he added, in a more lively tone, "And on top of all that, they take me aout of the line in the middle of the night, and drive me to Vadencourt, and I find aout I'm seein' the King of England, and my uniform's filthy, and they don't have any clean Australian Corps uniforms that fit me proper. So look what they did!"

He threw his arms out for emphasis, and Tommy remembered his initial mistake in the *château* hallway, when he'd thought Collins was talking to a British officer. "You're dressed like an Englishman!" the Doughboy exclaimed; then he started to laugh. "You're going to meet the King of England dressed like an Englishman."

"*Three times* today," Jamie reminded him, holding up three fingers for emphasis; then he, too, burst into gales of laughter. When, after a couple of minutes, they finally calmed down, it was Jamie who added, "Are you rested naow, Corp'ral Flaowuhs? We're goin' to be late for tea with His Royal Majesty."

Taking Colbeck's proffered hand so he could rise again, Flowers, quite overwhelmed, said, "When this is over, I wanna go back with you to the front."

"We'll see haow fast your leg heals. In the meantime, I don't want to leave the men with Dougherty for too long."

The mention of their least favorite sergeant unexpectedly caused them both to laugh again. Tommy tried to cool them off by asking, in all seriousness, "Do I look all right?"

"You look fit to meet a King, Tommy. Haow abaout me?"

To Tommy's surprise, Jamie also sounded serious, so the Yank assured him, "Like a proper English gentleman."

"Shut up, Flaowuhs," Colbeck said drily, and they both continued laughing as they made their way, Jamie slowing his pace to accommodate Tommy's leg.

# Chapter LIII

Out the back of the Château de Molliens and through the broad, open, relatively treeless space where Elsie Janis had cavorted three weeks earlier, the two walked until they reached a beautiful shady glade where dozens and dozens of American soldiers, mostly officers and all nattily attired, were milling about. Once again Tommy looked self-consciously down at his uniform. He decided he did, after all, hold his own in this gathering, and was again grateful he hadn't slept in his clothes, despite what sleeping out of them had led to with Glennon. Jamie, he thought, looked fine, too, however much the Aussie despised the English uniform he was wearing; it was clear they had cleaned him up at the hospital in Vadencourt, much as they had Tommy.

Though Jamie had said the three-hundred-man honor guard was drawn from every unit of the 33rd, Tommy didn't recognize a single soul among the crowd. Jamie was looking at a particularly large group clustered closer to the *château,* and he snarled to Tommy in a whisper, "Staff officers, ev'ry last one of 'em. They've never been aout from behind their desks, but on a day like this, here they all are. You'd think they were winnin' the war single-handed. That's one thing's the same in ev'ry army."

"Billy should be here instead of them," Tommy suggested back in a whisper.

"Damn right he should," said Colbeck, looking away from the coterie of staff officers, as if he truly couldn't stand the sight of them, and toward the other side of the glade. "You wanna meet the boys gettin' the medals?"

"Don't reckon I know any of 'em. Any from E Company?"

"I caounted nine that were, aout of abaout twenty medals. But not one from aour platoon."

"Really? Why?"

Jamie gave Tommy a look. "We sawr some hard action at Hamel, but they sawr worse."

"But Ski–" Tommy began, and Jamie cut him off:

"Don't even think that way, Tommy. They ain't bringin' the King of England all the way here to give Pom medals to dead Americans."

"Pom medals?"

"Yes, Pom medals. Did you think he'd be givin' aout American medals?"

That made sense when Tommy thought about it. "So you said there were twenty medals?"

"Yes, but not twenty men here to get 'em. Abaout twelve, I heard."

"Are the others–?"

"Their wounds are too bad. They're all in hospital."

"So the King'll go to the hospital to give 'em theirs, right?"

Jamie frowned. "He's the King, Tommy. He don't *have* to go anywhere."

"If men in the hospital can get medals, then why not Billy?–"

"These are for Hamel, remember? Not for what just happened – what's still goin' on. With all the paper-pushin' brass it takes to give aout these trinkets, it takes time."

"You shouldn't call them that, Jamie," Tommy said, meaning the medals, not the paper pushers.

"I call 'em what I please, Corp'ral," Colbeck said, spitting for emphasis.

That resurrected another thought in Flowers' mind: "Am I really a corporal, Jamie?"

Colbeck stared at him. "What a question."

"It's just – they gave me this uniform, and I don't know if Billy told anyone, or they just took my word for it."

Jamie shook his head. "When we had dinner with Billy that night in the trench at Gressaire, he'd already made you a corp'ral, right?"

"Right–"

"And he wasn't wounded 'til the next mornin', right?"

Tommy had to think about that; then he repeated, "Right."

"So that's probably twelve haours or more. Billy's famous among the officers for bein' efficient with his paperwork. We could probably all learn from him on that score."

Tommy laughed. "About paperwork?"

"Don't laugh, lad. Paperwork matters in a modern army, whether you and me like it or not." Tommy was duly chastened as Jamie looked about them. "They're gonna want us in line in a minute. Let's beat 'em to it."

"You know where we're supposed to stand?" asked Flowers, limping after him.

"Of course. Follow me."

"How come you know so much, Jamie?"

The Australian turned to his young American friend with a smirk. "Sometimes I do my paperwork. And, I have my ways."

Now it was Flower of Iowa who rolled his eyes and shook his head. "I don't know why I bothered to ask."

★

The sun nearly did Tommy in. The glorious early morning had turned downright hot as noontime drew near, and the honor guard was standing at attention well before a certain amount of clamor made it clear the royal visitor was drawing near. Sweating under his field cap, Tommy could hear a band strike up "America," then remembered it was also "God Save the King." There was more patriotic music, and then there was simply more waiting at attention in the hot sun. After minutes on end, Tommy couldn't stand it, and he whispered to Jamie, on his left, "What are they doing?"

"I told you, takin' tea," Jamie muttered back; and just at that moment, they heard a great commotion coming from the direction of the *château.*

Flowers and Colbeck were not well placed within the three-sided hollow square formed by the honor guard; they were near one of the farthest corners, which put them a long way from the dozen Doughboys uneasily awaiting their rewards at the other end. Tommy had seen pictures of King George V, but he was so engrossed at the sight of General Pershing, a tall, imposing man with a mustache, that he didn't take much notice of the shorter, bearded man in the British military uniform to the general's right until the King, Pershing and another man in British khaki ("Rawly," Jamie whispered) drew up to the tables where the decorations were placed. As each of the lucky dozen was called up, the dignitaries' faces were mostly obscured to Colbeck and Flowers' line of sight, and yet they didn't have a good view of the decorated men, either; and they couldn't hear a thing.

Tommy felt Jamie glance over at him once during the medal-awarding ceremony, which was concluded with dispatch. He thought maybe the King would come over afterward to inspect the honor guard, or at least that Pershing and Rawlinson would, but the entourage left as quickly as it came. Once the King and the generals left, the honor guard quickly dispersed, with many of the men rushing over to the decorated soldiers to offer their congratulations and admire the medals.

Jamie turned to Tommy and informed him, "I'm gonna have to follow His Royal Majesty."

"He's going to Querrieu next, isn't he? Can I come?"

Jamie laughed a little at Tommy's eagerness. "You're not invited. And anyhaow, ain't you been disappointed enough for one day?"

"I wasn't disappointed, Jamie, I just–"

"–and you got a commandin' officer waitin' to see you in Vadencourt. Lieutenant Collins will make sure you get a ride there. And Tommy?"

"What?"

"I know you're the last person I need to tell to mind his manners, but – don't tell Billy haow this really went."

"Why not, Jamie? I got to see a King!"

Jamie's response was to glance heavenward and offer a perfectly sincere "Thank God for you, lad.

"Now I really have to get aout of here," the lieutenant added. "You can take your time, of course. The way things look, you got no choice, anywise."

"Are you going right back to the front?"

"I daoubt it. Prob'ly see you later in Querrieu," Jamie replied as he hurried away.

★

Alighting in Vadencourt about an hour after the sun had been directly overhead, Flowers had to stop and scratch his head as he remembered it hadn't been twenty-four hours since he'd first arrived here at the hospital. Since then he'd seen a King, slept with Michael Glennon, and decided to marry Nicole Lacroix. Holy smoke, he thought, Jamie better be in Querrieu later; I never asked him about what Madame said.

He was struck, too, as he wandered inside, by the contrast of the two *châteaux* he'd shuttled between the past two days, the one now a divisional headquarters, the other a medical facility. Limping along, he abruptly saw a familiar face: the medical corporal whose kindness and efficiency had impressed him the day before. Tommy called out to him, and the young man swung his head around and peered at Flowers, trying to place him.

"You helped me out yesterday," Tommy reminded him. "I was asking about Captain Sand?"

The medic returned Flowers' level gaze and nodded. "I remember. So you're back to see him?"

"I have orders to see him."

The medical corporal allowed a slight smile. "At least I know where he is today. He's been giving orders ever since he came to. I'll take you there." As Tommy walked over to follow his lead, the man noted Flowers' limp and said, "You haven't been keeping off that leg."

"I tried. I had to stand at attention this morning for the King of England."

"Go on."

"Really. Hey," Tommy added as the man began walking away and he followed, "don't you have a name?"

"Cline," he called over his shoulder.

Corporal Cline led Flowers down a couple of corridors to an open, sunny courtyard out back of the *château,* a place greener, shadier, and more full of casual life than its counterpart at Molliens. There, out from underneath a linden tree, conspicuously removed from its shade, a pale blond man in a bathrobe lay napping in a wheelchair. The medical corporal tapped the captain's shoulder, cleared his throat and said, "Sir. You should be in the shade. And you have a visitor." Turning to Tommy as Billy came awake, Cline added, "Think you can take it from here?"

"I'm sure of it." Flowers watched Cline walk away, then swung his head back, and drank in the picture of his captain alive and alert. He couldn't think of anything to say, was afraid he might say or do something unsoldierly, and finally Sand spoke in that calm voice of his:

"Hello, Tommy."

Smiling broadly, Tommy slowly saluted, deliberately taking his time, and said, "Sir." They just regarded each other for a moment, then Tommy found his voice: "My orders are to take you into the shade, sir."

"Then do it." As Tommy grasped the wheelchair from behind, Billy added, "Even though I was enjoying the sun."

"Orders are orders, Captain."

Sand laughed lightly, then began to cough a little as Tommy parked him under the linden. When the cough didn't stop, Flowers became alarmed and asked, "Should I call for the doctor?"

Billy's cough subsided even as Tommy asked this, and he shook his head. "I'm all right."

"Are you, sir? Are you really?"

Sand looked up at him and said, "I have two orders for you, to start with, Corporal. One, quit calling me 'sir,' for the time being at least. And two, stop standing there and come sit down next to me. I'm getting tired of looking up at you."

"Yes, sir," Tommy said, placing himself on the cool grass, to Sand's front and right. It felt good to get both off his feet and out of the sun. But most of all it felt good to be talking to Billy.

"I suppose you'll never learn to obey orders properly," Sand added wearily. "Now, how's your leg?"

"I asked you first, Billy."

That made Sand laugh again, without a cough. "*Touché,* Tommy. All right, we'll talk about me first. I'm going to need some more operations. But they say this probably won't kill me."

"So Captain Block was wrong?"

"Not necessarily. Seems some of the shrapnel shifted the other way, closer to the surface, during our little voyage."

"Do you – do you remember any of it, Captain?"

"Very little, Tommy. Very little. But I do remember you saved my life."

Tommy flushed at this, and looked at the ground. "I – uh – ah – thank you for getting me in to see the King, sir. It was the most exciting thing that's ever happened to me."

"Tommy," came a stern voice, "look at me." Flowers obediently looked up; Sand was leaning forward somewhat in his wheelchair, in a fashion that Tommy still found alarming in terms of the shrapnel. "I was thanking you for saving my life, soldier," the captain went on. "Now, I know you don't want the credit. But don't deny me the chance to thank you."

"Yes, sir."

"Quiet, Tommy; I'm not finished." Sand leaned back in his wheelchair, paused a bit, then said, "You know, when we were in that trench, you cared more about saving my life than anyone–"

"I couldn't just let you die, Billy!" Flowers cried out with considerable feeling, and Sand smiled indulgently at the interruption:

"But I was ready to, Tommy. I was really resigning myself to dying. But now that you've done… what you did… I'm so glad. I want to live. I want to see Mrs. Sand again, and my parents, too." It seemed odd to Flowers, picturing Billy with parents, since he thought of Sand as such an adult himself. The captain continued, "So I'll say thank you once and for all, here and now, and then I'll leave you alone about it."

"Beg pardon, sir, but Private Pearson deserves as much credit as me. And then there was Private Sleziniak, and even the prisoner–"

"–and Captain Block, too. Yes, I know. But you were the one who figured it all out." Sand raised his good hand, rubbed his chin. "It always comes back to Pearson with you, doesn't it?"

Tommy froze, tried not to show it. "Sir?"

"You two are just tight as ticks." Tommy was afraid to say anything in reply to that, and when he didn't, Sand went on, "Is he all right, do you know?"

"He's probably seeing his King about now, Captain."

"Aha. And how was seeing the King?"

"Like I told you, Billy, it was the most exciting thing! I can't wait to write… home." Davey and home one right after the other were too much for Tommy, who stumbled on: "And Captain?"

"Yes?"

"You remember that French girl, Nicole?"

"From the *estaminet?* Yes."

"I'm – I'm gonna marry her, sir."

"You are?" he asked, surprised. "Where did this come from?"

"I – I have to, sir."

"What do you mean, you have to?" Sand asked jovially; but then he caught Flowers' look. "Tommy, you… *have* behaved honorably toward this girl, haven't you?"

At that, the Doughboy turned crimson, stammering, "I – sir, I…"

The captain's face darkened. "I take it that means otherwise."

"Sir, I…"

"Just tell me if it's not true."

Now ashen, Tommy looked down at his shoes. "I – can't, sir."

Sand's warm tone had turned chillier. "I see. I expected better of you, Tommy. You know you should do right by this young lady."

"Yes, sir." Tommy said, looking up. "I intend to."

Billy nodded in apparent approval. "Have you asked her yet?"

"No, sir."

"And you do love her?"

It was a question Flowers didn't want to hear, but he answered it honestly. "No, sir, I don't."

Sand sighed, and his expression clouded further. "Do you think you can learn to?"

"I hope so, sir."

"I hope so, too, Tommy," said Sand, the doubt palpable in his voice. There was a short, uncomfortable silence, then Billy changed the subject: "You never told me: how's your leg?"

"I need to stay off it for a while, they say… Captain?"

"Now what?"

"Do you still need me to write Gillis' folks for you?"

Sand shook his head. "No, Tommy. I did that almost as soon as I was able."

"So, I reckon you don't need me as your adjutant any more."

Sand arched one eyebrow. "I thought you promised me the rest of the war, Tommy."

Flowers smiled back at him. "I thought you hardly remembered anything, Billy."

Sand smiled at that in return; but then he looked away and said, "I don't think I'll be going back to the front." He looked back at Flowers. "And that's where you want to be, isn't it?"

Now Tommy looked down again. "As long as there's a war, sir." Looking back up, he said, "But if they tell me I can't because of my leg, there's nothing more I'd rather do than be your adjutant."

"Even if it meant going back to America?"

"Even, sir."

Billy flashed one of those large, unexpected smiles, and now it was Tommy who had to look away. Flowers was suddenly a bit restless; he needed to see Jamie in Querrieu, to find out what Madame had meant about Nicole, and of course David was there, too. Almost as if he were David, reading Tommy's thoughts, Billy said, "You're in a hurry to get somewhere, aren't you?"

Flower of Iowa redirected his attention to Billy Sand. "Captain, I feel like I waited a long time to see you sitting up and well. I'm in no hurry."

Sand yawned in reply. "Well, you won't see me sitting up much longer. I've been awake since midnight or so."

"You want me to wheel you back to your bed?"

"Yes, Corporal, why don't you do that? Then I'm ordering you to report to

Querrieu – and then back here, tomorrow. And stay off that leg!"

Rising and grabbing the chair from behind again, and pushing it playfully, a little too fast, Tommy, full of high spirits, gave the only possible reply: "Aye aye, Captain."

★

After he'd seen Billy to his hospital bed, Tommy remembered there was at least one other patient at Vadencourt he should check on, so once again he sought out Corporal Cline. "It's about the other man I came here with–" he began.

"That German kid? He's gone. We don't know what happens to prisoners once they leave here."

Tommy hadn't even thought about Hans, but he found Cline's comment unsettling. Still he persisted, "I meant Sleaze. Private Sleziniak."

"Oh. The shell-shock case. No one's allowed to see him."

Flowers was stunned – not least by the ease with which Cline used this term, given Captain Block's reaction when Tommy had dared use it in his presence. "Can you at least tell me if he's all right?" he eventually managed to ask.

Cline visibly considered his answer. "Well, he's not dead," he finally said, in a voice from which Tommy inferred that death might be preferable.

# Chapter LIV

Tommy could tell by the sun that it was already past midafternoon when he disembarked from a British ambulance in the village of Querrieu, in front of a large, bare, square building he was told went by the name of the "Prison Cage." There he reported, for the second time that day, to Lieutenant Collins, who sat somewhat flustered at a desk so disorganized that it seemed it should have been manned by somebody else. As he lifted his countenance at the sight of the freshly arrived soldier, Collins looked considerably more harried than he had that morning. "What are you doing here, Corporal?" he snapped. "You were supposed to go to Vadencourt."

"I did, sir. My captain ordered me here, and then back there tomorrow."

Collins exhaled in apparent irritation, surveyed his desk, and muttered, "One more thing to do." Then he looked back up at Flowers and added, "I can't possibly handle your billets right now, Corporal. I only just got here myself."

Tommy, all sympathy, said, "They moved you here, sir?"

"They're in the process of moving the entire 66th Brigade here."

It took only about a second to register. "You mean we're leaving Pierregot and Molliens?"

"Division headquarters is staying at Molliens. The 65th Brigade, which has been moving from place to place while your brigade stayed at Pierregot, is moving to Pierregot. And your brigade is coming here."

"But, sir, why? That doesn't make any sense."

Collins regarded Flowers balefully. "Soldier, weren't you ever taught not to ask why?"

"Y-yes, sir. It's just that, to leave Pierregot, after all this time–"

"All this time? Seven weeks?"

Seven weeks? Could that really be all, Tommy thought, but Collins was still talking: "If you must look for an explanation, Corporal Flowers, you might consider the fact that your battalion has helped to push the front forward. The front goes forward, brigade HQ goes forward."

"Wow!" was Tommy's inadvertent reaction.

One would have thought he had spoken in French, the way Collins repeated, "'Wow'?"

"Yes, sir. When you're out there, at the front, you don't think about how what you do could change things in the back areas."

"Isn't that what this is all about?" Collins responded, almost cheerfully. "Making the world safe for democracy, one village at a time?"

Tommy couldn't believe the Wilson lookalike had actually used that phrase. "Yes, sir," he replied. "I reckon you're right."

"Oh, and speaking of the larger world, Corporal Flowers, I almost forgot. There was some Tommy came looking for you a while ago. I told him you were in Vadencourt, not here, but he asked if he might come back again later, to see if you showed up here."

Flowers wasn't surprised; indeed, at this point the greater surprise would have been Pearson not making an appearance. "Would you remember, sir, when that was? Or did he say when he might come back?"

Collins frowned. "No on both counts, soldier. Although he couldn't have been here too long ago. I haven't been here that long myself."

"Would it be all right if I waited for him here, sir?"

The frown deepened. "I'm very busy, Corporal."

"Oh, I wouldn't wait *here,* sir. Somewhere out front."

The frustrated lieutenant pursed his lips and regarded the corporal. "That might work," he conceded. "Since, as I told you, it will be a little while before I can get things in order here. What about your leg?"

"I'll find someplace to sit and rest it while I wait."

"All right," Collins, clearly glad to be rid of Flowers for the moment, said with a quick, dismissive wave of his hand. For his part, Tommy was glad for Collins' vagueness, which left him free to formulate his own plans as soon as either David or Jamie, or both, caught up with him.

There wasn't anywhere immediately outside the Prison Cage that met Tommy's requirements of a place where he could sit and rest his leg – an order he was now taking quite seriously – and also stay out of the sun (though that was past its peak for the day) and keep clear of the dust being kicked up by the passing traffic. Ultimately he did spot a spindly sapling across the road, which provided a little bit of shade if he sat under it just right – a position that still gave him a line of sight to the HQ door, in case Davey or Jamie returned there.

As he watched the road that lay between him and HQ, the volume of traffic – human, animal, and mechanical – seemed incredible to Tommy. Querrieu lay athwart the road from Amiens to Albert, a far more principal thoroughfare than those which ran through either Pierregot or Molliens. As he regarded the men, the mules, the caissons – which caused him to start whistling the song about caissons rolling along – he thought, when they talk about the "machinery of war," this is what they mean: all these men and all this equipment in motion, keeping up with the front as it surges back and forth. Somehow the thought of it left him as awestruck as the sight of a battlefield. Who decided to move all these people? No wonder Lieutenant Collins couldn't straighten up his desk, much less find somewhere for a mere misplaced corporal to sleep.

He hadn't sat there for ten minutes, though it was more than five, when a motorcar pulled up in front of the Prison Cage and discharged a particularly smart-looking English leftenant who, Tommy knew, was no English leftenant at all. Tossing aside decorum as Colbeck had taught him, Flowers hollered "Jamie!" out from under his sapling, and the Aussie turned, smiled, and walked away from the Prison Cage, seating himself next to his young friend, but in the sun.

"Where'd you come from?" Tommy asked congenially, and Jamie answered in a similar mood, "Villers-Bretonneux. I've just been talkin' to Gen'ral Monash."

It no longer seemed unusual to Flowers that his lieutenant friend might be taking tea with the head of the Australian Army. "And?" he asked.

Jamie picked a blade of grass, stuck the better part of it between his lips, and said, "I hate to say it, but maybe we really did do somethin' this time."

Tommy sat up a little straighter, hugging the knees of both his good and bad legs. "You reckon so?"

"Maybe. Sir John wanted to hear my accaount of the front. But he said it just confirmed what he already knew."

"Which was–?"

Colbeck seemed to be looking off toward the front. "German deserters by the hundreds. Jerry pushed back all along this line. And Foch has the sense not to give them a rest. It could be what we've waited for… though we've thought *that* before, too." Looking back to Tommy, Jamie added, "He also asked what I thought abaout aour American allies."

"And you said–?"

"Good fighters. Don't let it go to your head, though – not good enough to win the war all by yourselves. But maybe, along with the rest of us, good enough to make the diff'rence." Tommy gaped at this version of high praise from Jamie, and Colbeck hastened to add, "Of course, I could be all wrong abaout all of this."

"You and General Monash?"

"Maybe. And even if we ain't, Jerry won't stay on the run. He'll hit back, fight for ev'ry yard, all the way back to the Rhine if it comes to that. Plenty more men will die, even if we do finally win. Which we may not, anywise."

Flowers rolled his eyes. "God forbid you should bring too much good news, Jamie."

"You watch your smart maouth," the Australian said without rancor. Then, as if it were part of the same conversation, he said, "Haow's Billy?"

"Good," Tommy replied. "Good." Trying to get used to the idea, he added, "But if we do have to fight all the way to the Rhine, I reckon he won't be with us."

Jamie, understanding, nodded. "Still, what you did–"

"Would you be our captain then?"

"Hah! What an imagination you have – me, a captain–"

"I can remember when you didn't want to be a lieutenant."

"And like I said, you have a smart maouth." Jamie took a long pause, then, not looking at Tommy, continued in an unusually low voice, "Pershing wants his own army, y'know. He don't like it when you American boys fight in units attached to the French, the British, even us Australians. He wants his own army – and his own officers."

Tommy was not as slow to grasp some things as he once had been. "You mean – we might go forward without you *or* Billy?"

Jamie gave a mirthless grin. "You'd still have Dougherty."

"That's not funny, Jamie."

"No. But it may happen."

Tommy contemplated this, couldn't stand it, and asked, "Jamie?"

"I hate it when you say 'Jamie?' like that. What is it naow?"

"Promise you won't get mad if I ask you something?"

Not at all kindly, Colbeck replied, "What's it matter if I do?"

It was enough to make Tommy want to take back his next question, but he couldn't, not now. Drawing a deep breath, he began, "Last night, Mike Glennon and I stayed at Madame's *estaminet*."

Tommy thought he saw the slightest tremor run through Jamie, but he couldn't be sure. Impassively the lieutenant said, "I figured that from what you said before. You stayed in Nicole's room, I suppose?"

Jamie, Tommy knew, would not be casting aspersions on Nicole the way Mike had. "So you knew she went away?"

"Of course." Not until after Jamie said it did he realize maybe Tommy hadn't.

"Do you think it was because of me?"

Very cautiously, Jamie said, "What do you mean, 'because of me'?"

Tommy did not want to be discussing this with Jamie of all people, and he could feel himself turning red, and hating himself for it. "Because of I, uh – of what we..." He faltered.

"Because you fucked her?" Jamie offered, his tone deadly.

The language caused a snapping within Tommy; in a voice he'd never used with Jamie, or few others for that matter, he cried, "Stop talking like that! That's my future wife you're talking about!"

Jamie seemed to freeze for many long seconds. Finally he said calmly, "Does she know this?"

Colbeck relaxed somewhat in response to Flowers' negative shake of the head. Jamie let the ensuing silence just sit between them, until at last Tommy said, "I don't know where they sent her. Do you?"

"No," Jamie said flatly.

"I thought you might. Mike asked her – Madame – in French, and all she would say was 'Tell him Jacques was right.' What did she mean by that, Jamie?"

Jamie took a beat, asked Tommy to repeat: "What did she say?"

"'Tell him Jacques was right.'"

Instead of answering, Jamie suddenly said, "Do you love her?"

"I'll – I'll learn to love her, Jamie–"

"And what abaout your Susan?"

"I'm – trying to do what's right–"

"What's *right?*" Colbeck said, his voice rising. "You already failed to do what's right."

"I know," Tommy agreed, but he added, "I'm trying to set it right." Colbeck merely glowered in response, and Flowers desperately continued, "Billy says it's the right thing to do."

"Billy? Billy already has a wife he loves! What does he know?"

"He knows about honor."

Colbeck could not hide his fury. "And I don't? And you do?"

"I didn't say that, Jamie!" Tommy insisted. "Look, I'm sorry, I know you love her, but I'm the one who has to make it right–"

*"But do you love her?"*

*"No!"* Tommy admitted in a near-shout that attracted attention from passersby, and he added, almost in a whisper, "No, not yet. But there are some things that are more important–"

"Listen to the expert! We're talkin' abaout marriage here! When you're talkin' abaout that, there ain't nothin' more important."

They looked away from each other, and a cold silence fell between them, though neither one made a move to leave. At length Tommy swallowed and said, "Jamie?"

"I told you, I hate it when you do that."

"Jamie, will you ask Madame what she meant? If not for me, then for Nicole?"

Jamie turned and held Tommy's gaze. Very, very slowly, his aspect changed, though Tommy couldn't describe just how. "Not for your sake," he finally said with a slight nod. "For Nicole's."

Tommy smiled with relief. "Thanks, Jamie. Thanks. Maybe we could even go tonight–"

"Not 'we,' Corp'ral. Not you. Just me."

"But–"

"You're confined to quarters," Colbeck, suddenly rising to his feet, ordered.

"But I don't have any quarters–"

"So stay right here, then. You're supposed to stay off that leg anywise, and I'm going to have to walk all the way to Rainneville." Seeming to relent slightly, Jamie added, "Maybe your little English playmate will come along and have a better idear."

Jamie's choice of words stirred Tommy's resentment, even as he asked, "What's – is something wrong?"

"Nothin's wrong, Flaowuhs. Nothin'. You've given me *my* mission, for a change. And naow I'm off on it." Colbeck smirked, almost like Dougherty. "So wish us both luck."

"But what am I supposed to–?" Tommy began.

"Why don't you work on the letter you're goin' to have to write your dear Susan?" Jamie said acidly, before turning on his heel and taking off at a virtual run in the direction of – Tommy could only assume – Rainneville.

# Chapter LV

The distance between Querrieu and Rainneville was not a considerable one – about seven miles to the northwest, with the way angling through the village of St-Gratien – but Colbeck had, after all, started the day shortly after midnight, moving his platoons into position on the Somme near Étinehem; then he'd taken the long ride back to Vadencourt, where he'd seen Billy and gotten cleaned up; and since then, he'd been through no less than three royal ceremonies, at Molliens, Querrieu, and Villers-Bretonneux, not to mention his meeting with General Monash at that last village… and then it had been back to Querrieu, and Tommy's quite unexpected announcement. All that, and Jamie couldn't remember when he'd last slept; in fact, he couldn't have remembered had he been posed the same question at midnight, before the day's marathon had begun. Trench life in general was hardly conducive to sleep, but trench life in command of inexperienced troops who depended on you, with no one worth the trusting to spell you, made the very thought of rest impossible, at least to an officer like Colbeck.

All of these circumstances converged on Jamie as he plodded on toward Rainneville. He recognized the feeling; when you allowed yourself to relax even a little, after being at such a state of high alert for so long, the resulting fatigue was of an order unimaginable to a civilian. Even being a man possessed – a man, as he'd told Tommy, on a mission – couldn't save the Aussie from bone weariness. As a result, the journey (all on foot, as he'd predicted; with the action of the war flowing eastward, there was no vehicular traffic between the two villages to take advantage of) took him the better part of two hours.

The sun was low in the sky, though it hadn't set, when he finally trudged up to the hilltop main street of Rainneville… which turned out to be full of strange Doughboys. This initially came as a surprise, until Jamie thought about the situation: he knew the 65th Brigade was moving into the 66th's old haunts in Pierregot, and he also knew anytime soldiers hit new billets, at the first spare moment they would make a reconnaissance of the nearest *estaminet*. Madame, he thought to his chagrin, would be in her element, her place overrun with customers after a long drought. This was not the scenario he'd bargained for when he'd set out from Querrieu.

And sure enough, the line outside her establishment was long and full with Doughboys, none of whom was familiar to Jamie. The Australian wearily took his place at the end, contemplating stratagems for improving his position, and thereby hastening his admittance to the *estaminet*. Even if it meant falling asleep on his feet or getting into a fight, he wasn't leaving Rainneville until he spoke with the old woman.

★

Back in Querrieu, Flowers sat numb beneath his assigned sapling, still smarting over Colbeck's once again turning on him after the subject of Nicole surfaced. It was, Tommy thought, as if Jamie became a completely different person, some kind of lunatic he didn't recognize. The Doughboy realized, of course, that his lieutenant loved the girl he planned to marry, probably far more than he himself ever could; but he also had expected the Aussie to be rational and understanding of his own intention to be honorable, however belated. At least Tommy could count on David to behave more sensibly – if he ever showed up.

The afternoon shadows were stretching longer, and Tommy was beginning to contemplate how well he would be able to sleep under this skinny tree, next to this busy road. He had been trying, with no success, to compose in his head the very letter Jamie had taunted him about, the one telling Susan he was marrying a French girl. All that did was make his head ache; and when he thought about writing the same news to his folks, his head ached even worse. Lying down full-length on the sparse grass, he closed his eyes against the sun, but could feel himself inhaling the dust from the road, so he sat up again and looked around in despair. The sapling was too weak for leaning; where could he sleep tonight without choking?

"Are you lost, Sammy?"

Tommy looked up, temporarily dazzled by the light, and replied, "No, sir, I–"

"'Oo you calling 'sir'?" came a warm and familiar voice as the inquisitive Englishman crouched down to face him. As he finally focused on David, Tommy's first thought was, he looks so wonderful. And indeed Pearson, who was wearing his own crisp, clean dress uniform and had his hair carefully combed, looked every inch the proper soldier, fit to participate in a royal ceremony. "'Ello? Tommy? Is there anyone at 'ome?" he continued, cocking his head from side to side.

Simply repeating what was on his mind, Tommy stated in a low voice, "You look wonderful."

"'Ere," David scolded in a similar register. "You shou'n't be talking like that 'ere."

"Sorry. But you do. And I'm just so glad you're here–"

"And I'm glad to find you 'ere. But why were you looking like a little lost lad just now?"

"Jamie's ordered me to stay right here, 'til he gets back. And I don't know if he'll be back before tomorrow."

"Tomorrow? Where'd 'e go?"

"To Rainneville. To Madame's."

Pearson, still crouching, straightened his cap and grinned. "Busy place, that Madame's. I 'ear you and Mike stayed there last night." Tommy flushed, feeling for the first time he'd betrayed David; but he could only assume Glennon hadn't told the whole story of their evening, and rather than respond, he let David go on: "But it does seem a bit rude of Jamie to go there to stay the night, and leave you 'ere all by yusself like this."

It was a perfect opportunity for Tommy to inform David of his decision to marry Nicole, but something stopped him from doing so. Instead he told the Briton, "He said if you could come up with someplace for me to stay, that was the one exception to his order."

David broke into one of his sunny smiles, and suddenly Tommy realized why he hadn't been able to tell him: it was the American's own selfishness; he wanted to keep things the same with Pearson as long as he could. Oblivious, David said, "Per'aps I can arrange something. I was coming to tell you, Mike's got wind the Rangers are to be relieved. They'll be on the march tonight, to the Bois d'Escardonneuse. By tomorrow, we'll bivouac there–"

Several thoughts stormed through Flowers' head at once, but the uppermost, to which he first gave voice, was "'We' who?"

"Why, Mike and me, of course."

"I don't wanna sleep with Mike tonight," Tommy blurted out, and David looked puzzled – and troubled.

"'Ere, that's not a very nice thing to say, after 'e put you up at 'is own expense last night. And 'twasn't what I meant, anyways." Pearson stared at Flowers, who tried to look away, but not quickly enough. "What is it, Tommy? Did something 'appen between you two?"

It was all happening too fast for Tommy, who swung his head back to David and pleaded in a soft voice, "I just wanna be with you tonight, all right? Just you."

David blushed slightly, but he looked pleased, and glanced at the ground as he answered quietly, "Cor, Tommy, mind 'ow you talk out in public." Looking up and looking cautiously about, he added, "I thought we agreed that 'ere in France–"

"We already broke that one, Davey, remember?"

His gaze now steady, Pearson responded, "Yes, love, I remember."

"So, if you're off to the Bois de – Bois de–"

"D'Escardonneuse."

"–whatever, tomorrow, and we're moving from Pierregot, who knows when we'll see each other again?"

"'Tisn't so far, Tommy. Just the other side of Querrieu, between 'ere and Bonnay. Not so much more than it was between Pierregot and Molliens."

"Oh." Tommy made no effort to conceal his relief. "Still–"

"Still, every night at liberty is precious. I understand."

"So you are at liberty?"

David smiled once more. "I suppose I am. If Mike covers for me."

With a newfound cold practicality, Tommy declared, “He will.” If he doesn’t, thought Flowers, I’ve got something I can tell his superiors.

David didn’t argue with Tommy’s confident prediction; instead, taking Glennon’s cooperation as a given, he went on in a near whisper, “Are you sure about this, love?”

“Absolutely, Davey. Absolutely.”

Pearson slowly nodded, then with equal deliberation rose to his feet. “All right. You stay ’ere and I’ll see what I can find. ’Twon’t be easy, y’know. I’ll be back soon’s I can.”

Without another word from either of them, Pearson walked away – or rather, limped away, Flower of Iowa realized as he watched. Here everyone’s worrying about my leg, he thought, and Davey’s probably had that much pain every day. Tommy wasn’t sure if he’d insisted on this plan of action on his own behalf or David’s, but suddenly it seemed the most important thing in the world, and Nicole, Susan, and his folks were a long way from his thoughts.

Jamie was no longer the last man in line, but he was still a goodly way from the *estaminet* door, and it was growing dark. He knew Madame would do her best to skirt the closing rules in order to make a maximum profit, but soon enough even she would have to close the place for the evening, perhaps without ever catching sight of him. He had tried to figure out various clever gambits for jumping the line, but none of them held together long enough in his now-fuzzy brain to even justify the attempt. Worn out and frustrated, he sighed to himself, “God, I’m so tired.”

“You’re English, aren’t you?”

Jamie hadn’t quite been aware he’d spoken out loud. His eyes focused on the Doughboy who stood in line in front of him, who had turned around to ask him this question. “No, you silly bugger, I’m Australian,” Colbeck said, his voice more civil than his words.

The Doughboy, who looked like Tommy, or Frank Gillis, or any number of men Jamie had commanded, asked with a combination of awe and friendliness, “Were you at the front?”

“Up ’til this mornin.’”

At this, the young Doughboy simply stood aside, in a clear motion for Colbeck to move ahead of him. The gesture was so like what Gillis had once done that Jamie was surprised to feel a momentary stab over the loss of the Pennsylvanian. Poor Frank. But then, he had known so many poor Franks over the past four years. To the Aussie’s amazement, this deferential American went still further, calling to his friends ahead of him, “Hey, fellas, our ally here is just back from the front.”

The assorted Doughboys turned around and, within seconds, Jamie found himself standing at the front door of the *estaminet.* It rarely happened to him, but Colbeck was dumbfounded; in trying to gain the front of the line, it had never occurred to him to prevail on the decency of these Yanks. Biting his lip, he turned back to them, forced a smile, and said, "Thanks, mates." Turning around once more to face the door, he thought about the American boys he commanded, the lads he'd left behind on the Somme, and it was almost too much, even for him.

Fortunately, at that moment a rowdy crew of Doughboys noisily exited the *estaminet,* and Jamie, again focused on his mission, wasted no time elbowing into the familiar place, and headed straight for the bar. Madame saw him coming; and rather than dismay like the last time he'd been there, or the surprise or joy of earlier days, her face reflected a simple satisfaction. As he reached the bar, she leaned forward and said, *"Je t'ai t'attendu, M'sieu Jacques."* It did not escape his notice that she used the intimate form of "you" as she told him she'd been waiting for him.

*"Il faut que je vois Nicole,"* he demanded inelegantly, but the old woman unexpectedly and enigmatically smiled before replying, *"Pourquoi?"*

Why indeed did he need to see Nicole? *"Parce que je voudrais l'épouser."*

Fortunately the *estaminet* was chock-a-block full of Americans, none of whom – at least those nearby – had Billy Sand's facility for French; so none of the Doughboys surrounding the Australian and the Frenchwoman understood he had announced his attention to marry her niece. And Mme. Lacroix had no interest in betraying the gist of their conversation; she looked coolly at Colbeck while serving more drinks to the Yanks, and said, *"Nicole ne vas pas aller en Australie."*

*"Je resterais ici,"* Jamie said flatly, evoking another smile – but nothing more than that – from Madame, at the news he would be willing to stay in France to become Nicole's husband, rather than take her back to Australia.

She paid attention to a couple of more customers, while Colbeck's attention never left her. Finally, she came back over to him and said, *"Il faut le lui demande à elle."*

Hastening to assure her that he had always meant to ask Nicole herself, and not just arrange a marriage, Jamie answered, *"Mais bien sûr."*

A look of even greater satisfaction spread across Madame's face. *"Alors, M'sieu Jacques, tu lui demanderas toi-même, plus tard."*

Jamie's heart soared and his pulse raced: "Ask her yourself – later," Madame had told him. He slumped against the counter and tried to concentrate; he had the whole trip to Villers-Bocage to figure out just how he was going to persuade Nicole to agree to his proposal. As he stood there pondering, a young female voice came from behind him, inquiring, *"Une bière, m'sieur?"* and he turned to tell Odile that yes, he could use a beer.

Only it wasn't the glum young Belgian. It was the woman he wanted to marry, who Flowers wanted to marry, too. Dazed, Colbeck merely gave his order, *"Oui. S'il vous plaît."*

Nicole Lacroix did a slight curtsy in return, said, *"Mais bien sûr,"* then giggled and practically ran to the other side of the bar, the crowd of Doughboys notwithstanding. How much had she heard? Jamie Colbeck wondered. Had she been there all along? Or was *"Mais bien sûr"* just a coincidence?

★

Tommy still lay beneath the same scrawny tree as the last light began to fade. Once, during his long wait, an American lieutenant had stopped and demanded to know what he was doing there; but the officer was concerned mostly about malingerers and, upon hearing Flowers' story, didn't even offer to check with Lieutenant Collins to see if some arrangement had been made for the corporal. That was just as well for Tommy at the time, but as darkness began to close in, he was beginning to wonder. Even as he did, a familiar figure, looking rather less crisp than before, returned with a large kit in tow, and plopped down heavily on the dusty ground next to him.

"'Ere's the story," David began without introduction, speaking low and not looking at Tommy, as if they were planning a raid on an enemy trench so close by that the Germans were within earshot. "There's no place in town, or anywheres nearby; it's simple as that. The officers took them all, and anyplace else would be too far for me to walk tonight, far less you."

There was a brief quiet, then Tommy said, "Will you stay here with me, Davey?"

Pearson looked over at Flowers in the growing dark. "Per'aps we can do better than that, love. I sawr the Bois d'Escardonneuse. Tomorrow it will be full of Rangers, but tonight there's plenty of room there to pitch a two-man tent, like I 'ave 'ere with me. Even some pretty, out-of-the-way patches – peaceful, if the artillery from the front isn't too loud."

Flowers edged a little closer to Pearson. "And you know the way to them exactly, don't you?"

David nodded. "There's some problems with it, though."

"What?"

"It's a bit of a ways for you to walk, with that leg, for one."

"I'll chance it. What else?"

Now it was David who moved in closer to Tommy, so that their faces were mere inches from each other. "If Mike is right, the first Rangers won't be back there 'til morning. But if 'e's wrong, and they come back in the middle of the night and find us… well, you could imagine 'ow much trouble we'd be in then. They could put us both in prison. Per'aps even shoot us."

Tommy was particularly uneasy at the thought of trusting Glennon. "So where's Mike in all this?"

David drew a deep breath. "Mike's taking 'is own chances. 'E 'eard about a – a bawdy 'ouse, back on the ways to Amiens. 'E said 'e was going to try to find it, and stay there all night if he could."

Tommy felt a shiver of revulsion as he thought, last night, for Mike, it was me; tonight…

"Per'aps it's not worth it, love" came David's urgent whisper.

Tommy needed no time to think it over. "Oh, yes it is," he said decisively. "I say it is."

It was too dark for the American to really see the Englishman's smile in return, but Tommy felt it nonetheless. "All right, then, Corporal," David whispered. "Let's be off."

The wait in Gallipoli, with the barbed wire stuck in his back, seemed no longer and no more excruciating for Jamie than the wait for the *estaminet* to empty. The Doughboys of the 65th were particularly eager to sample the wares and atmosphere of Madame's establishment, and thus were in no hurry to leave, even after the proprietress announced she was no longer serving any more *bière* or *vin*. (Since none of the Americans spoke French, Jamie assisted in translating this, though Madame's emphatic gestures probably obviated the need for it.) In the meantime, Colbeck was making a conscious effort not to watch Nicole, even though she came back twice to ask if he wanted another beer, which he declined.

When at last the final Doughboy had been none-too-gently shoved out the front door, Mme. Eglantine placed the long wooden bolt across it, wiped her hands, then turned to Jamie and said, *"Un moment."* Only then did he realize Nicole was nowhere in sight. Madame smiled at him encouragingly as she ascended the stairs, presumably to summon her niece.

As he awaited the Frenchwomen's next move, Jamie sat and drummed his fingers on the bar, looking around the *estaminet* and thinking about his parents. Although, unlike his younger charges, he never talked about his mother and father, they were in fact alive, and he did write them, albeit infrequently. He considered their reaction if and when they learned their errant son had finally married. That would make for the second thing he'd done in his life (along with joining the army when the war broke out) that pleased them – at least, until they found out his wife was a French girl, who was having a baby sooner after the wedding than was respectable. That is, if Nicole was in fact pregnant. He had to wonder after seeing her so hard at work tonight; would even someone as avaricious as Mme. Lacroix make her own niece labor under such conditions? And then there was that other "if," of Nicole saying yes to him, which was no sure thing, especially if she wasn't actually carrying Flowers' child.

A noise at the top of the stairs – the slight clearing of a throat – interrupted his thoughts, and he glanced up to see the woman he loved, who seemed some sort of apparition, until she gave him a fluttering, nervous smile. She had changed her clothes, to a blue summer dress, and brushed her hair, which suddenly had a strange blue flower in it – a cornflower, he thought, as he watched her descend. Where had it come from?

He rose as she crossed over to him, and she gestured with assurance to one of the smaller tables. As they both sat down, she inquired politely after his health, as if seeing him for the first time that evening: "*Vous allez bien, M'sieur Jacques?*"

"*Oui,*" he said, a little breathlessly. "*Et vous, Mademoiselle?*"

"*Moi, je vais bien,*" she replied, and all he could think of was how beautiful she was, and how thoroughly in control of herself in such a difficult situation. There ensued an awkward silence, which Nicole broke by saying, "*Ma tante m'a dit que vous vouliez me dire quelque chose.*"

Emboldened by her boldness, he replied, "*Oui. Je voudrais que vous considérez vous faire ma femme.*"

Despite her own directness, she flushed at his, and her first response to his proposal of marriage was to gently correct his French, as she murmured, "*Devenir, Jacques. Pas faire.*"

"*Devenir,*" he repeated, and then suggested, "*Tu m'apprends. J'apprendrais.*"

"*J'y réfléchirai.*" Jamie understood; rather than responding to the idea that she teach him to improve his French, she was answering his first proposal, telling him she would think about it. But before he could say anything more, she continued, her voice halting, "*Mais… il y a… quelqelque chose.…*"

Her tone told him his original assessment of her situation had been right all along. "*Ce n'est pas nécessaire,*" he began.

She had paled, but her voice was strong as she interrupted him: "*Non. Vous avez le droit de savoir.*"

He didn't want the right to know, didn't want her to have to say it. He shook his head and said, "*Mais–*"

But she would not be stopped. "*Il y aura un bébé,*" she declared stoutly; then, having announced there would be a baby, she lifted her eyes to him in a mixture of defiance, hope, but above all fear.

He could see that, and he was ready with his answer. "*Je sais,*" he said plainly. "*C'est à moi.*"

Her eyes grew wide at his incredible statement, one they both knew to be untrue. Shaking her head, she insisted, "*Ce n'est pas possible,*" which was of course accurate; it was not possible that it could be his baby.

But when Colbeck simply repeated, more slowly, *"C'est à moi,"* Nicole threw her hands up to cover her face. He moved to comfort her, but with sudden resolution she broke free, running from the table and up the stairs.

Exercising an inordinate self-control he had learned at the front, Jamie did not follow her. He knew that Eglantine had been eavesdropping on them, even if the old woman was nowhere in sight. There was the slamming of a door, then the opening of a door, then the quieter closing of a door, then the muffled sound of the two women's voices. He couldn't tell what they were saying, but the pitches of both indicated high emotion.

The Australian sat back from the table and exhaled deeply. He'd done what he could, he thought. His mind moved in rapid, practical strides. He was determined to be ready for either answer. If she said yes, they would have to move quickly, because he had to be back in camp tomorrow. If she said no, he'd have to move even faster, proposing again to her, this time on Flowers' behalf – and then he'd drag the Doughboy back here bodily to ensure the marriage, if that was what it took.

David's scouting was as peerless as ever. A fair part of the Bois d'Escardonneuse was damaged after so much time so close to the front, and according to Pearson it was also crawling with MPs, so they skirted the northern edge of the forest and then made a dash, to avoid detection, across a road that ran between the villages of Bonnay and Lahoussoye. All of this appealed to Tommy's sense of adventure, so much so that he forgot about his leg.

On the other side of the road lay an escarpment with a panoramic view that faced the direction of the front. Looking at the considerable drop, discernible even in the darkness, Flower of Iowa, catching his breath, said, "We better not pitch our tent too close to the edge."

"We're not done, Tommy. We're too close to the road 'ere. We're going down there. I found a path."

No wonder David had been gone so long. It looked a foolhardy thing to try with his leg, and in the dark, but Flowers trusted Pearson completely. A tortuous descent led them down to a secluded glen – a site that, in addition to being at the bottom of the ravine, seemed surrounded on all sides by vegetation; yet the glen itself was clear, covered with soft grass. "How do you find these places?" Tommy asked, mostly rhetorically, as he finally sat himself down, exhausted, his leg aching.

"I have me ways," Davey replied laconically; then he added, with a worried glance at Tommy, "You're knackered. Let me pitch the tent."

"Come here first," Tommy commanded, in a tone that did not allow for a negative answer. Davey had chosen exceptionally well, even for Davey; though they were two to three miles closer to the front than when they'd started out, it felt here as though they were far away from the world, both the world of the war and the world they'd come from. Tommy had no fear they were just over a rise from a graveyard this time. Instead he was seized with a wild sense of freedom, and when Davey came over in response to his call, he seized him in that same spirit, to their mutual delight.

★

Jamie awoke from a dreamless sleep and peered at an expanse of wood, which turned out to be the table where he'd been sitting at the *estaminet*. How could he possibly have dozed off at a time like this? Then he thought again about his powerful fatigue on the walk over, and had the answer to his own question.

Looking up, he suddenly realized he hadn't just drifted awake; somebody had shaken him by the shoulder. His eyes focused on Madame; her eyes were red, and so his heart plummeted. He tried hard to concentrate, even as he dreaded hearing her words: *"Le curé est venu, M'sieu Jacques."*

The priest? he thought. What is she talking about?

Tears escaping her eyes, Eglantine added, *"Tu es un saint, Jacques. Un saint."*

Abruptly he understood, and was wide awake and roaring with laughter… until he saw the look on the face of his future – what would you call her, he thought, aunt-in-law? – and the dour mien of an old man in long black robes, standing behind her. Sobering instantly, he said gravely to Mme. Lacroix, *"Non, Madame, seulement un homme."* He was not a saint, only a man, but right now he felt he was a mighty lucky one.

Though Flowers and Pearson had finally pitched their tent, they lay, from the waist up, outside the enclosure, looking up at the stars, David's head in the crook of Tommy's arm. A sudden blast – artillery from the front, less than ten miles away – shook the night, and a tremor ran through Flowers, though not Pearson. "Ssh, ssh, love," David whispered, reaching his hand over to caress Tommy's face. "'Tis far away."

"It's close enough," said Tommy, holding the other man tighter. "What if a stray shell found us here?"

David shrugged in Tommy's arms. "We'd never 'ear it coming, remember?"

They both laughed, but the Doughboy went on, "They'd never find us."

"If there was any of us left to find. No, they probably wou'n't find us 'til long after the war was over. But we wou'n't care anymore, would we?"

Gently kissing Pearson's forehead, Flowers responded, "No, I reckon we wouldn't."

They lay in happy quiet until David suggested, "Per'aps we should put our togs back on, just in case–"

"No."

"I di'n't want to meself," the Briton conceded cheerfully.

A longer silence passed, until Tommy wasn't sure if David was asleep or not. Watching the star-spangled night sky, he whispered, "Davey?" not really expecting an answer.

But Pearson replied, "What, love?"

Looking at the stars rather than the man he loved and held in his arms, Flowers said, "I want it to always be like this."

David rose on one elbow, his face suddenly blocking Tommy's view of the stars. "If 'twas always like this, we wou'n't appreciate it, would we? It would just be ordinary." They touched noses, then Davey added, "Why don't you turn over onto your side? I want to 'old you for a while."

"OK by me, pal," Tommy replied affably, and he shifted himself accordingly, and enjoyed the feeling of Davey's strong arms wrapping around him.

The ceremony had been nothing to write home to Melbourne about, but Jamie had to credit Eglantine – she insisted, the moment the wedding was complete, that he now call her that – for being even more practical than he was. Not that this was a surprise, coming from a woman who would make her own pregnant niece wait tables; but the moment Madame had obtained Nicole's consent for the marriage, she had dispatched a neighbor with a wagon to Villers-Bocage, to fetch the priest from the convent where the girl had been staying. She also let Jamie sleep while she got the bride ready; he was just thankful he'd gotten himself cleaned up earlier that day. The wedding was held at some wee hour of the morning, but what mattered to everybody, including the civil and religious authorities, was that Nicole Lacroix had become the bride of Lieutenant James Colbeck on August 13, 1918, and that they were now man and wife in the eyes of the Lord and the law.

Now, having slipped some francs to the clearly disapproving priest and taken his leave of Eglantine, who was all too obviously envious of her niece's "catch," Jamie knocked on the door of the bedroom belonging to his new wife, with whom he had shared not a single private moment since she'd fled from him in tears. As Nicole cracked open the door, he saw she was wearing only a slip, and not looking the part of the shy and blushing bride at all. With the door closed behind them, he moved tentatively to kiss her, and she responded easily, making it simple for him to take command. Breaking off, he began to say something, spoke her name, but she cut him off: *"Je vous aime, M'sieur Jacques. Vous êtes un homme bon."*

Jamie's French might not have been perfect, but at that moment, he felt he knew too much about the language. He knew she could have meant either "I love you" or "I like you," but since she used the formal "you," and went on to say he was a good man, it was probably the latter. *"S'il vous plaît, Nicole, 'te.' Je t'aime, Nicole."*

To his surprise and relief, she looked at him, eyes bright and sparkling in the low candlelight, and said, *"Ah, oui. Je t'aime, Jacques."*

There was no resistance as he kissed her again, then lifted her slip over head and took her bare, firm, supple body in his arms, and then to the absurdly small bed. He tried hard not to think about the fact she'd done this at least once before, and as he entered her and she shuddered, then relaxed, he thought, it really is all going to be fine.

Jamie had fallen fast asleep soon after their lovemaking – so soon, in fact, that they hadn't put the candle out. Eventually, Nicole realized, she would have to waken him to move, or they would all burn down along with the *estaminet.*

But she was in no rush just right now, as she was taking advantage of this opportunity to survey the body of her new husband, the man who had saved her from a life of disgrace at the convent at Villers-Bocage. He wasn't ugly, she thought; she was fascinated by how much hair he had on him, as opposed to Fleur, even if every here and there a bit of that hair was gray, reminding her how much older he was than either herself or Fleur. And the lovemaking – the sex – with him had not been a bad thing. Nicole had, after all, her aunt's practical streak, and since her Fleur hadn't come to rescue her, still she could *considérer* a life with Jacques, including sharing his bed, as a reasonable alternative.

But it also hadn't been the same as with Fleur. She was trying hard not to think about that, not to think about Fleur at all tonight, out of respect and genuine affection for her new husband. But it wasn't easy. She could even swear that she caught his scent on the sheets of her bed; but that, she told herself, was ridiculous.

# Chapter LVI

The lightening sky – the same sky that Tommy had fallen asleep watching – awoke him. They were back in their original position, David's head on Tommy's chest, having shifted again sometime during the night. It must have been a quiet night at the front, Flowers mused, or else we were both more tired than we thought.

He hadn't just been jawing when he'd told Pearson he wanted it to be this way forever. He no longer had any doubt – maybe he never had – about that being his first choice. But life, he now realized, wasn't about first choices. Knowing what he had to do, at length he grew impatient with David's continued sleeping, and eventually he tapped his companion on the shoulder with an accompanying "Davey?"

David stirred languidly, smiled up at the sight of him, and mumbled, "Morning, love."

"Davey, there's something we've got to talk about."

So ominous was the tone that David snapped wide-awake, lifting his head and anxiously demanding, "What, are we late? Is it the Germans?"

"No, Davey," replied Tommy, doing the calming for once. "The sun ain't even up yet, and there's no one around."

Pearson relaxed, lowering his head back onto Flowers' chest. "So, what is it?"

"Davey" – Tommy seemed compelled to keep repeating the nickname – "I've decided to ask Nicole to marry me."

Tommy was looking at David's upturned face as he said this, but the Englishman quickly cast his eyes downward at the announcement, simultaneously tensing a little; then he simply uttered a low "Oh."

When it became apparent that was all David had to say, Tommy prodded, "You understand, don't you, Davey? It is the right thing for me to do."

There was a pause. David didn't look up. Then he said, "I suppose 'tis." There was a longer pause, and Pearson murmured, "Poor Susan."

Flowers let loose a sigh of relief upon hearing this, which seemed a sure sign that David was being practical about it all. But Pearson still hadn't looked back up at him. The Doughboy began to re-entwine his arms around his mate, but abruptly, the same arms that had held him close last night shoved him away, and David sat up, his back to Tommy, and said in a sharp voice, "Don't."

Tommy was so stunned, he could think of nothing to say or do in reply. After a few more interminable seconds, David got up and quickly began pulling on his clothes. "We best be off," he finally said, his tone preoccupied.

He began to break down the tent, with Tommy still lying half beneath it, and finally Flowers found enough of a voice to begin, "Davey–"

"Don't let's talk about it, Tommy," Pearson interrupted, his voice all business. "I still must guide you back to Querrieu." Striking the tent, he pulled away the canvas to reveal Flowers' body in the pre-dawn light. He looked away quickly and said in a tone near contempt, "For God's sake, Tommy, put some clothes on. You look ridiculous lying there."

Suddenly embarrassed – as Pearson had intended – Flowers moved quickly to don his own uniform as David continued to gather up their gear. Tommy wanted to say something, anything, to get David to take back his surly reaction; but he was afraid to rile Pearson any further, lest the Englishman abandon him there. He'd never find his way back on his own.

The brightness of dawn found Jamie and Nicole awake and making love again, long and slow, both enjoying it, though Nicole once again was doing her best not to think about Fleur. When it was over, Jamie did not fall asleep this time; instead he held her close and, after a short while, gently whispered in her ear, *"Il faut que je depars bientôt."*

*"Pars,"* she automatically corrected, *"Pas depars."* His announcement should have come as no surprise to her, of all people, the war's disruptions being such a regular feature of her life; even so, the thought of Jacques leaving, just as she was getting used to the idea of having him with her, was a jolt. As he repeated her correction, she said, *"Si tôt?"*

*"Oui,"* Jamie said, adding, with a smile Nicole found inappropriate, *"C'est la guerre."* Although it obviously was the war forcing his departure, she rebelled at the cliché, making that *"Pfff!"* sound Colbeck had come to recognize all too well. *"Je revenirais,"* he hastily assured her. *"Nous resterions ici."*

Agitated, she wriggled from his grasp and reached for her slip. As she stood up to throw it over her head, he watched her body admiringly in the new sunlight of morning. She might have reveled in that, but for their discussion. She had no desire to stay in Rainneville after the war – if there were ever to be such a thing as after the war – so she ignored his clumsy French and retorted, *"Je ne veux pas rester ici."*

Pleased enough to hear she didn't want to stay there, Jamie didn't think about what she really meant, and asked, *"Tu voudrais aller en Australie?"*

She turned on him in a fury, shouting, *"Non! Non! Vous avez promis!"*

*"Alors, alors,"* he replied, in such a hurry to reiterate his promise not to take her to Australia that he chose the wrong word; he'd meant to reassure her with "All right, all right."

For her part, Nicole interrupted her rage with a perplexed *"Quoi?"*

This is going to be harder than I thought, all of it, Jamie realized. *"Nous allons où que tu veux aller,*" he told her as plainly as he could: we will go where you want to go.

"*Cumières,*" she said decisively. "*Je veux que nous allions à Cumières.*"

Of course. He should have known. And he should tell her, right now, that the village of her birth no longer existed. But Jamie had had enough for the time being; he simply couldn't do it. So he told her, "*Trés bien. Nous nous la reveniri-ons,*" and was rewarded with his wife's throwing her arms around his neck, pouring out her gratitude.

A short time later, after Eglantine had made him a hearty country breakfast and served it to him downstairs in the estaminet, Jamie took his leave of Nicole with some parting words for her aunt: "*Il faut que Nicole ne travaille pas ici. Comprenez?*"

Both women understood him fine; Colbeck didn't want his pregnant wife working at a place like this. They both nodded gravely and murmured agreement; but a look passed between aunt and niece. Madame still needed the help, and Nicole had no intention of returning to the convent, or sitting bored in her room upstairs. The birth of the baby was still months away. What Jacques didn't know would be of no concern to him. Men were so foolish and impractical.

In stony silence, David led Tommy back up the escarpment, across the Bonnay-Lahoussoye road, and around the northern edge of the Bois d'Escardonneuse. Their luck was holding out on at least one account: the Rangers were not yet back from the front, and so nobody spotted them. Past the woods, they reached a rise where Querrieu came into view, and Pearson finally spoke, though his tone remained unchanged: "You can make it the rest of the ways from 'ere, can't you?"

"Yes, but–"

"All right, then," Pearson pronounced, turning back around to face the woods, but Flowers cried out in sheer desperation, "Davey!" and Pearson froze, but did not say anything. Flowers took a step toward him and said, his voice faint, "Please, Davey. I can't just walk away from you like – I can't leave it like this."

David's face was still turned away. "But I can walk away from you."

"I'll follow you," Flowers threatened.

"I'll walk faster." At last Pearson turned to face Flowers. "I know what you want, Tommy," he added. "You want me to tell you it's all right. Well, it may be the right thing for you to do, but it's *not all right!*"

Despite David's anger and resolve, his face conveyed something else Tommy couldn't miss. "I hurt you," Tommy said, his voice low, his tone anguished. "Oh, God, I'm sorry, Davey, I didn't mean–""

"Oh, shut up!" David shouted back. "I don't want to 'ear it. I don't want to 'ear 'ow sorry you are. I don't want to 'ear 'ow you di'n't mean it–"

David's voice caught on this last, and Tommy inserted a quick, quiet but firm, "I love you, Davey."

"–and I specially don't want to 'ear that!" Pearson yelled; then he turned determinedly about and stalked away.

"Davey!" Tommy called after him, and Pearson slowed his step, but kept walking, and Flowers added, "Thanks for bringing me back here. I couldn't have found it myself, and you could have just left me there."

David whirled back around, a malignant smile on his face, and snapped, *"I* wou'n't do that to *you"*; then he turned and more or less ran, his own game leg notwithstanding. Tommy wanted to call out to him once more, and remind him that if they left it like this, they might never see each other again. But of course, they both already knew that.

Pulling himself together, Tommy limped on into Querrieu, and Lieutenant Collins' office in the Prison Cage. To his relief, the fussy officer didn't even ask where he'd spent the night. At Flowers' request for transportation to Vadencourt, Collins responded with a sigh, "That'll take at least an hour. There's too much going on this morning."

"I'll wait across the road," Flowers offered, and his luck held out, as he was able to retire to his favorite sapling.

Far too much was going through Tommy's mind for him to fall asleep again. He was ready now to write Susan, and even his folks – after his talk with David, all that would be easy by comparison – and so, without pen or paper, he began to do so in his head, as the sun climbed in the mid-morning sky. Perhaps twenty minutes had passed when he heard a jaunty voice call out, "Tommy!"

Flowers snapped out of his trance, looked up, and felt a twinge of repugnance: it was Mike Glennon. Restraining his newfound dislike of the Welsh sergeant, he gave a reasonably hearty "Hello, Mike" in return and, feeling he had no choice, inquired, "How was your night at liberty?"

A wicked glint shone in the bright blue eyes as Glennon made himself comfortable on the ground next to Flowers. "You should have come with me, Tommy, you and David. I started out toward Amiens, but then I heard about a very friendly *mademoiselle* up in St-Gratien. And she turned out to be *very* friendly, if you know what I mean."

Mike winked at Tommy, who felt his gorge rising; how could this man talk to him this way, after what they'd done? Still, he was glad their conversation hadn't lingered on the subject of David. He was about to bring up the Bois d'Escardonneuse, in an effort to encourage Mike to move on to his next camp, but Glennon spoke first: "Say, that's really something about Jamie, isn't it?"

Despite his determination to carry through on his resolution to marry Nicole, Tommy had quite forgotten, temporarily, about the friend who was carrying his message to her. "What about him?" he asked unthinkingly. "Did they promote him to captain?"

"Wouldn't know anything about that," said Mike, who was clearly relishing playing the role of messenger, "but I did run into him on the road this morning, and he had some other news, the rascal. You really don't know?"

Something about Glennon's chatter finally set off a distant alarm in Flowers' head. "No, I don't," he said, now apprehensive. "What news?"

"Seems Nicole was just away for a time," Mike said, which surprised Tommy twice over, for the news itself, and because Glennon's bringing it up meant at least an oblique reference to their night at Madame's. Then the Welshman paused dramatically and added, "And now our Jamie's up and married her."

"*WHAT???*"

The strength of Tommy's reaction startled, maybe even frightened Mike, who backed away as the American repeated, "*What??*"

"Sorry," said Mike, trying to keep his voice light. "I – I don't think I realized–"

Tommy's head was swimming – and at that very moment, he saw Lieutenant Collins come striding across the road, calling out to him. The Doughboy suddenly found himself grateful for the regimentation of military life; he sprang to his feet, ignoring the pain it caused his leg, saluted, and barked, "Yes, sir!" Mike, he noticed out of the corner of his eye, reluctantly followed suit, minus the "Yes, sir."

"There's an ambulance on its way, heading for Vadencourt," Collins informed him. "It'll be here any minute."

"Thank you, sir!" Tommy practically shouted, with another salute; but Collins already had turned on his heel and was on his way back to his office. Flowers felt the briefest bit of sympathy and admiration for the lieutenant; everyone spoke poorly of desk officers, but Collins did his job well and kept things moving.

Clearly glad to get out of there himself, Mike said, "Well, then, be seeing you, Tommy"; but as the sergeant turned to walk away, Flowers snapped to and, overriding how he felt about touching the man, grabbed him by the sleeve and implored, "Mike, you've got to tell Davey, I've got to talk to him!"

Shaking off Tommy in a manner that indicated he didn't like being touched by Flowers, either, Mike casually rejoindered, "And what is there new about that?"

Tommy was anything but casual in his turn: "Will you do it, Mike? Please say you'll do it!"

Mike frowned. "You don't have to beg me, Tommy. Of course I'll tell him. But where will you be?" Before Flowers could answer, Glennon glanced up the road and added, "That would be your ambulance, I imagine."

Tommy swiveled about, saw how close the vehicle was, checked traffic from the other side, and dashed across the busy road. As he did, he shouted after Mike, "I don't know where I'll be. Vadencourt, maybe. But, *please,* tell Davey I've *got* to see him." As the ambulance pulled up and blocked Flowers' view, Glennon was walking away, shaking his head.

# Chapter LVII

At Vadencourt, Tommy returned to Billy's room to find the captain sitting in his wheelchair. Two of Sand's wardmates had returned, and the captain pointedly introduced Tommy to them as "my adjutant, Corporal Flowers." After a polite exchange of pleasantries, Flowers wheeled Sand outdoors, back into the garden, under the same linden.

It was a particularly gorgeous summer day, milder than the day before. When they had settled in their places, with Tommy seated on the ground next to the captain's chair, Billy announced, "I've got something for you." He leaned over and handed Tommy several letters – letters addressed to Flowers, from Iowa. "Mail's had trouble catching up with us, since we're scattered all over the front," the captain said. "Aren't you going to open them?"

"Don't you have work for me to do first?"

"It can wait," said Sand, sounding puzzled.

"So can these," replied Flowers, almost rudely.

A look of comprehension crossed the captain's face. "Oh. I see. Your marriage to the French girl. You don't know how you're going to tell her."

Tommy kept forgetting: just because he'd heard certain items of news didn't mean everyone else had. "There's not going to be any marriage to the French girl, sir."

Sand frowned at this, no doubt regarding it as Flowers reneging on a promise. "Oh? And why is that?"

There was no need to guard his words. "Because Jamie already up and married her, sir."

For once Tommy had succeeded in shocking Billy. After a long pause, Sand said, "You're joking."

"I wouldn't joke about something like that, sir."

"When did this happen?"

"Last night. I thought Lieutenant Colbeck went to Rainneville to find out where Nicole was, so I could ask her to marry me. Well, sir, he found her all right – and he married her himself."

Sand stared at Flowers. "He told you all this?"

"No, sir, but… it's reliable intelligence."

"Amazing!" the captain said to himself as he sat back in his wheelchair. Then he returned his attention to the man on the ground next to him: "I'm sorry, Tommy."

Feeling safe with his captain, Tommy said, tentatively, "Maybe – maybe you shouldn't be, Billy. Jamie was the one who always really loved Nicole. He knows… he knows what… I did to her… and he must not care. She's probably better off with him. He really loves her."

"You sound awfully certain you know love when you see it, Corporal." Sand's tone bordered on the playful.

Looking up at Billy, Tommy answered, "I reckon I do, sir."

Somewhat bemused, Billy asked, "And is this from personal experience?"

Flower of Iowa swallowed hard and said, "Yes, sir, it is. I just hope it's not too late for me."

Billy Sand laughed heartily at this. "At your age, Tommy, I'm quite sure it's not too late. Your girl in Iowa doesn't even know this happened with the French girl. I don't encourage my men to lie, but in this instance, I don't see why she ever needs to–"

"But it isn't Susan, sir." There. He'd said it out loud at last. Sort of.

"Oh." There was a long pause. "Somebody else, then?"

"Yes, sir."

"I see. Anyone I'd know? Though for the life of me, I can't think of any other women out here–"

"I'd rather not say, sir," Tommy replied, a little too swiftly and sharply. For a second he'd been tempted to say who, since he felt so safe with Billy. But the way his captain had mentioned "other women" caused Flowers to pull back at the very last moment. He thought about how ridiculous it would all sound to Billy. He knew he was offending Sand slightly, but that seemed preferable to the risks involved in telling his captain the truth.

And, in fact, Sand did seem a bit miffed as he said, "Very well, then, Corporal. Let's get to work."

Over the next couple of hours, as the sun climbed in the sky, Tommy had to move Billy's wheelchair a couple of times to keep them in the shade, as the corporal helped the captain clear out a backlog of that all-important paperwork. Flowers tucked the letters from home in his tunic, content to look at them later, and tackled his work for Sand with zeal. Everything was proceeding fine until, early in the afternoon, his concentration was shattered by an all-too-familiar voice calling out, "Haow naow, Billy!"

Flowers squinted harder at his paperwork and purposely remained seated on the ground as his lieutenant loped over and gave a desultory salute to their captain, who himself had stiffened in his wheelchair. Sand wasted no time in getting to the point. "Lieutenant Colbeck," he said coldly, not bothering to return the salute, "I understand congratulations are in order."

Jamie stepped back a pace and a half, looked down at Tommy, who offered him no clues, then over to Billy. "Sir?"

Showing more confidence in Flowers' information than he might have felt, Sand said, "You *are* a married man now, aren't you, Lieutenant?"

"Ahhhhh… yes, sir… but haow?–"

"It really doesn't matter how I know, Jamie," Billy interrupted, his voice raised. Taking a sheet of paper off his lap, he offered it to the speechless Australian: "Perhaps you'd like to give the United States Army your wife's name and forwarding address. In case anything happens to you." Colbeck took the form dumbly, and Sand continued, "I'm sure your intentions towards this girl were completely honorable, Lieutenant – admirable, even. But I believe I'll leave you here alone with Corporal Flowers for a few minutes, so you can explain how your behavior towards *him* was honorable." Billy thrust the rest of his paperwork at Tommy, who took it; and then, for the first time, Flowers watched his captain grab the wheels of his chair and set off on his own.

Rousing himself, Jamie almost snarled at his departing commanding officer, "You can't do this, Billy–"

Sand stopped his chair in its course and shifted his body sharply to face Colbeck. "Lieutenant, that was an *order* – not a request," he told the Australian in a voice full of menace. In a completely different tone, he added, "I'll be back in a few minutes. We have some other matters to discuss." Then he wheeled off, toward the far end of the courtyard.

During this entire exchange, Tommy had never left his position seated on the ground. Jamie turned back to him, and they finally looked each other in the eye. In a clear tone of conciliation, the Aussie said, "Mind if I sit daown?"

Tommy looked away. "You're the officer. You can do what you want," he said, adding in a mutter, "and you do."

Flowers heard Colbeck sit down heavily next to him. "Tommy, look at me," Jamie ordered. "I ain't gonna talk to your back."

Flower of Iowa would have been happy to disobey, but the pull of military protocol was stronger. He didn't say anything, though, so Colbeck continued, starting with a note of defiance: "I ain't sorry for what I done, Tommy. But I did mean to tell you myself. You shouldn't have faound aout any other way."

"I did, though."

"Who told you?"

"Mike."

"Ah, that big maouth–" Jamie began, but Tommy cut him off:

"We're not talking about Mike, Jamie. We're talking about you. The captain said so."

"And I told you, I ain't sorry."

"You oughta be."

"Why? Because I stopped Nicole from marryin' someone who doesn't love her, but was ready enough to fuck her?"

Just as Jamie wanted, Tommy reacted as if he'd been slapped, looking away in contradiction to the lieutenant's order; but Colbeck, satisfied, didn't command him a second time. After a long, uncomfortable silence, Flower of Iowa, picking at blades of grass, said, "If it was such a good idea, why didn't you tell me about it last night?"

"'Cos you'd have said no. And not because you love her; because you were so damned determined to do right by her, whether it was right *for* her or not."

"Where'd you find her?"

Jamie sighed, said, "Right there at the just-a-minute, as it turned aout."

"She wasn't there night before last. But you knew she'd be there last night, didn't you?"

"No, Tommy, I didn't. I was sure she'd be at the convent–"

"Convent!" Tommy said, finally looking up and over, and giving Jamie a hard stare. "What convent?" For once, it was the Australian who shrank back from the American. "So you knew where she was all along! That old biddy put her in a nunnery?"

Deliberately passing on the opportunity to point out to Flowers who was responsible for that – and exactly to what extent – Colbeck found his voice: "Why are we arguin' abaout all these details, Tommy? I did what I did. It's over. Nicole married *me*. You're aout of the picture – hon'rably."

There was another pause, then Tommy asked, "Is she all right?"

For a moment Jamie was seized with a terrible uncertainty. "Did you… did you really love her, lad?"

Tommy looked down again. "No," he said, accentuating it with a shake of his head. "No, I didn't. I don't." Glancing back up at Jamie, he added, "But I do care about her. And I asked you if she was all right."

Jamie slowly nodded as he replied, "Yes. Yes, she's all right."

"That's good," Tommy said as he looked away yet again, determined to say no more.

The silence eventually coaxed Jamie into saying, "Lad?"

"I don't want to talk about it anymore, Jamie. Ever."

"All right." After a pause, Tommy heard his lieutenant add, "But I'm ord'rin' you to look at me again, Corp'ral."

Tommy obeyed with another glum "What?"

"Ain't there anything else for us to talk abaout?"

Tommy couldn't decide what he wanted to do more – tell Jamie off, or tell him they could still be friends after all. Thrashing about in his mind, the Doughboy hit upon something he had meant to ask his lieutenant when he saw him again: "When we were carrying Billy back here–"

"That was a fine piece of solj'rin', lad," Jamie put in eagerly. "A fine piece of solj'rin'."

Ignoring the praise, Flowers continued, "–there was this Gerrman prisoner – Hans?"

"I know. I was there when you captured him."

"Oh. Right. But, he was just like you or me, Jamie, when we were his age–"

"Of course he was, Tommy." Jamie considered his words, then added, "We can kill as many of them as we want, and they can do the same to us. But we're all still men, or boys. We forget that, but you learn it all over again when you get to know one."

"Yes, yes, I know all that," Tommy said, eager to make it clear that that wasn't his point, or his question. "But – Hans was – a prisoner – with the French, before, and – and they did something to him. Something so awful no one will say what it was."

Jamie worried his lip a little. "The French, you say?"

"French – Colonials. Moroccans?"

"Ah," the Aussie said knowledgeably.

"'Ah,' what? What did they do to him, Jamie?"

One more time, Colbeck seemed to select his words with great caution. "Well, they might have cut him–"

"He had his ears. I heard about that. They didn't cut him."

Jamie regarded Tommy closely. "He was young, wasn't he? Very young."

"You know he was."

"I'm pretty sure what they did, then," Colbeck said flatly, nodding.

"What, Jamie?"

"Yes, what, Jamie?" The slightly mocking tone came from above both of them, as their captain re-materialized. "What did they do? And what are we talking about?"

Tommy gaped at his captain, then said, "About… what the Moroccans did to Hans."

Sand's eyes flashed, and he looked over to Colbeck. "You told him?"

"No, Billy. But I was abaout to."

A look of pure disgust came over Sand. "Some things do not need to be said." Jamie shrugged, and Billy continued, "But since you seem to enjoy exploring the seamy side of life, Lieutenant–"

Jamie shot to his feet, fists clenched, and only Flowers calling out his name seemed to interrupt the Australian's momentum; otherwise he might have hit the captain, wheelchair or no. "Go ahead, Jamie," Billy said coolly. "Tell him." To Tommy he added, "Since you want to know so badly."

Turning about to face Flowers, Colbeck spat out, "They prob'ly raped him."

"Huh?"

"They – Don't they teach you *anything* in America?" Colbeck bellowed. Seeing

Flowers' incomprehension, the lieutenant knelt down to face the Doughboy, and said with a sudden, strange intensity, "Tommy, they probably – *used* him. Used his… body. D'y'understand?"

The concept was almost too much for Tommy to grasp – almost, but not quite. "They *m-m-made him* – ?" he stuttered.

"I ain't gonna draw you a picture, Tommy. The Moroccans do that, y'know. They're savages. They cut the ears off most of their prisoners, but they keep the young ones for themselves, since there ain't no women araound."

*"Enough,* Lieutenant!" It was Sand reasserting himself, and he addressed Flowers: "You see what happens, Corporal, when you ask too many questions? I told you it wasn't fit to talk about–"

"Poor Hans," Tommy said involuntarily.

"Poor Hans will never be a man now," Sand said, with no particular tone of compassion for the German who had helped save his life. "He'd've been much better off if the Moroccans'd killed him. What revolts me is they're supposed to be on our side. Our allies seem to be willing to fight alongside any savages they can find. This is supposed to be a war for civilization."

Tommy still sat there in shock, not daring to say anything more. Jamie had returned to a standing position, waiting for Sand's next order. "Now, Lieutenant," Billy continued, looking up at the Australian, "if we're quite finished with this disgusting discussion, you and I have some real business to attend to. Tommy, why don't you go read your letters?"

Tommy barely heard his commanding officer, but stood up automatically, saluted and said, "Yes, sir," then blindly set off without looking back at either Billy or Jamie.

# Chapter LVIII

There wasn't much to Vadencourt outside the *château* complex, but Tommy had to get out of the hospital right then and there. The afternoon sun was at its zenith, making him almost dizzy, as if the images racing through his mind weren't enough. Pushing them aside, he sat down behind a small abandoned building and tried to focus on his mail. There were two pieces from Susan and two from his mother. He noted the postmarks – almost three weeks old – and put the letters in chronological order. The first, from Susan, was a short one:

July 24, 1918
Dearest Tommy,
I am so very worried about not hearing from you. I know this letter will take a long time to reach you, but when you get it, do you think you could send me one in return, just to let me know you are all right? I would so appreciate it, as it would so ease my mind.

Very truly yours,
Susan

The second, from his mother, struck a similar theme, if not tone:

July 26, 1918
Dear Tommy,
It seems so very long since we have heard from you. You have such a very important job to do, defending our country and our freedoms, and we are so proud of you. But we do worry about you so. Your sisters and I would be ever so grateful to get a letter or note – your Dad, too, altho' he won't admit he worries about you. We all hope you are keeping warm and dry and safe.

Love,
Mama

Tommy carefully replaced both letters in their envelopes, though part of him wanted to crumple and toss them both, especially Susan's. They were demanding correspondence from him while he was fighting a war! As if he had nothing more important to do! But of course, the notes also made him feel guilty; and the way his day had gone so far, he didn't need any more emotional turmoil.

Before he could even concentrate on the next two letters, however, the conversation with Billy and Jamie came flooding back. Tommy might have been naive, but in view of his recent experiences, the pictures that formed in his mind when he thought about what had happened to Hans were all too vivid. He couldn't stop himself from thinking it: he, Tommy Flowers, was just like the Moroccans… and Billy and Jamie thought the Moroccans were the lowest form of human life – not even human, really. And he was like Hans, too – he would, as Billy had put it, never be a man. If either of the officers knew about what he'd done with David – and Mike – they'd put him in a real Prison Cage and throw away the key.

And Hans – Hans had known, from the very beginning! That was why the German had been so scared of Tommy; he was afraid Tommy would do to him what the Moroccans had.

But Tommy's train of thought came to a dead halt with Davey. He wasn't prepared to see the Englishman as evil like the Moroccans, and David was a real man; Tommy was sure of that. The only problem with David, Tommy decided, was Tommy. He should leave David alone, and David would be all right. Maybe what had happened between them this morning actually had been a good thing – maybe it would save David from him, Tommy.

He wished he had never been born. He wished the Germans would launch a surprise attack and kill him, right now.

And then he went back to his mail. The remaining two pieces were sent the same day, so he read the one from his mother first:

July 27, 1918

Dear Tommy:

We were all so excited to hear from you, a postcard from England! How exciting for you! And you've made friends with an English soldier. It's so kind of him to take you home to meet his family – and so wonderful to know you're safe in England, at least for a time. The stories you'll have to tell us when you come back, Tommy!

It is a hot summer here, and there is not much news, altho' the 'flu is getting worse, and so keeping your Dad busy down at the pharmacy. Old Mr. Fowler caught it and died. Isn't that terrible?

We all hope you are very well. Your sisters say to tell your friend David hello – your Dad and me, too.

Love,

Mama

This letter made Tommy homesick, and more importantly, it made him smile, but for the news about Mr. Fowler, who he remembered as a nice old man who sat every day on a bench on Jackson Street and commented on the passing scene. He recalled Sister Jean's warnings about the 'flu in London, but this was all the way over in Iowa.

The final note, from Susan, was a little different yet:

July 27, 1918
Dearest Tommy,

It was such a relief to hear from you at last. I know I should be green with envy. Everyone always dreams of going to England, don't they? But as for myself, I am quite content to stay here in Brooklyn. It is world enough for me.

I am so glad to hear you are well. Everyone is well here. I still miss Brownie, though.

Very truly yours,
Susan

It seemed to him such a strange note that he looked through all his mail twice to make sure he had not misplaced a page. When it became apparent there was no more, he did crumple this letter and toss it over the wall, into the abandoned building. It was too late, he thought; there was no chance of going back to Susan, as if nothing had ever happened to him here. He was no longer sure what he had ever seen in her – or she in him. Fishing out the paper and pencil he had gotten from Billy, he amazed himself by dashing off two quick letters. The first one, to Susan, he deliberately dated the day before:

August 12, 1918
Dear Susan,

Thank you for your letters. I am well.

This is going to be a very hard thing for me to write, but I have to tell you something, and tell it to you plain. I have met someone else that I wish to be my wife – someone from this side of the ocean. I don't know if she'll have me, but I mean to ask her. And even if she tells me no, we should not cling to notions from long ago, when we were very young. You need to find a good boy in Brooklyn, and I know you will.

I am so sorry, Susan, but this is for the best.

Yours truly,
Tommy

He re-read it, saw how cruel it was in its directness, and resolved to send it anyway. If he could be so cruel and direct with David, the one he really loved, he could be that way with Susan, couldn't he?

But sending it to Susan meant he must also send a letter at the same time to his family. And so he did, dating this one correctly:

August 13, 1918
Dear Mama, Dad, Annie, Lidey, and Peg,

I am sorry it has been so long since I last wrote. Much has happened, but I have been thinking about each one of you every day.

We have been at the front, fighting against the Germans. I am well and have not been hurt. We won a great victory with our British and Australian allies. (David is also well and was not hurt. He says hello to everyone.)

We will be going back to the front soon. I have seen what it is like there, and I am not afraid to go back. I know we will win this war. I only hope we do it soon, so the Doughboys can come marching home.

When that happens, and it will, I am not sure I will come right back home myself. I know this may come as a shock to you, but I fell in love with a French girl, and I asked her to marry me. She said no, and married another. But I have sent a letter to Susan, to let her know. It was hard, but anything else would not be fair to her. I hope you understand.

I love you all very much, and I miss you, too. I am very well, and hope you are all the same.

Your loving son and brother,
Tommy

He re-read this one, too, and was much more satisfied with it. Now, he thought, he could mail them both, go back to the front, and get killed. It didn't matter anymore.

Later that evening, Corporal Cline, having posted Flowers' letters for him among many other small and useful tasks, was staffing a quiet front desk at the Vadencourt *château,* unmindful of how long he'd been on duty. He watched as a small motorcar pulled up in front and discharged a Tommy. Another runty Englishman, he thought with an annoyance born equally of fatigue and chauvinism; this one also sported a slight limp. The British private saluted the American corporal and introduced himself as "David Pearson, Private, London Rangers."

"Yes, Private?" Cline asked expectantly.

"Beg pardon, but you wou'n't 'appen to know the whereabouts of a Corporal Thomas Flowers of the 33rd American Division? I b'lieve 'e was 'ere earlier, and there's no one's seen 'im at Querrieu–"

"You can save your breath, Tommy. I know where Corporal Flowers is. He's gone back to the front."

To Cline, Pearson looked as if he'd taken a punch. "To the front, y'say?"

"Yes, Private, I do say."

"Did 'e – 'e di'n't leave any message for me, per'aps?"

"Perhaps not."

Only a little daunted by Cline's rudeness, Pearson hesitated, then asked,

"Would 'is leftenant, Jamie Colbeck, be about, then?"

"His lieutenant's about in the same place – at the front. Look here, Private Pearson, this is–"

"And Captain Sand?–"

"–highly irregular – and now you're inquiring about a captain? How do you English put it? You've got cheek!"

Patiently, the Tommy explained, "Captain Sand knows 'oo I am, Corporal. If I could just 'ave a word with 'im–"

"Captain Sand is sleeping, and the last thing he needs is to be disturbed by some Tommy private."

"Could I leave a message for 'im, then?"

"No!"

"What's going on, Corporal?" Both enlisted men turned to see a figure in a robe, in a wheelchair, gliding down the hallway toward them. "I thought I heard my name."

"Sir," Cline began, "you're supposed to be in bed."

"I was restless… Oh! Why, hello, David," Sand said with great familiarity, even warmth.

That effectively silenced Cline, who watched dumbfounded as Pearson replied, "'Ello, Billy. It's so good to see you up and about. Are you feeling in the pink?"

"Yes and no, David," Sand said with a game smile. "That's partly why I'm still awake. What are you doing here?"

"I 'ad a message Tommy wanted to see me, but I can't find 'im anywheres."

"That's because he and Jamie were sent back to the front."

"So I 'ear. Did 'e 'appen to mention to you what 'e wanted with me?"

Sand thought, shook his head. "No, David. I'm sorry. They left in a hurry. Lieutenant Colbeck didn't even have time to see his wife again."

"'Is – wife, sir?" asked the perplexed Pearson.

"Yes. Sergeant Glennon didn't tell you?"

"'E – 'e only told me Tommy wanted to see me, Captain."

Drawing himself up in his wheelchair, Sand pronounced, "Lieutenant Colbeck has married Nicole Lacroix, David." When Pearson failed to respond, he added, "She's–"

"Oh, I know 'oo she is, sir… but I must say, I'm speechless, I am."

"So was I," Billy said with a small laugh. Then he grew serious. "But of course, you're Tommy's friend. So you must have known that–"

"I thought 'e–" David began, and Billy nodded.

"He thought he was going to, too. But Jamie beat him to it."

"I – I wou'n't know what to say about this, Billy."

"You don't have to say anything about it, David. But it wouldn't surprise me if Tommy wanted to see you because of it." David jerked slightly, startled by the comment, but Billy took no notice and went on, "When something like this happens to a man, I'm sure he'd want to talk to his best friend."

"Per'aps so, sir."

Billy broke from his own reverie. "Anyhow, David, can I ask *you* to carry a message for *me?*"

"Certainly, Captain Sand."

"I got my orders late today, after Tommy and Jamie left for the front. They're moving me out of here tomorrow. If all goes well, I may be back in the States within the month."

David grinned. "I'm glad for it, sir. Really I am."

Billy smiled in return. "I'm glad, too, David. But will you do me a favor? Will you tell Tommy for me, when you see him, that I wish him all the luck in the world, and that I'll write him?"

"'deed I will, Captain. If I see him."

"You'll see him," Sand said confidently. "You two always end up together somehow. And David?"

"Yes, Billy?"

The captain offered his hand. David took it, and Billy shook it. "Thank you, too. Thank you from the bottom of my heart. God bless you, David Pearson."

Even in the dim light of the hospital corridor at night, Cline could see Pearson redden. "You – ah – you give the likes o'me too much credit, sir," David demurred, breaking off the handshake. "But," he added, "if nothing else good 'appens from 'ere on out, at least we'll all know we did one thing right in this bloody war. So good luck to you, too, Billy Sand. And God bless you, too."

# Chapter LIX

The star shells bursting overhead, far from unnerving him as they once did, only gave Tommy more confidence as he and three others, including Daniel Dougherty, crawled on their stomachs across the foreshortened no-man's-land between the Allied and German trenches. It hadn't rained since well before the Allied attack at Gressaire Wood a week ago, so the chalky Picardy clay was hard and dry, a far cry from the mud he'd encountered the last time he'd been on a trench raid with Dougherty. The problem now was in kicking up too much dust, and thereby betraying, even at night, the patrol's presence to the Germans just across the way.

The enemy had not been obliging of Tommy's death wish in the four days since he'd returned to the front. Although the German trenches were barely twenty feet from those the Americans shared with the Australians – the Allies were fighting side by side here, just north of the Somme, and Colbeck seemed particularly at home – the Boche hadn't been much in evidence. Flowers had been relieved, therefore, when Jamie had ordered this small squad out on patrol; he hadn't even minded when Dougherty turned out to be the leader of the party. For his part, the sergeant, who had been his usual self toward Flowers when the corporal returned to the front, had seemed to mellow somewhat upon discovering Tommy's new imperviousness to his baiting.

The two privates with them were raw recruits, even though they were both older than Tommy. Both were farm boys from central Illinois, and the younger and smaller of the two, Carl Wegman, reminded Tommy a little of himself or, more painfully, Frank Gillis. But Tommy was feeling very little pain or anything else these days. The surest sign of that was the other private's name – Pearson (first name: George) – a coincidence Flowers found more an irritation than anything else. He had no interest in getting to know new men too well; either they would be dead soon, he figured, or with luck, he would be.

Tommy watched in admiration as his sergeant scuttled silently under the wire; then, bringing up the rear, he coaxed the two green privates through, ever mindful of Jamie's Gallipoli story – no men under his command were going to get caught on the wire. As Flowers himself cleared the obstacle, he saw Dougherty come to a sudden halt up ahead: the NCO was motioning him forward. Tapping both privates on their calves, the corporal motioned them to scoot apart from each other, then scrambled between them and up to Dougherty, who said to him in the lowest of whispers, "Hear that?"

Tommy, flat on the ground, cocked his ear and actually was able to listen, since there was a lull in the artillery, which at times seemed endless up here. Concentrating hard, he could hear the soft murmurs of conversation – words he couldn't understand, since they were in German. But like Dougherty, who faced him grinning, he understood the import: the enemy soldiers, no more than a few yards away, were totally oblivious to any sense of threat.

As Flowers and Dougherty motioned the other two men farther forward, the artillery conveniently broke out again, its racket thereby covering any noise the less-experienced men might make. Dougherty had placed a knife in his teeth and a pistol in his hand. A star shell burst and faded; and as it did, other shells burst loudly, closer than before but still a good distance away. The sergeant shot to his feet, and Flowers and the two privates did likewise; then the NCO charged straight toward the enemy trench at a full clip, letting out a war whoop that would have been terrifying had anyone been able to hear it.

Flowers followed swiftly in Dougherty's wake, with the privates not far behind. In the brief few seconds it took for Tommy to reach the lip of the German trench, another star shell began to rise, virtually lighting the way for him. As he hurtled himself into the now brightly illuminated trench, he landed on the body of a very young private – probably no older than Hans – whose throat had been slashed. Staggering to his feet, he saw another young man about his age, wearing glasses, charging toward him, pistol in hand. Tommy's reaction was quicker, and he shot first, rather wildly; but a geyser of red from the Boche's forehead told the Doughboy he had found his mark. As the German crumpled to the duckboards, his glasses fell off and shattered, and it briefly occurred to Flowers that men with bad eyes were being turned away from the American Army.

There were no other enemy soldiers ahead of him, so he swiveled about, and caught sight of total mayhem: Wegman and Pearson also had each killed a German with their guns, while Dougherty, his knife bloody, stood proudly grinning over the corpses of two more, including a much older officer. Scattered about among the bodies and blood were the remains of some rations; they'd interrupted the Jerries' dinner. There had been six Germans to their four, and now all the Huns were dead, half of them at Dougherty's hand. The sergeant let out a triumphant whoop, in which George Pearson joined. With the last flash of light from the star shell, Tommy could see Carl Wegman turn to him with a far different emotion on his face; but when Wegman saw Flowers looking back at him, his expression changed and he joined in the impromptu celebration.

"Sergeant!" Tommy yelled impatiently over the din. "What do we do now?"

"Let's search them and get out of here," ordered the jubilant Dougherty, who did have enough sense to realize that more of the enemy could show up momentarily.

They quickly rifled through the bodies, and Private Pearson called out, "I found something!" He handed Dougherty a sheaf of papers from the officer's coat.

"Let's *go!*" the sergeant commanded, and they all scrambled back out of the German trench. With no star shells or Very lights for the moment, they took advantage of the darkness, scrambling to the wire and then madly under it, returning at a dead run to their trench, where all four made clean landings (Tommy was amazed how his leg had healed better and more quickly since he'd come back to the front). "Where's Colbeck?" the NCO demanded, and a voice came from down the darkened trench, "I'm here, Dougherty. You and Flaowuhs report to me at once." As Flowers followed his sergeant, he heard the two new privates behind them bragging about their first kills to their comrades.

Jamie met them halfway with a simple "Well, Sergeant?"

"Six dead Heinies, Lieutenant! And this!" Dougherty thrust the captured papers at Colbeck, who addressed Flowers:

"Was that your caount, too, Corp'ral? Six dead Germans?"

"Yes, Lieutenant."

"Good work," Jamie tersely told Dougherty; then he added to them both, "Follow me."

The trenches here were extremely narrow and deep, with only the occasional zigzag back to a second line. The lieutenant led them down one of these communication trenches, to a slightly deeper dugout. There he was able to light a lantern and peer at the papers while the sergeant and corporal anxiously watched. Had they found secret plans for a German attack? A map of the enemy trenches?

After poring over the papers awhile, Jamie scratched his head and said, "It's a map of Paris."

"Paris!" Dougherty said excitedly. "You think they're planning an attack?"

"I daoubt it," Jamie said, his tone withering. "They're in retreat ev'rywhere."

"Maybe they're planning to bomb it," Tommy suggested.

"They already bombed it," Jamie said, still dubious. "I told you, they're in retreat." He looked at the papers carefully again, nodded to himself, then added, "I'll send this on back, so the boys in intelligence can take a look, but I can tell you right naow what it is. This officer thought he was goin' to see Paris someday. There's a letter here from his wife. She was there once, before the war, and she gave him a map, tellin' him what to see when he got there."

Dougherty was manifestly unhappy at this explanation, but said with grim satisfaction, "At least he'll never get to see Paris now."

"No," Jamie agreed with a chuckle, "I don't suppose he will." Out of the corner of his eye, he perceived Tommy's reaction to their conversation.

"Somethin' wrong, Flaowuhs?"

"No, Jamie, nothing."

Colbeck gave them both a look, then said to Dougherty, "Sergeant, check to see if aour rations have arrived yet. The men are hungry."

Without his usual insolence, Dougherty saluted and said "Yes, sir." They hadn't had a ration delivery for an entire day, and all of them were feeling hunger pangs.

Once the sergeant was gone, Jamie, his jaw set, turned to Tommy and said, "Corp'ral, when I ask you what's wrong, I expect a better answer than 'nothin.'"

"Beg pardon, sir, but there's nothing to–"

"Goddamn it, Tommy!" Jamie shouted, smashing his fist into the side of the little dugout and causing all of its walls to tremble, "You're lyin'! I can read you like a book. Naow tell me what's both'rin' you."

But Flowers gave a bland, simple response: "I'm sorry, Jamie. There's nothing to tell."

Colbeck frowned, deeply, then said in a snarl, "Get aout of here."

Tommy's salute was simultaneous with a cry of alarm from outside the dugout:

*"Gas!!!"*

His tone totally changed, Jamie began to say, "Make sure–"; but Tommy was already on his way, pulling on his mask and running down the communication trench, heading for the main fire trench. In the zigzag, he ran into a masked, barely recognizable Harry Carson.

"What is it?" Flowers asked, the sound of his voice echoing inside his stuffy headgear.

"Gas shells. Direct hit" came Carson's muffled reply.

"Everyone get their masks on in time?"

"One of the new boys didn't."

Tommy sped past Carson at this news. Reaching the fire trench, he cut sharply to his left, pushing past several Doughboys and Aussies, all of whom looked like huge insects in their headgear, and discovered a small group gathered around a prone figure. He pushed through and crouched down to find the soldier on the ground gasping for breath inside his mask, which clearly had been put on too late. "Medic!" he shouted, and the man standing nearest him said, "We already sent for one, sir."

Tommy stood and addressed this masked soldier: "What happened?"

"We weren't fast enough, sir."

The voice, garbled though it was, sounded vaguely recognizable. "Is that you, Private Wegman?"

"Yes, sir, Corporal Flowers, it is."

"And–?" Flowers began, turning back around to look at the choking, prostrate man.

"It's Private Pearson, sir."

Hearing these words, Tommy suddenly forgot completely where he was and what he was doing. In confusion and horror, he whirled about and demanded, "Private *Pearson?*"

"Y-yes, sir. He and me was tellin' the boys all about the raid, and then–"

"Oh. Right. Of course."

Two medics pushed through the group of soldiers as George Pearson continued writhing on the ground. Tommy thought he heard one of them say "He's frothing" as they took command of the situation.

Needing to be useful, Flowers barked, "All right, men, move aside, give 'em room. And keep your masks on until the all-clear."

Leaning against the parados, pressed up against Wegman and several other men he didn't know very well, all of them breathing in heavy gulps of fear, it suddenly hit Tommy: He didn't want to die, after all. He wanted to make it back from the front. He wanted to see *David* Pearson again. He didn't want to die at all.

Long minutes elapsed before word passed down that the men could remove their masks. As soon as the signal came, Flowers hurried back down the communication trench to Jamie's dugout. He got there at the same time as Colbeck himself, who arrived from the opposite direction, and Dougherty, who was right behind Tommy. "What's the report, men?" the lieutenant asked.

"Private Pearson took in some gas, Jamie."

Now it was Colbeck who seemed confused. "Peahson?" he said quizzically.

"Private George Pearson, 33rd," Tommy replied, his voice steady despite the renewed racing of his pulse.

"Sir!" Dougherty interrupted.

His attention diverted, Colbeck asked, "Sergeant?"

"The rations are here... but they're spoiled. The gas."

"Shit!" Colbeck swore; then he repeated, "Shit! Shit!"

All three tried not to think about their growling stomachs. As sergeant and corporal stood there waiting for their lieutenant to calm down and give them their next order, Dougherty whispered an aside to Flowers: "Should've eaten those Jerries' rations when we had the chance."

Flowers could only look at Dougherty in revulsion, and Colbeck, noticing it, said to the latter, "Thank you, Sergeant. You're dismissed." The lieutenant ducked into his dugout, adding with a come-hither motion, "Corp'ral."

As Tommy dutifully followed Jamie into the dugout, his lieutenant turned around to face him. "I ain't gonna ask you again, Flaowuhs. If you got somethin' to say–"

"Yes, sir," Tommy said hurriedly, then slowed his tempo and repeated, "Yes, sir. I reckon I do have something to say."

Visibly relieved, Colbeck eased himself against the back of the dugout. "Sit daown and tell me, then."

"I'll stand, if you don't mind."

Jamie lit a cigarette. "Suit yourself. So?"

Tommy wasn't sure where to begin, so he just blurted it out: "Jamie, what are we doing here?"

"What do you mean, what are we doin' here?"

"What I mean is, why did we risk our lives to go kill six Germans who had no good information or anything else of use to us?"

"What do you mean, why? They're the enemy."

Flowers no longer cared what Colbeck thought about what he said. "I'm sorry, but that's not good enough. They were just sitting there eating their rations – I reckon they just got 'em, like we've been waiting all day for ours. Then we jump in and kill them all. And for what? So we can come back and bring you some officer's tourist map of Paris, and then a new man can choke to death on gas while he's bragging about the raid? Christ, Jamie, what are we *doing* here?"

Jamie took another puff, licked his lips, then said in a low, dangerous voice, "You talkin' treason, lad?"

His passion seemingly spent, Tommy replied, "I – No, sir. Never. I love my country, and–"

"Good," Jamie interrupted, cutting him off. "'Cos as long as you ain't talkin' treason, I agree with you. I don't know what we're doin' here. I don't know why I had to send you over to kill some Germans while they were havin' their dinner, and then their gas spoils aour dinner – except that's six less Germans that'll ever have the chance to jump in aour trench and kill you and me."

Unsatisfied, Tommy crossed his arms and said, "I repeat, Jamie: what are we doing here?"

Colbeck sighed and said, "Sit daown. That's an order." Tommy obediently seated himself, cross-legged, directly opposite his lieutenant in the small space. "We're here to keep each other alive," Jamie continued in a voice suddenly filled with urgency. "Nothin' else matters. They were there to keep each other alive. They didn't do their jobs. Naow they're dead. It was all of aour job to keep this new private alive. We didn't do aour jobs. Naow he may be dead." The Australian shook his head as he added, "There ain't nothin' more to it than that."

Flowers sat there numb, not saying a word, until Colbeck prodded him with "Penny for your thoughts, Tommy."

Impulsively Flowers responded, "I just want out of here."

Genuinely surprised, Colbeck retorted, "You thinkin' of desertin'?"

Tommy gave Jamie an angry look in return. "You know me better than that."

Jamie was slow to reply, but the look he gave back to Tommy was fraught with significance. "I ain't been sure, these past few days," he finally admitted. "But naow I think I'm hearin' the Flaowuh of Iowa I know."

"A traitor? A deserter? A coward?"

Colbeck, still calmly puffing, shook his head once more. "No. A lad who speaks his mind, and keeps the rest of us honest – maybe even human. I was wond'rin' where he'd gone to."

Flowers stared at the ground, then said, "Me too, Jamie."

"Well, thank God you're here." Tommy looked up, and Jamie went on, "'Cos you may not believe it, but I want to get aout of here, too. Alive. I'd like to see my wife again. So, maybe if we all watch aout for each other, we won't end up like those Germans. Haow abaout it, Corp'ral?"

Though a bit dazed, Tommy nodded. "All right, sir. Can I go now?"

"Yes, Corp'ral. Go back to your men. They need you." But as Flowers rose, Colbeck added, "Tommy?"

"Yes, Jamie?"

"You weren't wrong. You know that, don't you? You just called this game for what it is." The lieutenant stubbed out his cigarette. "Of course, there ain't no reward for bein' right. But you weren't wrong."

Serious, unsmiling, Flowers replied, "Yes, sir, I know that."

# Chapter LX

Flowers awoke to a strange shade of daylight – and a great deal of noise. Blinking into full consciousness, he realized the odd, greenish color was the result of sunlight filtering through the closed flaps of his tent. The first sound he was able to place was a loud snoring emanating from Harry Carson; one bit of paperwork Billy Sand hadn't accomplished was a change in Tommy's tentmate assignment. But in fact Harry's snoring was the least of the noise: from outside the tent came a welter of sounds, none particularly identifiable, though, importantly, none seemed to be combat related. How, Flowers wondered, could Carson be sleeping through all this… until he realized that he himself had been doing the same thing; he'd simply awakened because his body was ready, not because of any external stimulus.

It was no wonder they were all exhausted. Last night, after another couple of days and nights during which they were only fitfully fed and remained under fairly constant gun- and shellfire, the entire 131st had been marched out of the front-line trenches and back, back, back, somewhere in the dark, to who knew where.

But when Tommy stepped out of the tent to greet the morning – actually, from the look of the sun, it was already afternoon – he had a distinct feeling he'd been here before. They were partway up a long, grassy slope with tents pitched all over it, willy-nilly. Many soldiers were now up and about, and that was the source of most of the noise, though there was yet more racket behind him, farther up the ridge, in a mostly ruined village where, he guessed, the officers' quarters might be. As Tommy surveyed the remnants of the old French town, then again regarded the sweep of the slope, his sense of *déjà vu* increased, and then suddenly he knew, or thought he knew, where he was. Had he been David, he'd have been 100 percent sure; since he wasn't, he set off to find someone who could confirm his suspicions. Wandering up close to the town, he caught sight of the first soldier he recognized – Carl Wegman, somewhat to his dismay, as the green Illinoisan was looking to Tommy all too frequently for leadership, especially since the gas had killed George Pearson.

"Morning, Carl." Despite Tommy's casual greeting, Wegman's response was a formal "Sir" and a salute. "Have you seen Lieutenant Colbeck?"

"I thought I saw him up thataways a while back, sir," replied Wegman, pointing to the ruins of the village.

Wearily Tommy told the private, "Carl, my name is Tommy, OK?"

"OK, Tommy."

After a moment's hesitation, Flowers added, "Why'n't you come with me to look for Jamie?"

"OK, Tommy," Carl repeated; his expression betrayed his pleasure at being asked to join the corporal. As they reached the edge of the village, Wegman asked, "Do you know where we are?"

"Reckon I do," Flowers replied grimly. "I reckon this is a village called Le Hamel. If it is, I fought here, back on the Fourth of July."

"Kill any Germans?" Wegman asked eagerly.

"One," Tommy answered tonelessly; then, having a second thought, he turned on Carl: "Now, why'd you ask me that that way? You know what it's like to kill a German."

Looking as though he'd been caught out at something, Wegman responded uncertainly, "Sir?"

"You know there's not a goddamn thing noble about it," said Flowers, surprised by his own language, his tone serious but not angry. Wegman smiled, quite winningly, then quickly frowned and looked down. "What is it, Private?" the corporal asked.

Wegman looked back up, but away, as he said, "I thought I was the only one felt that way."

"Well, you're not."

Wegman looked back at Flowers and smiled again. "Thanks for letting me know."

Tommy smiled back, and there was a moment of quiet between them, until he said, "So, tell me, Carl: why did you ask me that?"

Carl shrugged. "Don't know why. Thought that was what I was supposed to say."

"It would have been," said Tommy, "if I was Sergeant Dougherty."

Wegman's smile dimmed a bit at the mention of the name. "Tell the truth, sir, the sergeant gives me the willies."

At that comment, Tommy burst into laughter, and Carl once more looked unsure of how to react. Tommy threw an arm around the smaller man's shoulder while using his other arm to make a sweeping motion downslope. "Look here, Carl," he began. "See all the way down to the bottom of this hill?" Wegman nodded. "If I'm right, that's where we were lying on the ground when the battle started. Ski – Andy Kopinski – and Maple – Eddie Maple, he was my sergeant then – got hit right there, before we could even stand up–"

"Did they – die?"

"Yes, Carl, they did. And it was our own artillery."

Carl broke from under Tommy's arm and turned around to face him. "No!"

Nodding, Tommy replied, "It's true."

"Didn't – did somebody do something about it?"

"Sure we did. We slowed down, so it wouldn't happen again. And then we marched up this hill."

"So it was their own fault?" asked the evidently confused Carl.

Tommy swallowed his anger at the question, but it informed his tone: "Not on your life. They were brave fellows doing the best they could." Wegman looked abashed and said no more, and Flowers concluded mildly, "It was nobody's fault. It was just the war, you know?"

The pair turned away from the slope and strolled into the remains of the village. In short order they encountered their lieutenant, who greeted Flowers with "Welcome back to Hamel, Corp'ral!"

"I thought that's where we were," Flowers replied. "I can't believe they had us put down here."

It was Jamie's turn to shrug. "There's only so many taowns back of the front. And since we helped make this place *back* of the front instead of *at* the front, I'd say it's only proper for us to camp here."

"Will we march back to Querrieu today?" Flowers asked, "or are we going back to the front?"

Glancing at Wegman, as if he wanted to share some information with Flowers only, Colbeck said warily, "I hear it might be neither one."

"Oh?" said Tommy, wishing Jamie would tell them more, but it was apparent the Aussie wasn't going to, at least for now; so he inquired instead, "Are there any orders for the day?"

"Not that I've heard. Ev'rything seems to still be in an uproar over the whole area."

"Is something up?"

"Maybe."

Since Jamie was still being so evasive, again Tommy switched topics: "How far do you reckon we are from the Bois d'Escardonneuse?"

"The what?" asked a puzzled Colbeck.

"Where the British were, other side of Querrieu?"

The lieutenant briefly rubbed his chin. "I should've known. We're maybe, oh, three miles from Corbie and Bonnay. It's not too far to Querrieu from there."

At this, Tommy grew more animated. "If we don't have orders, do you think I could–"

"Tell you what," Jamie interrupted. "Go back to your tent. I'll find aout what's goin' on and come raound to let you know."

Flowers ambled back down the slope, in the process shedding Wegman, who had stood there silently throughout his conversation with Colbeck. He returned to his tent to find Carson just stirring. "Where are we, Tommy?" his tentmate greeted him as he poked his head out between the flaps.

"You don't recognize this place, Harry?"

Carson emerged completely from the tent, looked blankly about him, up and down the slope, then answered, “No.”

“Really?”

Exasperated, Carson insisted, “Yes, Flower, really.”

“Harry! You don’t remember Hamel?”

Carson’s expression darkened, and he said sourly, “Hamel! Why the hell did they have to bring us back *here?*”

Something crossed Tommy’s mind, and he said to Harry, who had turned away from him, “You ever hear from Vern?”

“No, I didn’t,” Carson replied, biting off the words.

“You reckon he–”

“Shut up, Tommy! Will you just shut up?” Carson shouted, and he stormed away.

But Tommy’s tentmate was back there with him a little while later when Colbeck came by to inform them, “There’s no orders for the day. Except we’re goin’ to move again later.”

“Where?” both corporal and private asked at once.

“Not far. Aubigny. It’s, maybe, three or four miles due west.”

“Closer to Querrieu?” Flowers asked eagerly.

“Closer to Rainneville, too,” Colbeck answered with a grin and a nod. Like somebody who’d been hiding a Christmas present, he winked as he added, “And I faound a motorcar.”

“You did?” Tommy cried, continuing in the same tone as before; then, with admiration, “Of course, you would.”

“Meet me at the edge of taown in abaout five minutes,” Jamie said cheerfully, turning about.

“Can I come, too?”

They had both conversed as if Carson weren’t there. Jamie glanced at Tommy, then told Harry with a marked lack of enthusiasm, “Sure. There’s room for another.”

“You’re going to the just-a-minute in Rainneville, aren’t you?” Carson continued.

“I am,” Jamie said evenly, and Tommy stressed, “To see his *wife*. Nicole?”

Neither man had mentioned Colbeck’s marriage to Carson, but the private seemed unsurprised as he responded, “Well, they still serve drinks there, don’t they? And maybe that little Belgian gal’s still there.”

“She better be,” said Jamie, leaving the other two puzzled by the remark as he strode away.

★

The particular vehicle Jamie had commandeered was not in good condition, and the level of discomfort riding in it was in direct proportion to the number of passengers. As the smaller passenger this time, Tommy rode squashed in the middle, silently resenting Harry's presence. Jamie didn't speak, either; the motor's noisiness made for a good excuse, but the Doughboy corporal was sure he and his Aussie lieutenant friend would have chatted away, notwithstanding, had they been left to themselves.

It was another fair summer day as they bumped down a pitted road away from Le Hamel and the Somme, eventually turning onto a larger road filled with military as well as some civilian traffic in both directions. The dust was nearly stifling, and the going slow, but still they rode on in silence, finally crossing the river into the village of Corbie, which was full of Tommies and Aussies, plus a few Doughboys. Jamie broke the long quiet in their vehicle by shouting an inquiry to one of his countrymen as to the whereabouts of the Bois d'Escardonneuse; the Australian soldier helpfully identified the road they would want, out the other side of town. As they moved on through the village, Carson ventured, "Is this a short-cut to Rainneville?"

"No. Tommy's got a mate he's meeting," Jamie said simply as he navigated them to the outskirts of Corbie.

Carson turned to Flowers in surprise. "You ain't coming along to the just-a-minute?" he asked, and Colbeck supplied the answer for his friend:

"No. We're leavin' him here, and we'll meet him on aour way back from Rainneville."

"Aw, c'mon, Tommy. What am I supposed to do while Jamie sees Nicole?"

"Sorry, Harry," Tommy said coolly; then, feeling a little guilty, he added incautiously, "But I haven't seen David for a week."

"David? Oh, you mean your little limey pal, Pearson? Why can't he just come along with us?"

"There ain't room, and there ain't time," Jamie interjected. "We're goin' to have to leave Tommy off at the junction as it is. He'll have to walk the rest of the way to the Pom camp."

Carson still pouted. "We could see that Belgian gal, if she's there. I can't believe you wanna see your limey friend instead–"

Smashed together as they were, Jamie could feel Tommy tense up and, since he had his own reasons for not wanting Flowers at the *estaminet,* the officer continued to speak up for the corporal, reprimanding the private with "Mind your own business, Cahson."

As they reached the junction with the road leading into the Bois d'Escardonneuse, Jamie slowed the vehicle to a complete halt. Turning to Tommy, he said, "This is all takin' more time than I thought. Be back here in two haours, or you'll have to find your own way back."

"Sure, Jamie. Thanks," said Flower of Iowa, still wedged in the center of the seat.

"Well, get aout, Cahson," Colbeck said impatiently, "so Flaowuhs can."

Harry, still sullen, swore but complied. As Tommy jumped out and began heading up the road, Carson called after him, "Have *fun,* Flower."

Deliberately ignoring the ever-so-slight feminine lilt Carson had added to his tone, Flowers retorted, "You too, Harry," without feeling; to Colbeck, he added, with greater sincerity, "Tell Nicole I said *bonjour.*" But Jamie merely grunted as Carson leapt back into the motorcar and they sped off toward Rainneville.

Walking double time up the dusty road that led into the Bois d'Escardonneuse, Flowers began occasionally to encounter Tommies. From the first of these he received assurances that the London Rangers had not returned to the front, but were still bivouacked in reserve somewhere in the woods. Encouraged, he quickened his pace further and met still more British soldiers, but none of them seemed familiar – until about fifteen minutes after he had started walking, when Flowers, striding alone in a fairly intact part of the woods, spied a lone Tommy, tall with wavy blond hair and puffing away on a cigarette, loping toward him from the opposite direction. Completely setting aside their entire history, the American shouted with something like joy, "Private Hardison! You're alive!"

Hardison, taken aback by the Doughboy's happy greeting, stopped short as Tommy rushed toward him, narrowing his eyes, then held up his hand to arrest the other man's progress. "So it's you, Yank," he finally said. "It's *Corporal* Hardison now, thank you very much."

"It's Corporal Flowers, too," Tommy replied.

"Why are you so glad to see me? We're 'ardly mates–"

"Who cares, Hardison? We've both been to the front. We've both lost mates," Tommy pointed out, deliberately using the British term. "You lost most of your squad. We know who the real enemy is."

Hardison stared at Flowers briefly, then, apparently and improbably touched, forced a smile. "I daresay you're right. It's decent of you to put it that way."

Tommy moved on to his real priority: "So, have you seen Davey?"

"Davey, is it?" The British corporal took a long, slow puff, and his smile broadened. "Of course I've seen Peahson. And you've come to see 'im, 'aven't you?"

"Yes, but I don't have much time."

Hardison hesitated, seeming to think; then he positively grinned. "A pity, that. But you're not all that far. 'E's – back there, from the way I came. Round the next bend, you'll see a fork in the road. Be sure to take the one that runs to the left."

"Thanks, Corporal Hardison," said Corporal Flowers, taking the other man's hand and shaking it, though it hadn't been offered. "And congratulations on your promotion."

"There was an opening," Hardison said as Flowers began to pass him. "And they wouldn't promote Pearson, now, would they?"

The man couldn't seem to contain his nastiness. Under any other circumstances, Tommy would have been tempted to defend David's honor, with words and maybe with fists, but he had more pressing matters involving Pearson.

Almost running to the next bend, he found Hardison true to his word, and took the left side of the promised fork. After about five minutes, during which Flowers met no one coming the other way, the path began to narrow and become increasingly overgrown; this part of the forest appeared virtually untouched by the war. Another five minutes and there was scarcely a path at all, and Tommy stopped, out of breath, only to notice that just ahead, the trail widened slightly – and forked again. Tommy chose the larger fork, and proceeded to walk and walk – another twenty minutes at least, puffing and sweating in the warm summer woods. He felt a little dizzy, like he might be going in circles, and he was beginning to worry he wouldn't be able to retrace his steps; pretty soon he should be turning back. Hardison hadn't mentioned how long the walk was, only that it wasn't far. Had Tommy taken the wrong fork?

*"Halt!"*

Abruptly, Flowers found himself face-to-face with a British soldier about his age – and more specifically, the business end of the soldier's gun, leveled directly at him. "'Oo goes there?" cried this slightly built lad, whose hands, Tommy noticed, were shaking; so, therefore, was his weapon.

"Don't shoot!" Tommy cried out in return, holding up his hands in a gesture of surrender. "I'm Corporal Thomas Flowers, 33rd U.S. Division–"

"Tommy!" came an unexpected, familiar voice from the brush. "Drop your gun, Foster." The voice was followed by the appearance of the man himself; and suddenly Tommy wasn't so unhappy after all to see Mike Glennon. "What in the hell are you doing *here?*" the sergeant angrily demanded.

"I was – looking for Davey–"

"In this part of the wood?" Glennon's tone continued to be heated.

"Well – yes. What's going on, Mike?"

The sergeant spat on the ground for emphasis, just like Jamie. "We had a report of an escaped Jerry in this part of the wood. You could've been killed. Why would you be looking for David here?"

"I – met Corporal Hardison on the main road, and he–"

"Hardison!" The blue eyes flashed, and the Welshman turned to the young English private and snapped, "When did we get that report over the field telephone? About the escaped German?"

"I'd say over an hour ago, Sergeant."

Mike returned his attention to Tommy. "And when was it you met Hardison?"

"Half an hour ago, at least. Maybe closer to an hour."

In a cold fury, Glennon said to himself, "This is a bleedin' war. We've got no bleedin' time for this." Looking over to Flowers, he added, "This was Hardison's doing, I know it. He'll deny it, and I can't prove it, but he tried to get you killed."

The color drained from Tommy's face, but he did manage to ask, "What about David? Is he all right?"

"David went to Querrieu, looking for you. He heard a rumor you were back. You missed each other."

Tommy sighed heavily. "I'm gonna miss my ride back, too. I was supposed to meet Jamie on the road to Corbie."

"When?"

"About three-quarters of an hour from now. Maybe less."

"We'll escort you there, then. We know the way – and knowing Hardison, he might be out here somewheres, waiting to make sure the job's done. We'll get you back, and then I'll deal with Corporal Hardison." Flashing a smile, he added, "I may even know of a certain leftenant from Australia who'd be happy to help me."

By the time the extremely frustrated Colbeck finally arrived in Rainneville with Carson in tow, he knew he would have very few minutes to spend at the *estaminet.* Fortunately, there was no line this afternoon; but when Jamie burst through the door, he saw the place was nearly full – and then he spied his wife, loaded down with a tray full of mugs. With no time to waste, he stalked over to her; as he did, she caught sight of him and broke into an apparently genuine smile and cried, *"Jacques!"*

*"Pourquoi travailles-tu?"* he demanded, so fiercely that it brought all other conversation in the estaminet to a halt.

*"M'sieu Jacques! M'sieu Jacques!"* an anxious Madame Eglantine called out to him from behind the bar.

Her diversion tactic was successful: Jamie turned his fury on her. *"Pourquoi ma femme travaille-t-elle?"* he shouted; then his anger overtook his command of French, and he completed the thought in English: "One thing! I ask one thing of you while I'm gone, and you can't do it. You greedy old caow!"

Nicole had taken advantage of Jamie's distraction to complete serving her orders. The highest-ranking of her customers, a British captain, rose as Jamie refocused on her. "See here, leftenant," this man began, "what do you mean by–"

"She's my *wife,* Pom, that's what I mean by it!" Jamie almost said something else, giving the exact reason for his anger, but he stopped himself.

*"Pfff!"* sniffed Nicole, clearly demonstrating for the whole crowd her disapproval of her husband's behavior, and carrying herself regally past him to the safety of her aunt and the bar.

But Eglantine wasn't a reliable ally for her niece. She called out again, *"M'sieu Jacques!"* and made a motion indicating the upstairs.

*"Cinq minutes,"* said Jamie, holding up a flat hand to indicate five minutes and adding, *"C'est tout,"* as it truly was all the time he had. As Eglantine surrendered Nicole to him and he hustled his wife up the stairs as quickly as his concern for the baby allowed, his unwanted companion called out to him:

"Lieutenant, how long we stayin'? The Belgian girl ain't here."

"Shut up and have a beer, Cahson. I'll be right daown." There was general amusement in the bar over the entire scene, and Colbeck knew he was the butt of it. But that really was the least of his concerns.

# Chapter LXI

After all they'd been through, the nighttime march to Aubigny should have been easy, even with the Doughboys loaded down with so much equipment. But Flowers and Colbeck plodded wearily alongside each other, each lost in his own thoughts.

Tommy had forgiven Mike Glennon for what had happened between them, and the Welsh sergeant for his part seemed not even to remember it. With their rift healed, Tommy knew he could count on Mike to tell David his American friend had come looking for him. And he'd discovered anew that Glennon was almost as astute as Colbeck: on their way back down the blind alley where Hardison had sent him, they had encountered the arrogant corporal himself, with a couple of cronies (Hardison seemed never to lack for cronies). That lent credence to Glennon's theory about Hardison lying in wait; and as Mike had predicted, Hardison denied any knowledge of the mysterious message about the escaped German prisoner, claiming that Tommy had misunderstood his directions.

Tommy worried about David fighting alongside such a man, but something else Mike told him worried him more: today, Glennon pointed out, had been the Rangers' sixth in reserve, and under the British system, after six days in reserve a unit traditionally rotated back to the front lines. Flowers couldn't stand the idea that he had missed seeing Pearson before his mate's return to the front, and all because of Hardison.

On the other hand, the Doughboy's Australian friend found himself wishing he hadn't seen his wife at all. Nicole had been unremittingly defiant throughout their brief interview, refusing him so much as a kiss, and declining, too, to apologize for continuing to work, thus endangering the baby. Their argument had been conducted with only the utmost difficulty, as Jamie's grasp of French kept slipping as his temper rose. When, all too soon, he had to take his leave, with nothing between them remotely resolved, Colbeck in his frustration made his worst mistake, conveying Flowers' greeting by sarcastically informing her, *"Fleur te dit 'Bonjour'."*

The resulting spectrum of emotions that crossed Nicole's face, ranging from hurt and sadness to sheer joy, compounded by the way she uttered the single word *"Fleur,"* had given him a sick feeling that persisted still. He held no anger toward Flowers this time. But he wasn't particularly eager to see Nicole again soon.

★

Determined to connect with David if he was still about, Tommy intended to rise early the next morning; but the nighttime march and his own fatigue conspired against him, and he awoke late in the morning, though once again before Carson, who had managed two mugs of beer in Rainneville over the short duration of Jamie and Nicole's argument. Emerging from their tent wide-awake, Flowers focused on yet another small, damaged French village and, just beyond it, a creek. Tommy could only assume this was Aubigny, and behind it the Somme.

There was no one about – yet again – to give orders, so he ambled down to the bank of the river. As he reached the water he spied, off to his right and on the opposite side, another, larger village which, thanks to its twin-towered church, he recognized as Corbie. He realized if he shifted his vision slightly to the left, he would, for all intents and purposes, be staring straight into the heart of the Bois d'Escardonneuse, where the Rangers were camped (if they hadn't decamped). It had to be less than an hour's walk from here as the crow flew.

"Strange, ain't it, Tommy?" came a voice close behind him, and Flowers, startled, swung his head about, only to be startled anew; it was Daniel Dougherty, addressing him familiarly, and with something approaching friendliness.

With extreme caution, the corporal answered, "What's that, Sarge?"

Looking across the river instead of at Flowers, Dougherty continued, "The way they just keep moving us around, with no orders, not even for training or shooting practice."

That was a fair observation; so Tommy countered, "You think something's afoot?"

Dougherty looked over at him. "There better be. This is a hell of a way to fight a war." Grinning, the sergeant added, "There's plenty more Huns to kill."

The German youth whose throat Dougherty had slashed, staring lifelessly up at Tommy from the trench floor, crossed Flowers' thoughts, but the corporal simply grunted "Hm"; then, assuming it was safe to move on to a new topic, he asked his NCO, "Do you reckon we're free to come and go?"

Both Dougherty's expression and voice changed. "I wouldn't reckon any such thing, soldier. You should stay with your platoon. Don't wander off – and don't go running to *him* to get permission, either." Tommy noticed his sergeant couldn't bring himself to say their lieutenant's name, but the corporal said nothing in response – which simply raised the NCO's level of irritation: "You hear me, soldier?"

Well, thought Flower of Iowa, I tried to be obedient, but what's the point. "You can't order me not to talk to Lieutenant Colbeck… *sir*," he snapped at Dougherty, then walked away, back toward his tent.

Jamie, however, was nowhere in sight, and so Tommy remained bound by Dougherty's order, and spent the next couple of hours fraternizing with his squad mates, first over a game of cards and then in a spontaneous attempt at a baseball contest, which was difficult without proper equipment – rifle butts made clumsy bats, chunks of Picardy clay even worse balls – but Tommy's heart wasn't in it, anyway, and he played at both poorly. About two o'clock, Staff Sergeant Searles, the postal officer, came round and immediately brought the game to a halt by distributing the Doughboys' mail. To Flowers' surprise, Searles called his name. Tommy's first thought was that Susan or his parents were responding to his last letters; but no, that would be too soon. The mystery increased with the unfamiliar handwriting and London postmark. Tommy hurried away from the crowd of Doughboys to his tent, carefully seating himself outside and tearing open the envelope.

First London General Hospital,
Camberwell
Dear Tommy:

I gather from the letter I received today from David that the two of you are no longer fighting side by side. I am sorry to hear that. He asked me to write you, to tell you he is all right, and you are in his thoughts. I suppose there is no way for him to reach you. I only hope this letter does.

The casualties from last week's push are here now – the hard ones, anyway. They seem optimistic about the war, and so do the papers. I do hope they are all right this time.

And I hope you are well, too.

Sincerely,
Jean Anderson

He re-read the note several times. The Canadian nurse had once again selflessly reached out to help them; Tommy noted she said nothing about herself, tired though she no doubt was. But then, David specifically had asked her to write him. Tommy thought he knew why: Davey had written Sister Jean in case he, Pearson, went back to the front and got killed before he saw Flowers again. But what did it mean, that the Englishman was all right and Tommy was in his thoughts? That everything was all right between the two of them, since by the time David wrote Sister Jean, he must have known from Mike about Jamie and Nicole's marriage? Or did David mean he just didn't care anymore about everything that had happened between him and Tommy? While Sister Jean's intention clearly had been to reassure, Flowers was less certain about Pearson's, and so his anxiety increased instead. Reading the letter one last time, he jammed it in his tunic and set off in search of Colbeck; he had to get leave to go across the river.

Tommy made a complete circuit of the 131st's area, which took nearly half an hour, without finding Jamie. By the time he had circled back to the vicinity of his tent, there was Vinny Giannelli, who exclaimed, "Been looking all over for you, Flower! Jamie's called us all down to the river. Something big is up."

And indeed there was. When Tommy and Vinny reached the riverbank, Jamie had assembled all the men of Company E. That was too big an assembly for him to address easily, so he delegated his sergeants to help, but the lieutenant himself was in earshot of Tommy and most of his squadmates: "Gentlemen, there's a field order comin' daown today that's goin' to change all of aour lives a little bit. Your division is being transferred to another army." Colbeck paused to let this sink in. "What that means is, you'll be leaving this area entirely. Over the next couple of days, you'll have to turn in all your rifles and all your other English equipment. Then you'll be issued new, American equipment… and then you'll leave." Offhandedly he added, "Of course this ain't official quite yet, but it will be shortly. And you can't hide an operation like this. I figured you might as well know what it's all abaout."

"Where are we going, Jamie?" asked Young, the married private.

"Can't tell you that," Colbeck countered. "You're being transferred to another army, that's all I can say."

The reality – that the 33rd was not going to be attached anymore to Rawlinson's Third Army – finally hit Tommy – Tommy, who had so blithely assured David they would fight side by side for the rest of the war. Though dazed, he had the presence of mind to ask the next question: "Will you be coming with us, Jamie?"

For a second Colbeck appeared annoyed; then he seemed to decide there was no point in that. He smiled slightly and said, "I don't know. But if I don't, I know this: I haven't worked with a finer group of soljuhs in this war." There was a stunned silence, and Jamie could tell the men of Company E were trying to imagine their lives without their brash Australian lieutenant. They still, he thought, had a lot to learn about this war. But he addressed them like an indulgent parent: "Naow, go back to your tents. I'll be araound when the orders are firm."

Tommy could barely see as he trudged back to his tent, his mind spinning. They were moving! Pierregot, Molliens, Querrieu – they were abandoning it all for some completely different place. He wouldn't see David again 'til the war was over, and then only if… No, he couldn't think that way.

"What's the matter, Tommy?" It was his unwanted tentmate, Harry Carson, the lilt in his voice unmistakable this time, no mere hint. They were close by their tent, and Giannelli, Young, Wegman, and some others were with them.

"Nothing," Flowers said stonily.

"Oh, I think there is," Carson continued in the same vein, and to make matters infinitely worse, at that point Dougherty caught up with the group. "What do you think, Sarge?" Harry asked the NCO, his tone surprisingly chummy.

"About what?"

"Don't our Flower of Iowa look down in the dumps?"

To Tommy's surprise, Dougherty came to his defense, sort of: "Maybe. So what?"

But Carson wouldn't let go of it: "Our Tommy's all sad because of this transfer business."

"Why?" said Wegman. "We're all transferring together."

The new private had obviously meant well, but he had given Carson just the opening the big man needed to take things too far: "Not all of us," said Carson, his tone almost mincing. "Tommy's gonna have to leave behind his British boyfriend."

At that, Flowers, who had been trying to walk away, froze – as did the others, except for Carson and Dougherty. Turning back to face Harry, Tommy asked, in a low, dangerous voice no one had ever heard from him before, "*What* did you say?"

Undaunted, Harry began, "I said, you're going to have to leave behind your British boyfr–"

It was all too much for Flower of Iowa, and at that moment it all ran together in his mind: Hardison's treachery, Carson killing those unarmed Germans, Dougherty's bloodthirsty behavior, and now the two of them holding him and Davey up for ridicule. His fists moved faster than his mind, and he landed a roundhouse punch on Carson's jaw, sending the dark-haired giant crashing to the ground. When Dougherty stepped forward to intervene, Tommy socked the sergeant in the stomach, wiping the smirk from the man's face and bringing him to his knees; then, without interrupting his motions, Flowers turned back to the prone Carson and began pummeling him savagely. Though there was by now much excitement and shouting around him, he was oblivious to it, simply reveling in the pleasure of beating his tentmate to a bloody pulp.

He had no sense of how long it took – it could have been seconds or hours, but more likely it was minutes – before several MPs roughly pulled him off Carson, whose own screaming had ceased. When Tommy continued to struggle with them, for good measure one of the MPs smashed his rifle butt against the side of the corporal's head, sending Flower of Iowa into blackness.

Tommy awoke to a buzzing in his ears and an aching on the side of his face. He could tell he was in a dark room, but beyond that, he had no idea where he was. A dim figure – an MP, he thought – appeared at the door, then slammed it shut behind him, causing Tommy's head to ache some more. A few minutes – or maybe many – passed, and then Jamie entered the room, dressed in a clean, formal-looking uniform. Flowers heard Colbeck tell the MP, "That will be all, soljuh," his voice a little testy. Taking a chair Tommy hadn't noticed before and pulling it up next to the cot where the corporal lay, Jamie said without ceremony, "Well, Tommy, what do you have to say for yourself?"

Slowly Tommy answered, "Nothing, Jamie. I feel too–"

"Well, you better come up with somethin'," the lieutenant said sharply, "'cos you're in a maountain of trouble."

Flowers sighed. "I don't care. I don't care anymore."

This was stated with such conviction that it gave Colbeck pause. Trying to restrain the anger in his voice, the Aussie told the Doughboy, "Tommy, do you realize what you did? We're at the hospital in Vadencourt. Cahson is fightin' for his *life,* you beat him so bad–"

This news did not have the effect Jamie desired, as Tommy replied solemnly, "Carson is a cold-blooded killer. God will judge him."

Jamie sputtered, then countered, "That's right. God. Not you." When that drew no response from Flowers, the frustrated Colbeck asked the obvious: "Why, Tommy? Why did you do it?"

Shaking his head although it hurt to do so, then grabbing his forehead, Flowers said, "I can't tell you."

"Tommy, I have witnesses, remember? I already talked to them. They all say Cahson and Dougherty were goadin' you. But, Christ, lad, that's just words. You don't nearly kill a man over words."

Tommy turned to face Jamie more directly, then said, "Isn't that what we're doing every day? Killing men over words?"

It was Jamie's turn to sigh. "No, Flaowuhs, we're killin' them because they're tryin' to kill us." Then, when nothing more was forthcoming from Tommy, he snapped: "God *damn* you! You're more trouble than all the others combined! You're more trouble than the Germans! You ain't fit to be a soljuh! Do you know haow much trouble you've caused?–"

"I know. I almost killed Carson," Tommy repeated in an exhausted tone, as if by rote. "Is Dougherty almost dead, too?"

"Dougherty? No, he's fine."

"Too bad. So, what else did I do?"

Flowers' flippant attitude further infuriated Colbeck, and it showed in the latter's voice: "Look, you, we're leavin' here in two days, and there's a lot of work to be done. I don't even know yet if I'm goin' with your division. If I am, I'd like to see my wife first. But naow I have to fill aout a report and make a recommendation abaout this incident, so, here I am–"

"I'm sorry, Jamie," Flowers interrupted, with considerable sincerity.

Colbeck had been shouting, but that stopped him cold. "Did you keep up your manners even when you were beatin' Cahson bloody?" he asked, incredulous. But Tommy wasn't amused; he turned away from Jamie on his cot, even though the maneuver was quite painful. "Tell me what he said, Tommy," the lieutenant ordered, but the corporal was defiant:

"I can't and I won't."

"The others would only say it was disgusting." Colbeck regarded the American soldier, who had his back to him; the witnesses had all had convenient memory lapses about exactly what Carson had said. On instinct, Jamie took a stab: "Was it something abaout Susan?" Tommy slowly, slowly shook his head, and Jamie continued, "Was it Nicole, then? Is that why nobody can tell me? It's abaout my own wife, ain't it?"

"No, Jamie, it's not about Nicole" came Tommy's muffled voice.

"Well, then, what?" A random thought hit Colbeck. "Couldn't have been Peahson, could it?"

Tommy didn't answer, but Jamie could hardly have missed the body language; the Doughboy seemed to shrink into himself. Hardening his voice, the Aussie said, "Flaowuhs, I *order* you to turn araound and sit up and face me."

With great reluctance, the American eventually pulled himself up and around to face his lieutenant, who for his part was mystified by what he saw on the boy's face: sheer terror, as one glimpsed in some men on the eve or in the midst of battle. Having achieved a good part of what he needed, Jamie let his voice grow softer. "What is it, Tommy? What did Harry Cahson say abaout David?"

"About me and David," Flowers corrected, more quickly than either of them had expected.

"What abaout you and David, then?" Colbeck could see Flowers working his jaw, trying to form an answer, and suddenly it almost came to the lieutenant, who went on, "It don't matter what they say, Tommy, if it ain't true. Why worry abaout things other people make up?"

Jamie had thought that a comforting explanation, but Tommy looked more agitated than ever, and still seemed unable to speak. But finally Tommy swallowed hard, blinked, and whispered, "Don't make me say it, Jamie. What you'll think of me… are you going to make me say it?"

"Make you say what?" Jamie replied automatically, and then he stopped, amazed at the violence with which Flowers was trembling, even while managing to maintain a last shred of self-control. Pulling himself back mentally, Colbeck thought about their fragmented discussion, and then about many, many things he'd seen and heard since knowing Flower of Iowa. When the notion finally came to him, it was like finding water spurting from a well in the middle of the Outback – a sudden richness of understanding that colored everything surrounding it. "Oh, my God," Jamie said slowly, and then he repeated, "My God." In astonishment he looked directly into the miserable face of his friend, and said simply, "You're sweet on him, aren't you?"

Tommy winced, once, then tentatively found his voice: "I – I–"

But Jamie could not stop himself from expounding on his discovery. "Of course. It all makes sense naow. It explains ev'rything, from the way you treated Nicole to your fight with Cahson. You're sweet on David Peahson, and he's sweet on you. Haow could I have missed that–?"

Tommy interrupted: "It isn't Davey's fault, Jamie. If I'm gonna be court-martialed, please don't let them–"

The desperation in Tommy's tone snapped Jamie's reverie. "Court-martial? Why would I recommend a court-martial?" the lieutenant asked in genuine bewilderment. "You ain't *done* anything, except to Cahson–"

Now Tommy grew alert and intense. "But, Jamie, we – we *have.*"

"Oh." Colbeck seemed taken aback for a second, but only that; then he said, "Well, that's nothin' new, neither."

It was Flowers' turn to be flabbergasted. "It's not?"

"Of course not. You think you're the first two soljuhs in this war ever got sweet on each other? Why, I can remember two lads back in '15 were so tight, they went into ev'ry battle hand in hand, always. Last time they did that, neither one came back." Flowers didn't know what to say, and Colbeck continued, "It's the war, Tommy. They're ain't no women araound. It does strange things to a man–"

"But there *was* a woman around. And still–"

Irritated by the reference to Nicole, Jamie gave his voice an edge: "I still say it's the war." There was a silence, and the lieutenant surveyed the younger man's face, then said in a calmer tone, "Anywise, you're askin' me to call this a court-martial offense after ev'rythin' else that goes on in this war?"

"But – the Moroccans–"

Jamie wrinkled his brow. "Moroccans? What do Moroccans have to do with this?"

"Because I'm – like them."

Colbeck frowned and spat on the floor. "No, you're not! Where'd you get that idea?"

"Well, because of – what they did with Hans–"

Jamie shook his head vigorously. "Tommy, maybe you and David are sweet on each other; maybe you've even done somethin' you ain't supposed to do. But I know you'd lay daown your lives for each other. The Moroccans would've thrown Hans to the wolves; Christ, they *were* the wolves! You're nothin' like them."

"But – Billy said–"

"Billy!" Jamie said with a snort, again angered. "Billy Sand is a man with very high standards. Maybe that made him a better officer than me – but it's your misfortune to have me here naow, not him. I'm not goin' to recommend you for court-martial. You had a fight with another soljuh who was spreadin' tales abaout you. You got carried away. Case closed – *Private* Flaowuhs… 'Cos I will have to bust you for this."

Reverting to his previous tone, Tommy lay back down and said, "I don't care. I don't care about anything anymore."

Jamie cleared his throat and stared at Tommy, perplexed. "Lad, I just let you off the hook. You could at least be grateful."

"I am, Jamie. But – nothing matters anymore."

Colbeck exploded at the continuation of this attitude. "Christ, Tommy, why? Maybe you and David will both live through this war. Then you can have all the time together you want – if you still do, which I daoubt–"

"I want to see him *now*," Tommy, staring at the ceiling, said plainly. "I *have* to see him now."

"So what!" Jamie exclaimed. "I want to see Nicole naow. We can't always have–"

"Will you see her before we leave? If you go with us?"

"I – I told you, Tommy, I should be seein' her right naow. But this little fight of yours–"

With sudden energy Flowers sat up again and looked at Colbeck. "Then let's go, Jamie. Right now. Go see your wife, and let me find David, if the Rangers didn't already go back to the front–"

"They ain't gone. I sawr Mike today, and–"

Now Flowers lurched forward and grabbed Colbeck's sleeve. "Then *please,* Jamie! Please."

Jamie backed off a little from Tommy's intensity, and Tommy let go of the lieutenant's sleeve. Regarding his own arm, Colbeck said, "You are a very determined young man when you want to be, Tommy Flaowuhs. Very determined. I always thought that abaout you." Then he looked up at Flowers and added, "You're still a prisoner. It would be highly irregular for me to escort araound a prisoner in my custody. Dougherty would try to cause me trouble abaout that, for one. So, what's in it for me?"

"Seeing Nicole again."

"Yes, but I can do that withaout you." Jamie pondered a bit; then slowly a smile spread across his face. "But there's somethin' I *can't* do withaout your help. Let me think abaout this." He did, while Tommy regarded him closely, anxiously. At length Jamie made a proposal: "Tommy, supposin' you came with me to Rainneville, and you told my wife – to her face – that you don't love her. That you're sweet on someone else. You don't have to say who; she wouldn't understand that, anywise."

The very thought made Tommy swallow hard again; then he said, "Maybe I don't love her, Jamie, but I don't want to hurt her, either."

"You're hurtin' her more if she thinks she has any chance with you." For half a second, Jamie considered mentioning the baby, then decided against it one last time.

Tommy thought about what Jamie had said, then brought up another problem: "But I – don't speak French."

"I do."

"She won't believe you."

That stung, but Colbeck conceded Flowers' point. "You're right. Too bad Billy's gone back home."

"Billy would've had me court-martialed," Flowers noted archly.

The Australian smiled. "Maybe." He pondered a little bit more, then said, "I know. I know. Mike! Mike speaks good French. We'll get word to him. He can bring David with him to the just-a-minute, and–"

"I don't want David there."

Colbeck raised his eyebrows. "I thought you just said you wanted to see him more than anything else in the world–"

"I do. But not there, not at Madame's. Tell Mike to drop David off, and to tell David I'll meet him at the usual place when I'm done at the just-a-minute."

There was a long pause; then Colbeck, tacitly agreeing to Flowers' scenario, said, "So, you'll do it, Tommy?"

"Yes, Jamie, I'll do it. If you'll let me meet with David while you spend the night with your wife."

Colbeck folded his arms behind his head. "It's a crazy plan. But this war's full of crazy plans. And ev'rythin's a balls-up here right naow anywise. It just might work." Again looking at Tommy directly, he said, "We might have more time to work this aout tomorrow night. The trains don't start leavin' 'til after midnight Friday–"

"For where?"

Jamie shook his head. "I ain't tellin'."

Tommy shook his in return. "The Rangers could leave tomorrow – or tonight. It's got to be tonight."

Jamie seemed to give it one last thought, then stood up. "All right, Corp – sorry, *Private* Flaowuhs. Tonight it is."

# Chapter LXII

When Jamie and Tommy arrived at the *estaminet,* it was quite dark outside, but the place was still full, in brazen defiance of official closing hours. Mike Glennon, who had managed to arrive earlier, waved them over to where he stood by the bar, nursing a fresh beer. "Good evening, mates," the Welshman said cheerily. "This is quite a party, is it not?"

Jamie frowned as he noticed Nicole across the room, waiting on a crowd of Doughboys. "Why are they still servin'?" Colbeck (who didn't really mean "they") asked, mostly to himself.

"Last chance to get you Yanks' money," Mike glibly told Tommy. "Or close to it."

"Some secret these orders are," the Aussie muttered, and then he spotted Odile, who had evidently returned to Madame's employ. He shouted a quick *"Deux bières"* at her, showing an accompanying pair of fingers, and reached for his money as he said to Glennon, "Ev'rything all right gettin' here?"

"Couldn't get a motorcar. But the Yanks are turning in their motorbikes, so we pinched one of those for the evening. Felt strange not bringing David in here, but those were your orders, and he didn't seem to mind."

"Hm," Colbeck grunted. "Good work, Mike. As always."

"So will you be staying, Jamie, or will you go with the Yanks?"

Colbeck shook his head and gave his standard answer. "Don't know yet. But if I do, I especially need your help tonight."

Mike laughed and said, "What, with Nicole?"

There was an unmistakable bawdiness to Glennon's tone, and Flowers waited for an angry reaction from Colbeck, but the lieutenant was all business: "In a manner o'speakin', yes. Tommy needs to take his leave of her tonight, and he doesn't speak French."

"But – I don't understand. You can take care o'that."

"No, Mike, I can't. I need you to."

Mike turned to Tommy – who realized with concern that the Welshman had had too many beers already – and asked, "What's he talking about? He can't translate for you with his own wife?"

Tommy had remained silent up to this point. Now he told Glennon, "It's personal, Mike, between her and me. The translator should be neutral."

The Welshman turned back to the Australian in amazement. "And you're letting him *do* this?"

Colbeck was not amused by Glennon's beery inquisitiveness. "Let me be straight with you, Mike," he shot back. "It was my idear. Nicole has always carried a torch for Tommy. But he's never loved her, because – because there's someone else. I've asked him to tell her that, so my wife can understand, once and for all, that there's no chance for her with him." In the wake of this frank talk, the Welsh sergeant was staring at the Aussie lieutenant and looking aghast, but Colbeck paid no mind as he concluded, "So y'see, Mike, I'd be the wrong one for the job. I'm askin' you for your help – as a friend."

Mike Glennon took two, three beats, then said in a much more sober voice, "No." He looked over at Tommy, then back to Jamie, and repeated, "No. You must be daft, the both of you. I'm the one she'll end up hating. The bearer of the bad news. Why should I put myself through that? No."

There was a heavy silence among them. Tommy almost said something, with Jamie right there, then thought better of it. Instead he asked Colbeck, "Jamie, can I talk to Mike for a minute?"

The lieutenant was clearly deflated by the unanticipated refusal from his friend – and mystified by the American's request. "Sure," he said. "I need to talk to my wife anywise."

As Colbeck moved away, Glennon turned to Flowers and said peremptorily, "I don't know what you think this is all about, Tommy, but the answer is still no."

"The answer will be yes, Mike," Tommy said, his voice steady.

"Says who? You and what – army?" Glennon started giggling at his own joke.

Flowers' tone didn't change. "Mike, this is very important to Jamie, and to me. And after all he's done for you–"

"Forget it, Tommy," Mike said dismissively, but the American cut to the point:

"Who do you think you're talking to, Mike? I didn't want to bring this up, but if you don't do it, I'll tell Jamie what happened between you and me. Right upstairs."

For a moment Glennon looked shocked and stricken, but only for a moment; then he recovered himself and said, "You'd never."

"What makes you so sure?"

"'Cause if you did, he'd know you did, too."

"Mike, he already knows about me." Flowers watched the color drain from Glennon's face as he added, "He knows about *me*, but he doesn't know about *you*. Do you aim to keep it that way?"

In a final burst of defiance, Glennon sneered, "If he knows about you, why should he believe you?"

"He will," Tommy said confidently, "...and then there's Madame. She adores him. And *she* probably changed the bed."

Glennon's jaw dropped at this last remark. "I never thought you could be like this, Tommy Flowers. What's got into you?"

Tommy felt himself wavering at the last second. "It won't be so bad, Mike. Maybe she won't blame the messenger."

That was a weak comeback, and Flowers feared he'd lost Glennon. But the Welshman took a long, slow draught of the rest of his beer, then slammed it down on the counter, a gesture that drew little attention in the crowded tavern. "I should never have fallen in with your lot," he said bitterly.

Realizing he'd won, Tommy continued his conciliatory tone. "C'mon, Mike, we're not that bad. You could've met worse."

Jamie returned a little bit later, as the place began to clear out at last. "Well?" he asked them both.

"He'll do it," Tommy informed the Aussie.

"Thanks, Mike," Colbeck said with sincerity.

"What mates are for," Glennon mumbled sullenly.

*"M'sieu Fleur!"* The voice came from behind them, from behind the bar, and it wasn't Nicole but her aunt, who had just now come to their end of the bar and spotted them in the thinning crowd. *"Bienvenue, M'sieu Fleur,"* she said to Tommy, her voice a bit shaky, and her eyes darted anxiously to Jamie as she asked him tremulously, "Jacques?"

*"C'est ça va,"* Colbeck reassured her. *"Il est ici pour dire 'Au revoir' à Nicole."*

*"Ohh – ahh, c'est dommage,"* Madame Eglantine proclaimed, trying too hard to persuade them she thought it was a shame Tommy had come to tell Nicole goodbye. So overdone was her performance that Glennon, fighting laughter despite his own mood, had to turn away. She aimed the next question at her new nephew: *"Et toi, Jacques? Tu pars aussi?"*

*"Je ne sais pas, Eglantine. Peut-être. Mais je ne sais pas."* If Jamie really knew whether he would be going with the Americans, his denials were as convincing in French as in English.

Turning back to Flowers, Madame asked, *"Vous voudriez parler à Nicole maintenant?"*

Tommy looked in confusion at Mike, who in turn looked at Colbeck, to gauge the lieutenant's reaction to the offer that Flowers speak to his wife right away. Quickly divining Jamie's wishes, Glennon asked the old woman, *"C'est possible?"*

*"Oui. Odile peut finir ici."*

Glennon shrugged and translated, "She says Odile can finish up, and we can talk to Nicole now."

"Good," said Tommy, adding to Madame, *"Oui."*

Madame nodded, then beckoned them to one of the empty small tables in the corner – the very table where Tommy had sat with David and Jamie the first time he and Nicole had laid eyes on each other. This wasn't how any of them had pictured it; there were still other people in the *estaminet.* But it was too late. Eglantine had no sooner seated Colbeck, Flowers, and Glennon than she went and collared her niece, and brought Nicole over to the table. Catching sight of Tommy for the first time in nearly a month, the young woman smiled in a friendly fashion, and reacted as if she were merely greeting a favorite customer: *"Fleur! C'est toi! Bienvenue."*

*"Bonjour, Nicole,"* replied a half-rising Tommy, ignorant of the proper French term for the time of day.

The Australian rose completely, saying, "I'm gettin' aout of here."

His wife turned to him solicitously and asked, *"Jacques? Tu ne restes pas?"*

Gruffly Jamie pointed to the upstairs and said, *"Je t'attendrais."*

Tommy turned to Glennon and whispered, "What was that?"

His duties as translator underway, Mike whispered in return, "He says he'll wait for her upstairs."

Thus reassured – perhaps – by her husband, Nicole seated herself opposite the other two men, beaming at the American. Mike threw a few words of French at her, to introduce himself, Tommy presumed. She said something back to him, and though it was hardly necessary, Glennon told Flowers, "She is very glad to see you."

"Please tell her I congratulate her on her marriage," Tommy said. He watched as Mike did so: a slight flush and an equally slight shake of the head. Before she could say anything, Tommy added, "Tell her I said Jamie's a good man."

There was an exchange between Nicole and Mike, then the translator told Tommy, "You're in agreement on that point."

Tommy was taking a good look at Nicole. She was so beautiful, and so happy to see him, and it was so unfair to talk to her like this with other people around. Yet he had to do it. Drawing a deep breath, he continued, "Tell her she picked the right man."

Mike did, but he wasn't enjoying his job at all: "She says – ah – *he* picked *her.*"

"Tell her I wasn't the right man for her. That I'll never be the right man. Tell her I'm sorry, but that I'm also happy for her, because she'll never have a better man than Jamie."

Glennon stared at him for several seconds, then turned back and aimed a rapid stream of French at the girl. Tommy watched her closely; she neither flinched nor showed any outward sign of surprise. She merely paused, then said evenly to Tommy, *"Pourquoi?"*

"She wants to know why."

"I know," said Tommy, who took another breath, then said, "There's someone else."

Mike rolled his eyes. "Aw, Tommy, you don't expect me to tell her *that?*"

"Tell her, Mike. Just *tell* her."

And so he did, and Tommy saw Nicole's composure slip a fraction, but only that. *"Qui?"*

"She says who, which I was rather wondering myself."

"I'm – sorry. I can't say. But I do want Nicole to understand that I like her very much. But Jamie loves her, and Jamie's a good man."

"We've already said that–"

"Mike–"

"All *right,* then!" This time when Mike translated, there was a flash in her eyes. Nicole uttered something lengthy in French that ended with a phrase no more comprehensible to Tommy than the rest – *"Il y aura un bébé."* Glennon appeared stunned, then finally turned to Tommy, his aspect much changed; but before he could speak, Nicole cried out to him, *"Non!"*

Mike again turned back to Nicole, and there ensued some sort of additional terrific discussion, until Tommy asked, almost shouting, "What's she talking about? Why won't you tell me what she's saying?"

But the French conversation continued for a few more sentences; then Glennon turned to Flowers with a strange look in his eye, and told the American, "She says she hopes you'll be very happy with the girl you love. And – and she says she will always love you." Mike turned away from Tommy as he said this last, and his voice almost caught.

Dumbstruck, Tommy slowly got up, then rounded the table and knelt next to her. *"Merci, Nicole,"* he said, his voice full of emotion, and he added in English, "I don't deserve it," a sentiment Mike quickly translated.

Nicole nodded in apparent agreement. Both she and Tommy were trembling; and though there were a few stragglers in the *estaminet,* not to mention the prying eyes of her aunt and Odile, Nicole drew herself up, leaned over and kissed Tommy gently on the forehead – eliciting gasps from the onlookers, that a married woman would behave so – then said quietly, *"Il faut que je voie mon mari."*

"She says she has to go see her husband."

Tommy stood as she began to walk away, and called after her, *"Au revoir, Nicole."* Turning quickly to Glennon, he whispered, "What's 'Good luck'?"

*"Bonne chance."*

"Bone chance."

She paused on the stair and looked back at him without really looking at him. *"Au revoir, Fleur,"* she said with an unnatural brightness. *"Bonne chance."* Then Nicole Colbeck turned and hurried up the stairs.

Shaking slightly again, ignoring the stares from the others in the room, Flowers turned back to Glennon with a heartfelt "Thank you, Mike, you don't know–"

"I'd rather go blind again than do that again," the Welshman said savagely, rising unsteadily to his feet. "And with luck I will, tonight. I'm taking the motorbike over to St-Gratien, where I can get blind drunk with a certain young lady of my acquaintance. Tell Jamie I did what he wanted, so he should make sure Pearson gets back to camp tomorrow, wherever the hell *he* is. As for you, Tommy Flowers, I trust we're truly even now. Because I never want to see you again."

Flowers knew Glennon was quite drunk, and so was not especially hurt by this, but he did wonder, as he watched the Welsh sergeant stagger out the door, whether the man's heightened anger had anything to do with that long exchange in French with Nicole. Turning to face the bar, he saw Madame regarding him with a mixture of sadness and disapproval. Unlike Glennon and the few other remaining customers, Tommy was perfectly sober. He strode over to the bar and, with no hesitation, took the old woman's hand and kissed it. *"Merci, Madame,"* he told her, then repeated, "Thank you for everything," and bowed deeply.

As he walked away toward the door, he heard a voice call after him, *"M'sieu Fleur!"* He turned to see the old woman still standing behind the bar, tears in her eyes but a smile on her face. Echoing her niece, she said, *"Bonne chance, M'sieu Fleur."*

Flowers nodded, said, *"Au revoir, Madame."* Then he was out the door, back into the Picardy night, hurrying northward down the main street of Rainneville, down the hill toward Pierregot, and a short-cut off the main road between the two villages.

# CHAPTER LXIII

The night was another fair and warm one, and Tommy worked up a light sweat as he hurried down the hill, still not confident he could find the short-cut. Rather than trotting all the way to the Molliens fork, though, he tried recalling the way as David would, from the last time he'd been here. He therefore headed down the first side-path leading off to the right that he could find; but after less than a minute on this narrow thoroughfare, he was suddenly seized with the conviction that it was totally unfamiliar, and retraced his steps back to the main road. He then took the very next fork after that; and although a couple of minutes passed without Tommy spotting any familiar landmarks, he became certain he was literally on the right track this time.

Rounding one more bend, it all appeared at once, off to his right: the rise, the copse, the stable beyond. He tore up the slope, past the trees and then toward the building; but as he approached it, he saw the stable was dark and apparently empty, its door still wrenched off, the whole place looking much the worse for the wear. Yet he could tell it was the right structure. Could David have misunderstood? Or had he deliberately stood Tommy up? On the verge of despair, Flowers stepped gingerly into the doorway, and then the faintest of glows caught his eye, and a voice called out softly from within: "'Aven't been keeping the place up to snuff, 'ave they?"

An enormous wave of relief welled up from within as the Doughboy spotted Pearson silhouetted in the dim light of the lamp. But now, having bent every fiber of his being toward the goal of reuniting with his mate, Tommy was suddenly unsure what to do. Still standing in the doorway, he finally said, "Have you heard? We're leaving."

"Yes, I 'eard," Pearson acknowledged with a tone of slight disinterest, as if Flowers had given him a weather report.

There ensued a long, awkward silence, and then Tommy began tentatively, "How–?" and David rushed his response:

"Oh, me, I'm in the pink, I am." Seeming to strain for politeness, Pearson added, "And you?"

"Me?" Tommy didn't like the way they were speaking to one another, so he repeated, "Me?" then added, "I – I haven't been able to think of anything but you since–"

David turned away as he cut the American off: "Don't let's start this way, Tommy." Flowers nevertheless took a hesitant step forward; but, as he had their last morning together, Pearson stopped him with "Don't."

At a loss, Tommy just stood there dumbly, until at length he tried to start anew: "I'm sorry, David. I – I made such a terrible mistake–"

For the first time, David turned to face Tommy directly, his expression hard in the lamplight. "Jamie's right, you know. You're always apologizing for things you shou'n't. You did what was best. You did what you 'ad to do – the proper thing–"

"No!" Tommy cut in, with unexpected ferocity. "No, it wasn't. You're wrong! You're both wrong. *I* was wrong–"

Abruptly David's voice rose, too. "What, because Jamie got to Nicole and married 'er first? You wanted to do right by 'er. You tried. And that's what's important."

"What about *you,* Davey?" Tommy asked wildly; then he added, more quietly but with considerable emotion, "You're leaving something out. There was something more important I didn't do. I didn't do right by *you*… and you're more important to me than anybody."

David was sitting cross-legged on the stable floor, and at this, he looked down, seeming to examine his knees as, voice suddenly lighter, he reminded Tommy, "Di'n't I ask you not to talk that way?"

"What else am I supposed to say, Davey? It's the way things are."

Pearson looked completely away again, and it was a long while before he spoke: "Please, Tommy, just stop this? I cou'n't bear it twice. I 'ardly did oncet. The only thing is for you to marry Nicole, or since you can't now, your Susan. We shou'n't ever 'ave talked about anything else. It's not what we did was so terrible, it's what we said."

Tommy, who was still several paces away, knelt down and implored him, "Why?"

The Englishman still looked away, and his voice was quite thick as he continued, "It was as much me own foolishness as anything. I knew better. Thinking the likes o'me could ever 'ave that kind of 'appiness…." David shook his head. "It's impossible, Tommy. You know it well as I do."

Now it was Tommy's voice which grew lighter. "Don't you – care that I'm leaving, Davey?"

"What's it matter to me now?" came the reply. "I've lost you anyways."

At that, Tommy rose and took another couple of steps forward. "You're never gonna lose me, David Pearson," he said in a strong, clear voice. "Never again. Not ever. No matter how far we're apart, no matter how hard you try. Not… not as long as we both shall live." Tommy thought he saw David tremble at this very deliberate turn of phrase, but there was no verbal response, and the American went on, his voice maintaining its conviction while growing gentler, "Because it isn't Nicole I love, Davey, or Susan. It's you. Just you. I don't *want* anybody else but you. And that's all there is to it." He took another step and a half, drawing close enough to see that Pearson's shoulders were in fact shaking, and to hear the other man's shallow gulps as he tried to maintain his composure, even as Tommy resumed, "Unless you don't love me anymore. I could understand if you didn't. I know I hurt you, Davey. I can't stand it that I did, but I know I did. It's something I'll regret to my dying day, and if you don't love me anymore because of it, I know it's what I deserve–"

"Oh, will you shut up!" David interrupted, finally turning to face him, his voice low but clear. Tommy did, and after a pause David said, almost in a whisper, "I never stopped loving you, Tommy. I wou'n't know 'ow, not anymore."

Tommy closed the brief gap between them like a man running for his life, and David rose to greet him, his arms outstretched. The American scooped up the Englishman in a powerful embrace, lifting Pearson off his feet and whirling him around for one long, slow, complete circuit. As they both touched down, David, dizzy and out of breath, asked, "Cou'n't we sit down?"

"I don't want to let go of you. Ever again."

"Di'n't say you 'ad to," David noted with a small laugh. "Di'n't say I wanted you to."

They stumbled down together onto the messy stable floor – the place was, in fact, much more disheveled than the last time they'd left it – and then, out of the blue, Tommy buried his head on David's shoulder and began crying. "Oh, God, I'm sorry, Davey. I'm so, so s-sorry–"

Stroking his hair, wiping his own eyes, David responded, "Ssh, ssh. Leave it, love. Just leave it."

"But I c-can't. I hur–hurt you–"

David kissed the top of Tommy's head and said, "Yes, you did. But I've forgiven it. If I can, you can, too."

They held tight to each other, and eventually they both calmed down; then, after a time, Tommy stirred and began to pluck at David's clothing – but the latter pushed his hand away. "You don't–?" the Doughboy began.

"'Tisn't that, love. It's just I feel all mucky." Noting the reaction on Tommy's face, David went on, "We went to the bath'ouse when the Rangers first came back from the front. But that's been seven days. I'm all dirty again."

"Well, so am I. But we're leaving, Davey. We're leaving! Who knows when we'll see each other again?"

David hesitated. "It's just – it doesn't feel right–"

Now Tommy's voice was heavy with passion. "I don't care! Do you understand? I don't care! I want to – to..."

But Tommy didn't have the words for what he wanted to, so without warning he lunged and took David in his arms again, and this time David offered no more resistance.

★

Much later, they lay together quietly on the stable floor, and Tommy told David about everything – his confrontation with Jamie after the marriage, the last time he'd seen Billy, the letters to Susan and his parents, how he himself had wanted to die and then changed his mind during the gas attack, the incident with Hardison, the fight with Carson, the confession to Jamie, being busted back to private, the painful interview with Nicole. Having recounted all this, of a sudden he turned to Pearson and said, "You're awfully quiet. And I've done it again."

"You 'ad a lot to say, love. You 'ad a lot 'appen to you."

Tommy pulled David closer. "And through it all, I just wanted to be with you." There was quiet, and then he asked, "What was it like for you, Davey? The last week?"

"Eight days," the Englishman corrected, "almost nine." He pondered and finally answered, "I – ah – I 'ardly remember any of it. I knew, oncet Mike told me, that you wanted to see me again. But still I thought I'd lost you."

"Did you want to die?" Tommy asked.

David wrinkled his nose. "Cor, not! I've been un'appy before. I could be un'appy again."

"Are you happy now?"

David slowly exhaled, then touched noses with Tommy, and deliberately used a fancy word: "Ecstatic."

"But are you happy?" They both got a laugh out of that one, but then grew quietly serious again. "Are you going to be all right," Tommy asked, "with me somewhere else?"

"I 'ate to say it, love, but in some ways I'll be better off, per'aps. You, too. Until this war is truly over."

With an optimistic tone to match his words, Tommy said, "I reckon it'll be over soon."

"That's what they all said in '14," David demurred.

"It has to end soon. So we can be together all the time."

"Oh, you," David said playfully.

"Me, what?" Tommy asked in similar fashion.

"You… daft Yank." David's tone changed again as he added, "It's growing light, Tommy. 'Ere, I want to give you something."

"What?"

"It's Sister Jean's address. We'll write each other, with 'er 'elp. But mind what you say. There's censors all about."

Tommy took the address from David and carefully placed it in the pocket of his trousers, which were lying next to him. "How will I know you're all right? How can I tell you that I am?"

David thought briefly, then suggested, "We'll say we're in the pink."

Tommy laughed. "But you say that all the time."

"Yes, but we'll only *write* it to each other if we're truly all right."

"And every time I call you Davey in a letter, you'll know it means I love you," Tommy said, emphasizing the point with a caress.

"And every time I call you Tommy, you'll know the same."

Tommy laughed again. "But everybody calls me Tommy."

"So they do. But when I call you Tommy in a letter, it will mean something different."

They settled back into each other, even though Tommy had heard perfectly well the comment about the growing light. "I'd rather not have to write," he mused. "I'd rather stay here with you. I don't ever want to leave here, Davey."

"I feel the same way, love. So, now we've both said it, let's not say it again."

Davey always knew the right thing to say and do, Tommy thought as he wrapped his arms around his mate. The war had to be over soon. There was so much world they could explore together, and as long as he could be with Davey, he didn't care what anybody thought about him not getting married.

# Chapter LXIV

Less than a mile away from where Tommy and David lay together on the stable floor, Mr. and Mrs. James Colbeck also lay together, in somewhat more comfortable circumstances, give or take their small bed. Jamie was no longer sure what he'd expected from Nicole following her talk with Flowers, but whatever it had been, her reaction was different. She had come to her room – their room – calm and collected, and to all appearances genuinely glad to see and be with him; and once he had gently guided her to the bed, she was a willing, even eager, partner. It was she, not he, who had fallen fast asleep after their lovemaking; so as Jamie, too, noted the brightening sky with apprehension, he felt a considerable reluctance about interrupting the peace and quiet of his spouse. But he had to, because he still didn't know what he would be doing and where he would be going next, and therefore didn't know if and when he'd be seeing Nicole again.

As unobtrusively as he could, he began to rock her, at first so easily it probably deepened her slumber, but then with an increasing force and rhythm. And slowly, gradually, she returned from wherever she was, at last fluttering open her eyes and regarding him dreamily. But her first words were practical ones: *"Il faut que tu dois partir, n'est-ce pas?"*

*"Bientôt,"* he replied, concurring that he did indeed need to leave soon.

*"C'est dommage,"* she said, and somehow this simple statement, that his leaving would be too bad, gladdened Colbeck far beyond reason.

*"Tu voudrais que je reste ici?"* he asked, and she replied, *"Mais bien sûr"*; of course she wanted him to stay here.

*"C'est possible–"* he began, eliciting a sharp *"Comment?"* from her.

*"C'est possible,"* he repeated, *"que je resterais ici."* She looked at him in utter confusion, and he emphasized, *"Pas ici,"* his index finger stabbing the bed, *"mais près d'ici. Tu comprends?"*

She confirmed her understanding that he really might stay in the area, if not her bed, by replying *"Oui, je comprends."* Then, in an apparent afterthought, she hastily added, *"C'est bon…"*

But there was something about the way she completed her response, or rather didn't, that Colbeck couldn't help noticing. Staring at her, he eventually said, *"Mais?–"*

She shook her head vigorously, prettily, and said, *"Rien."*

Jamie tried to control a rising – what? Anger? Panic? Both? He'd clearly heard the "but…" in her tone, yet she denied it. And he didn't want to start a fight with her, not now. But just as he turned to her to say *"ça va,"* she asked, with seeming distraction:

*"Que penses-tu qu'il va lui arriver?"*

Jamie's mouth turned dry. She had said, "What do you think will happen to him?" – and there was no need to ask who "him" was. After all that he, Colbeck, had so carefully orchestrated, Nicole seemed not even to be angry with Tommy; far less was she prepared to forget him. Reluctantly, and rather sternly, Jamie answered her, *"Je ne sais pas. Et toi non plus. Tu le sais."*

She nodded, conceding his point: neither one of them could know what was going to happen to her Fleur, and she should know better than to ask. Still she persisted, *"Tu ne va pas avec lui?"*

She didn't see the question as one of whether Jamie would go away or stay, but whether or not he would be accompanying Flowers. He struggled to keep his voice steady as he asked her if she wanted him to leave with Tommy: *"Tu préféres que je pars avec lui?"*

She looked away from him at this too-direct question, then, rather than reply, asked him something else: *"Tu sais où est-ce qu'ils vont?"*

Everyone had been asking Jamie this for several days: did he know where the Americans were headed. This time, he responded with what he knew – *"Près de Toul."*

*"Ah,"* she said, and with amazing clarity he suddenly could see her mind working – Toul was close to Cumières… but not close enough; about fifty miles.

*"Tu n'as pas répondu à mon question,"* he reminded her.

But she answered his question now, with more guile than he thought she had in her: *"Il faut que tu fais ton devoir."* He should do, would do, what was right. As Jamie climbed out of their bed and began to get dressed, he found himself still wondering what that was.

Nicole's farewell in the full light of morning was affectionate enough – as, of course, was Eglantine's – and Jamie started his motorcar down the hill toward Pierregot in reasonably good spirits. But their good-bye was overshadowed by muffled rumbles off to the north, which had begun shortly before dawn. It sounded like the start of another big offensive, not only to the veteran Aussie but also to the less experienced Doughboy and Tommy who were standing ready and waiting for him by the side of the road, partway down the hill.

Colbeck greeted them with a cautious, civil "Mornin', lads," but the boys were all business. As they piled into the seat next to him, Pearson, who as usual took the middle by dint of being smaller, immediately asked, "Would that be artillery we've been 'earing, Jamie?"

"You ain't the only one's heard it," Colbeck said enigmatically as their vehicle began to pick up speed again.

"So there's a new push?"

"Maybe. But whether it's theirs or aours…" Jamie didn't finish the thought; instead he changed subjects, if only slightly, telling the Englishman, "We better get you back to camp as soon as possible. Your battalion's been aout of the line so long, you'll be the first ones they want when they need reinforcements."

If Jamie had any thought that this scenario might bother either of the younger men, there was no indication it did. David merely nodded in assent, while Tommy finally spoke, asking, "What about us? Do you reckon our orders will change?"

They had turned and were now on the road to Molliens. "They might not," Jamie said after a pause. "Once they make up their minds to move a whole division… They could, but I daoubt it." To David he added, "I have to stop at Molliens first, but we'll get you back as soon as we can."

"What about Mike?" David asked.

"Mike's a good soljuh. Even if he woke up three sheets to the wind, he'll make his way back."

That was the end of their conversation for the moment. Colbeck didn't ask the two if they'd had a good night, and neither one of them asked it of him.

Molliens seemed calm despite the apparent gathering of another storm. Tommy and David were instructed to wait in the vehicle while Jamie went inside the *château*. The two would have been happy to share some more private time together, but under the watchful eyes of the MPs, who just then seemed to have little else to do, they sat together silently, each lost in his own thoughts, for a good five minutes, until Colbeck returned in an evident hurry.

"Tommy, get aout," the lieutenant said peremptorily – so abruptly, in fact, that Flowers just sat there for long seconds before he began to respond. Incensed at the delay, Jamie repeated, "I said get *aout*. Naow! I've got to take David back. Quit wastin' aour time."

Dazed, looking at Pearson, Flowers obediently dismounted from the vehicle, carefully closing the door behind him, then slipped into military mode, saluting and saying to Colbeck, "Sir! Do I have further orders, sir?"

Jamie was already at the wheel, starting the ignition, but he stopped, sighed, and said in a rapid but more rational tone, "They've got some civilian brass visiting the 65th in an haour or so." Rolling his eyes for both boys' benefit, he added, "He's makin' some kind of speech to the troops. Rawly and Monash and some of the others were supposed to be here, and naow they ain't goin' to be, 'cos of this new fightin'. But they want the craowd of soljuhs to look as big as possible." Addressing Tommy directly, he continued, "Since you ain't busy, I volunteered you to be a member of the 65th for the duration of their little ceremony. Naow, go inside and report to the lieutenant there–"

"But, Jamie–" Tommy began as Colbeck flung the car into reverse.

"What are you *arguin'* abaout, soljuh?" Jamie said fiercely. "Those are your orders!"

Tommy stiffened, saluted, and snapped, "Yes, sir!" As the vehicle wheeled about in a cloud of dust, he caught sight of David, who sat up a little straighter, turned to face him, and saluted, following up the gesture with a quick smile. Tommy could only hope David saw his wink in return.

For most of their way back to the Bois d'Escardonneuse, Colbeck and Pearson rode in silence – not that it was quiet, as there was suddenly a great deal of traffic in both directions on every road they took; but they barely spoke to each other, even when they made a brief stop in St-Gratien to discover that Mike Glennon had, indeed, already headed back on his own. They had cleared Querrieu and were on the last mile or so to the Rangers' camp when David finally addressed Jamie with what he assumed to be an innocuous question: "D'you suppose you'll be moving out with Tommy?"

It was just the wrong question, wrongly phrased. The anger in his voice all too evident, Colbeck replied, "Not you too, Peahson."

If the Aussie's intent was to intimidate the Briton, it didn't work. "What d'you mean, me too?" David asked evenly. "Meself and 'oo else?"

Gritting his teeth, Jamie responded, "You and my *wife,* that's who." David stared at him in surprise as Jamie snarled, "That's all either one of you wants to know. Will I ship aout and look after your precious Flaowuhs."

David didn't waver. "I can't speak for your wife, Leftenant. But as for me, per'aps it's because I know you're such a good officer… and that you care what 'appens to 'im, too."

The lieutenant spat – out the driver's side – then angrily redirected his attention to the English private. "Listen, Peahson, if you're sayin' I'm like you are–"

Faced for the first time with someone else voicing outright the truth about himself and Tommy, David didn't flinch. "I di'n't say that, Jamie. I know you don't – you don't love Tommy like I do. But you 'ave taken good care of 'im, and–"

"I take care of all my men!" the Aussie protested.

"So there you 'ave it," said Pearson, throwing up his hands the way he might if he'd just won a friendly argument at his favorite pub. "Why wou'n't somebody 'oo cares for Tommy want you as 'is leftenant?"

"Somebody like my wife?" Jamie said bitterly.

"I told you, Jamie, I can't speak for Nicole. Only for meself."

Colbeck gave Pearson a strange, dangerous look. "I could have you court-martialed for talkin' like this."

Lowering his eyes, David retorted, "I know you know, Jamie." Then he looked back up. "I wou'n't insult you, pretending it was some other way."

Colbeck slowly shook his head – banishing, for the moment, his brooding thoughts about Nicole – and then, finally, smiled. "You got guts, David. I've said it before, and I'll say it again: you've really got guts."

"And I 'ope to keep them," David said brightly. "There's some blokes I know 'aven't." They both laughed at that, then David added, "'Ere, 'ere's me camp." Before Jamie had even brought the motorcar to a complete halt, the little Tommy jumped out, landing on his game leg; but he turned about smartly and saluted. "Thank you, leftenant. And wherever you do fight next, good luck to you."

For a few seconds, Jamie sat idling the motor. "You know, you're all right for a Pom, Peahson," he said. "Who knows? Maybe I'll end up back in your army."

"I wou'n't mind," David said with a shrug and a cheeky grin; then he turned around again and headed into camp, as Jamie swerved the vehicle back toward the direction from which they'd come.

Back in Molliens, the brass was thoroughly distracted with arrangements for this latest state visit on the eve of the whole division's departure for distant parts unknown; so Tommy was turned over to the charge of a large, ebullient, easygoing sergeant who immediately addressed him as "Corporal Flowers." The Iowan realized he was still wearing his stripe, despite being busted. He hesitated for a second, wondering if he should tell his true rank to this bluff, friendly NCO; then he thought of Billy Sand's practical streak: maybe one more corporal in this crowd would look better than one more private. Besides, he'd be gone before anyone knew different.

As Flowers and the sergeant were ambling at an easy pace away from the *château*, toward Molliens Wood, he asked the NCO, "So who's this brass?"

"You mean our visitor? He's from President Wilson's Cabinet. Almost."

"Almost?"

"*Assistant* Secretary of the Navy."

"The *Navy?*" Tommy laughed, and the other man laughed with him. "What's the Assistant Secretary of the Navy doing this far from the sea?"

"Damned if I know," the sergeant said with a chuckle. "Maybe they're planning to send the fleet up the Somme." This caused even more hilarity between them, and then he added, "Queerest thing, too. This man's name is Roosevelt."

That caused Tommy to come to a complete stop. "As in Teddy?" he began incredulously.

"Can't be too much like TR, can he, if he's one of Wilson's men?"

"That is queer," Tommy agreed, "a Roosevelt, and a Democrat."

"Must be some kind of black sheep of the family."

They had reached the section of the Bois de Molliens where the 65th Brigade was gathering in formation for the state visit. Tommy inevitably experienced a strong sense of *déjà vu;* at least the sun seemed a little less strong than for the King's appearance, which had been only ten days ago, but seemed yet another lifetime away. The low, dull thuds of the artillery to the north could still be heard, and Flowers couldn't help thinking: why are we here for this silly ceremony when there's fighting to be done, and then they're going to send us away. It made no sense to him, and he still hadn't quite learned to dismiss from his mind all the things in this war that made no sense. Oh well, he thought, at least he would have something else to write home about, seeing a relative of President Roosevelt's who worked for President Wilson.

They stood at attention for the better part of an hour before the distinguished visitor finally arrived. This time Tommy was close to the front of the mass formation, and as a result he could see and hear this Mr. Roosevelt much better than he had the King – and much better than most of the 65th Infantry today. The almost-Cabinet member was a tall, thin, elegant man who seemed old by the soldiers' standards but young for a politician. He looked rich, Tommy thought, and his speaking voice, with a heavy Eastern accent, was hard at times for Flowers' Midwestern ears to follow. Roosevelt seemed to think he was addressing the entire 33rd Division, as that was whom he thanked in his speech, telling them they had "shed luster upon American arms.

"I have heard on all sides of your prowess as fighting men," the Assistant Secretary told the soldiers, "and I have heard of your achievements at Le Hamel, from the King of England himself." Tommy started at this; every one of the soldiers from the 33rd who had fought at Hamel, he knew, was from the 66th Brigade, not the 65th. Why was he congratulating these troops? Of course, Flowers himself was here; he might be the only man present who actually had fought at Hamel. He wasn't sure if he felt flattered, personally thanked by Mr. Roosevelt, or just awkward, the only one there to represent all those others, including Ski and Eddie Maple.

When at last the speech was over, and the Assistant Secretary had departed and the mass formation of the 65th was breaking up, the friendly sergeant offered to walk with Tommy back to the *château,* to make sure Flowers got back to his camp. "He's a pretty good speaker, ain't he?" the NCO ventured. "It'll be something to write to the folks about."

"I reckon," Tommy agreed with a nod. "But it's not like telling 'em you saw a King."

★

The next forty-eight hours were rife with as much confusion as Tommy had encountered in his entire army life – more, even, than in the two battles he'd experienced. Weapons had to be turned in, and various pieces of equipment checked and rechecked, but most of all it seemed everyone in the 33rd, the enlisted men especially, sat about and waited and waited, for… nothing in particular, even as the distant clamor of the fighting continued.

It would have been a good period to spend more time with David, but that wasn't possible; through a harried Jamie, Tommy had gotten word that the Rangers had marched back across the River Ancre, assembling with other British and Australian troops near Morlancourt in anticipation of an enemy counterattack. "They're on stand-to," Colbeck had told Flowers.

"All the time?" the Doughboy asked.

Jamie nodded. "That means they're all but certain the Germans will strike back there."

That had been late yesterday afternoon, the day after Tommy had stood at attention with the 65th Brigade and listened to Mr. Roosevelt's speech. This morning, at last, Flowers' battalion had received their orders to move out, and had marched through the outskirts of Amiens – which seemed to him an enormous city after all this time in tiny, mostly destroyed villages – to the St-Roch train station, where they awaited their turn to board another of those dreaded *"Hommes 40, Cheveaux 8"* specials. Dougherty was at the head of Tommy's group, but Colbeck was nowhere in sight; and when the Iowan took a moment and thought about all the other squadmates who had come with him to Picardy, it made him shiver: hardly any of them were joining him on this journey. Besides those who were dead, there was Vern Sanders, who might be, and Walt Sleziniak, who might as well be, not to mention Harry Carson, who still lay recovering in Vadencourt from the beating administered him by Flowers. Other than Giannelli and Young, there were only the newcomers, notably Carl Wegman, who had become Tommy's shadow of late. Remembering Frank Gillis, Flower of Iowa consciously brushed aside his irritation over this and let Carl tag along.

Thus lost in his thoughts as they moved, single file, in a seemingly interminable line to board their train, Tommy didn't hear his name the first two times it was called. Only when a loud voice cut through the din with "Tommy Flaowuhs!" did he snap to and see, coming toward him, not only his Australian friend but his friend's French wife, who was distracting many a Doughboy despite being dressed in her subdued Sunday best and clinging to her husband's arm.

Tommy glanced quickly, apprehensively, toward Dougherty, but his sergeant, several men ahead of him, rapidly assessed the situation, then merely called back, "Make it fast."

"I'll wait for you," Carl told Tommy as the latter stepped out of line, and Flowers nodded to the Illinoisan in appreciation. A bit dazed, the Iowan contemplated Jamie and Nicole as they drew up to him, looking for all the world like some smart couple, with the husband home on leave to see his wife.

"*Bonjour,*" he said to them both, and he was surprised to hear Nicole respond haltingly, "Hello."

"We've been workin' on English," Colbeck said with a satisfied grin.

Tommy, terribly conscious of time, asked him flat out: "Any news?"

Though he had to have known the question was coming, Jamie's face changed completely, assuming a stricken look. As if he'd practiced, he recited woodenly, "The caounterattack came araound midnight. I'm afraid they were hit very, very hard. There's a report of heavy casualties. That's as much as I know right naow." Tommy stared back at him, stunned, and Jamie took a deep breath and said in a much different tone, "I'm sorry, Tommy."

Jamie and Nicole watched as a sharp, highly visible tremor ran through Tommy, just once; then Flowers seemed to brace himself and said to Colbeck, not as a question, "You're staying here."

"Yes."

"That's good," he said kindly, directing his comment to Nicole. "Tell her–" But before he could complete the request, Jamie had already translated for her, and she nodded in agreement.

"Tommy!"

That was Carl, calling for him. Working his jaw, Tommy began, "Thank you, Jamie. Thanks for everything–"

"Good-bye, Tommy." But that wasn't Jamie; that was Nicole, who obviously had carefully rehearsed this phrase.

A bit short of breath, Tommy asked Jamie, "Permission to kiss your wife good-bye, sir?"

"Granted."

Tommy and Nicole quickly kissed each other on the cheek, French style, and the American whispered, "Good luck, Nicole," which her husband quickly translated.

"*Tommy!*" Carl cried, more insistently.

"I just thought of something," Tommy said as he turned to go. "He's got to be all right. The counterattack came around midnight, and yesterday was a Friday. And it's 'rotten bad luck to get kilt on a Friday.'"

"Better catch your train, Tommy."

"Yes… well… thanks again."

He turned swiftly away without looking at them again, and caught up with the near-frantic Wegman, but then he heard his friend call out once more, "Hey,

Flaowuhs!" Tommy swiveled his head to catch sight of Jamie and Nicole one last time, and the Aussie said with a slight, crooked grin, "Be sure to mind your manners, naow." Flower of Iowa flashed a smile back to the couple, and then he disappeared into the crowd of Doughboys boarding their trains.

# SEPTEMBER 1918

# Chapter LXV

The rain, which had been nonstop since their most recent relocation, to a forest close to Verdun, had lifted for the time being, and Searles had come up the line with the men's mail, sent, perhaps, by some officer smart enough to understand that, having been moved wholesale twice in less than three weeks, the soldiers of the 33rd might be impatient to receive their post, which kept trying to catch up with them; that this might, in fact, be good for their morale.

The last two and a half weeks had left Flowers simply numb, and in a different way from his battlefield experiences: all this mass moving about and nothing to show for it, save a single terrain exercise that amounted to… nothing; they had been moved again the next day, so what did it matter what they had learned about that particular terrain? He had the sense, impossible to prove, that great, titanic battles were being fought all along the front – everywhere, that is, except where the 33rd had been sent.

The lack of real activity made it all the more difficult for Flowers to keep his mind off not hearing from Pearson, not knowing whether his beloved David had perished even before Tommy had left Picardy. There had been no post for several days, what with all their moving; and what little had arrived before that included no word from Davey, or for that matter anyone from Iowa. Now he really knew how the folks back home felt, understood so much better the agony of their helpless waiting, and as one result, regretted the way he had handled his letter to Susan, occasionally even the fact he had sent it at all. He might well be killed, after all, before getting back home; if that happened, why shouldn't she be left believing things between them were as they always had been? Too late, though, to change that.

His heart rose to his throat, therefore, when Searles ambled down the trench, stopped directly in front of him, and told him, "You hit the jackpot, Flower. Three letters! Wegman and Dougherty each got two from home, and so did you. But you got one from England, too!"

For a moment all Tommy could do was ponder the bizarre possibility that there was someone back home who cared about Daniel Dougherty, that maybe Dougherty had a girl, maybe even a mother. But then his thoughts raced straightaway to the letter from England, which lay on top of the packet proffered by Searles. He was gripped by the notion that it would be from Betty or Mrs. Pearson, announcing the loss of the last of their male line. Yet before he so much as read the return address, he recognized the graceful skirl of Sister Jean Anderson's hand. He tried not to let his own hand tremble as he took the letters.

"Who's writin' you from England, Tommy?" That was the ever-eager, ever-curious Carl. It was soldierly etiquette to share mail from home. But Flowers was afraid of his reaction to reading these letters in private, much less in public. Grunting as politely and noncommittally as he could in reply to Wegman, he set off, as hastily as the mud-clogged trench would allow, in search of someplace to open his letters in comparative solitude. This in itself proved not to be easy, but eventually, after maybe ten minutes, he found an unoccupied bay in a rear trench.

The top letter, he noted, was postmarked 31.8.18. Eleven days. Letters from England, he knew from David and from his own infrequent experience, often reached Tommies by the third day; but since the 33rd had left the British sector, this was how long it was taking. He glanced at the letters from America to determine their ages: August 17, August 19. That meant, almost certainly, that they had been mailed before his letters from Vadencourt, breaking things off with Susan, had arrived. Tommy sighed in frustration; then he closed his eyes, said a prayer, and opened the first letter.

> First London General Hospital,
> Camberwell
> Dear Tommy:
>
> I am writing this as soon as I can, as the letter I received today from David made it clear he was most anxious to "let Tommy know I'm in the pink." And he was very clear that I was to use those exact words.

He could read no further than this without letting loose a long, slow breath and closing his eyes against hot tears; the relief was past description. But fast upon this reaction came the thought: when did David send her his letter? Could it have been *before* the battle Jamie had described at the Amiens station – itself a mere week before her letter? Seized up once more with dread, he forced himself to look again at Sister Jean's writing.

> From the sound of his letter, it's a miracle that he is. He said to tell you – I don't know how to say this, Tommy, because I don't know whether these men were good friends of yours or not – that Sergeant Glennon and Corporal Hardison have both gone west. Perhaps he thought he was sparing me by putting it that way, but I've known too many soldiers not to understand what that means.
>
> I'm sorry, Tommy, if I've written this too directly. I'm no good at this sort of thing.

Oh yes you are, thought Tommy; he was not accustomed to women who stated facts so plainly. But hard upon that thought, to his astonishment, his feelings of admiration for Sister Jean, and even his overwhelming relief about Davey, were eclipsed by the memory of the hairs on Mike Glennon's chest tickling his bare back – a sense memory so powerful and so explicit it caused Tommy to redden, even though there was no one else in his immediate vicinity. Was this what it was like, he wondered, when you learned of the death of someone who'd touched you that way, who you'd touched that way? For that was all that differentiated Mike from other, better friends he'd lost, whose deaths had not occasioned such a pronounced physical reaction.

He closed his eyes and, temporarily, could see nothing but the Welshman's bright blue eyes, the ones he and David had saved from blindness. What good was that now? He dared not allow himself a reaction to Hardison's death, for he knew it wouldn't be a kind one. But he profoundly regretted that Glennon had died carrying such a low opinion of him, and he hoped the end for him had been quick and painless, not all horrible like with Muffett. "I'm sorry, Mike," he heard himself whisper.

And then it passed. Far more calmly than before, he looked back down and read the rest of Sister Jean's letter.

> Summer is lingering here in London, and the days are still quite fair. The papers say that the war is going well, altho' we never seem to lack for new patients. I wonder.
>
> David says you will be writing me as well. I shall look forward to your letters, too. Perhaps the girls will tease me about having two beaux at the front! A bad joke, I'm afraid. But I don't mind it at all, really I don't.
>
> I do hope you are well and safe. God watch over you.
>
> Sincerely,
> Jean Anderson

Tommy looked twice at her comment about "having two beaux" and couldn't convince himself that he was imagining the tone of self-mockery. It was as if she knew exactly what her role was in this exchange – down to the most important detail – and didn't care. He thought of how she had surprised them together that last morning in London, how she had seemed far less embarrassed than they. But it simply wasn't possible she really understood about him and Davey. She could never be so matter-of-fact about such a thing.

With a start, he realized he'd been thinking about Sister Jean, Mike – and not about the one who'd so thoroughly occupied his thoughts, awake and asleep, for the past three weeks. David was alive! – or at least, he'd made it through that dreadful counterattack the morning Tommy had left Picardy. How many times since then had Tommy said silently, if You just let him live…? As the full exhilaration over the reality of David's survival overtook him, he counted himself ready for anything.

The letters from home were, as he had anticipated, from Susan and from one of his sisters, full of the most inconsequential bits of information. And so it went for the next week: now that they were apparently staying in one place – indeed, it seemed they were destined to stay in this particular trench, in close reserve, forever – the mail began arriving regularly, with a message almost daily from Sister Jean to "tell Tommy I'm in the pink" (prompting daily letters back to tell Davey likewise), and also, nearly every day, a letter from home with little of substance to report. He began to wonder if his fateful communication to Susan, and the accompanying one to his parents, had gotten lost somewhere between France and Iowa.

Command of the 33rd, which had technically belonged to the French Army since they'd been moved to this sector, passed back to the American Army, with little effect on their day-to-day lives. Rumor had many, many Doughboys coming into the general area; but, stuck in their little trench, which clearly had seen a lot of use from their *poilu* predecessors, the soldiers of Tommy's unit could not confirm these distant reports. Dougherty, transparently bucking for lieutenant, was doing his best to keep his men motivated, but they were all feeling restless in the leadership vacuum left by Sand and Colbeck.

The rain had finally gone away, and it was the third day of fair weather. In what had become the highlight of his routine to alleviate the boredom, Tommy picked up his two letters, the one from England and the one from home, in the midafternoon, and then retired to the nearest unoccupied place, in this case a funk hole barely scraped out of a trench wall. He scratched himself in discomfort as he settled in; it had been many days since he'd had a bath, and the sunny weather seemed to make the chats more active.

The date on the letter from Sister Jean surprised him: 13.9.18. That meant she had posted it Thursday, a mere four days ago. Perhaps the American Army's mails were catching up with the British after all. But what was inside surprised him more. The terse note read:

First London General Hospital,
Camberwell

12.9.18

Dear Tommy:

I am sending you something rather different today. I do hope it reaches you in satisfactory condition.

I am well, and hoping you are the same.

Sincerely,
Jean Anderson

It seemed a missive designed to provoke anxiety. There had been no accompanying package, nor was there anything else in the envelope; Tommy quickly re-examined that, to assure himself he hadn't missed something. No, nothing but the single sheet of paper, which he read and re-read, 'til he ceased scratching his body and began to scratch his head. Just one sheet of paper, he repeated to himself, albeit a little thicker than the stationery Sister Jean usually used....

He flipped the page over; nothing on the back. Then some instinct caused him to hold the letter up to the sunlight that had so providentially reappeared the past few days, and his eye caught the faintest hint of something....

Excited now, and intrigued, Tommy glanced around to verify he was alone; then he turned the letter sideways, so that he was looking straight down at the top of it. He brought it very close to his eyes, and only then could he discern that this rather thick sheet of stationery was actually three sheets of paper carefully pressed together. He knew, or thought he knew, what that meant, and his elation soared. Although it had been only a few seconds, once again he looked about him; if this was indeed a soldier-to-soldier communication, uncensored, they were breaking the rules. He felt like a spy in a book. He thought about using a lucifer to get the leaves to separate, but feared burning them entirely in the process.

After some hesitation, he took out the blade of his bayonet, and began patiently paring at the edge of the paper. Every few moments he would look up, fearful someone might come by and catch him at this suspicious activity; then he would return to the task, tongue set between his lips in concentration. The work was as laborious as trying to thread a fine needle – something he'd often watched his sisters attempt – but even more painstaking. After many long minutes, he'd made no progress other than to fray one corner of the letter – and then he heard a noise, and replaced his blade just as he heard someone coming around the corner of the trench.

He certainly wasn't prepared for who it was. He shook his head and looked a second time as the familiar face broke into a grin and said, "Why, hello, Flaowuhs. Fancy meetin' you here."

Tommy's astonishment was so complete that he pitched forward out of his shallow funk hole and toppled unceremoniously to the trench floor which, fortunately, was mostly dry. He heard Jamie's raucous laughter, then felt the Australian's strong hand grab him by the collar to aid him to his feet. When the American had staggered back to a more dignified position, his first remark was "I ain't dreaming, am I?"

"No, Tommy," Colbeck said affably, "it's me. I'm really here."

"But – how–?"

"It's a long, long story, lad."

"I wanna hear it!"

"And you will. But there's somethin' important I got to tell you first. Peahson's alive and all right – at least, as far as I know–"

"You saw him?"

Colbeck, looking pleased with himself, nodded. "Abaout two weeks ago, saouth of Maricourt. The Rangers were in reserve there."

"Thanks, Jamie," Tommy said, gripping the Aussie's hand as he tried to sound more surprised at the information than he was. Then he recalled Colbeck's friendship with Glennon, and proceeded to give himself away: "You must know about Mike, then. I'm sorry."

For a second, Colbeck appeared genuinely unsettled at the mention of the Welshman; but then he closed up, saying, "It happens all the time in a war like this. But he was a good man." The lieutenant's eyes narrowed. "Haow did you know abaout that, anywise?"

"I just… heard." Tommy didn't think his evasion tactic was very effective, particularly with Jamie, who so often bragged he could read Flowers "like a book." But Colbeck merely nodded again, and didn't question him further. Feeling free to move on to another topic, the Doughboy eagerly asked, "Are you here for good?"

"For the duration," Jamie said with one more nod. "Have we lost anyone?"

"Hah! How could we? We ain't been doin' a thing–"

The Australian would have been hard put to miss the disgust in the Doughboy's voice. "You weren't at St-Mihiel, were you." It was a statement, not a question.

"What's that?"

"St-Mihiel. The Americans just won a big vict'ry there. Closed up a salient. Close to where they first took you, after Picardy."

His dander up, Tommy demanded, "Then why did they move us again? It was a great victory? We could have been in it!"

"But you weren't. So, forget abaout it." Having succeeded in cutting Tommy off, Jamie went on, "Besides, they've got other idears. Bigger idears. St-Mihiel was just a skirmish by comparison. That's why I'm back. Though I didn't expect to be, and it wasn't easy for me to do it."

Flowers shook his head. "I still don't understand."

Jamie's voice dropped. "Pershing's gath'rin' up the whole American Army. Ev'ryone knows he'll attack somewhere soon – Jerry knows it, too. Only question is when and where."

"So that's why you're back with us?"

"Yes and no. When I faound aout where they'd sent your crew, I had no choice. Especially once I told my wife, who always wants to know where you are."

Ignoring the implications of that, Tommy simply asked, "How is Nicole?"

Jamie smiled, though he didn't seem all that amused. "She's all right, thank you for askin'. And she's thrilled naow we're both here."

"She is? Why?"

"Do you know where you are, Tommy?"

"Somewhere near Verdun? The Bois Bourrus?"

The French was primitive, but the information was correct, as Colbeck acknowledged with a slight tilt of his head. "Just over the hill from here, just east of aour front lines, is a place called Cumières. Nicole grew up there."

"My God," Tommy said. "Nicole's hometown?"

"I called it a place, not a taown. Actually, it's just rubble naow. I sawr it not more than an haour ago. The village is gone. She don't know it, but I knew it even before I sawr it for myself."

Jamie watched the look on Tommy's face as he related this, and he judged the boy's reaction completely appropriate. But then the Yank grew ebullient, saying,"We'll get it back for her!"

"Tommy, you don't understand. It's already in aour hands. There's nothin' left to save."

"Then – then we'll get revenge for her!"

"That's all right with me. That's what we're here for, much as anything else. Hard to say, though, haow much it was Boche shells, and haow much it was her own people's artil'ry."

"Oh." There was a silence between them, then Tommy changed the subject yet again, saying, "Dougherty know you're back?"

At that, Jamie went instantly from grim-faced seriousness to full-fledged laughter. "Should have seen his face," Colbeck said as Flowers joined in with him, "like I was a ghost from Hell!"

Only much later – the next morning, in fact – did Flowers' attention return to his letters, the one he hadn't opened at all and the one within the letter that he was still trying to uncover. Sensing he had little time before he would be interrupted, he opened the mail from Iowa.

August 31, 1918
Dear Tommy:

Yesterday we received your letter about the French girl, telling us about your letter to Susan. Lidey went right over to Susan's house, but she didn't stay long. I don't think she felt particularly welcome.

I suppose I need hardly tell you that Susan is pretty broken up by your letter. I surely hope you know what you are doing, Tommy, and that you haven't let your head get turned by foreign ways. That happens to a boy sometimes. Your papa and I always thought you and Susan were a good match, and you said yourself this French girl turned you down flat. But of course, it is your life.

We all hope you are keeping safe.

Love,
Mama

It was as reproachful as she had ever been in writing him, but he realized it was probably the best he could hope for under the circumstances. Again he regretted the way he had broken the news, both to them and to Susan.

Without worrying about it any further, he shifted his attention to the other letter, holding it up to the light to reassure himself he hadn't imagined its secret contents. But this morning was a bit more cloudy than yesterday, and he couldn't make out the letter-within-a-letter.

"Flowers!" The voice was so near and so loud, it startled Tommy into dropping Sister Jean's letter. As he came to attention, he saw it was his sergeant. Dougherty had been unexpectedly circumspect with Tommy since Flowers had punched him during the fight with Carson; he also had been in a predictably foul mood since learning of their lieutenant's return. "Report to the front trench immediately!" the sergeant commanded.

Since their battalion was still in reserve, whatever was prompting the order was likely to be less pressing than Dougherty's tone; but Tommy snapped a salute in return, augmented with a crisp "Yes, sir!" Then he hesitated a fraction, and said in the same businesslike tone, "Permission to retrieve my letter, sir!"

Dougherty glanced down at the sheet of paper lying facedown in the dirt, and then, in horror, Flowers watched him pick it up. Tommy held his breath, waiting for his NCO to read it, possibly aloud, or maybe even tear it to pieces.

"Here," said the sergeant in a wholly unanticipated mild tone, as he tendered the letter; then, as Tommy took it from him, his voice reverted: "Now, get going! Double time!"

"Yes, *sir!*"

# Chapter LXVI

The relentless rain returned a few days later, but with the reappearance of Colbeck a certain comfort had returned to their routine; even the ancient friction between the Aussie and Dougherty was reassuringly familiar for the men of Flowers' unit. And there was also a growing sense that something big was indeed impending.

Tommy's post now consisted exclusively of letters from home, with each of the various members of his family adding their two cents' worth to the already established position that they all thought he had made a mistake with Susan. The last letter of this sort came from his youngest sister, Peg; it was also the kindest:

Dear Tommy,

How are you? I hope you are well and safe.

I am sure by now you must be weary of hearing from everyone about your letter to Susan. I must confess I don't understand, myself. She is like a sister to us all, and I think we were all expecting she would actually become our sister, someday. But you are doing the job of a man, and you are entitled to make a man's decisions. I only hope it is the right one for you. If we seem harsh in our judgments, please understand we are afraid you have done something you will regret. But we still all love you very much.

Your affectionate sister,
Peg

Each day Tommy also spent what little time he could out of the sight of the other Doughboys teasing the edges of Sister Jean's letter. He eventually succeeded in prying open one corner, thus confirming what he'd suspected; but the inner letter was glued, or waxed, between the other two all the way around, and when he tried to rush the process of separating them, all three tore a little, so he slowed the pace of his own efforts accordingly. The tedious task was difficult enough, but the lack of post from London worried him, and made his efforts to pry loose the inside letter all the more imperative.

The third day after the resumption of the rain was both unusually quiet, in the sense that there were no special orders to change their daily routine, and unusually hectic, in that more and more soldiers seemed to be crowding into their trenches. Colbeck was there when Searles made his way along the muddy, slimy duckboards, half lost in puddles, and handed Tommy two pieces of mail with the brief comment, "Something different for you, Flower." Then the postal officer was gone. Tommy quickly glanced at the postmarks and stuffed the letters in his tunic, next to the now nearly week-old post from Sister Jean, in order to keep all of them dry.

"What's the matter, Flaowuhs?"

Tommy turned to face his lieutenant in the downpour. "Nothing, sir."

"Tommy. I know you better."

The American gave a slight shrug. "I just wish I had a dry place to open my letters and read them… by myself."

"Demandin' little bugger, ain'tcha?" Tommy looked down at the muddy trench floor, and Jamie added, "Hey! That was a *joke*, Flaowuhs!"

Tommy looked back up. "Sorry. Couldn't see your face for the rain to tell."

Jamie seemed to make up his mind about something. "Come along," he said with an easy toss of his head, and he splashed off a couple of steps in the opposite direction; when Flowers failed to follow, he turned back and added, "That's an order!"

The Doughboy followed Colbeck through several muddy, rain-drenched mazes until they reached slightly higher ground. Off the main trench there, on the parados, were several – well, they looked like doors. Jamie knocked on one, got no response, then said to Tommy, "After you, Private."

Tommy entered the blackness beyond the door as he heard Jamie say behind him, "Careful of your step." The warning came none too soon, as the American almost stumbled; then Jamie struck a lucifer behind him, and it illuminated a small, dank – but dry – area, with a few blankets on the floor. There was an old wine bottle with a candle stuck in it; Colbeck lit the wick just as his own source of light was about to expire.

"What is this place?" Flowers asked in wonder.

"It's an officers' dugaout. They built this one a little deeper when the Jerries were bombardin' the area. The French give their officers a little more in the way of creature comforts than they give their men. So do the Germans and the English." Jamie's tone was not one of approval. "Several of us sleep here naow when we can, but I knew today, right naow, no one would be here. Of course, I'm not even supposed to show this to one of the rankers, let alone have you here. They could accuse me of playin' fav'rites."

"Then maybe we should leave. You don't have to–"

"'Course I don't have to, lad. I wanted to." Tommy stared in confusion at Jamie, whose tone grew more solemn as he said, "They're goin' to put us in the front lines tonight. There'll be a big show very soon naow. I don't think we'll see Sergeant Searles again 'til it's over. Least you can do for naow is read your post in peace."

"Thanks, Jamie," Tommy said, all sincerity. Pulling the letters – all three – safe and dry from his soggy tunic, he added, "There's one here I reckon you should hear, too."

Jamie raised an eyebrow. "You don't say?"

"It's from Chicago."

Jamie's tone remained bemused. He crossed his arms, leaned against the walls of the dugout. "Chicago? Someone been writin' you letters from there?"

"Not 'til now." Tommy opened the letter and, accepting Jamie's tacit acknowledgment that he'd like to hear the contents, too, read aloud:

September 5, 1918
Dear Tommy,

I apologize for not writing sooner. Today is my second day out of surgery, and on the first day they would not let me do anything as strenuous as writing a letter!

The voyage home was a hard one – quite a few cases of sea-sickness, and I don't mind telling you your old captain was one of them. But, oh, when we made it into New York harbor! I've always loved this country, but until now, I believe I never knew how much.

They put me on a train to Chicago, and I had a fine homecoming with Weezy–

"Such a strange name for Billy's wife," interrupted Jamie, though he already knew it. "Weezy!"

–but then they decided to operate on me right away, to get some more of the shrapnel out. And they got quite a lot, 'though not all of it, of course. I don't suppose they'll ever get all of it.

Today they wheeled me outside, which reminded me of your wheeling me around at the hospital in Vadencourt. Tommy, words cannot describe how wonderful it is for me to be alive and home. I know I thanked you already, and I told you I wouldn't again, but I do. And tell David Pearson the same when you see him.

The war news is very positive. When you come marching home, I hope you'll stop in Chicago, and we can have a drink together. I won't give you all that malarkey you usually get in letters about hoping you're safe and warm, because I'm sure you'll be all right. And I know you will come marching home, because you have a good head and a good heart.

Best regards,
Billy Sand
P.S. – Weezy and I are expecting our first child early next summer.

"Well, that was quick," Jamie said with studied lewdness. "And that's one part the shrapnel obviously missed."

"There's something more," Tommy said, and his voice caught as he read:

If it's a boy, we mean to name him Tommy.

Jamie cleared his throat, then said, "Actually, Weezy ain't the only one."

"You mean–?" Jamie nodded, and Tommy's face, dimly illuminated by the candle, lit further with pure joy. "Jamie!" the American cried, and he stood and reached over to his friend, pumping his arm. "Congratulations! That's wonderful!"

"Yeah," Colbeck said in an odd, clipped tone. Then, in a hurry to change the subject, he added, "That Billy Sand writes a nice letter. But then, I'm not surprised."

"Sorry he didn't mention you," said Flowers, re-seating himself.

"Ah, listen, Mister Manners, I'm not the one who saved his life. That was your doin' – yours and David's. That's somethin' you ought to be praoud of – savin' the life of a good man."

"I am. We are. But I reckon you saved the life of more than one good man in your time."

"I have," Jamie acknowledged. "Naow, what abaout your other letters?"

"I – uh–"

"–want to read them in peace, I know. Go ahead. I won't read over your shoulder."

"Does… Nicole write you?"

"Of course she does. So does her auntie. Only diff'rence between their letters is Nicole always asks abaout you. Auntie never does."

"I'm glad you're getting mail, too."

"Go on. I get mail. From Australia sometimes, too."

"Really?"

"Yes, really. I wasn't born an orphan, y'know." There was a pause, then Jamie added, "You're puttin' off readin' your other letters. I'm sorry, lad, but I can't leave you here alone–"

"I don't expect you to. You've done more than enough for me already." Flowers pondered for a second, then made a decision. "Jamie – you promise not to tell anyone something?"

Colbeck's laughter was rather harsh. "What is there left for me to know abaout you, lad?"

Without a word, Tommy took the old letter from Sister Jean out of his tunic and presented it to Jamie, who simply said, "What's this?" He didn't read the writing, just noted its torn condition.

"There's a letter inside the letter, I think."

Jamie examined it more carefully. "There's – Well, I'll be!" he exclaimed, with something that sounded like real admiration. "From David, is it?"

"I reckon so. Hope so."

"Who's your middle man?"

"Someone we met in London. Uh, a woman, actually."

"Hah. Either she's very clever, or Peahson is." The Aussie's tone changed momentarily: "This is totally against regulations, you understand." Then, in his original tone: "Which is why it's so clever... but you ain't opened it all the way."

"No. It's taking a long time."

"A long time? Why?"

"I've been – using the blade from my bayonet–"

Jamie burst into laughter again, good-natured this time. "Lad, that ain't no way to open a letter like this! The war'll be over before you get it done."

He looked closely at the edges of the three-in-one letter, obviously more interested in the mechanics of the ruse than the contents of the note. "This is wax," he stated. "That's easy." Without asking Tommy, he picked up the bottle with the glowing candle inserted in it.

"Hey!" Tommy said impetuously.

"Hey what?"

A bit abashed, Flowers said, "Be careful, that's all."

"Hardly even need to be. But don't you worry." Colbeck held the candle flame about two inches from the edge of the letter and rhythmically moved it – over, down, over, up. After three full passes like this, he gingerly peeled the top and backing papers right off, replaced the candle, and offered all three sheets to Tommy with an accompanying "There you are."

"Wow, Jamie, I don't know how to thank–"

"So don't. I just happened to know haow. You, obviously, didn't." Before Flowers could say anything more, the Aussie added, "I could use a short nap. That'll leave you time to read your letters. But if you hear anyone comin' in, kick me awake. And I mean kick me." Jamie threw himself inelegantly on one of the blankets, and Tommy took the candle and the secret letter he was free at last to read.

8.9.18

Love,

Tis a foolish, foolish thing I do, but I can't help myself. Sister Jean has been wonderful, and now I ask even more from her, to send this on to you without reading it herself. But as good as it is for her to send messages between us, I miss so very much talking to you. And this is as near as I can get.

We are in another little town, in reserve, though we could go back up the line any time. The last two weeks have been bloody awful. The battle the day your lot shipped out was terrible, I thought I was going to die, and as you know, Mike and Hardison both got it. But we hit the Jerries back as hard as they hit us.

We've been in reserve most of the time since, but like I said, it's been bloody awful all the same. And I must tell you the truth, love. It's because I worry so after you. I know I said we might be better off apart til the war is over. But I believe I was wrong about that. I so miss seeing your face, hearing your voice. I'm being soft, I know, and in writing beside. But I believe you will understand. Because you always understand me, Tommy. You're the only one ever has.

Keep your head down, love. It's all I live for.

Yr loving Davey

By the time he reached the end, Tommy could feel his pulse racing and his breath coming in great gulps. So strange to read David's writing, with all the h's that he'd never pronounce in place, and words like "myself" and "awful" spelled right, not like he said them. But his heart and soul were in it – Pearson, who could be so reticent sometimes. And the risk for the both of them, but especially to himself, in sending it! The trust in Sister Jean!

Tommy's eyes were full, but inside him there was a wild exultation. He felt himself the luckiest man in the world. Shaking, he folded the letter and put it back inside his tunic, right over his heart. As he did, he withdrew Jean's letter that had arrived today. He was amazed to note the date – only three days ago.

First London General Hospital,
Camberwell
19.9.18
Dear Tommy,

I heard from David today – the same as always. He said to "tell Tommy I'm in the pink." His unit has been in another battle, but they came through all right, at least he did, and now they are reserve again.

My last letter from you, which I related to him, was an interesting one. I am sure they are moving you about so constantly for a reason. Or at least they must believe so. Be patient, and be careful.

Sincerely,

Jean Anderson
PS – Did you get the special delivery?

He was glad to get the letter, of course, but it also revived his sense of frustration about the time that lay between and among them all. David had already been back to the front, in another battle, and back to reserve since writing his letter to Tommy. And Sister Jean was sitting in London thinking they were still constantly shifting Tommy about, when his unit hadn't moved now for nearly two weeks!

He had to write a reply suitable to David's letter, though somehow he felt he could never match its rough eloquence. But with time running down – he knew he should soon waken Colbeck, who was now snoring loudly – it behooved him to try, anyway, so he could leave something for Searles when they went up the line.

9/22/18

Dear Sister Jean:

Yes, I got the special delivery. You are an angel, you know. Please tell David I said that now I believe in angels. And please tell Davey I'm in the pink, thanks to the special delivery – more in the pink than ever, in fact. Tell him that, please.

We are about to go up the line, and that's good, because we have been here doing nothing for almost two weeks. It is time to win this war and be done with it. Do not worry, I will keep my head down. Please tell Davey I will always keep my head down, because I have so much to live for. Please tell him I said that.

And thank you for everything, Sister. Thank you.

Sincerely,

Tommy Flowers

# Chapter LXVII

Jamie's information was accurate as usual; that night, Tommy's battalion, the 2nd, moved up the line to join his regiment's 3rd Battalion in trenches the latter group already occupied. The considerable discomfort of these crowded conditions was outweighed, though just barely, by the palpable excitement attendant to the now-obvious fact that an American thrust (and a purely American thrust, give or take the presence of a few men like Jamie) against the Germans was imminent, perhaps even that very night, and that they were to be a part of it.

But the attack didn't commence that night, nor the next. The day after that the rain stopped, but the trenches stank of too many men literally on top of each other for too long. And still more soldiers seemed to be pouring in, giving rise to jokes about how many Doughboys could be fit into one trench system.

The next day was also a fine one, and that afternoon Jamie squeezed his way to where Tommy stood at the ready at the parapet, and ordered Flowers to stand down from the firebay. Since his particular tour of duty was being cut short, Flower of Iowa shot his lieutenant a quizzical look; but the Aussie simply said, "Follow me," so the Doughboy did, through one jammed trench after another, and then another, and another. Eventually they came aboveground to a sheltered clearing, a place with a sudden, sweeping view, though that was partially obscured by a low-clinging light fog. Only then did Jamie speak again: "Do you remember this drill, from Hamel?"

Tommy hadn't, until the question was asked. With some confidence, he replied, "The battle's tonight, isn't it? You're gonna show me the field of battle, so I'll know it in case you fall. Or in case I do."

"Huh," Jamie grunted. "You remember too well. I don't expect to 'fall,' as you so delicately put it, and I don't expect you to neither." His tone was gruff and very officer-like, but then he added, "I should only be showin' this to Dougherty, but I don't trust that bastard. So, even if I was the one who busted you back to private..."

He let the sentence drift, and Tommy put in, "I deserved it."

"Yes. Yes, you did deserve it." A pause, and then, "Anywise, look here. Right naow we're on the far slope of Le Mort-Homme – you heard of it?" Tommy shook his head. "You should have. It means 'Dead Man's Hill' in French. It was called that before the *poilus* and the Boche *really* made it Dead Man's Hill, araound the time of Verdun. French have held on to it ever since, though it's blasted to bits more than not – that's Cumières over there, on aour far right."

It was a short, sharp aside; Tommy merely nodded at the sight of the rubble where Nicole's family had once lived, and Jamie continued, "Below is the Ruisseau de Forges – we'd call it a brook, or maybe you Americans would call it a creek. It ain't much, but it'll be hell to cross with all the rains we've had." He pointed ahead, beyond the creek, to the ruins of two more villages. "That's Bethincourt on the left, and Forges on the right. Aour division will attack between them. The Jerries are in the hills just beyond." The hills looked more like gentle ridges to Tommy. "We're goin' to drive 'em aout o'there." Tommy was taking it all in, and Jamie looked over to gauge his reaction. "Any questions?"

"No, sir," Flowers responded, feeling for once that a "sir" was appropriate with Colbeck. "Seems clear and simple enough."

Jamie seemed to relax a shade. "It is and it ain't. Y'see, this is just the little part aour division is takin'. The whole *army* is moving forwards."

Again Tommy reacted on impulse, whistling and saying, "No!"

Jamie merely nodded and smiled. "It's as big as the Somme," he said. Then the smile vanished. "And it better be better."

A heavy ground mist settled over everything that evening, and Tommy wondered if the generals would postpone the attack. But in fact, though he couldn't know it, the mist was helping, as it obscured efforts by American engineers to put pontoon bridges over Forges Creek. At 3:30 in the morning, Tommy's unit – and everybody else, it seemed – moved all at once to their forward positions on the far slope of the Mort-Homme.

The weather was fairly warm for late September, and the mist was thinning. Tommy lay quietly amid the terrible congestion of men and equipment, his mind at ease, David's letter still where he'd placed it over his heart. Carl Wegman, of course, was right by his side; and as it grew light and close to zero hour, Flowers remembered that, the trench raid notwithstanding, Wegman really hadn't been through anything like this before, and he briefly patted the Illinoisan on the shoulder and whispered, "It'll be all right."

"It will, won't it," agreed Carl, trying to imitate Tommy's can-do tone.

At 5:30 the Americans' opening barrage went off – and judging from the noise, Tommy could tell Jamie was right again; it wasn't just in their little sector, but all along this front. With shouts from Colbeck, Dougherty, and their other leaders, the men of E Company set off from their forward trenches, down into the marshy valley of the Forges, crowding with their fellow soldiers of the 33rd onto the bridges which had been so miraculously constructed overnight, and which, equal miracle, held.

Once across the creek they tried to re-form, egged on by their officers. "Let's go let's go *let's go!*" came the familiar cry of Dougherty out of the din and confusion, and this time Tommy was glad the sergeant was there, as Flowers himself led

Wegman, Giannelli, Young, and several others up to the road that ran between Forges and Bethincourt, where they stopped to reassemble.

"Hold on, men!" Jamie called out. "Wait for aour barrage." Remembering Hamel, Tommy prayed it wouldn't fall short this time. As his lieutenant trotted past him, Colbeck casually turned to Flowers and said, "Piece o'cake so far. When the smoke lifts, you'll see Jerries runnin' the other way." He laughed then, but the laugh was drowned out by the buzz of an aeroplane soaring from out of nowhere, spraying machine-gun bullets in their general direction. They all hit the dirt, but by the time they did, the infernal machine had moved on and it was over. Jamie stood up again, called out, "Anyone hit?" and, receiving no responses in the affirmative, chortled, "They ain't shootin' sharp, neither."

Shortly after that, up in front of them about a hundred yards, there came a tremendous roar – the rolling barrage, on time and in perfect position. *"Vivent les Français!"* Jamie cried, and his American charges, whether they knew French or not, understood he was saluting the army that had provided such perfect artillery. "Let's go, boys!" he shouted to his group, and they headed up the foggy, smoky slope, the sound of artillery, aeroplanes, and machine guns blasting, buzzing, and rattling in their ears.

They had advanced about a hundred yards, maybe less, when suddenly they broke through the fog and smokescreen to a wondrous sight – a splendidly beautiful, sunny September morning, with Doughboys on all sides moving up the gentle grassy slopes beyond the Bethincourt-Forges road. Much of the area was still green, and it was clear the land had been cultivated for many, many years, maybe even for centuries.

It looks like Iowa, Tommy thought. What a grand thing to be here, he exulted, and to help win this war, to help Nicole's people reclaim this land that looks so much like my own home.

As was generally the case with the German Army in the area that morning, things were not going very well for the artillery battery just across the River Meuse, which marked the edge of the American Army's advance. In frustration and fear, the once well-disciplined crew had begun to launch their shells wildly into the air. Few of the projectiles were hitting their marks; almost all were falling harmlessly behind or in front of the oncoming Doughboys – almost all, but not quite. As the men of E Company confidently picked up the pace of their ascent of that first slope past the Bethincourt-Forges road, one of these deadly strays suddenly came shrieking from off to their right, and exploded directly in their midst.

Following procedure, they had been sufficiently spread out to avoid a resulting massacre; indeed, at first, as he scrambled back to his feet and tried to assess the damage wrought by the missile, Jamie was sure it had managed to miss them all – not even any shrapnel wounds. But then he heard Carl Wegman's piercing cry of *"TOMMY!"* – and saw the young Illinoisan gaping in horror over the new crater the shell had created.

As fast as he could remember running on a battlefield, Colbeck tore over to the spot where the shaking Wegman stood rooted. The private's terror was beginning to affect the other men, causing them to slow down, and as Jamie reached Carl's side, he heard Daniel Dougherty shout to them all, "C'mon, men, keep moving. Let's go let's go *let's go!"*

Out of nowhere, an old promise resurfaced in Colbeck's mind: You are responsible for this man's safety. Either you both make it through this war, or neither one does. He turned and focused on his sergeant, and he could tell by the unprecedented fear in Dougherty's eyes that the NCO suddenly recalled the threat, too. It would be so easy, Colbeck thought, to shoot this man dead right here; these green Americans would take his word that it was a necessary action because Dougherty was making too much noise.

But then, the Australian thought, he can't be called to account for a stray shell. Besides, Dougherty was right; the only thing to do was to keep moving forward, to kill and capture more of the enemy. Turning back to Wegman and firmly gripping the private's heaving shoulders, he cried out to the group, "The sarge is right, men. Let's go!"

How on earth, Jamie wondered, was he ever going to find the words to tell Nicole.

As for Carl Wegman, before Colbeck's steadying hand literally swiveled his head forward, to face up the hill, he took one long last look at the gaping hole where Flower of Iowa had so cheerfully stood only moments before. Hanging over the crater now there was only a fine red mist, minute droplets suspended for seconds before they fell back to earth.

Tommy, of course, had never heard it coming.

The next day, about 150 miles to the northwest, Sister Anne Simpson was busy trying to bring some sort of order to the army hospital in Peronne, a small city athwart the Somme that had, until earlier in the month, been occupied by the Germans. With the British offensive now seven weeks old and continuing its successes, the front had moved far enough forward that it was deemed safe for a woman to be in Peronne, although Sister Anne was still one of only a few around.

This particular hospital was serving as a way station for men whose wounds were too serious to be cared for properly at a casualty clearing station. Some of the wounded were passing through on their way to England; others mended here and were sent back east, to the ever-advancing front; still others never left. Sister Anne, a stout, no-nonsense, sixtyish native of Belfast, had been brought down to help reorganize the Peronne hospital in view of her long, hard experience – about three years' worth – behind the front in the Ypres sector, in Belgium. She had truly seen it all, and as a result was uncommonly good at forecasting a patient's fate from the moment he first came under her care.

But not always. For example, five days ago, upon his admittance to the Peronne hospital, Sister Anne had immediately pegged as a born survivor a little Tommy who had been wounded in the thigh in an action at Epehy. While the inside of his groin area – though not the most vital parts – had looked horrifying to the untrained eye, and his entire left leg bore witness to a fairly severe injury earlier on, she noted with approval that his wounds had been thoroughly cleansed – agony though it must have been for the patient – at the casualty clearing station. There was no sign of sepsis, and the patient had seemed to be responding well, with typical Tommy cheer, even if he was a bit on the quiet and subdued side.

Last night, though, he had sprung a fever; and this morning he had a deep cough and a few other symptoms that both perplexed Sister Anne and struck her with dread on the young man's behalf, for they all seemed to add up to the Plague of the Spanish Lady. Such a diagnosis would not have surprised her this past spring, when she had watched as many Tommies falling before the 'flu as from bullets and shells. But this autumn, General Haig's men seemed almost impervious to it; all the cases she had seen lately were either German prisoners, who clearly had been eating poorly, or, conversely, those hearty Doughboys newly arrived from America. It usually killed them both with equal disdain.

By mid-morning the little Tommy's symptoms had become so pronounced that his hot, writhing body was confined to a barren isolation ward. Most of the doctors and medical corpsmen with whom Sister Anne worked could not be much bothered with a 'flu case, whether from a sense of priorities or from plain fear; but she had no terror of the Spanish Lady for herself, and although he was just one more dying Tommy in a long line she would never forget, should she live to be a hundred, still he seemed so small and alone that she took up a sporadic vigil at his bedside. Toward evening, she stopped by once again and found him awake; but the sheets were drenched, and when she touched his forehead, he was burning up, being consumed alive. Pulling up a chair alongside this private, whose identity disc read "D. Pearson," she asked him gently, hoping she wouldn't alarm him, "Private Pearson, is there anyone you'd like me to write for you?"

His voice was throaty and far away, and his speech a bit slurred. "One."

"Your mum?"

He shook his head slightly, with great effort. "No. Sis–"

"Your sister, then?"

"Not… me sis, neither. Sister… Jean."

"Sister Jean?" In a flash it added up for Sister Anne. "A nurse?" He nodded, very weakly. "Your sweetheart's a nurse?" she suggested kindly.

But he used his sapping strength to shake his head. "No," he wheezed. "That's Flower."

Confused, she repeated, "Flower," and he nodded, adding, "Iowa."

She almost didn't catch the word. "Ioway? But that's in America, isn't it?" The poor boy was obviously delirious.

With his greatest effort yet, Pearson said, "Tell… Sister… write Flower."

Though it was obviously important to him, Sister Anne had no idea who or where this Sister Jean was, and she was reluctant to press the soldier any further, he was in such a poor state. Perhaps he'd fallen in love with some American nurse, from Iowa. She quietly told him "I will," patted the dying lad on the head, stroked his soaking hair.

She thought she heard him whisper "Tommy." Poor thing, she thought with an aching heart, he really is confused. *He's* the Tommy.

Just as she turned to go, Sister Anne heard a horrible hacking sound, and when she looked back she saw he was coughing up black blood. She ran to get a towel, and came back to absolutely no hope: it was indeed the Spanish 'flu, and he was near the end. After the hemorrhage, he was quiet, pale and still, and although Sister Anne was due for a period of rest, she was certain he would not last the night, and she made a pact with herself not to leave him there to die alone. She was still there, dozing, when shortly after midnight, he quietly slipped away.

By the time Sister Anne returned later the next morning, the cross-wallahs already had whisked away Private Pearson's body for a proper burial in a nearby British war cemetery. She supervised the familiar but always melancholy task of ensuring that a telegram would be sent to his family, who were from some town in Somerset she'd never heard of. Going through the boy's personal effects, she discovered several letters from the mysterious Sister Jean, who apparently really did exist; she worked at First London General in Camberwell, a hospital Sister Anne knew very well. Sister Anne resolved to write this fellow nursing sister, and to send her letters to Pearson back to his family. But, straitlaced though she was, the woman from Belfast's curiosity got the better of her, and she decided she should take a look at the letters to make certain she had the situation right.

And the letters were very odd – friendly, but definitely not romantic. They kept carrying the same message over and over again: "Tommy says, 'Tell Davey I'm in the pink.'" It seemed almost a code. Their strangeness caused Sister Anne to hesitate on her resolve; then she got distracted by the many other demands of her work, and two days passed before one final letter, forwarded to Private Pearson, arrived at the hospital in Peronne. Rather than simply marking it "Deceased" and returning it, Sister Anne, hoping to solve this small mystery, opened and read it:

> First London General Hospital,
> Camberwell
> 26.9.18
> Dear David:
>
> Another letter from Tommy today – a bit different. He said to tell you he received the special delivery, to "please tell David I said that I now believe in angels," that he is "more in the pink than ever" because of the delivery, and that you shouldn't worry, that he will always keep his head down, as "I have so much to live for."
>
> Our Private Flowers – your Flower of Iowa – has got quite chatty, hasn't he?
>
> And I hope and trust you are well and safe.
>
> Sincerely,
> Jean Anderson

"Our Private Flowers – your Flower of Iowa." Sister Anne froze when she encountered this phrasing, and then she read and re-read the letter several times, hoping to divine a different meaning. "That's Flower," the dying David had said, using the last of his strength to correct her suggestion as to who his sweetheart was. Given everything she had seen and heard, the import was now quite clear to her. She had half a mind to write this silly Sister Jean and tell her what a foolish, naive girl she was, letting herself be a party to something like…

In a fit of disgust, she picked up the other letters and tied them in a packet with this latest one, then crept down to a part of the hospital where they always kept a fire stoked, now the nights were colder, with October on the morrow. As she watched the letters with their damning contents burn, she thought, and he seemed such a nice lad. At least, this way, both the boys' families shall never know.

# EPILOGUE
# OCTOBER 1993

Jack Intaglia's after-college vacation, postponed from the summer while he worked and saved up more money for the trip, hadn't been going all that well. He had felt a bit let down by his first couple of days and nights in Amsterdam; it was a beautiful city, to be sure, but the fabled red-light district was a little intense for his tastes, and the loud, bad music and dark, smoky ambience of the discos made him think he might as well be back home at the local watering hole in Danbury, Connecticut.

But then, yesterday at lunchtime, he'd checked out a tavern listed in his guidebook, and his luck had turned. The place oozed comfortable charm, with the unlikely atmosphere of an English pub; and as Jack sat himself down at one of its sidewalk tables in the cool sunshine of early October, watching the boat traffic on the Singel canal, another young man, a breathtaking brown-eyed blond, wandered, rather tentatively, into the bar, then came back out and seated himself two tables away. After a minute or so, Jack stole a nervous glance at that fabulous face – and found a shy smile aimed, improbably, back at him. Jack had thought the apparition was German or Dutch or something, but when Sandy Hampton spoke to him, he turned out to be English, of all things, from the Midlands near Manchester, though he was currently going to school in Amsterdam.

Best of all, what followed wasn't merely a matter of scoring for an evening; Jack and Sandy had clicked in a way neither young man had experienced before, in a way both were longing for. Even when Jack told Sandy that, unfortunately, he had to leave town the next morning, to drive to Luxembourg and discharge the family obligation that had caused his parents to help pay for his trip, the Briton had said, to the American's surprise and pleasure, that he would be willing to go with Jack, if the latter thought it appropriate.

So there they were, together on the *autoroute,* first speeding through the flat Dutch countryside and then through the gently rolling Ardennes of eastern Belgium, the two of them still getting to know each other in the first flush of maybe-this-could-turn-into-something. "Tell me again who it is we're seeing?" Sandy asked Jack.

"The whole thing is really for my great-grandmother. She's ninety-two, ninety-three later this month."

Sandy whistled. "And still getting 'round? God bless the old bird. But how did a Yank named Intaglia end up with a great-granny in Luxembourg?"

"It's a long story."

"We've a long enough ride," Sandy pointed out amiably.

Jack collected his thoughts, looked at the road as the cars with German plates whizzed past them. "My great-grandmother – we all call her Grand-mère – is French. Her oldest daughter – that's my Grandma McCaffrey – married an American, a G.I. who came to France during the war. That was my Grandpa McCaffrey."

"Think I could've figured that one out," Sandy said lightly. "That's World War II, I presume?"

"Of course. Anyway, they came back to America, to Florida, and settled there, and had my mom and my two uncles. And my mom went to school in Connecticut, where she met and married my dad, who was from Hartford."

"So you're Irish and Italian, and a bit French, too. No wonder you're so handsome."

Jack blushed to the roots of his dark hair, shot a look with his green eyes over to Sandy. "You should talk."

Sandy laughed and patted Jack's knee, and the American put his hand over the Briton's, then went on, "I'm named Jack, after Grandpa McCaffrey, but also for my great-grandfather. His name was Jack, too."

"This is the great-grandfather who married your Grand-mère?"

"That's right."

"'Jack' doesn't sound very French."

"He wasn't. He was Australian. They met in the war."

"World War II?"

"No. The first one."

"The Great War, you mean?"

"Yes, World War I."

"He's probably dead, then?"

Jack nodded. "A long time ago. He was shot by the Nazis for fighting with the French Resistance. In the second war."

A little bemused, Sandy said, "Aren't you the international lot?"

"It gets better. My great-grandpa and Grand-mère had another daughter, my great-aunt Lizette. *She* married a Frenchman, but *he* was killed in the war – the second one – and their daughter did the ultimate when she grew up: she married a German! They're the ones we're going to see, got a couple of daughters about our age – twins, but they're not identical."

Sandy pondered all this, said, "So your great-grandmother, who lost a husband and a son-in-law to the Germans, is now living under the roof of a German?"

"That's one way you might put it. And actually, she lost more than that. All but one of her brothers were killed in the war – the first war."

An hour or so later, the two pulled into the driveway of Klaus and Eglantine Sternberg's home overlooking Luxembourg City. Their arrival had the air of a family reunion, and Sandy would have felt uncomfortable had it not been for the warm hospitality of the entire clan, especially Jack's cousins Annik and Monika, who seemed happy to have a pair of good-looking young men around – a point re-emphasized by the family's oldest member, for when Grand-mère was introduced to the young Mr. Hampton, she surveyed him with bright, alert eyes and pronounced, *"Mais tu es beau!"* using the familiar French and not caring; the license of the very old.

After the whole group had enjoyed a hearty dinner, Annik led the young men down the hall to a small computer room, and pointed to the floor there. "You can sleep there together, it's OK?" she said; both sisters' English was charmingly accented by French.

"It's OK," Jack agreed, and he stole a devilish look at Sandy, just as Monika came down the hall to join them.

"Grand-mère is right, Jack. You chose a beauty. And such a nice boy, too."

Sandy, who had been increasingly concerned that the girls might have the wrong impression and be too interested in the boys, colored at this comment as Annik joined in the giggling. "As you can see, they know," Jack said in his easygoing, American way. "It's cool."

"Grand-mère, too?" Sandy asked.

"Well, I don't know about *her*–"

"But, as you mention Grand-mère, we do wish to ask of you a favor," Monika interrupted.

"Sure," said Jack. "What is it?"

They had moved out onto the back terrace, where they could admire the soft gold of the lindens of Luxembourg's lovely, muted autumn. Annik spoke next: "Every year Grand-mère wants to go to her old village, Cumières, for – 'ow do you call it, Armistice Day?"

"Veterans Day, we call it now," Jack said. "November 11th."

"Remembrance Day, in my country," Sandy put in.

*"Oui,"* Annik agreed. "But, by then it is cold, many years, and Grand-mère is not so strong as she was. And – this is important to her, but for our parents, it is something they would rather forget."

Monika spoke up. "Cumières is not even there, not since Grand-mère was our age, when the Germans and the French fought over Verdun. It was so long ago." She paused, added, "We do not much think of ourselves as French or German anymore, only as Europeans. Is that not so, Sandy?"

"That's how I see it," the young Englishman concurred.

"So you see," Annik said to Jack, "it is all a little awkward for us. If tomorrow is beautiful, like today, perhaps you will take Grand-mère this year, while the weather is still fine, *hein?*"

Jack looked uncertainly over to Sandy, who simply gave him the slightest of nods – which gave the American a flush of unexpected satisfaction; it was like they were already a couple, making decisions together like that. "Sure, we'll do it," he said. "But my French isn't so hot. I don't know about Sandy's."

"*Très pauvre,*" the Englishman put in, and they all laughed.

"It will be all right," Annik said with certainty. "She mostly sleeps in the car. And she knows more English than she lets on. After all, her husband was from Australia."

"I remember," said Jack.

"Oh," Monika added, "and she will, probably, want to stop at the American cemetery in Romagne, too. That is usually her wish."

"The American cemetery?" Jack asked. "Why?"

Monika shrugged. "She has never said. When we were little girls, we used to pretend she had a secret lover there."

"Sounds like a bit of schoolgirl fantasy," Sandy chided them good-naturedly.

"I am sure you are right," Annik conceded, and she shrugged. "Who knows why old people do the things they do, sometimes?"

The next day dawned sunny, cool, and sublime, and Jack and Sandy, in the afterglow of another perfect night together, carefully escorted the old lady into the back seat of Jack's rented Opel, then breezed across the French frontier (as easily, Jack thought, as if he were driving from Connecticut to New York), armed with directions from the grateful Sternbergs. As the girls had predicted, Grand-mère promptly fell asleep in the back, and the two young men were able to quietly enjoy the drive through the rolling countryside that straddled the River Meuse, Jack driving and Sandy, who admitted to being a keen map reader, navigating. As they drove south past the village of Forges, the easy swell of the agricultural landscape gave way to the cathedral hush of a tall pine forest.

"This should be it," Sandy said. "Look, isn't that a sign up ahead for Cumières?"

But all there was, was a parking lot on the right side of the road. In a small clearing on the left-hand side, a low brick wall formed the backdrop for a medium-sized stone column emblazoned with crosses and marble plaques on each of its four sides. The monument was surrounded by four short obelisks connected by chains, and they in turn were surrounded by a low iron fence.

"Grand-mère," Jack called to the back seat, "we're here."

Nicole Lacroix Colbeck stirred from her dreamless sleep and beheld the same spot to which she had made an annual pilgrimage for nearly as long as the monument had been there. Her American great-grandson, Jack, was a nice boy, she mused, and so was this English boy he'd brought with him. She had no trouble closing her eyes and envisioning them in the uniforms of their great-grandfathers, in their varying shades of khaki. Indeed, sometimes, when she took the sun in Luxembourg City – she was still spry enough to go downtown on her own occasionally – she would look at a German boy and imagine him in the gray of *Feldgrau,* with a spiked Pickelhaube helmet; or suddenly dress, in her mind's eye, a French boy in horizon blue. It was all too easy for her to do, and a perverse game, too, she knew, but when you lived as long as she had, you had to be permitted your perverse games.

Escorted by the two boys, she made her way across the road and over to the monument, whose plaques bore the names of the men and boys of Cumières – including her brothers Lucien, Richard, and Philippe – who had given their lives for the glory of France. She closed her eyes while touching the iron fence around it, and the village where she had grown up materialized perfectly in her mind – the church; the *mairie;* the straw-and-chalk, stone, and stucco houses and stores. In a matter of weeks, there would be seventy-fifth anniversary observances of the end of the Great War of her girlhood, but to her they would seem as small and pitiful as the few flowers around the base of this monument, to which she now added her own; everyone's attention remained fixed on the second war, the one that had taken her husband, the more recent war, the bigger war. But for her, it was not bigger, would never be bigger, because it had not been the war that totally overturned lives thought settled. It was from the Great War she had learned there would never be such a certainty to life again. And there wasn't, not even now.

With their schoolboy French, Sandy and Jack were translating aloud the inscription on the monument:

CUMIÈRES
CE VILLAGE
A ÉTÉ
COMPLÈTEMENT ANÉANTI
PENDANT
LA GRANDE GUERRE

"'This village was completely' – is that 'destroyed'?" Jack asked.

"Closer to 'annihilated,'" Sandy suggested.

"'– annihilated'," Jack continued, drawing out the full, awful power of the English word, "'during the Great War.'"

After a pause, Sandy said, "It's really appalling... You have to ask yourself, how could people do this?"

"But we know better than to ask, don't we?" Jack shifted his attention to his great-grandmother, who appeared finished with her devotions. In his best French, he asked her, *"Grand-mère, vous voudriez aller à la cimetière américaine?"*

Pleased to be asked about the American cemetery, Nicole replied, *"Oui, mon enfant. Merci."*

Across the road again, as they were helping her back into the car, Jack realized she had left all her floral tributes at the Cumières monument. *"Grand-mère?"*

*"Oui?"*

As Jack had indicated, his French was OK, but now he stumbled in trying to express himself, and he left out an article. *"Pour la cimetière. Vous n'avez pas fleurs."*

Her great-grandson's phrasing almost caused Nicole to swoon, for she heard it two ways, both of them true. She saw the looks of concern on both boys' faces in reaction to the look on hers, and the concern only grew when she said with an unexpected laugh, *"Ah, oui, c'est vrai. Mais je n'ai jamais de fleurs."*

Which was also true.

"For the cemetery," her great-grandson had said, "you have no Fleur." That was how she'd heard it, and it was true; she knew how her Fleur had died; she knew there was no body there at the American cemetery, only a cross with his name on it. What her great-grandson had meant, of course, was, "For the cemetery, you have no flowers," and that was true, too; she never brought flowers to the cross that bore Fleur's name, because to do so would have been disloyal to the man who, after all, had been the love of her life, though to her everlasting regret he had died still not quite believing it. For he, too, had no grave; her Jacques had simply disappeared in that second war, and his death was only confirmed when it was over, by the Nazis' own records, kept with typical Teutonic precision, noting he had been summarily shot, but not mentioning disposition of the body.

So she had answered her great-grandson, "Yes, it's true. But I never have flowers" – which was absolutely the case – and also, perhaps, "But I never have Fleur." Because, despite the secret bloodline of this American boy who spoke to her in halting French as his great-grandfather once had, she never really *had* had Fleur, in life or in death, and she knew it. Someone else had, and she had never known who. Once it had mattered, just as once it had seemed a teenage girl could never get beyond her first love. But she was old now, very old; and she excused herself her youthful follies. She only wished Jacques had known before he, too, was taken.

Sandy had determined that the most scenic way to the American cemetery at Romagne, with or without flowers, was to drive back up to Forges and then go via Bethincourt. In the front seat, the two young men murmured quietly together, sharing their apprehension that maybe Jack's great-grandmother really was, in the American's term, "losing it." "I'm sorry I dragged you along to all this," Jack added.

"Why?" Sandy immediately demanded. "Family is part of life."

It was a statement pregnant with the possibility of a future together, and Jack paused, then whispered back, "I think I'm in love here."

"Restrain yourself," Sandy said drily; but he was clearly delighted. Looking to the back seat, where Jack's great-grandmother was once again dozing, he added, "Strange, isn't it, how much something that happened so long ago can still affect the people who lived through it? All four of my great-granddads fought in the Great War, even the American one."

"The American one?"

Sandy nodded. "Yes. My grandmum was American. *Her* dad fought in the Great War, too. I'm named for him, in fact."

"He was named Alexander?"

"No, my real name is Sandy. His surname was Sand. He sent both my grandmum and her brother, my great-uncle Tommy, to school in Europe, and that's where my grandmum met my granddad. Actually, my American great-granddad lived to be even older than your Grand-mère is now. He was still alive when I was sixteen and came out to my family. Not everyone took it well, and they tried to keep it from him, but at the end of the day he was just wonderful about it – said I had a good head and a good heart, and that was all that mattered."

"Wow! So – *all* of your great-grandfathers fought in World War I."

"Yes. Though on my mother's mother's side, he didn't make it back. But even for the ones who did, I think they never got past it. I think as long as they lived, it was the defining event of their lives."

They were nearing the village of Bethincourt, and Jack glanced appreciatively at Sandy before making his reply; then his gaze briefly shifted past to admire the lush, undulating green of the upward slope beyond the road, as he said, "Probably. But that was then, and this is now.... I think my cousins are right. It was such a long time ago, and when you get right down to it, this" – he jerked his head toward his sleeping great-grandmother in the back seat – "really doesn't have much to do with our lives."

# About the Author

Lance Ringel has enjoyed a four-decade career as a journalist and writer. He first published his novel *Flower of Iowa* as an eBook in 2014. This debut met with unexpected success in the United States and Europe.

Concurrently, Ringel's reputation as a playwright was growing. His play *In Love with the Arrow Collar Man*, based on the true story of famed illustrator J.C. Leyendecker and his muse-lover Charles Beach, premiered at New York's Theatre 80 St. Marks. Both *Arrow Collar Man* and the musical *Animal Story*, for which Ringel wrote books and lyrics, with music by Chuck Muckle, made the semifinals of the New York New Works Film Festival, and his stage adaptation of *Flower of Iowa* subsequently made the finals of the festival.

At Vassar College, where he has worked for 20 years, Ringel wrote *Vassar Voices*, which premiered at Jazz at Lincoln Center with Meryl Streep, Frances Sternhagen and Lisa Kudrow. He also wrote the narrative for *At Home in the World*, which played in Tokyo, New York, Washington, and Kampala, under the direction of John Caird.

Ringel has also distinguished himself with an impressive career in politics. He served as Assistant Commissioner of Human Rights under New York Governor Mario Cuomo, and at the National Gay Task Force under veteran LGBTQ advocate Virginia Apuzzo.

A native of central Illinois, Ringel currently resides in both New York City and in Poughkeepsie, NY, with his spouse of 43 years, actor-composer-director Chuck Muckle.

CPSIA information can be obtained
at www.ICGtesting.com
Printed in the USA
BVHW030819230320
575296BV00022B/25/J